2235

THE WORLD IS BROKEN

KENNETH TAM

2235

THE WORLD IS BROKEN

MARTIAN WAR - OMNIBUS 5

KENNETH TAM

ICEBERG

Published in Canada by Iceberg Publishing, Waterloo

Library and Archives Canada Cataloguing in Publication

Tam, Kenneth, 1984-
    2235 : the world is broken / Kenneth Tam.

(Martian War ; omnibus 5)
Contents: Tapestries of blood -- Memories of
    angels -- Acts of war -- Enemies of empire.
ISBN 978-1-926817-45-3

    I. Title. II. Series: Martian War ; omnibus 5.
PS8589.A7676T85 2012   C813.6   C2012-904156-4

Iceberg Publishing
55 Northfield Drive East, Suite 171
Waterloo ON N2K 3T6
contact@icebergpublishing.com
www.icebergpublishing.com

Cover Image: Wesley Prewer
Cover Design: Kenneth Tam

INSCRIPTIONS

TAPESTRIES OF BLOOD

"Assassination has never changed the history of the world."

- Benjamin Disraeli

MEMORIES OF ANGELS

"The distinction between Chinese and barbarian is most strict...
Do not say that you were not warned in due time!
Tremblingly obey and show no negligence!"

- The Qianlong Emperor, in an edict to King George III

ACTS OF WAR

"For the strength of the Pack is the Wolf,
and the strength of the Wolf is the Pack."

- Rudyard Kipling

ENEMIES OF EMPIRE

"You have enemies? Good. That means you've
stood up for something, sometime in your life."

- Winston Churchill

TAPESTRIES
OF
BLOOD

THE AUTOBIOGRAPHICAL REMINISCENCES OF
ADMIRAL THE LORD KEN BARRON FOR 2235

THE MARTIAN WAR - 17

KENNETH TAM

FROM THE AUTHOR

Foreign relations is a difficult game, and though today we're all accustomed to watching summits between different nations on 24-hour news channels, at points in our history even relatively friendly relations between great powers have been colored by some difficult practices.

A fine example: for centuries, China tried to keep the world at bay, not even recognizing the existence of some rather notable European powers (like England). To accomplish this, the Qing dynasty developed a system of international trade centered around 'Cantons' — a series of authorized ports, through which European traders could operate with state-authorized counterparts. By keeping the 'barbarians' confined, the Qing figured they would prevent outside contamination of their culture.

That, I'll admit, is a quick summary of a very complex concept for relations between a great Empire and those seeking to do business with it... but the principle is simple: when the government wants to control the way its people see the world, and the way other nations see its people, one tempting solution is to limit access.

In the Chinese case, the system sort of worked for a while... but because of the demand for goods from China, it was ultimately broken. The British wanted to sell opium without limit, and after the First Opium War ended with a British victory in 1842, the system was shut down, and China was opened to European intervention.

I'd probably argue that the Canton system never could have lasted permanently. One side or another would eventually get fed up with the relationships being built out of these Canton ports, and full diplomatic relations... or military interactions... would likely be the result. How that happened simply depended on who held the most military power... in that case, it was the industrialized European states.

What might happen if the playing field was more level? This year, we explore that question... in amongst a few other minor goings-on within the universe of Defense Command.

Before we get to that, I have the usual thanks to give.

Once again, numerous characters in this book are based on real-world friends of mine, so my thanks to all of those people... I hope this year, your characters meet your expectations.

Peter Caron is my best friend and has long helped me sort out my plans for 2235; massive thanks to him, and for all his character does. By the same token, Wes Prewer's continued efforts both towards the art for this series, and in providing the moral compass for a certain character, warrant much gratitude. I'm indebted to such great friends.

Finally, of course, I nod to my parents; this is my tenth year working with Jacqui and Peter at Iceberg, and each year it just gets more brilliant. Thanks too, Atlas.

– Kenneth Tam

PREFACE

It's about time we set the record straight about 2235. I know there have been unauthorized movies, many books, and plenty of space legends about the events of this year. I also know there have been considerable real-world consequences to what happened. No one has ever prosecuted me — no one can — and many people don't blame me, or even look the slightest bit critically at my actions.

They should. I want one thing to be clear from the outset: I'm one of the villains in this story. Perhaps not the only one, but I'll be the first to tell you this isn't my good-guy moment.

And it might be fair to suggest I'm not alone in this position.

What happened at the start of 2235 was different than anything in the history of the Empire. An attack by an outside force at a gala held by an Emperor… targeting celebrity heroes of the Black Sun with intent to punish them, and to do so on a solar system-wide stage.

On the face of it, it was a terrible idea — poking a bear that had just recently begun to doze off, but which was still strong and fierce after its last fight. Still, the risks were, to the man who conceived of the plan, quite reasonable. He knew what we'd do, and he knew how he'd use it to his advantage.

There's no point being coy anymore: Grant Merger had been behind this — his plot for revenge, hatched after his defeat at Deep Black. While we fought the Martians, he installed himself in the Solar Asteroid Union, and with incredible speed he gained a reputation and station there.

How and why, we'll examine throughout this year. We'll be able to spend some time with him, thanks to the spying efforts of Haley Briand and others… we'll get to see how well and truly evil his plans were.

And how largely brilliant.

But of course, right now, I suppose your first thought is for the fate of Karen McMaster. It's not something I want to write about, you understand — not something I enjoy. But we've come this far, so I might as well. Just as you might as well know what it meant to lose her, and leave her, and go after the man who I'd once thought of as a friend.

In order for any of that to really make sense, the first place I'm going to take you isn't the Terra Nova Palace on 31 December 2234… it's to the beginning.

Without that, nothing will make sense.

CHAPTER ONE

HEROES OF THE FUTURE

We liked going to the Academy pub.

The fact that we were two of the brainier sorts in our first year of studies meant that we found the place fascinating — enjoyable for reasons that other people didn't comprehend. We were, you understand, smarter than the average cadets, and quite superior to those young would-be officers who came to the pub for the purposes of intoxication, fornication and fighting.

Watching those people entertained us, and always made us feel superior, no matter how old or young they happened to be.

"She's well fit," my friend observed of a woman sitting at the bar as we entered the *Sunburst Arms* — that's what the pub was called.

I was coming through the door and unbuttoning my overcoat as he spoke, so it took me a moment to follow his view across the dimly-lit room, and to pick out a golden-haired woman at the bar. She sat there alone, staring at a drink she was stirring with her straw.

I recognized this girl from somewhere, and I said as much, "I think she's in my history lecture. Sits near the front, pretty intelligent."

That was praise, and my friend smiled thoughtfully, "Interesting. Perhaps she's having a bad day."

If that sounds a bit boorish, it shouldn't — my friend was not the womanizing type. Maybe that was his problem… his affections and attention tended to be intensely devoted to whatever woman he fancied, and in his experience so far in life, young women had not been ready to accept his mature concern for them.

My crimes were, I suppose, no different than his — we were both young and full of idealistic, happily-ever-after notions. If only the beautiful girls of the Academy realized that we were the ones they wanted to be with — the good guys they lamented not having when their idiot boyfriends mistreated them — then we'd be set.

Together, my friend and I moved to a table in the back corner of the *Sunburst Arms*, then ordered ourselves a couple of non-alcoholic drinks from a passing waitress. As we settled in, our eyes turned back to the blond at the bar, and my friend chuckled to himself.

"I guess I could go say something to her," he supposed aloud, and I nodded.

"Looks as though she might need someone to talk to."

This was a familiar refrain for the two of us — it was easy to talk about chatting with beautiful young officer cadets, and this girl certainly qualified, but actually doing so was not a skill we'd yet added to our repertoires.

For a while we continued to watch the lonesome cadet, but eventually other things began to distract us. As our drinks came, a couple of guys at the pool tables started shoving each other — another fight between cadets who'd had too much to drink. Bouncers moved in to break it up immediately, though both the guys involved in the shoving were large and muscled… the sorts of fellows who'd come to Defense Command specifically to be a part of Special Branch, not realizing that Branchers need brains more than they need brawn.

A scuffle ensued, and one of the bouncers ended up with a broken nose.

"Break a bottle and sever his windpipe," my friend clinically recited that killing blow as he looked towards the bruiser who'd done the damage.

I nodded slowly, then countered, "Steak knife from the table next to the door… into the femoral artery."

"Oof!" my friend laughed, then sipped his drink before praising my ruthlessness. "Remind me not to get on your bad side."

"Like you ever would," I shot back, drinking as well.

This was one of our pastimes at the *Sunburst Arms*; we were not brawlers by any means, but by our own reckoning we were worse. Though we were deeply sensitive young men, we also fancied ourselves to be cold-blooded killers. We didn't speak of it to anyone, of course, but somehow we wore that identity with pride…

Kill someone for looking at you the wrong way? Sure, if you could get away with it. Why not? Good people died every day, so why not a bad one?

Perhaps it was just because we were young and didn't understand the gravity of such callous thinking… perhaps it was because there was something deeply wrong with us. We didn't care, though; we felt satisfaction at the thought that we were so much more dangerous than every big idiot in this room who could throw a powerful haymaker. They were bruisers, but we were killers (albeit without track records) — and if they ever crossed us, they'd regret it.

The bouncers finally wrestled the two bruisers out of the pub, and then the guard with the broken nose left for treatment. That meant only one was left to police the establishment, until a replacement could be called in.

Since this was a pub full of Academy cadets looking to blow off steam, that almost inevitably meant there was going to be another fight. My friend and I could feel it, and as we watched from the back corner we started picking out possible contenders.

Neither of us thought the blond at the bar would have any involvement whatsoever.

Both of us were paying attention to a couple of loud-talking apes who were yelling at each other about cricket when something drew my attention back to the bar. The blond suddenly had company.

Nudging my friend I nodded in her direction, and we both watched as she, still minding her own business as she sat so elegantly on a stool, was set upon by another female — one we'd seen around a bit, and was the sort who looked like trouble.

The sort, I guess, who came to the Academy because the judge gave her a choice between the military or prison.

This attacker had short, dirty-blond hair… quite a juxtaposition to the quiet girl's wispy, long and elegant golden locks. Her face was twisted, and though we couldn't make out the words, we could tell that she was saying something harsh.

The intelligent girl at the bar could probably handle herself — I think we automatically hoped that she was like us, understated but lethal — so our first reaction was not to intervene… but then the newcomer pushed her.

It was the sort of moment that young heroes-in-training dream of. A damsel in distress, a chance to swoop in and prove to everyone how tough you are, but how civilized at the same time. I looked at my friend, he looked at me, and we stood immediately.

Unfortunately, we weren't the only two to have that idea. A couple of third-year cadets were closer, and they got to their feet as well.

The blond at the bar, meanwhile, slid off the stool she'd occupied, and stood opposite her attacker with clenched fists and a stern glare.

She said something we couldn't quite hear, and then the two third-year cadets came to her aid, presumably saying supportive but ultimately unsophisticated things about how they were there to help.

But the bully — who would have no future in a fleet like Defense Command — wasn't about to stand down before three adversaries.

By the time my friend and I stepped a little closer to the situation, we could hear the third years talking to her: "This is stupid, we're all here for a good time, so just let it go..."

The guy who said that weighed at least twice what the short-haired woman did, but when the bar stool hit him in the side of the head he didn't stay upright. My friend and I were shocked; Academy bar fights usually started with bluster and poor coordination. This bitch had some skills.

As the first fellow staggered back and collapsed onto someone's dinner, his buddy came forward swinging his mighty fists. He was fast, and I would normally have given him an even chance, but the bitch stepped out of his way, hooked his leg with her foot, and drove him head first into the bar top.

He went down too, and that just left the blond girl to face this monster alone.

That was enough to get us moving again, even if we hadn't yet decided on a course of action.

Would we have to?

The elegant blond was, we realized, no slouch. Pulling a stool from behind her, she launched an attack, and as my friend and I closed in we realized she might not need saving at all.

But at least it'd look like we'd tried...

The blond's stool was knocked from her hands, and then iron fists pounded into her ribs, cracking several of them. Staggering back, she hit the floor hard, and her attacker dropped right on top of her. Grabbing a handful of the blond's hair, the bitch pulled hard to expose her neck, then reached down and began to throttle her one-handed.

Good thing we were there.

My friend was first in, since he'd been interested in the victim. He didn't mess about, either; grabbing the fallen bar stool, he brought it down hard across the bitch's back. The blow flattened her out atop the blond, and for a second he and I both figured that was the end of it.

Then her foot found a way to hit his, and as he stumbled sideways off balance, she rolled to her feet, grabbed the stool, wrenched it from his hands and hit him with it. He buckled and fell to his knees, just in time for her foot to meet his groin with force.

She followed that first kick with a second to his face, and blood sprayed from his mouth all over the fallen cadet, who was still too stunned to notice until he basically fell across her.

The bitch then loomed over both of them, stool in hand, ready to finish her work.

Just as I started to move, the lone bouncer on duty finally brushed past me, yelling for the fight to stop… then he was sailing past me in the other direction, until he landed on a table and was knocked out by the impact.

The bitch was like a fighting machine, and she finally turned on me, eyes angry and a smile on her face. Charming.

I looked quickly from her to my friend. He was trying to regain his wits, and the blond he'd been protecting was sitting up slowly, fumbling to find a weapon of some sort. I caught her gaze quickly, nodded my head towards my friend, and basically hoped she understood the message: look after him until he was on his feet again.

I'd deal with this problem.

To be perfectly honest, in that moment, I had no idea what to do — none whatsoever. But as unsure as I was, I did know that I'd be fine. I was arrogantly confident, you see, like all the other guys who'd tried to intervene. But unlike them, I believed my cold, callous lack of humanity would help me. I'd do things that none of them were willing to do, and this bitch would go down.

Save the girl, prove to the Academy that they should never mess with the quiet ones.

As those thoughts flashed through my head, the short-haired bitch came on, winding up the stool for a big swing. Instinct took command and I moved in to meet her, so when the swing came there was no chance to follow through. It hit me, but not as hard as I hit her.

My fist missed her chin, but hit her collar bone with a lot of force, and she staggered. When she did, I didn't wait; I grabbed the stool from her hand and stabbed its legs into her abdomen, forcing her to double over. My hands landed on her collar and her belt respectively, and with all the strength I could muster, I spun and threw her head first into the bar. She got her arms up just in time to protect her skull.

She crumpled to the floor in front of the bar, and for a second I believed that was it. But she was too mean to be put down so easily. I moved around her towards the bar and her eyes immediately found me as I came into range.

They were furious, cold, and yet at the same time pleased. It seemed she wanted someone to hurt her, because that would add to the satisfaction when she ultimately won the fight.

I'd never seen anyone get back on their feet so quickly, and then she came at me fast. I backed off with equal speed, and as I did, my hand found a steak knife on one of the tables I passed. She surged ahead, kicked once and missed, then my back hit the wall of the bar and she came in with fists flying.

She was too slow. My left hand intercepted her right cross, grabbed her wrist, and then with my left hand I stabbed her. The blade went through her right forearm, easily parting skin and flesh, glancing off her bone and then projecting out the other side. She didn't even feel it at first, but I used the knife as a leverage point, stepping out and spinning her so that it was her back against the wall.

Then I pulled the knife free, which earned me a grunt from her, and at last I laid the point of the blade against the inside of her thigh. The femoral artery, as planned earlier.

She knew what was happening by then — knew that I had her at the point of my steak knife — and her eyes found mine as soon as our positions settled, my free arm across her neck to keep her from wrestling too much.

I expected to see rage in her gaze, but instead I found something more complex. She was interested, not angry.

Behind me there were sounds of commotion, and for some reason I felt comfortable enough with the situation to take my eyes off her. My friend had sufficiently recovered to help the blond to her feet, but she was staggering. I'd later learn she'd hit her head in the fall, damaging her inner ear — her sense of balance was anything but stable, so my bloodied friend put his arm around her and started leading her to the door.

"Shore Patrol is coming," the bartender declared at that moment, angrily looking at the short-haired woman I'd pinned to the wall.

So I just had to hold her long enough for some full-timers to show up…

I looked back at my prisoner, and she looked at me. It almost appeared as though those words — that the Patrol was coming — were the ones she had wanted to hear. That maybe…

All of a sudden, she made sense.

I wanted to ask her something, to confirm my assessment of what was malfunctioning in her brain, but this wasn't the time or place. Not after everything that had just happened. She was bleeding out, there would be consequences…

"You alright?" I directed that question to my buddy.

He was almost at the door with the blond, but he glanced at me and managed to nod before glaring at the woman on the wall. He considered saying something to her, but instead turned back to me, spitting blood before talking, "Get out of here before the Shore Patrol."

"Get her to hospital," I replied, and with a nod my friend Grant Merger took the blond cadet out of the *Sunburst Arms*.

Looking back to my prisoner, I studied her for a few seconds, then said the most important words of my life: "Stop this charade, and I won't kill you."

She stared at me with some surprise. Then I stepped back, tucked the knife in my belt and released her. I turned away — actually showed her my back — and collected my coat from the table where Grant and I had been sitting. I then returned to her and asked: "You have a coat?"

Her answer was a slow shake of her head, so I pulled her roughly away from the wall and put mine over her shoulders. Then I took her by the now-bloody wrist of her stabbed arm and pulled her towards the door. She winced and let out a hiss of pain, but didn't try to stop me.

"Where are you going?" the bartender demanded, but I met him with a glare that shut him up.

We stepped out of the *Sunburst Arms* into the cold Friday night air, and then she finally planted her feet on the ground, "What is this?"

I stopped, turned to her and stepped in close, coming almost nose to nose, "What's your name?"

"Karen McMaster."

I studied her face for a moment, then my fingers tightened around her wounded forearm. She hissed and tried to wrench away, throwing her knee in my direction as she did. My free hand landed immediately on her throat, and I drove her off balance and slammed her up against the outside wall of the pub.

"You're not getting out of this that easily," my voice was cold.

In case you're wondering, I didn't really know what I was doing at this point. But instinct was driving, and sometimes you just have to sit back and watch the scenery until you get there.

Karen stared at me, struggled a little more, and then decided she was better off seeing what I had in mind than waiting around for Shore Patrol.

"Fine," she didn't sound pleased, but I didn't care. I released her throat and started pulling her down the street. We moved away from the *Sunburst Arms*, and wandered into a whole different future.

One that ended with her bleeding out in my arms.

CHAPTER TWO
THE CHAOS

It was really happening.

I had Karen in my arms and I was wailing for help while blood flowed out of her in an entirely inexplicable manner. She had a swollen shoulder, the blood was pouring out of her mouth… more than you might think possible.

Medics were fast to arrive, because this was the Terra Nova Palace, and with them came equipment and a stretcher and all manner of things meant to save Karen's life. I was peripherally aware of their existence.

Wes and Mik pried me away from Karen as the medics took her. They say I didn't fight them, but I don't remember. I can see her being loaded onto a hover stretcher and taken away, through the growing crowd of shocked onlookers. I can remember following… I think Wes was keeping me from chasing too fast, from crowding the medics as they tried to figure out what was happening.

They didn't know — the blood kept coming — but they were saying things and doing things. Someone hooked up an IV of plasma to replace the fluids that kept pouring out of her, and someone else used a spider bot to intubate her, to make sure oxygen had a chance to continue reaching her lungs.

Their concern, I know now, was that there was significant internal bleeding too… that she was drowning in her own blood, as if this was some sort of terrible Phosgene poisoning.

It wasn't Phosgene this time. They didn't know what it was, so all they could do was wrestle with the symptoms.

We walked for an eternity – forty-six seconds, it turned out to be — to get to the building's surgery. This was a fully-equipped operating theater located within Terra Nova Palace — if the Emperor was ever to be injured, it was vital that the best doctors be present and able to take action on short notice.

This was a blessing, of course — from injection to operating table was less than two minutes for Karen — but that didn't change the fact that no one knew what was causing the bleeding. Not the doctors, not the medics, and certainly not me.

Karen's blood was pouring from her body, and we assumed that was the worst of it. We were wrong.

I remember the doors of the operating theater closing behind Karen and her medics. I can see Wes' face in my mind, because he stepped in front of me to stop me pushing them open and following the stretcher inside. I remember Mik pulling me around a corner to a viewing window, and once there I was able to stare at the medics and the rapidly-sterilizing doctors who were hurrying to get to work.

The whole surgery was recorded by internal cameras, but I've never been able to bring myself to watch the feeds. I never will watch them.

They were saying things like: "We don't know where the bleed is..."

"It was immediate... we don't know what she was hit with..."

"Be watchful for contamination..."

These doctors, Daragh's personal surgeons, were brave men and women. It didn't strike me until much later, but they had no idea what they were dealing with — a chemical attack, or a biological one. If it was some sort of fast-acting hemorrhagic virus, they could all be exposing themselves to Karen's fate by just being in the lab with her.

They didn't care; they went to work immediately. To be a doctor on the Emperor's staff, you must be willing to take such risks, and these men and women were.

That didn't change the fact that they didn't know what was happening, though. All they could do was search for the source of the blood and do whatever they could to fuse the rupture before their efforts to pump in replacement plasma fell behind.

More spider bots were dropped into Karen's mouth so they could go hunting. I watched this without any grip on reality, as my friends Wes and Mik kept me upright.

It was all we could do.

Andrea spotted the waiter who'd hit Karen with the injector gun, and our Irish skipper who'd been so bent on a one-night stand with an MP called Rousseau instantly lost interest in lust. She kicked off her impractical shoes and chased, and as she bolted out into the corridor, she drew the attention of two SF.

The pair were from the Constabulary branch, and had come to this event expecting to be on drunk duty. Detective Inspector Dave Highdeck was a bearded man who was two weeks from retirement, and Detective Inspector Jon Finn was new to the job and learning the ropes. Neither really knew what was happening, but when Andrea waved to them they followed.

All the way down the corridor from them, and making progress at a very fast run, was the waiter. Andrea meant to catch the man, to cut pieces off him and then kill him once he revealed who had sent him... she just had to get her hands on him first.

Barefoot she ran, the plush carpets of the palace making the going soft on her feet. She felt great burning in her lungs and in her muscles, but she didn't stop or slow.

Hidgheck and Finn kept up, too — no mean feat considering the anger that was fueling Andrea's sprint — and as they reached a bend in the corridor that led towards the landing fields, the trio swept around it.

A mag bolt on full power was their greeting, and the shot caught Highdeck in the foot. Cost him three toes in the end, and as he went down hard the shock of the blast stopped his heart. Fortunately he had an implanted defibrillator bot, and that zapped him back to life... but as he fell, Jon Finn had to take a knee and draw his mag to return fire, while Andrea slid to a stop behind a chair for concealment.

Looking down the corridor she saw the waiter had joined up with a woman in similar dress, and that they were now both carrying mags.

Someone would stop them — there were SF all over the grounds — but Andrea was in no position to do it. She was in a ball gown with no shoes and no mag...

Jon Finn tossed Highdeck's mag across the floor to her, which solved one of the three shortages. Picking it up, she quickly turned and started sending shots down the long corridor… but the waiters were already running.

"He alive?" our Irish skipper turned to Finn and Highdeck, and the downed veteran managed a groan.

"Stay with him," *Wolf's* Captain ordered, and then she rose and ran again, chasing the waiters to the back exit.

When she reached that door she could see just beyond that an SF Constable was down. She waited a second, pushed the door open and swung out low, trying to cover every direction. Unfortunately the landscaping was in the way — there were too many walls and hedges around, and the assassins could have ducked behind any of them.

More Constables were hurrying to the area, and one of them checked to find that the guard on the ground, Elisa Cui, was dead. She had been stabbed through the heart from behind.

Andrea hurried out over the paved path towards the landing fields, looking every direction she could. Rocks cut the bottoms of her feet, but she felt nothing. The assassins… where were they?

Then the sounds of a warming engine drew her attention, and the attention of the two dozen SF who had joined the search. A pinnace from the nearest row of landed craft was doing a crash launch, shooting up into the sky. There was nothing Andrea could do as it flew away except turn to the nearest Constable and bark her orders: "Contact Admiralty House, we need that shuttle intercepted!"

In that moment she didn't think it possible the shuttle was a decoy. Nor did she even consider the notion that two of the more than twenty SF constables now with her, staring up at the sky in seeming frustration, were indeed the assassins in disguise — using the chaos to their advantage so they could slip away.

She continues to blame herself for that lack of clairvoyance. She shouldn't; this hit team was professional — good enough to break into the palace, and good enough to get out.

Except when they ran into a superagent.

Melissa Samuels let the Constables cuff the two servers who'd tried to kill her. She didn't know what precisely had happened on the far side of the massive ballroom — it had sounded bad, but there were too many people in the way for her to get a clear sense of what was going on. Eventually she'd find out.

For now, she watched the Constables pick up the man she'd shot — who was out cold — and then drag the battered woman to her feet.

Before they could take that second assassin away, Mel took a napkin off a nearby table, rolled it into a cylinder and jammed it into the woman's mouth as a gag. It was not comfortable, I'd assume, but it would prevent the would-be killer from cracking any poison teeth that might have been in her head.

Old school, but Mel figured it was better to be safe than sorry. She was right; they pulled a cyanide capsule out of the woman's mouth as soon as they got her to the guardhouse.

There would be no easy escape for this creature, or for her partner. They would tell us what was happening. They would answer to the Empire, and lead us to more who would answer even more miserably.

As the Constables dragged the woman away, Marshal came up beside his wife. Noting the injector gun on the floor, Marshal pointed to one of the SF and had him collect it, "We'll need to see what they're using."

He had no idea how right he was.

As the weapon was carried away, the PM and the Foreign Secretary approached as well. It was Pope who spoke first, "Thank you, Melissa… if they'd gotten to us…"

Mel's brow was creased by a very dark frown, and she shook her head as she turned to the PM, "They weren't after you, they were here for me."

Pope blinked, then looked at Macdonald. If Mel was the target, then the suspect pool was inevitably quite small, with a single name dominating it.

"But… if it was him…" Marshal began to try to analyze the possibility, but the whispers finally reached them.

"Karen… they got Karen McMaster!" someone nearby said it.

Marshal's eyes widened, as did Mel's. They looked at each other, then completely forgot the politicians they were with and ran towards the center of the commotion.

We weren't there.

Chapter Three

Autopilot

Word traveled fast. The ball was being closely covered by the press, so live news feeds broadcast the attack in real time. As soon as it happened, the fleet went to General Quarters in orbit — any attack carried out in a palace of the Emperor was reason for everyone to stand to alert.

Rufus Chang had, perhaps unsurprisingly, been field-stripping his MAG-90 that evening, because he found that activity more enjoyable than being herded into a massive ballroom full of people he didn't know.

As he worked on the underslung grenade launcher, the screen in the wall of his quarters flashed on, Felicia Khalid's face appearing as she overrode his privacy lockout.

"Major Chang!" her greeting was urgent, her expression grave.

Rufus looked up with a frown, and immediately predicted trouble at the party — though that trouble, he assumed, would be centered around either Emperor Ryan or one of the politicians in attendance.

"Commodore McMaster was attacked with an injector gun... she's in critical condition and the assassins are being chased or caught right now..."

It was as coherent a summary of the situation as anyone might have managed, and Rufus stared at the screen for an entire second as he listened. Then he reassembled his MAG-90 in eleven seconds, speaking as he did: "Alert my team and have our shuttle prepared for launch. They'll probably be locking down the Capital Island airspace momentarily, so put a call into Admiralty House and get me permission to land, please. Don't take no for an answer."

Felicia nodded immediately, then switched off the feed as Rufus came to his feet and moved to his closet. Pulling on his combat gear took no time at all, nor did hooking up his rifle. He'd have to go to the armory for power cells and grenades, but with his team in tow he could make it to the palace in twenty minutes or less.

It would be too late, he realized, to do much good... but he needed to be there. It was his responsibility to be there.

He wondered then — for the only time — whether he should have gone to the ball with us. But there was no point thinking such a thing, so he shelved his concern and left his cabin.

At least he was closer than a certain other Brancher...

Luna, the Belt and Venus were sent word of the attack almost as soon as Earth learned of it — as were neighbors like the Hawke Protectorate. Everyone our Empire dealt with on a regular basis, except for the Martians, knew within an hour just what was happening.

There were many good people out there listening to the news, but only two — and really, just one — were relevant to what was to come.

Charlie Peters was asleep with his arm around Lia when the klaxon in their private quarters on Hawke One began to sound. He woke up instantly, and true to his Special Branch talents he was instantly focused — his mind had none of the cobwebs of fatigue that most of us can suffer from when woken unexpectedly.

He reached for the remote to the wallscreen, and then activated it to find an urgent message at the top of their inbox. As Lia began to sit up and get her own mind going, Charlie opened the note and found it was simple text.

The message was unpretentious, and entirely disastrous: "Assassins attacked Daragh Ryan's Empire Day ball. Attempted to inject Melissa Samuels with unknown compound. Succeeded in injecting Karen McMaster with unknown compound. Condition critical as of sending."

Lia didn't manage to read the note in its entirety until after Charlie was out of bed and pulling on a pair of combat pants. She frowned at him, then looked at the note, then looked back at him with wide eyes.

Our elite Lord Major was on complete autopilot. His face was set, his mind working with all possible haste in putting together a variety of pieces of information. If the attack had been targeted against Mel and Karen when there were so many other important targets in the room, it had to be Grant Merger.

If the assassins had managed to get into the Imperial Palace, it meant they were well-organized professionals, the sort that Merger would hire.

If the chosen weapon was an unknown injected compound, the point of the attack was to cause lasting harm in as torturous a manner as possible, which was Merger's typical approach to revenge.

If Karen died, he knew what would happen, and that meant to have any chance at stopping a war, he needed to leave immediately.

Being a Hawke Lord could wait, he decided. Because he's my best friend, and he knows me well.

Lia needed a few more minutes than Charlie to realize all this — it was the middle of the night, and she didn't have enough history with Grant Merger to really fathom all of it so easily. She did realize, though, that her consort had to leave... that if she asked him not to it would be like asking a planet to halt its orbit for a little while.

"Orbital season means you'll be there in twelve days, maybe a little less," she offered.

It seemed a very long time, but if that's what it took, so be it.

Charlie nodded as he pulled on one of his old DC Special Branch shirts, and Lia took a breath, "I'll call ahead and have them put a corvette at your disposal."

Charlie sat on the edge of the bed and put on his boots.

"Tell Ken I'm sorry I can't come," she watched his back as she spoke, and she bit her bottom lip uneasily at his continued silence. He was completely on autopilot, and as she rolled onto her side and propped her head up on her hand, she just hoped that whatever came next was not dangerous... and that it didn't mean the death of Karen.

When Lord Peters finished dressing, he stopped and remained still on the edge of the bed, his head hung for a moment as his mind continued to process information and interpretation. He would, of course, have plenty of time to ponder the situation during the long trip to Earth...

No time to waste here, then.

He made to move, and Lia let out a breath as she realized this was the last time she'd see him for a while — just like the old days, when they'd spent so much time apart. It wouldn't be easy for her, or for him…

Charlie turned towards her, climbed across the bed, and kissed her with no warning at all. This kiss was a powerful one, meant to last for as long as they were separated. Charlie made sure it was equal to that ambitious task.

Then he slid off the bed and headed out of their quarters, leaving Lia to call her fleet command. The corvette *Krystal* was made ready for Charlie's immediate departure.

CHAPTER FOUR
PAIN AND CHAOS

I have no sense of time for this period. I know that 31 December, 2234 and 1 January, 2235, together became the longest day of my life. I know that the doctors worked on Karen through the night, chasing the rupture that had sent so much of her precious blood out onto her body, and onto my arms and hands.

It took hours, I understand. And then as soon as they found the bleed new problems arose… they never stopped working. Not for an instant.

But their chase was in some ways a hopeless one, because the weapon that had been used on Karen was more alien than any of us realized. This wasn't a Schedule 1 or Schedule 2 compound, or even an older one that had been forgotten, as Phosgene had been…

No, as the SF delivered the unused injector gun to a doctor in the palace's labs for analysis, the mystery grew only more insidious. The palace lab wasn't as robust as its operating theater, but it was state-of-the-art nonetheless… and when the specialists started examining the guilty compound, they recognized none of it.

It was the middle of the night so they assumed the stress and shock was interfering with their assessment. No doubt there was some truth to this, but still their equipment could make no sense of the compound that was ravaging Karen. When the doctors in the theater called to the central DC lab for whatever instructions they could provide, none came back.

We didn't know what was happening to her. We could only watch to find out.

And I couldn't watch any longer.

I don't remember exactly why I left the viewing window. Hours and hours had passed, and the doctors still seemed to be working on her, but for some reason I just felt an uncontrollable need to stop being there. Wes and Mik had remained nearby throughout, keeping an eye on me in shifts while they hurried to and from the entrance to the medical section for conversation with SF and other officers…

Now both looked up in surprise as I staggered away from the theater window, heading for the door. I was loosening the collar of my court dress… I must have needed air, or water, or to vomit. I needed the quiet of the corridor outside the medical chamber, just for a moment.

As I opened the door, I was greeted by no quiet of any kind.

Jim Hannigan and Kris Jacobs were leading the efforts to keep cameras and civilians away. All around the entrance, and across the wide hallway, Belt Squadron officers and SF had set up a human chain to keep people back, but the bright lights of news cameras were still pounding into the cordon.

You may have seen the footage of me staggering out of that medical bay — you don't need me to describe how I looked.

Mercifully, in my state of mind I didn't hear anything when reporters started demanding updates on Karen's condition. I staggered around in a circle, looking like I was going to fall, until Greg Noyce got a hold of me and pulled me to a chair that Marlene Stoll dragged over. I wasn't even really aware of the two of them, I just sat in the chair for a second, staring at the wall.

Then, without saying anything, I pushed myself to my feet and went back inside.

John Fiora and Daragh Ryan together stormed into the palace guardhouse's interrogation room. In that cold chamber, Andrea Kiley was already sitting opposite the spy who Mel Samuels had beaten, and whose poisoned tooth had been removed.

"Ye fuckin' bitch is dead!" Daragh's explosion was thunder, but the assassin seemed immune.

John Fiora's own Irish — on his mother's side, if you recall — was up too, and he slammed his fists into the table, "You attack an Imperial event in a palace? You understand you've committed a hanging offense?"

As both men came to a stop on either side of the bound assassin, the woman kept her eyes fixed on Andrea, and let a small smile appear on her face.

It was not the reaction John and Daragh wanted. The Emperor was about ready to go get his shotgun, and to load it with slugs. A test of pain for this creature — a test of agony to see how long she could keep smiling.

"We'll have your identity, and that of your accomplices, in no time at all," John leaned down so his mouth was beside the woman's ear.

She turned her head so she could look at him, and then she tried to spit in his face. She didn't succeed, but the intent was enough. Neither John nor Daragh had the facility to hit a woman, even like this. They were quite capable, however, of other things that were probably crueler.

Stepping away from the assassin, John looked across the table at Andrea Kiley, who appeared almost like a living weapon in her gunmetal-color ball gown. Daragh's gaze fell on *Wolf's* skipper as well, and the Emperor decided she was the answer.

"Captain Kiley is Irish, and she will make you answer," the former Second Lord declared coolly.

The assassin wasn't impressed, and that's understandable. To her, Andrea was just another Defense Command officer — one of the weak regulars who had so often been easy to outwit.

Looking across at John, Daragh bobbed his head towards the door. The pair then made their way to the hatch, the Emperor stopping beside Andrea just long enough to ask one question: "You've read the Articles of Empire?"

He didn't mean the last book in this series, obviously. He meant the real ones.

Andrea nodded.

"Good. Use them."

With that he left... and had Andrea not been completely on the same page with our Irish Emperor, she might not have understood what he meant. Fortunately — if that's the right word — she completely understood. She got to her feet, followed the two men out of the interrogation chamber, then came back in with a knife.

This was not a particularly special knife, you understand — just a sharp combat blade that had been in the weapons locker in the guardroom.

Watching her approach with the implement, the assassin put on an indignant face, "I'm so afraid…"

Andrea pulled the woman's bound hands forward onto the table, flattened the right one out, then drove the knife through it — and through the table itself.

The assassin managed to keep her scream short — tough murderers have their pride — but Andrea wasn't done. This was no random act; the blade had been turned so that it went between the bones of her hand, with its sharp edge facing the tips of her fingers.

As soon as the blade went in, Andrea came around the table and kicked the assassin's chair out from under her. This was a shock, and the woman wasn't ready to fall. The only thing keeping her off the ground would have been her hand… but the only thing securing it to the table was the knife.

When she fell, her hand pulled against the blade, and the sharp edge was unforgiving. Her hand was mostly cut in two.

That drew a much more pronounced scream, and Andrea felt no remorse whatsoever. Instead, she gripped the knife and tore it out of the table, then reached down and hefted the assassin up again, pulling her farther across the now-bloody tabletop and extending her hands forward. The assassin was thus lying on her stomach, feet dangling in the air… and then Andrea put the knife though the back of her left hand, blade oriented in the same direction.

Because the assassin was on a flat surface — not falling — there was nothing to drag the blade through her flesh. Nothing, that is, until Andrea moved around the table, and began lifting it from the other end. As soon as the assassin started to slide, the knife began making progress through her hand, and she wailed.

"Stop it… no!"

Not so tough after all.

Andrea lowered the table again, and the wailing assassin tried to shuffle forward across the bloody top to relieve the pressure on her hand. As she did this, Andrea leaned down close to the woman's face, "Want to explain this situation to me?"

The assassin hadn't cracked yet, though. Just starting. It took a few seconds, but she worked up a defiant glare, then spat out the rather unimpressive words: "Fuck you, Defcom."

That brought a smile to Andrea's face, and she leaned in close with her next words, "Just so you know, when you do tell me — and you will — I'm going to cut your cheeks out of your face, and then with this knife I'm going to dig every tooth out of your head. Prepare yourself for that, and hold out as long as you can. Because I'm going to do it."

Something in Andrea's tone made the threat seem all too genuine, and as the color drained from the assassin's face, Andrea went back to the end of the table.

"This is why you don't commit high crimes against an Empire with a constitution that sanctions torture," *Wolf's* Irish skipper said, and then she raised the table.

Fiery mutilator of doom and excruciating pain. Not so funny any more, is it?

+++

Marshal and Mel were giving the assassin who'd been shot a quick once-over for clues. This was more a job for the Constables than a spy and a Commodore, but under these circumstances everyone with sense was staying out of the way of the Belt Squadron elite.

No one, for instance, offered to take over the interrogation of the conscious prisoner from Andrea.

As Marshal collected all the contents of the assassins' pockets and dropped them onto a tray beside the unconscious man's gurney, Melissa started cutting off his clothes. Those would have to be saved for analysis by the forensic people, but it seemed likely that the server uniform had been stolen from in the building… they'd have better luck finding identifying marks on his person than from generic clothes.

She got the guy stripped down and started looking for markings they could send to DCI for referencing. Tattoos were the most obvious thing you could look for, but any sort of body modifications might help identify who he was aligned with — where Grant Merger had found him.

There was nothing to find, however — nothing except a pale complexion and a skin texture that suggested he wasn't born or raised on Earth. That didn't mean much, but it was something…

"I don't think there's much here…" Marshal said as he moved through the contents of the man's pocket with his gloved hands. Except… "Wait a minute. Seen something like this before?"

Mel turned away from the stripped criminal and joined her husband, just as he held up a slim cylinder about three inches long.

There were bands around one end of the cylinder… it looked like some sort of key.

"Maybe a key for a lock box?" she wondered aloud, and Marshal nodded. Seemed possible — the killer wouldn't have carried anything that could have identified him, but the tools of his escape might be somewhere nearby, secured in a box that could only be opened by an innocuous key.

Turning away from the tray, Mel waved to a Constable who was staying near the door of the guardhouse medical room, "We need a full search of the grounds, starting with the waiters' lockers… and anywhere near an exit. Look for some sort of lockbox that might contain clothes, weapons and travel documents."

It was a tall order, even for the massive SF contingent at the palace. Nevertheless, they had to try.

These assassins needed to be identified. Two had already managed to get away.

CHAPTER FIVE
EASY PROGRESS

When the sun came up the boxes were found. Some SF constables who were scouring the grounds near the exit used by the two escapees located the silver metal containers, each about the size of a bread box, hidden beneath camo nets in hedges near the door.

They were locked, so when they were brought back to the guardhouse, Mel, Marshal, John and the Emperor weren't allowed in the room with them until they were swept and re-swept for booby traps.

In the bloody pockets of the female assassin, a second key had been found, so once the all clear was given, a volunteer went in to start trying the locks. That volunteer was, of course, Rufus Chang. Though he was too focused to be frustrated, it's safe to say he would have preferred to have been of more use in the situation so far — he felt he'd arrived late, and done little. But now he was the one to enter the interrogation room where the boxes had been brought.

From the other side of the blast-proof glass, four watchers waited anxiously.

"She said her name was Dejana Soeur?" Mel Samuels was asking Andrea about her interrogation. The mess in the next room over had been hard for all of these watchers to ignore, but none had commented on it explicitly.

Nodding, *Wolf's* skipper kept her eyes on Rufus as the Major studied the two keys he had been given, and tried to determine which belonged to which box.

"The one we have is called Ludwig Grenfell, and the other two were the Connaughts — Angelo and Sylvia."

"The gall of the fuckers to use Irish names for themselves..." Daragh spat those words mercilessly.

By now the Emperor had his jacket off and the collar of his fancy shirt wide open — he was in no mood to act posh when this sort of thing was happening in his own palace. In point of fact, he was angrier now than he'd been in years — angrier than he'd been during the coup, or anything else.

Because though he hated his job in many respects, this party had been a chance for him to welcome friends, and show them a properly good time. He had hosted them in his home, done everything he could to make them comfortable... and some fuckers had come in to kill them?

"I was surprised she talked so quickly," Andrea continued, and then paused as Rufus prepared to try the first key in the first box. Everyone fell silent as he inserted the cylinder into its receiver... and then the box popped open.

No explosion, no flash burn inside or other interference. They'd have a chance to look at the contents, to corroborate the information that had come out of Andrea's interrogation.

"People can be more open to discussion when they're losing so much blood," Mel replied, casting a sideways glance at Andrea. "And... no, nevermind."

Mel was thinking something, but she didn't want to say it just yet. First they'd see what was in the boxes, and as Rufus opened the second one without incident, he turned back to the glass and frowned.

The audio was switched on from the room, so when he folded his arms and spoke, the assembled officers could hear him, "That seemed a little too easy."

It did, and while none of these people were the sort to look a gift horse in the mouth, they certainly found it interesting that professional assassins who'd had the wherewithal to penetrate the Emperor's security, hack the badgelink database, and then launch attacks in a room full of officers, would be clumsy enough to leave their escape boxes where they could be found... and to give up information after only a couple of hours of torture by a non-professional.

Now, that skepticism might be unfair. It was entirely possible the attackers were arrogant and had assumed they would escape... as two of them indeed had. It was also possible they weren't as tough as they thought they were.

Hell, maybe Miss Soeur just really wanted to keep one cheek.

But the answers had come too quickly for the wise and experienced officers standing on either side of that glass. They expected to have to work harder for them...

"He knows we know it's him," Mel decided aloud after a long and thoughtful pause. "He knows I'd figure it out as soon as they came for me. And maybe... he's leaving breadcrumbs for us. Maybe he wants us to follow..."

John, Daragh and Marshal shared uncomfortable glances — Grant Merger was playing a game with all of us, but we didn't know to what end.

Once the open boxes cleared extra quarantine scans, everyone crowded into the room and their contents were laid out on the interrogation table. Constabulary crime scene technicians should have been the first to look through the contents, to avoid inadvertent contamination of evidence... but no one was willing to wait.

Something from these boxes had to give an indication of how the assassins were planning to leave the planet. I should have actually explained this earlier, but the pinnace that had taken off from the palace landing field had entered orbit and been plucked by *Hokkaido*. It had made the trip on automatic pilot; the assassins who got away had done so by other means.

How this was accomplished became immediately clear: the boxes had held green SF tunics. Andrea realized her error as soon as she saw the garments — in all her haste, she hadn't thought to check the guards who'd come to help her find the attackers.

No point dwelling on that, though; there had to be another clue that would help reveal how the bastards meant to get out of Earth space. Though it was unlikely that either of them would have a ticket on a commercial vessel destined for safer territory, any documentation that would get them out of Earth space... or even just into orbit... would have given a helpful direction.

But nothing jumped out at them as they looked through the items. The escape route was probably known only to the assassins themselves... not committed to writing anywhere. They could have fled to a certain space terminal and booked passage up to an orbital station, or even to Luna, and from there they could have hopped a transport anywhere.

The only chance to catch them would be visual and DNA records, but the coverage within the palace wasn't great. Constables from SF were working on getting pictures to the necessary authorities now, but if the attackers had hit orbit within an hour of the attack, there was every chance they'd already escaped.

How, then, could we possibly catch up to them?

There were ways… if we could just find out where they were going.

After several minutes of fruitless sifting, the five informal investigators gave up.

"They're going somewhere in the non-aligned belt, perhaps?" Marshal suggested as he folded his arms.

Mel began to nod, but stopped: "Thea Fostopolos mentioned that Haley Briand was on Grant's trail. And that she had disappeared into the Union of Solar Asteroids."

"Solar Asteroid Union," Daragh corrected sharply, shaking his head. "Those fuckers who built the *Tharsises* for Mars… they stuck their nose in during the war. Could be that they want to pick a fight they can't win now…"

John recognized Daragh's growing anger and moved to block it: "That's a possibility, but we can't really know. Maybe more interrogation…"

He didn't enjoy saying that last word, having seen exactly what Andrea had done to the assassin Soeur. Not common Defense Command practice, but dictated by the circumstances… Turning back to the Irish Captain, the First Lord leveled a stern question: "Can you get a destination out of her, you think?"

Andrea stared at him for a moment, then glanced at Rufus, "Could you help me hold her down?"

Rufus is a man who knows something about violence, though there are lines he will not cross. This seemed to be skirting such a line very closely… but he knew the importance of the answer they were seeking, and that Andrea's work was within the limits of the law.

At this point, it was vital to be entirely certain of who was responsible for the attack — not just to allow us to catch them, but to make sure this assault wasn't the first attack of many. If there were other targets on Earth, or in the Empire, we needed to know (of course we know now that there were no other targets, but at the time it was still a serious possibility to consider).

Rufus thus nodded to *Wolf's* Captain, and they turned and headed back to the interrogation room containing the butchered assassin.

A medic was changing Soeur's IV bag when the pair arrived, and he glared at them both, "Which one of you monsters did this?"

Andrea glared back: "I did. Get out."

The horrified medic opened his mouth to protest, and then found himself pierced by the mismatched eyes of Rufus Chang. That was enough to deflate any humanitarian protest, and the medic moved past them without looking over his shoulder.

He couldn't bear to imagine what was coming next — and what shape the criminal would be in when Andrea finished her work.

Soeur was only partially conscious when Andrea leaned down, almost pressing their noses together, "I've come for your tongue this time."

Hearing the voice, Soeur seemed to come out of her stupor, then began to struggle against the restraints that held her in her chair.

"I don't think she likes you," Rufus interjected, purposefully reminding Andrea that she wasn't alone in the room.

Rufus was not the sort to butcher anyone when they were tied to a chair, so he rather hoped that threats and fears based on the work Andrea had already carried out would get the required information.

Stepping away from her prisoner, Andrea moved over to a tray in the corner of the room, then picked up a pair of pliers and the knife she'd already used to great effect. Rufus swooped in at this point, grabbing Soeur by the collar, "I'll stop her if you answer one question for me."

His words were hard, and the assassin turned her wide eyes on the Chinese Major. Perhaps this would work.

"Where are you based? Where are your friends running to?"

That was two questions, but Rufus needed only one answer. He turned the assassin's head so she'd be forced to watch Andrea approach with her latest implements, and that sight was sufficiently chilling.

"Etat… Concord…" the woman moaned, and on the first try those words — which were French — didn't make sense.

"What was that?" Rufus asked, jerking Soeur's head and drawing a yelp.

"Etat Concord!"

"And where's Grant Merger?" Andrea Kiley came to a stop right in front of Soeur's knees as she asked the question, letting the tools she'd collected hang down at her sides.

At this moment, in her gunmetal grey dress and with her hair still looking surprisingly fancy, Rufus believed this Irishwoman was in fact the angel of death.

"Who… Grant Merger?" Soeur struggled, and Andrea didn't accept the answer.

Crouching down, she raised the pliers, "Open her mouth…"

"No! No! Who?"

Andrea had no patience for games, but Rufus was mindful that there might be some barriers to understanding here. That in mind, he asked another question: "Who hired you?"

Eyes turning back to the Chinese Major, Soeur's fear seemed to intensify, "He… it's… the Governor. The Governor of Etat Valcour."

"Name?" Andrea's insistent tone was backed by the pliers pressing gently against Soeur's busted lip.

"George Madison."

Andrea looked up at Rufus as the assassin blurted the words. Remember that we didn't know where Grant had gone, or what alias he might be using. He'd always arrogantly preferred to work under his own name in past… perhaps this time he was a villain reborn. The name 'George Madison' had the same initials, and of course, was also a mix of names of the American founding fathers.

So perhaps that was the game… Grant had reinvented himself as a politician in the Solar Asteroid Union, and was trying to use his resources to get revenge.

Still, there were too many questions… just none that this assassin could answer.

"Good, now I suppose you don't need your tongue anymore," Andrea was pleased, and she started to roughly push the pliers into the prisoner's mouth.

The squeal was immediate, and Soeur struggled as panic set in. Andrea smiled at the discomfort — at last, someone who had earned the punishment she hadn't been allowed to carry out against any of Egesta's criminals.

Rufus' hand closed on Andrea's wrist, "Not now."

Andrea looked up at *Wolf's* Special Branch commander and considered ordering him to leave... then recalled a time when she'd tried to get around Charlie Peters to kill some Martian prisoners. He'd stopped her, and rightly so.

That had been after the Phosgene attack on *Idaho*. Phosgene... and a supposedly alien spacecraft that said 'Made in the USA'.

Could Grant have... but why...

"Not now," Rufus repeated his order, and Andrea slowly straightened up, her eyes turning away from the prisoner at last.

With that the pair left the room, and outside they found the rest of the investigating party waiting for them. They'd all been watching through the window, and none were terribly overjoyed at Andrea's willingness to do whatever she saw fit... but, it appeared, they had answers — answers derived from torture, which civilized observers (like I often pretend to be) will instruct you might be inaccurate...

But these were true.

"If they're from the Asteroid Union, they'll be running back. We didn't stop traffic leaving Earth zone, did we?" Daragh turned to John with the question, and the First Lord shook his head.

There was no way all traffic leaving Earth space could have been halted overnight — the commerce that came and went from the central world of the Empire amounted to trillions a second.

So two assassins had probably already gotten out of our defense zone, and were heading for a part of the Belt that we hadn't charted so they could report back to the Governor of 'Etat Valcour'... a man named George Madison.

A man who either was, or worked for, Grant Merger.

My former friend had attacked us, and as that conclusion settled over these five most important individuals, it brought with it both a certain kind of calm... and a complete despair over what to do next.

"If they're leaving breadcrumbs, do we follow?" Mel asked eventually, the question directed mainly to John and Daragh.

The two men looked at each other silently for a moment. They didn't know — none of us did. Was this attack at an Imperial Ball sufficient provocation for us to send out warships...

Too much to decide. And for all the time they'd spent dealing with questions of who and how, none of them had been able to check in on the person at the heart of the attack.

I'd like to say Karen was fighting for her life, but I can't. There was no way she could fight the unknown enemy that had been injected into her body.

Chapter Six

Coma

A coma at this point was good news, but I remained altogether too numb to understand that. Actually, I was too divorced from rational thought to process much of anything. As I sat in a chair in the medical bay and looked at Karen, who was now in an isolation chamber on the far side of the room, I could hear words... and probably understand them... but I retained nothing.

This wasn't a situation like Io or the Fleet Clash, where I was reportedly appearing rational and decisive on the outside, while I was in turmoil within. Here I was just plain out of my mind, and Wes and Mik, joined alternately by Matt, Jim, Greg, Marlene and Kris, simply kept me company while trying to understand the situation themselves.

The ruptures throughout Karen's body had all been found and fused, which meant she was no longer bleeding internally. Transfusions were replacing the blood she'd lost, but none of that really mattered now. The damage to her body seemed only to be the most outwardly visible sign of her attack.

"I've never seen anything do this before," Doctor Imogen Imahara was the surgeon who'd done most of the work to keep Karen from dying on the table, and she stood not too far from me and explained what she was seeing to Wes, Mik and Greg. "The compound seems to have stopped causing bleeds, but we don't know why. And it's definitely not gone — we're seeing it in every blood scan. It's not dormant at all... looks like it's just wandering around, waiting to do something else."

To Wes in particular, that sounded very disconcerting — during his last year at the Academy he'd done a paper on the supposedly-intelligent 'Omega virus' from the twenty-first century. Had that plague been released, the whole human race might have been driven from the Earth... so the thought of any sort of bio-weapon that had the ability to *wait* was not one he was comfortable with.

Maybe it was just Doctor Imahara's choice of words...

"Right now it seems to be focusing in her brain. We don't know what it's doing there, but it looks as though it may have gotten through the blood-brain barrier... it's in the frontal lobe now."

None of the three listening Naval officers knew much about brain physiology, but that seemed irrelevant — the key was that the compound was still doing harm, still working its way through Karen.

"Can you scrub her blood?" Mik asked that question, and Imahara shook her head.

"It's not just in her blood, it's parking in tissue and muscle... we might be able to purge it, but figuring out how will take time. We're hoping that the transfusions will help in the meantime, though there are signs that the compound is just contaminating the new blood as well."

It sounded like a medical nightmare, and that's largely because it was. Karen was being afflicted by something insidious and entirely unlike any compound one of the best surgeons in the Empire had ever seen.

"Now I'm not a specialist… we've got the lab working, and I've sent scans to London, Sydney, Luna and Venus. We're getting the best eyes in the Empire on this thing, and we're also tracking its progress. Whatever damage it does, we think we can undo with gene therapy… as long as it doesn't turn a corner and kill her."

That sounded hopeful. You know, like knowing how to swim would make you hopeful if your ship went down in the middle of the Pacific.

"Surely the risk of her dying now has decreased…" Greg asked evenly, and Imahara simply shrugged.

"Normally I might think so, but we haven't actually done anything to stop the compound's progress. We can't get at it. So as long as it doesn't launch any more attacks on her system, we don't think she'll die. But we just spent hours stopping the bleeds it started. If it starts causing more, or goes after entirely different systems… well. Without knowing what it is, we can't get ahead of it. She's at its mercy. That won't change until it either burns up, or we figure out something new."

Hopeful like knowing how to swim would make you hopeful when you're being depth-charged in a submarine.

The bottom line was that our doctors didn't know what Karen was up against. How the hell could you fight an enemy you didn't know? The fact that we had a sample of the compound should have helped, but it was too soon for any results to come back, and even knowing what the offending agent was didn't mean a cure was easy — remember how hard Doctor Conrad Rhee had tried to create a Phosgene scrubber at short notice aboard *Artemis Agrotera*?

This was different of course — we had the whole infrastructure of the Earth medical system behind us — but the challenge was greater too.

So many questions. And there were no answers.

For now, the only thing that Doctor Imahara could recommend was movement.

"At this point, she's stable. I think we take the opportunity to get her to Terra Nova Hospital. A full medical suite backed up by a few shifts of doctors give us the best chance."

That made sense to Wes, Greg and Mik, though none of them were sure how I'd react. I hadn't said two coherent words since entering this medical bay… would I even understand what Imahara was saying?

I got to my feet immediately, "Let's go."

Guess part of my brain was starting to check back into reality.

Terra Nova Hospital is an impressive facility. To this day, TNH offers one of the highest standards of care in the Empire, and I would be lying if I suggested that had nothing to do with the number of politicians who passed through its doors.

As much as I hate to admit it, the proximity of influential people definitely did make for a high-class hospital… and this was one day where my usual self-righteous populism would yield no complaints about the disproportionate level of expertise to be found in the building.

Karen was transported very carefully from the palace to the hospital — her condition was stable, but no one had any idea how long it would remain so, or what might trigger a change. They erred very much on the side of caution.

A special isolation chamber was set aside for her on arrival — a place where the doctors would have absolute control over the environment, and would have the ability to seal her off from the rest of the world if she became infectious (sorry, forgot to mention they'd established that she wasn't so far). As I suppose I keep saying, no one knew what to expect next — all we knew was that Karen required intensive care, so she'd get it.

I stayed with her for hours. I don't know how long. Nothing else really mattered to me, you understand — I was incredibly fortunate to have so many good men and women close at hand, finding answers about the assassins and also talking to the doctors about Karen's care. If not for them, all might have been lost early on… the information they gathered in those first twelve hours proved vital.

I just wasn't part of the team.

Standing outside the glass walls of the isolation chamber, I watched masked doctors supervise Karen, take samples of her blood and tissue, scan her, send bots into her… do anything and everything they could to learn more about her situation. But these doctors were no more successful in their venture than Doctor Imahara had been — there were no answers to be had.

Our science was the best in the solar system, but that didn't matter. The most intelligent person in the world can't answer a question asked of her in a language she doesn't speak.

By midday the sky had clouded and some snow had begun to fall. It had been, up until this point, a relatively mild December on the North Atlantic coast. Now it was as though the island I was born on was trying to send down a peaceful blanket — something to calm nerves, restore faith.

I love my homeland, but this effort was not a successful one. I stood there, in that spot outside Karen's window for the rest of the day.

Standing on bridges for years helped make this possible — any skipper in our fleet knows how to remain on his or her feet for long periods, because sitting down on the bridge is generally not done.

So I stood, and watched, with no sense of time at all.

Perhaps that was a blessing, or perhaps it was sheer cowardice. Perhaps if I'd tried to participate in any of the efforts to catch the attackers I'd have been in a poorer state for it… whatever, I just stood. I must have eaten and drank, too, but I don't recall.

Different officers took turns standing vigil with me — Mik and Wes were first, but rotating through were literally all the officers you could name from the Belt Squadron and our extended family. I wasn't really conscious of them, I'm sorry to say, but they were there.

And I know they were there because my parents were too, and told me so. You haven't met my mom and dad in these books, but of course they're the only people closer to me than my Belt Squadron family. They lived twenty minutes from the hospital, so they came almost immediately, and they didn't seem to leave. I was incredibly fortunate to have them, as was Karen… because her parents didn't exist in any real sense, and they certainly didn't come.

That afternoon, though, one person did arrive… one person who shook me out of my catatonia.

Karen, I may once have mentioned, hated her sister. They hadn't gotten along since their childhoods had taken them in different directions; Kath had ended up living her adolescent and teenage years in a startlingly different environment than the one Karen had experienced, and while that in itself was no reason for them to fall out, Kath was also a stupid ignorant bitch.

I didn't hear her arrive — or if I did, it didn't register. I certainly didn't notice her stride up beside me, and I didn't notice her husband Rick, who was trailing behind as he focused on the comm in his hands.

No one had stopped these two from getting into the hospital because they were, of course, family. No nurse at a checkpoint, or SF guard, would see anything wrong with them coming up to see Karen under these circumstances — indeed, not knowing the family history, the guards and nurses might have assumed we'd be angry if they were held up in any way.

But it would have been better if they had been stopped.

"So you finally got her killed!" was Kath's greeting.

Andrea Kiley (of all people) was the one keeping vigil for the Belt Squadron at this point, and she was sitting beside my dad. Trust me when I explain to you that this was a poor combination of mediators. To make matters worse, my mom was off at that particular moment, making arrangements at Shewfelt House for me to rest there (whenever I finally collapsed).

Kath came around in front of me and got in my face, her perfect makeup, coiffed hair and stylish clothes eclipsing part of my view of Karen's bed.

At this point husband Rick was holding up his comm, because of course he was recording the scene — this was going to be Kath's coming out party for the tabloids. She'd only ever cared about Karen after the media had started taking an interest… only appreciated her as a ticket to personal fame.

Seriously. The media — even the most salacious tabloids — had stopped caring about Kath not long after it became clear that she was an attention whore, and that Karen was in no way supportive of her. But now she had a chance to show the whole Empire that she loved Karen more than I did, and that everyone should give a shit about her heartbreak.

"Say something! Stop pouting, you put her in there and you better own up to it!" I remember thinking that line sounded rehearsed — which it was. Most importantly, though, I *noticed* it sounded rehearsed.

Finally my eyes focused, and I looked down at the face of Karen's sister. They looked a lot alike, but if ever you needed proof that goddess-like beauty runs far deeper than just skin and bones, Kath was it. This woman's face made me angry. In the midst of all the numbness, I actually did begin to feel *anger*.

But it was different than I was used to… different than any anger I'd felt in a long time. That should have been a warning… but let's not get ahead of ourselves.

"I think you should be going, Miss McMaster," Captain Kiley had changed into her uniform, by the way, though her hair and makeup were leftover from the ball — she'd had no time to shower. It must have been odd to see her so finely done up while wearing ship fatigues.

That was irrelevant; the woman who'd spent a night cutting open an assassin in all the ways allowed by the Articles of Empire was not to be trifled with. Any person with a brain would have realized as much.

"Stay out of this, Captain Kiley," Kath's words rang with insolence, and they drew a smile to Andrea's face.

By this time, my dad — who didn't have much to say during this situation — had gone to shake Rick's hand. Since Rick's hand was occupied by the comm, my dad took the comm, and accidentally threw it straight at the floor, and then stepped on it. Funny how that happened.

Rick started to puff up about this, but my dad — who was not as young at this point as when last he'd been obliged to do anyone harm — succeeded in convincing him to shut his stupid fucking face. All it took was a glare.

Kath required a little more effort. Finally my brain began to formulate a response, and I realized too that Andrea was looming over my shoulder.

Andrea who was known for her very sympathetic nature.

Mindful of my responsibility to keep Karen's family safe, I smiled — smiled — and reached up and cupped Kath's face in my hands, "So good to see you."

She wasn't having any of it, "Don't try to sweet talk me you bastard, because of you my sister..."

I leaned in close to Kath, so that my mouth was right beside her ear, "Are you familiar with fertility drugs? You must be, I know you and Rick want kids."

That quieted her. She did want kids — very badly — but there had been some poor decisions during her younger years, and that had made things rather difficult for them as they'd tried to start a family. This, I think you'll agree, is a very serious and frankly rather sacrosanct problem — you don't needle someone about procreation trouble. It's as low as you can get.

"It's really a shame they're not more effective. Did you know, there are certain types of damage to your reproductive system that even drugs won't offset? Must be tragic, never being able to have kids. Never being able to send your legacy out into the world. I hope you never have to go through that."

I released her face, then watched as she stepped back, her expression contorted with both rage and desperation. Tears started to form in her eyes, and then just because I was able to, I decided to be a little more pointed.

"I've always meant to ask, when you did all that cocaine while you were knocked up... did you not read the warning on the package, or were you trying to kill your baby? I mean, you clearly didn't know who the father was, so it might have seemed like a good idea to just 'accidentally' murder the only child you could ever have."

Andrea was actually surprised by my words — I got a wide-eyed look from her, which gave me some satisfaction.

"You monster!"

It was a predictable retort, I think you'll agree — and also a very accurate one.

I simply smiled, then shrugged: "Well like you said, I *did* put Karen into intensive care, after all. But tell me, do you dream about that child? Imagine what he'd have grown up to be? I bet he'd have been a waste of oxygen like you, so you probably did us all a favor."

Shockingly, Kath didn't take that very well. She struggled for words but found none. Her idiot husband attempted to puff up... but was deflated by glares from me, Andrea and my father. The two of them fled, and neither of them came back.

This, you see, is how I began 2235.

As Kath ran away I found myself taking deep breaths. My spiking emotions began to level off, and rather suddenly I was overcome by incredible physical fatigue. For the first time I needed to sit down, and as I did my mind started to function properly.

Taking the seat beside the one my dad had occupied, I looked up at Andrea, "I've retained pieces of things I've heard, I think... but I need to know everything we know. Killers, how they got here... what we can do..."

A massive headache hit me all at once, then, and had there been anything in my stomach I probably would have needed to vomit. Instead it became quickly apparent that I needed sleep — no matter how much I wanted to stay, I couldn't function. I'd used up the last of my strength being unimaginably cruel.

My mom returned not long after this, having secured accommodation for me at Shewfelt House. I don't especially remember how I got there, but when I did I passed out on one of their beds, putting an end to the longest day of my life.

The worst year of my life was just beginning.

Chapter Seven

Latitude

While I slept, my friends didn't. Some of them had managed to catch a few hours of rest during that day I spent staring at Karen, others were just superhuman. Whatever the particular case, they had a meeting to discuss the implications of everything that had happened.

Admiralty House played host to this meeting, and when Daragh Ryan attended he very much was seeing himself in the role of Second Lord of the Admiralty. It had been a couple of months since his coronation, so he should have been cured of that notion... but he wasn't. Because Emperor or no, the man had spent his life in Defense Command.

Which changed things.

Crowding around a meeting room table were Daragh, John Fiora, Marshal Samuels, Mel Samuels, Wes Pellew, and from the government side, Gabriel Pope and Craig B. Macdonald. Everyone else was back at the hospital, keeping a vigil over Karen... so these few would decide what to do with the information that had been gathered.

You'll have to forgive me if what they'd found so far hasn't been clearly explained in the preceding pages... it's difficult when writing about this to be conscious of the exposition, and I was a bad enough writer to begin with. To review, here's what was known:

The Governor of a state within the Union of Solar Asteroids (a self-styled 'USA', trying to steal American traditions in a bid for legitimacy) had sent four assassins to attack Daragh's ball, targeting Melissa Samuels and Karen McMaster. Considering these were two people with very sharp histories with a certain Grant Merger, it seemed entirely obvious that the governor of Etat Valcour (Valcour State) was Grant in disguise.

Grant had been my friend... before he'd turned into a pirate, created his Syndicate bent on overthrowing Imperial power, and attacked Earth. Under Greg Noyce's command, the Belt Squadron had hunted him down in 2230 (with the help of Mel Samuels, who had worked her way into his confidence as a pirate ship skipper), and we destroyed the Syndicate at the Battle of Deep Black.

Now Grant was a declared enemy of the Empire, so it was the duty of any and every Imperial citizen to do him harm. For those unfamiliar, 'harm' meant anything up to and including killing him. Anyone harboring or assisting him could be declared an enemy of the Empire as well, though there were a few shades of gray on that subject.

If the USA (or SAU as I will call them, because I think their name is disrespectful of the real United States) was harboring Grant Merger, and indeed, making him a leading political figure, they were clearly not trying to be our friends — unless he was completely hiding his history, which was possible.

But the SAU was still not exactly in the Empire's good books: Union yards and laborers had built the *Tharsis*-class battleships used so effectively against us by Bort McWebsbert in 2233. The fact that the SAU was willing to build ships for our enemies had not been well-received by the Second Lord during the war, but it hadn't mattered much at that time. After all, how likely was it that the mad Irishman would ever have the power, opportunity or reason to vent his frustration?

You might be able to see where this is going. Andrea had been able to acquire the rough location of one the SAU's rocks — a place called Etat Concord, where the assassins hailed from — and that meant there were decisions to make.

As the meeting attendees settled into their chairs, Daragh was the last man left standing, and with his anger only slightly reduced from earlier hours, the Irishman said his piece: "So the Solar Asteroid Union fuckers start off by building superbattleships for our enemies, and then they send assassins to *my* party, to attack Defense Command officers. I'd almost have respected the fuckers more if they'd tried to kill me or Douglas."

He nodded towards the PM as he said that, then lowered himself into a chair, "I'm declaring the whole fucking lot of those renegades to be enemies of the Empire."

That was a privilege the Emperor did technically enjoy — he could make such a declaration, though whether it would be upheld by the government was an entirely separate question. If it was, though, you can see how it was in some respects as good as a declaration of war.

The forcefulness of Daragh's anger meant that the next comment had to come from the Prime Minister, and Pope was not eager to follow the new Emperor's words. He and Macdonald had spent their day at PMO, trying to figure out what options they really had — an attack like this could theoretically be written off... or calmly responded to by diplomatic overtures. But we had no relationship with the SAU at that time, which raised a whole lot of questions... and the fact that the Union hadn't taken the necessary steps to introduce itself into the established system of solar states left much ambiguity.

Touchy stuff — delicate and political — but if handled properly, this first encounter between the Empire and the Union could potentially end with a civilized outcome.

Problem was, there was absolutely no chance of that happening. Civilized responses weren't going to cut it, because public opinion had turned positively warlike over the course of the day. You'd think the recent end of the Martian War would have made people wary of fighting, but it was rather the opposite. We had a huge fleet in orbit (including the most powerful warships in human history), we had a proven track record of victory, and to quote one newscaster, we'd just had two of our most popular heroes sucker-punched by some upstarts who'd sold ships to the Martians.

A public opinion poll conducted on the afternoon of 1 January had some sort of violent response favored by more than seventy percent of the population.

So Pope and Macdonald had to be aware of the implications of the public mood — so soon after an attempted coup, the people wanted to go out and kick the SAU in its pants. The government, which had retained its place in our society by wordlessly pledging that it was indeed the representative of the people, was going to need to do something.

But total war couldn't be the answer, at least not as far as Pope saw it. Leaning forward and lacing his fingers together, the Prime Minister locked eyes with Daragh Ryan, "We cannot launch an outright attack, Emperor. If we send a force for a punitive response, the parameters of the mission must be laid out explicitly, and protocol followed by whoever commands it."

That was the start of the real tension in the room — because Daragh fiercely wanted to put the SAU down.

"If we're going to get their help in finding out what's happening to Karen McMaster, we have to give them a carrot to go with the stick," Craig B. Macdonald weighed in with heavy words. "I want to cut the fuckers down too, Daragh, but we can't just start shooting them."

The Emperor's eyes moved between the two politicians at the table — two men he didn't hate — and then he shook his head, "We're not just going to let them off with a slapped wrist. I won't be so trite as to say we'd be setting a dangerous precedent... most *sane* governments know better than to fuck with us... but I'm not having it. Public opinion won't have it!"

Well, at least the Emperor was speaking for the people...

"We could go in there and rattle some cages... demonstrate our ability against their military targets only. Compel their assistance in getting Merger into custody," John suggested, trying to sooth the atmosphere.

It didn't really help, because Pope had a clear concern: "No, because this wasn't an attack by uniformed members of their military, we don't have cause. If we do anything it's an effective act of war. We're just trying to repair the damage after Egesta... this would be proof that we're as bad the Imperial Army was."

The problem was obvious: if our Empire attacked another government because of actions taken by some of its presumed citizens, we'd either start a war or be labeled as rather self-important bullies... something that the Empire was probably considered to be anyway, but which we couldn't afford to play up to.

It was a difficult dilemma, but some folks at the table were beginning to see it from a different perspective.

"We need to get in there to find out more about the compound Grant used, right?" Mel spoke for the first time, and as eyes turned to her John was first to nod.

"The analysts haven't been able to make any sense of it," he replied. He didn't need to elaborate because everyone present was well-informed, but I will for you.

The compound that Karen had been hit with was, to quote one of Fengate Hospital's specialists, either completely engineered or of alien origins. Considering how unlikely the latter possibility was, everyone had settled on the former — this weapon had been genetically constructed from the ground up to be unlike anything we'd ever seen. Our people could pick it apart, analyze it and try to guess its purpose, but fully decoding it could take months, or longer.

If we were to get answers on exactly what it was, how it was designed to operate, and how it was shielding itself in Karen's tissue, we might be able to counter it much more quickly. Hell, the bastard who'd created it might even have come up with an antidote... but the only way we'd find out was by going out there and getting answers.

Had an attack been carried out in another state in the solar system, with Earth Empire citizens as the assassins, we'd have unleashed Defense Command on the guilty parties and turned them over to the victim government immediately... so our first instinct was to insist that the SAU government do the same...

After we smacked them around a bit, because they and their citizens had fucked with the Empire one time too many.

But that's why the role-reversal play doesn't work so well in this case: if Imperial citizens had done this to an independent asteroid, there wasn't much that asteroid could do to punish the Black Sun for the actions of its citizens. We could do a whole lot. Disproportionate amounts of destruction, in fact.

The question was whether we should or shouldn't… gunboat diplomacy or the path of peace.

Getting back to that day, public opinion clearly favored action — favored war…

"What if we don't recognize the Solar Asteroid Union government?"

It was Marshal Samuels, soon to be joining Pope and Macdonald in the Empire Party, who asked that milestone question.

"But…" Craig started to question the notion, then stopped.

What Marshal had suggested was entirely brilliant, and again the people at the table didn't need as much context as I want to provide, so here we go: despite existing for years, and setting up formal relations with the Martians, the SAU had never approached the Empire — never asked for formal relations between our states. Hell, they'd more or less kept their existence an official secret.

So what if we didn't bother recognizing them as a legitimate government — what if we simply treated them the way they wanted to want to be treated, as non-existent?

"They didn't start relations with us… if not for our interrogations and our intelligence service, we wouldn't even know they exist," John caught onto the idea immediately, looking to Daragh as he did so.

At the same time, Pope was looking to Craig B. Macdonald, and as master of the foreign relations of the Empire, the Scotsman was leaning forward with interest, "If we… officially, they've never declared themselves as a state. We only know they exist because of information we've gathered. So if we were to send out a mission to investigate the assassins, and to find their base and locate information that will help us with Commodore McMaster…"

He trailed off, and John picked up, "Then they can decide if they want to request official relations with the Empire, once they see how we treat pirate asteroids that shelter those who attack us."

You'd be fair in calling this disingenuous — us officially pretending that we didn't know the SAU was a multi-rock solar state. However, again, this was something they'd well and truly brought on themselves. You might not be familiar, but one of the first treaties ever negotiated at the neutral asteroid Ceres was the Meester Accord (named for Ambassador Yolanda Meester), which laid out the provisions for official recognition of any government within the solar system.

The government of every independent asteroid that we knew about had registered under the Meester provisions at Ceres — the Hawke Protectorate, the Coalition of Unaligned Asteroids, the Martians… hell, even Egesta's government had registered there.

Not the Solar Asteroid Union (or the Union of Solar Asteroids, for that matter).

From an official diplomatic standpoint, their government didn't exist. They'd never tried to deal with us, never so much as said hello. That being the case, they couldn't expect the same protections that an officially-understood government was granted (fairly or unfairly) under the diplomatic rules that had replaced the Westphalian State system back in 2087.

Which is a long and complicated way of saying: they weren't 'real' until they bothered to tell us they were. And if they only decided to tell us while a squadron of our ships was traipsing through their territory, breaking fragile things while we looked for Grant Merger, that was their tough luck.

"It gives us diplomatic cover," Craig B. Macdonald looked from the Emperor back to Pope, and the Prime Minister took a deep breath, then laid out the next question.

"If we were sending a squadron out after attackers believed to be returning to Grant Merger's lair... what would the normal collateral damage protocol be?"

That was a fair question, and everyone turned to John. Our First Lord narrowed his eyes thoughtfully as he sat back in his chair, "If they're declared enemies of the Empire, our commanding officer would have the authority to take whatever action necessary to capture or kill them. Any persons actively involved in attempting to protect those individuals *could* be treated as enemies of the Empire themselves, at the discretion of the commanding officer."

In other words the Articles of Empire, and the fleet standing orders that had been spawned by them, left the mission commander as much latitude as she or he needed under circumstances when a designated enemy of the Empire was involved. A recipe for disaster, unless you could give the job to the right commanding officer.

That was Pope's conclusion: "So if the squadron got out there, and the government of the SAU cooperated, there'd be latitude to begin diplomatic relations in a... more pleasant fashion. And if they resisted, there'd be latitude to punish them."

"And if we punish them, because we don't recognize them as a government, it's not war," Daragh concluded. "Best of all fucking worlds. Do it."

It was far from the best of any worlds, fucking or otherwise. But it was a compromise — a way to send out a force for 'retribution', but one that wouldn't have to necessarily attack the SAU, if the SAU government was truly ignorant and willing to cooperate.

If they wanted to help us catch Grant Merger, that'd be great... but if not, they'd have to get out of the way or be destroyed.

"The mission mandate is to capture the assassins, and their master, and to gather information that might assist in the treatment of Commodore McMaster," John said slowly. "No mention of the government. That'll be incidental."

His words drew nods from everybody around the table save one — and that person was soon the focus of stares from the rest of the attendees.

Realizing people were looking at him, Wes took a breath, "Is that the glare of me being volunteered?"

"You're a popular hero and a combat veteran. You going will appease the people," Pope said plainly.

"And you're also someone we can trust to use the right amount of latitude," Craig B. Macdonald added.

There are times when too much latitude is a bad thing, and Wes got the distinct feeling this was one of those moments.

"Fine, so we declare the assassins enemies of the Empire, then send Wes out there with what… the Belt Squadron? And some *Bonnies*…" Daragh was thinking out loud, but Pope shook his head.

"We send only what we'd send if we didn't know the Union existed. No battleships."

"Fuck," Daragh spat the word, but nodded. "Fine."

They'd spend a couple of hours sorting out the details — right down to the best time for the squadron to depart, based on orbital seasons. I think we've had enough of this though — you have the information you need, that Wes was going out there after the bastards, and that whatever he did would be perfectly legal.

You could hear the weight of the Empire shifting at that table. The sheer, lethal might of the Black Sun was going to move, but at least with Wes at the helm, it would move deftly.

CHAPTER EIGHT

UNRESPONSIVE

I should be telling you more about what was happening to Karen. All of the political ramifications, the plans, the implications… none of that matters compared to the very latest information about Karen's situation.

But Karen's situation didn't change. Not one bit. That was the worst part. She was stable, but she was in a coma. The doctors had no idea if she'd stay that way, but as every hour passed, it seemed less and less likely that she would simply die suddenly.

Still, there were no changes, and no answers. What afflicted her was a mystery, and what might restore her was unknown. All we could do was wait… the hated waiting that you never get used to, even when you're in the Navy and you travel long distances on a regular basis.

Sleep, at least, had briefly interrupted this torture, but that wasn't destined to last. I woke up in the middle of the night — I'd slumbered enough by then for the pounding in my head to have eased marginally. Rising from the cot I'd occupied in Shewfelt House, I popped a teeth-cleaning tablet into my mouth, changed into the uniform that my parents had left for me, and made for the door.

If you don't know, Shewfelt House is attached to Terra Nova Hospital — part of a chain of facilities that provide quarters for families when their loved ones are being treated. Attached to hospitals around the world, and with some freestanding care facilities, the Shewfelt Houses are homes away from home for parents, siblings, and children, young or old. This was the first time I'd ever needed to use one, and I can say nothing but thank god it was there.

I think we all recognize a good cause when we see one, and Shewfelt House qualifies. But when you're in a situation where you can't really conceive of being more than a three-minute walk from someone, you really appreciate the benefits a whole lot more.

As I left the room I'd been settled in, the hallways of the house were quite dark. I didn't know my way around exactly, but a sign on the wall directed me towards the walkway back to the hospital, and as quietly as possible (because there were undoubtedly children asleep in the rooms near mine) I headed that way.

When I reached the entrance to the glass-enclosed walkway that crossed over a dark strip of grass to the hospital, I found someone on duty at the check-in desk. This was interesting, as I expected the place to be shut down… well, it was shut down, but a staff person was still at the desk, ready to deal with any emergencies.

Noticing my arrival, she smiled and stood: "I'm Tracy, the owner of this place."

No kidding.

"I came over from Toronto when I heard what had happened. Wanted to make sure you and your family were personally taken care of."

Little things that strangers do can be incredibly affecting under circumstances like these. Had I not been on the verge of a psychotic episode, I might well have become genuinely emotional. As it was, I hope my gratitude was sufficiently evident.

"Thank you… I… thank you. I can't say I've spent too much time conscious here, but the fact that this place exists at all…" my words fell off, and Tracy nodded.

"Of course, but you and your family, and all of your officers, will have whatever you need. Everyone's pulling for Karen… and I mean *everyone*."

Yeah, seventy percent of the population wanted us to go out there to kill the people who'd done this — and to wipe out anyone who got in our way.

Tracy appeared far too compassionate to fall quite into that camp, but nevertheless her genuine support struck a chord inside me: I had spent the whole longest day staring at Karen in isolation, completely absorbed by what was happening, and missing the fact that others were shocked too. I wasn't going to feel guilty over my preoccupation — it was very honest — but going forward, I had to remember that others needed to be included.

Sounds clinical, perhaps — like the analysis of a psychologist or social worker — but I distinctly recall having that rational thought. Sleep combined with a bit of distance from the event was starting to have a profound effect on my state of mind, and while I could plunge into a review of what I think was happening to me, it's probably better that I just keep showing you.

Keep in mind, though, that from this point forward, any reaction you think seems odd… well, it's the reaction I had. For better or for worse.

Back to Tracy.

"I really appreciate that," I said. "I think… I think she's going to need everyone pulling for her, as much as they can. So thank you."

I meant it, though I felt rather more like a politician saying it than anything else. Say the right thing, the gracious thing — don't reveal emotional turmoil. Don't reveal anger.

With those words, I left Tracy behind, and returned to the hospital. It didn't take long to reach Karen's isolation chamber, and as I arrived there I found the only thing that had changed was who was on the vigil: Matt Baxter had taken over, and with him was Wes Pellew, arms folded tight as he stared through the glass.

Matt was the first to notice my arrival, and he moved over to me immediately to share the most vital information: "No changes. They did another battery of tests, but none of them have been able to establish anything about the compound in her system. All they know is it's in the frontal cortex of her brain right now."

I nodded slowly as I carefully processed those words, then turned towards the glass and advanced in its direction. I stared at Karen, and I remember forcing myself to feel numb.

"I take it there's no point to me encouraging the lab techs?" I asked quietly, and Matt's reply was clipped.

"Already tried, but they don't need coaching. This is a science issue: Grant designed this thing to be a mystery."

I blinked when I heard that name, then I looked back over my shoulder, "Why, so he can force us to go out there after him? Fall into some trap he's setting?"

Though Melissa had earlier suggested that Grant might be leaving breadcrumbs, the whole debate about how a mission could be politically sent out to the SAU had eclipsed such concerns. Knowing Grant, though, I had to assume the only reason he'd hit Karen with something that hadn't killed her by now, and which was apparently designed to baffle the Empire's science, was to draw us to him.

At this point Wes moved over to me, and with a strained expression he nodded, "I'm taking the Belt Squadron out. We're going to go find the assassins… get some answers. We think we know where they're bound for, and we'll find them.."

"Where?" I asked, not sure if I knew the answer after my catatonic listening of the previous day.

"Union of Solar Asteroids… a place called Etat Concord. They think Grant is tied up with another rock in that system… Etat Valcour."

I stared at Wes for a moment — a long moment, which he recalls as being uncomfortable, though I didn't notice. Then I nodded, "That's good."

I didn't specify what was good, or why. I let the words hang there, then looked back at Karen, nodding slowly. If there was a trap, Wes could handle it. He'd have the Belt Squadron with him. And if there were answers… ways to help Karen… yes, he'd find them. Wes wouldn't let her down.

Because I said nothing more for several minutes, Wes eventually drifted away, sharing a concerned glance with Matt Baxter. Both men had wondered whether I'd want to be part of the mission, or whether I'd be content to stay on Earth with Karen, to watch her lie in a hospital bed with a tube stuck down her throat.

Governed by reason, perhaps I would have thought it better to go — to help find answers that could save her. Governed by emotion, I would have to stay with her, even if my presence provided nothing but a spiritual balm.

At this time, though, I was governed by neither. I was switched off. High-functioning numbness that could quickly transform into other sorts of feelings, but hadn't just yet. And since it hadn't, I'd simply abide by the decisions of others. Wes was going, and I was staying with Karen.

Better that way.

CHAPTER NINE

THE BELT SQUADRON

Everyone on Earth expected the Belt Squadron to chase Karen's attackers, and everyone on Earth was obviously right. Though *Cheetah* and *Alberta* weren't with the squadron now sitting in orbit, *Nova Scotia* would join up for the mission, since Wes was commanding.

Now's the time for me to pause and reflect on exactly what that meant — or more precisely, *who* that meant.

Starting at the top, with *Nova Scotia*: Wes Pellew and his skipper Rozy Young would be heading up the operation, aiming to make sure that whatever passions had been inflamed weren't allowed to override good, sensible decision-making when the squadron got out to the SAU.

With *Nova Scotia* would be the frigates *Wolf* and *Lion*, obviously skippered by Andrea and Kris Jacobs respectively, and the corvettes *Friendly* (Matt Baxter), *Generous* (Isoruku Togo), *Sackville* (Katya Romanov) and *Lady Grace* (Kate Levec). If you look back to *The Rogue Commodore*, that list will seem largely familiar, and that was both a good and bad thing. These ships had long histories together, and while some of them had been split apart during the war, it would be beyond foolish to think that they were anything but formidable now.

That was the good thing. The bad: every senior officer aboard each of these ships had taken the attack on Karen personally. Some were obviously not that close to her — it's a big family — but others were very close. And none of these people, not even the sensible ones, were above thoughts of revenge.

Considering the potential for excessive force, Wes Pellew knew he was going to need to meet with his senior officers, and on the morning after he spoke with me outside Karen's room, he set up a face-to-face meeting aboard *Nova Scotia*, to lay down the rules for the mission to come.

All the ship commanders attended, including Andrea. Tension still existed between her and Wes, of course, but that hardly mattered under the circumstances — their personal battles were completely sidelined.

As the skippers gathered at the briefing table, Andrea sat furthest down from Wes. The Independent Squadron's Commodore — the Belt Squadron's Commodore for this mission — took the chair at the head of the table, and as he sat he wasted no time in beginning the discussion.

"As you know, I've been officially tasked with taking over the squadron for this mission… for now *Nova Scotia* will join in place of *Alberta*. Based on information Andrea was able to gather, we're going out after the assassins. The destination is a rock called 'Etat Concord'. Departure will be in forty-eight hours, and our intelligence about what we'll find is sketchy… but we'll get them. We'll get them and they'll pay."

Wes tells me this was perhaps the most stressful briefing he'd ever given as a squadron commander, but he handled it very well according to the veteran skippers whose dark eyes had settled upon him.

He continued: "We have unofficial reason to believe that Grant Merger is a Governor of a rock state in something called the Union of Solar Asteroids. But that Union isn't a recognized government under the Meester System, and they've never reached out to us diplomatically… so we're going in there as heavy as we need to, to get the assassins, and to capture him. He may be the only one who knows exactly what's in Karen's system… and even if he doesn't, he planned this and we're going to bring him in."

Everyone at the table stirred with those words — people were hungry to get their revenge on an old enemy who they'd beaten at Deep Black… but who had slunk away, rallied, and sent a back-stabbing attack against our family.

Recognizing the dark intentions behind many of the glares at the table, Wes went on, "We do have carte blanche to treat anyone supporting Merger as an enemy of the Empire, but that will be at my discretion. And as angry about this as you all are, and as I am, we have to remember what we stand for. I'm not going to let us get out of hand. My word will be law on this mission, and if I say we *don't* fire on something, we *do not*."

It was an incredibly rare thing, to reiterate that basic sort of order to the officers in this briefing room. The notion that any of them would be trigger-happy was largely alien… but at this moment, it was wise to ensure there was no misunderstanding.

No one responded to Wes' orders, so he pressed on, "We're going to make this a speed run, fast as we can. We probably won't be able to send any intel back to Karen's aid for weeks and that's a pretty grim thought. But if the doctors can keep her stable that long, we might make a difference. Our priority is to get answers, and to get Grant Merger. We'll decide how to accomplish that when we get out there."

They certainly would.

"Questions?"

Wes had covered everything he felt he needed to put on the table, so now he opened it up.

"Will Mark and *Cheetah* be back in time to join us?"

Even with the addition of *Nova Scotia*, the squadron was down by a frigate from its pre-war complement. Unfortunately, no matter how badly he wanted to, Mark Gunney couldn't get himself or his ship back online in time for the scheduled departure.

Shaking his head, Wes leaned forward in his chair, "Afraid not. And we're not going to take any other ships with us to replace *Cheetah*… or to fill in for *Honesty*, for that matter."

That was another good point: recall that we'd lost Mark's old corvette, *Honesty*, out at Io — along with its crew and skipper Aaron Ashby. Nancy Whitehorse and *Trusty* had joined us at Io, filling the gap in our line of battle, but that ship had been lost in 2233 as well. So the Belt Squadron numbered two ships less than it would have in 2231.

No matter.

"Grant Merger came after our family when he sent his assassins," Wes said with some finality. "That doesn't go unanswered. We're going to find him, find out what he did to Karen, and we're going to do so with as much force as is necessary. I know you'll all give better than your best for this… he's going to get more than even his plans could fathom."

Nods rounded the table with those confident words, and then Wes dismissed all the skippers save one. As the door shut behind Isoruku Togo, Matt Baxter stopped at the far end of the briefing table and the two men locked eyes.

"Matt, I know you were meant to retire, so I wanted to thank you for staying on. I think I'm going to have to rely on your sense most of all," Wes said. "You always know how... how to stop people doing stupid stuff."

A sad smile twitched at the corners of Wes' mouth as he finished his statement, but the words were almost like a dagger to *Friendly's* British Commander. For a moment he stood silent, and then he looked down.

"There was no chance of me retiring under these circumstances, so no thanks required," he said softly. "As for the other thing... Grant Merger just tried to kill... maybe he *has* killed... one of the two people I've spent my career protecting. If you're counting on me to be sensible, I'm afraid I'm going to disappoint you."

Sobering words from the man who'd for so long been like a parent to Karen and me... words that made Wes realize exactly how tough his job was going to be. Every one of those officers had a personal stake in this, and they were going to struggle with the discipline needed to do the job right.

Don't imagine that Wes had no stake in it either... but remember that he'd been through his own dark period of vengefulness. He knew precisely how destructive it could be to oneself and one's friends.

Taking a breath, Wes nodded, allowing Matt to depart and return to *Friendly*. Alone in the briefing room, the new Commodore of the Belt Squadron sat on the edge of the table and folded his arms, wondering how he'd keep the calm.

It was going to be difficult.

More difficult than he knew.

CHAPTER TEN

EMOTIONAL DISCONNECTS

They only let me in the room with Karen once. Again, due to the many unknowns about her condition, the doctors at Terra Nova thought it best not to insert too many presences into her isolated environment, for fear that one of us might inadvertently trigger a reaction. My editors think that sounds over-cautious, but I accepted it — the last thing I wanted was to watch Karen die because I sneezed.

All of that said, I think my constant presence outside the glass concerned them. So they decided to offer me a chance to go in with her... and I had to take it.

It was late afternoon on 4 January when they did — a few hours after Wes' meeting with the squadron, and my parents had the vigil, along with Shelby McLaws. I had become a more engaged member of the vigil team — talking to them, even trying to make sure I occasionally seemed upbeat — but when I had to start kitting up to go into the isolation chamber, my silence returned.

I had to put on a special set of medical scrubs, and stand in a disinfecting field for five full minutes before I was allowed to step inside. The scrubs, I should add, were equipped with monofilament bags similar to those in our uniforms... the difference was these bags would deploy if any sudden release of airborne pathogens was detected by the hospital AI. I also had to wear a mask and gloves, because the old-school ways of preventing contamination still worked.

All in all, it wasn't the most comfortable visit. The movies that boldly suggest I was able to sit next to Karen's bed and hold her hand while she lay in beautiful slumber are completely off-base... when I stepped into that isolation chamber, I looked like I was in a biohazard lab.

Approaching the side of Karen's bed slowly, I tried to see as much as I could without feeling anything about it. Without wondering about what was going to happen next, and most certainly without thinking of why. If my mind was allowed to focus on anything beyond the simple facts of her condition, I wasn't entirely sure what would happen.

I could break down, or I could *not* break down — and the latter possibility was the worse of the two. Either way, I was terrifyingly close to answering the question that I've posed in passing so many times during these reminiscences: what would I be without Karen McMaster?

Eventually I reached the side of Karen's bed, and this is where the movies would have you believe there was a touching moment — in both senses of the word. Some suggest that I took her hand in mine, others that I just let my hand hover over hers, and that somehow we shared a psychic moment through the coma.

Nothing of the sort happened. Even with the surgical gloves I was wearing, I couldn't stand the thought of touching her hand now. I was under orders not to for medical reasons, and that made for an awfully good excuse... but consciously or unconsciously, I was quite afraid that if I held her hand, it would be cold and stiff.

The hand of a corpse.

Karen was a goddess, at least in my mind. Had been since the beginning. Goddesses could be slain, they could be lost, and I'd faced that fear during the war. But this time was different… this time she was being destroyed. It was worse than the Phosgene, worse than the Fleet Clash. This time I knew someone had made specific plans to take her away and that those plans had been successfully carried out.

I knew that the man who'd been my best friend, and my single most formidable foe, had gotten to her.

But I wasn't thinking that as I stared at her. The ease with which, even now, I can spin off into long passages about what this felt like is a clear indication of how dangerous it was for me to be near her — recalling it still profoundly affects me.

As I stood there, I had to force myself to stop such thoughts. My eyes traveled from her still-pale body to the screens with her vital signs, then back again. I could barely make out her face behind the tube apparatus and the sensor leads… I couldn't see her neck either, because there were too many tubes and cables in the way.

This was Karen McMaster in a state of complete lifelessness. At least she was still alive… that was a blessing, surely?

Or is it better when someone dies suddenly, without suffering?

I know my answer to that question, but it doesn't bear repeating at this point. It's too self-indulgent.

Once I planted my feet inside the isolation room, I didn't move for twenty minutes. Outside the observers watched me through the glass, wondering what I was thinking. Eventually, the doctors came in for the next set of checks, and I made my retreat.

It was a generally unsatisfying experience. I can understand why the movies go out of their way to try to make this more emotionally engaging… why me staring at Karen's comatose form would not make for the best viewing. People need to be pulled into the feelings of the moment, right?

But the true emotions were the last thing I wanted in those hours, so I did everything possible to lock them down. I was somewhat successful, but under the circumstances, you could never be successful enough.

I was still maintaining the vigil when the sun set over Terra Nova. Shelby departed at that point, and because she'd be shipping out with the Belt Squadron about thirty-six hours later, she said her final goodbye to me. It was unlikely she'd be able to come down again, given all the pre-departure work that would need to be done.

My parents went to get dinner as well, leaving me on my own for a while… but that didn't last, because Andrea came to see me. She seemed different after the events of the ball, though I didn't know if that was her changing or me. Either way, I did feel she and I were much closer all of a sudden, and I was glad to see her when she arrived.

"Wes will be taking the squadron out," I said as she came to a stop beside me, and she nodded.

"He's… determined that we don't overreact. But according to the Emperor, the PM and the First Lord, we'll have as much latitude as we need."

Her words carried with them an unmistakable hunger.

"Good," I replied, then fell silent for a long moment before looking at her. "You will do whatever it takes?"

That was a question for her personally, not one meant to include the rest of the Belt Squadron. I knew that, perhaps alone of the officers with that elite formation, Andrea could do *whatever* was needed to make Grant Merger accountable. The mission had been granted full latitude, and she would be willing to use all of it to resolve the situation.

Andrea understood my meaning completely, and she concurred very simply: "I will."

It was a promise with immense consequences — one that might set her against Wes, against other skippers in the squadron, and even against some of *Wolf's* crew. Who would follow her into blackness, if that was where the capture lay?

But that was not something I'd have to worry about. My destiny lay in the hospital, watching helplessly over Karen McMaster. I continued to do that, accompanied by Andrea for many more hours until eventually I felt the irrepressible force of fatigue working against my brain.

"I need to go put my head down for an hour," I looked to *Wolf's* skipper with that admission of defeat. "Will you be here when I get back… or are you up prepping the ship?"

A few seconds of thought preceded Andrea's answer, "I need to get back to the ship."

Of course she did, because everything had to be made ready for the mission. The one I wasn't going on. I nodded slowly at her words, then turned to her, "Well thanks for the company. Go… go and do what is necessary."

A real thread of emotion was creeping through with those words, though what emotion in particular I can't now define. It was just difficult not to think about the implications… the notion that these people, my Belt Squadron, were going out there to try to save Karen, and to catch or kill Grant Merger.

Andrea turned to me as I turned to her, and she nodded at my instruction, "I will."

Then, in a move that surprised us both, we hugged each other. This was most strange, because neither of us was in any way healthily connected to our emotions in that moment. But we needed to hug. Perhaps it was the only way I could safely convey thanks, and the only way she could assure me that she understood without risking words.

It may not make sense, but it was appreciated. And once it was done, and we stepped apart, Andrea went in one direction and I went in the other, heading back to Shewfelt House for a nap.

Many days of observation lay ahead, so I couldn't afford to burn myself out early.

The Belt Squadron would soon leave without me.

CHAPTER ELEVEN

THE BLADE

That night I dreamed of Karen. This is perhaps understandable, even predictable. The dreams were vivid and mostly realistic — memories from the past, with some strange random elements occasionally wading through. I remember these dreams clearly, even after all this time, and for once I'm really going to build a chapter on them… because you need to understand how it began. I can't put that off any longer.

I dreamed of the night in the alley, when I'd pulled Karen out of the pub after the fight I recounted in Chapter One. I remember that night so clearly, and I lived it again in my sleep.

I dragged Karen roughly away from the *Sunburst Arms*, despite her resistance. She was bleeding from the stab wound to her arm, but it wasn't life-threatening, nor would it cost her a career. Being caught by the Shore Patrol, on the other hand, might have been quite expensive. I wasn't going to let her off so easy.

We hadn't gone very far before her resistance to my uncivilized handling became more pronounced, "Listen, I'm not going to sleep with you, so just let me go…"

This was what she thought my agenda was, you see — that, in some twisted way, me beating her in a bar fight was part of a mating ritual. Such had been her experiences in life… not pleasant, and certainly not healthy.

I shot a look at her after she raised her objection, realizing that she was beginning to lose the curiosity that had let me take her this far. It was necessary for me to get straight to the point. I was taking a chance here — a huge chance — that underneath the brashness and fury, she was what for a moment she had appeared to be.

An alley was ahead — we were coming up the main drag towards the Academy grounds, and between two sets of buildings was a narrow lane. I dragged her in there, and as soon as we stepped off the main street her resistance became less notional.

"I said *stop*," she finally wrenched her wounded arm from my grip, then stood and hit me with a sharp glare that was illuminated by a few yellow lights on the side of one of the buildings. "Thanks for the exit, but that doesn't buy you anything."

She sounded profoundly insolent. She wanted to make sure I knew she was not to be toyed with, that my ability to kill her in the pub hadn't made her into some sort of quivering girl. She thought she knew what I was about.

She didn't understand yet, though.

"I can't fault your performance in any way. You actually believe your own story, don't you?" For my part, I sounded like a smug student who'd read a book too many on the subject of psychology, and presumed myself to be an expert. This was what she picked up on, and the chance to deconstruct a self-important idiot tweaked her interest.

"Oh so you're going to screw with my head if you can't get me in bed?" she smiled and took her eyes off me as she began to pick at the wound in her arm with her opposite hand.

"Your hair isn't attractive. You should get a ponytail."

She looked up at my answer, though only for a second before returning her gaze to her wound, "You flirt a lot, obviously. You're a real player with lines like that."

I stared at her for a moment, then my eyes narrowed, "Catch."

Drawing the knife I'd taken with me from the pub, I tossed it gently towards her. Surprised, she just managed to catch it, and then as she turned it over in her palm she looked up at me with a frown.

I said: "You're smarter than most other people, and you like it. I know this because I'm smarter than most other people, and I like it too. Difference is I don't wander into a pub and try to get myself thrown out of the Academy. And I don't know why you do."

Karen looked from the knife to me with a frown, "What's this for?"

I tilted my head slightly, eyebrow climbing, "You want out, use it. Kill me."

It was either an unorthodox suggestion or a reckless one, and she puzzled over it for a moment before I helped her.

"That way, when I cut out your eyes and leave you here to die, it'll be self defense. I tried to help her, really, but she was crazed. I had to do it."

I sure sounded smug, but at least this time it was intentional.

Karen's eyes hardened, "Think you're some sort of killer?"

"You sure think you're one. Or maybe you're just trying to make everyone else think that. I don't know which, but I figure handing you a knife is the best way to find out. What's your move, you going to teach me a lesson or run away?"

I was goading her quite intentionally, and she knew it.

"No," she shook her head, then lowered the knife to her side. "I don't know what book you read which qualifies you to be a pretentious bastard, but I'm not having this discussion."

Of course she wasn't, because I was right.

"Then answer one question: why are you trying to get yourself thrown out? You're smarter than everyone else here, smart enough to see through my bullshit, so why not stay here and do a brilliant job and start a career that could make a difference?"

From smug to recruiting-vid narrator, and Karen rolled her eyes, "Seriously? What I do is my own business, and you stabbing me doesn't exactly grant you the right to have any input."

"Because you don't care if you die. Because your life is worthless."

Those two statements came out of my mouth sharply, and Karen began to fume.

"You seriously can't pretend to know anything about my life."

I shook my head, "Just what I've seen tonight. And it's been a joke. The old 'I'm misunderstood by the world and therefore will be self-destructive to prove how wounded I am' routine."

Karen's glare was piercing, and as I watched her fist tighten around her knife, I got ready.

"You wander into a pub, pick a fight for no good reason, and keep letting the odds pile on. Why? To prove you can? My friend Grant and I got involved to prove we were knights in shining armor, and to prove to ourselves we're as cold-blooded as we think we are… but you did it because you're being self-destructive. Because you think your life doesn't matter, and you'd rather do something ridiculous and get ejected from an Academy that's threatening to turn you into something useful."

As you can see, I was pretending I knew something about her life... turned out I was pretending pretty well. She took two steps forward as her eyes bore into me, "Really? That's your conclusion based on our long history together?"

"That's my conclusion based on the fact that you're still in this discussion. You're too smart to be that reckless without good reason."

The confidence in my words was a product of my youthfulness. I was so sure I knew what I was talking about... so convinced that I was as smart as she was. Later in life, I'd be far less decisive. The joys of inexperience...

Karen was losing this argument, or at least she thought she was — largely because I was actually on to something, something that she hadn't fully admitted to herself. She knew she needed to change the rules of the contest, needed to wrong-foot me, so she came up with a strategy that was either very unexpected, or entirely predictable.

Circling me, she backed up against the wall of one of the buildings, "You're right, my life is worthless."

With that, she raised the knife to her throat, pressing the blade up against the soft tissue on the side of her neck.

"Want to see me do something about it?"

Threatening to kill yourself is a pretty juvenile way to stop an argument, but this was different. You see, Karen wasn't actually kidding about this; she'd cut her own throat, as best she could, just to prove she was indeed the winner of the debate. Because I wasn't wrong: she didn't consider her life terribly valuable.

She'd come to the Academy because it spited the parents she despised — the ones who had never favored her the way they had Kath — and because some of the previous behaviors she's undertaken to defy them had forced the courts to send her somewhere with discipline. But discipline was not something she'd accept easily — not when she was right, and no one else was — so instead of playing along, she'd determined it best to destroy everything she could, including herself, hoping that it would finally cause her parents to realize what they'd so casually taken for granted, and ignored.

Dying by her own hand in an alley with a stranger was not exactly the most compelling way to go, but she'd be willing to give it a try. She didn't have much else to do.

This was Karen McMaster. Young, smart... arrogant, childish, self-important, deeply wounded and a complete fool. The only thing that separated me from her was simple: I loved my parents, and we'd always gotten along. I'd had the chance to grow up with their support.

And that, I believed, qualified me to help this girl now.

"I'll actually cut my own throat," Karen promised me sternly, and I stared at her, then nodded once in agreement.

"I believe you will."

"Even if I don't succeed... I'll seriously damage myself trying," she added, clearly wanting me to know that she was aware of the practicalities, almost daring me to try to stop her.

I continued to stare as she pressed the blade against her throat, and contemplated the logical courses of action. I could walk away and let her off the hook or I could go for the knife, and continue the conversation. I knew those were my two main options, and she did too. Either one of them would have fit neatly into some planned response she had — I would either be the coward who, like so many others, lacked the constitution required to deal with her anger... or I'd be a do-gooder hero who lacked the anger necessary to comprehend how profoundly wounded she was.

The third option was thus the one I preferred — and it was probably the single most important decision I made in my life.

I closed the distance to Karen in slow, even strides, and she watched me come with a defiant glare. She wasn't going to do anything until she saw my answer, and as soon as she did I knew she'd have words ready — something to prove she'd thought one step ahead and thus was smarter than me.

But in this moment, she wasn't smarter than me. When my hand reached up and closed over the knife, she started to smirk. Before she could speak, though, I drove my fist into her stomach, slipped one foot between her legs, and forced her to slide down the wall she'd been leaning against.

I crouched beside her as she fell, my knee across her thighs to keep her down, and one hand gripping her collar while the other stayed on the knife at her throat.

The surprise of my blows wore off quickly, and she looked up at me with venom... but stopped when she realized I wasn't trying to pry the knife away.

"Suicide is a sin. I'm Catholic... lapsed, but I'm Catholic. So it would be wrong of me to let you commit a sin you can't repent."

I pushed the knife into her neck.

She didn't believe it was happening at first. I took it slow — very slow — and there was nothing at all she could do. My weight was across her legs, and only her wounded arm was partly free. My other hand was locking her to the wall, and the way she'd been holding the knife to her throat, there was no way she could resist when I pressed my weight against her.

Blood began to trickle down from the blade, the steel not having crept down far enough to carry through the flesh into her jugular. At first she thought this was a bluff, but apparently my eyes said differently. Apparently my eyes were too cold, and my pressure too firm, to be anything but real. One jerk of my hand and she'd be dead... and as she realized this — and realized that I didn't seem the least bit concerned — she really started to struggle.

Well, tried to struggle. There's not a lot you can do when a blade is at your throat, you have no free hands and your body is pinned between the ground and the wall by someone who outweighs you.

I pressed the blade further, and the blood started to run a little more — but still only from her flesh, not from any of the vital arteries or veins beneath.

And that, at last, was enough: "Stop."

I didn't respond at first, though I halted the pressure.

"Stop it," she repeated, and there was something different in her voice.

"Why?" I asked her. "You have to say it, or I'll kill you."

She stared at me, then twisted her neck away from the blade a little. I made sure the blade followed, and she ground her jaw in frustration before speaking, "I don't plan on dying tonight."

"Why?"

I wasn't letting her off without a complete admission, and she blinked in anger a few more times before she finally conceded, "Because. I don't want to."

"Your life?"

"Worth keeping."

It's easy to think your life is cheap when you're the only one threatening it. That's just self-indulgent angst. Life becomes a whole lot more valuable when someone else is trying to take it from you. Under those circumstances, I think you're much more inclined to drop the pretenses and get over yourself.

Karen had reached that conclusion, and as she did I wrenched the knife away from her neck, then shifted myself off her, falling onto my backside on the ground. Her hand reached up and covered the gash, which was starting to bleed a little more profusely, but wasn't gushing as it would have been had I not stopped.

"You were going to do it," Karen's words were not in the form of a question.

I looked down at the knife in my hand, then looked back up at her, "You think so?"

She nodded, not taking her eyes off me, "I do."

In that moment with Karen, I could have become a murderer, and she could have become a corpse. Imagine how different everything would have been if my hand had slipped. How terrible was that idea? How irresponsible and arrogant, foolish and ridiculous?

"You took a huge chance," Karen had grasped the consequences, and her words had softened. "Why?"

I blinked, then gave my reason: "Because you're worth it."

I don't know how I knew that — obviously I had very little evidence to support such a claim. But I knew. I just knew... and she did too. Knew there was something that connected the two of us — something intangible, beyond intelligence or anger or emotion. We were just... together. And pretty much from that moment, the rule between the two of us was that if someone tried to take one of us away, the other's responsibility was to intervene.

In this case, it had been Karen trying to take herself away. In future, there would be others... many others.

Grant Merger was just the last and best of them. The only one who'd succeeded.

I dreamed about that night, and that alley. The only difference in my dream came at the end, when a wolf in a blue uniform appeared at the end of the lane. I was standing in front of him, frowning and wondering why he was upright and folding his arms.

"We're connected," he told me. "And we're going to leave her behind for a mission more important than you realize."

A talking wolf in my dream. Really.

Of course, it doesn't take a lot to interpret the meaning: my subconscious was telling me that I had to go out on the mission with *Wolf* — that to keep the pledge to Karen that had started that night, I had to leave her behind.

Fortunately, I don't get swayed by dreams so easily. When I woke up in the darkness of my room at Shewfelt House, I shook my head against the intense emotions that had built up during my slumber, and then took a few breaths to try restore the numbness that I was going to need to endure the wait until the Belt Squadron returned.

It was slow going, though — the dream had been intense.

Eventually I noticed the red light beside the screen in my room was flashing; someone had left me a message, so I looked around for the remote and then activated the display.

A message was indeed in my inbox, from a garbled address — probably junk mail, since I was in a civilian facility lacking Defense Command's powerful filters. A low-rate mortgage was undoubtedly mine, so I opened the message for a lark.

I shouldn't have.

"I know by now your scientists must have told you what mine told me: this compound is completely undecipherable if you don't have the key. But I have the key. I know how to save her. And I know what will happen if you don't get the key, and you don't save her. I hope you can find me. I don't want her to die. But then, I'm willing to risk killing her, as you once did, because that risk serves a much greater good. You probably can't understand that now, but I hope you will. I'll see you soon, Ken. I'll see you and together we'll change history."

The message froze, and sitting on my cot in the darkness of my room in Shewfelt House, I stared at the face of Grant Merger.

That was the moment everything changed.

CHAPTER TWELVE

VENDETTA

It didn't really matter how I got into the Terra Nova Palace's private kitchen. Even had the grounds been protected by blockheads instead of SF (who were obliged to answer to an Admiral because they had no orders to the contrary) it would not have been difficult.

What mattered was that I was there when Daragh dragged his feet into the bright room, and began to make himself a cup of coffee. The Emperor, you see, still wasn't accustomed to having staff — 100 of them, in fact — whose job it was to make food and drink for him, and to serve him wherever he pleased.

He came to the kitchen himself, and as I sat at the relatively plain table and watched his back, I distantly appreciated that the Irishman remained the man he'd been, not some self-righteous monarch who'd lost sight of what mattered.

I assumed, too, that he'd noticed me when he came into the room. I'd made no attempt to conceal my presence, and typically in these sorts of scenarios, the wily old warrior wouldn't miss the presence of an intruder in his space.

I was wrong; when Daragh turned towards the table he stopped with a jolt, causing his coffee to spill over the rim of his cup and drawing a line of Daragh-esque dialogue: "Fuck dammit hell!"

I didn't react to the words in any way, and then Daragh turned back to the kitchen counter for a cloth. He proceeded to wipe the sides and rim of his cup, then he dropped the cloth into the small puddle of coffee on the granite floor, "I'll deal with that later."

Crossing to the table, he pulled out the chair facing me and sat down. He didn't ask what I was doing there, or start any sort of conversation, he simply started to drink his coffee. He'd just woken after too little sleep, and he knew better than to try to manage a conversation of any consequence before the caffeine had come to his aid.

I waited patiently, because a delay of a few minutes was irrelevant. I did watch as a couple of the household staff swept in — alerted somehow to the coffee spill — and cleaned it up in barely two dozen seconds.

"Bah," Daragh waved a dismissive hand at them as they finished. "I'd have gotten to it."

The elder of the two household staff looked up at the Emperor and scowled, "Yes, Your Majesty..."

"The Emperor isn't supposed to wipe up his own spills, is what he wants to say," I offered the translation — a flat comment that no self-respecting palace servant would dare declare to his monarch. As a Defense Command officer, I had no problem saying it, especially not now.

Daragh turned his eyes to me as the staff departed, and then finished his coffee in a long gulp. Putting the cup down on the table before him, the Irish ruler of the Empire finally decided to open the discussion: "What happened? I hope she's not dead."

You could make the argument that his words were a bit too brusque, or perhaps insensitive, but I hardly noticed.

Shaking my head, I answered: "Grant Merger sent me a message last night. DCI is trying to figure out how he got it to me."

The Irishman kept his eyes on me, looking for any signs of emotion in my expression. Apparently there were none.

"I figured this might happen," he said after a time, leaning back in his chair. "Why me?"

I'll explain the implications of his question in a minute.

"Because you're not going to tell me no. Because you want to say yes, and even if you didn't, you owe me… you owe us both… for the coup. I'm calling in the favor."

Daragh's face remained impassive as his mind assessed my answer, and I waited patiently again. He knew I'd come to him because once he approved my request, it would be incredibly difficult for anyone to overturn him. Given the public opinion, and the sensitivities, this was a moment when Daragh's influence really was considerable.

That was good for me. And terrible at the same time.

"I don't think I'll make you turn in that favor for this," the Irishman said eventually. "I think it'd be indecent of me not to agree to your demands. But I'll make you tell everyone else."

Fair enough; I was ready to tell John, Greg, Marlene, the PM and Craig B. Macdonald, as well as Wes and the whole squadron… no problem at all.

"You realize, though, that if Merger called you, it's because he wants this?" Daragh's question was flat, and it drew a nod in reply.

"I know. But this trap of his… it's going to be as intricate as all of his old plans, and he's built it on imperfect information."

Daragh's eyebrow went up at that, and he leaned forward, "Oh?"

I smiled, and it wasn't even that cold a smile, "In order to start things in motion to get this attack mounted… to get all the conditions in place… he'd have to have planned it before our coup. He can't have expected that you'd be the Emperor. He'd have known Luther Gregory had lost, but he can't have known that you'd be sitting here, ready to sanction as much latitude as you have."

That sounded thin to Daragh, and it might sound thin to you too, but I was certain of what I was saying. I knew Grant Merger — knew the way he built his schemes. There was always flexibility, but you could wrongfoot him if his assumptions were incorrect.

He'd sent a message to draw me to him… but he couldn't have realized how much force, and how much latitude, Defense Command would be allowed to deploy.

"I can't promise you any more firepower. That's John's decision. I'll support you if you want to ask, but…"

I shook my head, "I don't need more firepower, just permission to use what I have. And you've granted that already."

He had… and as his mind settled on that fact, Daragh realized that the deft discussions of days past were all for naught. Because sending Wes out there to walk softly with a big stick was sensible, reasonable, and likely to yield a fair outcome.

But Wes would no longer be commanding the mission.

And as Daragh studied my face, he realized my command could lead to something very different than what had been discussed.

He wasn't the only one to think as much.

"You're going to leave Karen?"

John's question was incredulous, but it drew only a nod from me in reply.

"I don't think we can go along with this," the First Lord of the Admiralty was my friend, and that's why his voice was raised and his resistance so obvious. Sitting behind his desk, with Greg Noyce leaning against the wall beside the window and Marlene Stoll seated at the meeting table in the corner, the First Lord was grappling with what sounded like a plan for suicidal revenge.

"This is a trap," Greg added, folding his arms as he spoke. Remember that Greg had fought Grant Merger extensively — he knew the man's ways almost as well as I did. "Either he'll be waiting for you with bait that will make you fight on his terms... or he will let you destroy yourself."

"Wes wouldn't be baited the same way, he'll have a clearer view..." Marlene put in, her tone kind and her words wise.

None of it mattered: "I'm fully aware of the situation. The risks. But standing in a hospital and watching Karen is not going to help anyone. Especially not her. I'll lead this mission, I'll find him, and we'll have some answers."

"They could figure out something here," John shook his head. "Karen could wake up any day and need you. Or, she could..."

He stopped in mid-sentence, and it actually took a second for me to guess what had been coming next, then shake my head, "She won't die while I'm gone."

I sounded awfully confident, though looking back I can't manage to fathom any rational reasons why. I suppose I believed Grant would be too smart to actually kill Karen... to unleash that anger. Maybe I was just convinced that, had the compound in Karen been meant to kill, it would have done so already. Either way, I was certain Karen would not be lost while I was away finding her attacker, and the cure that he held.

Grant knew me too well... and I knew him too well.

But my certainty did nothing to reduce the resistance in the room. The three Admirals present had been friends and mentors throughout my career, and they were rightly reluctant to see me throw my life away with some sort of vendetta.

John finally put words to that notion, knowing he couldn't skirt the subject any longer: "If you go out there, it will be nothing more than a quest for revenge. You won't be thinking clearly, you'll get yourself into a tough spot... or people will be killed... or both. I can't authorize it."

I seemed to pause for a moment, then nodded and looked down, turning my wrist so I could see my watch. I was actually running late, but that didn't matter.

"Turn on the news," I said, nodding my head in the direction of John's office wall screen.

The First Lord frowned, immediately realizing what I must have done...

As the screen flipped on and John switched to a news station, he, Greg and Marlene all fell silent. Daragh was giving a press conference from the lawn of the Terra Nova Palace, and though he was already taking questions, the text at the bottom of the screen revealed what his announcement had been: *Barron to lead Belt Squadron in search for assassins.*

"I won't disrespect you by apologizing for this. And you can still try to overturn the order… he has no legal authority to give it, after all. But after the coup, and given the state of public opinion, I suggest you don't try to go against the Emperor, or me, on this one. Because if you or the PM try, I will personally, and publicly, destroy you all. And then I'll go find Grant."

This, you'll agree, was dirty. It was unacceptably arrogant, dripping with hubris, and completely insensitive to the friendships I had with the three elite officers in the room.

And I didn't care.

John looked from me to Greg, then Marlene, and back. He knew he was in a bind now; it would be a public relations nightmare to reneg on the Emperor's promise, because the people wanted their vengeance as much as I did. And I was the best public figure to get it for them.

Some upstart asteroid would be blown out of space, and the plot for a good action movie established — not reasonable, or sensible, or right… but entertaining. To three out of four Imperial citizens, that was most important.

And I'd leverage their support for all it was worth.

"I can't stop you," John said eventually, anger rightly bubbling beneath his words.

Just for the record, I'd betrayed him, and by extension had betrayed Greg and Marlene. These were some of our finest and wisest officers, but they were human… and they were angry.

"No," I replied. "I'm sorry to put you in a position like this, but needs must. I'm going to launch a personal vendetta using our fleet. I'm going to kill some people, maybe a lot of people, and then I'm going to come home and give our doctors the best chance at pulling Karen out of her coma. When all of that is done, I'll start trying to make things up to the three of you, though I may never succeed."

I feel like I sounded young again — smug and certain of the way things would turn out, just as I'd been that night with Karen. I can't quite tell you why or how, but that version of me had come back. Perhaps all the parts of me that had grown wiser with Karen were too busy grieving her, leaving only youthful anger and arrogance to govern.

Whatever the case, there was no stopping me now: I was leaving Karen, and going after Grant Merger. Just as he wanted.

CHAPTER THIRTEEN

DEPARTURE

According to the movies, I went back to see Karen one more time — I sat beside her hospital bed, either bathed in warm sunlight or clouded in gloom, and held her hand while I explained to her comatose body why I had to leave her. In one movie (the one with the sunlight) she even squeezed my hand — a way for the writers to show that she understood me leaving... because virtually no one else did.

The reality was very different. There were no exterior windows in Karen's isolation chamber — no sunlight, or clouds — and I certainly wouldn't have been able to sit with her, or hold her hand. She definitely couldn't have squeezed mine.

And she wouldn't have needed me to explain my reasons for leaving. Grant Merger was trying to play me after hurting her... and I had no doubt what she'd want me to do in that case.

Standing around wasn't an option.

I didn't go back to Terra Nova Hospital, then — didn't even get close. I left Admiralty House and headed directly to one place where we've never been in these books: my parents' house. There I sat with my mom and dad in the reading room. We filled three of the four chairs that were set up in a ring facing inward... what we've always called the 'circle of chairs'. Not terribly creative, perhaps, but a comfortable place where we had always talked.

And talk is what we did. With Karen gone, they alone had any notion of what was going on in my mind, and though there was no real way for them to change my plans, it was important that they understood them.

That's not to say the plans were concrete — I had no specific designs, no critical path to follow... I just knew that I'd go and find Grant Merger, and they understood that.

Most importantly, I left them in charge of Karen. As a military officer, her treatment was actually at the discretion of the highest-ranking officer who took an interest (she'd named Defense Command the executor in her living will, as many of us do). Since John was the one watching her closest, and since he knew my parents, I was basically asking my mother and father to exercise moral authority in her care... to make sure he did the right thing.

I know I've talked very little about my parents in these books, so my absolute trust of them might come out of left field, but in a matter like this they were the ones I could count on the most.

I was fortunate to have them; Karen was too.

After we talked in the circle of chairs, my parents and I had lunch together, then I headed for the Admiralty landing field where a shuttle was supposed to meet me. As I arrived outside Admiralty House, a dense fog had begun to move in — quite thick, as Capital Island fogs can be. It came because of an unseasonably warm spell that had hit Terra Nova during the afternoon; melting snow had sent moisture into the air, and with the milder temperatures that fog clung to the ground, and indeed began to freeze.

I could barely see three meters in front of my face as I walked down the path from the street into Admiralty House. When I stepped inside I found Greg was there to meet me — he had been nominated as the one to see me off.

"The shuttle is on its way, but it'll have to circle a few times and land with instruments due to the fog," he said to me.

That blanket was very thick, and even modern craft had to be respectful of it. Fog had grounded me on Capital Island a few times over the years, and this was no different. It was as though the island, which had previously tried to cast calm over itself with a blanket of snow, was now trying to keep me from running off on a wild mission of revenge.

Unfortunately, even the land I grew up in was not going to make a sufficiently compelling argument to satisfy me.

"You... need to be careful. We both know how well Grant can foresee possible threats," Greg offered that wisdom thoughtfully, and I nodded. It was nothing I didn't know, but I'd hardly discredit my friend and superior for offering supportive advice.

"We'll be cautious. I think he expects a certain reaction, but you know how intricate his plans are. If we break out of the expected mold, we can pin him."

Again I sounded confident, though this time less smug — I had won the necessary battles already, so there was no need to posture before Greg.

His observation after my point was sober: "He wants you to believe you can pin him."

That was true, and I didn't mind the reminder. This was chess now — from here until I found the villain and extracted penance from him, it was all chess. Plans within plans, games of strategy, cunning and guile. Grant Merger was one man who wouldn't give us the gift of stupidity... perhaps arrogance, but not stupidity.

And I had to be cold and sharp to meet him.

At last the shuttle was able to land outside Admiralty House, and when it did Greg shook my hand, "Come back safe. Remember who you've become."

I appreciated his sentiments, replied with a simple nod, and then stepped out of Admiralty House and into the freezing damp fog. The shuttle was not easy to find, but eventually I reached it and went aboard. With no further delay, I was carried away from Capital Island to *Wolf* and my vendetta.

The last time I'd seen Karen had been the night before.

Such was the way of things.

Andrea Kiley met me on the flight deck when my shuttle touched down. She'd been waiting in the observation lounge, of course, and when the space doors closed and the bay repressurized, she alone came out to meet me. There was no fanfare, no special attention; *Wolf* was preparing to cruise into a fight, and every man and woman aboard was keeping focused on his or her duties.

As I descended the ramp and came to a stop on the deck before our Irish skipper, her expression seemed warm. That, at least, was my interpretation of the look in her eyes. Whether she actually was warm, or whether it was just a matter of me coming ever-closer to her post-Egesta state of mind, I don't know. And it doesn't matter.

"Ship and squadron are ready to depart," she said.

I nodded, then turned for the hatch, "Let's not waste time."

Heading through the ship towards the bridge, we passed many spacers, and they all seemed to be looking at me. I nodded to each of them, and every one of them nodded back. Their faces were cool — professional, determined, and certain of the job at hand. There would be no hand-wringing from the crew. We might be cruising into a trap set by our old enemy, but the Belt Squadron was used to great peril, and our wartime experience could only make us more ready for trouble.

The fact that Karen wasn't aboard, and the *reason* for her absence… that was something different. I hadn't been aboard ship to experience any of the immediate fallout of the attack — hadn't talked to this family. They weren't pleased about what had happened, and they'd go wherever they needed to in order to make it right.

Wherever was necessary, or wherever I took them.

When Andrea and I reached the bridge it was quite alive with energy — not enthusiasm, but all the usual activity that came when a squadron was readying to put to space after months of orbital duty. Every department had its full top-line staff on deck, every section officer was preparing the departure systems.

My arrival changed none of that, though Jim, Shelby and Felicia did turn their eyes to me for a moment, perhaps wondering if I'd say anything momentous. I had no desire to do anything of the sort, and once my silence was confirmed, they went back to their respective duties.

Striding to the front of the bridge, I found that Battlelink was already up with the entire squadron. It somehow felt like an eternity since I'd stood before an entire wall of screens with Battlelink feeds on them… not since the flight to the Mars Convention had I been in charge of a squadron. It would have felt good to be back, had circumstances been different.

And actually, circumstances aside, it *did* feel good.

The skippers on the screens were all familiar faces, all knew me very well, but when I came into range of the bridge viewfinder and popped up on their screens, no one wanted to say anything.

"All ships ready to depart?" I put that question to them even though Andrea had already told me the answer.

There were nods on every screen, and as I looked across the faces I noted that with one exception, everyone bore the same grim certainty that I'd observed among the spacers of *Wolf's* crew. Kris, Matt, Isoruku, Katya, Kate… they were all ready to do this. When my eyes stopped on Wes Pellew, though, I could read something else in his eyes. Again, he'd seen this sort of thing before.

I should point out, actually, that Wes was still joining the mission, even though I was to be in command. Daragh had made that much clear in the press conference, and John had confirmed the orders while I'd lunched with my parents.

The First Lord hoped that Wes would be a voice of reason during stressful times, and keep me from getting too far ahead of myself. John was right. But there would be plenty to work out on the way to the SAU, and I wanted to let my friend know now that I'd be willing to take part in those conversations.

"Wes, you and I will need to talk separately about our strategy and principles. We can discuss them on the way. In the meantime, ladies and gentlemen, it is obvious to all of you that I am here, and not in Terra Nova Hospital right now. I am here and we are leaving Earth on a mission that might save the life of one of our own. I'm personally grateful for all of your support. We all know that it could be a trap, set by our old enemy Grant Merger. I suggest that you assume this *is* a trap. Assume that he's trying to get revenge for Deep Black. And I suggest that we all work together to make sure he's disappointed. I don't care what he has in store for us; whether it's a fleet or some sort of espionage, he will not find us so vulnerable as he expects. I will look to each of you for your best — your best fighting, your best thinking, and your best judgment. I promise you the best of my own, no matter what has brought us to this place and time."

It was more of a speech than I'd ever given prior to a mission, but it was important; I knew these people, these members of the Belt Squadron family, would be wondering how ready I was.

At this point, I'm reliably informed, they were all completely convinced I was capable. All except Wes, because he heard in my tone something he remembered from his own past, and he worried.

But I had no plans to fight DNR duels with anyone. Just the opposite, really: I was much more inclined to torpedo a dome and kill everyone inside it. That, you see, was much quicker than shooting each of them one by one. It also came with the added benefit of murdering their families.

So Wes needn't have worried at all.

Or, perhaps, he had to worry a great deal. Because thinking murderous and vengeful thoughts is no crime, particularly under such strained circumstances. The question he had to grapple with — and that I had to actually ask myself, if I bothered to — was whether I'd act on such thoughts.

That answer could change the fate of many.

For now, though, there was no one to kill; we had a week's cruise ahead of us to reach the SAU, and much to discuss and learn on the way. That being the case, I took a breath, then nodded.

"*Wolf* to lead, let's break orbit."

The Belt Squadron boosted away from Earth. Karen was left behind.

Let me put that another way: I left Karen behind.

I left Karen behind.

CHAPTER FOURTEEN
THE FOE

The thing Grant Merger missed most about Earth was bacon.

Growing up in Britain, bacon had been one of his favorite foods, and no matter what the scientists did, they couldn't make simbacon — a staple of asteroid breakfast cooking inside and outside the Empire — live up to the texture and flavor of the original.

Of course, real bacon, which comes from pigs, was not easy to come by anywhere away from Earth. Some domes on Venus reportedly kept pig farms to provide fresh-packed bacon for the Lords there, but for the most part the only bacon one could find in the Empire was simulated. It only got worse when you left the borders of the Black Sun and headed for parts less known; Grant hadn't tasted real bacon in six years, and he missed it.

That didn't stop him from trying to make the most out of simbacon, though. Today's plan: more salt.

"I think this is going to do it," he declared as he worked over the stove in his kitchen. It was early morning — the best bacon-making time — and he was shaking salt all over the strips of bacon that were frying up in the pan in front of him.

Sitting at the kitchen table behind him was Sonia Hart, wrapped up in a fluffy white bathrobe and reading pads that outlined the day's agenda. She looked up at Grant's declaration, then looked down again with a smile, "You're just going to give yourself high blood pressure."

Smiling at Sonia's quip, Grant turned to her, "And you high blood pressure as well."

"Goes without saying, but you do that anyway," Sonia's own smile was warm.

She wasn't just responding to Grant's comment as he bobbed around the kitchen and made her another hot breakfast... her entire situation was different than anything she could have imagined years before. The story, I believe, is one I've told you already: she'd come from Egesta on one of the transports that Mark Gunney had pulled out of there in 2231, escaped to the Union of Solar Asteroids, and now found herself the beloved consort of a man who would soon be President.

A man who loved her passionately and who made breakfast for her.

She knew Grant Merger in a way no other woman had. Grant was never the womanizing type — he'd tried to love others, but none had been able to keep up with him. He'd thought Melissa Fox could, but she'd never let him close to her — she'd been a spy, after all, and not the sort to falsify her affections in any way that would lead to Grant's bed.

Nevertheless, he'd been profoundly wounded when Melissa had turned out to be one of DCI's finest. As soon as she'd learned of that part of his history, Sonia had understood why Grant had remained so guarded for so long. But now, after her years with him, she knew he'd gotten past his regrets and fears. Every morning they spent some intimate time together, which was something she'd never expected to enjoy but which had proved very compelling, and then he made her breakfast.

The most powerful man in the Union of Solar Asteroids, and he loved her and made her breakfast every day.

"Alright, we're ready," Grant declared from the stove, and as he switched off the range he started loading two plates with the simbacon. The toast and eggs were already getting cool on those plates, but that was fine — perfect bacon would cover all other deficiencies.

As soon as the plates were loaded, Grant hefted them and turned for the table, while Sonia pushed aside a couple of pads to make space. When one plate landed before her she breathed in the aroma and smiled, "Smells great."

"The proof is in the taste, though," Grant replied as he sat opposite her, and then together (a little absurdly) they each took up a piece of bacon and began to nibble it.

They were like silly food critics... and unfortunately, salt wasn't the thing that the simbacon had been missing.

Sonia tried not to screw up her face, but it was tough. She was Belt-born, after all, so she would have had only limited experience with salty foods. British-raised Grant was more of a veteran in that area, but even he winced before laughing.

"That's not gone well."

Nodding, Sonia rotated the plate in front of her, bringing the toast to bear. She'd start with that, "I'll have the bread."

Grant grinned, but gamely he kept at the simbacon — it wasn't good, but it was edible, and he'd always believed it best to eat what you cook. Kept you honest.

"The reports this morning are that the Belt Squadron has boosted, and that Ken Barron is personally in command."

Sonia's news was a mood-changer by any definition, and Grant slowed his chewing as it sunk in. He'd expected this, of course — it had been his plan all along. But to know that it was happening was simultaneously a relief and a source of apprehension.

Now there was no turning back. The Union of Solar Asteroids, which for so long had buried its head in the sand and refused to consider how it could exist in a solar system that was increasingly under the thumb of the Empire, was going to get a visit from a hero of the Black Sun. And that hero was going to make a real case for the USA getting its act together.

Grant knew all this because he was genuinely brilliant. He knew what he was doing, knew the risks, and knew what was likely to come out of them.

If there was any chance of helping these asteroid states prepare themselves, he had to get control of them, and he needed them to prepare. Only a close encounter would drive home the need... only a crossing of swords with someone he knew, someone whose reactions he could manipulate...

"Everything's going to plan, right?" Sonia had noticed the change in Grant's mood, and his eyes remained on his plate for a moment before he looked up.

"Yes... yes. Ken's coming, and... it's to plan."

Sonia had learned enough about Ken Barron to know the sort of man he... I... was. She knew that having an Imperial hero coming in this direction, fueled by anger and revenge, was going to be dangerous, no matter how much control over the circumstances Grant had.

"You're sure this is the best way, I know," she said softly, then sighed. "Just... promise me this is going to end the right way."

Grant's eyes found hers, and the Imperial renegade's protective-gentleman streak immediately kicked in: "We're taking a real risk, Sonia. But I know Ken, and I know what I had to do to get him to come out here. He's a good man, he's just... well he's spent too much time in the Empire. He can't see the forest for the trees anymore. We might be able to change that... and if not, at least I know how to deal with him. But however dangerous, we must bring him here. We must prove to all of these people that the Empire's threat is *real*. Because if we don't, God only knows how long it will be until their talons sink into the Union. Until our last chance at a just society is destroyed."

He always spoke with conviction, and the passion behind his words appealed to Sonia. She wasn't like many others — not like the voters of Etat Valcour, who'd been seduced by George Madison's energy to the point that they'd made him Governor. No, she was his lover, and she was the only person he trusted when he had to say something for the benefit of his own ears.

She knew this risky plan was the only way he felt he could wake up the slumbering people of the Union of Solar Asteroids... and the only way he could, at the same time, draw his old friend Ken Barron to this place. One last chance to win a long-standing argument, and perhaps to save his friend.

It was a cruel world that made such steps necessary, but Grant had the courage to take them, and she admired his clarity of purpose more than anything else.

Especially his bacon.

She reached out across the table and closed her hand around his arm. Grant took a breath when he felt her grip, and then he finished eating the last piece of bacon and pushed back his chair. It was an invitation, and Sonia rose and came around the table to seat herself on his lap. This wasn't an erotic move — that part of the morning came before breakfast — but as she put her arms around him and pulled his head onto her shoulder, she closed her eyes.

"These are dangerous times now," she whispered. "Whatever happens, I'm going to be with you. Promise me you won't leave me behind anywhere, even if it's to protect me."

Grant had closed his eyes too, and as he breathed the clean-smelling air off Sonia's robe, the real weight of the day ahead seemed to settle on his shoulders.

"You stay with me," he agreed.

Sonia tightened her grip around him as he spoke, and hoped he meant it. She didn't want to think about the possibility of being left behind. Tipping her head back, she looked to the ceiling and offered a silent prayer.

She should have smiled, because the surveillance bugs that were infesting Grant's house (and just about every part of the Governor's complex on Etat Valcour) got a great closeup of her. The records are still locked, but I assure you, she was the picture of tragic-lover-of-a-freedom-fighter angst.

Makes your heart melt.

CHAPTER FIFTEEN

HELP FROM A FRIEND

"I don't really want to ask this question, but I have to: what are you planning?"

Wes Pellew's tone carried with it a sort of knowing concern that could be possessed only by a man who'd experienced great loss, and great rage, and now was seeing the prospect of the same in a friend.

That's a very specific kind of knowing concern, I think you'll agree, and it made me smile.

"Ah Wes, trust me when I say I'm not planning anything. We just have to go find the cure to whatever Karen has. That's my plan."

Those words were contradictory, but I didn't care. They were reflective of my purpose, and my intent, and as I sat in my cabin and watched Wes on the screen, he looked as though he understood. My declared intention was simple, and how it would be brought about was going to be a matter of improvisation.

"I suppose we can't really make firm plans until we see what Grant has in mind for us," he confirmed after a moment. "But that's not the only thing I was asking about."

Of course it wasn't. He was reading my expression, my mood, and sensing danger.

"You know I'm not going to be able to stand aside if you get... too involved."

He was trying to be diplomatic, and I think by any objective standard the Independent Squadron's Commodore was doing an admirable job of that. But he and I had known each other too long, so I cut to the chase, "Wes, trust me, I don't plan to kill anyone just *because*."

"Don't *plan* to? And what did we just say?"

My smile broadened, and Wes tells me that was rather unsettling. Of course he was paying close attention to my words — was very aware when I failed to explicitly commit to conducting myself in a manner that would be respectful of my previous standards for Defense Command.

Made it easy to needle with him, "Come now, Wes, it's just a turn of phrase."

It was and it wasn't, but there was little point to us debating. Wes knew I could circle on semantics endlessly, and I knew that I could never actually convince my old friend that he had nothing to fear. Why bother talking about such things, then? Instead, we'd simply speak of the mechanics of this mission, and how we'd deal with a variety of challenges, all the while silently knowing that we could come to a clash later.

"I'm not going to argue about this stuff now," Wes said eventually. "You and I both know what this is. I just hope that, deep down, you decide what you don't want it to be. No point saying anything more right now."

He was right, and I appreciated his candor.

"Good," I replied. "So, let's talk about what we do know. I didn't get the full briefing, but I hope DCI actually has useful intel for us?"

That should have been a pretty reasonable hope... but unfortunately Thea Fostopolos hadn't been able to volunteer very much. We knew what Andrea and others had managed to get out of the assassins who'd been captured, which was enough to point us in a certain direction (to Etat Concord), but in terms of what we were really facing, there wasn't much detail.

"DCI has no idea what we're cruising into. At all," Wes' tone was flat. "And I don't just mean Grant's involvement. They have a basic notion that the Union built the *Tharsises* for Mars, but they have no idea if the technology behind those monsters was actually native to the USA, or came in with the Martians."

"I like to call them the SAU... the *sow*..." I said absently, narrowing my eyes in thought. "So we could be up against a well-militarized asteroid state, or we could be up against a low-cost labor pool that the Martians tapped into. Interesting."

It *was* interesting, and my thoughtfulness at least didn't seem too sinister.

"Either way, they're a government that hasn't requested any official recognition from us or from Ceres. And they're harboring an enemy of the Empire. We have the latitude to do whatever we need to do... thing is, we'll be the first official contact between the Empire and these people. What we do could resonate for a long time."

With those words Wes was drifting sideways towards the subject that we'd decided we weren't going to address, and I tilted my head slightly and smiled again, "Of course it will. Wouldn't be any fun if we weren't getting to make history, now would it?"

Wes chose not to take the bait, instead moving to another technical concern, "Now, when we get out there, communications with Earth likely won't work. We're talking about a part of the Belt that's never been covered by DCC's network. We might be able to reach out to a comm ship for a while... but eventually we'll be too far."

Ah, something to explain: the Defense Command Communications grid that so nobly served the Empire (when it wasn't being hamstrung by the acolytes of Dave Caldecott) was not an omniscient presence. While we might all be accustomed to confidently sending messages to the farthest-flung corners of the solar system, the reality at this time was far from certain when signals were sent beyond the borders of the Empire. Depending on where in the Belt our chase took us, we were likely to fall out of range of the communications ships that would allow us to relay messages back home.

That meant we'd be entirely on our own out there — another reason why measured and sensible decisions would be vital from the mission commander.

"So we don't know what we're cruising into, and we have no certain way to call for help," I repeated, my unwavering smile seeming increasingly unhealthy. "Our only definite information is that Grant Merger is running part of the government of the place we're headed."

Wes didn't sound anywhere near as enthusiastic: "Yes."

I clapped my hands together and shook my head, "Can't wait."

I think Wes' reaction at this point was most fair: he stared at me, the crease in his brow deepening as he tried to imagine what was going through my head... and tried to imagine how it could turn out. More than anyone else besides me, he would be responsible for what happened on this mission... and he'd fight the uphill battle for as long as he could to keep our squadron within the realms of good conduct.

"There's one person I can call for advice," I said after a long silence, my mind tracking back to conversations I'd had the previous year. "Better send the message before we get out into the great unknown. I'll let you know if I hear anything useful."

Wes didn't answer at first, then he found the words he was looking for: "I think you'll let me know if you hear anything *at all*. Won't you."

The reason there's no question mark there is because those last two words weren't a question; my old friend was telling me that he wasn't going to allow any secrecy, any misbehavior. He was putting me on notice, and now I appreciate his effort. Then I just laughed.

"I most certainly will, of course!"

It was not a positive note on which to end our conversation. Indeed, it was arrogant, rude, and disrespectful — but that was fine. Wes wasn't buying into my agenda, and he thought he could stop me going out of control. How delightfully idealistic.

For now he'd heard enough, so he closed the realtime link from *Nova Scotia*. As he vanished, so did my smile, and then I sat in silence in my cabin for close to twenty minutes as my mind started churning over a variety of factors. When I plugged back into reality, I opened a new message window and started recording a signal to a friend who might be able to help with this mess.

If Defense Command Intelligence couldn't give me answers, maybe he could…

CHAPTER SIXTEEN

FRIENDS AFAR

While I was jousting unfairly with one friend who was riding shotgun on my most important mission, another friend was in a ship running hard for Earth. Charlie Peters was doing his level best not to overreact to the situation that was playing out... but it wasn't easy.

See, as is standard protocol for a warship in transit, the Hawke corvette *Krystal* was checking in twice a day with its allied comm ships from DCC, and that meant the news of the Belt Squadron's departure reached my best friend on the very day we left.

Imagine how thrilled he was.

Charlie was one of the very few people who had a realistic expectation of my response to this situation. He didn't have to try too hard to be able to figure out the state of mind I'd be in, and he knew that sending me out at the head of a squadron loaded up with people personally loyal to me, and to Karen, was probably a bad idea for the wellbeing of humanity.

As someone who'd been learning the skills of government so he could help Lia run the Protectorate, and someone who's naturally smarter than me to begin with, Charlie immediately recognized that a brash show of gunboat diplomacy against a heretofore undeclared government could lead to a state of war... and if the SAU-types had friends among the Martian fleet, then perhaps there would be a danger of stirring a new conflict with the Red Banner.

Granted, after the thumping we'd given the Martians, it did seem unlikely that those bastards would so much as raise their voices if the Empire crushed the Union of Solar Asteroids like a bug... but it was a possibility that wouldn't have existed at all had Wes been running the mission to Etat Concord.

And what about the Empire's reputation with the unaligned asteroids, or the independent belt? Acting like vengeful fools could do a lot of damage to Imperial relations for years...

So you see, there were plenty of things I could completely demolish if the opportunity presented itself.

Knowing as much, Charlie was faced with a difficult decision; *Krystal* was still bound for Earth, but it would just take one order to the corvette's skipper to see the blue vessel redirected to pursue the Belt Squadron. Because of the relative vectors, it wouldn't have been an easy chase... if you want to visualize our relative courses, imagine a letter 'V' but flatten it right down so there's a 140 degree angle between the arms.

Hmm. I don't know if that helps at all, but suffice to say that he could have ordered the ship to bypass Earth altogether, and given himself a better chance to catch up to the Belt Squadron before we disappeared into parts unknown.

It was a tempting option, but as Charlie reflected on it, something told him not to take that route. To this day, he can't rationally explain what possessed him not to give direct chase. He's told me that he's tried various rational justifications — tried to make the decision make sense — but ultimately he says it came down to a gut feeling.

"I was supposed to go to Earth," he told me when I last asked him, and then he shrugged. "Sorry."

If you think that seems odd for him, it really is, and he'll be the first to tell you as much. Maybe it was a matter of wanting to gather more intelligence from DCI, or to talk to John and Daragh, or to interrogate the captured assassins himself.

But none of that is enough of a reason for someone like Charlie.

Don't tell him, but I do know what possessed him to go to Earth. This is going to sound like mystical bullshit, because frankly it probably is… but I think he was going to right the imbalance caused when I abandoned Karen.

Someone from the old days had to be with her, and it wasn't me. Thank God he went. I will forever be grateful that he did.

Whether his absence from *Wolf* and the Belt Squadron condemned people to die as a result of poor decisions on my part… well, he cannot ever be accountable for my mistakes. And if you think different, send me a list of all your relatives, then put your affairs in order.

There's not a whole lot more I can say about Charlie here… he was on his way to Earth aboard *Krystal*, and there wasn't even anyone aboard the ship he could talk to about this mess, so he basically spent his time alone in his cabin, or working out, or reading… nothing exciting enough to carry this narrative.

Just know that he was on his way. Just know that, as had been the case so many times before, he'd be in a crucial place at a crucial time. Even though there was nothing he could do to change what would happen…

Meanwhile, a much newer friend of mine was having a tough time in the post-war world. Having come home in disgrace, and facing threats of all sorts of retribution, Bort McWebsbert had called upon the many friends and supporters he had on the Martian Asteroid Epsilon to protect him and his soon-to-be-bride Casey Flynnboldak.

At this particular time, Bort was unemployed, and Casey was making very little as a dance instructor at one of the smaller community centres on the Asteroid. They were living for free in an apartment owned by Casey's parents, and enjoying a modest existence.

If I say now that they were nevertheless the happiest they'd perhaps ever been, please don't throw this book across the room in frustration. I know it sounds sappy, but it's true: they were together, Casey didn't have to worry about Bort getting murdered in space by me or my officers, and they were largely safe because they were on Bort's home rock — a place where the Imperium's much-maligned 'common people' would never be convinced that he wasn't a hero.

One of my editors has pointed out that it seems unlikely anyone would toss this book across the room because of some sappy happiness on Bort's part. Hm. Perhaps my implication that readers might have that reaction was a passive-aggressive jab based on the fact that I'm not writing about happy and sappy things for Karen and me.

Apologies to Bort and Casey.

Anyway, Bort was home on this particular afternoon, trying as best he could to straighten up the apartment while Casey taught her class. This was a struggle for him, I don't think he'll mind me saying: in Martian society clearing up was the work of a woman, and though Casey was hardly typical of the Martian female, she did make a point of doing certain things.

But being underutilized, Bort felt like he had to contribute somehow, and the scrubbing of a kitchen floor seemed to fit the bill. Until about five minutes after he started, at which point he wondered how the hell any woman survived the ordeal.

Taking a break after fifteen minutes, Bort drifted over to his computer unit (no wallscreen in this place) and opened up his mail. A lot of what he found was of little interest — fan mail from local citizens, a couple of dubious job offers, and a lot of junk mail. Even the Martians in their authoritarian society get messages offering great interest rates on mortgages... and other, less wholesome things.

One message, though, stood out. It was highlighted red, indicating it had come from outside the safe confines of the Martian Imperium. If not for a few friends Bort still had in the military, it's possible the censors wouldn't have even let it into his box.

But it got through, and he opened it.

When I appeared on the screen, Bort was surprised... and then as he read my expression, his surprise dissolved into something closer to concern.

"Bort, my old enemy Grant Merger attacked a ball put on by our new Emperor, Daragh Ryan. I don't know if you know any of this, but during the attack his agent injected Karen with some compound that we can't identify, let alone stop. I need to find him to get a cure, or any sort of treatment. And we've learned that he's in the Union of Solar Asteroids."

That was a lot of information and it hadn't been blurted out in an easily-processable fashion. Nevertheless, Bort kept up as best he could.

"The assassins Grant sent came from Etat Concord, and I'm taking the Belt Squadron after them. What I need, though, is any information you can provide from the time you spent with these SAU people while you were building *Olympus Mons*. Anything. Their defensive abilities, their population, their political leaders... I am going to be insisting on their cooperation, so anything you can tell me that might help them understand they need to be compliant... anything."

I remember this being the point in the message where I began to lose any semblance of coherence. Pausing with a deep breath, I tried to focus and make sure I asked the right questions.

"We're going out there, and we probably won't be accessible through our own DCC networks when we get far enough away. If you know something, please send it as soon as you can. Let me know anything that might get me to Grant Merger soon enough to save Karen. I appreciate whatever you can do."

That was the end of my message, and you might agree that the whole thing was a bit of a mess. Fortunately, Bort got the point, and his immediate reaction was simple: he pulled up his personal copy of the file Martian Military Intelligence had put together about the USA before and during the construction of the *Tharsis*-class battleships, then attached it to a new message addressed to me.

The whole MMI file, which he wasn't supposed to have. Information gathered after years of shipbuilding partnerships between the Imperium and the Union. Bort bundled that with a message he recorded, including his personal insights, and he sent it straight back to me.

If there had been any question that this man was my friend, it would have ended right there and then. He'd just committed treason against his (admittedly stupid and impotent) government in an attempt to help save Karen.

We can get into the particulars of what he sent later — the package was exhaustive, and it would take me most of the flight to Etat Concord to digest it all — but for now I just want to emphasize the last part of the message he recorded for me, to go with this treasure trove of information.

Said Bort McWebsbert: "You told me once that you and Karen helped make each other better. At the time I thought I was glad not to have fought a battle against either of you without the other, because you'd both probably be hard to kill, and good at killing. Now I'll just say one thing: if you're going out there to save Karen, don't turn into something she can't make better when you return to her. Good luck."

It was a noble and honorable sentiment — the words of a man who had liked many of the people he'd met in the Solar Asteroid Union, and had liked Karen and me even more. He was concerned that I not turn into some sort of monster too dastardly for her to accept, once I got back with the treatment which would save her life.

Now I'm going to ask you to find the big problem in his thinking. The Asteroid Admiral was a hell of an optimist.

But all that said, he was also a good friend, despite the fact that our friendship was young and relatively untested. I remain thankful to this day that he was able to provide as much as he did… it made a difference.

And once he finished sending this vital message to me, he stopped for a moment, considered if there was anything else he could do, and then opened a new message window. He'd become an outsider within his own Imperium, but he was an outsider of the most dangerous kind — one with a loyal network of people throughout the territories he'd once sailed.

In the future, those contacts would serve him in the greatest cause of his life… for now, one of them might be able to help me in mine.

CHAPTER SEVENTEEN
PULLING ASIDE THE CURTAIN

When I found Bort's reply in my inbox a couple of days later, my jaw literally dropped. For two days I'd been keeping busy — touring *Wolf*, accepting statements of support from members of the crew who were hurting because one of their own had been so nastily attacked by their old enemy, and then waiting in my cabin around the time of every comm check with Earth.

If news came from Terra Nova that something had happened to Karen, I'd want to be alone to hear about it.

That being the case, I was alone when I started going through the files on the Union of Solar Asteroids — I scanned a dozen pages on my wallscreen at first viewing, but as it became clear that the information was too in depth for me to sift on my own, I knew I'd need to employ a group of minds to get through it all. And to figure out how to use it.

Fortunately I had the Belt Squadron with me, and in addition to being great fighters, the skippers, officers and crew of this formation were some of the brightest in the service. I know, I keep lauding the Belt Squadron and you're probably sick of it. But they were the best, and I'm afraid that you'll just have to put up with that fact. Sorry.

We were about halfway to Etat Concord by the time I distributed the file to the rest of the ships, without telling them how I'd come by it. I gave everyone another day to go through it, then I scheduled a meeting in *Wolf's* briefing room so we could all bring our heads together to review what we'd found, and come up with some possible plans of action.

This was all very sensible, which given my state of mind might seem surprising... but approaching a squadron operation this way was simply habitual. You can whirl off into an enraged and chaotic vendetta by yourself, but if you plan to use a whole squadron to get your revenge, it's important to talk it over first.

Also important: not saying to anyone 'we're here for revenge'.

"I want revenge, and these are the people who are probably going to get in the way," was my opening statement in the meeting — and I said it with a smile and a little bit of swagger. I was trying to make light of the notion that this cruise might be a murderous vendetta, and as a result there were a few smiles from the assembled officers.

And a glare from Wes.

Now I should explain: in the briefing room with me were Andrea Kiley, Rufus Chang and Jim Hannigan. The rest of the people in the meeting were connecting via realtime comm, and we'd brought in a bunch of free-standing screens and placed them around the table to try to create the feeling that they were actually in the room.

This might seem daft, but it was largely because there were so many skippers to link in that the briefing room's wall screen would have been cut up into a checkerboard to get them all.

A few printed copies of the Martian files were spread out on the briefing table for the benefit of those of us actually in the room; all the other skippers had the files with them, in whatever format suited them best.

The first question was a pretty logical one from Kris Jacobs: "So can I ask how exactly we got hold of all this pretty information?"

As I said, I hadn't mentioned the source of my intel when I sent it around, so the question resonated — a lot of people were wondering exactly where it had come from. And before I finish that thought, I should interject again and remind you exactly who 'people' were. On the screens were Wes and his Flag Captain, Rozy Young, as well as Kris, Matt Baxter, Isoruku Togo, Katya Romanov, and Kate Levec.

I was sitting at the table by the time the question was asked, so I shrugged and smiled, "Bort McWebsbert, actually. Don't tell anyone, or Martian Military Intelligence might have a problem with him."

While it was obviously unlikely that any of the people in this meeting would blab to the Martians about anything, I thought it rather important to emphasize that Bort was standing out on a limb for me and Karen.

Matt Baxter took that news with some surprise, as did Wes Pellew — though not nearly as much surprise as Katya, Isoruku, and especially Kate and Kris. Few people knew how well Bort, Karen and I had gotten along during the late days of 2233 and the first part of 2234, so there would have seemed no logical reason for him to be helpful.

"You... have some dirt on him?" Kris asked that question with a frown, and I shook my head.

"You'd like him if you met him, Kris. Truly. And he quite understands how serious it is that we find the people behind the attack on Karen, so he did me a favor."

That, as far as I was concerned, should have been the end of any discussion of Bort — he'd done a great favor for me and all of us, providing information that Grant Merger probably didn't expect us to have...

"But... can we trust information from a *Martian?*" Kate Levec asked a little bit sharply. "They were getting ships from these USA folks, right? Why would they help us take them down? Especially one of their Admirals?"

My immediate reaction was a flush of frustration, and I very nearly retorted in a fashion that would have been both unbecoming and unreasonable... but Jim Hannigan got there first. Fortunately.

"You didn't meet him, Kate," he said evenly. "I was besieged on Mars with him — he was very reasonable. He's Asteroid-born, not Martian, and I don't think he has any great love for the Imperium. We should all feel lucky that he got away from Mars safely after the treaty... I think they were going to try to hang him for losing the Fleet Clash."

All of that was correct, and I remember being surprised that Jim had those details — including Bort's need to escape — at his fingertips. But I wasn't going to complain; as my long-time shipmate looked from Kate's screen to me, he nodded once as if to tell me to continue — calmly. I did as instructed.

"We can rely on this intel," was my summary statement, and then I reached out to the table in front of me and pulled one of the printed stacks in my direction. It was a briefing document covering most of the main points about the Union of Solar Asteroids, meant to educate diplomats and military personnel on the political entity they were going to encounter.

I won't actually include passages from the report here, because the language is typical Martian bureaucrat speak... alright, *one* example because my editors are curious:

The structuring of the state of the Union of Solar Asteroids is fundamentally at odds with the structuring of the states of other states in our solar system, and this is largely due to a desire by the leadership to maximize the quality of those permitted to make the decisions by vote within the structure of the system, and with the recognition of the inferiority of the common people, and with the need for a cheap labor force, because of which we are able to leverage lower labor costs and sufficient production methods for the ships of our own Navy, even though heretofore we only built such ships domestically, but now we can leverage the construction abilities of these new builders to increase our production and to do so without attracting attention to our new hulls that might come if our counterparts in the tyrannical Earth Empire are capable of sensing what we build in our own yards, which is something we suspect as related in report 0X14452 issued last year relating to the fact that Defense Command seems aware of most new warships before we even launch them, and the need we observed to have the new battleships constructed in secret. This is good.

Yes, that was a paragraph of two sentences, the second of which was three words. You know I'm a crap writer, but even I'm better than that.

Anyway, the data from the briefing package was itself very useful: what the Martians had discovered was an asteroid state that was consciously built to be very different than the Empire or the Imperium... and they were cultivating a relationship with that state.

We, on the other hand, were getting ready to slap them like troublemaking cowards who were sheltering the declared enemies of our Empire.

"So we're talking about a society that's based around an elite and a laboring... class..." Matt chewed at that last word, because he's always found theoretical discussions of social class to be a bit unpleasant.

"Indentured servants," Wes Pellew agreed from his screen, sounding no less displeased with the notion. "Come here and work as slaves for ten years, then get your freedom and maybe the right to vote... if you live that long. Thought we got rid of that."

I have to divert into a bit of a history lesson here: indentured servitude in human history was a precursor to slavery, at least in the American colonies. The idea was simple: if you wanted to leave Britain and go to America, you could have your way paid if you agreed to basically be a slave for whoever paid your travel bill, for a period of around seven years.

This system didn't work so well, because the servants always knew that once they got through their period of service, they'd be free citizens again — perhaps even able to have their own indentured servants, though I somehow doubt that worked out too often. Anyway, when you knew that the guy who 'owned' you would eventually lose the deed to your life, you could be less inclined to do ridiculous amounts of work, or to suffer mistreatment.

After a rebellion led by a guy called 'Bacon' (seriously), the system was plunged into danger in the American colonies... so the plantation owners switched from indentured servants to African slaves. Those poor souls were an ocean away from their homes, with no legal prospects of freedom, so they were a more effective labor force.

Charming.

Anyway, the Solar Asteroid Union, in its unending quest to try to make itself into a new set of American colonies, seemed to have adopted indentured service as an immigration policy... though with a few differences.

"So let me follow this," Kate Levec spoke up for some clarification, which is convenient for us now: "You want to get out of wherever you're living. You either have the money to pay your way to USA... and you arrive unindentured and free... or you go to a USA immigration mission in one of the independent rocks..."

"They probably have some inside the Empire, too," Kris interjected quickly, drawing a nod from Kate. Then *Lady Grace's* new skipper continued.

"If they pay your way, then you're property of the government for ten years. A ward of the state, and also a laborer for the state?"

That drew nods from around the table. Old American indentured service was, I believe, a private matter... but if you came to the SAU with nothing, the government of that state would put you to work until you paid off your debt to their society.

Small wonder the SAU yards were able to build the *Tharsis*-class battleships more cost-effectively and secretly than any Martian yards would have managed — the SAUs had a limitless labor pool.

And just to finish the picture for you: while you were indentured you couldn't vote. Only once you completed your time serving the state were you set free, at which point you could be considered for citizenship if you applied. It wasn't guaranteed.

Sound like a backwards way to run a society? I think so too, and if you're currently reading this from the USA, consider my opinion to be another reason to hate me. But contrast the experience of an indentured servant with that of a person who shows up in the SAU with money: citizenship can be purchased for a downpayment and an agreement to abide by the state tax schedule.

Alternately, if you can be sponsored by an existing citizen in good standing, you can be brought in as a citizen without a downpayment... provided you have some skill or quality to offer the broader society.

All of this adds up to a culture in which 'people of quality' are granted the ability to become citizens and contribute quickly to the SAU state, while people looking for an escape to a different realm are expected to work as slaves for a decade to earn their right to simply live as free individuals.

And after that, they *might* gain voting rights.

"Amazing this hasn't led to a revolution," Isoruku Togo made that observation after Kate finished her summary, and it was Andrea Kiley's bitter response that highlighted what I think is the secret to the SAU's survival.

"Military service guarantees citizenship," she said sharply. "Anyone serving in their military probably wouldn't have much sympathy for any indentured servants trying to jump the queue."

Talk about different cultures found in different armed forces... the SAU military would support its government because all of its members had a real shot at being *part* of that government.

It all left a bad taste in my mouth then, and it still does now. And while I think it's fair to say that in practice the whole system didn't work as brutally as it looked on paper, I still had (and have) a tough time understanding why anyone would hate our Empire so much as to flee to such a place.

In this Empire, you are *free*. You can do whatever you want to do and live however you want to live, provided you don't interfere in someone else's right to do the same. Yes there are some exceptions to that broad principle, but not many. Equality is mandated by the Articles of Empire, and for all our constitution's flaws, I think Luther Gordon the Great got that completely right.

Anyway, all of this knowledge was useful as we cruised into SAU space, but we had far more to discuss.

"The question is how much control one Governor can have over all their military," Matt Baxter put that subject on the table, and as we all were drawn back to more pertinent matters, I flipped open one of the files before me.

The Asteroid Union had a dozen colonies, and Etat Valcour belonged to George Madison, the man we knew had to be Grant.

Unfortunately, the Martian files didn't include any navigation information. We couldn't simply go straight to him, but we did have some data about the place he'd been elected to run.

"Valcour… seems to be one of the smaller rocks. Mining based, no shipyards… largely harmless…" Katya Romanov was reading that from the same page I was looking at, and her words drew nods from everyone again.

"I'm guessing if anything, he'd be pulling strings from behind a curtain," Kris commented, and there were more nods. Lots of agreeing, it seemed.

"Why do you think the Martians don't have nav data for the Union?" Kate was asking a lot of questions — helpful questions, frankly — and that caused many of us to look up from what we were reading.

Matt answered, "Seems to me that the fact the Martians needed their intelligence folks to put together a report like this in the first place suggests the USA is being pretty secretive about their makeup."

"Like the Chinese after contact with the west," Rufus contributed quietly. "Confine relations to the outside world to certain authorized cantons. Etat Concord."

Sorry, I know this chapter is already heavy on explanation, but it's all important — especially Rufus' point. The SAU strategy to make sure their state was largely safe from the boorish Empire, and even from the seemingly-friendly Imperium, was to limit interaction with all outside traders to just one of their member colonies, Etat Concord.

No nav data for the rest of the Union was distributed to outsiders, and indeed, it was rather closely guarded. This makes sense, I suppose — if you're trying to become a serious player in the Meester State System, being secretive gives you the chance to increase your strength and your economy to a significant level before tipping your hand to the other major powers.

Also, if your Navy is a pathetic piece of shit, discretion protects your stupid colonies from attack by governments who might want your resources.

That last point is daft, though, because no serious government — particularly not ours — starts a war for asteroid resources. If we even wanted more asteroids, we'd just go claim the damned things. It's not like there's a shortage. You'd have to be pretty full of yourself to assume that some big government would want to come along and take your rocks, just because you'd put a dome on them. Nevertheless, those are the sorts of worries that could be kept at bay by remaining secretive.

"So we get to Concord, find the assassins, then acquire some nav data from them that will lead us to Grant?" Kris got to the point, and I paused for a second.

As I contemplated what to say, I felt Wes' stare settling one me... though, of course, because this was over comm, his stare could have been settling on any of the people on his screen. No, he was staring at me.

"Maybe," I said eventually. "Or we could find the capital... do we know what the capital is called?"

"Lexington," Matt replied dryly. "They're hardly subtle."

I grunted my agreement, though there were confused looks from a few skippers who hadn't specialized in history.

"They're naming their colonies after battles from the American Revolution," Matt explained, again saying the words as if they tasted sour. "Lexington, Concord, Valcour, Saratoga, Johnstown..."

It was yet another sign of how determined these asteroid people were to make themselves into the second coming of the United States — rather an unfair tactic, since the first coming of the USA was still doing fine on Earth. Just ask Shelby McLaws, our resident American.

I suppose that shouldn't irritate me as much as it does — when they were creating their own national iconography, the Americans did borrow liberally from previous greats, like the Greeks. All their capitol-style architecture was right out of Herodotus, Plutarch, and the rest.

Anyway, sorry about the continued tangents.

"We may not go straight for Grant," I said, getting back to the original question that was still earning me Wes' glare. "We'll see how cooperative the locals are, and if I think there's a chance we can do this more diplomatically, we might go to Lexington. See the President. Maybe if he realizes how dangerous one of his Governors is, he'll offer state cooperation."

Nobody looked too convinced when I said that last part, but Wes seemed slightly relieved — it appeared that I was willing to possibly consider a more sensible approach that might not start a war... provided these SAU types weren't a bunch of fools.

And provided I wasn't lying.

"There's one wrinkle," Matt Baxter added after a moment's pause. "Look at the notes about Concord's defensive arrangements... page seventy-three."

Every officer in the meeting started flipping or scrolling to the page Matt had indicated, but Rufus Chang was well ahead of us all: "Part of the deal for the *Tharsises* was that the Martians would guard Concord."

I stopped flipping as Rufus spoke, then continued to the page he mentioned. At first I saw no mention of such arrangement, and I hadn't noticed it during my earlier scans of the file... but as with so many things, the devil was in the fine print, near the bottom.

"A guardship," Isoruku said as he read it. "Do you think that agreement is still in force?"

The file we were reviewing wasn't necessarily up-to-date — it certainly hadn't been revised since the treaty had been signed — so it was possible the arrangement had ended. But if it hadn't...

"We should assume that the Martians will still be there," Wes advised wisely from his screen.

"Why would they..." Katya started to ask, then stopped. There was no point asking, and indeed, I've done more than enough explaining in this chapter — I'll leave a discussion of the SAU defensive strategy for later.

For now, I could feel Wes staring at me hard again, "We'll have to be even more cautious. It's not likely that anything we do would re-start the war... but still, that's not a chance we can take."

"They'd be fools to pick a fight they'd lose," Andrea said that as much to disagree with Wes as to make the observation, and the venom in her tone earned some awkward looks of surprise from people on screens.

I didn't notice.

"Tell that to the spacers who have to leave home to start fighting all over again," the Commodore of the Independent Squadron countered immediately, his tone hardening.

Andrea was about to come back with something, but I had tuned out the exchange and began issuing directives instead, "We're going to get what we need. Before the war, we used to be awfully good at coercing Martian ships into getting out of our way, so we'll just have to do that again. For now I'm not worried about a red guardship, I'm worried about what Grant might have waiting for us. Ideas?"

That, in the end, was the biggest question — because we all had to assume that Grant knew he'd have left sufficient breadcrumbs for us to find Concord. Would he have a trap there waiting for us, or would he be counting on us to come all the way to him?

No way to know, so we'd have to consider as many possibilities as we could imagine.

Unfortunately, instead of imaginings, it was silence that came after my question — no one knew quite what to suggest.

"That's what I was afraid of," I said, then smiled. "Guess we'll have to wing it, eh Wes?"

If he could have, I think Wes would have punched me. Glad we were on different ships.

The meeting went on, and eventually we started to come up with a list of things we figured Grant might try. But as was always the case when my old friend planned something, the cards all seemed to be in his hand. We'd have to wait and see.

You, however, won't have to wait for his next words...

Chapter Eighteen

Noble Governor

Julie Pichot had been asked to come into the main office to take notes during an important meeting. For the youngish staffer in the Governor's office on Etat Valcour, this was a major opportunity — and proof that she'd earned her place on what was a very tight-knit team.

And since Julie was actually a DCI spy, whose name wasn't really Julie, it was even better. Of course she'd seeded the entire Governor's complex with all sorts of bugs that were undetectable to Grant Merger's science, so she could have probably viewed the meeting later from the clean room she'd set up in her modest quarters... but the fact that she'd be inside, taking the notes, was a major sign of confidence.

It also meant that finally, for the first time, she got to experience firsthand how Grant Merger ran a meeting of his key people.

"So we've confirmed he's brought the entire Belt Squadron?" the Governor who went by the moniker George Madison asked his Chief Security Advisor, a man named Fletcher Karadzic, who I'd shot at a few times in my life, and who'd managed to escape Deep Black along with Grant.

He had done well for himself since then, it seemed — and apparently he didn't feel the need to use an alias in his new life.

Now Fletcher nodded, "The whole surviving squadron, but short one frigate because *Alberta* was back at the Belt. And they replaced *Cheetah* with *Nova Scotia*, from the Independent Squadron."

It was good intelligence, though not that difficult to come by if one had access to any news broadcasts coming out of the Empire. We hadn't exactly departed in secrecy, which might have been an error, or might just have been a courtesy. No matter what Grant would have known we were coming; might as well make sure he knew we wanted him to know we were coming. If that makes any sense.

Grant sat back in his chair as he digested the information.

Eventually he glanced at Sonia Hart, a frown creasing his brow, and she responded with a not-too-firm question: "More than you were expecting?"

The movies will teach you that villains don't like to be questioned in front of others. You can usually identify a hero — or at least a good person — by the way he or she handles real or perceived challenges to his or her authority. If an innocent question sets that person off, you know you're dealing with a baddie.

Grant, for his part, shrugged and then nodded, "I didn't factor in the mood of the people after the coup. And Daragh. That's a key factor I couldn't predict. I should have changed the attack plan when I learned he was the new Emperor... but too late now..."

Pausing, my old friend let thoughts work over in his head before letting out a sigh, "Yes, any other Emperor would have fought against sending such a strong force out here.

But Daragh has taken this personally. That's fine, though. It doesn't change the main structure. In fact, it might even help us. The more damage they do, the stronger our case is to the citizens."

Julie had worked out much of what Grant was up to by this point, but it struck her as both odd and uncomfortable to hear him speak so plainly about his plans. He wanted a Defense Command incursion into Union space, so that he could lead the effort to turn it back, and then later be lauded by voters as the one with the ability to stop the evil forces of the Black Sun.

He'd be president within months, provided he *could* control my rage.

"The fleet is ready… and its commander is confident…" Karadzic offered that observation with a fairly skeptical tone, drawing a smile from Grant.

"I'm sure he's eager. I'm still not convinced he's competent."

"Who do we have who is, aside from you?" Sonia interjected, and she wasn't sucking up. One of the problems with the Union of Solar Asteroids was talent. So many of the SAU leaders were failed bureaucrats looking to start over, so many of its military officers were disgraced egotists who had sought out the only place where their 'skills' could purchase them the rank they sorely wanted.

A few of these people proved to be excellent, but none of them were experienced fleet commanders. Eventually Grant had been able to recruit one, but still, the man in question (who I won't yet name) was hardly the combat officer that I was, or the battle commander that Grant had been before taking up his desk.

Still, it was a task he had to delegate — because the desk was more important.

"He'll have to do," Grant said eventually. "And I want our escape routes well guarded, checked and re-checked. If Ken does get through, we operationalize the escape narrative. If we contain him, we use the narrative about recognizing the threat, and positioning the resources to defend the Union."

You have to understand, Grant has plans for every eventuality. Okay, perhaps not *every* eventuality — if humanoid wolves, cats and bears showed up in his Union, he'd likely need twenty minutes to figure out what to do with them — but just about anything that could actually happen was covered, no matter how unlikely. If we beat his fleet, there was one plan… if his fleet beat us, there was another.

"Where do you think Barron goes first?" Karadzic put that question to his leader, knowing that no intelligence harvested by his nascent network of spies could compare to Grant's opinion.

The Governor paused again — he likes his pauses — and then shrugged, "He could come directly here, or he could try a stop at Lexington. Either way will work to our advantage, as long as we know which he's chosen."

The Security Advisor nodded at the words — he was confident, as many of Grant's followers were, that the Briton had the situation well in hand. They had reason for their confidence.

"So, no warning to the shooters on Concord?" Sonia posed that question directly, and Grant shook his head.

"They've been good operatives, but now's the time to put them down. We'll let Ken do that for us…" Grant replied casually, because killing was no major issue for him. "We'll also need to triple check our security here... because I know Ken may have tried to send ahead a spy. Any new arrivals will need to be checked closely."

Julie was careful not to react visibly to that comment, but immediately her mind began reviewing all her measures for secrecy. There was no reasonable way anyone could find her out... she'd even had cosmetic surgery to make certain she didn't look the same way she once had. That's dedication, and an understanding of how dangerous this environment could be.

But as those concerns began to play out in her mind, Julie's ears picked up one more comment that, I think, is rather important.

"And we need to prepare the signal. The Belt Squadron will be doing their last effective comm check with Earth tomorrow," Sonia said.

Julie had no idea what signal the woman was referring to, but Grant obviously did, and he began to nod.

"Right."

Then he paused, taking a deep breath and frowning as he looked down his desk. It was clear this next decision was a tough one for him, but nevertheless it was essential — he couldn't come this far and turn back now.

"So when Ken gets the last word from the Empire, Karen will have died," my old friend said quietly.

Julie again succeeded in showing no reaction, which was good, because Grant's eyes rose from his desk and crossed hers before returning to Sonia.

"We're sure he's not going to hear that news and turn around?" Karadzic asked, and Grant shook his head.

"He couldn't do that. No, he'll come looking for me. We'll have to be ready."

Of course they would, because of all the people you've read about in this series, with the exception of my parents, Grant knew me the longest. Obviously we hadn't kept in touch, but he knew what I'd be like in a world with Karen dead.

"All I can hope," Grant said after a time, "is that he realizes this was for a greater cause. Maybe he'll even see reason to join us..."

It was hopelessly wishful thinking, and Sonia looked at Julie with sad eyes when she heard the words. Of course Grant hoped that his oldest friend might be redeemed... but such redemption, while appealing to one part of his character, had taken a back seat to the villain's life mission: to try to stop the Empire, before it shattered human civilization.

Such a massive task demanded sacrifices.

As I was about to learn.

CHAPTER NINETEEN
NO POINT WAITING

Why should I draw this out, except for the fact that I don't want to write it? Grant Merger made me wait… made me hope… made me think that maybe I could get to Concord without receiving the one message, the only message, that would change everything.

I'd left Earth with the sort confidence that usually accompanies rage; if I could make it all the way to the SAU without hearing that Karen's condition had worsened, then clearly that meant she'd survive for however long it took for me to come back with answers.

I held onto that certainty, and I believe it was the only thing that partially countered the anger that was swelling inside. The spitefulness and irrationality that you've been seeing… the aspects of my personality that had long been dormant, but which had never truly disappeared.

Karen's presence had made me bury those old ways — made me a better officer. But now her absence allowed them to resurface… and the news itself…

No coyness.

I was sitting in my cabin, thinking about the SAU and occasionally flipping through the Martian intel file, learning all I could. There would be no time to waste when we reached our destination — no time to stop to do our homework — so I wanted to know as much as I could know, as quickly as I could know it.

That was a good distraction, and I hoped it would get me through the final comm check before we crossed out of the natural range for our comm network. No such luck.

I knew something was wrong when I turned on my screen, to find no mail had been deposited in my box by Felicia Khalid's staff. There was always something for me in an Earth communiqué — not always something important, but trust me when I tell you that, once you hit Admiral, the spam mail starts to get pretty tremendous.

But there was nothing.

I started to worry… though I made every effort to control that worry. There could be plenty of reasons for a delay in receiving messages… or maybe we'd lost contact without realizing it until our scheduled final check-in. Maybe I was in the clear, could proceed with uninformed clarity about Karen's condition — could remain certain for the rest of the cruise…

Andrea Kiley knocked on my door.

I opened the door.

She stepped in.

She looked grave.

She spoke exactly these words: "We have a report from Admiralty House. Karen passed away last night."

She then fell silent, and she stared at me.

I stared at her. I stared at Andrea Kiley and I didn't process the words she said at all. I didn't understand what she meant when she said that Karen had passed away. Because that hadn't happened.

"There was also a news report. Jessica Qing did the news report."

It hadn't happened. Andrea was mistaken because Karen could not have passed away.

What did 'passed away' even mean? It meant something that Karen was not capable of doing, especially not when I wasn't there with her.

Not all alone, after a war when they'd tried so often to kill her. That was not possible. Impossible. Unpossible.

Not happening.

No. I didn't accept it. Could not.

I stared at Andrea Kiley, and I wanted to say to her: 'No, sorry, you have that wrong.' Because no. No no.

No no no my God.

My God, my God.

I stared at Andrea Kiley, and I began to feel ill. My feet stopped feeling the ground, my eyes stopped seeing, but I still somehow registered Andrea's face, and its sadness. She was sad. After being totally destroyed by Egesta this still made her sad.

No no no no not possible. My God no.

"She never... never regained consciousness," Andrea said. It was meant to console me, but it couldn't console me because I still didn't know Karen was dead.

How could news like that cross into my mind? Not possible. No sir.

Karen didn't know how to die. She couldn't do that. The woman could do everything, but not that, because that wasn't what she should have done.

No. No.

Please no.

Perhaps... maybe it was a mistake. That was a possibility. Just an error. The wrong person, the wrong bed. A mix up. Jessica getting her story wrong.

No. No please.

It was all going to be okay, and Karen was alive, and I was going to bring back the information that would cure her.

Why was I suddenly sitting? I was sitting beside Andrea because I'd started to fall. She was too small a woman to keep me from falling, but she slowed the fall so now I was sitting on the floor with her.

I was staring at the floor, I was lying on the floor. Then I was sitting up again, and staring at the wall.

Andrea didn't say anything, she just stayed beside me and watched me because my mind wasn't working yet.

No. No no no.

Not Karen.

Karen passed away.

No it was a mistake. But Andrea never made these kinds of mistakes.

Never regained consciousness. So I hadn't missed anything by not being there. Now I could find Grant and he would pay. That would be my mission. And anyone between me and him would…

I stopped thinking for a moment. I stared at the gray wall of my cabin, and a wolf stared back at me with sad eyes. *Wolf* stared back at me, though without eyes. I was alone all of a sudden, but the wolf I saw in *Wolf's* wall shook his head.

I stopped thinking altogether.

And then it hit me.

Karen McMaster, goddess and champion, that woman, that lady.

My Karen.

My Karen.

September 10, 2222.

No more.

Not any more.

No God no. Please God no.

"The world is broken."

Andrea can't describe the sound I made when it finally sunk in. At first she tried to get her arms around me, hoping I wouldn't feel alone… but nothing she could do would help, and as soon as she realized that she backed away.

I struggled. Lying on the floor, I tried to claw myself back through time. To tear myself free of reality, to find a way back into the recent past to get to that palace ball, or to before that ball… to some place or time where I could stop all this madness.

Because it couldn't be real. But it was real. Now, before the Empire and history, I was alone without Karen.

No matter how I struggled, no matter how deep I tried to dig my fingers into the past, nothing worked. I lacked that power. Karen was gone, and I hadn't been there.

"The world is broken."

CHAPTER TWENTY

LOST ANGEL

Word spread through the Belt Squadron like fire. At first no one could believe it — someone had to be playing a sick joke, or perhaps Grant Merger had planted a false signal to disrupt us...

But the signal, and the news report that came with it, bore authenticated DCC stamps. And while it was possible to fake a news story, having Jessica Qing on screen made it tough to doubt.

There was no hiding from it. There was no denying any of it. Karen was dead.

She'd died while I'd been out chasing my old friend Grant. I hadn't been there in the end. None of us had.

The pain was palpable across the Belt Squadron. Karen had been loved by everyone — whether they had good reasons to love her, or they just did because everyone else loved her — and the reactions were predictably grave. For those who hadn't met her, hadn't worked with her, it was more the principle of the loss... the idea of it. The way people feel when a hero, or a public face, is needlessly killed.

Those people felt pain, and sorrow, and anger when the news reached them. But I don't know many of those people, haven't spoken to many of them, because as you might imagine, the people I know and speak to often are ones who knew me and Karen well.

And for those people, it was difficult.

I won't try to catalogue every reaction here. Why bother? But some bear mentioning, because they changed perspectives... they affected what was to come.

Matt Baxter, for instance, retreated to his day cabin. A British officer so close to his planned departure from the service is not the sort to become emotional, and Matt didn't, but as soon as the cabin door shut behind him the roar he released was incredible. It was heard through the bulkhead, which shouldn't be possible because the bulkhead is atmosphere-tight... but multiple people on *Friendly's* bridge heard it. Perhaps it came through the ventilation shafts.

You must understand that this was the moment Matt had always feared most. He'd always had within him that instinct, perhaps a genetic imperative, to be the responsible one — the one who'd guarantee safety for those who held his loyalty.

Karen had been one of his charges, one he'd always lectured to keep from doing stupid stuff... and yet she'd been doing nothing stupid at all, save for dancing with me, when Grant Merger had come like a coward to kill her.

Matt Baxter's anger at this was intense. Whatever notions he'd had of leaving the service had long been shelved, but now they ceased to exist. He would do whatever was necessary — *whatever* was necessary — to find Grant Merger, and see justice done. God help anyone who stood in the way.

♦♦♦

Kris Jacobs' reaction was less furious at first. She cried, and has no reason to say otherwise. Karen had never been as close to Kris as I had — certainly, they had *Lion* in common, but Kris had been my XO, so the relationship with me was naturally closer.

And Kris was devastated for both Karen, and for me. That devastation was the only thing that kept her anger under control, because after all she'd struggled through to come back to us, she hadn't been able to do anything to stop Grant Merger's last attack.

She'd known that when she returned from her recovery, the squadron would be different... the whole solar system might be different. But she'd expected that some people would remain untouched.

Such a great crime had happened, though, to rob her of her comfort. And now, like Matt, her thoughts could hardly part from the new reality, and the need to do something to avenge the loss of Karen.

On *Wolf* if was bad. Very bad. The ship stopped breathing I think. Somehow, throughout the entire hull, everyone just stopped when the word reached them. Because Karen had spent the war on the decks with all these people. She'd suffered with them, led them, laughed with them and killed with them.

She was to them a symbol... someone they chose to believe was special, both because she was, and because they needed her to be. Because war is easier when you believe your leader is a goddess — a goddess who cares about you.

People like Andy Jensen and Alicia Morgan simply didn't know what to say. Shelby and Adrienne could do little other than hug in grief. Felicia Khalid stood watch in tears, not leaving her post but feeling it nonetheless.

Jim and Bunny sat on their bed and held onto each other, both seemingly numbed by the absolute waste of what was going on.

Rufus Chang wore armor of ice. He had no choice; he locked down any hint of emotion and realized that he would need to have a very active part in the justice to come. As I think I've said before, for Rufus the calculus surrounding many complicated moral questions is simple. Getting the perpetrator of an attack like the one Grant Merger had launched was a worthy and necessary cause... and making certain the villain paid whatever price was warranted would be beyond just. It would be divine.

Andrea Kiley retreated to her own cabin after she left mine, and there found herself in tears that she couldn't feel. This confused her as much as it might confuse you — she was crying, but not fully processing the emotions that went with the physical reaction. In fact, the only real feeling she seemed to notice was one of dizziness... thoughts seemed to slip into and out of her grasp, as did feelings.

Such an unstable woman, at least by her own reckoning. Karen had been a friend — not especially close, but they'd been together through the war, and that mattered. Now... Andrea was saddened and numb, but also angry and impassive, and full of rage and peace as the room spun around her.

She was not well, she tells me. She didn't know how to grieve any more, and though she doesn't believe it was sane, she almost began worrying more about her emotional limitations than she did about the loss of Karen McMaster.

I say this advisedly: she's right, she should have been more upset about Karen.

But I won't hold that against her.

And speaking of someone who wasn't as worried about Karen's death as something else, there was Wes. Because Wes had known Karen a long time, but he'd been my friend more than hers. Because he'd been through a loss very much like the one I was now suddenly coping with. Because he knew damned well what I could start feeling... how I could start divorcing myself from any brand of morality... and how much harm I could do.

When Wes had lost his perspective all those years ago, it had been as a young officer with relatively little command authority. The only thing he could do to vent his rage was fight duels, and that was dangerous enough.

Since becoming a ship skipper, and especially since becoming a squadron commander, he'd known that losing his perspective in a similar manner could be far more dire. And as if you need me to explain this to you, he knew that my current circumstances, and the resources I had at my command, made the upcoming scenario positively disastrous.

I had an elite squadron — a bunch of officers who were similarly feeling unkind towards the SAU. And I had nothing to lose.

Wes knew what was coming — he saw what was soon to be painted in blood.

A whole tapestry of blood...

CHAPTER TWENTY-ONE

CRUCIBLE

My crew wisely left me alone. Any of them trying to help would have simply reminded me that Karen was gone.

As you can probably tell from the ravings of chapter nineteen, my ability to think and reason had completely evaporated as soon as Andrea had reached me with the news. I'm not terribly proud of that, and I'm sure it makes for crap narrative, but nevertheless that's how I coped. Or failed to cope.

Whatever way you slice it, I ended up on the floor, sleeping.

I did dream, though. Another dream, as if you need to hear another one... but I remember this one so vividly too. And it was perhaps a portent of things to come. I don't know.

I remember distinctly that I was standing on a beach on Capital Island — a rocky beach that I think was near Terra Nova. But the place was different; where the city had been, there were trees. It was as if I was there in a time before the city existed, when the place was just a national park.

Standing on this beach, with trees to my back and the sea to my front, I was watching a couple of people I'd never seen before. They were standing down by the water, and it looked as though they were unhappy about something.

All of that might not seem cause for me to remember the dream, but there were other elements... disturbing elements. The ocean, for instance, seemed still. The people were moving, talking to each other, seemingly upset... but the sea we were facing was as calm as if it was in a photo.

There was no wind, either. No sounds of life at all around me on the beach, or coming from the woods.

The only living thing besides myself and the two strangers seemed to be my friend Charlie Peters. He was standing next to me with his hands thrust into his pockets, and as I glanced at him he shook his head.

"I don't remember what Lia looks like all the time either."

I stared at him as he said that, and then in the dream I remember *remembering* being in my cabin, on the floor in the moments after hearing of Karen's death. That probably sounds as confusing as it was: it was as though the dream was happening in the future, and I was remembering what was actually happening in the present.

Very strange, and for some reason that fact made me wake.

When my eyes opened I saw the baseboards of my cabin not far in front of me. I also felt... numb. I think numb is the word. All the rage that had been surging through me before... all that loosely-controlled, petulant and self-righteous anger seemed gone.

Whether it had actually left me behind remained to be seen, but no more did I put much value in spitting my venom at anyone... in toying with Wes when he tried to rein in my brusque and self-indulgent commentary. None of that seemed to matter.

I tried to picture Karen's face, and was relieved when I could.

Perhaps a time was coming when I no longer would be able to.

Sitting up, I took a breath and tried to figure out who I was. Ken Barron, Rear Admiral commanding a mission to the Union of Solar Asteroids. Hunting Grant Merger, now to arrest him and bring him home for trial, since any information he could have provided would come too late.

Yes, that was me, and that was my job.

I looked to the chronometer on the wall and it was very unhelpful: it said 0450. I didn't know what day it was… couldn't remember how close we'd been to Etat Concord when Andrea had come with the news. But I could find out. First I'd have to rise, and clean up, and prepare for a day's duty.

So I did that. I got ready for duty, as if everything was normal.

When I stepped out onto the bridge at 0600, all eyes turned to me. The watch was in the hands of Jim Hannigan, and he turned with surprise as I appeared. His gaze found mine, and I could see him studying my face, wondering what to make of me.

What was there to make?

I nodded to him, not seeing the need to volunteer any commentary related to the unasked questions. As I strode towards the front of the bridge, hands linked behind my back, I simply asked a question: "What's our ETA now, Jim?"

It was my calmness that surprised him the most. It didn't sound forced or in any way artificial. I sounded tired, very tired, but not at all angry. Maybe that's what I was… and if I was, then what did it mean?

Jim could have dwelled on the question, but instead he answered me, "We'll be there this afternoon, based on the information we have. No sign of picket ships yet."

I nodded, "Good. Pass orders to the squadron, standby action stations at noon. Make sure everyone gets a good lunch at 1130."

"Aye," Jim replied, then took a moment to relay the orders to Sensors and Communications for transmission. After the message began sending, he came up alongside me and lowered his voice, "Is there anything you need?"

I blinked, my eyes settling on the main screen as it showed a sensor reading of the empty space we were passing though.

"I don't think so," I replied. "I'll let you know."

Taking a breath, Jim agreed, "Alright. We're all here."

Of course they were, because this was a family — a massive, powerful, Belt Squadron family. Cut one of us, we all felt it. Stab us collectively in the heart, and we all pulled together to survive as best we could. I never doubted that, and now I would benefit from it. People to lean on, if I needed to lean.

Who knew what I'd need.

When Wes got to his bridge at 0730 and called over to *Wolf* to check in, I hadn't left the command deck. Felicia Khalid had taken over the Sensors and Communications section, so when the signal came in she looked up from the appropriate console and gently asked: "Commodore Pellew signaling… would you like to speak with him, sir?"

My hands remained linked behind my back as I paced back and forth — very, very slowly — at the front of the bridge. I was facing Felicia when she asked the question, so I nodded to her.

"Of course."

Why wouldn't I want to talk to Wes? He was my friend.

Felicia accepted my answer with a nod of her own, then she patted the shoulder of the technician responsible for routing the message to one of the bridge displays. A *WolfNet* loading graphic popped up on screen three, and I moved over to face it, making sure I'd be in range of the viewfinder.

Wes appeared after only a short wait, and it was clear he hadn't been expecting to see me; his stern expression jumped slightly, then his eyes narrowed as he began to study my face, trying to determine what state of mind I was in.

"Ken?" was his introduction, and for a moment I simply looked at him — I presumed he would say more.

Eventually it became clear he had nothing else to add, so I answered, "Yes?"

My tone, my demeanor, my expression… nothing suggested anger to him. Only weariness. To explain it the way he described it to me later: 'you seemed disconnected'. He didn't know whether that was a good thing or a bad thing, but in the short term, perhaps it would be better than having me acting an idiot and prancing about in a pathetic, predictable, and hedonistic rage.

"We're due to reach Etat Concord this afternoon," my friend the Commodore said eventually, finding a proper way to start a conversation now that his observations were complete. "Was that you who passed out the order for standby action stations?"

I nodded, but didn't speak.

Wes continued studying me suspiciously, though he pushed the conversation forward, "Thanks. I was going to suggest the same."

He fell silent for a moment, because my expression remained unchanged.

"Do you want to chat in private for a minute, maybe?" he asked next, conscious of the fact that we were both on bridges and in front of the people we commanded.

I considered his offer, but I realized that if we paused this conversation and then picked it up in private, we'd probably only circle uneasily around one question. It was a question others in the squadron would have as well, so it was probably for the best that we just answered it here.

"I'm not fine, Wes," I said. "But I will remain in command, as is my responsibility."

According to everyone I've asked, I sounded almost defeated as I said that. Tired, weary… whatever, there are too many words, but none of them seem to capture the futility I was projecting. Why bother caring now?

Those words compelled Wes to nod and say, "Okay. We're here for you."

But that's not really what he was thinking, because as he assessed my probable state of mind, he realized he might have a completely different reason for concern than the one he'd predicted. Perhaps he wasn't going to spend this mission reining in a hot-headed monster… perhaps he'd have to be the aggressive one. By the sounds of things, I was just going through the motions, staggering along because I didn't know what else to do.

He'd have to be ready to jump in if I proved incapable of fighting.

Whether that was a better problem, or a worse one, he didn't want to guess. But he'd be ready.

Good thing too.

I continued to stand watch, lost in my own silence.

CHAPTER TWENTY-TWO

FIRST CONTACT

After all this, you'd almost expect our arrival at Etat Concord to be a dramatic affair, though in reality it was far from exciting. The rock was just like all the others in the Belt: lonely and dark. A few domes stood on it, and some commercial traffic was cruising to and fro as we arrived. A bunch of small craft were buzzing around as well, but mostly it just seemed like an independent asteroid.

Nothing at all to write home about.

In point of fact, the only interesting thing we noticed as we cruised in was the guardship: a Martian destroyer was sitting in orbit around the slim asteroid, and as the seven-ship Belt Squadron approached, that red hull turned and came out to meet us.

Not much of a threat, I think you agree.

I'm sure everyone in our formation was tense because we'd arrived and were about to begin operations and seek our revenge... but I remained relatively sedate.

Andrea Kiley was standing beside me at the front of the bridge by this time, her arms folded while mine remained linked behind my back. She was keeping an eye on me, just like everyone else, because my seeming calm wasn't consistent with her own rage any more than it was consistent with Wes' anxiety.

I didn't make sense. What else is new.

"We probably just made a lot of people very nervous," *Wolf's* Irish skipper said as she watched the icon of the Martian ship crossing space to challenge us.

"Hi there, we're the Empire," Kris Jacobs muttered from the screen she was occupying — Battlelink, I should have mentioned, was up and running between all ships once again.

The point both women were making was certainly a sound one; imagine for a moment that you're the Governor of the only asteroid in your state that is allowed contact with the outside solar system, and you're accustomed to dealing with the odd unaligned trader, or with the Martians who came to you for cheap labor.

Now imagine you're sitting in your office one afternoon when a whole squadron suddenly arrives. A squadron from the government you'd essentially sided against when you'd built warships for the Martians.

Just about the only piece of good news for you would be the fact that there were no battleships with the squadron. Not that we needed them to cope with a single Martian destroyer.

"Should we target the Martian?" Kate Levec asked from *Lady Grace*.

Before I could say anything, Wes' expression tightened, "No need to jump to a belligerent posture. It's peace now, so let's give him a chance to talk first."

It was a very reasonable instruction, but because I was in charge, everyone had to wait for me to confirm the order. I suppose all gazes shifted to me; because they were on Battlelink there was no way to tell.

Nevertheless, I knew they wanted my perspective.

"As Wes says, we've no reason to be unreasonable," I confirmed softly, and I could certainly detect surprise, and uncertainty, on a few faces. Didn't sound like I really had the hard edge I'd need... but it was so soon since the news, I had time to get it back. They didn't lose faith in me, just wondered whether I needed more rest before I'd be ready to lead the first incursion.

No, I could get by.

"He'll be in weapons range in four minutes," Felicia Khalid informed me (and every listening skipper) at that point.

And then she had another useful addition: "Wait... getting a signal from the Martian ship. Directed to... Admiral Ken Barron, sir."

That was unexpected, and even in the midst of my lethargy, I found my interest tweaked. Our force had been recognized. Was this Martian a veteran who had fought us before, or had he been tipped off about our impending arrival by Grant or his people?

Either way, we didn't quite have the surprise on our side that we'd thought we *might* have had.

Wes picked up on the threat immediately: "They know it's us... General Quarters?"

A prudent suggestion, and I nodded, "Yes, probably for the best."

That might have been the most ambiguous order for action stations I ever gave, but it worked all the same — every skipper on *Wolf's* screens turned away from his or her viewfinder and called his or her ship to alert. Andrea did the same beside me.

Even though there was only one Martian on our scopes, it made sense to be cautious. I turned to Felicia and offered a gentle nod, "I'll see the Martian now."

Our Sensors and Communications Officer frowned and hesitated at that order — did I really seem like I was ready to deal with a potentially belligerent Martian?

That was for me to decide, and I'd given my order, so Felicia did as I'd asked; a new loading screen appeared and I moved over to stand before it.

As usual, the buffering time was longer when our comm computers had to translate a signal sent by the Martian Vantage OS — patently inferior to our own OS XX — but I didn't mind the wait. No need to hurry now.

A Martian skipper appeared.

It had been a while since I'd seen any Martians. Remember it was back during *The Mars Convention* that we'd really crossed paths with the Imperium's finest — we were all at Mars and dealing with the unfortunately-named Germaine Blovuspaco. Perhaps I was out of practice, then, because on first viewing this one didn't strike me as incompetent.

He had the uniform, but his hair was a bit disheveled, and his shaving effort hadn't been completely crisp. Either he'd rushed to his bridge half-groomed when his ship detected our arrival, or he just wasn't the sort to maintain the Martian officer cadre stereotype.

Interesting.

"You asked to speak with me, Captain?" my question was again largely benign, and the Martian considered me briefly before answering with a nod.

"Captain Gerhard Franspaldov, of the destroyer *Daedalia Planum*, Admiral Barron. Welcome to Etat Concord."

It was a cordial greeting, but one that could be loaded with all sorts of meanings. I waited for a few seconds before replying, suspecting that the man might have more to say... he did not.

As that became clear, I decided to push forward a bit, "I hope you don't mind, Captain, but we have business here. A couple of fugitives we're pursuing have probably come this way. Perhaps you've seen them."

Franspaldov nodded as I was speaking, and then he answered in a manner that surprised both me and everyone else who was eavesdropping, "Give us their names, or their aliases, and we might be able to find them for you. But before we do that, Admiral, I suggest we discuss a few matters in person. There are questions that I best not try to answer over open comms, so if you'll have me, I'll come aboard *Wolf*. Alone."

That was a whole lot at once, and the offer to come to our ship was intriguing. A few officers... actually, most of our officers... bristled at the suggestion, fearing a trap. He could fly over in a shuttle loaded with explosives and detonate when he got inside our flight bay... or something equally vicious and unlikely, just because we'd recently been wartime enemies.

Or maybe he had something valuable to add.

"What's prompted such a gracious offer, Captain?" I asked gently, tilting my head.

Franspaldov tipped his head as well, then shrugged, "I heard from a mutual friend that your ship has a very interesting drink called scotch. Goes well with poetry — poetry that might be a song to you."

No one had any idea what the Martian Captain was talking about, and indeed, Gerhard himself didn't understand the significance of his words. Like so many other proofs of affiliation, this one was ambiguous but effective: I knew at once that Franspaldov — clearly from the Martian lower class — was one of Bort's people.

The second message our Asteroid Admiral had sent that day — after sending the all-important intel package to me — had been to Gerhard.

"Come aboard, certainly. And if you need a pilot, I don't see the danger to that either. See you shortly, Captain."

With that confirmation, Gerhard nodded and then killed the link. As I turned away from the screen I saw a stern glare on Andrea's face, and as I crossed the bridge back to a more central point, I realized her expression was shared by many of the people on Battlelink.

None of them knew what Gerhard had meant, you see — they'd all been patched in, but the only other person who would have understood the importance of drinking scotch and reciting the words to *Parting Glass* was Karen, because I had told her about it.

And now she wasn't in a position to remember anything, was she?

"What's all this about?" Matt Baxter's question was firm. "We shouldn't be led around by the nose by some damned Martian..."

The Briton's frustration was evident in his tone, and it drew nods from other screens. Our people were ready to lash out, and a Martian seemed an awfully convenient target. Recent-enemy guarding current probable-enemies...

"I don't have any problem with diplomacy," Wes interjected, his aim clearly meant to mute the belligerence. "I'm not so sure it's wise to have him aboard *Wolf*, though. What could he have to tell you that can't be explained over comm?"

That question was aimed squarely at me, and I shrugged, "I'll find out."

With that, I turned and strode from the bridge, pausing at the hatch only to call back to Andrea, "I'll wait outside bay two, bring him in there."

And I was gone.

In my wake, surprised and dismayed Belt Squadron skippers wondered what I was about. These were all good people, you understand — good and trusted and the best. But they were still in the same state of mind they'd been in before... their anger perhaps heightened by Karen's death.

While I seemed to be entirely neutralized.

Was I ready to lead this mission? Wes wasn't the only one wondering.

The Martian shuttle seemed tentative as it put its feet down on the deck in bay two. I leaned against the wall of the observation lounge with folded arms, watching as the craft's pilot went through a seemingly complex shutdown routine, and then waiting for the space doors to close so I could go out to greet our guest.

This was, I believe, the first time that a Martian shuttle had ever landed on *Wolf's* deck, and many of the crew working the bay weren't too pleased to see it. There were also Starlights on launch standby, with pilots looking out from their canopies in some disbelief as the craft's hatch opened, and its ladder lowered to the deck.

Only one person climbed out, unarmed, and as his boots hit the deck Captain Franspaldov paused for a moment to take in his surroundings. There was nothing on his destroyer to compare to this flight bay, and we had two of the them. It was as impressive as Bort McWebsbert had told him it would be, and by the time I crossed the deck to him, his eyes had begun to fill with that same sort of discomfort that had punctuated Bort's tour with Karen back in *The Fleet Clash*.

No wonder we'd won the war.

"Captain, welcome aboard," I interrupted such thoughts with my greeting, and Gerhard turned to me and saluted quickly.

I returned the gesture very easily, then nodded in the direction of the hatch, "You'll appreciate we don't have too much time. The Officers Club?"

He nodded, still a little too overwhelmed by his surroundings to speak. That was fine; we began our march to the lift in silence. We passed through wide, bright, clean corridors, and passed many spacers and officers — both male and female.

The women of *Wolf's* crew presented an even greater surprise to Gerhard than they had to Bort, as Gerhard's wife was a devoted homemaker with no aspirations to work outside the home, let alone go to war. At least Casey Flynnboldak's character had given Bort some preview of what he might expect.

When we reached the lift and I ordered it to the rec deck, Gerhard finally managed to get some words out, "I... thank you for having me aboard, sir. I got a call from Admiral McWebsbert a few days ago, and he advised me of the situation. I hope Commodore McMaster remains stable."

That he hadn't heard about her death was interesting; perhaps it meant that Etat Concord didn't get news from the Empire very promptly. Surprise could be on our side after all… the assassins wouldn't know what to expect from us.

"I'm afraid Karen passed away while we were on our way here," I answered, my voice not so much as quivering. Gerhard's head turned sharply as I spoke; he seemed to expect a different reaction.

Why did *everyone* expect a different reaction?

"I'm so sorry," he stammered, and I glanced at him with a nod.

"Thank you."

The hatch opened and we emerged onto *Wolf's* rec deck. The place was abandoned because the ship was at General Quarters, so we were very much on our own when we reached the Officers Club. I went behind the bar myself to collect a bottle of scotch, as well as a bottle of beer — I recalled that Bort hadn't cared for JW twelve-year-old blend.

Gerhard took a seat at a table as I collected our drinks, and in the interest of saving time, he continued to explain himself, "We have a precarious role here, sir. My understanding of our purpose isn't completely clear… I think it's considered imperative that the Imperium maintain an alliance with the Union of Solar Asteroids… I suppose to offset alliances that your Empire has with the Hawke Protectorate and so forth… but we have little latitude to operate in this place."

He was volunteering a lot, and had I been in a different frame of mind I'd probably have been even more suspicious of him now. But because I trusted Bort, and because Gerhard was as much one of Bort's people as Andrea and Kris and Matt were my people, I figured he was genuine. And I was right.

"You defend Concord against its enemies?" I asked as I set the drinks and glasses on the table, and the Captain nodded and quickly thanked me before continuing.

"The USA doesn't tell us much. I must make that clear: I don't even have nav data for their capital asteroid. Our alliance has existed for eight years, and yet they still confine us to Etat Concord. We also lack authority for ground operations, though over time we've developed some contacts down there. I think we can probably help you find whoever you're after."

That was a very generous offer, and I raised a glass of scotch to it. Gerhard mirrored the gesture with the glass of scotch I'd brought him, and then we both drank. The Martian Captain didn't seem to react to the strong drink at all; his taste in liquor was obviously different than Bort's. Fair enough.

"We appreciate the help. My Captain will send over the information we have on the assassins, and when we suspect they arrived here. Based on the intelligence we gathered from the pair we did capture, we know this was their destination."

Gerhard nodded slowly at my words, "That will help. This place has all sorts… the wealthy and the poor… and the mercenaries. Because it's the gateway to the Union, they all come here."

"Fascinating," I said, because it was. The notion of a whole new state, with all sorts of new rules, customs and ideas would normally have appealed to me. Obviously not now.

"The next question I have for you, Captain, is what their military is like. I presume they must have one."

That question came a little out of left field for Gerhard, because as far as he knew our only objective in this mission was to find the assassins — not to dive further into the Union to find and deal with Grant Merger. Nevertheless, he'd been instructed to be helpful, and he'd do just that, as best he could.

"We've never come across one of their warships, or at least I haven't," the Captain replied. "I've seen bits and pieces of technology, but nothing that I can clearly relate to you as intelligence. My sense is these people don't have the resources they'd need to foster an advanced warship design and building project. We brought in all our own plans and special materials for the *Tharsis* battleships… they contributed mostly the labor and crude metals. That said, their locally-built non-military ships seemed very effective to me. I wouldn't underestimate them."

More fascinating information. Though the SAU was doing business with the Martians, they were still keeping their military abilities far from the light. That was sensible; recall, the arms race that brought about the Martian *Tharsis*-class had begun when we'd loudly publicized the *Bonaventure* project. If we'd kept *Bonnie* secret, perhaps we could have completely blindsided the Martians during a war.

But that in itself raised a question about the SAU's ultimate intentions. Consider; we had publicized the power and might of our *Bonnies* because we'd wanted to scare the Martians and everyone else away — they were as powerful as pre-war deterrents as they had been as wartime combatants.

Building warships in secret suggested you'd need them to surprise your enemy with a major attack. So the fact that the SAUs wouldn't even show their powerful allies their line of battle suggested that they either didn't have much to show… or that the Union one day expected war with at least one of the major human civilizations.

"We may have to find their capital before this is over," I returned to the conversation with that comment, and Gerhard winced slightly.

"Don't have that for you, sorry sir. And believe me, we've asked. They don't give that out to anyone. You'd have to take it forcefully."

"I'd rather not," I shook my head. "If it came to that, though, would you not be obliged to intervene against us?"

Gerhard Franspaldov had clearly thought about that particular question already — he'd probably been wondering about it since Bort's message had reached him. If we decided to start pushing around the locals at Etat Concord, what was his top priority: protect the alliance with the SAU, or protect the peace with Earth?

"My orders don't cover the possibility," Gerhard said eventually. "But I suspect keeping the peace between our two governments is much more important than this alliance. I'm afraid we'd have to remain unengaged."

So much for our recent enemy; the Martians were going to stay out of the way, in no small part thanks to the judgment of this one Captain. I appreciated that, and also carried a concern: "Are they likely to hang you for that?"

Franspaldov shrugged, "They can try. But I'm an Asteroid Beta boy, I'll just go home and the locals will protect me."

Like Bort from Asteroid Epsilon… that was interesting for a couple of reasons, neither terribly pertinent for the moment.

"We appreciate your assistance, Captain. It makes our continuing in this mission much easier."

That was true. Gerhard and I shared one more drink, then I escorted him back to his shuttle and he went back to his ship. Minutes after he left, Andrea transmitted the information we had about the two assassins we were hunting, and then *Daedalia Planum* escorted the Belt Squadron into Etat Concord local space.

Altogether a pleasant arrival.

CHAPTER TWENTY-THREE

TARGETS

We were after Angelo and Sylvia Connaught, but we didn't have any information on them. In point of fact, we didn't even know what they really looked like. Though many cameras had tracked them over the course of the evening at Daragh's ball, it was standard practice for assassins to do some quick cosmetic surgery to disguise themselves when on a job. It's surprising how much you can do to thwart security identification software with a simple off-the-shelf nose job kit.

Still, thanks to Bort's assets we had more of an advantage than Grant Merger could have figured possible, and I had high hopes that Captain Franspaldov would come through.

Rufus was less certain of the Asteroid officer, though like a few of us who had been down on the surface of Mars for the lovely Convention kickoff, he did acknowledge it was quite possible the destroyer skipper could be genuine.

He hoped so, anyway, as he briefed his half-sized team — the same group of six who had been with us on Mars, on Egesta, and during the coup. At this point I don't think we could call them the 'new guys' any longer — they may not have been with us for quite so long or through quite so much as Charlie and Carly had been, but they'd seen their share of messes, and I was more than confident in every one of them.

"The Connaughts… it might be an alias, but it sounds to us like they're actually a husband and wife team. Means we could find them together, and means they could be nasty," Rufus was standing in the Special Branch ready room with a screen behind him, showing surveillance images and vids from the Terra Nova Palace.

He didn't need to narrate too much of what was being shown on that screen; the operators in the room could see it clearly enough for themselves. As they'd fled, the Connaughts had moved and shot very effectively, as though they'd done a lot of this sort of work. That dexterity suggested that if Special Branch came looking for them, the assassins would have at least some idea of how to make trouble.

"We'll need to be concerned about traps, bombs… all of it. We find their home, or their usual hangouts… they're going to know exactly how to hurt us and get away. So we'll need to be extra cautious," Rufus continued. "But we still have to get them. Understood?"

The officers of the squad nodded. Clarissa, Selma, Bobby, Simon and Maggie weren't going to let us down.

"Local security?" Clarissa Hutchinson asked that prudent question, and Rufus nodded.

"They exist, from what we know. But there's no strict access control on the spaceport, and we don't think they have a heavy presence on the ground. If they show up we'll be courteous, but this will be our operation."

If you're not familiar with how the Empire tends to operate on rocks in the independent belt, that disconnect might sound strange to you… but it's how we do things.

If we don't have a relationship with your asteroid's local law enforcement (perhaps because you haven't bothered to establish any sort of diplomatic relations with our government), we simply move in and do what we need to do, trying to be polite as we go.

That was the plan now — we weren't going to waste time playing nice with the local SAU authorities, and if they didn't like it, they'd have to cope with a seven-ship squadron in orbit of their little asteroid.

This was one of the times it was helpful to be from the Empire — to have all sorts of weight to throw around.

"Backup?" Simon Keynes asked the next question.

"Obviously we're going down there solo, along with Ken, but we'll have backup ready to fly down if there's trouble. We're keeping things tight to begin with — to minimize the chances that we'll be noticed on the way in."

Being noticed was always the big concern on an operation like this one; we could have attempted to go in disguise, but that would have been a waste of time — any assassin with a decent network of contacts would have noticed the presence of the Belt Squadron, and would be keeping an eye on arrivals. We wouldn't have a chance to blend in with the scenery; we'd just have to roll in hard and catch them before they realized we'd found them.

And that, I should make clear, was the key. Assassins couldn't expect us to have anything on them, but thanks to Franspaldov's contacts we hopefully would know a great deal. There would be no searching for leads, no visiting the local sheriff to do some browbeating for intel… we'd land and go straight to their homes. Catch them before they were quite ready, if not entirely unawares.

Provided the Asteroid-born skipper came through.

We'd know about that soon enough; in the meantime, there was one other target to consider.

"Since they don't want to share their nav data, we're going to have to appropriate some," Andrea Kiley's words were predictably cold as she explained her part of the mission to Master-At-Arms Eugene Sengooba. "That's us."

It certainly was them; one concern we obviously had was finding an accurate chart of the SAU, so that we could continue our quest deeper into their space once we had the Connaughts. Unfortunately there was no help from Franspaldov on that front — he couldn't get the information, and if the SAUs wouldn't give it to him, there was little chance of us getting it by asking nicely.

So it had been decided that Andrea would take charge of finding some data for us, while Rufus and the team dealt with the killers.

"Commodore Pellew will make an official request with the Governor's office, but he's not going to get anywhere. So you and I are going to find a black market spot somewhere. The Martians have told us what parts of the main dome are sketchiest, and we're going to get the information."

Andrea and Eugene were meeting in her day cabin, I should add, and as he heard the nature of the mission, our African Master-At-Arms raised his eyebrows in surprise: "You're saying we're going into the bad part of town, ma'am. Just the two of us?"

"Back-up team of whoever you like from our SF, but Rufus has to be focused on the assassins. Either way, we need that data."

More context is undoubtedly necessary here: we had left Earth with only Rufus' team of Special Branch officers. The rest of our ships had *no one*, seriously, because after the coup and the rapid reorganization of Earth's Special Branch complements, we'd been stripped. I know it's an old refrain by now, but the problem of using up so many of our operators on Mercury was still wearing on us, damned near two years later.

Definitely grounds to talk 'Marine Corps', but in the meantime it meant Eugene and his regular SF were going to be tapped for a job that they certainly had the ability to do, but which was normally in the province of the black-clad Branchers.

"We'll get it done, ma'am," the Master-At-Arms said evenly after a moment's thought, and Andrea nodded.

"Never doubted it."

"Where are you going to be? You waiting on your bridge the way you should?"

Wes' question was frank, and it drew a shrug from me, "I think I should probably be down there with Rufus."

We were going over the broader plan as we waited for Gerhard to get back to us, and now that we'd confirmed the two prongs of our intended operation — Rufus' hunt of the Connaughts, and Andrea's plan to acquire nav data — Wes needed to know where I'd be.

He didn't want me on the ground.

"If you're on the ground, I should come too," he began to shake his head as he spoke. "I don't think it's a good idea for you to be down there on your own."

"I'll be with Rufus and the team."

"You know what I mean."

I did know what he meant, or at least I thought I did. Now as before, he was worried about two possibilities — either I'd go nuts and kill Karen's assassins, or I'd collapse into a weeping mess when I saw them.

His concerns were undoubtedly reasonable, but I shook my head, "You know Rufus will look out for me. I think it's best for you to be up here with the squadron. I trust Franspaldov, but maybe I'm wrong to. And if a SAU squadron shows up while we're down there, you'll have to stand off against it. I trust you in command of this squadron, so you really should stay."

Those were valid points, but what struck Wes was how I said them — like I was negotiating, not demanding. Didn't sound like I was unstable, maybe not even close to cracking… so he let out a sigh and nodded.

"Okay. You're going to work within the parameters down there."

That was a statement — perhaps a demand — and it led me to dip my chin, "What else could I do?"

As we all prepared for the missions ahead, Captain Franspaldov was speaking to his contacts on Etat Concord. Depending on how much you like to romanticize things, you could make the case that the place was either delightfully eclectic, vibrant and engaging, or a complete mish-mash of the worst trash one could find in the solar system.

The garbage piles up at the gate, you see. Everyone who'd heard of the SAU and wanted to do business with it (legitimate or otherwise) came here, and then sent their proposals, their wares or their monies through accepted channels into the Union. They weren't allowed in themselves, so they all camped out in Concord.

Quite an arrangement — a real canton system, to again invoke the example of Imperial China. That system hadn't worked so well for the Chinese in the longer term, but then they were in a different context, and suffered from having things that the wider world desperately wanted at that time.

No one knew exactly what the Union had, though perhaps we'd soon find out.

Anyway, in the midst of this garbage, Franspaldov's contacts were able to sniff out a pair of professional 'mechanics' (apparently a popular moniker for hit men in the Union) who were a married couple, did jobs together, and had just come back from some unknown mission.

It was not as hard to find those two as you might expect... but then remember that Grant undoubtedly wanted us to find them. Whether he made sure the information was out there, or simply had picked a pair he knew wouldn't cover their tracks very well, was irrelevant; Franspaldov's contact located them within hours of asking.

As soon as files on them were transferred up to *Daedalia Planum*, Bort's Captain took one look and then dumped them into a message bound for *Wolf*. No point wasting time; he'd just have to stand aside and watch us work... see how the Belt Squadron handled criminals.

It would be quite a sight...

"That was fast."

Before we all went on our operations, we gathered together in *Wolf's* briefing room — Andrea, Eugene, Rufus, and me, along with Wes on the screen. Whatever information Franspaldov had provided could help fill out our plan, so we called it up on pads and began sifting immediately.

It didn't take long for us to realize a few things.

I got stuck on the photos of the two killers — the un-cosmetically-altered photos on the first page of the digital file. I felt like I'd seen Angelo Connaught before, but I couldn't figure out where. Undoubtedly it was at the ball, before he'd injected Karen... but...

"They have two kids."

Andrea's words were hard as she read that from the slim dossier.

"That means it's less likely there will be trip wires at their place," Rufus commented, then scrolled to another page. "And we have their address here. This is an awful lot of information the Martians found."

"Found quickly," Eugene Sengooba concurred, the implication being fairly obvious.

Both Eugene and Rufus had been down on Mars with us, of course, and so again they had more reason to think well of certain Martians (or Asteroid-born officers) than most... but they were naturally suspicious of the fact that our targets were being so quickly served up.

Wes was similarly cautious, "We can reconsider this. We have seven ships... we can send down a lot of SF, good people who handled Egesta."

Prudence and common sense — caution was necessary in a time like this, because we were operating in a foreign dome, amongst people we'd never dealt with, and tracking some obviously dangerous individuals.

Why rush? Karen was dead — we could be methodical.

But I wasn't in the mood. And believe me when I tell you I know how bad a reason that is to do anything.

"Run Angelo Connaught's real photo through our recognition banks. I feel like I've seen him before," I decided to ignore the doubters and return to the point. He was so familiar...

"Already doing that," Andrea replied. Alone in this group, she was the only one not objecting. She didn't care any more than I did... indeed, the only disappointment she had with this whole operation was that she wasn't going to get a rematch with the assassin who eluded her at the palace.

But that wasn't a great concern; she knew she'd have plenty to do in acquiring the nav data.

"Alright, let's go," was the next thing I said — more than slightly out of the blue. I came to my feet and looked to the screen. "See you later, Wes."

With that I walked out, leaving the three people in the room and the one aboard *Nova Scotia* looking at each other with varying levels of surprise.

"We..." Wes started to speak, but Andrea interrupted him by standing too.

"Have work to do," she said, shooting a glare at him through the screen. Again, don't forget the unpleasantness between those two.

She exited the briefing room, so only Eugene and Rufus remained in Wes' remote presence. For a moment the three men were silent, then the Commodore of the Independent Squadron gave them their marching orders, "Don't pull any punches down there, but just be careful neither of them gets in over their heads."

"Yes sir," Eugene agreed immediately.

Rufus' expression was a little darker, "We'll make sure we get what we need."

It was as much as Wes could hope for; Rufus in particular would have no sympathy for those he was pursuing, but at the same time the Chinese Major would know excesses when he saw them, and hopefully intervene.

"Rufus," Wes added one more note, "make sure Ken's okay. Whatever happens."

Obviously that was a redundant request — remember, Rufus would have broken through the gates of the underworld to come kill Karen and me if we'd gotten ourselves killed... he wasn't going to default on that dedication just because one of us was dead now.

He rose with a nod, triggering Eugene to do the same. Wes took a breath and then cut the feed. That was it: off to Etat Concord.

CHAPTER TWENTY-FOUR

A DIFFERENT WORLD

There was nothing exotic about getting down to Etat Concord's main dome; you'd find the same technology in the independent belt — lots of universally-compatible docking ports and landing decks to ensure that traders from all over could come to the rock for business.

Of course, we weren't traders.

Now I must apologize for jumping past this point earlier: in the files Bort had sent, it became clear to us that Concord had no customs apparatus. This was not a place where visitors were carefully screened, it was a free port where all could come and trade, whether they were pirates or military or just plain civilians. That's one of the reasons it was so laden with trash. The Martians suspected that other colonies in the SAU were more careful about controlling admissions, but not here. In order to attract all sorts of commerce, the Concord SAUs maintained an open door policy.

As we disembarked from our Special Branch assault shuttle (I flew down with Rufus instead of taking my plane, because I didn't want to fly), we therefore expected to simply take the lift down from the main docking tower and walk out into the dome.

Instead we were greeted by a military party.

This was the first time any of us had ever encountered members of the Union of Solar Asteroids Defense Force, or USADF. I call them SAUDF... pronounced like the female pig (sow) and 'deaf'. They don't like being referred to that way, but if it makes them feel better they can call us Defcoms.

The party was not large; four shooters headed up by an officer, all men and all rugged — the sorts who had been in plenty of fights over the years, and had learned how to win them. Their uniforms looked worn too; faded brown with sky-blue trims and facings... an interesting group.

As we came to a stop in front of this welcoming committee, the posturing began immediately. The locals wanted us to know they were tough and professional, while Rufus' team wanted the locals to know that if they tried anything, death would come to their rock like an apocalyptic plague from whichever scriptures you prefer.

"Welcome to Etat Concord," the SAUDF officer at the front said before too much of that posturing could be completed, and then he stepped forward with a glare that was supposed to intimidate me. "First visit, isn't it?"

I raised an eyebrow, "Came to see the sights. Heard good things."

"Lots of hardware for sightseeing," the officer countered quickly, obviously meaning that six Branchers in tac gear with MAG-90s weren't the typical tourists one expected to see.

As he was speaking, Andrea Kiley and her team came down a nearby chute from her own landing shuttle, and seeing that we were having a little summit, she led her ten SF in our direction. They were all wearing tac vests and carrying MAG-90s as well — not to be trifled with, even if they weren't Branchers by training.

The SAU officer noted this arrival and two of his guards turned slightly to face the newly-approaching threat.

"We don't take kindly to trouble here," the officer continued. "Rest assured that I'm just an emissary, and there are a lot more guards where my men come from."

My eyebrow remained up, and I tilted my head, "You worried we're here to invade?"

The man's eyes narrowed, "I don't care what you say you're here for. You make trouble and you'll be asked to leave."

"And if we're asked to leave, we will," I answered with a gentle shrug. "If we were here to cause trouble, we wouldn't be chatting."

I was speaking in the same gentle tone that had seemed to come naturally since I'd heard of Karen's death, but it must have seemed condescending, because the officer took a step towards me.

"I know your kind. I recognize you from news feeds from back when I was in the independent belt. You don't belong in this Union, and if you try to throw your weight around here it's not going to be tolerated. The people in this state are tired of being treated like toys of your Empire. And even if you kill us all, we'd rather that than having to play by your rules."

A good summary of the generally illogical attitude towards the Empire possessed by the people of the SAU.

Considering the statement for a few seconds, I began to nod as I formulated a response, "Sounds fair to me. We're here for a very specific purpose. Trouble in our Empire came here to hide... we want to send a message that the trouble of our Black Sun should not impose itself on other states. So we'll get these two troublemakers, we'll tear them out of here, and the message will be clear to anyone else who considers hiding behind your Union. How's that sound?"

It probably wasn't the reply this officer was expecting — it might have even sounded in some sense logical, and reasonable.

"Either way," I added, "we'll be off your asteroid by the end of today, and we have no intention of coming back. Or hurting any bystanders in the process."

Definitely reasonable. That's not to say it was fair — here was a perfect example of the Empire showing up somewhere it had no authority, and expecting to get its way. But perhaps the reason we so often got away with such tactics was because, on those occasions when we did show up and brusquely demand that the locals allow us autonomy, we tended not to abuse it.

Doesn't make it right, but nevertheless, it had a history of working. And it worked now.

The officer's initial anger was dulled, though certainly not erased. He remained silent, so I smiled and nodded, "If you're here, we'll see you on the way out. If not, a pleasure to have met you."

And that was that. I stepped around the SAUDF man, nodded to his guards, and then proceeded out of the departure lounge followed by Andrea, Rufus, and our two teams. I'm sure that officer called into his dome HQ with warning that we'd arrived — if he didn't he'd have been a fool — but the question asked by the SAU senior officers was simple: dare they intervene when we had committed no crimes, knowing that seven of our warships were in orbit?

This was gunboat diplomacy… come to think of it, it smacks of the arrogance with which the Empires had ultimately treated the Chinese cantons that I keep comparing to Etat Concord.

However you slice it, we were in without so much as having to make a threat. Now we just got to enjoy the sights.

Our teams split up as soon as we reached the ground floor of the spaceport tower, and as we emerged out into the earthgreen main dome of Etat Concord, it struck me as being basically the same as the independent rocks I'd visited. This place definitely didn't seem to have any defining characteristics… whether that was because it was supposed to feel welcoming to people from all over, or whether it was because the Union had grown out of normal independent rocks, I'm not qualified to guess.

Rufus came to a stop beside me as we stood on the sidewalk just outside the spaceport doors, then he pulled a small pad from his vest and checked the address and map we'd been given by Franspaldov.

"About four kilometers to the Connaught house. Walk or acquire transport?"

I thought about that for a second, then decided against calling a cab; I'd rather walk the streets to get a feel for the texture of this place.

"Foot is fine," I said, and with that Rufus nodded and did some hand gestures to deploy his team in a formation fit for walking down a busy sidewalk.

The walk itself was incredible in a few ways. People's reactions were the most interesting part; some were clearly recent-arrivals who had history with the Empire, because they greeted us with looks of recognition. Some were nervous, others just surprised. All of these people, I assume, had left sins behind in the Empire, and more than a few wondered if we'd made a trip all this way to take them back.

The people who didn't know us were obvious too. I didn't know how long the SAU had been around, but obviously it (or its constituent rocks) had spawned entire generations of adults who had never seen Defense Command personnel, and may not even have heard of us. Those people eyed us with suspicion or disinterest… they saw a party of well-armed, uniformed individuals and wondered where we hailed from. For all they knew, we seven could have been from some small rock in the independent belt.

Being unknown to those people was a liberating feeling, I think. I wished Karen could have shared it.

But she couldn't.

As we passed open street markets, and commercial districts, and inner city slums, I was able to distract myself from any thought about her… though I expected she'd be on my mind when I reached the Connaught house.

For the moment, I breathed in the smells of the main dome of Etat Concord, and the more I saw and heard the more I became convinced that this was a rough place to make a go of life. A raw, desperate colony. A place you came to in hopes of getting a new start… and where you could die very easily. The worst parts of the Belt colonies were a hundred times more civilized, as were most of the independent rocks...

Beggars, panhandlers, street prostitutes... so many people trying to survive with nothing. I wondered if the entire Union was as encouraging... but there was no point wondering, because I'd find out soon.

"Left up here," Rufus finally broke our silence as he checked his map. He and his officers were having a tough time keeping eyes on everything as we walked — there were so many possible threats, so many dangerous-looking individuals, that their heads were constantly swiveling around.

No trouble came at us, though, and as we turned off the main drag and onto a more residential street, things seemed a little less chaotic. The place was run-down but not disastrous, and the only people we saw were out on their porches, drinking or smoking as they chatted with each other.

We were noticed, of course, but I didn't care; even if the neighbors warned the Connaughts we were coming, we'd find a way to catch them. Rufus wouldn't fail.

In the meantime, I kept walking.

While our team skirted and then bypassed the seediest parts of the main dome, Andrea Kiley and Eugene Sengooba dove straight in. For the Master-At-Arms this was a revival of old skills he hadn't relied upon since before the war, when it was more common for SF to barge into the Belt Widow side of a town to do a little shaking up.

He was out of practice, but then, he was also now a veteran of war, Pion Rock, and Egesta. None of the troublesome people he saw concerned him too much.

That didn't mean he wasn't going to be cautious, though.

Behind the Master-At-Arms were the other eight guards he had insisted on bringing along, but they were hanging back a ways. No one on the crowded market streets missed their presence, which was part of the intent, but it became clear to all observers that Andrea was the leader, Eugene was the heavy, and they were the guards.

Posturing of a kind — a message to local criminals that there was firepower on the move, and it probably wasn't worth taking a shot.

Andrea's ultimate destination was not fixed; *Wolf's* Captain had done her time chasing pirates, so she had an idea of where to look for centers of information. She was paying careful attention to her surroundings as they passed through the crowded streets, noting the occasional brothel, gambling house, and drug den. She didn't want to start with those... she needed someone who sold weapons.

The people who could get you weapons could also get you the high-level sort of information she wanted... and they tended to have fewer scruples about trading official secrets.

But where...

Ah. Andrea slowed to a stop in the middle of the busy street, spotting an older man sitting at a table outside a café up the road. Now, if you're imagining a picturesque café with fine furniture and dapper serving staff, please replace that image with one of a filthy street in the worst inner-dome district you can imagine. There was feces on the ground not far from this man's table, and what appeared to be a dead man lying in the street near him.

But this older fellow with silver hair was wearing what Andrea describes as comfortable retirement clothes — khaki pants and a yellow shirt with a knitted cardigan draped over his shoulders. He was sipping coffee from a tiny cup while he read a magazine pad... and if Andrea's distance vision wasn't fooling her, it looked like the pad was showing tips for knitting.

The fellow, as you can tell, didn't belong in an environment like this... and he wasn't being bothered by anyone — the panhandlers, the hookers, even the pickpockets were leaving him alone.

Andrea studied the area around the café for a moment, looking for obvious signs of security. None were present, which meant the fellow was either so influential he could walk these dangerous streets without protection, or he could afford the best and most invisible guards in town. Either way, he was the one she wanted.

Touching Eugene on the arm, Andrea pointed at the older gentleman, and the Master-At-Arms nodded immediately. His hand slipped down to the grip of the mag on his hip, but he didn't draw the weapon — just got ready.

Then Andrea started moving again, and he trailed not too far behind. She could speak to this man alone, he'd just have to watch for trouble. He looked back to his guards and nodded for them to move up and take positions all around her, then started crowd-watching. Trouble could be anywhere...

When Andrea pulled out the chair opposite the old man, he didn't look up from his knitting magazine, "That's taken, I'm afraid."

He had a very faint Martian accent, but it sounded as though it had been significantly dulled by time away.

"It is now," Andrea answered as she sat. The chair was sticky and the smell of defecation was intense around the table. After two Egesta tours, though, she was immune to such things — her focus was entirely on the man who didn't belong.

He didn't acknowledge her again for a few moments so she waited, knowing he was testing her. How quickly she jumped into her demands would indicate to him what position she was truly in... he could see that there were SF all around the café now, and whatever security he had in place, this many Defense Command personnel were still intimidating.

"I didn't think your kind came out this way," the man said eventually, lowering his pad.

Andrea tilted her head but remained silent. She knew that speaking to a creature like this would put him a little more at ease. Too often, rookie DC officers would turn up in places like this and start issuing threats... experience teaches us that sometimes the best thing you can do is shut up, because people with the power to do anything rarely need to announce themselves.

Even though Andrea wasn't so advantaged here, that was the tack she chose. It worked.

"What can I do for you?" he asked eventually, carefully making certain to sound calm and at ease.

Continuing to stare, Andrea wondered whether she'd be better off remaining silent... but no, there was little value to over-playing her intimidating hand.

"We need nav data for the entire Union of Solar Asteroids."

It was the man's turn to stare at her, thoughts clearly racing behind his eyes. Defense Command was showing up and asking for something very valuable — and very difficult to access — and he had to consider whether it was worth risking his well-established position to give them what they wanted.

"Difficult to come by," he said eventually, tentatively.

"Irrelevant," Andrea's sharp reply was immediate, and the man took a deep breath. "Expensive."

"You'll do it for free," Andrea replied. "And you'll do it now."

He didn't like the sound of that — few people would. Andrea watched as he placed his pad on the filthy tabletop, then shifted in his seat, "I know where you're from. You don't have influence here. And you never will, particularly if I don't give you that data. So if there's nothing in it for me, why exactly would I assist you?"

Andrea studied his face for a moment, "Well, if you don't help me, I'll cut your head off and take it with me through the streets of this rock. I'll find the next person like you at a café, I'll put your head on that person's table, and suggest that they shouldn't fuck around with me about price and timeline. And you know what, they'll give me what I need."

I'm sure any major player in a place like Concord had heard many such threats — talk is cheap. The difference with this particular threat, though, was who it came from, and how little room her tone left for doubt. Andrea didn't have a blade in hand and she didn't reach for her mag... she didn't need to.

The older gentleman locked eyes with her for a moment, then responded with a small smile, "That would ruin my dinner plans."

"The information," Andrea wasn't going to acknowledge his attempts at charm, and realizing he was in a no-win scenario, the man nodded and came to his feet. "Join me inside."

He turned for the café and found Eugene was already standing by the doorway. The Master-At-Arms let the gentleman step inside, followed by Andrea, and then he entered as well. The rest of the SF who had been standing watch closed in around the structure too — being mindful not to step on the dead body, or the shit.

Inside the café, the older man led Andrea and Eugene to a back room loaded with weapons and other interesting items. Seeing the many opportunities for danger, Eugene drew his mag and kept it on the fellow while he sat at a computer terminal and brought up the nav data Andrea had requested.

He loaded it onto a disc — old school — and handed it to her, "Here you are."

It seemed very simple, so Andrea looked from the disc to the man with her icy eyes, "And if this turns out to be anything other than what we needed..."

"I have no interest in leaving this place, I am in a good position here," the man answered. "I can arrange for someone else to take the blame for you getting this data... but if I give you wrong information, you'll kill me now."

That was a fair argument, though certainly not one Andrea would count on. She thus handed the disc to Eugene and drew her own mag, covering the gentleman with it.

"Transmit that up, have it checked for signs of authenticity," she ordered, and holstering his mag, Eugene nodded.

Drawing his comm, the Master-At-Arms quickly scanned the disc, then sent the enclosed information up to Felicia Khalid. She, in turn, passed the telemetry over to Shelby McLaws, who spent five minutes checking the master celestial marks. It was always possible to forge nav data, but bad forgeries could be caught because they usually missed the nuances of the orbital seasons.

After five minutes, Shelby called back down, "Looks good to me."

Satisfied, Andrea nodded, then lowered her weapon, "Thank you."

The gentleman smiled, "My pleasure to be of service. See you again?"

Andrea paused, then shook her head, "Never."

With that, she and Eugene departed. Their part of the mission was done.

Only two targets left.

CHAPTER TWENTY-FIVE

CONNAUGHTS

Rufus insisted he be the one to knock on the door. His reasoning was sound; the Connaughts had to have friends who would have told them we were in orbit, and if they were home they might start shooting at the first sign someone had come to see them.

We had an advantage, though; we had passed a school on our way to their house, and knowing they had school-aged children, we figured their kids might be in that facility. Imagine, assassins raising two youngsters to be just like them. What a wonderful contribution to humanity.

Clarissa and Maggie had been left to watch the school area, keeping out of sight in an alley between two abandoned buildings across the street from it. If the assassins came to pick up their kids, they'd be tailed home.

Rufus, Simon, Bobby and Selma thus went to the house, and I joined them.

The Connaught home was a bungalow set back from the street. It had a front yard but no fence, so there were plenty of ways in and out, all of them possibly containing traps for us. Rufus and Selma took the front door, Bobby and Simon took the back, and I was told to wait. Familiar instructions, but where I might previously have argued with Rufus about being sidelined, I accepted his orders quietly.

Others would be first through the doors.

The plan wasn't complex; force was in order, so Rufus started by banging on the door, "Open up! Angelo and Sylvia Connaught, open this door!"

As he did this, he half-wondered if the house would explode in his face, as that liquor store on Mercury had exploded on his team and Charlie... but this was the Connaughts' home, where they raised their kids. Rigging the place to blow would be unwise.

That's what we chose to assume, anyway.

Predictably, there was no answer. Unfamiliar voice and banging on the door? Not something you open up to when you're just back from attacking the Emperor's ball.

Rufus had expected silence, so he stepped back from the front door, leveled his MAG-90, and racked a grenade into its underslung launcher.

"Fire in the hole!" he called over his comm headset, and all his officers crouched slightly.

Finally Rufus got to blow something up — it had been far too long. The launched explosive did exactly what was intended, blasting the front door into shards and taking much of the wall with it.

I wonder if Keith Pine ever researched how much Rufus' presence increased the likelihood of a building being destroyed... ten times more likely, perhaps.

Rufus and Selma then swept in fast and hard, while on the other side of the house, Simon and Bobby made sure nobody escaped through the windows or the back door.

If the Connaughts were inside, they'd be captured... if not... we'd have to get them at the school…

But they were in the house, and for just a moment I'm going to try to switch to their point of view.

Neither of them had been expecting to be found so soon. They had known they'd be chased — George Madison's girl, Julie Pichot, who had sent them the instructions for this job had also warned that the Empire could come for them.

Fair enough, if things got bad they'd just retreat from Concord back to Valcour, because no one knew where Valcour was.

But then the Defense Command ships had shown up just days after their own return. That was a surprise, but still they had breathing room — they'd left nothing behind to point to their actual identities, so it would take the newcomers at least a day or two to find them, by which time they and their kids could have moved into a safehouse, and ultimately made their way onto a transport for one of the other Union colonies.

Leaving behind what they'd built on Concord would be disappointing, but necessary. Certainly nothing they hadn't done before, or wouldn't do again. The kids would have to make new friends, but they'd tough it out. They always did…

Except that Defense Command had landed and come straight to their house. How the fuck had the Empire managed to find out exactly where they lived? They hadn't been too careful about protecting their identities from the local network… but Defense Command wasn't supposed to have any plugins to that network. And they hadn't been here long enough to make the necessary inroads.

It didn't matter, because when their front door exploded, Angelo and Sylvia had no time to think about why they had become such pathetically easy prey.

They simply headed for the basement, and to the escape tunnels they'd long ago dug to get them out of a situation like this. Slamming a heavy security door at the top of the basement stairs, Angelo led the way as they hurtled down into the darkness. They didn't touch the lights as they arrived — there was actually enough light coming in from the two basement windows to allow them to move the shelf that concealed their tunnel access.

Neither of them noticed that there was more light than the windows should have provided — not, at least, until I blew Angelo's left leg off at the knee.

I'd been leaning against the wall beside the basement stairs, and in their panic the two assassins had somehow missed me. This was a surprise — even a disappointment — because you'd expect hired killers to be better than that. You'd expect them to notice that one of their basement windows had been blasted open by a full power mag bolt, the noise concealed by Rufus' explosion upstairs.

You'd expect them to look both ways when entering a room.

They didn't, and as Angelo collapsed to the floor screaming, Sylvia tried to turn. It didn't work because I was already right up behind her, and a knife I'd pulled off one of the basement shelves was in my hand.

"Stop!" she barked as soon as she felt the blade come up to her throat. I'd pulled her against me and turned with her to face Angelo, who realized just in time what was happening. He stopped wailing.

"You don't have to do this," he basically screamed, half-delirious with agony. Apparently that was supposed to be a distraction — Sylvia tried to wrench herself free of my grip.

Foolishly, this meant she forced her windpipe against a blade that she herself had probably sharpened, and then slid fast away from me. It's sort of like she cut her own throat, though I'd like to take some credit too. After all, I'd been holding the knife.

Her eyes must have been wide and wild with surprise, but I only saw Angelo's reaction to them, not the eyes themselves. She was doing all the things you'd expect, though — clutching her throat and writhing as she hit the floor and blood flowed from her.

It was disappointingly quick. But at least Angelo wasn't dead.

He was screaming like a pathetic banshee — watching his wife die on the floor next to him while he gripped the stump that had previously been a leg. The mag bolt had cauterized that wound, so he wasn't actually losing as much blood as I'd have liked... but that would soon change.

As Sylvia stopped struggling for life, Angelo started roaring a variety of threats, curses, oaths, pleas... he was about as coherent as I'd been after he and the now-dead woman on the floor had killed Karen. Funny how that works.

At one point I saw him flailing for something on the shelf he'd previously been trying to move — the one with the tunnel behind it. I shot his arm off as punishment, and he didn't like that either.

Given the injuries I was inflicting on him, I knew he'd be going into shock shortly, which was a problem. I didn't have much time, so I moved around Sylvia's body and stepped on his remaining hand, which had been sliding back and forth over the floor.

"What files do you have about who hired you?" I asked quietly, and his wild eyes found mine as he writhed on the floor. He wasn't really coherent enough to talk, so I put more weight down on the foot crushing his hand.

It didn't help. He wasn't going to answer any questions, which was disappointing but not disastrous. I didn't care if he knew anything about the compound that had killed Karen — that wasn't the priority anymore. And I knew where Grant Merger was, and Andrea would find me a map...

I stopped thinking about those things, because I recognized this man all of a sudden.

Carl Devoir.

Lieutenant Carl Devoir.

Supposedly.

"You... recorded a message for us and left it aboard *Idaho*, didn't you?"

Again the man was too much in shock to answer, but I knew it was him. This man, if you go all the way back to *The Dark Cruise*, had been in the fake message left for us claiming *Idaho* had been overrun by an alien. And if he'd been the fellow in that message, it meant Grant had been behind that attack. Bort had been right: the Martians had not been involved at all.

Grant had tried to kill Karen before. With Phosgene he'd killed many of my crew, including people like Kyle Stranks and, of course, Jocko Kent and two of his camera crew... that had been Grant. And this fellow, Angelo Connaught.

I smiled.

"Dear me, I didn't recognize you before. Glad to have met you, Mister Connaught," I took my foot off the flailing man's hand, and I could tell he would soon lose consciousness.

That being the case, I retrieved the knife and crouched at his side.

"Sorry this went more quickly than I'd planned," I said to him softly, then I leaned down beside his ear, figuring there was one thing I could say that might get through to him. "I was going to let you watch when I killed your children. Guess they won't have their daddy to hold their hand while the pieces come off."

Then I stuck the knife into his inner thigh — the femoral artery — stood up, and let him flail for a few seconds. I think at one point he tried to say 'Please', but it was too late.

After he died, I climbed the stairs from the basement and opened the security door for Rufus. He was not pleased to see that I'd come into the house, but his angry words were preempted by three things. First, I was smiling. Second, I was covered in blood. Third, it wasn't my blood.

"Didn't get anything out of them," I said with a shrug, then walked past both our Chinese Major and Selma Koestecki as I headed out into the simulated sunny afternoon.

Rufus looked back to Selma with wide, mismatched eyes, then descended the stairs to the basement. The mess was more than he expected, but then he didn't know me as well as Charlie did.

Guess I still had the edge.

Our Chinese Major called Wes immediately, just to let him know. Then he realized I'd left the house, and that I hadn't mentioned where I was heading. This was a problem on many levels, so he left Bobby and Simon to do a quick intel search, and took Selma as he went after me. He figured the school was the best place to look.

There had been a printed photo of the Connaught kids — one son and one daughter — on the fridge in the house, and I'd taken it on my way out. I didn't know their names, but they looked to be around ten or eleven years old. I held this picture as I sat on a bench just outside the front door of the school, legs crossed and mag sitting on the bench beside me.

Clarissa and Maggie had seen me arrive, and though neither knew what I was doing, they called in my presence. Unfortunately, timing was on my side, not theirs; as soon as they reached Rufus, the bell rang, and in a fashion which I believe is universal across human civilizations with formalized school systems, children spilled from the doors almost immediately.

It was interesting here on Etat Concord, though: not every child on this rock had access to school. It was a paid proposition, so indentured servants couldn't send their kids. Only the children of citizens, or at least free people with means, could attend.

If you think about it, the Connaughts had come to our Empire and killed Karen so they could send their kids to school. Heartwarming.

As the kids spilled out, I spotted the Connaught pair pretty quickly. I'm not really sure how — it just worked out that way — and as I saw them I got to my feet and moved into the crowd to intercept them. A couple of the teachers at the front doors of the school took notice of this and, I think it's fair to say, freaked out: a blood-covered man with a gun was approaching their students, and they started hurrying forward to do something about it… as if they could have.

Another did a smarter thing, going inside to call security… not that that would have changed anything either.

The Connaught children came to a stop and looked up with wide eyes at the tall, blood-stained form blocking their path. I smiled at them, then held out the picture I'd stolen, "Borrowed this from your house."

The Connaught daughter was eldest, and she took the picture from me with a frown. She was an intelligent-looking child, and she was clearly frightened. I didn't like that she or her brother were frightened, so I decided to crouch down to be less intimidating.

This was when the first teacher arrived and screamed with the desperation of a mother protecting children, "Get away!"

Clarissa Hutchinson and Maggie Joyce reached me in the same instant, though, and while neither woman quite knew what I was doing, their instincts directed them to cover me against any possible attack. The teacher was suddenly staring down the barrels of two MAG-90s, and she froze.

I looked from the face of the daughter to the face of the son and smiled, "You look like your mom and dad. I just wanted to come and tell you that I killed your parents. They were bad people, and they killed someone I care about a lot. Killed a lot of people, actually. So I came out here and found them and killed them. They're back at your house."

The young boy's eyes went wide, but he said nothing. The girl — clearly the smarter child — was wide-eyed but angry at the same time.

"I know, me killing them makes me a bad person too. You're right. But I just wanted to let you know. My name is Ken Barron. Will you remember that?"

Neither child responded, which was understandable.

"Good. Ken Barron. From the Earth Empire. When you're old enough, if you want to, you can come try to kill me for revenge. If you challenge me to a duel, it's even legal. So remember my name. Can you say my name?"

"Ken Barron," the Connaught daughter repeated.

"Good job. So eight or ten years from now, you can come to the Empire and challenge me to a duel. If you want revenge. The only thing is that if you come, I'll kill you. Trust me, you won't live, and I will. But it's up to you if you want to try."

If you're wondering, yes, I know exactly how fucked up this was… though I didn't necessarily appreciate that just then. By the time I stood up Rufus had arrived behind me, and he was relieved that I hadn't physically harmed the children. Kids do not factor into Rufus' calculus of revenge, because he's a good person. He was less pleased later, when Clarissa told him what I'd said.

"You're a monster," the teacher who had charged forward spat at me, moving to put herself between me and the kids.

I frowned, "Obviously. Listen, I don't know if this shitty Union of yours has a foster care program, but you should definitely make sure they get looked after. We'll leave you to it."

With that I smiled, turned, and walked away.

This was just the beginning of my revenge. The two Connaughts had physically done the deed — they had killed Karen. It was time to work my way up the ladder.

Rufus, Clarissa, Selma and Maggie followed as I strode away from the school covered in blood. Behind, two terrified, devastated, orphaned children clung to their teacher and began to learn to hate my name.

That was the first day of our Empire's relationship with the Solar Asteroid Union. I'm not sure who made a better first impression on who, but however you slice it, we weren't exactly reciting poetry to each other.

Chapter Twenty-Six

Gawkers

By the time I got back to *Wolf*, it seemed everyone knew how the mission had gone down. Others had been listening on the frequency when Rufus had reported to Wes, and the whispers had started immediately: don't worry, he hasn't lost his edge.

Oh yes, he cut her throat and stabbed him in the groin.

Oh yes, he named himself to their kids, but he's a good guy because he didn't actually murder their kids.

Right. So many of us were so angry that my actions apparently fell within the parameters of cold-but-acceptable. If you think about it, all I did was kill two named enemies of the Empire — people who had broken into the Capital Palace, killed Karen, and then killed SF as they made their escape.

It was the duty of every Imperial citizen to do harm to enemies of the Empire, so I was acting completely within the laws of our land. Of course I hadn't had a chance for a follow-up conversation with that SAUDF officer on my way out, to find out whether I'd abided by the laws of his land. But his laws didn't matter.

Perhaps I had been messier than I needed to be in the way the killing had been done, and in the taunting of the children. I had taken a little too much joy in the process, don't you think? But why not — these people were assassins, and the main actors in the death of Karen McMaster. And, in case I needed more justification, they had also played a role in the murder of the crew of *Idaho*.

To answer one of my editors, I can honestly say I've never lost sleep about this. I don't know if that means there's something wrong with me, but I didn't then, and I never will.

I've lost too much sleep remembering the moment Karen collapsed in the ballroom. That's what matters.

Of course, Wes didn't necessarily see it that way, and as I peeled off my bloody tunic and tossed it in the laundry hamper, it was his message that came up on the screen in my quarters, "What did you do?"

His question was urgent and uncomfortable, and as I glanced at the screen I found my tone had reverted to something approaching normal, "Killed the people who killed Karen."

"You went in alone with a knife and cut them up?" Wes wasn't going to offer me any slack, and I answered honestly.

"Well, I won't split hairs with you about the 'alone' thing, and I did use my mag too… but basically, yes."

Wes fell silent and stared at me. He'd killed dozens of Belt Widows in personal DNR duels; he felt no particular humanitarian anxiety at the fact that two assassins were dead. But the way it had happened concerned him — because there was no question now that I was very much in a vengeful frame of mind.

Killing two assassins? Fine. Do it. Even taunting their kids wasn't the end of the world in a strictly limited sense. But what would my liberal attitude mean when the Belt Squadron arrived at the SAU's capital rock?

"Don't worry, Wes, I haven't ordered us to laser open their dome or anything," I predicted my friend's thought process, and interjected with that supposed assurance. "I'll murder anyone individually who had a part in killing Karen, but it would be overkill to exterminate all of them, wouldn't it?"

Imagine how much Wes didn't like the sound of that question, "I don't know, would it?"

I smiled at him, "It would be overkill. Trust me."

Wes remained silent after I said that, and as I fished another tunic out of my closet I finally moved on to more pressing matters, "Now, we have the nav data we need. Let's set course for Etat Lexington. I wonder if the government will play ball with us."

I was still talking about bringing the Union government on side, which theoretically should have been a good thing. Wes was no longer buying it, but I was saying the correct things. He couldn't fault my orders, and maybe now that the people responsible for injecting Karen were gone, my rage would be reserved for Grant Merger himself.

Maybe we wouldn't start a war with the Union of Solar Asteroids after all.

"Alright," he said eventually. "I'll get us underway. Clean up and I'll talk to you later."

He didn't wait for me to say anything else before he disappeared.

As the screen went blank I stopped what I was doing and took a deep breath. I won't lie to charm anyone here: it felt good to have killed the Connaughts. I was honestly enjoying a certain sense of satisfaction when my wall screen chimed again.

As I turned away from the closet and grabbed the remote, I saw a signal was coming in from *Daedalia Planum*. I accepted it immediately, and as Gerhard Franspaldov appeared on my screen I smiled.

"Thanks for the intel, it was exactly right," I said brightly, and the Captain eyed me.

"We're just hearing. Those two… were directly involved in the killing of Commodore McMaster?"

I nodded, "They were the trigger-pullers, so to speak."

"I see… fair play then."

He didn't sound like he thought it was terribly fair, but at least there had been no collateral damage. That was probably best — if things had escalated they might have threatened to draw in his guardship.

"We'll be leaving for Lexington momentarily, thanks to some information we found. If you'd like, I can have our Sensors and Communications section transfer the chart, for your information. Mightn't hurt to know where things stand out here."

That was a generous offer by any measure — the least I could provide considering all the help Gerhard had given us.

He nodded slowly, "Yes, that would be appreciated."

"Good…" I paused, then thought of something else. "You can get signals out here?"

It was an unexpected question, and not an entirely clear one, so Gerhard only answered tentatively, "Yes…"

"Could you relay one to Bort for me? And ask him to pass it on to Earth when he can?

Our comm ships aren't aligned to receive from us out here."

Gerhard blinked with some surprise — he'd assumed the far-reaching Empire would have comm access everywhere. But he nodded; of course he'd relay a note for me.

"Thanks... send the charts for the Union to him, and ask him to send them to Admiralty House. Ask him to tell them that I've killed the two people who were responsible for killing Karen, and that we're going to Etat Lexington to ask for Union governmental support before we go to Valcour for Grant Merger. Tell him to tell them it'll be fun."

Gerhard actually made notes of what I said, which I appreciated, and then he nodded one more time, "I'll send that, and I'm sure Admiral McWebsbert will forward it along promptly."

"Thanks. It's been good working with you, Captain Franspaldov. Hope to do it again sometime."

"Likewise, Admiral Barron. Good hunting."

That was the end of the message. My screen darkened again, and moments later *Wolf* and the Belt Squadron turned and burned for Etat Lexington. There was much more revenge still to come.

CHAPTER TWENTY-SEVEN
CHARLIE COMES HOME

The situation was not quite as bad as Charlie could have imagined, but it was close. Very close, in fact. As Greg Noyce walked him through the corridors of Terra Nova Hospital, and explained to him the message that Admiralty House had received from Bort McWebsbert, the gravity of the situation was all too clear to my old friend.

With the news of Karen's death, I had slipped out from under the sensible restrictions I'd placed on myself. I'd allowed pain, despair and self-indulgence to guide my decisions, and though for now that had just meant I'd been mean about killing a couple of people I was within my rights to kill, the potential consequences when I got to Lexington were severe.

"You think he might start a war?" Charlie asked Greg as they walked through the hospital corridors, and my mentor Admiral nodded.

"We shouldn't have let him go. Daragh twisted us into it... no, I should take responsibility, I let him go as well. We all did. But now we're all regretting it."

Rightly so. They realized, as Wes did, how dangerous it could be to have a rogue like me throwing the weight of the Belt Squadron around...

"Wes will do what he can to control the situation, but Ken's persuasive, and he can get a lot done," Charlie observed after a moment of silence. "He's not going to slow down... we need to get someone out there to stop him. I can go direct to Lexington, try to meet him there..."

Because Bort had sent back the charts, along with news of what I'd done upon hearing of Karen's death, it was possible now for another force to be dispatched, directly from Earth to Etat Lexington. It would take them longer to reach the Union's capital than it would take the Belt Squadron to get there from Concord... but still, it was worth a try.

Greg agreed, "We're getting *Cheetah* back online, and we've briefed Mark Gunney about the situation. He's walking with a cane, but he's determined to take over and get out there. So we'll send him, and you can go with him. Probably be best if you didn't take a Hawke ship out there right now — last thing I'm sure Lia would need is to begin diplomatic relations with the Union on this note."

He was right, of course, so Charlie would transfer to Mark Gunney's restored *Cheetah* for a voyage of redemption. I know that last part sounds melodramatic, but it seemed an accurate descriptor.

What a fucking mess this all was — and my fault, just to be clear. Well, my fault and Grant Merger's fault.

For now, though, I can't put off why Charlie had come to the hospital. Greg turned the corner to the corridor I'd been tirelessly occupying just days before. The area was abandoned now, as there was no need for observers.

When Charlie came to a stop at the glass containment wall, he stared at the bed that had once held Karen, and now as empty.

He took a deep breath, then shook his head.

"Ken should have waited…"

Greg agreed, though knew it was complicated: "Grant pulled his strings. Pulled all of our strings."

So totally right.

"Can I see her?" Charlie asked eventually, and Greg nodded. He led my friend from the empty hospital room down a corridor and around a corner, to a cold part of the hospital reserved for patient decontamination… and the treatment of cadavers.

"They should be finished processing her, through there," Greg pointed to one of the doors ahead, and with a nod of thanks, Charlie proceeded that way. This was the mystical reason why my friend had come home, instead of chasing us. Because if a war happened that was fine, but someone needed to be here with Karen. She couldn't be alone.

As Charlie moved through the antiseptic corridors, they reminded him of his own convalescence with Lia at Venus. He distracted himself with that thought until he came to the cold room in which the decontamination took place. The light over the door was green, meaning it was safe to enter without scrubs. Charlie went in.

Karen was on the table and two nurses were cleaning up around the room when Lord Peters arrived. He nodded to them and they nodded back, then kept doing what they were doing, as was appropriate.

Charlie approached Karen's table slowly, taking tentative steps because he wasn't sure precisely what was appropriate under the circumstances. A lot of it would depend on how exactly Karen felt about all this.

He got the sense that something was wrong the moment she looked at him.

Sitting up, she was just in the process of wrapping a blanket around herself — she was cold and shivering after they'd scrubbed her during the decontamination. Now she turned so that she was sitting obliquely to him on the table, and as her eyes landed on his, she seemed different.

"Charlie?"

He nodded, "Just arrived from the Protectorate. Greg was filling me in… he said he'd already told you."

She was frowning at him, but she managed one single nod, "Grant Merger is a Governor of something called the Union of Solar Asteroids. Ken's out there looking for a cure for this thing I had. He now thinks I'm dead because of some false signal we assume Grant sent. He's killed the people who attacked me, and now we think he might start a war."

A perfect summary of the situation.

Charlie met it with a nod, and then took a deep breath, "If you're willing, we can take *Cheetah* out there to find him. Put a stop to this."

Karen stared at him, then looked towards the nurses on either side of the room. Charlie followed her gaze and got the message, "Could you give us a moment?"

Both nurses looked to Charlie at the same time, then to each other. They weren't really supposed to leave the patient under these circumstances — the doctors were still trying to figure out exactly why she'd woken up when she had. But this was Charlie Peters, the known hero, and he was a friend of Karen's. A bit of time alone for the two would be alright, especially since she was about to be discharged anyway.

Without a word, then, the pair of nurses departed, and Karen watched them go.

Turning back to Charlie once they were alone, she started to shake her head. She tells me now the confusion was beyond immense… nothing seemed to make sense, and here, finally, was someone she could admit that to. No one else could be trusted enough to know what was going on in her head.

Or more precisely, what *wasn't* there anymore.

"Greg told me that *Rear Admiral* Ken is going out after Grant. That I'm *Commodore* me. And apparently you're at the Hawke Protectorate as a Lord. And *Cheetah*… has obviously been built…"

What she was saying didn't make any sense to Charlie, so he frowned, "Yes… I don't…"

Karen held up her hand, "Last thing I remember… *really* remember… you and Ken had just taken over *Friendly*, and you were heading for the Hawke Protectorate. And I'd just taken over *Lady Grace*, and we were bound for the Coalition of Unaligned Asteroids."

Charlie blinked, but said nothing.

Surely not — surely this was some stupid joke…

"I keep playing along so I don't get confined… but what year is it?"

It wasn't a joke. You know it wasn't. And Charlie figured that out too.

The compound… Greg had told my friend that the stuff she'd been injected with had been messing with her frontal lobe. Her memory. But there hadn't been time for an in-depth interview yet.

Dear God.

"It's 2235," he said. "We just finished a war with Mars."

Karen stared at him, then she started blinking very quickly. Her breathing and her blood pressure both spiked — good thing she wasn't hooked up to monitors anymore, or the doctors would have started panicking.

She sure as hell was…

"But…" she tried to get out words between breaths, and Charlie quickly realized it wasn't working. He leaned forward and put his hand on her shoulder.

"It's okay… it's…"

"No it's *not*," she snapped. "Who… but… if this is 2235… who am I? Who did I actually become?"

Only me, Charlie and a handful of people in the universe could possibly realize what a terrifying question that was for Karen… for Karen of years before. And as soon as he heard it, Charlie understood why he was there.

"You…" he started, then stopped. "You became the only person who can save Ken from himself right now. And I need you to do that with me."

Karen McMaster — Commander Karen McMaster, for all she knew — locked eyes with Charlie after he said that, and then through shivers and a desperate desire to hyperventilate, she managed one nod.

As she's told me many times since, she was thankful in that moment. Because for all the things that didn't make sense anymore, one still did. She reached up and gathered her hair onto her left shoulder, then pulled it tight against her neck.

Nothing that came next would be easy… but she was alive.
She just wasn't the same woman she had been.

AFTERWORD

Now, at last, we acknowledge what Grant did to Karen. It is not an easy time to remember, though — for any of us.

I'm sorry if I shocked you with how frank I was about what happened on Concord… I refuse to glamorize this the way so many movies have. In drama, the avenging hero always seems a bit nobler than I think is genuine. Killing because justice compels him or her to do so, not because it feels good.

Wouldn't want to make anyone think that we enjoy the killing of those who have harmed us, right?

Maybe, maybe not. But more frankness lies ahead, because Etat Lexington, and the government of the Solar Asteroid Union, are soon to get a visit.

See you then. In the meantime, take care.

MEMORIES
OF
ANGELS

THE AUTOBIOGRAPHICAL REMINISCENCES OF
ADMIRAL THE LORD KEN BARRON FOR 2235

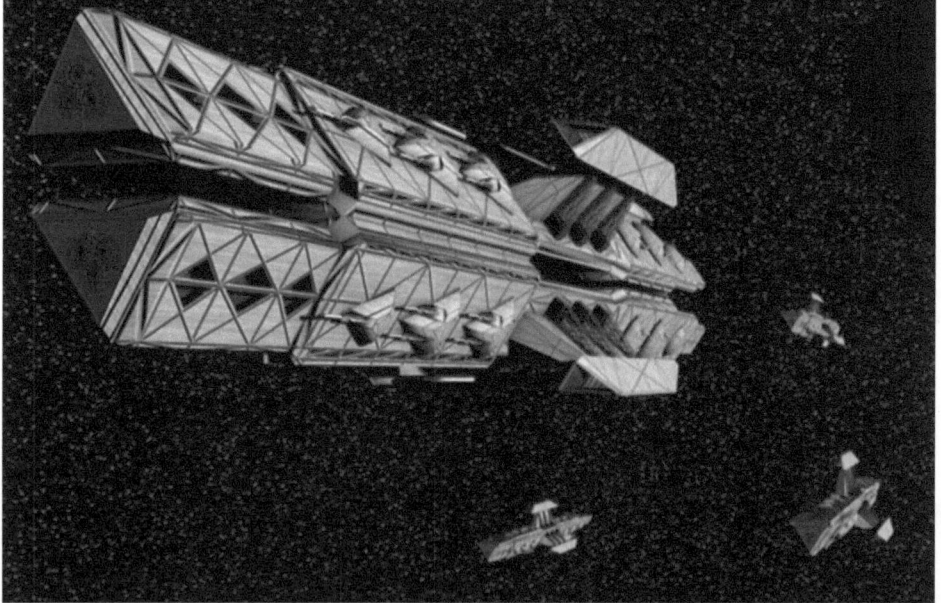

THE MARTIAN WAR - 18

KENNETH TAM

FROM THE AUTHOR

Gunboat diplomacy was perhaps one of the defining arts of nineteenth-century foreign policy. A powerful Empire with its industrially-built Navy could show up in a certain part of the world and use the firepower of one ship (or if the locals were particularly unlucky, an entire squadron) to force a government to do whatever was in the Empire's best interest.

As with the Canton system from last book, this was a common practice in certain waters in Asia, but the reach of a Navy could be worldwide, so many places suffered. An infamous example of gunboats taking matters too far has already been mentioned in this series: at the Battle of Sinope, the somewhat modern Russian Navy wiped out a squadron of Ottoman frigates that hailed from a previous era of war at sea, and did so in such brutal fashion that they triggered French and British intervention, effectively starting the Crimean War. Had not the destruction been so heavy-handed, one might wonder if that conflict would have happened... but that's secondary to the point.

I suppose the power of gunboat diplomacy speaks to the fact that, as implements of war, warships are often some of the most advanced tools in a nation's arsenal. Rifles and muskets are very different, but compare far more favorably to each other than do wooden men of war and steam-powered ironclads.

Indeed, things always became more complicated for the Empires when their would-be target operated on the same Naval technological plane. I've previously written about the defeat of the Imperial Russian Navy in 1905 by the Japanese, and though that's not a perfect example of gunboat diplomacy gone wrong (few would have suggested by that time that the Japanese were a 'primitive' naval power), it illustrates what can happen if an Empire's gunboats show up assuming superiority, when in fact they're not so far ahead of their opponents as their hubris would like to suggest.

That in mind, how much the Earth Empire can 'accomplish' in its first encounter with the Union of Solar Asteroids could depend largely on where the Union's Navy falls on the technological scale: closer to the Ottomans, or the Japanese. We'll find out shortly, but of course, I must give thanks first.

Many of the characters in this book are based on real-world friends of mine, so my thanks to all of those people. In the midst of these dark events, I hope those who have appropriated your identities do right by you.

Once again, the input of my friend Peter Caron was invaluable to everything staged for 2235, and I am indebted to him for his patience and contributions. Similarly, Wes Prewer's design of the Union ships, his assistance developing their fighting doctrine, and his ongoing friendship have helped immensely. Thanks again, Wes.

And at last, my parents and Iceberg Partners for ten years now: thanks Jacqui and Peter. Also, Atlas.

– Kenneth Tam

PREFACE

I have never been drunk.

This is something that perhaps makes me alien to all of you. Not one night, not one occasion of waking up the next morning in utter confusion. No hunting through pictures to see how I'd embarrassed myself. No walk of shame. No drama. No excitement.

Some think this is because I'm no fun, while others wrongly assume it's because I think I'm better than other people.

I know it's neither. When all is said and done, it's a question of memory. Always has been.

I won't discuss my family history just now, but suffice to say I know what a visceral tragedy it is to forget who you are — to not be able to recognize the person staring at you in the mirror. Imagine waking up one day and looking at yourself… and seeing a stranger.

For much of my life, I had known one person who had experienced that. It had killed him when I was a boy, and that profoundly affected me. I became terrified of not remembering. My mind had to be as well-cared-for as was possible, so such a fate did not one day befall me. Of course, we cannot control who such conditions afflict. My number could come up one day, and everything that I am, and everything that I have been, could go away…

But before I would have to face that possibility, the horror befell someone else.

It befell Karen.

For the books to come, I will do all I can to convey the helpless confusion she felt after waking up in that hospital. After learning she'd succeeded in becoming everything she'd one day hoped she would be… and then losing it all in a single fell swoop.

Perhaps for some people that sounds desirable… imagine waking up and discovering it's fifteen years later, and all your dreams came true… would you be satisfied?

Maybe you would. But then what if someone asked you to do something — even one small thing — that you didn't know how to do? That you'd known how to do a short time ago, but forgotten.

What if people were depending on you?

What if *you* were depending on you?

Could you become again the person you no longer were?

And what if you hated the person you had started off as… and that you were again. What if you hated that person so much?

None of this is easy, and I want you all to understand that. Too many people have assumed that the punishment Grant Merger inflicted onto Karen was mild, or not really so serious because it left her able to physically function. She wasn't dead, after all.

But despite what some people and some movies have suggested, this wasn't a case of melodramatic amnesia. She wouldn't get a hit on the head, or a zap from a power relay, and suddenly be alright again. The compound Grant had attacked her with was vicious and persistent. It had moved into her brain and started attacking her frontal lobe. As I am not a neuro-scientist, I can't tell you how it did its job... I just know it was brutally thorough.

We think now that it stopped when it did because the medical staff had started her on an advanced type of hemodialysis... it somehow reached the compound on the other side of her blood-brain barrier, thus keeping her from regressing further.

That's what we think, anyway. Knowing Grant, it's also entirely possible he knew how far back he wanted the compound to take her, then programmed it with a genetic off switch.

Whatever the reason, the memories were gone. All gone. And we didn't know if they would ever come back.

It is not, in fact, wrong to suggest that the Karen I had gone with to the ball was now dead. Part of her was there, but not all of her. And whatever came next — whoever she was now, would be different. As if a writer had completed a book, but then lost the last two thirds, and had been forced to rewrite them all again for the same deadline.

Karen had a great challenge ahead of her... and the first task (because I'm an idiot) was to come out to the Solar Asteroid Union. Whether she'd be coming to rein in my anger... or to vent her own... no one quite knew.

We'd soon find out.

Chapter One
I Remember

The friendship that Karen and I formed after the night in the alley had been an intense one. From the beginning, no one quite knew if we were together in a romantic sense, or just joined at the hip as friends. She grew her hair and started wearing it in a ponytail, always keeping it on her left shoulder because she was sure there was a scar where my knife had been.

She also stopped being quite so outwardly aggressive. Her marks rose, her attendance improved… she started to realize her potential.

Also, instead of looking like a feral quasi-felon, her appearance became that of an officer. A beautiful one.

I allow myself to take credit for some of this, but really I know the change happened because she had found an excuse, or maybe a reason, to start doing what she'd known she was supposed to be doing all along. These days she bats her eyelashes and claims it was just hormones that encouraged her civility… but I can assure you, it was much more than that.

She and I both got ourselves onto the same interesting path.

And Grant, grudgingly, came along with us.

Karen and Grant weren't natural friends; I was the glue in our trio — the common ground. Grant did go on to date the girl Karen had savaged on the night we met, but Megan Dunne was never the same after the pummeling she'd taken. Her injuries had been considerable, and the violent experience had convinced her that joining the fighting arm of Defense Command wasn't really what she wanted.

She focused on teaching at the Academy instead, and the results were very good — as you might remember from *The Articles of Empire*, she trained some of the most notable up-and-comers in the fleet.

Meanwhile, Grant, Karen and I set the Academy alight, and it was no different one evening when we booked ourselves into the war-games simulator for a duel with the computer.

At this point in time, the bridge simulator — now often-replicated by video games, though never as good as the real thing — was running battle scenarios written by Commandant John Fiora, based on the pirate-fighting experiences of people like Daragh Ryan at the Forge. The scenarios were endless, and some of them were billed as quite difficult.

One of the very toughest was our sport for that night: a scenario with the innocuous name '00124', which pit three *Canada*-class corvettes against a pirate base. Sound like fun? It was.

Karen, Grant and I each took a ship, and in we went. I won't bore you with our tactical acumen — we used every trick we could imagine, doing everything possible to demonstrate how creative and formidable we were. How deadly we could be. We were all killers of the first order, you understand, and so a pirate squadron crumpled before us, despite the fact that it was skippered by AIs that had been programmed by John to kill impetuous cadets.

It was a fine outing, and then our three simulated corvettes closed in on the pirate base. Fairly modest as an installation, it still had to be dealt with, and this was when the differences between us really became clear.

"Lasers?" I asked hungrily over comm as I looked at Grant and Karen over Battlelink screens.

My suggestion was rooted in a simple set of principles that I had entertained as a young man: if the enemy was left alive, he or she could come find you later. And if you were going to kill, there was no point trying to get fancy about it, just use the most effective means at your disposal.

A laser shot to a pirate asteroid base? We could put an end to them once and for all, and if any survived the strike by hiding in pressure-tight buildings in the dome, they'd soon be out of air and food. They'd die a painful, lingering death as punishment for their choices in life.

It was their fault they were criminals, after all. No one had prevented them from getting jobs, living honest lives.

I still harbor some of those sentiments now, but back then I had a very uncomplicated view, and I readily applied it to any situation. That being the case, the choice seemed simple: these corvettes had the latest in laser technology, they could carve up the pirates like a roast.

But Karen disagreed: "We can go down there and look for intel, though. And leave some survivors with stories to tell."

I could hear her smile as she said it; she remembers very clearly smiling about the prospect (though she knew the simulator wasn't sophisticated enough to let her go anywhere and punch anyone).

Karen still loved the feeling of walking into a room, and knowing — just knowing — that she could kill most of the people in it. This was not something she'd later be proud of, but the certainty of superiority was a crutch she'd leaned on throughout her young life... one that a couple of years with me wasn't going to change. She was still deeply insecure, extraordinarily angry with her parents, and eager to pass along her pain to anyone she believed had earned it.

Of the three of us, Grant had the most interesting answer — or at least, in retrospect, I think it was the most interesting.

"You ever think we should stop and ask them what their agenda is?" his voice interjected, and to Karen and I both, he sounded far too reasonable — damned near pacifistic.

"The raping and pillaging agenda?" Karen shot back.

"I was also going to suggest it is a raping and pillaging agenda," I added smartly, and Grant laughed.

"Yes I suppose. Criminals are criminals, but are all of these pirates out for that purpose, do you think? We're an Empire, after all. You'd assume at some point we're going to run into freedom-fighters."

Now, given what happened later, this might seem to you like a rather large red flag — why didn't we immediately realize Grant was going to turn traitor, form the Syndicate of pirates and attack Earth?

Because we were kids. We all said things we didn't mean, up to and including Grant's suggestion that there might be freedom-fighters out there, who didn't like the fact that the Empire was big, strong and successful.

"Well, that might make sense if they weren't free to begin with," I decided to answer philosophically. "But those pesky Articles of Empire make it kind of hard to argue."

Karen chuckled, and I could imagine Grant rolling his eyes before smiling as well, "You two are always on the team. It's charming."

"As long as we're on the same team," Karen agreed. "We even share a room for road games."

Okay, so maybe there were some hormones involved, but I assure you they were mostly on Karen's side. I was a brooding young psychopath, innocent in the ways of the world.

"We even share a *shower* for road games," I added.

Right, so you can go ahead and choose how you define 'innocent'. Keep in mind that this was banter, and doesn't necessarily imply anything.

Grant just shook his head, "So I'm the deciding vote between 'laser them from orbit, because it's the only way to be sure'... or 'go down there and cut off their faces with spoons'?"

Karen answered that giddily, "I like the spoons!"

"Laser," Grant replied flatly, just to interrupt her fun, and then the three of us ordered up laser strikes to cut the dome right off that pirate rock. The simulation ended as soon as the place was destroyed, and we emerged from our booking fifteen minutes early. The next set of cadets (coming in because they actually needed the practice) grumbled as they watched us swagger away. They didn't like us — we three always set the high scores and impressed the instructors... and we had the egos to prove it.

But some who watched us bitterly assured themselves that when we got out into the real world, our lack of field experience would get us killed.

Those jealous kids were wrong. We never got ourselves killed. Just a lot of other people.

And more very soon.

CHAPTER TWO
NECESSARY OMISSIONS

The first question Karen and Charlie faced was simple: should they tell anyone Karen couldn't remember anything that had happened in the last dozen years? The answer to this might seem equally simple: of course they should tell.

But no, it wasn't that simple at all.

What if the doctors, or the officers... someone... anyone... tried to stop Karen from leaving on *Cheetah*. According to everything the medical staff saw on their screens, she was fit and ready to go out after the Belt Squadron, albeit with careful supervision from *Cheetah's* shipboard doctor.

But this particular lingering symptom might rightfully scare the medical people, and equally would concern John, Greg and Marlene. They might wonder whether Karen was ready to cruise... if she was mentally stable after the compound... if more memories could vanish... and if she had the experience she needed to help calm the situation, instead of inflame it.

Because inflaming things was still very much in her repertoire when she'd started as commander of *Lady Grace*. Hard lessons as a Commander had cured her of most of that, but those lessons were nonexistent now.

Charlie considered this carefully as Karen got dressed. Someone had retrieved a uniform for her, and after the pair left that cold decontamination chamber and headed to a warmer, private room where she could change, he rolled the question over in his mind.

For him this was a problem: Karen was wounded... but she *was* breathing.

And there was no way even he could convince me of that without bringing her to me.

That is to say, if he turned up aboard *Cheetah* and told me 'not to worry, Karen's alive'... even if he showed me a recorded message from her... I might not believe him. I might think it was a desperate forgery meant to stop my madness, and disregard it altogether.

Far better if Karen arrived, and proved herself to be alive... because surely that would calm me down.

Unless she was as eager to kill as I was, in which case it could be a disaster.

Better with her or without... how was Charlie to know? He couldn't, but as he analyzed the situation more, he realized there would be additional options with her aboard *Cheetah*.

Karen pondered the same question as she dressed, but her mind wasn't completely focused on the mission. In fact, the more clothes she shed, the less she thought of it. Because she was standing in front of a mirror, and she was getting her first look at herself in more than a decade.

She was older... but quite fit (coma notwithstanding). That was good — she'd never wanted Naval duty to kill her figure, and it hadn't.

But she wasn't twenty-something anymore. There were scars in places she'd never expected to see them. She noticed the one in the palm of her left hand, and the one that ran up and down her left side. Her knee ached in a way she didn't remember, suggesting she'd damaged it acutely at one point, or perhaps was damaging it repeatedly over time.

And there were lines around her eyes... lines that meant she'd suffered, and fought, and killed...

She was older than when she'd gone to sleep the night before. Her body felt different... firmer, and stronger... but thicker too. And not as flexible. She'd grown into her ears, to use one of her favorite puppy-related phrases... and of course, she couldn't remember doing so.

What the hell was she going to do?

Karen knew she needed to avoid that question until at least after they got away from Earth. She knew nothing about the time she was now in... nothing except for Charlie, who was also older... so she'd go wherever she had to with him, to find someone else she could trust.

She knew she could trust me — knew that, despite the years that had passed, I had to be at least somewhat the same, because if I'd changed too much I wouldn't be out there hunting Grant.

And, of course, Grant had apparently gone rogue. That one piece of information didn't surprise her. She'd always had a feeling about him, dating back to the day he walked out of Defense Command. She'd known he was trouble, even if I wouldn't believe it.

Trouble indeed. He'd destroyed her memory.

As that thought crossed her mind, Karen paused to stare at herself in the mirror again, then took a deep breath and tried to focus on adjusting to her body. She slid into her pants, which were a couple of sizes bigger than she was accustomed to, and then tucked in her ship fatigues. She was still attractive, and no point being coy, that was important to her.

Now, though, she couldn't let her circumstances change the way she carried herself — she could not be some failing, amnesia-suffering victim. While she might no longer bear the moral authority of a true Commodore, she knew everyone expected her to act like one. So she would — and she'd do her best to be convincing.

If she was found out, and forced to stay in a hospital while I was out getting the guy who'd done this to her... out teaching Grant that he hadn't really won those arguments... she'd go insane.

Not an option.

So when Karen opened the door to the changing room and emerged in uniform, Charlie was one of only a few people in existence who could have noticed the difference between who she'd been, and who she was.

Fortunately, the slight change in her posture and the way she moved could be blamed on her weeks in a coma.

"I'm ready to cruise," she said firmly, and a smile played at the corners of her mouth. "And I'm a Commodore?"

Charlie recognized a bit of swagger in her tone, "Alright. But let's play this carefully: you pretend you're not feeling completely well. Don't answer questions... don't do anything that will tip anyone off to what you can't remember. We'll get you out of here and then we'll fill Mark in on the way."

"Mark?" Karen asked immediately, and Charlie winced.

Mark Gunney had probably been around the Belt Squadron as an Ensign by the time Karen took over *Lady Grace*, but they wouldn't have crossed paths.

"Belt Squadron, skipper of *Cheetah*. One of yours."

"Oh," Karen's smile faded a little. It was all very easy to say she was going to play the part, she realized, but even the Captain of her new ship was going to know who she'd become better than she did.

"Like I said, keep quiet until we can get you out of here. I'll also make sure we carry a lot of files and extra histories... you're going to have to go to school. Maybe you'll start to get your memories back as we cruise, but if not, we're going to make sure you've read up on what's going on."

That sounded less appealing, and Karen's expression soured, "Once people know, I can just ask what I've missed."

Charlie locked a firm stare on her, then took a step forward and put his hands on her shoulders, "Doesn't matter if they know or not. You need to have as much information as you can if you're going to be able to contribute. And I expect you to be able to contribute."

Karen's expression darkened, not so much at the lecturing tone — she wouldn't accept that from many, but from the first time they'd worked together on *Alberta*, Karen and Charlie had gotten along — but more at her own impetuousness. She wanted to go out and find me and then shoot some things. That's what a Commander on her first mission is apt to want.

But that wasn't her role now. She had to get used to being a decision maker of a different order.

She felt entirely unprepared... because she was.

Charlie eventually let go her shoulders, and then the pair made their escape. They had to get to *Cheetah* and get out of orbit.

CHAPTER THREE

SUSPICIONS

Grant Merger was leaning back in his desk chair, a frown on his brow as he steepled his fingers in front of him.

"They must have been able to buy charts from someone. There's no reports of any threats to the local nav authorities," Sonia Hart was making her report about the events at Etat Concord, and though she wasn't terribly convinced by that assessment of how the Belt Squadron had so quickly gotten in and out of the canton colony, she was at least trying to make sense of all that was happening.

As you know, Grant Merger builds complex plans with many moving parts, and that leaves plenty of room for things to go off the rails. The reason Grant has usually gotten away with these operations, though, is because of his flexibility; when one plan stops working, he's usually able to tweak it so it can accommodate the new factors.

In this case, the fact that the Belt Squadron had spent less than a day at Etat Concord was a concern — Grant had figured it would have taken us at least two or three days to nab the assassins, and then browbeat someone into giving us the nav data we needed.

There were a few reasons we'd been able to go faster than Grant had planned. First and foremost, Bort McWebsbert had called ahead on our behalf, and basically put the resources of the Martian guardship at our disposal. Given our public hatred for the Martians, Grant would have had no way to suspect that I had a contact on that front.

Second, I suppose he'd overestimated the discretion of the criminals on Etat Concord — they weren't so willing to put their lives on the line for Union security as he might have thought. Or perhaps Andrea was just much scarier than he would have expected.

But Grant had no way to know either of those things, so he was left to frown and wonder whether I was getting information from another source... perhaps one closer to him.

"I find it more interesting that they got a message back to the Empire," Fletcher Karadzic, Grant's long-time security man and current chief security advisor made that point in a grim tone. "We still don't know where the signal came from, or where it went to... wondering if they detoured one of their ships back towards the Empire..."

"But the fact that they don't know the truth about Karen suggests they don't have two-way contact. Well, assuming they don't know..." Grant shook his head as he agreed with Karadzic's concern, then paused in silence again for a moment.

Thanks to Grant's connections in DCC, he still had the ability to know most of what Defense Command was saying to its ships. That ability had served him very well since he'd obtained it in 2233, and because of it he knew that Admiralty House had gotten a message from me, declaring my intention to go to Etat Lexington to request the support of the Union government.

Fortunately, being sensitive to my source and their communications conduit, the folks at Admiralty House hadn't mentioned in their messages who had passed along my information — they kept Bort McWebsbert's name right out of it. That meant Grant was left to wonder where they were getting their news, and indeed, who was giving the Belt Squadron the information we needed to move ahead faster than he anticipated.

Grant certainly didn't mistake me or any of us for fools; he had a healthy respect for the fact that we had defeated him at Deep Black, and that we'd fought a hard war in the years since. We weren't rookies… but he still knew how long things were supposed to take. We were moving faster, and that suggested…

Taking a deep breath, my old friend shook his head again and looked up at Sonia and Karadzic. They were alone in his office, I should say — aside from the constantly-watching surveillance bugs on the ceiling — so he knew he could speak freely.

"I think we have a mole."

Though Grant's tone was relatively relaxed, the implication was anything but casual.

"You think so?" Karadzic scowled. He'd checked the staff forward and backward, and none of them seemed suspicious… but he never doubted Grant's intuition. The villain was a genius, and a man like Karadzic was big enough to respect that.

After another heavy sigh, Grant affirmed his suspicion, "I do. It feels like the way they came after us just before Deep Black. Remember how they seemed to catch our scent, and we couldn't figure out why?"

Karadzic had been aboard *Guy Fawkes* with Grant during that last fight, so he knew exactly what the Briton was referring to — somehow Greg had managed to keep the Belt Squadron on the Syndicate's tail even though Grant had taken his ships out into open space, away from the asteroids. Deep Black had been the result… and if you'll recall, we owed that success to Mel Fox, who'd been one of Grant's skippers at the time.

And one of our superspies.

Fool me once, the saying goes…

"Want another audit of the staff?" Sonia asked, looking from Karadzic to Grant.

After a moment the Governor nodded, "We have to…"

He trailed off, then the frown on his face deepened as he looked back up at his lover. Sonia wasn't sure what revelation he was having, but like Karadzic she knew that when he had a revelation, it was necessary to pay attention — he tended to be right. It was one of the reasons he was here, and she was with him.

"The new girl. I know it would be foolish for them to send another woman… same type even… but we know DCI isn't as well-run as it should be. Fletch, take a close look at her. And whoever it is, call Renault. We're going to need him to deal with the problem."

As Grant gave those orders, Karadzic nodded, but Sonia looked confused. The 'new girl' was most likely Julie Pichot, the survivor of the Forge she'd recruited from an office at Venus… but Renault wasn't a name she'd heard in these offices before.

Picking up on the uncertainty, Grant sought to offer some consolation, "Don't worry, Sonia… these spies are very good. If it's Julie, it's not your fault. Believe me. And Renault is just an old colleague of ours. Tends to be immune to the abilities of DCI superagents."

That's putting it mildly; if you've never heard of Augustin Renault, you might want to look him up. Born in Paris and very proud to be French, he became known early as a spykiller for hire, and eventually he ended up on retainer for the Syndicate. Of course he wasn't good at *identifying* spies — that was the business of men like Karadzic — but once he was pointed at a target, he had an excellent kill record.

He's the sort of person Mel Samuels actually spares the odd concerned thought over — the reason she'd been so completely under cover in the years following Deep Black.

If Julie Pichot was a spy, and if Renault was sent after her, it was bad news indeed.

And since we know she was a spy, I guess that means we can declare right now that the news was bad.

More on that later; aside from putting his own house in order, Grant had other concerns. He'd been prepared for the possibility that we'd go to Lexington and seek the support of President Fabian Kohl, but now that we were moving so quickly — just five days away from the place — he'd have to make sure the defensive arrangements there were appropriate.

"Where's the Admiral? I'll need to talk to him about the ships at Lexington..." Grant changed the subject smoothly.

"He's waiting outside. Should I show him in?" Sonia replied.

Grant nodded, though he didn't do so eagerly. He didn't care for the style of the man he'd employed in this position, but sometimes needs demanded compromise.

"Go check out Julie, Fletch. Sonia, stay in the meeting with me and Dave."

With those orders issued, Grant took a breath and straightened in his chair, adjusting the appropriate lever to stop it reclining. Fletcher Karadzic departed, and behind him Sonia stepped out, spoke to the Admiral, then stood aside as he walked in.

Waddled in, I should say.

"Admiral, take a seat," Grant gestured to the chair opposite him, and the short, round creature with the stupid face and beard did as he was told.

"About time," he muttered. "I hear we have Barron coming right at us."

"At Lexington first, Dave. And you're going to wait here... we just need to decide who we're putting out there to draw his fire."

Those words might have chilled the enthusiasm of Admiral Dave Caldecott, but he still clapped his hands and then rubbed them together eagerly.

Yes, it was Dave Caldecott. Alcibiades, I called him back in *The Almost Coup* — and if you'll remember, he disappeared from his supervised exile near the end of 2233. Guess who recruited him. Guess how Grant Merger had gotten access to the DCC network. It wasn't just the Emperor's acolytes who still had friends in there... some of the same people who'd been monitoring our signals during the coup were still talking secretly to Dave, passing along information and planting messages for him.

Now, when they were later tried, these people claimed they had no idea Dave was actually working for Grant Merger when he gave them those instructions — they thought he was still working for the Emperor. Nevertheless, he was a declared enemy of the Empire, which meant he and Grant had some strange common ground.

The Empire hated them both, and they both hated aspects of the Empire... though for Dave, his bitterness was obviously much more personal, and tied to the fact that he hated we Fiora Ring officers for our cavalier ways and our irresponsibility. We were turning the Empire and Defense Command into a circus, and we'd destroyed his life in the process.

That dovetailed well enough with Grant, whose personal feelings about us were somewhat different, but whose perception of the Empire as a whole had led him to do everything you're reading about.

Strange bedfellows, but Grant would work with whoever fit within his plans. He'd plucked Dave from his exile in the Coalition as soon as he'd been able to, and then used his influence with the USAN (SAUN or 'shaun' if you choose to use my derogatory acronym which voids their feigned connection to the real American States) to get Caldecott catapulted into the top job.

His resume, appropriately massaged, had been sufficient to make that appointment fairly easy... and it gave Grant the control he needed. The nascent Union fleet went wherever the villain desired.

Now he'd need to deploy part of the twenty-four-ship force around Lexington.

"The fleet is scattered around the Union," Dave described the strategic situation without being prompted. "I figure I can have five ships in position over Lexington in three days. Nine if you can give me six days."

Grant knew more than a little about Naval strategy, obviously, and he'd already thought about what he wanted. Considering the SAU fleet, he had three battleships (one much more powerful than the other two) and twenty-one cruisers. None of these vessels were standardized into proper classes at this point in time, but four of those cruisers were the first ships crudely built for the SAUN. The rest were newer and progressively better.

That said, because of the standardized construction methods used in the Union, they all looked very similar to each other. An uninformed observer could mistake a first-generation ship for a fifth-generation ship quite easily, but could be surprised by the vast difference in survivability between the two.

"Send *Freedom, Republic, Independence, Justice* and *Trincomalee*. And only those five," Grant said, naming the four oldest ships in the fleet, and arguably the least formidable of the three battleships.

The fact that those five were precisely the ones Dave Caldecott had promised could be deployed within three days was no accident; Grant had previously suggested their deployments, knowing they were the ones he'd want at Lexington if I headed there.

He'd have his wish.

"No more than those?" Dave Caldecott asked in his squeaky way, somewhat surprised that his master wasn't inclined to make more of a stand against the Belt Squadron.

Shaking his head, Grant explained his position — or at least elaborated in a manner that would make some sense to the fool facing him: "You know how Kohl feels about me. He might try to sell me out to Barron, and if he does, I don't want him to be able to seize any of our best and most loyal ships right away."

"Aha," Caldecott nodded, then tapped the side of his nose with the index finger of his right hand.

Idiot.

That was enough, so Grant nodded to Caldecott to go, "Get those ships deployed, Dave, and then make sure our core squadron is here over Valcour. Spread the rest out however is best to continue to protect the Union. We can't forget our responsibilities just because the Empire has come."

"Of course!" Caldecott rose, and then he saluted before waddling out of the office. Sonia closed the door behind him and let out a long sigh.

"I don't like that man," she said very honestly, and Grant laughed as he adjusted his chair to lean back again.

"No one does. And he's not even good at his job. But his contacts... they're valuable."

It was the simple truth, and Sonia was one of the few who could hear it. I think it's fair to say that, in Sonia Hart, Grant finally felt like he had someone to match my relationship with Karen... though he didn't. He really didn't.

Compare the two... before the attack and after... and you'll see very, very different relationships. Nevertheless, my old friend enjoyed something like what he'd taken away from me, and if I found out about Sonia, he knew I'd be determined to take her away from him, in the cruelest way possible.

And I can be cruel.

For now Sonia lowered herself into one of the chairs opposite Grant's desk and closed her eyes, "So if he goes to Lexington, he's going to find out pretty quickly about the election. He might figure out what you're doing."

It was possible... indeed, it was probable, and Grant acknowledged the truth behind Sonia's words, "You're right. But it won't matter. Whatever Ken does, and importantly, whatever Fabian does, will all work within our narrative. The key for us is to stay out of his grip. Best case scenario is we stop the Belt Squadron cold... but if we don't, you and I need to get clear. Which means we need to be careful of a spy..."

Right. Sonia had managed to turn her mind away from the possibility that the young woman she'd recruited from Venus could now be up for extermination. But it was possible, and there was no keeping the discomfort off her face as she thought of Renault waiting for Julie in a darkened room.

"Hey," Grant spotted Sonia's unease, then rose and rounded his desk to crouch beside her chair. "I know it's tough, but it's worth it. We'll be safer."

He took Sonia's hands in his as he spoke, then leaned forward and kissed her. That always got the reaction he wanted; Sonia seemed to uncoil. Then she coiled again, but for a different reason.

Grant wasn't a womanizer at all, but when he found one he truly appreciated, he tended to be very enthusiastic. He locked his office door, confident in their privacy because of the soundproofing he'd had installed. But as I've mentioned, the surveillance bugs didn't miss anything.

He loved Sonia Hart, in whatever way you choose to take that term. Perhaps that was a vulnerability he should have reconsidered.

CHAPTER FOUR
SEEKING ALLIES

To say Wes Pellew was concerned would be, of course, an understatement. Since we'd left on our cruise he'd had the feeling that things could all go very badly, and the events on Concord had done little to dissuade him of the notion.

My quiet demeanor since learning of Karen's death had been misleading — perhaps intentionally, perhaps not. Either way, the Independent Squadron's Commodore now knew for certain that I needed to be closely monitored, and he was the only one who seemed to be of that mind.

He needed some allies, but who to ask?

Despite their previous conversation, Matt Baxter was the first person who came to mind, so Wes called him on realtime the evening after we departed from Concord. The discussion had been lengthy — a lot of checking in and catching up — but the pertinent part was this:

"So... how do you think Ken is holding up?"

Matt frowned at Wes' question, not picking up on the intention behind it, "Seemed pretty effective down there. I was worried this was going to take him right off his feet, but he's proved he can do the job."

It was a firm endorsement, and left Wes feeling like he didn't have many places to go with the conversation. Still, he made one more attempt: "Indeed. We'll have to be ready to back him if he decides to be as decisive when there's a bigger threat around."

He was obviously fishing, though interestingly, Matt doesn't remember getting that sense. Instead he simply nodded, "Anything we can do to put these bastards in their place. I still may retire when this is done, and if I do, at least I'll know I helped end Grant Merger's bloody little fiefdom."

Matt will openly acknowledge now that his anger at Karen's death had completely shifted his moral compass. Where before he was the champion of avoiding 'stupid stuff', now he just wanted revenge. They had taken Karen and he wanted them all to pay.

It was not rational or reasonable, but that's how he felt.

And that meant Wes didn't have an ally in *Friendly's* skipper. If I ordered the squadron to open fire, Matt clearly would.

After Matt, Wes tried Katya Romanov and Isoruku Togo. Both officers had been separated from us during at least part of the war, so there seemed some possibility that their commitment to this vendetta would be less solid. It wasn't. If anything, the time away made them more determined to be involved now. To use Isoruku's explanation, being part of this mission seemed almost like penance to him... a way to make up for the days he'd missed during the last stages of the war.

Hardly necessary for him to make up for anything, I think you'll agree, but that's how he felt.

Wes had no allies there either.

The next attempt was with Kate Levec, recently made Commander and given *Lady Grace*. I can very simply sum up her conversation with Wes.

Her words: "I know... I shouldn't hope this, but I'd love to be the one to kill Grant Merger. It should be Ken's right, but I'd love to do it. He's got it coming, and I've never had the chance to do something like that. Maybe I'll settle for whoever he's got with him..."

Kate wasn't going to be talking anyone down from violent action — at least not unless it gave her a chance to do the killing herself.

That left just one more Captain: Kris Jacobs, who had been through enough suffering during the war to perhaps be sympathetic to the harm the Belt Squadron could do if it became reckless.

"How do you think Ken's holding up?" Wes asked that same question, and Kris sighed and then shook her head.

"I think he's very angry," she answered. "I just hope that keeps his head clear. I know Grant must have a trap waiting for us out here... I'm not good enough to see it. I know you probably could catch it... but Ken and Grant have so much history. He's the one you want to have sniffing for it, you know?"

It seemed a less-complete endorsement than the one Matt had given, so Wes probed a little more.

"You think his emotions might get in the way of seeing it?" he asked gently, and Kris' eyebrows raised.

"They could. But... no, I don't think he's the kind to lose his head when he's charged up like this. I'll trust his judgment... I know he'll tell us to shoot when we need to."

Kris had been my XO on *Wolf* for enough years to trust me implicitly, and though I fear those quotes might make her sound indecisive, she wasn't at all. She was just certain that she could trust me... another miss when it came to a possible friend for Wes on a day of excesses.

By this time the Independent Squadron Commodore was feeling quite alone. There was no one in this force who saw the situation the way he did — who was able to set himself or herself far enough back to consider the ten- or twenty-year consequences of their actions. This was, to be honest, a criticism of our Belt Squadron — a flaw we'd all admit now.

We were all hurting from the loss of one of our own, and that had reduced our perspective.

Wes alone had suffered something similar, and for him it was worse than Karen's death. When it had been his wife Sara, I'd helped keep him from harming himself or those who needed him.

But circumstances were different now. We weren't pilots, we were squadron commanders. We weren't talking about individual duels, we were talking about grand military action.

This was not the place to lose perspective, and he was the only one of us who'd kept his. He'd talked to every skipper, and...

Every skipper but one.

There was no rational reason to expect that Andrea Kiley would be Wes' ally in anything. He had no interest in speaking with her — not after the disgusting display she'd put on at the ball, not after she'd invoked his dead wife's name in a sorry bid to win an argument with him.

But she was aboard *Wolf*, cheek by jowl with me every day. Perhaps the best-positioned person to make a difference, and she did have enough genuinely awful experiences in her recent past to mean she might have a different perspective than the others.

Perhaps she was worth speaking to.

For about twenty minutes, Wes contemplated that possibility. In the end he brought himself to a simple question: was he reluctant to speak to Andrea because he didn't expect she would be of any use, or because he just didn't want to interact with her?

Knowing which answer was more likely, he sent a signal to *Wolf*.

When Andrea answered the hail from her day cabin, she appeared not at all pleased to see who was calling. She didn't so much as open her mouth to greet the Commodore of the Independent Squadron, she just stared at him through the screen.

For a moment this silence endured, and then Wes finally decided to break it. He almost began asking the same question he'd put to everyone else… but he stopped before sound came out of his mouth.

No, Andrea didn't need to be handled diplomatically.

"You want him to turn out like you?" his question was sharp, and the Irish skipper on the receiving end let her eyes narrow.

"Excuse me?"

"Ken. Let him be broken. Let him go as far as his anger wants him to go. Let him be broken like you are, and maybe that'll validate your own problems."

This was pretty much a pickup of the fight they'd had at the end of Egesta, many months prior — just with a new focal point (me).

Andrea was surprised by the aggression, but more than capable of countering it, "You expect everyone to cope with loss the way you do? Or perhaps you won't let them cope the way you did, because you're ashamed of yourself and it's easier to criticize others than to accept responsibility for what you did."

Though she knew Wes had hardly shirked responsibility for his earlier vengeful excesses, Andrea decided that was a good place to attack him. And if by 'good' she meant it would make him even angrier, she was on to something.

Wes started to snap back, but managed to catch himself. This call wasn't about him, it was about me and the Empire. And as much as Andrea was willing to push his buttons because he'd called her out, he couldn't let himself fall into her trap.

"I'm not the issue. You're not even the issue," he said. "I want you to ask yourself just one question the next time you see Ken making a decision about revenge. One question only."

Andrea fell silent at that, not sure how to respond. Wes felt like he'd regained the upper hand, so he pressed home his advantage: "You don't care what happens to you, I get that. But doesn't Ken deserve better than you? Ask yourself that."

It was a question to which he figured he knew her answer. He believed that, though Andrea might enjoy company in the world of bloody retribution and bitter unhappiness without respite, she wouldn't want me to suffer there with her.

Maybe deep down she even knew it wasn't a place for her, though that was a separate question.

Having burdened *Wolf's* Captain with that loaded line of thought, Wes immediately killed the realtime connection — he wouldn't endure talking to her any longer than was required. They both got too emotional. They needed to keep their distance from each other. Enough had been said.

That was the end of Wes' hunt for allies; there were no more friends around to help control the situation, so he resigned himself to the fact that he alone would have to calm the fires, when the time came.

Perhaps he'd have to challenge me to a duel. That might be the only way to get through, unless help arrived.

And Wes didn't think there was any help coming.

Chapter Five
Finding The Ground

Getting Karen safely aboard *Cheetah* was, rather surprisingly, a simple affair. Charlie had expected many questions from Greg, or John, or even Daragh… but aside from the briefest of farewells, there were no lengthy interviews. The doctors had given Karen clearance to cruise, Charlie himself had arrived to escort her, and a Belt Squadron frigate with a Belt Squadron Captain was ready to take them both to Etat Lexington.

It would be a trip of close to seven days, so basically there was no time to waste; Karen and Charlie got aboard, and minutes later Mark Gunney ordered his shiny and recently-restored frigate to break orbit and run like hell for Lexington.

No one was aware of Karen's condition, and Charlie thought it best to keep it that way until they were a day away from Earth, when it would be too late to turn back. Mark might be informed sooner (because he'd know better than to turn around with so much at stake) but not until he was finished with departure commands… so basically, Karen and Charlie stayed put in her new cabin, waiting for the next thing… whatever that would be.

"Did I get good at waiting?" Karen asked him after a prolonged silence.

Charlie was sitting in the chair beside the bed in this cabin — *my typical place* — but Karen wasn't in her normal spot; she was sitting on the far side of the bed, her arms folded against the chill she was still feeling.

Decontamination was a cold affair, believe me.

In answer to her question, Charlie simply shrugged, "I don't think anyone ever gets *good* at it. But you did seem to grow more comfortable with long cruises over the years."

"If I was aboard ship with Ken all the time, I bet I did," she raised her eyebrows, then glanced slightly sheepishly at Charlie as if she hadn't really meant to say that out loud.

The Hawke Lord raised his eyebrows, "You two are big celebrities now. And everyone wants to know the details of your relationship. It's getting a bit ridiculous, and you two have fed the fires by keeping things mysterious. Though the hints lately have been getting a little bit less ambiguous."

Karen frowned, "People want to know if Ken and I are…"

"Intimate," Charlie found the word for her, and Karen's expression clouded.

Another new reality for which she simply had no base of reference — why would the press care how she and I related to each other? What sort of personal life could you have when the public at large was asking such direct questions?

And more importantly, were we?

"So… you must know. How are things between Ken and me?"

"No change," Charlie shook his head, and that ambiguous answer led to a deepening of Karen's frown.

"Meaning?"

Charlie chuckled at himself — he too had become quite accustomed to keeping his answers unclear, even more now that he was a Lord: "I mean whatever you remember as being the case, that hasn't change at all."

"Ah," Karen answered, looking back down at her feet.

"Pretty much," Charlie agreed, and then another silence fell before a question that had been pressing at Karen's mind finally escaped her mouth.

"He's a different man than I knew, though, isn't he?"

Charlie had been hoping to avoid such inquiries, because he saw no way in which they could be adequately answered. Of course people changed over time, but what had happened over the course of a dozen years was very difficult to catalogue and describe to someone who would want — need — a very detailed perspective.

And Charlie knew full well that his own recollections of how I'd been, how Karen had been... all of it could be easily colored by his more recent experiences. To try to explain to Karen what I had become... even what she had become... was going to be incredibly difficult. It would be better to let her learn for herself... but the wait of a week and the need for answers made that impossible.

So the incomparable Special Branch master Lord Peters would have to try.

"I don't know if you remember this, but you once told me that the reason you were always with Ken... the reason you two partnered up at the Academy and stayed together ever since... was because he helped you see yourself as someone you wanted to be. That sound familiar?"

Karen stared at her feet as she listened, and then eventually she nodded in reply.

"Right. And he's told me many times, then and since, that that's exactly what you do for him. You both seem to have an irrational hatred for yourselves and for what you might become... but you both keep each other away from that hated place. You've been together so much, and know each other so well, that you've rarely ever strayed towards the limits. You've gotten comfortable together. That's who he is now... except he just lost you."

It was as good an explanation as anyone could have hoped to provide — a summary not unlike the one I'd given Bort the year before. Charlie knew us both well, and understood us. He wasn't like us, thank God — his quiet brilliance made him so much more human, and so much wiser than either Karen or me.

But he seemed to tolerate us, me especially, for reasons that remain beyond my grasp. And now his clear observations left Karen with a slightly better handle on the things she'd missed... the things that, for her, had never been.

That revelation in particular sent a shiver through her cold body. She remembers very well her feelings as she reflected on Charlie's words — fear being chief among them.

She was bound for the Union of Solar Asteroids on a mission to bring me back from the brink with her calming presence. Except she wasn't calm now, and hardly a presence. What if I saw her, and tried to connect with her the way I would have just weeks before, and it broke down?

What if, after all of this, the Karen I got back was damaged goods and I didn't want anything else to do with her?

It hardly sounds like an insecurity you'd expect from Karen McMaster, but it was what she was feeling. Because she couldn't remember how she'd coped with the stresses, how she'd achieved the things that had built her confidence, how we'd always been a team.

She started to wonder if I was some sort of philosopher-warrior type now... someone who would no longer be willing to tolerate her impetuousness. It worried her. It terrified her. Just as those things had concerned her back in the old days, they tormented her... now more than ever, because of the circumstances.

And fear led to frustration, and anger. Because she was not some useless little dandy. She was strong and smart and better than every other officer she'd known in her young career, save one or two, and she didn't need to be coddled to be effective.

But. She sort of did need someone she could say that to, someone who'd understand her ego. Dammit.

She was trying hard not to get swept away by the situation she was in, but it wasn't easy. It was quite impossible, actually. She was a mess, and that wasn't good... not good at all.

"I don't think you should try to cover too much ground too quickly," Charlie very wisely interrupted Karen's musing after her expression revealed her torment. "You've been attacked, you've lost a lot, and until we consult a doctor we won't have any idea how long this might last. No one can expect you to bounce back easily... just take some time to get acclimatized to this new environment, and then we'll take it from there."

Karen still didn't look at Charlie, though she listened to his words. He paused for a time before offering a last bit of advice.

"And don't start out thinking you need to try to behave exactly the way you would have before. Who you were was one version of yourself... but you're no less *you* now than you were a month ago. The core of you is the same."

That was one piece of helpful advice too far, and Karen finally looked up, "The core of me? The petulant, immature, self-indulgent, violent core of me?"

Charlie met her glare for a few moments, and then he said something which, well, I can't describe, only repeat: "You know one of the reasons why I think you two can never really part?" Karen didn't answer, so Charlie continued, "For all the good things, neither of you think much of yourselves... and you think a lot of each other."

Karen blinked a few times, but still said nothing. Charlie took a breath and elaborated on his thought, "He actually loves the one thing you hate the most: you. And you love the one thing he hates the most: him. It's dysfunctional, but it works."

Charlie had never said that to me. I don't know why, and he doesn't. But it's typical Charlie wisdom — so right, and making so much sense. Karen and I validated each other; that's the way we tried to explain it to people like Bort. Indeed, even Charlie used those terms when describing us.

This had been fundamental to us for a long time, and now if there was only one thing Karen could retain, Charlie figured it had to be that understanding. She had to know that, whatever our mutual doubts, we had an entire history of truly appreciating each other, beginning that night in the alley and ending, effectively, at Daragh's ball.

We had to begin again now — which was scary, but obviously there was a chance of success. She had to accept that fact, and as she stared holes in her feet, she wondered how difficult it would be.

Chapter Six

Positioning

Julie Pichot couldn't have gotten to where she was without being very, very good at her job. Defense Command Intelligence unquestionably had suffered from certain shortcomings during the years around the war, but one thing the service did not lack was effective field operatives. Ours were, and remain, the very best you can find in the solar system... or if you want to get a little lame, they were the best you could never ever find, no matter how hard you looked.

Unless you happened to be Grant Merger.

Because there were bugs crawling all over the Governor's House on Etat Valcour, Julie found out very quickly that she was under suspicion. It was an unsettling discovery, and a frustrating one — she had in no way been trying to send reports back to the Belt Squadron or the Empire, so the communication that had made Grant suspect her had nothing at all to do with her real mission.

But he suspected her all the same. That was a concern, because while agents did have a talent for extricating themselves from awfully difficult situations, he had said he wanted Renault to handle her. She'd never faced the notorious spy-killer... no one she'd ever met had crossed his path, in fact. If they had, they'd have been dead.

Julie was clearly concerned, and if you ask any spy who was active during those times (up to and including Melissa Samuels) you'll know they all took Renault seriously. He was one of the few bad guys whose reputation wasn't just fiction.

All of this concern was bubbling in Julie's mind as she sat at her desk in the Governor's outer office the day after Grant's orders to Karadzic to investigate her. The ghost trackers she'd planted in her apartment's computer had detected a security sweep the night before, so now she expected she'd receive more direct questioning from the man himself.

She just had to make sure she didn't display any of her concerns. She had to be the same Julie that had been working in this place for more than a year... who'd become comfortable but still felt out of her depth. Harmless, bashful, a little charming, and basically innocent.

People like Karadzic could be easily manipulated, she just needed the chance...

Julie had been staring at her screen, ostensibly working on meeting minutes as she thought about all of these things, and thus she didn't notice the new arrival at her desk — one of many in the Governor's outer office — until he lowered himself on its edge.

Blinking in surprise she turned, expecting to see Karadzic sitting there with his usual cold smile.

"How are things, Julie?" Grant asked gently as he looked down at her.

"I... they're good, sir. I'm just working on the minutes from yesterday's meeting with the mining—"

Grant held up his hand, then looked around the office to see if anyone was watching.

It seemed clear, so he stood up again, grabbed a nearby chair, and pulled it up to her desk. Julie watched in surprise as he settled down beside her, then leaned closer and lowered his voice.

"I need to tell you something that's going on. I need to trust you."

Not at all what Julie was expecting; Grant's tone lacked any coldness — it sounded as though he was planning to share a secret. Did this mean... was this how her mission, and perhaps her life, would end? A conspiratorial word with the Empire's greatest villain?

"Someone in this office is leaking information to Defense Command," he said very quietly. "I've pointed Fletcher Karadzic in your direction and I need you to play along a little. He's already probably started investigating you. I know he isn't going to find anything... because I think he's the leak. He's been with me a long time, but... but I think he may have received an offer that would let him go home to Earth. He left people there."

Julie's jaw dropped, and honestly that wasn't an act.

"I know it's a lot, and I need you to keep it to yourself. I need you to let him investigate you, and while he's distracted, I'm having a man called Renault look at him."

Grant stopped after that, letting Julie process his words. Eventually she nodded slowly, her wide eyes reflecting completely genuine surprise. Either Grant Merger wasn't actually worried about her, which would be good news... or he was up to something even more sinister than she'd anticipated.

Either way, she didn't have to falsify her confusion.

"I'm going to send you to Etat Lexington soon, Julie. We need someone we can trust there to observe how things go between Ken Barron and the President. It has to be someone the President won't really recognize as being from this office, and you haven't been here long enough for him to know about you. When you go, Fletch is probably going to use you as a scapegoat... he'll try to get a message to Barron, and make it look like you carried it. That'll be the chance we use to catch him."

"I..." Julie started to speak, but stopped when she realized that she still had nothing to say.

"I know, I'm so sorry, Julie. But can we depend on you for this?" Grant made it very difficult to say no. He was an intelligent, kind-seeming man when he wanted to be... and Julie could imagine how an impressionable refugee like she was supposed to be could fall into his orbit, and dedicate herself to him completely. Most of the staff in the Governor's Office were completely devoted to him — Julie had heard all sorts of things from the women in particular.

But Grant was always the gentleman. He was faithful to Sonia Hart, which made him all the more impressive, and he was always sensitive to the needs of his people.

No wonder he was such a dangerous enemy of the Empire.

Eventually Julie took a big breath, then began to nod again, "Okay. Whatever you need me to do."

Grant smiled, then reached out and took Julie's hands in his, "Thank you. I hope it turns out I'm wrong, that there's no spy... but I've learned that DCI can get its tendrils anywhere. I really appreciate your help."

"Of course..." Julie's nod became more emphatic, and Grant's smile grew. Then he slowly rose from his chair, lingering just long enough to kiss Julie gently on the forehead, as a father might kiss his daughter.

She turned red, and again that wasn't acting. Grant had mastered the skill of flattery, and it served him well.

Julie watched her boss — her target — walk off, then looked around quickly to confirm again that no one had been watching. It appeared everyone had been too focused on work to listen to their hushed words, but now more than ever she needed to be aware of possible observers. When she got back to the clean room in her flat, she would check the feed from the bugs. If Grant went back to his office and told Sonia that he'd set Julie up for Renault... well, he could be telling the truth, or would he be lying?

To be a good spy, you need to be able to see all sorts of possible angles, and keep them distinct in your head. As Mel once pointed out to me, if you start to get confused, you could easily end up dead. Julie was a good spy — a very good one to get this far — but Grant was brilliant in his own right.

Was he playing her? Was Karadzic under suspicion? Julie didn't know, and that did not bode well for her. Feeling quite uneasy, she went back to work on the minutes from the meeting with the miners, hoping time and distance from the Governor would help clear her head.

It didn't.

By the time she recorded all of this in her journal that night, it still wasn't clear.

Grant was very good.

Chapter Seven

Cheetah

Under just about any other circumstances I can imagine, the return of Mark Gunney and *Cheetah* to space duty would have warranted a great deal of enthusiasm. However, because of the way this book began, I didn't do much justice to the fact that Mark was getting his ship back... so now I'll try to make amends.

The story might seem a familiar one: as Kris Jacobs had gotten *Lion* back in *The Pax Terra*, Mark was now being restored to the frigate he'd taken over from Wes after 2231. It was a great occasion — a return home for one of our very best, and a chance for the ship that had suffered some serious punishment during the Fleet Clash to get back into action.

That said, there were differences — not least the fact that Mark was having a hell of a time getting around. The doctors had given him a cane, and Mark was determined to make that simple tool work for him, but his legs weren't back to their pre-frostbite capacity. He'd been in the middle of an extensive physiotherapy regime designed to teach his leg muscles to walk again, when this mess had arisen...

Now that the regime had been interrupted, he was making do.

It was painful and awkward, especially considering every Captain in the Defense Command Navy came up under the quarterdeck tradition — that notion we all have that Captains are supposed to walk their bridges the way Nelson's Captains walked the quarterdecks of their ships.

Captain's chairs? They're located at the back of the bridge, and there's nothing wrong with them... they just weren't for us. Maybe at the end of a twelve-hour watch after the hottest battle you can imagine, but at no other time should they really be used...

Unless you have absolutely no choice.

Mark grudgingly began to use his chair on *Cheetah's* bridge in the second hour of the frigate's cruise from Earth, and after that it became his usual place. The bridge looked very strange to him from so far back and so low down, but it was better to see it from there than not at all.

It was from his chair that Mark actually received the internal comm signal from Charlie.

"Lord Peters is looking for you, sir," *Cheetah's* Sensors and Communications Officer said, and Mark looked up, then nodded.

"Tell him I'm here... his legs are working better than mine, so if he wouldn't mind meeting me in my day cabin."

Nodding, the Sensors and Communications Officer replied to Charlie's message, and Mark took a deep breath before forcing himself to his feet. It was a struggle to get to the day cabin, and it took him so long that Charlie entered the small compartment off the bridge just a moment after he reached his desk.

Karen wasn't with the Hawke Lord, I should add: she'd agreed that it would be better for someone who remembered Mark Gunney to introduce the complex reality of her current situation.

"How's Karen?" Mark's first question was obviously for her wellbeing — I say obviously because that's just the sort of guy Mark is.

Charlie opened his mouth to answer, but felt the need to briefly deflect from that subject, "How are your legs? I know they pulled you out in mid-recovery."

With a laugh, Mark shook his head, "Ice crystals in your cells are not good for dancing, or any other activities best enjoyed with a woman."

"Fair to say," Charlie agreed. "You're still doing therapy now?"

Mark nodded, "As much as I can. They sent some physio instructions along for the med staff... basically I'm still trying to rebuild muscle mass after the regeneration they did to replace the destroyed cells. I've got the gravity turned down in my quarters, and that made life easier once I taped everything down. I'm doing the water-resistance therapy now as well. Twice daily I walk around in the pool."

It wasn't glamorous, but it certainly was necessary. And easy to overlook. A lot of the time we just assume that when you're back aboard ship, you're better... and I suppose if you look at someone like Kris, you *are*. But don't forget that getting back takes work... a great deal of hard work... and because Mark had been forced to come out after us, he was taking his homework with him.

We appreciate his efforts even more for that.

"Now you neatly avoided my question about Karen," Mark continued, smiling and lacing his hands together in his lap. "I'm guessing the reason she's not pacing around my bridge is because she's not all better?"

Charlie considered trying to be tactful, but nodding seemed the best answer, "She's not all back. Don't know if she ever will be. The doctors gave her a clean bill of health, but no one asked her what year it is."

Mark hadn't been expecting that answer, and he shifted slightly in his chair, "Brain injury?"

It was something he was familiar with — his own grandfather, a space fighter pilot from the pre-atmospace days, had suffered memory-related illnesses.

"She remembers everything up to the time she took command... of *Lady Grace*. Didn't want to tell any of the doctors before we left, in case they tried to keep her from coming," Charlie explained, and Mark's reaction was fair.

"Fuck."

He fell silent for a moment, and Charlie did the same. After that pause, Mark took a breath, "I don't know my doctor aboard ship now... they took away Kelly and gave me some recent graduate, I think. But we can get Karen down there for a look. Think the loss is permanent?"

Charlie shrugged, "No way for me to know. I can imagine two different ways this happens: the compound Grant hit her with either blocked access to those memories, or it went into the frontal lobes and started scrubbing. If it's the latter, she may not get them back."

"Shit," Mark wasn't shy with his word choice. "Well I hope it's the former, obviously. You said she still remembers things up to her first command?"

"Seems so. But she doesn't know you, or half the Captains from the Belt Squadron. Hell, she didn't even know Grant Merger was an enemy of the Empire… though she wasn't particularly surprised."

Mark nodded a few times, "And she remembers Ken?"

"She does. They go back a lot farther, to the Academy. But from a practical standpoint, she's not really a Commodore anymore. She's barely even a Commander. She doesn't remember any of her command experiences. She was great at the Academy, and aboard *Alberta* with Ken and me… but all that happened before she really got down to business. So… as a resource…"

"She's not ready to mind the store," Mark agreed. "Yeah, I get it. She understands that?"

Charlie nodded. Karen hadn't said it to him in so many words, but from the way she spoke and the things she asked, he could tell she wouldn't start trying to throw her rank around.

She was still fairly skeptical of how she'd gotten the rank in the first place…

"Good," Mark said eventually. "Well, I guess we'll have to let people know."

"True. But it will be important that we don't all start walking on eggshells when she's around. She's feeling uncertain enough as it is. We need to make sure people don't try to help her too much, too soon, or it's going to make her feel too damaged."

"Fair enough," Mark concurred. "I'll figure out how to manage that. For now, you better get her down to med bay. If the hugely qualified Terra Nova doctors gave her permission to go without noticing she's a decade behind where she was, it might be a good idea to get a second opinion."

It was a fair point. Mark's comparison to me later is a good one: 'It's like a house inspector finding that your foundation is okay, but forgetting to mention that there's a pile of half-eaten bodies in the yard, and a family of zombies in the living room.'

That said, it bears remembering that the doctors who saved Karen's life had been much more fixated on making certain the compound didn't destroy her body. They'd been remarkably successful at that, but there hadn't been time for them to check everything. That's where *Cheetah's* own medical staff would come in… so heeding Mark's advice, Charlie would take Karen to see them.

The new doctor on *Cheetah* was named Vanessa Hansen, and Mark wasn't wrong when he suggested she was just out of med school. Charlie wasn't sure if that was good or bad; Karen was frankly a bit glad she was younger, since it likely meant she'd be less inclined to lecture.

"Sir, ma'am," Hansen came to her feet as Charlie and Karen stepped into her office in *Cheetah's* sick bay. "What can I do for you?"

Charlie gestured for Hansen to resume her seat behind her desk, then he closed the door behind Karen as she stepped in and took one of the chairs opposite the good doctor.

"We have something to discuss," the Hawke Lord said, and according to Karen he sounded both dire and cryptic.

Hansen frowned immediately, and Karen could see the young doctor was starting to get nervous. It was an intimidating sort of scenario, she supposed — two senior officers march in and close the door. Of course, what Karen didn't have the context to fully grasp was that she wasn't just a senior officer, she was a celebrity war hero. Doubly imposing.

"It's about my... condition," she said, her tone strained. "I left Earth without admitting to some persistent side effects from my recent attack."

That probably wasn't the best way to medically introduce what they were about to explain, but as Charlie settled into the chair beside Karen, neither of the pair was in a hurry to clarify.

Hansen's frown deepened, and the nervous young doctor seemed to grow more concerned, "So... are you feeling alright, ma'am?"

Not the most precise question Vanessa Hansen had ever asked, but for her part she felt plenty anxious. This was her first posting as a ship's surgeon, and she was in no way an advanced specialist in... well... whatever field covered being poisoned by an unknown substance which seemed to have been designed in a genetic lab to baffle experts.

Tall order for the first day on the job.

"I'm feeling fine," Karen said gently, realizing she probably needed to cut the young doctor some slack. "Problem is, I can't remember anything after, oh, 2222 or so."

Hansen didn't seem to hear that admission at first. Then she processed it, but not fully. Her mouth opened, then closed, then opened again. Just to be clear, in 2222, she'd been in middle school.

"Woke up and everyone was calling me Commodore. But last I remember, I was Commander McMaster of *Lady Grace*. So that's been causing me to lose some sleep... because either I'm having a helluva dream right now, or my brain is partly screwed,"

"Uh... I..." Hansen struggled for words, and then she had to ask, "I don't mean to be rude, but this isn't some sort of... initiation? I've heard there are sometime jokes when officers join the Belt Squadron..."

Karen's eyebrow rose and she glanced at Charlie, "Still?"

"Older doesn't mean more mature," he answered Karen first, then looked back to the doc. "And no, it's serious. We need you to tell us as much as you can."

Hansen's jaw continued to hang slack, but she began to nod as she started reaching into her own memories for whatever she recalled from her brain-related studies. Unfortunately her recall wasn't working smoothly, so it took a moment before she blurted the next thing that came to mind.

"Well... if... do you recall if there was talk of your hippocampus... or your frontal lobe?" she asked, and Karen looked to Charlie for the answer to that question.

After all, she'd been in a coma for a lot of the doctor talk about her condition. Unfortunately, he'd been on his way to Earth for much of the same, but Greg had given him a quick briefing.

"Seemed that the compound focused on the frontal lobe, before they were able to scrub it out," he answered, and Hansen nodded again, her jaw shut now.

"Well... well that's the main repository for stored memories. So if the compound bypassed the hippocampus and went there..."

She was jumping into half-formed ideas and she knew it, so she stopped herself making assumptions and asked another question: "Have you experienced any difficulties remembering things since you've woken up?"

Karen paused at that one, thinking back through everything that had happened since Charlie had rescued her from the decon chamber. Her head began shaking as she tracked over those hours, and then she firmed up her conclusion with words, "So far I'm fine."

Hansen nodded again, then frowned, "If your ability to create new memories is okay, it sounds to me like the compound went in and wiped your memory for that period. But... well, that's very oversimplified. I need to scan your brain, and compare it with your file scan... and I need to talk to some specialists back on Earth. And I need to know if things like learned actions... muscle memory... if those things are still intact. I think they're a different part of the brain..."

It was all coming in an avalanche of thoughts, and realizing she was trying to say everything at once, Hansen stopped herself.

"One thing at a time... you need to scan my brain?" Karen asked, and Hansen nodded. "Yes, thank you, ma'am."

Karen smiled, "Of course. Let's get started... I want to know what marbles I have left."

That comment was meant to brighten the mood, but Karen couldn't control her tone enough to hide the anxiety beneath her words. What if she started forgetting things she'd learned since waking up? She hadn't even considered that possibility.

One worry at a time. Glancing at Charlie, she found his expression reassuring — whatever was going on, she had a Special Brancher on standby. She tells me that was nearly as good as having me there. Frankly, I think Charlie was handling this a lot better than I would... I was too emotionally vested in the situation.

Anyway, Hansen led Karen out of her office and started running the necessary tests. Time would tell whether the elusive memories were still somewhere to be found.

Chapter Eight

Guesswork

The nearer we got to Etat Lexington, the more carefully we needed to proceed. Wes was doing most of the squadron command work as we made our way — it seemed best for him to be the one who'd be in charge if we ran across a SAU warship.

He was therefore spending a lot of the time wondering how best to handle such an encounter... and worrying about the actual capabilities of the Union ships.

Worrying, remember, is a skill I had long since mastered. It's a necessary part of being a good Naval commander — you have to wonder, you have to worry. If you don't consider every possible outcome before you get into a battle, you're positioning yourself to be surprised.

Now, invariably, you won't be able to predict everything, but having worked through enough possible options you'll be better prepared than you would have been if you hadn't contemplated much at all.

And that is why I wasn't the one calling most of the shots on this cruise. My head wasn't in that game, I just wanted to find the next target. Wes, obviously, had different priorities — a different role to play. And a good thing too.

As he sat in his cabin on *Nova Scotia*, he was reviewing all sorts of data... the files that Bort had sent about the Union and the Martians' guesses about its military capabilities, the scans of the colony defenses we'd taken at Concord, and anything else that could be relevant to our mission.

He'd even pulled up our scans of *Idaho*, because our facial recognition AIs had confirmed that Angelo Connaught had indeed played the role of Carl Devoir in that gambit. A *North America*-class frigate making a lonely transit through deep space in 2232 had been overwhelmed by Connaught... and presumably it had been SAU warships that did the business in that case.

In fact, going back to that incident was perhaps one of the most informative things Wes could do, because *Idaho* had been mostly intact and undamaged. Knowing of course that the ship had been exhausted and alone, you could make a case that the crew was just surprised by an attack, and thus capitulated in the face of superior numbers of hostiles.

But Wes wasn't so sure. As he looked over the scans we'd taken before, during and after our encounters aboard that ship, he found no signs of fresh impact damage — no laser or torpedo strikes.

That suggested the use of mags... suggested that perhaps a flurry of electromagnetic energy had overwhelmed the frigate's power systems without doing any other noticeable collateral damage.

It wasn't much to go on, of course, but Wes paid attention. Using mags to overwhelm a solo ship... well, it couldn't happen the same way against the entire Belt Squadron, but we'd have to be conscious that our SAU friends might be able to disrupt our systems.

Beyond that, there were some rumors and guesses included in the Martian files that rounded out a picture of a SAUN that numbered at least twenty ships, and that seemed to be tasked with protecting the secretive Union against piracy. Not a line-of-battle fleet like ours, but a purpose-built pirate-hunting force.

If that's what they were, they were going to be in for a bad time... I don't know if this makes sense, and perhaps it's something you know already, but ships built exclusively for pirate hunting typically aren't what you need when a force of real warships turns up.

Consider: most pirates lack heavy firepower. Their raiding groups might include one ship adapted to carry a heavy laser, meant to attack domes, but for the most part light ship-to-ship weapons are easier to acquire, cheaper, and less onerous when it comes to maintenance. What you need to worry about when fighting pirates is speed and maneuverability.

Our Belt Squadron had speed and maneuverability in spades... but it wasn't all we had, because our ships had been engineered to be superior holistic combatants. We'd been meant for warfighting, which left us more than adequate to chasing pirates, and also positioned us well to fight the Martians.

Engineering like ours took money, experience, and huge numbers of ship designers and builders trying to one-up each other over the course of many years. Ships like *Wolf* don't happen overnight, they evolve... and the Union hadn't had time or need to evolve anything like them.

None of this is to suggest that Wes was feeling overconfident about the Belt Squadron's chances when we finally found the SAUN... just that he realistically knew that the quality of our ships would be different than anything the SAU had likely seen before. We'd leverage whatever advantage that gave us when the time came.

But, of course, they'd be different than anything we'd seen too. Something to worry about, but not be paralyzed by.

The good news in all of this was the fact that the Martians had, despite my earlier slamming of them, been mostly responsible for the design of the lasers that had made the *Tharsis*-class so effective. There had been a question before as to whether those powerful weapons had originated in the Imperium, or if they'd come from the SAU builders.

But based on Bort's file, they'd been designed on Mars, and were only built in the Union because they were complex and labor intensive... much cheaper to have slave (sorry, indentured) labor put them together.

So we were cruising into the unknown, but with seven of the best ships in the DCN, we had reason to be confident. Wes was at that stage — having read enough, and reasoned through enough, that he could be confident of our chances. Again, the usual disclaimer: not arrogant or assuming victory, just knowing we'd have an even chance in any fight we found. And when you give the Belt Squadron an even chance, you're basically giving me another chance to hit you over the head with how good these people are.

One set of worries thus passed into the 'addressed' pile in Wes' brain as he sat in his cabin. The other set of worries returned immediately, though, and this set was both different and familiar.

Since it was entirely likely that the Union would have nothing that could really stop us, what was to stop me? If the threat of the SAUN proved to be a paper tiger, what reasoning could Wes use to stop me doing something I would regret later?

It was a difficult situation. Wes was a student of history, and if you chose to extend the canton analogy from Etat Concord, you could look at the rest of the Union like China in the very late nineteenth century. During that time, the great nation was struggling to retool its might to fit within the context of European military technology, while continuing to jockey for position with Japan.

Japan, being smaller, had adapted more quickly — you could think of the island power sort of like the Hawke Protectorate, lean and well-protected by ships bought from or built by the yards of the most successful Empire of the time.

But China had been less able to redirect its resources, and in terms of a fleet, had acquired only a mixed bag of ships from whoever happened to be selling. The resulting fleet was a disaster, which the Japanese trounced when the two nations finally went to war in the 1890s.

The outcome was not good for China: the great nation continued to be menaced for years by those Empires with better fleets. It was clear abuse, and sitting aboard a warship from an even greater Empire, Wes got the feeling it could happen again very easily.

Now, you might wonder why that would be a bad thing; we're stronger, after all, and if the SAU wants to fight us why shouldn't we just let them?

For the pragmatists: because we're not always going to be the strongest — China certainly got its revenge.

For the moralists: because it's not the right thing to do — doing harm is often wrong.

For Wes: because there'd been enough killing.

But there hadn't been enough for me, and as Wes sat in his cabin and considered all of these possibilities, knowing he was likely to come head-to-head with some of them, he realized that the worst battle of his war years would not be against the Martians, but against me.

For some reason that thought caused him to look at the bottom drawer in his dresser, where his old flight gloves — his dueling gloves — were still tucked.

I'd won the last duel, could he win the next one?

CHAPTER NINE

MESSAGE

Julie Pichot was bound for Etat Lexington, and it was all she could do to keep from constantly looking over her shoulder. First-class passage had been booked for her on one of the transports that regularly made the run between the Etats — the SAUs call those 'runners', which is cute — so she wasn't obliged to share a berth with anyone else. That was both good and bad: it gave her the chance to prepare for the mission in private, but it also meant she had no roommate for Renault to deal with if he came for her.

She just didn't know what was coming next. Grant had wrong-footed her... she was either being given the chance to prove herself and be inducted into his inner circle, just in time for the final battle... or she was being sent to Lexington to be killed in sight of a Defense Command squadron that could, theoretically, provide her with safety.

Rather polarized options, and because of her uncertainty she'd treated her departure from Valcour as a full break. She'd wiped her clean room, disposed of her equipment (in a way that would leave it retrievable if she came back, but which pretty much guaranteed no one else would find it), and updated her secret logbook with all her suspicions.

Now she was travelling, and her anxiety was high.

Part of the problem for Julie was that she had no way to recognize Renault. The killer was very confident; word in the spy community was that he never bothered to modify his facial appearance... that he basically dared DCI to come after him.

But he was also good at not getting caught on camera, which meant she had no way to know if he was standing right in front of her. She'd have to go simply by instinct, and study every man on this runner for signs that he was a killer. Usually those were pretty obvious, but after so many spy kills, Renault would undoubtedly be able to deceive even the best DCI training.

Julie was justifiably worried.

The run from Valcour to Lexington took just two days — unlike Concord, the rest of the colonies of the Union were much closer together... another 'safety' measure in the design of the state. If ne're-do-wells used the canton as a starting point in a search for another Etat, the greater distance between it and the rest would make the exploration take that much longer.

So for two days, Julie would be cramped up on a ship with her possible killer.

She tried to put that thought aside, and because she was a spy she did have the ability to compartmentalize. As the runner departed Valcour with her aboard, the first thing she needed to do was scout it out... she'd taken these transports before, but the type of ship differed depending on the route. Some were as well-appointed as cruise liners, others were basically space buses with reclining seats.

The Lexington route was big business, so the runner was more in the 'liner' category — a couple of common areas, a supposed casino, a restaurant... and knowing food might help settle her nerves, Julie secured her gear, put a button cam in her blouse, and decided to track some down.

As soon as she stepped out into the corridor, she spotted Karadzic behind her. He was making some attempt to be covert, but there was no way he could escape her honed observation skills. Of course she didn't let on that she'd seen him; she was just the innocent new girl, after all, and he was no real threat anyway.

The corridors were narrow and low, because the runner wasn't built for comfort as much as it was for cramming in as many people as possible. She didn't even want to think what the steerage spaces were like — if the affluent ticketholders were so compressed on the upper decks, the recently-freed and the indentureds below had to be all over each other. Charming.

People were coming and going from their quarters, so a few times Julie had to stand aside to let them pass. Every time she halted, Karadzic had to appear casual while he did the same. It was mildly amusing.

Eventually she got out into the runner's largest common area, and then she crossed to the restaurant. It wasn't the sort of fine-dining you'd get on a proper cruise… a deli up front if you were looking for lunch sandwiches, then basically a pub-restaurant inside. The sort of place you find in a spaceport, come to think of it — a little bit of everything.

Stepping inside, Julie found an open table and took it immediately. She was facing the door, so she saw Karadzic slow before the entrance, then continue on as if he'd been heading somewhere else the entire time. The common space that the restaurant faced was quite small, so there was little chance of him being able to circle unnoticed… the security advisor's rudimentary tradecraft skills weren't up to working in such close quarters.

Not for the first time, Julie wondered why Grant would have such a seemingly clumsy person so high up in his organization… but you can never underestimate the value of a man like Karadzic. He may not be fancy but he gets the job done — and results matter.

A waitress came over with a menu, and after a quick glance through the choices Julie ordered a simple club sandwich. She was starting to feel better — the adrenaline of the chase was clearing the web of worry away. Certainly, Renault was a stiffer foe than Karadzic, but she was no slouch. Her skills had gotten her this far, and she figured they could get her the rest of the way.

She'd be taking over a desk at the Ministry of Agriculture in no time at all.

As that confidence built, the waitress returned with her mediocre-seeming food and she prepared to dig in.

Then the chair opposite her was pulled out, and Renault sat down.

So much for the confidence. Renault was… well, he's exactly what you'd expect a French killer to be: charming and easygoing. I think he took a lot of pleasure in actually living up to the silly stereotypes a lot of people hold about the French — enjoyed playing the role of the man who loved to love… but who just happened to be able to kill in the same evening.

Julie froze as he sat down, and his smile didn't help matters at all, "Good evening."

Somehow Julie managed not to react as she wanted to — she didn't try to get away from the table, or kill him. Instead her excellent training and her instincts kicked in, forcing a look of nervous confusion to her face.

"Hello…" she said meekly. "Are you… the one… the Governor told me about?"

Renault was definitely playing the French stereotype: "He did not tell me how beautiful my accomplice would be."

Julie blushed outwardly, then panicked inwardly. It sounded like he didn't suspect her, of course — he was a professional of the highest order. She lowered her sandwich back down to her plate and looked towards the door, "Are we supposed to… you know… be seen together?"

With a charming laugh, Renault shrugged his shoulders, "I do not care. Fletcher Karadzic is here on this runner, and he is trying to follow you around. But he does not like me, because I have always been able to kill the spies that he cannot. I think that is why he is now become a spy himself."

Blinking a few times, Julie leaned forward in a conspiratorial fashion, "So… so he will think you're here trying to interrogate me?"

Renault leaned down to match her, "He will think I have come to seduce you. He will think that, by the end of tonight, you will be lying sated in my bed."

Julie certainly turned redder at those words, and it wasn't necessarily an act. Renault had a lot of reputations, and this one is often forgotten. Sure he had the ability to kill spies, but a man who lives on the edge doesn't have to limit his fun to murder.

"He is not wrong about that," Renault continued, and Julie gasped the way a young and inexperienced member of staff would.

This was a difficult situation now. The man who represented the single greatest danger to her survival wanted a liaison with her… he was forcing her to choose a gambit. A simple secretary from the Governor's Office would be less likely to reject the supposed charms of a man like Renault, so if she rebuffed him now, his suspicions might spike.

If she did let him 'seduce' her, she might gain a chance to kill him while he was vulnerable, but that would pretty much declare her intentions to Karadzic and blow her cover. But if she did have the liaison, and Grant really had sent Renault after Karadzic, she might be able to return with her cover intact.

There were no good options. Such was the situation she was in.

Renault reached across the table, touching her arm with a smile, "You are the heroine in a spy thriller now, Julie. You should make the most of the opportunity."

If you'll allow me to interject for a moment with my own view: this guy was complete fucking slime.

But Julie was caught in no man's land… and unfortunately, the 'no man's' part was only metaphorical. She decided, for better or worse, to let this run… to see if she really was under the radar… and if she wasn't, to at least level the playing field in her duel with Renault. If he meant to kill her, she could get there first when he was most distracted.

The pair sat together and flirted suggestively while Julie ate half her sandwich. Her anxiety — which she hoped came across as excitement — prevented her finishing the other half. Then they went to her cabin.

I'm going to have a tough time handling the writing of this next part. Take it as a bad sign that, as Julie and Renault disrobed, the French killer picked up her fine blouse off the floor and laid it on the dresser in her cabin, adjusting it in such a way that the button cam she'd worn was pointed at the bed. So much for him staying off vid records.

He then set about his work, and Julie kept up.

I'm sure some people might be inclined to high-five at this point. Yes, copulation, awesome. Do it like Pions. Hell yeah. Superagents are invariably in great physical condition, and it's often suggested that because they're always living on the edge, they tend to be rather carnal when they become intimate.

None of that matters. This isn't a book for people who have fantasies about falling into bed with spies for wild, sweaty nights of passion. Because those fantasies aren't real.

I've seen the footage from the button cam, starting at the end. If you see the look on Julie's face at that point, it's obvious that she wasn't as attentive as she might usually be. She'd let her guard down; after sharing three hours in the cramped bed on the runner with Renault, she'd let go of her immediate anxieties about him, and she was briefly at her ease.

You could say it was the most foolish mistake of her life.

When Renault took her wrists in his hands, and raised them up over her head to touch the headboard, she smiled and expected one thing. He meant another.

Because Renault had somehow managed to get ties into the bed with them. Her wrists were suddenly bound together, and locked into the bed's frame.

As soon as she realized this, she started to struggle, but his full weight was crushing down on her legs, and then he somehow had a knife in his hands.

"I love spies," he said disgustingly. "You can always tell a spy, because she fakes the first few, but then the last one or two are the best of her life. A real lover knows the difference."

Julie started to scream for help — play the innocent-girl card… do anything to alter the situation until her hands got free. But it didn't matter. The quarters were atmosphere-proof in case of decompression, so her screams went no further than the locked door.

Then Renault cut out her tongue.

Yes, it's as horrifying as it sounds. She screamed and writhed, and somehow didn't pass out. As soon as Renault did this, he had the decency to hit the wound with cauterizing agent, to make sure she didn't drown in her own blood. The sounds Julie made are indescribable. Sounds I hadn't heard since Egesta, that no one should ever hear.

And then he cut off all her fingers.

Just… I'm going to stop trying to describe this because it's not human.

And then he leaned down and spoke into her ear as she drifted from consciousness, "If you are pregnant, call him Julian, eh?"

After that she passed out, thank God, and Renault spent some time tending to the stumps where her fingers had been. He didn't want her to bleed to death, you see, because he had other plans for her. Once he was satisfied she would continue to live minus the pieces that he'd causally dropped into glasses of water on the desk opposite the cot, he started going through her luggage.

Julie had used some classic tradecraft to hide a few key items for her trip, and after a bit of tearing apart he found what he was looking for: a makeup utensil that concealed a DCI emergency transponder.

He activated the beacon — designed to identify an agent in the midst of a messy situation (like if the Belt Squadron showed up and started shooting) — then planted it inside her, in a part of her anatomy that meant surgery would be necessary to get it out safely.

Sorry, but I don't have any words to get across how angry, how furious this still makes me.

Renault.

What can I say about him except that he had to die?

He got dressed after that, then put the missing pieces of Julie's body into the small freezer in the room. Just to be kind. Then, with a bold wave to the button camera, he headed for the door.

Grant Merger had cleaned house. And sent a message.

One of my editors asked an interesting question at this point: why does it seem that Grant Merger's worst violence is always directed at women? The attack at Daragh's ball had targeted Karen and Mel, and now Julie Pichot... you'd be forgiven for thinking that he particularly enjoyed doing violence and degradation to females.

Given a broader view, I can tell you Grant's violence doesn't really discriminate — he murdered everyone on *Idaho*, if you'll recall, and going back many years, there had been plenty of unspeakable crimes against men and women alike.

But if you've no other experience with Grant's designs than what you're reading in this series, you get a slanted view, and I'll tell you why: at this point, Grant was going after the people who'd managed to get closest to him, and then had betrayed him in one way or another. And in these three cases, the individuals who had succeeded at that were women.

The reality was that Grant was a man who appreciated women, and he was conscious of the fact that his passions sometimes made him miss the danger signs. That's how people like Mel, and then Julie, got close. Had it been Karadzic who'd managed to betray him, that man would undoubtedly have suffered similar destruction — missing pieces, anatomy rearranged... believe me, in the Syndicate days I often saw the results of Grant's revenge. It would turn your stomach just as much.

But since his flight from the Empire, it had been women who had gotten inside Grant's guard, and positioned themselves as his closest confidantes. Maybe that makes him old-fashioned, or a chauvinist. I don't really care. All I know is that my old friend was doing unspeakable things to people on my team... Defense Command people.

He was doing it because he believed we were wrong, and he was doing it to make sure I didn't relent.

He'd get his wish — but he would have gotten it anyway. I suppose the only positive thing about what you just read is that Grant had ordered Renault to keep Julie alive. Most traitors in Grant's inner circle didn't survive.

In any case, don't just try to dismiss Grant Merger as a woman-hater. Such a simple designation fails to comprehend the breadth of this inhumanity. He'd dehumanize and violate anyone who got in his way, and this time that had meant Julie Pichot.

Chapter Ten

The Agony Of Not Knowing

Karen will be the first to tell you that what she was suffering as a result of Grant's plan wasn't nearly so brutal as what Julie had just endured. I suppose she's right, too — she had suffered no physical rape, no blade, no mutilation. But it would be foolish to underestimate the sense of violation that came with the brain-tampering... to minimize what Grant had stolen from Karen would be grievous.

A sizeable part of her identity was missing, and she didn't know if she'd ever get it back.

Not knowing was almost as bad as... not knowing...

Sorry, this is not the right time to crack such a bad pun.

Vanessa Hansen needed a couple of days after taking her scans to consult with doctors on Earth, to go over her medical texts, and to figure out some possible outcomes. In that time, word of course got to Greg and John that Karen had been sent out minus her memories, and they weren't pleased that they hadn't been informed.

But at the same time, they still believed it vital that Karen was the one carrying news of her survival to the Union, so they didn't object too much... it just made everything more complicated from a command and control standpoint. They had to decide if she was to be put on some sort of medical leave, or expected to simply follow Mark's orders... or be left with theoretical control over this cruise.

That's not particularly topical to this chapter though. It was a couple of days after her tests, and Karen and Charlie were back in Hansen's office, waiting for the news. The doctor had popped out to collect one more piece of information just as Karen and Charlie arrived, so the pair waited for her return.

Time seemed to be moving slowly, at least for Karen.

Charlie's expression was stern; he had fallen fully into the role of big brother for this trial — just as I suppose I was Lia's big brother, Charlie was Karen's.

He was much older than her now, sort of, and his job was to project calm and certainty, two feelings that Karen wasn't enjoying in abundance. She was grinding her teeth, and her foot was tapping on the deck at a high cadence. She wanted to know what was happening to her.

Hansen returned to the office and closed the door behind her with an apology, "Sorry, sorry... had to get one last thing..."

The young doctor's anxious tone didn't strike either Karen or Charlie as positive, and as she sat down behind her desk Vanessa Hansen's expression basically told them everything they needed to know.

Or, more precisely, it told them just the opposite of what they wanted to hear.

"I'm sorry to say... that based on what we've seen... we just don't know whether your memory loss can be reversed..." her words were halting, starting and stopping as she struggled not to simply blurt everything out.

There was no immediate reaction on Karen's face — Charlie checked. Karen tells me no visible response was the best she could manage at that particular moment; she wanted answers, and not getting them spiked her frustration in a manner that demanded extreme self-control.

"Nothing we can find suggests that you'll naturally recover your memories, but no one has managed to gain a real understanding of that compound you were injected with. It's possible there could be... an antidote."

Frustration began to sink into a sea of gloom — even slight desperation — as Karen heard those words. Her only chance to retrieve what had been stolen was to find a mythical cure in Grant's lair. She knew that was doable — indeed, it had been my basic reason for coming out this way when I believed she was still alive — but it felt like a long shot nonetheless.

"There is some good news," Hansen moved to that positive note as she watched Karen's expression grow more somber. "There's no sign of structural damage. We don't think there's any chance you'll lose the new memories you've made since waking. Not unless you're exposed again, of course. But..."

"That won't happen," Charlie decided to interject at that moment, and taking that as the cue she'd said enough, the young doctor fell silent.

She wasn't wrong about that last part being good news — brain injuries are never to be taken lightly, and had the damage inflicted by this weapon been less targeted, the consequences could have been far worse, and ongoing.

Karen remained silent as she tried to come to terms with what she still didn't know. Charlie's own mind was racing through questions, though, and he voiced one: "What do the labs at home think... are we likely to unlock that compound, find our own antidote?"

It was a slightly more hopeful question than Charlie might normally have posed, and in retrospect, he tells me he regretted asking it without knowing the answer — or at least the doctor — better. He'd been counting on some sort of positive statement to buoy Karen's flagging hopes...

Unfortunately, Hansen missed the memo, "Well... maybe? But the genetic structure of that stuff is very strange. They're saying it's not actually native to Earth."

Any statement that unexpected — some might go so far as to suggest ridiculous — was inevitably going to raise Charlie's eyebrow, "Really?"

Hansen confirmed, "Must have been completely generated in a lab environment. And whoever came up with it must have a grasp on genetics that... well, we don't have anyone that I know of who can make genetic material like that. So unless it was harvested from some sort of alien creature, which we all know is ridiculous, Grant Merger is a genius. Or has a genius working for him."

For some reason Charlie flashed back to the guy in the suit who'd been on *Idaho* — remember, the one dressed up like an alien who they'd had to blast out an airlock because he was somehow immune to mag fire?

That had been enough bullshit about aliens for the Special Branch Lord... so he chose to believe the far more likely explanation for the compound used on Karen: Grant *was* a genius.

Whatever the case, it made the situation no easier, and as the reality of what she'd just learned gained a little more purchase, Karen's mood began to change. Charlie sensed it from his vantage point beside her, and he was about to speak to intervene... too late.

"Well I guess I just act as if I'm never getting my marbles back," she said, and there was no mistaking the bitterness in her tone. "Thanks doctor."

The venom wasn't directed at Hansen, but that didn't stop the young surgeon from feeling the sting — she winced as Karen stood and turned for the door. Charlie hurried to follow, adding his much less conflicted thanks before leaving Hansen's office.

Karen hurried out of the medical bay at a quick walk, and though Charlie had no trouble keeping up, the urgency struck him as a bad sign. As he came up behind her he saw other bad signs — her shoulders were tightening, fists clenching.

She'd managed to appear fairly cool up to this point, evening swaggering slightly from time to time. But as much as she had tried to conceal it, she was terrified of what she'd lost... or I suppose, terrified of what she might never recover. Afraid that she'd lost the most valuable thing she'd ever been given.

Now, one of my editors has suggested that she shouldn't have been so distraught by not knowing — at least she hadn't been given a definite 'no'. She *might* still get her memories back. That editor obviously hasn't had to endure the long wait for tests to come back... hasn't had to sit and wonder about the implications of positive or negative results.

That uncertainty is, in some ways, worse than knowing. At least when you know you can begin to cope — begin to grieve, or feel relief. While you wait, you're in limbo, worrying and wondering. It's like those hours before a battle, the ones I'd spend contemplating every possible outcome so I'd be ready, just in case. Stress like nothing else.

And stress that Karen had learned to cope with, before she'd lost twelve years of experience.

As Charlie caught up to her, he recognized that exact problem: Karen was young and impatient again. He didn't quite know how that would manifest itself, and he had to try to say something.

"You'll need to focus that frustration, and keep it in check," he said.

In retrospect he thinks that advice might have been too philosophical, but he was thinking on his feet.

Karen halted abruptly as soon as Charlie spoke, and as he came around in front of her he could see the storm cloud that had covered her face. Both he and she would later agree 'seething' was the best word to describe her reaction.

"I'm fine," she said sharply. "Give me space. I'm fine."

The words were carefully — tightly — controlled. She might have lost her capacity for waiting and worrying with grace, but she still did have the ability to manage her anger. It was a skill that had been essential to getting her to the bridge of *Lady Grace*.

Realizing that, Charlie decided to offer it as some sorely-needed positive reinforcement, even if it came out sounding flimsy: "Your anger will help. We need to find Grant, and your anger will help make that possible. Save it for him, because knowing his traps, we're going to need it."

After he said those words, Charlie stood aside and let Karen continue on. She didn't move at first, her eyes fixed on his as she worked on her breathing, and did her utmost to harness her rage. She needed to know her fate, and only one man had the answer. Now she had to get to him before I killed him. So she could kill him herself.

CHAPTER ELEVEN

MESSAGE FOUND

Jim Hannigan had the watch when the blip first appeared on *Wolf's* sensor track. We were just a day out of Lexington space, and every scanner in the squadron was banging away while every panel was carefully monitored. If there was a trap waiting for us, we intended to be ready.

So far we hadn't seen much of interest, though as we neared the central rock of the SAU, increased numbers of ships began to appear on our long range active sensor screens. Because we didn't have any real way to distinguish between civilian or military ships at the time, the whole squadron was holding at standby action stations.

Ready for any trap that tried to close on us.

But when Felicia Khalid was summoned to the comm panel, and then immediately after that to the sensor panel, it wasn't the prospect of a trap she was thinking about. There was a Defense Command Intelligence emergency beacon firing from one of the ships passing on the outer edge of our active sensor range.

I can't explain exactly how we were able to detect that signal over such a long range, because the technology involved still falls into the [square brackets] category... but we definitely saw it.

Felicia thus summoned Jim, "We have a DCI beacon on our scope."

Jim hurried over to the Sensors and Communications consoles at those words, a severe frown forming on his brow. As an expert in scanning and detecting, he reviewed the readings as well.

The signal was unmistakable — it was very similar, in fact, to the one that Mel Fox had used to let us track the Syndicate into the depths of the black.

We knew that Thea Fostopolos had sent spies out here... maybe one of them was coming good for us. Jim certainly hoped so, and with a nod to his replacement at Sensors and Communications, he directed the squadron to full readiness.

"Call the Captain and inform Wes on *Nova Scotia*. Let's go to General Quarters."

Wes reached his bridge just moments after the call came in, and by that time Rozy Young had put the sensor display up on *Nova Scotia's* main screen.

"Looks like a small transport ship... no signs that it has escort or armament," his Flag Captain explained as he came up beside her.

The pinging icon was not too far away... at full speed, the Belt Squadron could reach it within an hour. The question was whether we should — an emergency beacon could be a cry for help from a spy, or it could be meant to guide us somewhere. If we moved in fast and betrayed the identity of an agent, that could be quite a disaster. Imagine what the Governor of Etat Valcour would do to a spy caught in his midst.

Oh wait, you don't have to imagine. Because he fucking did it already.

But Wes didn't know that — none of us did. And while in hindsight it's obvious that we needed to get to that transport quickly, we had to be cautious.

Battlelink was going online as Wes contemplated the options, and within a moment every skipper in the squadron was on *Nova Scotia's* screen. Turning his attention to those familiar faces, Wes looked for me.

I wasn't there — Andrea held the spot on *Wolf's* bridge.

"Where's Ken?" he asked the obvious question, and Andrea shrugged coolly.

"Didn't answer. I suppose that puts you in charge until he gets here."

Wes was surprised by the reply, as you might be, but there was no time to dwell — a course of action needed to be mapped out, and if I wanted to change it when I arrived from wherever I was, so be it.

"Think it's a cry for help, or bait for a trap?" Kris Jacobs asked the straightforward question, and Matt Baxter was the first to answer.

"By the look of it, they're headed to Lexington same as we are. There might be something to be gained by shadowing them... but if that's a DCI agent in trouble, it'd probably be more valuable to get there while he's still alive. I'd rather have living intel than dead direction."

Matt's words were grim but logical, and Wes found himself nodding, "I tend to agree. Alter course to overtake that transport. We'll surround it and I'll speak to the master, get us permission to go aboard. Andrea, get Rufus' team ready to deploy... this'll probably be a job for Special Branch. And if Ken shows up, tell him our plan."

Wes felt odd saying that last part, but there was no time to worry. Helm and Navigation Officers across the squadron got their orders, then seven of the Empire's best warships turned and accelerated in the direction of the runner travelling from Valcour to Lexington.

"This is an act of piracy! You will suffer consequences for this!"

Rufus Chang was rechecking his MAG-90 as he listened to the master of the Union transport argue with Wes Pellew over the comm. The Major and his team were in their assault shuttle, already on their way over to the triangular-bodied vessel, a squadron of F-194s escorting them.

Obviously the warships were spooking the Union skipper, and Rufus supposed he sympathized. Out of nowhere a Defense Command squadron appeared and surrounded his vessel, and now the Empire was sending over boarders. The SAU skipper would have no idea there was a DCI agent aboard... perhaps an agent in trouble... so this really would look like piracy.

Too bad.

Rufus had no love for DCI superagents. He found many of them to be too arrogant, and altogether too reckless. Nevertheless, they wore the black sun of Defense Command (on those few occasions when they were actually in uniform) and that meant it was his job to look out for them — to save them from harm when they got in over their heads.

"If you resist our shuttle as it docks and the team boards your ship, we will open fire on you," Wes replied with those hard words, and though Rufus was fairly certain the Commodore was issuing an empty threat, the silence that followed over the comm line suggested the Union master wasn't going to chance it.

"They just cut their engines," Chet Srisai called from the assault shuttle cockpit. "I'm going to dock."

That was it; Rufus was going aboard a Union runner to find a spy.

Andrea had her arms folded as she paced the bridge. Rufus' shuttle was just getting ready to sidle up to the Union transport's lock, so new intelligence would undoubtedly be forthcoming.

And I was nowhere to be found.

This frustrated her for some reason. She shouldn't have cared, but perhaps it was a matter of not wanting Wes to be giving the orders right now. Better if I was there — someone she preferred to take command and make certain nothing was lost because of a misplaced sense of morality.

Where was I?

Finally deciding she'd better find out, Andrea headed for the operations consoles at the rear of the bridge, where she caught Jim Hannigan's attention, "Go find Ken. I don't know where he is... but make sure he's okay. And get him up here."

Her words were quiet — just loud enough to be heard by *Wolf's* XO — and Jim paused for a moment before nodding. He was one of the originals, which was why Andrea was taking him off his important station and sending him below on a goose chase.

If there was something wrong, better it be Jim who discovered it.

As had been the case at Concord, the lock on the runner was universal and mated seamlessly with the assault shuttle. As Chet locked on the clamps, Rufus and his team lined up at the hatch while the Major confirmed the plan.

"Chet stays on the shuttle. We don't know what to expect from these people, so be ready to open fire if they're hostile. Clarissa, you have the beacon on your screen?"

Clarissa Hutchinson had a handheld scanner, and on it she could see the beacon, along with various directional cues about its location relative to her position. Confirming that it was showing current data, the Captain nodded, and that was enough for Rufus.

"We're green," Chet called, and without delay the Chinese man with mismatched eyes hit the hatch button

He was then introduced to another aspect of the SAU.

The first thing that hit him was the smell. It was disgusting, and as he moved through the lock's chute and out onto the deck of the runner, he found himself bathed in dim light, with everything around him painted brown.

Well, he hoped it was paint... or if not paint, at least rust.

There were hundreds of people around him too. The compartment he'd entered had to be some sort of storage bay... but it was lined wall-to-wall with bunkbeds... beds rising all the way to the ceiling, five meters up... so the bunks were eleven high.

Some people leaned over their bunk rails and looked down at him, others were glaring at him from their positions on the ground floor. Rufus is a smart man, so it didn't take him long to realize that this was probably the Union equivalent of coach... steerage accommodations for those who didn't have money, or even freedom.

It was staggering.

Children were here, in these conditions. Children.

But the good news was that none of the people crammed into this hell were making any moves in Rufus' direction. Perhaps some had come from the Empire and knew what Special Branch could do.

Either way, the mass of humanity was haunting, and Rufus watched it until Clarissa called out movement orders, "We need to go up a few decks... or maybe just one, based on the height of this deckhead."

Rufus nodded, then looked around for obvious exits. None were apparent, so the Major declared his need: "Which way to the upper deck?"

No one answered. Perhaps it was defiance, perhaps it was fear, but either way, there was silence.

"Chet, do you think there are any locks on the upper part of this hull?" the Major asked, and the Special Branch pilot took a moment to scan using the shuttle's sensors before answering.

"Relative to our position... yes. I see one."

"We're moving," Rufus replied immediately, and then his squad quickly withdrew from the hellish conditions of steerage.

Come to the SAU to be free, everybody — they promise it's better than the Empire...

"Moving locks?" Wes Pellew asked with a frown as he overheard the conversation between Rufus and Chet. "Must have been something impassable."

Rozy Young shrugged at her Commodore, but made no comment.

They wouldn't get the full picture until after Rufus came back, and by then they'd have other things to occupy their minds.

The upper lock was as simple to open as the lower one, but the difference in what they found on the other side was staggering. Rufus led his team into a common area adjacent to a restaurant... full of civilians, a couple of quasi-uniformed officers, and four men who looked like private security bruisers.

"This is my ship," one of the men in a casual-looking uniform declared as Rufus arrived, and the Major trained his MAG-90 on the man before speaking to him over the barrel.

"Really. Did you notice there are hundreds of people on the next deck down, or did you mistake them for cattle?"

"They paid for steerage," the master of the ship didn't like the Major's tone, but he'd have to live with it — Rufus was armed, and again, whether the reputation of Special Branch had preceded them, or he and his team had the 'don't fuck with us' look, no one tried anything daft.

"This way..." Clarissa knew they were now on the same level as the signal so she led the way from the lock.

Rufus followed, along with the other four officers of his team — Bobby, Simon, Maggie and Selma.

And just in case any of the passengers decided to be mischievous, Chet Srisai stepped out of the lock with his own MAG-90 in hand. He was only one man with a rifle, but that was enough — no one was touching his ship.

People started retreating into their cabins as soon as Special Branch began barging down the narrow corridors. Anyone who didn't get out of the way was forcefully barked aside: "Defense Command! Make a hole! Move!"

Clarissa led the entire way to the door of the cabin she was sure held the beacon, and then moved a little further down to cover the corridor ahead. Maggie Joyce was at the back of the stack of Branchers, so she turned and covered the way they'd come, leaving Rufus, Selma, Bobby and Simon to enter the room.

They had no idea what they'd find, but knowing spies, Rufus prepared himself to get an earful if this was indeed an agent who claimed she didn't need to be rescued. Too bad.

"Entering the compartment," Rufus announced for the benefit of the listeners on the comm, and then he tried the hatch. It wouldn't open, so he adjusted his MAG-90 and shot out the lock.

And stepped into a smell worse than the one he'd found in steerage.

"Oh my God."

Wes was pacing the front of his bridge with folded arms, and he stopped abruptly at Rufus' exclamation, "What? Major Chang, what is it?"

Rufus didn't answer.

"Selma!" Rufus waved his medic forward, and to her complete credit Selma Koestecki — the medic with this team, if you'll recall — didn't hesitate, even despite the stench. It had been a day since Renault had done his work, so Julie wasn't just tied up and mutilated, she was delirious and she'd had no way to escape to get to the bathroom.

It was Egesta all over again, and Rufus Chang's blood flash-boiled.

There wasn't enough room in the cramped cabin for more than a couple of people to stand, so he waved for Bobby and Simon to step out, then stayed out of the way as Selma checked Julie's condition.

The spy was partially-conscious as she was examined, but completely unable to process reality. And even had she been able to, she couldn't have formed words, or even communicated with her hands. That was the whole point of her mutilation, wasn't it?

All she remembers from that time is staring up from her cot and seeing Rufus' mismatched eyes. That might sound otherwise sinister — I know how unsettling Rufus' glare can be — but somehow in this moment Julie found it to be a comfort. If the Major was a demon, then death was coming to claim her. But if the patch on his arm wasn't lying, then Julie was about to be rescued.

"She was probably raped. She has no tongue… and they cut off her fingers. They treated her though… she hasn't lost any more blood than… than was necessary…" Selma's clinical appraisal nearly cracked at that point, but her reaction was far more muted than that of the audience back in the squadron.

Wes Pellew froze. There were no pictures being beamed back from the transport, and that was a good thing, but he saw everything he needed to see in his mind's eye.

You know the pictures. You know how this sort of thing affected him. He didn't know enough about this situation — didn't know how Renault had managed to do all he'd done — but it didn't matter. Whether it was one spy killer, or a gang of blockheads, or the Belt Widows themselves, the notion that this had happened again...

The framework of reason and rationality that Wes relied upon started to collapse around him, and as his expression reflected the change, it became obvious to everyone watching him on Battlelink.

He fought back the memories and the words that came with them, then he swallowed hard and closed his eyes. This was no time to indulge himself.

"She's stable enough to move, if we can get a stretcher," Selma looked up at Rufus as she spoke, and immediately the Major turned to the door.

"Bobby, Simon, they must have a medical staff on this barge. Get their stretcher. Shoot anyone who gets in the way."

Our Chinese Major shouldn't have said that last part and he knew it.

"But try not to," he added, though Bobby and Simon were already on their way. Turned out they didn't need to shoot anyone, in case I fail to mention that later.

As they left, Selma sat on the end of Julie's cot, "I need you to help cut the cuffs. Then we should look for the... digits. And tongue. It looks like she's been here at least a day, but something might be salvageable."

The same regen we could do on people — like fixing Mark Gunney's frost-destroyed legs — could sometimes restore pieces of a person that had come off, reviving them sufficiently to be reattached. Nodding, Rufus did as Selma asked: he first shot out the bar on the headboard that was keeping Julie's arms over her head, then he started looking around as Selma brought the spy's arms back to her sides.

There was nothing visible on the floor, except for some scattered gear that had obviously come out of the secret compartments in her luggage. It was clearly DCI kit, so Rufus collected it and put it in one of Julie's bags. It would return to *Wolf* with them.

Other than that, there was no sign of anything... unless...

Why anyone who mutilated a spy so harshly would put the parts he'd taken off in a freezer — a place where, at least theoretically, they could be better preserved — escaped Rufus. Perhaps the killer had been sympathetic, or maybe the intent was to taunt Julie with the idea that even though the parts she'd lost were so near, they might never be restored to her.

Rufus didn't want to speculate because his blood was already boiling. Instead he took out the frozen blocks of ice containing ten digits and a tongue, and put them in another of Julie's bags.

It was, I expect you can tell, quite gruesome.

With that done, Rufus stood up and looked back to Julie. She was staring at him as though she was in a trance, while Selma sat with her and continued to examine various parts of her wrecked body.

Rufus could only take that stare for so long, then had to turn away and tap his comm headset, taking his team off the signal loop, "*Wolf*, is Ken up there yet?"

"Negative," Andrea's voice came back.

"Whoever did this is probably still aboard the transport. It's big, but with some extra bodies for crowd control we can find him," the Major said coolly. "Whoever could do this to a DCI agent has to be one of Merger's better killers. If we could take him out now, it'd help later."

That was a well-reasoned argument that supported what Rufus wanted to do, but the rational justification absolutely was not his motivation now. This was the second time he'd been late to a party at which Grant Merger's minions had horribly harmed or murdered one of the people who Special Branch was supposed to keep safe — first Karen, now this spy.

To be clear, Rufus didn't even know Julie Pichot's fake name, let alone her real one. But you don't need to know someone's name in order to feel fundamental rage at a brutalization like this.

"I can have Eugene and fifty SF over to you in twenty minutes," Andrea Kiley came back on the line, and Rufus nodded.

"Good, we'll get to the bottom of this."

Wes kept his eyes closed as he fought to clear his mind. He felt a fool — this was some stranger DCI agent, not his wife, and not some civilian.

But they'd cut out her tongue?

Her fingers?

There wasn't a wrench in the universe big enough... not nearly big enough.

And then the Commodore of the Independent Squadron heard Andrea Kiley's promise of more SF. More people going over to the transport... looking for a killer...

His mind took a minute to grasp that idea, then he realized what it would mean. He opened his eyes and fought through his anger, the cool calmness of command retaking control.

"Belay that. Rufus, get the agent off that ship, then we'll break contact and head for Lexington."

Immediately Wes could feel Andrea's glare, and sure enough, when he checked her face on the Battlelink screen she was wearing a look that could freeze neutrons.

"Excuse me... sir, what was that?" Rufus' question came back over the comm, and he was genuinely confused. "We have one of Merger's agents here on this ship."

Wes knew that, but he also knew something else: the master of the runner hadn't been wrong in saying this was an act of piracy. We had no authority to stop a Union transport, but we had done so anyway. An argument could be made that we were responding to a distress signal... but if we now detained the ship and all the people on it, looking for a supposed killer who was probably there but we had no way to find, what sort of position would that put us in?

There'd be no chance of getting the support of the Union government against Grant Merger, that was for sure. We could go to the President having done a rescue, and found one of Grant's victims, and reasonably ask for his assistance... but we if we captured a civilian ship and conducted a witch hunt, we'd be pirates.

Now, you might disagree with this assessment — our whole purpose for being here, after all, was to hunt Karen's killers, and Grant himself. But recall: we knew Grant and the killers to be named enemies of the Empire, and we had a clear sense of their whereabouts.

We had no specific evidence about this mutilation. Taking further action would have been piracy.

Wes wasn't going to let it happen, and he was the senior officer present in that moment.

"Ken will overrule you," Andrea said sharply, but Wes shook his head.

"He's not here right now. You'll follow my orders. Get your team off that ship immediately, Andrea. Get that agent to your med bay and make sure she survives," Wes left no room for interpretation.

Rufus was not pleased, but his grip on the chain of command was also unwavering, "Understood... sir."

That was it; as soon as a stretcher came for Julie, they were getting off the ship — leaving it to go on its way.

So long as I didn't turn up to change the orders.

Wes realized that was the greatest concern at this point, and in a moment which he now thinks didn't reflect the best of his judgment, he made a decision.

"I'm coming over to *Wolf* for this," he said, and then before anyone could object, he left his bridge.

Chapter Twelve

Disconnected

I don't know why I was dreaming so much.

I suppose those among you skilled in matters of the brain and psychology might be able to tell me. I suppose if I think about it a bit, the simplistic answer might be that my subconscious was dealing with the situation by trying to escape into other realms and do other things.

And, as is so often the case, the places my subconscious went bore little connection to reality. It was unsettling.

In this particular dream it felt as though I was walking on the red rock of Mars… marching across an island of red Martian rock, crumbling beneath my feet as a cold wind blew… But around me in the distance I could see green and gray cliffs, even some forests, as though I was back on Capital Island.

It was almost as if this recent stretch of war with Mars represented a strange interruption in the landscape of my life, and that I was nearly finished crossing it, because familiar green lands were near.

I had nearly reached them… and I was alone.

Maybe it all meant something, or maybe it was just a weird dream.

Anyway, I found a path that led to the edge of the red rock and down into the trees. As I started for the woods, I shook my head at myself; I had no business being asleep, but clearly I was dreaming. Something important was probably happening, and I was wandering around in a dream because I couldn't cope with being alone when I was awake.

That thought made me stop, and I turned back towards the red slopes before speaking: "I remember losing Karen. I remember what it did to me."

"And you survived. So will she, in time."

The voice came from the trees behind me, but at first I didn't look because I assumed it was Charlie who was speaking. It wasn't.

"It's easy to dwell on the pain. But it helps to know that good will come of it."

That definitely wasn't Charlie, so I glanced back at the trees and saw that I was again being visited by that personification of my ship — the wolfman in uniform, looking rather dapper.

I stared at the creature for a minute, then shook my head at the strange things my imagination generated. With a sigh, I replied to the apparition, "You're going to argue the greater good under circumstances like these?"

My ship's avatar smiled at me, then shook his head, "I'm not arguing. Just reminding you how we survived messes like these. She'll survive the same way."

I remember feeling distinctly disconcerted that my ship was delusional — that he was implying that Karen would survive. I also remember *remembering* this dream, as if this dream was of an event happening in the future.

It was all very strange... and I continued to dream. Mercifully, I can't remember the rest so vividly...

Jim Hannigan was getting concerned. He'd pounded on my cabin hatch and gotten no answer. He'd overridden the comm and broadcast a loud message asking me to wake up, but I hadn't. He'd therefore assumed that I was elsewhere, so he left my door and headed for the rec deck.

He checked anywhere I could have been... the pool, the clubs, the theatre, the firing range... he checked them all and found no sign of me. Of course there was no one around to ask because everyone was at General Quarters, and he certainly didn't want to broadcast the question on the intercom, because if I was off my rocker and wandering around, talking to my ship as though it was an Earther, it probably wouldn't be a good idea to call attention to that fact.

But Jim's concern was growing fast. No one had thought I needed to be on any sort of watch — I'd seemed well enough after leaving Concord, so why would I consider taking my own life, especially when we still had to deal with Grant Merger?

It didn't seem likely that I'd disappear under such circumstances... but what if I'd cracked, and decided to do myself harm? Jim didn't think that to be probable, but he was well aware that it was often a complete surprise to friends and family when certain people made such attempts.

He had to find out, so he returned to my cabin in a hurry, then pulled his comm from his belt and contacted the bridge.

"Hannigan to Ops," he said, and one of the officers from his station answered him.

"Here, boss. Go."

"Need to override the lock on the Admiral's door. Seems to be having a problem unbuttoning."

That was a lie — the lock worked fine. But in case I was alive and sitting catatonic on my bed, or in a difficult emotional state and unable to respond, his saying there was a lock malfunction might become part of a flimsy excuse for me missing the call to the bridge.

"I... alright boss," the officer on the other end of the line answered, and then took a few seconds before adding, "It's reset."

"Thanks," Jim replied, holstering his comm as he heard the lock on the door disengage.

He then looked both ways down the corridor, and when he was sure it was clear he opened the door.

All the lights were off, which made for a rather dark room. Jim stepped in, keeping his feet within the shaft of light that lanced through the door behind them, then spoke up into the darkness, "Hello?"

No answer. Also: no sounds of breathing, or snoring for that matter. No smell of death either, but sometimes that took a while.

Nothing to do but turn on the lights, so Jim reached back to the switch beside the wall and pressed it.

Light burst into the dark room, and Jim scanned it quickly.

Nothing. The bed hadn't been slept in, the chair was empty. He stepped further into the cabin and shut the hatch, ducked his head into the washroom, then crossed to the other side and checked the kitchen.

Where the hell was I?

Taking a breath, *Wolf's* XO started thinking of places he hadn't yet checked. The rec deck and my cabin were but two... what about somewhere like the briefing room? But there seemed no way that I'd have been in the briefing room, and heard all the announcements, and still not come to the bridge.

The same held for the rec deck, he supposed, but he'd tried there anyway. Otherwise, perhaps the flight bays... but no, Rufus had exited through one of those, and Starlights had scrambled from the other. I would have been seen, would have been involved.

What corner of this frigate was unoccupied, and would allow me to sequester myself without any interruption from outside forces?

Jim was stumped, so he opened my hatch and stepped out into the corridor again, looking both ways to see if anyone had noticed him. Everyone was still at General Quarters, so there was no one to see anything.

Taking a few steps down the corridor he stopped beside the hatch to what had been Karen's quarters, then planted his hand against the wall to brace himself as he considered the options. Where would I go to be alone, to think of Karen and not be interrupted? What place was like that on the whole ship...

Jim remains a bit embarrassed to this day that he needed a whole five minutes outside the hatch to Karen's cabin before he thought to try the door. It wasn't locked, of course, because there was no occupant for this cruise... no official occupant anyway. Though no one had packed up Karen's stuff. Her closet still held all her clothes, her sheets hadn't even been changed.

It still smelled like her, and felt like her, and would continue to for at least a while longer.

As he stepped in, Jim immediately heard breathing — he says breathing, I suspect snoring — and he hit the lights.

I was passed out in the chair beside her bed, my regular place. On the ground beside my chair was a tray with dinner dishes. Half-eaten rice and fish sticks.

Jim let out a noisy sigh of relief, which is the first thing I remember hearing when I awoke. And as soon as sleep — and its strange dreams — broke, I found myself perfectly alert. My eyes travelled to the chronometer as I wondered how long I'd been out, and why I'd even fallen asleep.

Then I looked up to Jim, "Something happening?"

"DCI emergency beacon found on a transport bound for Lexington. Rufus is pulling it off right now."

I was on my feet immediately, and Jim fell into step at my shoulder as we headed out of Karen's cabin. It was a very strange time to sleep, and stranger that I'd slept through the General Quarters alarm. Maybe *Wolf* had coaxed me to nod off, so that I wouldn't get to the bridge until Rufus' shuttle was already back aboard.

CHAPTER THIRTEEN

FRIENDS

Wolf's med bay went into a state of organized chaos as soon as Rufus and Selma came in carrying Julie Pichot. Alicia Morgan had met them in the flight bay's observation lounge, and had been checking vitals the whole way up, so as soon as she came through the door she was ready with orders.

"We have detached digits in ice in this bag," she called to her waiting staff, then held out the piece of Julie's luggage that Rufus had used to store her fingers, thumbs and tongue.

"Get them in preservation gels… hopefully we'll be able to save them in a regenerable state."

That was all Alicia said before the stretcher came up alongside the bed which had been prepared for Julie. As Rufus and Selma held it in place, the staff transferred Julie to the bed and began standard whole-body scans.

They had a beacon to locate, and undoubtedly a host of internal injuries to treat.

First, though, Alicia sought to put her new patient at ease — or as much at ease as was possible under the circumstances, "What's her name?"

Rufus shook his head, "Her ID was branded Julie Pichot. Don't have anything on her real name…"

"Julie," Alicia went with what she had. "Julie?"

Our spy was in and out of consciousness, but the second call of her adopted name was enough to spark some awareness. The pain was incredible… but suddenly there was an IV in her arm that instantly reduced it.

She tried to speak but couldn't. Her tongue was gone. She started to panic…

Alicia put her hands on Julie's cheeks, then held her gently so that she would pay attention to the words that followed, "You're aboard *Wolf*. We know you're DCI, but we don't know who. We'll call you Julie for now. You've lost all your fingers, and your tongue…"

Julie struggled as she heard that, but Alicia was firm.

"…but we have them. We saved them. We can regenerate them and give them back to you once we get home. I'm sorry we can't do it sooner, but right now I need you to just think of this as a nightmare. It's going to end and you're going to wake up as your whole self again, but until then I need you to be strong, okay?"

Julie stared at Alicia with wild eyes, but the steady gaze of the doctor somehow calmed her and she managed to nod in understanding before the drugs began to kick in. Her vision started to get fuzzy, and then the last thing she saw before losing active consciousness was Rufus' mismatched eyes staring at her.

"How is she?"

That question came from the door just as Julie drifted off, and turning, Alicia and Rufus were both surprised to see Wes Pellew standing in the hatch. He was wearing his flight suit, having just piloted his fighter over from *Nova Scotia*. He also had a mag on his hip, which made no sense, but Rufus didn't comment.

"We're trying to save her fingers and her tongue," Alicia answered. "Other than that, she's alive. I'll know more once we can do a full scan, but I expect there'll be more damage."

Wes swallowed hard as he looked at the shattered spy, but he consoled himself with the fact that, no matter how gruesomely she'd been treated, she was breathing and under excellent care.

"Good. I've ordered the transport to be sent on its way and we're resuming course," Wes said firmly, looking to Rufus.

Those orders, I should add, had been reaffirmed from his plane's cockpit on the way over. He'd taken a look at the Union runner and decided immediately that bullying such a small ship with seven Imperial combat vessels was about as big a mistake as one could make right now.

"We'll get whoever did this, Rufus," Wes added. These two didn't know each other that well, but he felt obliged to add something for the benefit of the Major. "He'll either be on Lexington, or we'll get him on Valcour. Either way, he's going to pay."

As I said before, the chain of command is something Rufus abides by, so he nodded again, "Yes sir."

Wes didn't get the sense his consolation prize sounded attractive enough, so he stepped back from the hatch, "Join me for a minute, Major?"

Rufus nodded, then took a last look at Alicia and Julie before stepping out into the corridor. Wes shut the hatch behind them and then looked quickly in both directions before adding: "We can't get distracted by this. It's what Grant wants. God knows I'd kill the man who did this myself, though you're likely better at killing his kind than I am. Either way, I know you're going to hold the line on this, I just want you to understand I don't walk away lightly. And some day soon, we're not going to walk away at all."

Wes didn't have any obligation to explain himself… but it was important in stressful times like these for a real leader to make sure the people trusting him understood what they were about. The big picture — getting Grant, and doing so without starting a war — mattered most of all.

Wes understood that.

At this moment, I didn't.

"I just countermanded that order, we're closing with the transport again. Rufus, take me to an arms locker, then let's suit up."

I was coming down the hall fast and hard, and the intent behind my words was pretty obvious. I glared at Wes as I passed him and got to the med bay hatch, then paused.

"Scratch that, Rufus, could you grab me a sidearm and meet me back here? Need to speak to Wes."

As I've already pointed out a few times, the Major respected the chain of command — Rear Admiral, unstable or not, outranked Commodore. He turned and strode off, and I waited until he was around the corner to open my mouth again.

"You want to let the assassin get away?"

"You want to eliminate any chance of getting a positive reaction at Lexington?" Wes countered. "You want to take a ship full of people hostage, in their territorial space, because there's a murderer or two aboard?"

I nodded immediately, "If this was the Empire, we would…"

"It isn't the Empire. These aren't our people to police."

"It was our operative they mutilated," I replied.

"So we're going to Lexington to admit we have spies in their ranks? You realize that if we admit we have agents out here, that means we know their state exists, even though we haven't extended diplomatic relations? And we want them to turn over one of their own Governors. That's a tough case. You want to make it tougher by capturing their civilians too?"

Wes was making a certain kind of sense, but I shook my head, "We're going to play it hard, we might as well add one more crime to the list. I'm not letting the one who did this get away."

"Because he mutilated this agent? Do you know her name?"

I blinked. No one had told me that, but fortunately I did remember my intel reports from before: "Haley Briand. She saved Greg and John from Caldecott's tribunal. She got us the information we needed to bring down the Emperor. And then some fucking ape cut out her tongue. Because Grant told him to. I don't care, I'm going to find that guy, and I'm going to make him tell me whatever I need to know."

Perhaps unsurprisingly I was seething. I knew I was right. I also knew Wes was right. Either option made sense… both had advantages and disadvantages. Wes certainly understood my way of thinking — that a search could yield information. But he was steadfast, and in the years since I've concluded that he was absolutely right to be.

Going over to that transport, sifting through all those people with no legal authority… it was, at the very least, a public relations mess. At worst, it really was piracy.

All the literary specialists can now point to the page and speak of role-reversals.

Rufus returned before I could even open the hatch to the medical bay, and as he handed me a mag with a holster, I nodded and drew my hand away from the door, "I'll visit her later. I've got Eugene prepping volunteers for crowd control. Let's go."

With that, Rufus and I stepped around Wes and headed for the flight bay. The Independent Squadron's Commodore watched us go for a moment, and then his mind filled with all the possible scenarios. None of them ended well.

He couldn't let this happen. Here was a moment when things could go too far out of hand — if something happened and we killed innocent civilians, all bets would be off. The SAU would have all the justification they needed… the Empire would be firmly in the wrong, instead of just surviving in a grey area. It had to stop.

So Wes followed us.

Eugene and twenty volunteers were waiting in the observation lounge for Rufus and me when we arrived. I nodded to him as I entered, "Team briefed?"

"Yes sir," the Master-At-Arms replied reassuringly. "We'll find this bastard."

"Good. Mags on low, don't want to cause an incident by killing someone… but be wary. Anyone who could do that to a DCI agent is a threat to all of us," I continued, heading straight for the exit hatch.

As I emerged onto the flight deck, I saw the rest of Rufus' team was already waiting there — Selma had rejoined from the med bay, and they were all stone-faced and ready to go back to the runner for a hunt.

Our Chinese Major took Eugene aside as soon as they stepped out onto the deck, then laid out the ground rules: "If you find the assassin, don't try to restrain him yourself. I'm guessing he'd have to be ex-Syndicate to know how to drop a spy, so he'll be ready for SF. Hell, he'll probably be ready for us too… but we have the better chance."

By 'we', Rufus meant Special Branch, and fair to say that he was more concerned about dealing with this nameless killer than he had been with most foes, probably since Pion Rock.

Neither of those two men paid any attention as Wes emerged from the observation lounge behind them. I was halfway across the deck by that time — a dozen meters away at least — and Wes spotted me immediately.

His heart was thumping. He knew what he was about to do was likely going to end his career, but he wasn't going to stop short of trying. He owed me a life save… well he thought he did, though I've told him many times he owed me nothing of the sort.

"Ken!" he bellowed my name loud enough to be heard over all the sounds of an active flight deck — no mean accomplishment.

I heard his voice and stopped, turning my head partway back in his direction.

"Don't do this," he called one more warning, and I narrowed my eyes.

"You coming or not, Wes?"

It was very dramatic, I think you'll agree. Some might say needlessly so, though honestly it is how things happened. I was running from his advice, so he chased me down.

And then he said something that made the hairs on the back of my neck stand up.

"I challenge you to a duel. Right now."

Wes was serious. Deadly serious. He had a mag on his hip, and a hush fell as everyone on the deck realized that. Rufus' attention immediately left Eugene and he placed his hands on his MAG-90… though he didn't know who to aim at, if anyone. A duel was… unexpected.

I didn't move, my back still to Wes. Then after a moment I looked over my shoulder, "No."

That simple. I started walking again, getting a little further away before Wes called after me.

"I challenge you to a duel!"

I shook my head and Wes stormed after me, his hand falling to the mag on his hip.

"*God damn you Ken, on Karen's name, and on Sara's, I challenge you to a duel!*"

"Accepted."

I turned and shot Wes Pellew in the chest. I don't really remember doing it, and that's the part that really scares me. From what I'm told, it was fast. I heard him invoke Karen's name, and just as I'd once triggered him to shoot at me, he'd managed to make me shoot him.

Problem was, I hadn't done it fairly; a duel requires you to stand and face off against someone directly. I've fought enough of them to know. Wes… I'd cheated Wes of the chance to save me the way I'd saved him.

And I realized that as soon as I found myself looking down the barrel of my mag, across the flightdeck, at his crumpling form.

In that moment I remembered that I hadn't checked the settings of my mag. I'd told Eugene to set them to low power, but hadn't checked the one Rufus had handed me. That wasn't part of the plan. If I even had a plan.

I suddenly found myself scrambling, trying to check the settings, while everyone on the deck stood and stared at me and Wes...

The settings were in the green. Stun. He might have burns.

Selma Koestecki hurried past me as I realized I hadn't actually killed my friend, and then I hurried after her. We reached Wes' side at the same time Rufus did, and I watched the Commodore grimace as she checked his pulse.

"Goddammit," he was groaning.

I just stared at him, realizing how close I'd come to killing him... then I fell back to sit on the floor of the flight bay.

Not what I'd intended.

What the hell had he meant by starting a duel on a flight deck? I didn't think it made sense, but it was Wes — he usually had a good reason. So I shook my head slightly. What were we doing again, and why?

Backing off from the runner... letting one of Grant's assassins escape for now... didn't seem like the right course of action.

But I'd just shot Wes without knowing if I'd be killing him. I needed to stop and check myself a bit.

As I came to this conclusion I saw Rufus was looming over us, his expression stern. He didn't know who to be more pissed at in this situation, so he was just broadcasting his displeasure.

I looked up at him, "Stand down for now. We'll tail them into Lexington and decide from there."

Seemed like a fair compromise to make after shooting my friend.

CHAPTER FOURTEEN
RIDICULOUS FOOLS

"Get off me…" Wes tried to slap one of the medic's hands away, but he groaned as the necessary twisting motion stretched the burned flesh on his torso. He didn't have any life-threatening injuries, but his flight suit had been insufficient protection against the heat of the mag bolt. Burns were the unpleasant side effect, though as soon as they got some topical anesthetic on them, they'd be less uncomfortable.

Not that Wes was cooperating.

"You need to…" the medic tried to put Wes in his place, but the Commodore wasn't having any of it.

"Ken! You son of a bitch, get over here!" he had spotted me across *Wolf's* med bay, and now he barked sharply. "You shot me!"

"Again," I added for him as I approached. "It wasn't sporting, I apologize."

Wes glared at me for a second, then let his head fall back down to his pillow with a grunt, "You remember, the psychopath on the killing spree is the one who's supposed to get shot. That's how this works."

"In a fair world," I agreed. "But if I'd given you an even chance, you'd have shot me and I wouldn't be able to tail that ship into Lexington."

Wes was entirely displeased, but in a testament to the sort of person he is, he wasn't angry at me in the way you'd expect. He'd known this was the sort of thing he was in for when he issued his challenge… and getting burned bothered him less than the chance of me going over to some Union transport and raising hell.

It wasn't a perspective I completely understood.

"You're confused, aren't you?" Wes looked at me again. "You *shot* me. But maybe next time you'll think twice before you decide to throw the weight of the Empire into a witch hunt."

"No, next time I'll check the settings on my mag before I shoot you. Was worried there for a moment."

Wes heard the cold edge on my tone and let out a sigh, then shook his head, "Dammit. If I got shot for nothing…"

"No, you got your way. I'm not over on that transport right now. Not over there hunting for the person who cut out her tongue," I pointed to the next bed over, where a sedated Julie Pichot was still being examined. They'd located the beacon, and Alicia would soon be scrubbing up to surgically remove it.

"And what would you do if you were over there?" Wes asked harshly as one of the medics finally started getting the treatment gel on his burns.

I shrugged, "I'd sift every person on that ship, find the killer, and do my best to get him back here. Or castrate him and space him. Whatever seemed more prudent at the time."

"And if the crew resisted the illegal arrest and possible execution?"

"We know how to subdue without killing, Wes," I countered, then winced slightly. "You just got a demonstration, actually."

Wes closed his eyes for a minute, "Okay, now I *am* getting angry. Did I seriously just get shot for nothing? Has this not gotten your damned attention yet? I know everyone else here seems to trust your judgment, but seriously, look at yourself. Decide if you're ready to play a subtle game on a civilian ship. Or with a President. You just *shot me* because I called you out and mentioned Karen's name. I've been there. You pulled me out of it. Now for God's sake, listen to me. Let me do the same."

This whole situation — duels and me shooting Wes — was beyond ridiculous. To preempt any questions, it wasn't strictly illegal, or even against regulations — duels in the fleet are only allowed by permission of a flag officer, but since it had been two flag officers doing the shooting, it was entirely above board. Not necessarily right or good, but allowed.

Sort of the story of this whole damned year, isn't it?

Anyway, how it would play with the squadron was an entirely separate question. Clearly there could be some division... people siding with one of us over another... but really, I doubted it would cause a rift. We were too close to Lexington, and in the end all Wes and I had been arguing about was methodology.

We'd put such arguments aside when we had a President in his crosshairs, surely?

Or perhaps that was part of Wes' point. Because he hadn't done this crazy thing without purpose: we were on a decidedly slippery slope and he wanted to make sure we didn't fall down it. Unfortunately, I wasn't cooperating nearly as much as he had years before, because there was one fundamental difference between his situation with Sara, and mine with Karen.

"Here's the difficulty, Wes," I said with that fact in mind. "You and I are a lot alike. But there's one difference: *good* is your natural state. It isn't mine. And even you can't change that."

That was perhaps the most self-indulgent bullshit I'd uttered in a very long time: 'look how bad I am. I'm so tortured you don't even know how tortured I am'.

Wes groaned again and rolled his eyes, before seeing Alicia passing by, "Doc!"

Alicia hurried over and Wes grabbed the hem of her coat, "Can I borrow a mag so I can shoot him? Please?"

He wasn't joking, but Alicia just wasn't in the headspace to process any such comments. She gave him a funny look, tugged her coat out of his hand and went back to dealing with Julie's condition.

"Dammit," Wes let out another breath. "I'm not going to have a war on my head, Ken. Promise me that when you do whatever you do next, you remember that my name, and the name of every other officer and spacer in this squadron, is going to be attached to it. You kill, you destroy... that'll be you *and* the Belt Squadron. You want to one-up Sean Cook, that's your decision. But remember it's about more than your anger."

Something he hadn't invoked before, because he thought it would be too callous — comparing us throwing our weight around to what the Independent Squadron had done at Egesta. It was a low blow, but an urgent warning too.

I considered it, reflecting on the things I'd done through the lens of my state of mind, and then shrugged, "The difference is I got the Emperor, the PM and the Admiralty on side before I left. And I have law on my side. I could kill everyone out here and go home a hero. Cook didn't think that far ahead."

The medic treating Wes' burns stopped as I said that, then looked at me with a surprised expression on his face. I smiled and patted him on the shoulder, which seemed to convince him that I was just kidding.

Wes wasn't reassured, and his expression hardened.

To put him at ease, then, I proved how far ahead I'd been thinking: "On the bright side, if I go so far off the reservation that they need to hang me, the Belt Squadron has a good Admiral-in-waiting. Make sure those burns heal up good, Wes. We might need you!"

I said it jovially, mainly for the benefit of the medic, who undoubtedly thought my joke was rather inappropriate... but still a joke. In that moment, Wes had a very different thought: next time he'd aim at me before asking for a duel.

I patted him on shoulder and then turned and left the med bay. That was the end of it.

Except that as I stepped out the hatch Andrea Kiley passed me, going in. I nodded to her, she nodded to me, but we said nothing. I didn't think twice about seeing her because I was too busy thinking of my next move.

Upon entering the med bay, she paused first to look at the savaged Julie Pichot, but the medical staff was just getting her ready to go into the surgical theatre. As that process was being undertaken, Andrea turned the other way and found that the medic had finished applying the gel to Wes' burns.

Nearing him silently, she found her eyes fixed on those wounds. He watched her approach and saw her lack of eye contact, but decided to say nothing. There wasn't much to say.

She stopped right beside his bed, stared at his wounds a little longer, and then shook her head, eyes finally travelling up to meet his, "You're a fool."

"Obviously," his reply was bitter.

"He's beyond your morality. Beyond stopping now. He has to run his course, and after that he might find peace," Andrea said, and in doing so she made a mistake: she admitted she knew what we were probably going to do wouldn't be, in the abstract sense, the best thing.

"I think I know something about what he's going through, actually," Wes countered. "And you have no idea. There is no course. You either stop the self destruction, or let it run into perpetuity."

Andrea shook her head immediately, "He knows what he's doing."

Wes actually laughed at that statement, "Of course he does. So did I. But knowing you're doing something doesn't make it right. I think I just proved that."

The words of the Independent Squadron's Commodore registered with Andrea, but she didn't react to them. Wes was turning out to be such a moral crusader... first with her, then with me... because he knew the things he'd done wrong, and could easily do wrong again. He'd do everything he could to keep his friends from repeating his mistakes, and he was willing to get shot trying.

He was a fool, Andrea concluded, as she left the side of his bed without taking hold of his hand. Even though she had wanted to.

Wes watched her go and let out a breath at the ridiculousness of this whole situation, then wondered how long before he'd be able to challenge me to a duel again.

It'd be a while — too late for Etat Lexington.

Chapter Fifteen

Lessons

Charlie knocked on Karen's door, wondering if she'd answer. It had been a day since the meeting with Hansen, and he'd basically given her space since the non-revelation. Somehow it seemed best to let her breathe.

Karen says it was exactly the thing to do. The only audience she had ever really accepted for her insecurities was me, and even then that was more of a grudging access — she knew I knew the worst of her insecurities already. And inexplicably I was still there.

But insecurities could only be allowed to dominate for so long, and that's why Charlie's knock on her door was well timed. It took her a little longer than usual to open the hatch, and when she did it appeared to Charlie that her mood had settled… if not improved.

"Mind if I come in?" he asked, and Karen shook her head.

"Help yourself."

She stepped aside to let him in and shut the hatch behind him… and then without any prompting whatsoever, she plunged straight into what she was thinking — she needed to talk to *someone*.

"I just keep pacing. Is that all I do to pass the time now, just pace?" she sounded frustrated with herself, and Charlie frowned and folded his arms, then leaned against the frame of the hatch.

"I believe Ken told me you dance. Around your cabin. To old music."

Karen had begun pacing again, but she stopped and turned to him with a frown, "*What?*"

Charlie shrugged, "That's what he says."

"Sounds ridiculous," Karen shook her head. "I can't even dance…"

She went back to pacing, the scowl no less dominant on her face. Dancing? She could hardly believe it. She'd feel like a fool just dancing alone. Besides, what self-respecting officer would be caught dead looking so stupid?

"Once you two even went and danced during some downtime in a battle. That was out at Io and I wasn't there, but you did."

Karen stopped again, opened her mouth to comment, but then decided against it. She just shook her head and returned to pacing, releasing a long sigh after a few more steps. Perhaps she'd gotten to a point in her life where all these silly diversions were entertaining, or good for the soul.

Maybe once she was a confident Captain, then Commodore, she'd realize that she could loosen up a little, not be so concerned about appearances, do what felt good no matter who was watching.

Yeah.

"You… you're with Ian Hawke's daughter, aren't you?" she asked Charlie after a period of silence, and our fine Lord was surprised by the subject change.

"They call me the official consort, at least until after the wedding. Lia is her name," Charlie replied, and Karen nodded.

"That's good. Good that you've got someone. And you were with her as a Lord before you came back here to pick me up and go after Ken. She must be pretty understanding."

Charlie wasn't sure where this line of thought was going, but he figured an honest answer was the best, "Yep. We've been through enough together... and she loves Ken like a brother. So there was no question."

The last part of that answer was nice, but it wasn't the part that Karen fixated on. The first part... the 'been through enough' part... was more relevant.

"So the last thing I remember, you and Ken were heading off to the Protectorate. That when you met her?"

Charlie nodded, "I guess it has been a while. Though we had to keep things long distance for years... right up until the war, actually. But that wasn't a bad thing. We both had some growing up and settling in to do."

He let his words trail off after that, because he suddenly realized what Karen was listening for. He kicked himself for not preempting her concern sooner.

"You don't need to worry about what you've missed. The main things that work between the two of you date back to the beginning."

Karen held her hand up to stop him, "Yeah I got that when you explained it to me last time. We both hate ourselves and love each other. It's delightfully dysfunctional. But the practicalities still exist. I have scars on my body I don't remember getting, Charlie. And I'm sure he'll know where they are and how I got them. And when he sees them on me, he's going to know something that I don't. And thanks to Grant, and our wonderfully young doctor, I don't know if that'll ever change. How exactly do I deal with that?"

The questions were fair, if bitter, and Charlie didn't have any immediate answers. Karen thus continued, "I shouldn't be obsessing over this, but I am. Maybe I should take up dancing, but until I do I have to wonder what's going to happen when we get out there. First of all he's been on a rage bender, and I'm going to show up and invalidate that.

"And then, if he needs me to actually be the other half of a partnership... to help him make decisions... what the hell am I going to do? Tell him to wait until we find Grant and then we'll figure out if I can still be useful? Right now I have *no* real command experience. I've never commanded a frigate, let alone a squadron. And wartime experiences? He was always better than me at all of this. And the only chance I had was to catch up through experience. Now I've lost all that, and I don't have his brain... suddenly I stop being a partner, and I start being a third wheel."

Insecurity. It was something Charlie hadn't seen from Karen in a very long time. He'd seen it more often than most back in the day, but she'd started dealing with hers very early on, and had been good at keeping it under wraps.

The fact that she was speaking about it to someone — to anyone — at this point was a great sign that she was trying to control it.

But it also clearly reflected her uncertainty. She wasn't going to remember the missing years when she saw me next... she might *never* remember them... and she didn't know where that would leave her, or us.

There wasn't a whole lot Charlie could say, either. He had no idea what would happen if Karen was asked for advice in her current state. Was she really just the sum of the memories she'd had up to that point, or was there more there than she realized? Was the wisdom she'd gained just a matter of memory, or was it also stored somewhere deeper — in a subconscious, perhaps. Either way, she had to have something to draw on, and Charlie decided he had to try to tap it.

"You want to know what sets you apart from a lot of people, at least in Ken's view?"

Karen nodded, "Sure. I'd love to know, preferably without you having to tell me."

Ouch, fair point. But Charlie was undaunted, "Fine. Tell yourself. What does he prize so much — to a maddening extent, even?"

"Intelligence?"

Charlie shook his head, "Not quite."

Karen thought for another minute, then shook her head, "Could be anything."

"He's the same man, just with more time on the clock. What did you see that made you take an interest in that alley?"

It was a simple question, but a tough one. Karen blinked a few times and then shrugged, "He knows… self-awareness."

"Right," Charlie agreed. "And what does that involve?"

"Analyzing your own reactions to things… figuring out your own problems and then mastering them as best you can. Knowing when you're going off the rails."

Charlie nodded again, "And what exactly are you doing right now?"

Karen had walked into that one — a positive, motivational comment about herself. She nearly cringed, "Honestly, does that shit work on me now?"

"Stop pouting and deal with it."

Turning her back and heaving yet another sigh, Karen pretended not to appreciate Charlie's observation… while silently hoping he was right. Maybe if she was clearly trying to get to grips with who she was… again… if she was demonstrating that she hadn't just floated all the way back to rage girl, and was in fact on a good path… that would help her last however long it took to find Grant and get her memories back.

Because she simply had to believe that they would be coming back. Being like this forever was… not an option.

"We're a day out of Etat Lexington," Charlie said after another period of silence. "Find some obnoxious music and try dancing around in here. Or don't, I don't care. But be ready, we're going to need you soon."

With that, he opened the hatch and walked out. It had been as good a visit as he could have hoped for. Karen agreed, though she wasn't desperate enough to try dancing. Instead she went back to her pacing, and wondered what else about herself she'd need to come to grips with before she saw me again.

CHAPTER SIXTEEN

ETAT LEXINGTON

Before the Solar Asteroid Union existed, Etat Lexington had been known as Wayfaren. It's a strange name, I know — Wayfarer with the 'r' plucked off the end and replaced with an 'n'. I suppose this was meant to convey the concept that it was a destination… Wayfaren, where the Wayfarers end up after their travels.

Didn't work. Name was stupid — so stupid that the replacement name of Etat Lexington looks good by comparison. That's a pretty low bar to set.

Anyway, Wayfaren had been founded on the principles of self-sufficiency: even before a dome was built on the rock, the plan was to have the place produce everything its colonists could possibly need. Sounds great, but it's one of those grand schemes which is always more doable on paper than in practice.

The attempt was a serious one, though, and it began with a small city not inside a dome, but on (and in) the asteroid itself. Those exterior structures — much like the control building back at Io, if you need a comparison — were crude, cold and cramped, but they'd contained the nascent form of Wayfaren's industry. Enough items were produced in them to keep the original settlers alive until a dome was ready, and more industry — and everything else — was built within it.

Many colonies have stories similar to Wayfaren's. Dome's aren't cheap to construct, so you find a lot of independent asteroids start with buildings and tunnels, then work their way up. Only domes with major backers — like the Empire, or certain major corporations — can be built at the start of a colony's life.

The interesting thing, though, is that most colonies move everything inside the dome as soon as possible. Earthgreen conditions continue to be popular with humans everywhere, even those who've never set foot on our home planet. Don't know why… maybe our species is just wired to want to have some notion of 'sky' over its head (instead of a reinforced and armored space roof). However you slice it, most independent colonies abandon their exterior buildings as soon as they have a dome. Some even tear them down for scrap.

I mention all of this for a simple reason: Wayfaren, now Etat Lexington, bucked the trend entirely.

Sitting on a rather large asteroid, the colony boasted five sizable domes, with its main one being by far the largest. But then, instead of a sixth and probably even seventh dome, the colony had spread out by putting exterior buildings on the rock's surface — like huge subdivisions spilling out of the dome cities.

As we arrived at Etat Lexington, it was the lights from all these buildings that gave the place a feeling of being lit up. I'd never seen anything like it, and I suppose if I'd been in a different state of mind, I might have been impressed.

Bad luck for them.

"I wonder if they expect that to impress people," Andrea muttered bitterly, folding her arms as live cam shots of the rock came up on *Wolf's* main screen.

We had Battlelink up because we were cruising into what we expected to be a thoroughly-protected defensive zone, so Matt Baxter weighed in after Andrea's comment: "Seems poorly conceived to me."

I agreed with him. Domes are not impenetrable, but at the same time they do provide incredible amounts of protection, putting two pressure-tight layers between their occupants and the vacuum. With few exceptions, domes have a good track record against meteor strikes… individual buildings just can't compete with the heavy construction.

But anyway, this is far too much about buildings. There were other things for us to worry about, and it was the outsider of our group, Captain Rozy Young, who first called attention to that fact.

"Those five ships look military."

She sounded irritated, which I suppose is rather understandable — Wes had called her from his bed in *Wolf's* medical bay to let her know his return flight would be delayed until Alicia Morgan decided to be less particular about treating him… and of course he'd told her what had happened.

By now, actually, the story had made its way around the entire squadron, and a lot of people were understandably uncomfortable. No one knew exactly why we'd shot it out in a landing bay — most of our squadron's skippers had joined long after those old days when Wes had been dueling, so they didn't know the history. But Wes was fine, he and I seemed to be on confusingly okay terms (no arrests, no recriminations), and we were still continuing the mission.

Some sort of disagreement over what to do with the runner had been resolved in a most unorthodox fashion, and no one was polled to see who's side they'd have been on during the discussion anyway. Basically, it was an unprecedented incident that was being overlooked, so long as it didn't repeat itself.

None of that changed the validity of Rozy Young's observation about a line of five ships that were on the far side of the rock from us, formed up in a column and seemingly at their ease.

Seemingly.

"Give me enhanced views on those," I glanced in Felicia Khalid's direction, and the camera that had been staring at Etat Lexington's poorly-planned settlement panned up from the rock to the line of ships. They were quite a ways out, but our cameras are excellent, and we started to see some clear detail.

They didn't look like any other combat vessels I'd seen. From the side they appeared to be long, thin, rectangular vessels with drive pods around the middle, on very short pod wings. But as we got in closer, we were able to see that the warships were similar to the transport we'd boarded in their triangular hull design — if you looked at one front-on, the whole ship would be in the shape of a triangle, and it would have only three drive pods.

If not for the fact that the ships were covered in what looked like giant tank turrets, it would have been impossible to tell these apart from larger transports, or Union freighters for that matter.

"They look… prefabbed," Kris Jacobs said from *Lion*, and I realized immediately that she was on to something with that observation.

If you think of prefabricated buildings, they have a very uniform look and feel. While the pieces that make up those structures can be assembled in different configurations, they're ultimately like building blocks… and everything you construct out of them has a similar quality.

These ships were absolutely the same — every one of them featured the same hull pieces, and not just in the way you see with multiple vessels of the same class. They were out-of-a-box warships… and we had no idea what they could do. As I came to that conclusion, I decided there was no point letting them get a drop on us.

"Let's go to General Quarters. Launch a Starlight screen, one squadron from each frigate. All other fighters on standby," I gave those orders coolly, and they came as something of a surprise to some of the people on the screens.

"Want to provoke them?" Matt asked with a frown, and I shrugged back.

"Don't want to them to think we're ordinary visitors. And in case they think they can jump us, I want them to know better."

What I didn't say, but which was equally true, was that I wanted to scare the shit out of everyone on Lexington. A Defense Command squadron coming in hot, having just enforced the real law of the solar system on Concord. They had to know we meant business, and by this time I was in no way against sending a strong message.

"One of those things looks like a battlewagon," Andrea Kiley was still looking at the ships on the screen, and I turned my focus back there as she said it.

Sure enough, one of the ships — which had previously been partly eclipsed by another — seemed to be double-hulled… it was like two of the other ships had been welded together, bottom to bottom. Presumably that made it more powerful…

"Bigger target," Isoruku Togo observed from his screen.

Right, or that.

"Either way, we'll keep to this side of the rock for now. Hold us just inside standard realtime range of the biggest dome out there… I'll want to chat with the local President before we decide what to do with his minions."

That was my last order for a little while. As the Belt Squadron approached the rock, we all watched with some inappropriate amusement as local civilian traffic scattered — no one wanted to be in our path.

The transport we'd followed in was keeping its course straight for the Etat, probably hoping to find safety in local space around the rock. We loomed behind it like a storm cloud, and I kept watching the warships, expecting them to at least turn in our direction — to do something to intervene.

But they did nothing at all. I wonder now whether they'd been under strict orders not to provoke us. Didn't matter; we weren't going to wait for someone to prod us into doing our jobs.

As we came to local space and it looked as though the transport was about to dock, I decided it was time to assume a less passive stance: "Alright, Matt and Kate, why don't you move up on either flank of that ship and send orders for it to stop short of the docking column."

Again with the piracy — I was certainly in that sort of mood on this particular day.

Matt blinked and then frowned slightly, "If they refuse?"

"We'll see," I answered. He was asking whether I was going to order him to open fire on a ship full of civilians. I hadn't decided yet, and one factor in the decision still needed to be understood. With that in mind I turned to Felicia Khalid again, "Let's see if we can get access to their network, and find a way to signal their President. If he doesn't call us."

She nodded, setting a few of her technicians to work on the challenge. This was the 'take me to your leader' part of the mission — we had to establish a line of communication with the top politico for this rock, so that we could have conversations with some actual value.

Historically, such occasions as these can be awkward ones. Returning yet again to our comparison between the Union and China of the nineteenth century... or in this case, China of the eighteenth century... we can see a disastrous first contact scenario. In 1792, the British sent a diplomatic mission led by Lord Macartney to open official China-Britain relations, but the Qianlong Emperor at the time hadn't heard much about Britain (they were barbarians from the west), and wasn't too impressed when Macartney refused to literally cowtow to him in court.

Relations didn't go well after that. A couple of Opium Wars, and ultimately the colonial invasion of Chinese territory by the British and others.

So you see, first contacts can be bad if either side decides to act unprofessionally.

"The transport is stopping engines," Matt Baxter spoke up over Battlelink. Only seconds before he'd had his Sensors and Communications Officer send the order for the runner to stop, and the craft now seemed eager to comply. Guess the master of the vessel was aware that we could have blown him out of space.

"Detecting signal traffic... the transport is calling the asteroid," Felicia warned us next, and I nodded.

Hopefully the fact that we were interfering with local shipping in the defense zone of the SAU's capital would compel *someone* to call us.

"Keep an eye on their warships," I warned as I waited. "They might be called over to see what we're about."

That had been directed to everyone in general, and there were nods. Then we finally received a signal... or more precisely, *Friendly* and *Lady Grace* received a signal. Matt looked off screen with a frown, then looked back to his Battlelink viewfinder: "Just got a 'cease and desist' from the 'Dockmaster'. Looks like a standardized message."

An automated wrist-slap? Good grief, what would it take to get some attention around here?

I considered a few options, including killing as many people as possible, but I thought of Wes and decided he'd probably need to be shot again if I went that far without better provocation.

"Felicia, you have any access to their comm grid yet?" I turned back to *Wolf's* Sensors and Communications Officer, and she started to nod.

"Just coming up now... I have basic access to their government services network. Looking for the executive offices..." she was leaning over the shoulder of one of her technicians as she went through the Union interweb, seeking the appropriate portal to the... "*Maison Blanc*. Their government head office seems to be called *Maison Blanc*."

My jaw dropped, and then I laughed hard. These kids weren't too subtle, were they? If you speak any amount of French, you might recognize that *Maison Blanc* is another way of saying White House — the historical and current building that houses the President of the United States of America.

These SAUs were so desperate to appropriate the American tradition that they'd even stolen the name (and partially, the design) of the seat of its government. Wow.

"There a contact code for them?" Andrea Kiley picked up the prudent questions while I exhibited my amusement, and Felicia nodded.

"I have a general switchboard number."

Perfect.

I collected myself rather eagerly, "Excellent, ring me through."

Felicia tapped another tech on the shoulder, then frowned as he started the comm link, "It's voice only."

"Works for me," I replied, then we all waited as our OSXX computers figured out a way to speak to the Union system. It only took a moment, and then the bridge speakers started projecting a ringing sound — like one from a telephone (look it up).

I folded my arms, and as so many people do when talking audio-only, I looked up at *Wolf's* bridge speakers, as though staring at them would help me talk to whoever picked up.

There were a half-dozen rings, then a click as the line engaged and a somewhat nasally female voice answered, "*Maison Blanc* operator, how may I direct your call?"

"Hi there, I'd like to speak to your President," I replied pleasantly.

Any humor in the woman's tone died a quick death, "Yeah, you and me both, hun."

Seriously, she was talking like a stereotypical operator from the long-lost past. This entertained me to no end — I nearly clapped with glee.

"What's your name?" I asked.

"That's none of your business, hun. You want to talk to someone then tell me, or I'm pulling the plug."

I looked down at Andrea, who was scowling, and grinned before continuing, "Like I said, your President. And he'll want to speak with me, I think."

"And why would he want to talk to you? You someone important?" her decidedly disinterested tone made her sound like she was chewing gum and had a beehive hairdo. It was epic.

"Well, I'm Rear Admiral Ken Barron. I'm sitting in orbit of your rock right now with seven warships from the Earth Empire, and if I don't speak to him within the hour, I'm going to kill everyone you know. Have him call me. He can just signal up here to *Wolf*, and ask for Ken."

There was a pause on the line, and then the most perfect answer ever: "Well I thought it was early to start drinking, but you have yourself a nice day there, hun."

Then the line clicked dead.

Smiling broadly, I looked from Andrea to the Battlelink screens, shaking my head, "Boy she's going to be embarrassed when we kill her and everyone else on her rock."

I was expecting laughs, but strangely I didn't get any.

Chapter Seventeen

Circling

It took twenty minutes for someone on Etat Lexington to put the pieces together, and in that time none of the rock's warships so much as moved. The transport remained similarly static, obviously not wanting to test whether two Defense Command corvettes would have the facility to stop it closing the last short distance to a docking column.

I paced the bridge with my arms folded, keeping an eye on the clock. The other skippers were similarly silent as they waited — everyone seemed almost afraid to start any sort of constructive conversation, thinking that as soon as they did, a message from the President would interrupt them.

We waited, and then finally a signal came in, though it was directed to *Nova Scotia*.

"We're getting a message from their White House," Rozy Young looked off screen and then reported the signal. "Should we route it over to *Wolf*?"

"Please do," I nodded, pacing back into range of the bridge viewfinder.

Rozy nodded to her technicians, and then the feed was redirected to our array, where Felicia's people took hold of it. The buffer was again able to translate the signal relatively easily — the Union seemed to be accustomed to communicating with comm systems from a variety of origins, so there wasn't a snag — and then a man in a suit appeared in a window on screen one.

"I am the Secretary of State for the Union of Solar Asteroids," he began with a declarative statement that didn't sound as obnoxious as I was expecting... but then, I'd started the previous year with Martian diplomats, so I was predisposed to expect a lot of hubris.

"Ken Barron, Rear Admiral with Defense Command. From the Earth Empire, which you've never heard of."

I wasn't going to be playing nice, in case you were expecting otherwise.

"Of course I've heard of it. What's your business in our space, *Rear* Admiral?"

Ooh, a 'rear' joke. I wasn't paying any attention to that part of his reply, though: "So you have heard of us. Shame you never dropped round to say hello."

The Secretary of State glared at me, but didn't launch into a petulant counteroffensive. Holding his tongue for a second, he assessed what he needed to accomplish and then repeated the second question, "Your business here, Rear Admiral?"

I narrowed my eyes slightly and considered how belligerent I wanted to get. It was a tough call, but ultimately...

"I'd like to discuss that in person with your President, Mister Secretary. I'm sure that defies all protocol, but this ends best if there's no mistaking our respective positions. And I'd certainly like it to end *best*."

The Secretary of State continued to study me while he listened. This probably hadn't been what he was expecting — he'd have to know by now how we'd basically stormed into Concord, and how we'd bullied and boarded the transport to rescue some unknown person… so he might have been expecting an immediate ultimatum.

But this was an offer for discussion, and politicos tend to love that sort of thing, so he was at least interested.

"You would be welcome at the *Maison Blanc*," he replied. "Sometime tomorrow, perhaps?"

I smiled, "Clear the nearest landing bay and send a car, I'll be landing with an escort shortly. I trust that I need not be concerned for my safety, but protocol doesn't allow me to travel unescorted."

That was a thinly veiled threat, wrapped up in a threatening demand. Not my best diplomacy, but still diplomacy.

"As a guest of our government, you will indeed be protected, Rear Admiral. And we may be able to arrange a meeting with the President for this afternoon. But we must also ask that you allow the ship you've been tailing to move in to dock."

He was bargaining, obviously, and he was doing it with a cool and collected sense of calm. His words were firm — he wasn't begging — and that meant he thought he was in a reasonable position… perhaps not a winning one, but one strong enough to give him some leverage.

I wasn't clear-headed enough to know whether he had that leverage or not; I just sensed pushback, and I didn't like it.

"The transport contains an assassin who mutilated an Imperial citizen. We'd like to search the passengers before they disembark. That in mind, I suggest you ask them to hold off docking until we can reach some arrangement for your law enforcement officers, and our security forces, to see justice done."

A whole other issue, and the Secretary of State again grew silent for a few seconds before taking up his next position, "All persons in our space are judged by our laws, Rear Admiral Barron. Your authority here has not been established."

He went out of his way to make that sound less rude than it could have been — more circling. And I was fine to keep it up.

"I'm sure there are provisions in your laws against rape, cutting off fingers, and cutting out tongues. We might defer to your laws on the subject, should justice be done."

The Secretary of State frowned immediately at the naming of the crimes, and then took a breath, "We'll order the ship not to dock until we discuss this further. You will be sent directions for docking momentarily. I look forward to seeing you."

It was a fair outcome, and I nodded: "Excellent. Thank you, Secretary of State… I'm sorry, I didn't get your name."

"Armin Deboer," he replied, and at the time that name meant nothing to me — he was just a reasonably competent Secretary of State.

"See you shortly, Secretary Deboer," I concluded, and with parting nods that seemed altogether civil, we cut our link.

Glancing at Andrea I gave the obvious order, "Have Rufus prep his shuttle. I'll take Eugene and five volunteers as well, just in case."

Having an extra six bodies with us might make no difference at all, but in the absence of a full Special Branch squad it seemed sensible. Hopefully things would turn out better than they had when last we landed in a capital dome.

Turning back to the Battlelink monitors, I scanned the faces of my skippers, then glanced at Andrea, "Since Wes is still in bed after I shot him, Andrea will have squadron command until I return. If anything happens to me, destroy this place. If those ships so much as look at you the wrong way, destroy this place. Stay at General Quarters and I'll keep you apprised."

There were nods again — the Wes part of the order notwithstanding — and then I left the bridge and the Belt Squadron to Andrea. Funny, doesn't seem like all that long ago when I would have been afraid to leave such a delicate situation in her hands.

Honestly, I may have been hoping that she'd do something with the opportunity.

Rufus was incredibly pleased that I was going down to the Etat Lexington main dome with virtually no preparation, and only a small escort. He told me several times on the flight how great an idea it was, and how much he looked forward to the chance to be diplomatic.

At least I think that's what he said. Or maybe it was the opposite of all that. Either way, he'd said a few things to me by the time Chet Srisai had the assault shuttle coasting into the lowest-level landing bay on the Union capital dome.

Assault shuttles don't have many passenger windows, and the ones they do have usually stay shuttered because sometimes assault shuttles have been known to receive fire. That being the case, I had no idea what we were flying into — Chet was the only one who could see where we were touching down.

"How's it looking out there?" I asked as the feet of our ship hit the deck, and the pilot paused before answering.

"Unremarkable, sir."

Sounds about right for the Union.

Rufus insisted on being the first one down the ramp to the deck of the landing bay, with his squad following before I could disembark. Eugene and his volunteers — all of whom had been with us for the events of *The Mars Convention* — followed right behind me.

And indeed, the bay we emerged into was like a lot of other bays I'd seen. There were a number of small craft coming and going on a broad, slightly worn metallic landing deck, and brown-painted walls with teal trim all around us.

At the bottom of the ramp was a platoon of Union troops, headed by an officer and seemingly escorting a General. All of them were in the same brown uniforms we'd seen on Concord, but the gray-haired General had various bits of trim covering his shoulders, cuffs and chest… and he wore a hat.

As I touched the deck, the officer commanding the platoon ordered his men — again, all men — to attention. As they snapped to, Rufus studied them carefully; like many wise warriors, Rufus was never one to allow even a hint arrogance to creep into his assessment of a potential adversary. He didn't like a lot of what he'd come across in the SAU so far… but these troops did seem professional, if somewhat vintage.

They might just be an honor guard with no combat aspirations, but something about them just felt a bit out-of-date. Not pushovers, but not necessarily as deadly as Special

Branch, or even good Martian marines.

Time would tell… or if things went peacefully, time wouldn't have to tell.

While Rufus studied the troops, I kept my gaze on the General. He sized me up too, and then came forward with a salute which I found odd — where Defense Command salutes palm-forward (facing the person, to show an empty and open hand), this salute was palm inward (facing the saluter's forehead).

"General Kelly Setoguchi," the officer said. "I am the Chairman of the Joint Chiefs of Staff."

Joint Chiefs instead of an Admiralty or even a General Staff. Seriously, if you ever need to cram for a test on the political systems of the SAU, and you can't find an SAU textbook, just look up American history. That's what the SAU founders did when they needed to come up with something that sounded smart.

"Rear Admiral Ken Barron," I replied, lowering my salute jauntily. "General, I believe my next words must be… and let me just assure you that I'm delighted to say this… *take me to your leader.*"

He didn't seem to find that amusing, but then by this time few people seemed to be appreciating my humor. Probably because I have terrible comedic timing — nothing to do with intentions or circumstances at all.

"The President is looking forward to meeting you," Setoguchi replied, and then he turned and led the way.

The SAU House (or *Maison Blanc*) wasn't that far from where we touched down, and I swear they did everything they could to make the approach and the exterior look like the White House. Of course, given the premium the SAUs put on ground space in a dome, there wasn't room for a bunch of fancy lawns… but there were columns out front, and lots of small windows… details someone had clearly included to evoke the feeling of the original.

As the cars they'd sent for us rolled (oh yes, they used wheeled vehicles for ground transport, and saved hovers only for public transit and special applications that required flight) through the SAU House gate and up the drive to the entrance, I surveyed the place carefully.

The rest of the town we'd passed through on the way there had been like Concord, but cleaner; the *Maison*, by contrast, had a feeling of cramped serenity, as well as and a bunch of suited guards (looking like Special Branchers on VIP security detail) prowling around, watching us.

Rufus emerged from his car as soon as it stopped, without waiting for anyone to open his door. The rest of his squad followed suit, and the sight of six black-clad, well-armed Branchers coming into the open got an immediate reaction.

Weapons weren't drawn, but every agent in sight turned quickly on our column, and I'm sure snipers we couldn't see were watching as well.

Once our elite Chinese Major scanned the surroundings and was sufficiently satisfied that it was safe (mostly) he nodded to me, and I opened my door too — again, before any of our hosts could do it for me. When I emerged, Eugene and his SF did as well, and we were thus unloaded.

General Setoguchi gestured to the front entrance as he approached me, "Please follow me."

There was no comment about my escort — the SAUs were being very accepting of a threatening presence within their tightest ring of security, probably expecting that I'd not respond well if they told me to lose Rufus' reassuring presence.

To be honest, I'm not sure what I would have said if I'd been asked…

The SAU House was not so carefully manipulated to look American on the inside. Some of the architectural touches definitely invoked the original, but most of the workspaces seemed decidedly practical as I passed them. Not too posh, not too worn — the place was working hard to convey the confidence you'd find in the Empire's PMO… the SAUs just weren't all the way to our standards yet.

Many eyes followed us as we headed deeper into the building, and at last we came to a stop in what was obviously an outer office. Four separate assistants were sitting at desks outside the door — all women, which struck me as odd — and that's where Setoguchi stopped us.

"We can only allow one armed escort with you in the Oblong Office," he said, his tone managing to be both conciliatory and firm.

I stared at him for a minute, then actually laughed, "Oh my God. Please tell me you didn't just call it an *Oblong* Office. Let me guess, it's an oval?"

I don't think he appreciated my humor, "It's named for its shape, sir. Are you quite finished?"

I wasn't really, but I held up my hand as I finished laughing, then tried to clear my throat, "Sorry, sorry. Right, just me and Rufus. You sure you want to let him keep his rifle?"

Setoguchi looked from me to *Wolf's* Major with mismatched eyes, then down to the MAG-90 harnessed to his vest.

"If you'll allow one of your other officers to hold it for you… that would be an appreciated gesture."

I glanced back at Rufus and he shrugged. He and I both knew he didn't need a MAG-90 to do harm in a close-quarters environment. We were also both still packing our sidearms, just in case. And besides all that, why would we need to be armed for a diplomatic meeting in the Oblong Office?

Rufus unclipped his rifle and handed it to Selma Koestecki, then moved up alongside me. As he did, Setoguchi turned to the office door, opened it, and stepped partway in to announce us.

"Any special instructions?" Rufus asked quietly as we waited for permission to enter.

I shook my head, "Nope, same as always."

Rufus seemed to like that answer. And without further ado, we were ushered into the Oblong Office.

This deserves a new chapter.

CHAPTER EIGHTEEN

LIKE MACARTNEY

The Oblong Office definitely made more of an effort to look like its American counterpart than the parts of the SAU House I'd just seen. The configuration was the giveaway: a desk facing couches and chairs, official-looking junk around the room...

But to be fair again, the place also looked like it was a functioning office, and as President Fabian Kohl stood up behind his desk at our arrival, I got the sense he had actually been doing a lot of work just before we'd arrived.

Advisors had probably just been shooed out another door — military and political people discussing how the Union should handle an incursion like the one being mounted by our fair Belt Squadron. Whatever those conversations had suggested, Kohl was a solid head of state: he pushed any concerns or frustrations off his face and moved from behind his desk to greet me.

I should mention that Armin Deboer was already standing in front of the desk, and both men offered their hands to me. I took them to be polite, and then the President gestured to the chair and two facing couches. Rufus continued to stand while I sat on the couch nearest the door, on the end closest to the President. Deboer sat opposite me, and Kohl took the chair. Setoguchi stood behind the President's chair, probably wary of Rufus... and right to be so.

"Thanks for seeing me on such short notice," I opened with a smile, crossing my legs and lacing my fingers together in my lap. "Long flight. Much to do."

Kohl undoubtedly hadn't known what to expect, and though I opened pleasantly he was hardly lulled, "Flexibility is necessary in the face of major events of state."

I could tell he might have wanted to say 'major threats', but had contained himself.

"Quite so," I agreed.

We then fell silent, sizing each other up. I also considered the Secretary of State — in this model of government, essentially a counterpart for Craig B. Macdonald — before looking back to the President.

Kohl finally cracked on the silence: "So tell me, Rear Admiral Barron, aside from rescuing someone from a transport under our flag... what brings you to the Union of Solar Asteroids?"

It was the sort of question he didn't like asking, because Presidents shouldn't have to inquire about the mundane issues. His people should have told him in advance why we were here, so he could cut to the chase. He was the most powerful person in these parts, after all.

I stared at him after he asked the question, wondering for a second how much he knew. Then I decided to simply come out with it: "Your Governor, George Madison, from Etat Valcour."

A stab of shock managed to break through to Kohl's face, and his eyes immediately jumped across to Deboer. The Secretary of State had a more muted reaction, but I think he was surprised as well.

"I see you know him," I added, then carried on. "Well he was a friend of mine, actually. He hails from our part of the solar system. He and I went through the Academy together..."

Kohl's eyes grew a little wider, and his concern was contagious; behind the chair, Setoguchi was tensing. This was an interesting reaction, so I continued to trundle along.

"...then he turned traitor, formed a Syndicate of pirates, and we had to put him down. Appears that he fled here after his defeat, but he's been named an enemy of the Empire by our government. It's our duty to do him harm... and he finally tipped us off as to where he was... when he sent assassins into a ball held by the Emperor on Empire Day. That's Earth standard calendar New Year's Eve, to be precise. We tracked the assassins to Etat Concord, then decided we'd come here for a chat before we go out to Etat Valcour to obtain him."

I hadn't thought through any of the possible ramifications of blurting all this out to the President and his senior advisors. I really didn't care. They couldn't stop me if they tried, so by being frank perhaps I was just giving them a chance to save something of the relationship between Empire and Union.

"George Madison did that?" Kohl asked, exasperated.

His reaction — open-mouthed shock — seemed genuine, and difficult to reconcile in that moment. I didn't think I'd given enough of an explanation to turn the President against one of his own so quickly.

"So you're not here by his request, to assist him?" Setoguchi asked sharply, and that question — a bit too revealing — earned a glare from Deboer.

I blinked — my turn to be surprised, "Well he wanted us to find him, I know that. But no, we're certainly not here to assist him."

Kohl and Deboer exchanged looks that spoke volumes. Then, following my example of simply blurting out information, Kohl leaned forward, "Admiral, Madison is my stiffest competition in an election scheduled for later this year. He has been making a name among voting citizens as being a strong leader who can protect us against the future aggressions of your Empire. He has spoken of a history of resistance, but never detailed it. He's polling well on his pledges... the citizens here chafe under authority... but there has never been a concrete threat by your Empire against our Union. At least, not until your arrival here."

I stared at Kohl, and in an instant the whole of Grant's design fell into place in my head. He had come here after Deep Black, created a quick-and-dirty new identity for himself and had managed to get elected Governor... probably picked the most desperate rock in the Union, just knowing that once he had the office, he could leverage it.

He'd then spun a story for himself — freedom fighter, wise leader, warrior — but in order for that narrative to have teeth, he needed the voting public to have some idea of the 'dangers' out there.

He'd needed to get someone from the Empire to show up in the SAU, and to throw around some heavy Imperial metal before going home again. And he'd known exactly who he could manipulate into playing the part for him.

Son of a bitch, brilliant and overcomplicated as usual.

Our presence here — the stories we'd already generated — would probably give him a huge boost in the polls over Kohl… and as I stared at the President, I realized the other elegant part of this whole situation: by us coming to Lexington and meeting the man, we'd created an impossible situation.

If Kohl cooperated with us to get Grant Merger, it would appear that he was trying to use the Empire to remove a political rival — playing right into the story Grant was spinning.

And if he didn't cooperate, and tried to fight us, we'd defeat him and he'd look too weak to stop us, also playing into Grant's narrative.

In either case, all the villain would have to do was escape us one more time… and he probably had a clever stratagem for that as well.

You don't see plans like Grant's very often, but it's like poetry when they work. He's a master at these sorts of things. He seems to get a lasso around all sorts of situations that appear uncontrollable.

And the worst part — or the best — is this: even when you're within the jaws of his trap, and you realize what's going on, you have no real choice but to continue forward.

Understanding that, I finally blinked myself out of my thoughts and returned my attention to Kohl. Perhaps he wasn't bright enough to realize that cooperating with us would undermine him…

"Well, we can take a problem off your hands then, Mister President," I tried it coyly, and Kohl's expression soured.

"You cannot swan in here and take one of our Governors on charges that we have no way of substantiating. Your Empire has a reputation, Admiral Barron, and such actions would play right into it."

He had no choice but to resist us. His only hope at this point was that he could resist us and win on his own, thus making Grant redundant. But I could tell from the look on his face that he wasn't confident. Even if he had no familiarity with his own fleet — which seemed unlikely — he must have known that Grant and Dave Caldecott effectively had taken control of the distribution of the SAUN… that if they knew I was bound for Lexington they wouldn't have sent him any good ships for protection.

But he had to try. He had no choice.

And I was sympathetic to his situation. I understood that this leader — whose politics, character and position I knew absolutely nothing about — had just been outmaneuvered in a manner rarely seen in human history. And that I was the weapon Grant was using to thrust him aside.

Unfortunately, sympathy couldn't change one thing: Grant had killed Karen. Grant had attacked Daragh's ball… he'd been responsible for *Idaho*… and he'd killed Karen.

Also, come to think of it, Kohl's government, or its predecessor, had also supplied the *Tharsis*-class battleships to the Martians. So they weren't exactly innocent and naïve either.

"I'm going to Valcour, and there I'm going to deal with him," I said firmly, my stare fixed right on Kohl. "I'm just here to let you know that, under our laws, any group that knowingly harbors an enemy of the Empire, that assists or protects him in any way, is subject to the same treatment as that enemy."

Strictly speaking that's true, though you might recall that the Coalition of Unaligned Asteroids had been looking after enemy of the Empire Dave Caldecott for us... most of the time we partnered with other states to keep an eye on our declared enemies.

This time, nope.

"You make threats against our Union, Admiral," Kohl's voice dropped, and now he aimed to mix menace with severity. "Would you really risk war between our two great states, just for a vendetta against one man? No matter who he is?"

I simply stared at Kohl, and I think he realized I was thinking about his words. He added one more idea: "What you say he did... if he is such a criminal, you would be descending to his level and doing to our Union what he did to your Empire. Is that worth it? Is that right? I ask you."

I had been in good spirits for the entire meeting — inappropriately so, in fact. And now, perhaps inevitably, a cloud began to gather over me. It was a fast change, and I think Kohl noticed as my expression grew darker.

If he didn't notice, he certainly heard.

"Risk war between our *two great states?*" I asked gently, and then tilted my head. "Mister President, understand what this is: a courtesy call. Your state is not great. It is far from great. It is like a dozen other states I've seen in a dozen other places around this Belt. You think I'm worried about starting a war with you? My own squadron could tear everything you've built here to pieces in a matter of weeks. If we summoned our battleships, we'd destroy you all in days. And when I got home I'd have to put up with a parade in my honor — thanks for being the hero who killed the criminals hiding an enemy of the Empire, a man who has done more to inflame our *great state* than your entire collection of rocks could manage in a decade. Mister President, you do not matter, and your *state* is a novelty. Do not mistake yourself for something of consequence."

Kohl didn't like that.

Setoguchi really didn't like it.

And Deboer just stared at me — his cold expression was not resentful, but thoughtful. He was the one I worried about most, because he wasn't reacting emotionally.

But he wasn't the problem for now.

Having delivered my statement, I came to my feet, and Kohl watched me rise without coming out of his chair.

"Now, that transport you stopped short of orbit has an assassin aboard. We're going to find that assassin. And we'll leave the rest of the crew aboard. If your warships try to intervene, we'll destroy them. If your dome tries to intervene, we'll deal with you as well. Use your imagination on that one."

I turned and rounded the couch I'd been sitting on, coming to a stop beside Rufus, whose stony expression was reinforcing my heartless words.

"And Mister President, one more thing: you think I've descended to the same level as Grant... as George Madison. I think you're right. And believe me, it's neither a surprise, nor something I'm particularly ashamed of. Good day."

With that, Rufus and I turned and left. Our immediate concern was getting back to *Wolf*, because while it would not be diplomatically wise for Kohl to try to take us prisoner, it was still possible he would.

But since there's no point building useless suspense, I'll tell you: they drove us back to our shuttle like perfectly decent and civilized human beings. As soon as we took off, President Kohl declared a state of alert for Etat Lexington.

CHAPTER NINETEEN

RUNNER

When I returned to *Wolf's* bridge, and got back in front of the Battlelink viewfinder, I was met by quite a few curious expressions. The question on everyone's mind was obvious: would it be cooperation or combat?

I didn't want to waste any time being coy on this subject — every minute we spent talking was one more during which the runner could get orders from the asteroid to do something that might impede our plans.

"Matt, you and Kate go ahead with the boarding operation on the transport. You'll have to do it with SF alone, but we'll cover you."

The first part of that order might have left room for the Belt Squadron elite to assume we'd been granted the latitude we needed to find Julie Pichot's attacker... the last few words made it entirely clear that we were in for some strife.

Matt Baxter's expression was stern, but he nodded, "We'll find Merger's man."

With that he turned away from the screen and started passing orders to his Sensors and Communications Officer — the transport had to be warned that boarders would be coming over, and instructed not to resist.

"I take it the President didn't approve our mission?" Kris Jacobs asked to make it official, and I shrugged.

"Pretty sure he couldn't if he wanted to. I'll explain what Grant's doing later, for now we need to be ready in case those warships intervene."

That was it; we'd tried to do it the 'right' way but there was no option in that direction, so once again the Belt Squadron would be called to action — this time against an enemy we'd never before seen.

If they decided to intervene...

"Sir, the transport is signaling the asteroid," Felicia Khalid passed along that warning as soon as the burst transmission turned up on one of her section's consoles.

I nodded, "To be expected. Watch for traffic to those warships..."

"Already on its way. Looks like they're being called by the main dome."

I didn't want to jump to conclusions about that signal — Kohl could be telling his ships to back off and let us do what we wanted to do — but I did get the feeling that it wasn't going to be so benign.

"We're standing by to launch the first boarding shuttles," Matt reported at that point, and I looked up at his face on the screen and opened my mouth.

Then I paused. I wanted whoever had done the mutilation of Julie Pichot, because that person would have to be one of Grant Merger's best. Any information from the villain's inner circle could be valuable beyond compare.

But what if those warships turned on us while Matt and Kate were sending over SF boarding parties? If it turned out the SAU actually were as tough as they wanted to be, we could end up being driven away from Lexington and leaving people behind at the mercy of their thugs.

Of all the things that could have made me reluctant about launching immediate boarding operations, it was the threat of marooning our Security Forces that actually convinced me to delay. Sovereign rights of the Union, comparisons to piracy... all of that could be damned.

If it put our people in undue danger, though, that would be entirely unacceptable.

So I shook my head, "Just hold a minute, Matt. If those things come at us now we may need you both."

Matt — and every other skipper — understood exactly what I meant. This was the Belt Squadron, of course, so I hardly needed to over-explain a concept as simple as 'keep your crew aboard in case of a possible fight'.

Would the warships take any action?

"Sir," Felicia Khalid was definitely working overtime as the narrator of these events, and she looked up at me as she offered more news: "Signal coming in from the larger Union warship out there."

A message that would undoubtedly declare intentions.

I nodded to her, "Main screen window."

"If they engage us, and we pull all ships off this transport, we could lose it," Kate Levec warned from the bridge of *Lady Grace*, and I nodded in acknowledgment.

"I know. But I'm not going to risk this squadron to catch that bastard. First priority is to make sure we win any—"

I stopped as the window to the SAU warship opened up in screen one. The man who appeared was in another brown uniform, and his eyes showed some experience despite his young age.

"I'm Group Captain Parm Harku of the USAN, red group. To commander of the Empire force facing me. Please respond."

Because of different ship-to-ship signaling protocols, the Group Captain didn't realize that he was on live with us, so I informed him, "We hear you. This is Rear Admiral Ken Barron. Something we can help you with?"

At this point Harku seemed to see me on his own screen, and his expression grew more concerned, "Admiral, I've been ordered to escort you and your ships out of Etat Lexington local space, and to instruct you to leave the Union of Solar Asteroids."

He didn't sound as though it was an order he necessarily liked, but it was one he would nevertheless obey. And from his point of view, why not? A bunch of bullies from some overbearing Empire show up around his capital, act like they own the place, show no respect for local authorities or the President himself... any self-respecting state would have a problem with such conduct.

Unfortunately, not to beat a dead horse, the Union hadn't registered under the Meester regulations as a state. So tough shit.

"Group Captain, we're hunting a fugitive. A man who's actually made himself one of your Governors, who's responsible for more chaos and death than I care to relate. We won't be leaving Union space without him in custody or dead. And we won't be leaving this asteroid without the agent he put aboard that transport. I advise you not to interfere."

My words were firm but polite enough, not that it mattered. Harku's expression tightened — he had no choice about what to do, any more than I'd have had in his position. His orders were to protect his asteroid.

"Sir, I hail from this colony. I will fight to defend it, no matter what your situation. And I will win. I command here four cruisers and a battleship. You seem to have no capital ships, and only smaller cruisers. Don't throw away your life and the lives of your crews for this purpose. Surely the hunt for this fugitive cannot be so personally necessary for you to make such sacrifices?"

I don't know what it was about the Union types at Lexington, but they sure liked to make declarative statements about how bad things *couldn't* be. Not the right approach to take when trying to talk down a mad man with a squadron.

As I heard the Group Captain's otherwise-reasonable case — and every other skipper in the squadron listened to it, and squinted at the last part — I tilted my head.

"Group Captain, I don't believe in talking about a fight. If you want to intervene, come ahead. You'll die in the shadow of the rock that bore you."

Harku's expression hardened, and again my spite seemed to bubble up: "Also, your pathetic ships are going to fold like tin for this squadron. Mark my words."

With that, I turned to Felicia and made a gesture for her to cut the line.

I only realized how angry I was when I looked back to the Battlelink screen, "They're going to threaten us? Let's prepare for combat. Launch all Starlights. Matt and Kate, form up... line abreast and advance towards their squadron. We'll deal with the transport later."

It was the wrong decision — it spoils nothing to tell you so now. But in the midst of everything that was happening I had no time for anyone trying to tell me I was wrong, or worse, trying to intervene.

Particularly if their intervention was prefaced by some sort of attempt to appeal to my humanity. That was such an insult — how could these people not realize that, with Karen gone, I had no humanity? They'd soon learn...

CHAPTER TWENTY

BETTER ANGELS

There's one thing a Captain (or Commodore) will never mistake when she or he is aboard a warship: the sound of battle. In space, of course, you can't hear anything at all — lasers, mags, even the explosions of torpedoes make no noise because there's no air to carry the sound waves to your receivers.

But within a ship there are all sorts of sounds. The pitch of the engines change as they build up power for maneuvers, the hum of the reactors alters when the weapons systems start drawing their share of the energy needed to make war, and the pressure hatches clunk shut and spin their locks as certain sections are isolated in case of decompression.

If you've ever been aboard a Defense Command ship in combat, and even during some drills, you've heard these noises, though often it's not until you've been in warships for years that you can really identify and understand all of them.

Wes Pellew had been in warships for a lot of years, and he knew all the sounds — even from a medical bed, and even when he wasn't on his own ship.

As he told me later, his exact thought when he heard *Wolf's* reactors go to battle output was unrepeatable (because Wes likes to avoid swearing). I might translate it into: 'Oh bother, that silly chap is flipping going to start another war'.

Burned though he was, Wes wasn't about to take such an event lying down. He looked up at the monitor above his head, which was tracking his vitals, and saw he wasn't in any immediate danger — at least not based on anything he knew about medicine. And he knew a lot because Sara had been a nurse, and had taught him plenty long ago.

Fine.

Swinging his legs off the bed, Wes staggered over to a nearby shelf and pulled a medical robe off it. He was still wearing his flight suit, but it had been unzipped and tied around his waist so the burns on his chest wouldn't be agitated by the singed fabric. The medical robe would double as his shirt.

Not exactly battle attire — robes don't have any decompression bags — but he didn't care. He'd risk going into a fight without the standard protective gear.

Alicia Morgan spotted Wes' intended escape and moved to intercept just as he was tying the robe, "You can't—"

"I don't want this bay any more crowded than it needs to be, Doc," he snapped at her, and then he opened the hatch and staggered out. Pain started radiating through his torso immediately, and he realized it was going to be a longer walk than he'd expected.

But he was going to the bridge.

With Starlights in the lead, we closed on the SAUN line quickly, and as we did I could only imagine Group Captain Harku's reaction. Perhaps he thought we were coming to be slaughtered by his disruptors… or maybe he realized he was about to be defeated by hardened veterans from a Navy that made his look like a collection of toys.

Either way, I wasn't going to give him the chance to get in the way — or the Unionists an opportunity to believe they could do anything to stop us getting to Grant Merger.

"We'll be in range in twenty-five seconds. No sign that they're preparing to engage," Felicia Khalid reported, and I nodded.

As we closed the range, each Captain was of course preparing his or her own ship. I did have some general thoughts for them, so I spoke up: "Don't want to go for the throat unless we see a serious danger. Start with mags and laser warning shots. See if we can spook them. If not, shoot to disable."

Those orders came straight out of my brain in its squadron-command mode, and I think it's fair to say they weren't really reflective of my broader state of mind. I find it interesting that, as I disconnected myself from the emotions that had been fueling my rage, and retreated to a more familiar place of ship-to-ship combat, I got a little less vindictive...

At least at first.

"Looks like they're training their guns on us," that observation came first from Katya Romanov on *Sackville*, and it was immediately confirmed by Felicia and every other Sensors and Communications Officer in the squadron.

That was sign enough for me: I watched on the main screen as the icons of our squadron moved into range of the enemy (ranges shown by Jim Hannigan's rings on the display, if you'll remember those from so long ago). As soon as our ring overlapped the icon of the first SAU ship, I gave the order.

"Mags open fire."

Wes hadn't gotten nearly as far as he'd hoped before he heard the telltale sounds of mag energy releases. From within a *Predator*-class hull, such sounds are very muted — barely noticeable — but Wes detected them, and he grunted and gritted his teeth as soon as he did.

He hoped the other guys had fired first... but he rather doubted that was the case.

He was correct.

The SAU warships didn't have lasers, and they didn't have mags. Instead, in between the two, they had massive weapons they called 'disruptors'. Turret-mounted on the outer hulls of their triangular ships, these weapons fired EM bolts that were several orders of magnitude more powerful than those that came out of our mags... but fired them at a much slower rate.

So while our mags rained golden energy on the SAU ships, they hurled much larger harpoons of blue energy in our direction. And we had no idea what to expect when those things hit us.

"Brace brace brace!" I heard Kris say from her screen, and I looked up just in time to see her lights flicker, and the feed get distorted.

"Direct hits on *Lion*," Felicia reported, and we all watched with bated breath — would our Aussie redhead be out of action all over again?

"Disruption to our systems... but... we're still online..." Kris was looking around her at the officers on her bridge as she spoke, getting nods and thumbs up from them as they listened to reports on *Lion's* critical systems.

The EM storm caused by a hit from a SAU disruptor was not insignificant — it stopped *Lion* firing its mags for several seconds as the power systems automatically interrupted themselves to prevent an overload — but it wasn't the same as being hit with a laser. Lasers cut deep and do damage; mags (whatever their size) are meant to fry your power grid.

And while they might have been devastating against unshielded pirates, or even against Martians, the SAU weapons were neutered against us for two reasons: first, the armor on our latest-generation warships was lined with grids that absorbed mag energy and redirected it into our outgoing buffers (I can't remember if I've even mentioned that since *The Rogue Commodore*, as it wasn't a major issue against the Martians), and second, during the war we'd learned our lessons and done upgrades to our secondary power grids, to avoid lethal overloads like *Lion* had suffered at Io.

Dave Caldecott would have known about the former advantage, but not the latter... so tough luck for his SAUN gunners. Their weapons, while certainly dangerous, would have to be used to full effect to stop us. And Group Captain Harku's ships weren't well-crewed enough to manage that.

"Let's be cautious," I ordered as the feed to *Lion's* bridge stabilized. "Lasers to target their drive wings. Katya, your armor isn't as well configured for this stuff, so turn back and go after the transport."

With a nod, Katya Romanov turned *Sackville* back to deal with the runner. We'd have the SAUN in hand soon enough.

The sound of a laser shot is surprisingly less obvious than that of the mags firing. It's probably because a laser is a single continuous beam of energy, not a bunch of rapid-fire bolts hosing space like some sort of cosmic machine gun.

Nevertheless, Wes recognized the noise of laser one firing just as he finally made it to the lift that could get him to the bridge deck. He'd been more hopeful when only mags had been firing, but if we were cutting someone up with lasers, it meant we were properly fighting.

He had to get to the bridge.

"One of their cruisers is now missing a drive pod," Matt Baxter was the first to make that observation, and I nodded to Kris.

"Good shooting. Let's see if we can disable the battleship next..." my words trailed off as three new icons originating from one of the SAU ships appeared on the main screen sensors plot.

Small icons, and fast.

"Torpedo separation! Three torpedoes inbound... track makes them for *Lion*."

The bastards seemed to have it in for Karen's old ship, and perhaps unsurprisingly, this was what started to drag my mind out of the more calculating mode of fleet combat, and back to where I'd been at the end of the Fleet Clash against Bort.

They were fixated on Kris, my friend who was just back from grievous war wounds, and in so doing they were trying to take away something Karen had loved. Rude of them.

"Commander Thompson is tracking the torpedoes," Felicia reported next, and I nodded as I also listened to Kris order a standby for evasive.

Three torpedoes from one ship... so the SAU had realized they might need to up their armaments to compete with real warships. Unfortunately, they hadn't launched any fighters of their own, and we had a bunch of Starlights out there basically doing loops, while they waited for something to shoot at.

Like three projectiles.

"Wolfstar squadron is locked on..." Felicia continued to narrate with her clear, firm tone. "Engaging."

Immediately, two of the torpedoes vanished from the sensor plot on the main screen... just one continued to race in against *Lion*, and it seemed to defy the efforts of our pilots to shoot it down.

"Sidestep to port... *now!*" Kris gave that order to her Helm and Navigation Officer, still Lieutenant Alek Nosov who joined the ship back in *The Pax Terra*, and he immediately moved the frigate.

The torpedo sailed right by. It was almost anti-climactic.

But I didn't quite see it that way.

My tone changed — or at least Andrea seemed to notice a difference — when I turned back from the screens and caught the attention of Jim Hannigan: "You see who fired those?"

He didn't realize I was talking to him at first, but when he did he looked up, "The torpedoes? Yes..."

"Laser shot to that ship, central hull. See how hard they are to kill."

No more toying about. They wanted to shoot torpedoes at us? At *Lion*?

Death.

"Shoot," Andrea gave that order as soon as Jim was ready, and the red beam sliced out.

Turning back to screens, I watched as a line crossed from our icon to that of the targeted cruiser... and then I watched the flashing of that icon to indicate it was a hit with noticeable damage. It wasn't until later (when we looked at footage from the enhanced camera views and the Starlights) that we realized how much damage that one shot did: we basically blew the front off the cruiser.

The SAU ships, you see, were mounting torpedo tubes the way old submarines used to — internally, bow and stern. They also carried more than we did, all in a relatively lightly armored (at least on these older ships) section of the hull.

Hit it with a hot laser, cut through the armor designed more to deal with mags than lasers, and detonate the torpedoes in their standby harnesses... you get the idea.

The cruiser was blown into a backward tumble by the sheer force of the explosion. Many were undoubtedly killed, and as soon as the other SAU ships in line realized what we'd been able to do with a single well-aimed laser shot, they started turning away and accelerating to get out of range.

I watched them go and spent a moment considering what to do next. Had I been angry, it would have made complete sense to go after the surviving ships. Some of them were damaged, the rest were poorly-equipped to face us. Right there we could have destroyed close to a quarter of the entire SAUN.

But I wasn't angry. The fact that they'd attacked *Lion* instead of *Wolf* had tugged on an irrational nerve, and I was stupidly rageful.

"Turn us back to Lexington. Let's get the President on the phone to plead for his life."

Wes staggered out of the lift onto the bridge deck, but he had a long walk left ahead of him if he intended to reach the bridge itself. He had started bleeding from one of the burns, and it hurt like hellfire, but he wasn't going to stop. They could smear him with more paste later.

He struggled on down the corridor, gritting his teeth with every step.

"The transport docked with the tower before we could intervene," Katya reported as our squadron crossed the short distance back to Lexington, and I frowned but nodded.

"Nothing you could do. They must have gotten orders to use the battle as cover. It's fine, there's always one way to make sure we kill the assassin," I replied quite reasonably, then gave an order which wasn't so balanced. "Start plotting targeting solutions for the domes on Lexington. We'll start with them, then work our way through all those exterior buildings."

That wasn't expected, and I got some surprised looks on Battlelink. Well, I shouldn't say some.

Matt Baxter asked the question first: "Sorry, repeat that? We're going to attack Lexington proper?"

I shrugged, "Might as well."

Matt didn't know quite what to say — no one did. I was giving an order that was really rather far off the path of goodness, and though a lot of people in this squadron were as angry as I was, it was something else entirely to start killing millions of people indiscriminately, just because we could.

"I'm all for teaching lessons," Kris spoke up next, trying to take a tactful approach to her question. "But is this what we should be doing?"

I shrugged again, "I don't see why not."

My answers were all like that — not just the ones I said aloud, but the ones rolling through my mind. We were the powerful squadron, the one with the ability to destroy. We represented an Empire that had been attacked by these people, these people who had protected and elected Grant Merger, and now were defending him even though they knew he was an enemy of the Empire.

We were within our rights, under the Articles of Empire, to murder every fucking one of these people. Citizens, freed persons, indentured servants… sure, bunches of them were innocent, but who cared? Sometimes it's not your lucky day. Sometimes you get the shit end of the deal, and it's not my problem.

In point of fact, it's my pleasure. Because as Grant and I had decided so long ago — before I'd had any reason not to be a self-indulging, spiteful fool — we were brutal, cold-blooded killers. In this case he'd set these bastards up, and I'd knock them down.

"No one actually going to refuse this order?" Rozy Young jumped in from *Nova Scotia*, and my eyes tracked to her as she spoke. She was one of Wes' officers, too humanitarian for what we needed right now.

Couldn't really fault her for that, though, so I offered her an out: "Feel free to back off, Rozy. If need be, *Wolf* can do the whole colony alone. It'll just take longer. Do watch our backs, will you?"

The look on her face suggested to me that she might not actually watch our backs. That was disappointing, but again I didn't mind.

"Do we have some laser tracks?" I asked, looking back at Jim Hannigan. He had the strangest look on his face.

"I have them. And I'll use them if you order me to. But I don't know if that would be any better than what we found on Egesta."

That was a good observation, so I nodded, "Good point. We wouldn't be torturing anyone. Except the people trapped in buildings who will eventually asphyxiate. So we're not as bad as Egesta on that count. But we'd also be killing everyone, without mercy. I'd actually tend to think that'd make us worse than Egesta." Jim just stared at me, so I shrugged and offered a final thought: "But no one on Egesta protected Grant Merger."

After that I turned back to the screens, and found a lot of eyes on me. Everyone wore an odd stare... the stare of officers from the Defense Command tradition. Officers who would never have allowed something like Egesta to happen, because they wouldn't have followed the orders to do harm to civilians.

These men and women were okay with necessary collateral damage... but we weren't talking about collateral damage here. We were talking about mass murder.

But why not?

Fortunately the bridge hatch opened at that moment, and Wes tumbled through. He managed to get an arm under him as he hit the floor, but it was still agony on the burns so he let out a grunt.

Everyone on the bridge turned back to look at him as he forced himself to his feet and staggered towards the front screens, his glare fixed on me, "Now who's shooting who?"

I answered him plainly: "We just drove off their defense squadron."

"They fire first?"

"We did, but they were targeting us. We were just faster on the trigger."

Wes wasn't impressed by the answer, "You start a war?"

"No idea," I replied. "But their President was manipulated into resisting as much as we were manipulated into being here. Grant's been busy."

Gritting his teeth, Wes began to step forward again, but his feet weren't working as well as they should have been. He stumbled again, but managed to drop to only one knee. Down on the deck as he was, he planted one hand on the cold plating and used the other to hold his robe shut over his chest. Blood was starting to seep through the fabric, making for a rather dramatic sight.

Well let's be clear, this whole situation was dramatic — verging on melodramatic — but Wes had no choice.

"We're targeting the domes of the planet. Possibly going to blow the whole rock to pieces," Jim Hannigan added helpfully, and my eyes jumped to him as he spoke. He didn't regret speaking out of turn — his expression basically said 'that's enough'.

And Wes found himself staring at the deck as he heard the words of *Wolf's* XO.

Targeting civilians. Targeting whole domes. It was exactly as bad as the Commodore of the Independent Squadron had imagined it might be.

He let out a very painful sigh and began shaking his head. I just watched him, and standing beside me, Andrea watched too — though I didn't notice her.

Wes then tried to force himself up onto his feet again, but he couldn't. Blood was starting to drip out from under his robes, and thanks to the new trauma his march had caused, the agony from his burned and now torn flesh was nearly sending him into shock.

Realizing he couldn't get upright, he turned his head towards Jim, "Arms box. Get me a mag."

Jim wasn't ready for that order either, and even had he been, it hardly seemed like a sensible one to follow.

Wes didn't wait, "I challenge you to a duel, Ken. I have to. I'm not going to live to see this happen to the Belt Squadron. Or to you."

It was impossibly noble. It was the sort of thing that would force me to roll my eyes if I read it in fiction. The wounded hero, so certain in his principles and so determined to save the innocent, that he'd dragged his torn body all the way to the bridge and now was demanding a duel so he could either die or save millions of lives.

I know, I wouldn't have believed it either.

I was still wearing my sidearm from the trip down to Lexington, and I felt my hand automatically drop to it. A shot now, at just about any strength, could actually kill Wes Pellew. He was wounded and had done himself much damage by coming all this way.

And yet I was ready to draw. On my friend.

I started to notice that fact... began to realize that it wasn't necessarily consistent with everything I believed... but noticing meant little at this point.

Jim Hannigan wasn't going to bring Wes a mag anyway.

"We're doing this, Wes. We might as well," I said, and then forcibly removed my hand from my mag. No need to shoot him, he couldn't stop me...

A hand closed on my wrist, and it tightened before I realized who it was.

"I'll be his second. And since he obviously can't stand for the duel, I'll have to put you down."

No one else was able to hear Andrea Kiley's words — she'd leaned in close to my ear and whispered them.

Then she stepped away from me and backed a few paces towards Wes. Her face was different. Something had happened, and I didn't know what because I didn't care about much of anything.

But while Wes had been focused on me, feeling like he had to do something to stop the Belt Squadron committing a most heinous crime... and I had been confused and trying to make sure he didn't end up shot by accident... Andrea had been staring at him.

She hated him deeply because of the sort of thing he was doing now. He was forcing himself to be too noble — to try to be everyone's conscience. He had once suffered, then erred, then found his way back... now he was hell-bent on helping everyone else around him do the same. He didn't seem to realize that everyone wasn't meant to heal the way he had.

Why wouldn't he just give up and let the wounded people have their way? And if he wouldn't give up on me, why had he given up on her?

Or had he?

Because Andrea knew that Wes hadn't stopped paying attention to her, even while she tortured him. Her only possible revenge after he'd defeated her in the argument including his wife's name was to be the things he wanted her not to be… but somehow she felt that he hadn't just abandoned her.

Such a fool…

A fool she needed, if she was honest with herself. A fool she would keep around, and somehow in this moment, would help to do the right thing.

That make sense to you? It certainly made no sense to Andrea then — she was acting mostly on instinct as she knelt beside Wes and started to help him sit back. She then told Jim to call for a medic while Wes struggled against her.

"Not going back down there."

"I know," she said.

It was the way she said it that mattered.

Wes noticed that her tone was different — just a little. He looked at the side of her face as she continued to watch me, and wondered if I'd shoot her the way I'd shot him.

Then she looked at him, and because of the way she was helping keep him upright, their faces were close together and they were staring at each other.

Andrea's eyes held an admonishment of Wes naïve nobility… and a plea for him to turn that irrepressible force on her again. It was the first moment that the two clearly realized how important they'd become to each other.

I saw the way they looked at each other. It was just the beginning, but I saw it.

For the first time I realized that they were going to be together. That for years to come, Wes was going to be the one sitting up with her in the middle of the night, talking her through cold sweats. The one helping her with coping strategies when they dropped their kids off at school in the mornings. The one she'd call her anchor to humanity.

None of that happened in one fell swoop, on the floor of *Wolf's* bridge. That was going to take them years and years — no matter how dramatic a situation they were currently in, it wasn't going to simply spring into existence.

But I *knew* it was going to happen, because I'd seen before what could happen when two similarly broken people came across each other at that right moment. I knew that look. I understood what it meant.

I'd seen it once in an alley.

And it had changed my life.

Normally at this point I'd say that a revelation such as this doesn't lead to those corny moments you see in movies — the ones where the tortured protagonist has a dramatic revelation, and looks stupidly into himself while violins play their mournful tune.

This was the exception. Hell, this whole situation with Wes and now Andrea was the exception. Because if there had to be one time in my life when I needed a story to work out like it does in the movies, this was it.

I watched Wes and Andrea together, just together, and I found myself feeling a bit lightheaded. There was no medical reason, just a feeling that I was spinning.

And then I remember a very distinct train of thought:

You promised Karen.

Now you're letting her down.

And whatever else you tell yourself, that matters.

I said this, but I don't remember it: "Cease targeting of the domes. Defensive posture in case the Union ships come back. Tell the President… we'll talk tomorrow."

Then I backed up to the railings before the screens at the front of the bridge, and leaned against them… or perhaps more precisely, found that they were holding me upright. I folded my arms and waited and watched as medics came to recollect Wes, who only agreed to leave with them after he took a look at my face, and saw something different there too.

So much for killing everyone on Lexington.

CHAPTER TWENTY-ONE

STAGNANT INTERLUDE

The next ten hours were very awkward ones. From the point of view of the Union crowd, they must have also been incredibly confusing. We'd mauled their local squadron without breaking a sweat — the half-blown cruiser had been abandoned from what our Starlights saw on recon patrol, and the other four ships had withdrawn out of the defensive zone... an interesting choice that left our squadron in complete control of Etat Lexington space.

Had I been clearheaded, I might have wondered why the SAUN would be so willing to throw in the towel — vulnerable to our lasers though they were, I would assume now that their first duty would be to protect their home asteroid, no matter the cost.

Then again, consider who'd assigned that particular 'red group' to this post. It undoubtedly played right into Grant's hands to have the local warships cut and run when they were fighting to protect their President... those defending Valcour would probably be a whole lot more determined.

It would add to Grant's narrative of being the freedom fighter.

For all the local space traffic, the flight of their own warships had to be disconcerting, but after several hours with the Belt Squadron simply sitting at their rock, literally doing nothing, some small civilian ships worked up the courage to start moving back and forth.

At one point I remember Kris Jacobs telling me that any one of those ships could be carrying the assassin from the transport away from Lexington, and back to Grant Merger. I nodded when she said it, but did absolutely nothing.

I was lost in my own world — entirely unfit to be in command, but nevertheless retaining that responsibility with Wes sedated in *Wolf's* medical bay. For a while I was on the bridge, but seemed disconnected from reality. After that I went to my cabin, leaving Andrea in charge with orders to hold position. Then I was back on the bridge again, and still we did nothing.

We should have perhaps talked to the President again, tried to find a way to locate the people who'd come off the transport (unlikely though that was when they'd had hours to escape). Or we could have turned and burned straight for Valcour, just a couple of days away and the home of our target.

All that we'd come here for — the hope of securing the cooperation of the SAU government in our hunt — was out of the question, so why linger?

I didn't have a good answer then and I don't now, but linger is what we did. And eventually we stood down from full General Quarters — our crews would only become exhausted if they were required to stand at their posts constantly, even with no threat in sight.

Looking back at this particular point in the mission, and as much of it as I can remember, I find our lack of direction quite shocking. Sorry, by 'our' I should say 'my'.

Because throughout the history of the Belt Squadron I don't think we'd ever been an indecisive force. Always had something to do, or somewhere to be… and if we didn't have that, it was because we were enjoying time off.

I'd screwed up that consistent clarity of purpose. That and many other things.

But as my grandmother would say, never an ill wind that doesn't blow some good.

"New contact… edge of sensor range, approaching Etat Lexington."

Felicia Khalid, who had stayed at her post even though she'd rotated most of her Sensors and Communications team off duty, made that report. I paid some attention because it seemed significant, though in reality it could be innocent… or it could be Grant Merger himself, come to make his fight a personal one, even if that seemed incredibly unlikely.

Whatever it was, it shook me out of my inexplicable inaction. Turning to the main screen, I watched as a new icon appeared. Only a few skippers were left up on Battlelink, but Matt Baxter was one of them and he frowned, "Think it's trouble?"

I had no way to know, so I said as much: "Could be. We may have earned some."

Those weren't remorseful words, in case you're wondering… I think I was actually hoping we were going to be attacked, because it would give us a chance for more shooting without wiping out a colony wholesale.

Our illusions didn't last long.

"I…" Felicia frowned and looked down over the shoulder of one of her technicians. Before she could say anything else the icon of the approaching ship changed on screen. It wasn't just any old vessel, it was *Cheetah*.

"Well I'll be damned… wonder how Mark broke out of that hospital," I smiled, and then as if to answer my question a signal came in, and Felicia put it up on screen two.

It wasn't from who I was expecting.

As the screen loaded up, Mark Gunney did appear, but with him was someone I never expected to see out here.

"By God Charlie, you came," my smile grew as I saw my friend, though his expression remained severe. "Mark, great to see you too. Thanks for bringing *Cheetah* to the party. Now we're all together again… eight ships against a new Syndicate…"

Charlie's expression was very grave, and I suddenly realized why: "Oh don't worry, I know about Karen. It's fine, Charlie. I promise, we haven't killed any civilians either. Was about to, but decided not to go through with it."

That didn't inspire a lot of confidence in my friend. He considered me humorlessly, then shook his head, "I'm coming over as soon as we're in range. And when I do, I don't want you to meet me on the landing deck. Head to your cabin, we're going to need to discuss something."

It was an unusual order, and I frowned. There was no mistaking Charlie's tone — no point arguing because he wasn't going to accept anything other than what he'd said.

With a shrug, I agreed, "Fine by me. See you shortly."

I would indeed.

CHAPTER TWENTY-TWO

ALMOST ASCENDANT

Karen had never seen *Wolf* before.

Well she obviously had, but you know what I mean... she didn't remember it. The ship was new to her, and though it was the same class as *Cheetah*, which had carried her all the way to Lexington, it was different.

This ship had been ours. She understood that from the files she'd read during the last couple of days. Throughout the Martian War we'd been together aboard *Wolf*, and that made it a mythical sort of place... it was the ship where we'd managed to realize some of the juvenile hopes we'd held back at the Academy.

We had served together on the same ship. Our ship. With cabins next door to each other.

And she didn't remember any of it.

Now, as she watched *Wolf* grow in the windows of the shuttle carrying her and Charlie, she wondered if being back would trigger a memory. She didn't want to hope for something so silly... Vanessa Hansen had been clear that without a cure it wasn't likely anything would come back.

But maybe, just maybe, Hansen was wrong.

"Ready for this?" Charlie Peters remained serious as he sat across from Karen, and she blinked before glancing at him. She was wringing her hands together and her stomach was in her throat... of course she was ready.

Terrified, anxious, excited and desperate. Also ready.

You might wonder why Charlie wasn't looking happier. This was to be a cheerful reunion, surely — the moment when we realized Karen wasn't gone, that Grant had failed... or at least that he hadn't killed her. Wouldn't that be a happy time?

He didn't know. He had no idea how I'd react in particular, or how anyone from the Belt Squadron would react in general. Would Karen coming back mean that things we'd done already were going to suddenly be unjustified? Would Karen coming back without all her memories make us less angry, or more?

And in my case, what would seeing Karen mean?

He wouldn't be happy until he knew... and he realized that might take a while.

"Coming in for landing now, sir, ma'am," *Cheetah's* shuttle pilot called back that warning as she directed the small craft into *Wolf's* bay one.

Charlie leaned down and looked out the window nearest him as they swept in and touched down. He wanted to see if there was a welcoming committee, though of course one wouldn't make itself apparent until the space doors closed and the bay repressurized.

He waited patiently until the atmosphere came back, continuing to watch. His eyes were fixed on the hatch to the observation lounge... and it didn't open. If anyone was waiting, they were inside there... probably just an escort, not a friend.

Karen had spotted that too, and it was one of the few things about this moment that reduced her stress level. Unfortunately, the weight of what was about to happen was sitting heavily on her shoulders, and she continued to feel physically ill.

Charlie had told her that I'd seemingly lost my cool, and that I'd made jokes about attacking domes. Like in the simulator that day back in chapter one, I'd suggested that lasering a civilian settlement was a good idea. It seemed obvious that I'd reverted to that mindset out of rage — rage that I thought was righteous.

So how would I handle seeing her again — losing the vindication for my anger? And how would I treat her once I realized she wasn't the same woman as before?

It's hard to overstate how worried she was. Whether she should or shouldn't have been is irrelevant: she was.

"Best not to overthink it. Now remember, everyone on this ship is going to be very glad to see you. Try to take it in stride... use the fact that we have to get to Ken's cabin to keep people from getting you into long conversations."

Charlie was suddenly standing beside Karen's seat, and his reassuring words were a small help. She nodded and slowly pushed herself up out of her chair, tugging at her tunic to straighten it, then following as Charlie led the way to the lowering ramp.

Some of the flight deck crew were paying attention as that ramp touched the deck — they knew Charlie Peters was back, and he was as popular on *Wolf* as Karen was, even though it'd been a long time since he'd been aboard. Remember, he'd left for the assault on Mercury, all the way back in 2233. So long ago.

When Charlie appeared on the ramp there were some smiles and a few calls of 'welcome back' and such things.

When Karen appeared behind him, there was stunned silence. The noisy landing bay seemed to stop in mid-breath.

Was that Karen? Not possible, because she was dead.

Before anyone could come to any conclusions, the arriving pair were stepping through the hatch to the observation lounge. The questions started loudly as soon as the door shut behind them.

In the lounge, Jim Hannigan looked up from the report he'd been working on, nodded to Charlie, looked down again... then his head snapped back up and his jaw literally dropped as the pad slipped from his fingers. He stared at Karen. She tried to smile at him, recognizing his photo from one of the files she'd reviewed — she'd done her best to memorize her old bridge crew.

Jim looked from her to Charlie, then back, then shook his head, "But... it was a lie..."

"Grant Merger has some sort of plant in our comm grid," Charlie replied. "But everything is not okay, Jim. We can't explain now. But we will soon."

Jim nodded mainly on instinct, because he had hardly processed anything our Hawke Lord had said, "Welcome home..."

He came forward with his hand extended, and Karen took it gently. Jim then reached out and clasped her shoulder.

"Thank God," he said next, mind seeming to skip gears. "Ken needs you... come on, let's get you up to his quarters..."

Jim let go of her, then hurried to the exit and led the way.

A dozen encounters like that one would come between Karen and my cabin, but I won't recount them all. Because all she could think about, and all I can think about now, was the one that mattered most.

I was sitting in the chair in my cabin, and the lights were on. I mention this because I know it would have been moodier, or more dramatic, if I was clad in shadow or there was some music playing... but I was just sitting in silence.

I was excited that Charlie was here, though I had no idea what news he might have brought. Hopefully it wasn't a cease-and-desist order. Whether I wiped out Lexington or not, I had no intention of backing away from this hunt until I'd dealt with Grant and every one of his acolytes.

But if Charlie tried to intervene... well, I wouldn't have much chance of surprising him in a duel. No offense to Wes, but Special Branch... you know.

Whatever, I'd figure out a solution. Because it was Charlie it wouldn't be difficult... he'd just be my conscience, and if I didn't listen then I could go to hell. Or stay in hell. In the end it would be a fool who didn't appreciate his presence — and didn't appreciate the fact that he'd come all this way even though he didn't have to. I'd just find a way to cope.

I was ready to see my friend again. When the hatch finally opened, I was ready for my friend Charlie.

Karen laughs now, because Charlie basically opened my hatch and pushed her through, then shut the door behind her. Like tossing in a grenade, this was the only act of cowardice I've ever witnessed from my friend the Hawke Lord... and really, I think it's fair enough. It's sort of in line with the act of cowardice Wes and Karen and I pulled with Lia, when we refused to tell her that Charlie had been wounded on Mercury until they were in the same hospital room.

In this case Charlie simply didn't want to get in the way, or to explain anything... he was going to make Karen do it all by herself.

The door shut behind Karen and I don't know what happened next. If you look at the movies — some of them well written, some of them poorly written — you'll see so many different pieces of dialogue. Some of it I wish I'd said, some of it I'm glad I didn't.

Here's what actually came out of my mouth, barely audible above a whisper: "Hello."

Karen was breathing. It sounds ridiculous, but breathing was the first thing I looked for.

She stood inside the door, breathing faster than she wanted to, one arm across her front with its hand holding onto the forearm of the other as it hung down at her side. She was breathing fast because she was anxious — anxious to the point of worrying she was actually going to be sick.

And I noticed she was breathing.

Dead people don't breathe. You can look that up if you doubt me.

They also don't stand, or look at you with anxious eyes. They don't bite down on their bottom lips, and they lack the ability to shed tears. Despite all that, the thing I noticed was that she was breathing.

I was also breathing. I don't remember doing it, but Karen tells me she was noticing the same... though her preoccupation wasn't with the fact that I was still with the living, it was the look on my face. I looked different than when last she'd seen me. Looked like I did in the photos she'd seen in the files.

I was a different person than the me she'd left behind... just as she was different than the Karen I'd just lost. And she had no idea what I was going to say.

I didn't either, but given what I'd noticed, it might not surprise you that I continued my quiet words with: "You're breathing."

I didn't know what else to say. Because of that, I did what any sane person would do when confronted with a situation like this: with as much haste as was possible, I got to my feet and wrapped my arms all the way around her. Somehow I don't think I believed she'd be there when I tried to do touch her. She had to be a phantom. She was gone and I was hallucinating.

But no, she was real.

When I squeezed her, my fingers were firm against her strong body. It was her cheek that pressed into the side of my face.

She smelled like Karen. Her skin felt like Karen. Her hair tangled in my fingers the same way it always had.

It was her.

She was breathing.

I can't remember if I laughed or cried. I probably did both, because they're not mutually exclusive. I lifted her up so her feet weren't on the deck anymore and I turned with her.

I felt her fingers pressing into my back. She was clearly controlling them, because she was breathing. That meant she was alive, and her hands could hold onto me. She did that — held onto me for dear life — but she wasn't laughing. She was happy — so happy — that my reaction was a human one. That, in fact, I was so glad to see her.

But her anxiety didn't go away, because I was welcoming a certain woman... and she wasn't that woman. And she knew this first embrace might mean nothing when I learned she was damaged goods in need of repair.

Her words, not mine.

Just for a second, though, she closed her eyes and breathed. I didn't smell quite the same way she remembered. I was different... a dozen years had made my shoulders bigger, because I'd apparently spent more time in the gym. My skin had aged, my hair was longer, and my grip on her was stronger, more intense.

She'd never thought it could be more intense than it had been, but that's the thing you never realize when you're young. No matter how strong your connection in the beginning, the trials of time will only make it more powerful. If you weather the storm together, the waves and winds of life will pound two people into one. And if you take away one part of that new person, what remains will be less than it had been to begin with.

So that was the question: was she now someone who could fill the gap left by the person she'd become?

"I'm not... it's not me... not who you knew..." she started to whisper, because she couldn't hold back that 'confession' (her word) any longer. If this was going to end badly, she needed it to happen sooner rather than later.

I loosened my grip and lowered her gently down to touch the floor, then she pulled back just enough to dip her chin — she didn't really want to make eye contact.

"The compound... It wiped out memories... I can't remember anything for twelve years... not since I got *Lady Grace*..." she blurted, and because of the way she was saying it — with very little context, she fully expected I'd be confused.

Somehow, and I don't understand this, I wasn't confused at all. In my mind it seemed to make immediate sense: Grant's compound had been in her frontal lobe, and it had wiped away many of her memories... but it hadn't taken her back to the very beginning.

It couldn't have, or else she wouldn't be this worried.

"Do you remember the tenth of September?" I asked softly, hoping I knew the answer.

"Of course," she whispered, and with that everything else was okay.

I mean, not *really* okay, but this was still Karen in the most important ways. That's what mattered now. Everything else could matter later.

I remember thinking all of that very clearly, then pulling Karen closer again, "Sorry for getting old on you."

Karen heard me say that and felt such relief that a genuine tremor passed through her. She pressed her face against mine, "What happened to your shoulders?"

No really, that's what she said. Shoulders.

"A decade in the gym," I answered earnestly. She didn't answer, so I continued — still somehow understanding: "You're... so. We have to go find Grant, and ask him nicely to give you back some memories?"

She tried to nod, but didn't elaborate with words — it was enough that I'd accepted who she was, at least for now. The most important things seemed to remain, and perhaps she could still get the rest back.

But that wasn't a worry for now.

One thing at a time. Just one thing at a time.

CHAPTER TWENTY-THREE

WILDFIRE

I expect you won't be surprised to learn that news of Karen's return spread like... well, pick your metaphor (or simile, I suppose) of choice. The deck crew started sending messages out across the ship as soon as the hatch shut behind her and Charlie. Jim Hannigan told the bridge, and since Battlelink was up other ships found out. And then more ships.

It was impossible. It was unbelievable. Or, if you prefer to say it the way Matt Baxter said it: "Thank God in heaven, there's a chance we won't blow up the universe now."

And you know what, he was probably on to something. We could all wonder later if Karen's survival meant that we'd gone too far when we'd stormed Concord and fought the SAUN at Lexington... but we weren't going to worry about that. Grant Merger had obviously made certain we thought she was dead, and the fact that he'd been able to accomplish that was a bigger concern. He had the means to control our communications with Admiralty House. What else had he influenced?

That was one question; another, perhaps bigger one was why he hadn't just gone through with it — why he hadn't actually killed her. Some people had theories about his motives, but I won't bother with them now, especially considering they'll matter more later.

No, in the midst of everything that had happened... the strange duel with Wes, his intervention on *Wolf's* bridge, the hours of inaction... none of it mattered now, because if I'd been spinning into oblivion for lack of Karen, that was over.

Now it was the real Belt Squadron, all together again. Mark Gunney had come back. Charlie Peters had come back.

Karen had come back.

And as soon as the first waves of elation finished surging through every ship in our formation, the smiles turned sharp. Now Grant Merger was going to pay — that was the realization. The fellow had no hope, because our determination would never waver. We had his scent, we knew his crimes, and he'd missed his one chance to actually hurt us.

So we'd hurt him.

He was as good as dead already, and he didn't even know it.

The only place such thoughts weren't resonating was in *Wolf's* medical bay. Alicia Morgan was very happy to hear Karen was back, of course, but she was also busy doing a bit more surgery on Julie Pichot — stopping some internal bleeding that had begun after the removal of the beacon.

With that very necessary work preoccupying most of the medical staff, it was only Wes who was left unattended, and he was in rough shape. He'd been sedated, but for some reason sedatives never work too well on him. Waking up before anyone anticipated he could have, he found he was pain free thanks to a new round of painkillers... and that one of his wrists was strapped to the medical bed.

That was Alicia's message to him: don't be stupid and try walking to the bridge again. He wasn't actually confined, of course — he had a free hand and could have undone the restraint — but she just wanted to make sure he knew she thought he needed his rest.

Looking down at his chest, he could see why. New layers of paste were all over his burns, and in the midst of the mess he could see some sealant that must have been closing nasty tears. Burns are messy, and he'd made his worse.

Sighing, he let his head fall back against the pillow of his bed, looking right and then left.

That's when he noticed Andrea Kiley. She was actually standing in the shadows in the corner beside Wes' bed, and with her hands laced together in front of her she looked down at him with heavy eyes.

Wes frowned, "You said something to Ken up there... stopped him."

Andrea's eyes shifted to meet his, "Don't want to discuss it, actually. *Cheetah* showed up an hour ago, carrying Charlie Peters."

Well that was good news; Wes had his ally at last. Someone who was an even better shot than he was — who wouldn't lose a duel even if I cheated. Not that the duel solution seeming like a good idea to him as he lay there.

"Good," he said.

"Karen was aboard too."

Wes heard that and instantly wondered why Charlie would bring Karen's body with him before his mind opened to the broader possibility. His frown deepened and he looked back at Andrea, "Wait."

She nodded, "We guess Grant must have planted the report. Because she's not dead at all."

"Not even a little bit?" Wes asked, and to this day he can't believe that question came out of his mouth. He was medicated, and despite what the drug companies tell you sometimes there are mild side-effects.

"Not even a little," Andrea confirmed.

Wes looked away from her, and then felt a sense of relief that was different than any he'd been expecting. After that relief came a feeling he didn't expect: envy. What he wouldn't have traded to have Sara come back from the dead. All he'd done for revenge... all those people he'd killed in the DNR duels... he'd have done a million times that much damage for just one chance to see her again.

He feels badly now, because in that moment he cursed my good luck. He's Karen's friend, and mine, and he feels bad for wishing it could have been him who learned Sara was alive.

But he shouldn't feel guilty. He had every right to wish for his lost wife, because I know how much he loved her. We'll never grudge him that.

"Happy ending when it works out that way, I suppose," Andrea's voice was low, her tone reflecting similar feelings on her part. My torment seemed to be at an end, but theirs would go on.

Two of our closest friends, it seems, were the least happy to see us back together. And again, we don't blame them... we understand.

They didn't. Wes sighed and shook his head, "What the hell are we doing?"

"No idea," Andrea answered honestly, looking down again as she said it.

"Right," Wes agreed. He fell silent for a moment after that, then looked up at her. "Are we in it together, at least?"

Andrea's gaze met his again, and she considered saying something she'd regret. An answer as simple as 'no' would have sufficed, but she didn't want that. Not if she was honest with herself. It had been a long time… too long… and she was tired of her enforced solitude.

She was tired of fighting.

So she nodded, "I guess so."

That was good news. Actually, that was the best news Wes had heard all day, including the fact that Karen was alive. Because he and Andrea had a long road ahead of them, and this was one of the most important steps on it.

It was a good day to renew relationships aboard *Wolf*. We all took some time to breathe, because we weren't dead and were thus able to do so. Once that was done we'd think about Grant Merger again.

CHAPTER TWENTY-FOUR

STILL TO PLAN

Grant Merger sat behind his desk and listened to the various reports Sonia Hart read aloud to him. As expected, the Belt Squadron had fallen onto Etat Lexington like a ton of bricks, had bullied the President, and had shot up the local defense force.

Grant knew they'd be coming to Etat Valcour next, and when they arrived there would be a lot to do.

But for now he just listened.

"Renault and Fletcher boarded a transport bound for us as soon as the civilian traffic began flowing again," Sonia continued, drawing a nod from Grant.

The timing of that message — the savaged and mutilated Julie Pichot — couldn't have been any better, and it was a bonus that both the operatives sent on the mission had managed to escape capture. Grant wouldn't have lost sleep if one or both of them had been taken by the Belt Squadron, but having them both still at his disposal was potentially valuable.

Especially with Charlie Peters back in the picture.

That thought captured Grant's attention for a moment, and he raised his hand towards Sonia, "Can you tell me again about the arrival of *Cheetah?*"

Sonia looked up at him and nodded. She was quieter today than he'd seen her in recent months... obviously she'd been fond of Julie Pichot, and now she was either upset that she'd been taken in by the DCI spy — which he'd told her repeatedly not to feel guilty about, as DCI spies were the best — or she didn't like Renault's mutilation.

Grant could understand if it was the latter, but as he'd told her, there was a difference between mutilated and dead. The former gave you another chance, and he thought that was fairer to the young girl who had no doubt been seduced by Defense Command before she'd even left high school.

Anyway, that all was irrelevant: quiet though she was, Sonia scrolled back through the reports until she reached one that had come from Etat Lexington's commanding General. "*Cheetah* arrived ten hours after the engagement between the Belt Squadron and red group."

Grant narrowed his eyes as he went over the implications of that again. The last intel he had received from Caldecott's people in Defense Command Communications suggested that Charlie Peters had made his way from the Protectorate to Earth, and then joined *Cheetah* for a fast run towards Lexington. There was no way to know for certain what his mission was — whether it was to join me in a quest for revenge, or to let me know that Karen wasn't dead.

Either way, there was a good chance I was going to know Karen was alive. There was no way the message Grant had planted would hold up against testimony from Charlie that he'd seen Karen breathing.

This changed things somewhat; instead of being ready for a reckless madman with nothing to lose, he was now up against someone with a cause and a woman to return to. He'd have to be more careful than he'd previously thought, just in case.

"The plan still holds, Sonia," Grant said quietly after a moment. "But we have to be ready for the fact now that when Ken Barron arrives, he's not going to be as aggressive. He knows Karen is back there, that he can go and see her, and that'll weigh on his mind."

Sonia lowered the pad she was reading and nodded slowly, "I understand."

Grant had been looking off at a piece of wall while he thought about the situation, but now he returned his gaze to her, "I'm sure you understand most of it, but..."

He paused for a moment, then looked his lover square in the eyes. He knew she was the one person he couldn't afford to lose, and that if I was on my game and coming for him it would probably be a lot more difficult for her to slip away using one of the usual escape routes that had long been ingrained into her.

If worst came to worst, and the entire defense of Etat Valcour crumbled, he had a way out — Grant always had a way out. He shared it with no one. The crews who built the necessary systems and tunnels died to keep them secret.

But it had been built for two, just in case. Now he was glad he'd had the foresight.

"Can you come with me for a moment, Sonia? I must show you something."

He rose, and though she was surprised Sonia Hart got to her feet as well. Grant then stepped out from behind his desk and led her to the bathroom adjacent to his office. For a moment she wondered if mid-afternoon lust was fueling her Governor — from time to time, they'd indulge — but instead he wanted to show her a secret doorway behind a towel rack.

A doorway she hadn't known about, which led into a corridor that no other living soul had yet seen.

When Grant had been elected, he'd immediately remodeled the Governor's House explicitly so he could install this corridor, and as he followed it all the way to a lift at the end, he looked over his shoulder to see Sonia staring in shock at everything around her.

"No one knows this exists, Sonia. It's just for me... and you."

The words actually made her blush, but she didn't have anything to say before they reached the lift. As Grant keyed the button the doors opened immediately. He was the only possible passenger and it had been waiting for him. Stepping in, he took one side of the cramped compartment while Sonia took the other. They had to press up against each other a little to allow the doors to shut, but neither minded.

With those doors closed, the lift began to drop down through the building and into the crust of the asteroid well below. It was a forty-second process, and when the doors parted again Grant nodded for Sonia to step out.

She emerged into a hollowed-out rock chamber with a metal floor, a couple of consoles, a few cases stacked against one wall, and a small shuttle unlike anything she'd ever seen before, sitting on a track and pointed towards what appeared to be space doors.

"What is it?" she asked as she came to a stop beside the black craft. Parts of the frame seemed to be made of metal, but the other parts seemed wrong. It was as though they were covered in some sort of strange black skin.

"The latest in our adopted technology designs. From the same samples we used to create the compound for Karen. This little ship will do… for a few hours at least… upwards of 300 kps. It's the perfect escape vehicle."

Grant approached the side of the small ship as he gave his explanation, but as she watched, Sonia started to shake her head. It was clear to my old friend that she didn't understand, and that was fine — he was keeping most of his work with this new type of technology secret, even from her, because the knowledge itself was rather dangerous.

Only Sonia could know.

Well, Sonia and Defense Command. Because as soon as the bugs in Grant's bathroom had detected the opening of a new space, they'd started racing through. Already they were roaming down the corridor towards the lift, and soon they would be in the shaft and down to the launch compartment.

But that's for the future — for now, Sonia took a breath, "I don't understand."

Grant smiled gently and came closer to her, then put his arms around her, "If it happens that Ken Barron and his attack force defeat every other plan we have in place to stop him, and every other avenue of escape is taken, I want you to come here. I'll meet you here, and we'll leave together."

Then Sonia realized — really realized — what Grant was saying, and what he was offering. He loved her. This proved it.

She began tearing up as she buried her face in his shoulder, "I… I…"

Her sniffles defied speech, but Grant didn't need her to say anything. He stroked the back of her neck and spoke with reassuring ease, "I need you with me. Don't let Ken Barron, or any of his people, take you. Come here and if it all goes wrong, we escape together."

For Grant there could be no better feeling than this; a beautiful woman who loved him was in his arms, moved to tears by the fact that he loved her back.

Whatever else came of this whole plan, at least he'd leave with Sonia.

As long as I didn't get to her first.

Or better yet, as long as *Karen* didn't get to her first. Because though his intelligence was generally excellent, Grant's spies in DCC had been found. Well, that's not completely accurate… but many suspects had been identified, all of whom had been isolated by John and Greg, and were now being fed incomplete information about what was going on.

This being the case, Grant Merger was missing a crucial piece of information — one that could mean the difference between life or death for himself, or for his beloved.

Karen was out here with us. And she would soon be ready to fight.

CHAPTER TWENTY-FIVE

ALLIES

After it became clear that the reunion with Karen was going well, Charlie decided the best way to utilize his time would be to track down the one ally he was confident he had in the Belt Squadron: Wes Pellew. Now, reading that sentence back it seems awfully dramatic — as though our elite Lord Major was aboard an enemy ship, surrounded by people who meant to do him harm… but hopefully you know what I mean.

Wes and Charlie had never really served together. They were both senior statesmen in our Belt Squadron family, but they'd become great friends of mine in different ways, at different times. They both knew what was going on — what I'd turned into — but for different reasons. And they both knew they'd need to team up to make sure no real harm was done.

If you could be so generous as to say what had happened so far wasn't 'real harm'.

Anyway, Charlie obviously had no way to know that I'd shot Wes, and that he was aboard *Wolf* under Alicia's care, so his first step in setting up this meeting was to pop by the bridge. To say he got a hero's welcome would be something of an understatement; there was enthusiastic cheering, backed up by handshakes — all, he assures me, quite inappropriate since his only contribution had been to show up late at Earth, making him the only guy conveniently in place to shepherd Karen back to us.

Nevertheless, the joy of the occasion mandated that he be congratulated, both in person by people like Shelby and even Andrea (no smile there), and by the people on the Battlelink screens.

After the few moments it took to get the formalities out of the way, our Lord Major finally got a chance to pay close attention to those screens… and he quickly found that Wes wasn't on any of them.

"So," he asked after things had died down sufficiently, "if I needed to talk to Wes…"

I suppose it's a testament to the level of elation in the air that the question didn't automatically sour everyone's mood.

Andrea cleared her throat, and as Charlie glanced back at her, she explained.

Charlie rapidly became even more relieved that he'd arrived in time to prevent the next blow up. With that in mind, he went to see the Commodore of the Independent Squadron.

"Glad you're here," Wes was pretty open about that sentiment, and perhaps you can understand why. If you need a hint, he added: "Ken shot me."

Charlie had come to a stop at the foot of Wes' bed, and now considered our elite Commodore with a frown, "Nearly did it twice, from what Andrea told me."

Wes nodded uncomfortably, "To his credit, he didn't actually do it the second time. Just don't challenge him to a duel unless you're ready to draw."

"I don't do duels," Charlie shrugged, and Wes snorted a laugh.

"Good point, can't imagine anyone saying yes if you offered one."

With that they tapered off for a moment, and had Charlie not been a Special Brancher (with the ability to know exactly where everyone was in the room without looking) he would have taken a few seconds to glance around and see who was within earshot.

There were a couple of medical techs, and Alicia was in her office... no one particularly close, but still Charlie didn't want to say the next part with any sort of volume. Taking a few steps up alongside Wes' bed, he folded his arms.

"He's as far gone as it appears?" he asked quietly.

"If it appears like he's completely broken from reality, then yes. I know what it's like, and it's an easy place to get comfortable. You decide the rules don't matter anymore and you start to enjoy things that you never should have enjoyed. You regret that later, in a certain way," Wes kept his tone equally low. "Even Andrea is starting to get it, at least a bit. It's clear that his rules have changed... and that's dangerous..."

"Especially because of this squadron," Charlie completed the thought. It was just as the Hawke Lord had imagined, and he took a deep breath before continuing, "Well, I don't know if anyone told you, but Karen isn't quite herself. Whatever Grant hit her with wiped out twelve years of memories. She's back to who she was when she took over *Lady Grace*."

Wes blinked, then looked right at Charlie, "Wait, what?"

"She's not the same woman who last stepped off this ship. We don't know if there's a cure to bring that woman back," our Lord Major confirmed, and Wes blinked again, then turned his eyes to look straight up at the ceiling as he contemplated the significance.

They'd both known Karen back then — she'd always struck them as resembling a caged animal, ready to strike at a moment's notice but reigned in by her relationship with me. Not necessarily the calming influence that was needed in a situation like this... and now motivated to find a cure for herself?

"So, do we have any idea how she's coping?" Wes asked the pertinent question, and Charlie sighed.

"As well as can be expected. The uncertainty is having a disproportionate affect on her, but she wants to find Grant, and a cure. And knowing her as she was... as she is... I expect that could be messy. I just hope putting the two of them back together encourages calm."

Wes frowned as he listened to Charlie's words, clearly detecting the skepticism behind them. He took a breath and then asked the question he didn't really want to ask: "You think that's the direction they're going to take?"

Charlie clenched his jaw and said nothing. He didn't want to answer. Because if it turned out that bringing Karen back didn't moderate the situation, both he and Wes might find themselves completely outgunned when we continued on our mission.

Taking Charlie's silence as an answer in itself, Wes groaned, "Shit. Can you please bring me a MAG-90 for my next duel? Maybe then I'll win..."

It was meant to be lighthearted, but under the circumstances neither of my good friends was ready to laugh. They had a lot to worry themselves about.

+++

Should they have worried? Well, if Charlie and Wes were now allies, perhaps Karen and I could be described that way too. After the initial wave of emotion that struck when she stepped into my cabin, she and I had both begun collecting ourselves, our brains functioning a bit better as we tried to express more than simple thoughts.

"They say it can never come back on its own. I mean, they could be wrong... but it looks like our only shot is to find Grant and get the antidote. And there might not be one, but I have to believe there is. And we have to find it so I'm not half of the person I'm supposed to be..." she was babbling a little as she sat on the end of my bed. I was sitting on the floor, back against the wall under my screen as I looked up at her.

She was obviously explaining the nature of her injury, and as I listened I was hit by a couple of reactions: I desperately wanted to get that cure, but at the same time I didn't want to sound as though it much mattered. If I'd come on too strong and said we'll find that antidote, no matter what, and one didn't exist, what would that leave her thinking? It might confirm her fears that I thought part of her was missing... that she was less than whole.

"Well, we'll see what Grant has to offer. It's probably part of his plan, come to think of it — make us chase him for the cure. The only way he can guarantee we won't just go home. But the antidote is secondary: the important part is you're back," my answer was clearly designed to be diplomatic, but however 'young' Karen's was, she could see through my attempts to handle her.

"Sounds like you want to help keep my hopes alive, without making me think I need those memories to satisfy you."

I stared at her for a second, and then the corners of my mouth twitched up into a smile, "Really? Is that what I'm doing?"

She shrugged, "I guess I was still anxious and insecure when you last saw me? Still needed to be coddled a little, to keep my blood pressure down?"

Those words were a test — a test of many things — and I found my eyes narrowing slightly, "You were someone who'd learned from experience that you didn't need to ask questions like that. But you probably still wished you could ask them now and then."

I almost felt like we were back in the alley... but it wasn't a bad feeling. Not bad at all. I could see the expression on Karen's face change... I could see a little lightness ease the furrow in her brow.

I was still me, and she still recognized that.

"So I quit trying? Doesn't sound like me."

"I wore you down. Broke you, really. Like a wild horse, I tamed you and made you civilized," was my answer.

I managed to keep a straight face for a half-dozen seconds after I said that last line, but then I started laughing — really, honestly laughing for the first time since I'd discovered that Karen was breathing again.

It was the old banter, like before — long before.

"Did I turn out to be a good ride?" was her answering question, and it came with a smile that could stop time. Her smile. The one from always.

"You did, actually. Can train an old horse to do anything..." I gasped between laughs, and she slid off the bed and down to the floor, giving me the most wonderful glare I've ever seen in my life.

"You keep going with this metaphor, I'm probably going to punch you."

I held up my hand as I struggled to breathe, and nodded a few times, "I know, I know. It's so perfect."

It was perfect. It was perfect because it was the break in the tension — the moment of honesty. The moment when Karen realized I was still the idiot I'd always been, and when I knew without a doubt she was the same woman I'd been welded to.

Would it be easy, saying things to her that she was supposed to know and realizing she didn't remember them? No. Would it be a challenge, trying to work with her when she lacked the experience she needed for her rank? Absolutely.

But could I sit on the floor of my cabin with her, and speak to her as though we were the closest of friends, because our relationship remained as tightly-woven as before? Yes.

That's a testament to who Karen McMaster had always been. And that was the reason why, no matter how many years she'd lost, Grant Merger was going to have a hell of a time winning.

He'd had his chance to shoot the old mare. Instead, she'd been saved from the glue factory and was galloping again...

Oh my God, Karen is going to kill me when she reads that paragraph. I'll have to finish this book as Zombie Ken Barron.

But finish it I will. And finish Grant? We'd find a way.

CHAPTER TWENTY-SIX

A HINT AT CONSEQUENCES

When I returned to *Wolf's* bridge (without Karen), there was a skip in my step, and I remember noticing how relieved people looked to see me. As I said before, they all knew Karen was alive — it wasn't a surprise that I was appearing to be more human. Hopefully this would mean no more awkward silences after my orders.

"How is she?" Andrea Kiley's question was flat, not quite reflecting the same pleasant emotions shared by her crew and her counterparts.

I smiled in answer, "Her *old* self. Long story. Right now we need to get this squadron out into the space lanes. Shelby, chart our course for Etat Valcour."

Striding up to the front of the bridge, I found the Battlelink screens were already active and took a quick scan of the faces of the Belt Squadron's elite skippers. It appeared everyone was in pretty good spirits... except for Rozy Young on *Nova Scotia*. She was still annoyed at me for shooting Wes and trying to wipe out Etat Lexington.

"We're going after Grant," I announced to them, then clapped my hands together in front of me a bit too enthusiastically. "We're *all* going after him."

"Thank God for that," Matt Baxter chimed in immediately.

"Will she be back on the bridge soon? We're all pretty fed up with you," Kris jabbed me pretty good with that one, and I grinned.

"Give her time. Some things to work out... but I'm still competent enough to get us started without her," I answered, sounding a little more like myself. The tension waned at last — tension I hadn't consciously been paying attention to, but which obviously had been there.

Boosting orders began when I fell silent — these were Belt Squadron veterans, so they hardly needed me to tell them how to prepare their ships for another run into the unknown. I'd say Grant had no idea what was about to turn up on his doorstep, but of course he did, because with the exception of *Nova Scotia*, these same ships had been responsible for his defeat at Deep Black.

It would be like déjà vu for him — if déjà vu had a sledge hammer and an inclination to hit you up side the head with it.

See look at that, my mood was even sufficiently bright for me to start using those sorts of metaphors again. Or similes. Whatever.

Anyway, all this positivity left just one more thing to do: we had to say our goodbyes to the President of the Solar Asteroid Union. Kohl and I obviously hadn't gotten off to the best start, but as you've no doubt noticed, that had happened while I thought Karen was dead. I'll admit, I might have handled my meeting with him better under different circumstances, so now I'd have to take steps to refocus our relationship.

"Felicia, can you call the *Maison Blanc* switchboard and ask for the President, please?" I put that question to *Wolf's* Sensors and Communications Officer with a smile and she nodded, then directed her staff to take the appropriate steps.

This time our call wasn't stopped at the switchboard; the *WolfNet* graphic popped up on the main screen almost as soon as the signal was received. Then the Oblong Office was revealed with Kohl sitting behind his desk, poorly shaven, and with DeBoer standing at his shoulder. Looking at the shot, I got the feeling that there were dozens of advisors just off camera — our little assault was probably the gravest threat the Union had ever faced, and all those smart people Kohl had surrounded himself with were probably explaining to him how hopeless the situation was.

"Admiral Barron, your attack on our warships was not warranted, but we are prepared to dismiss this entire situation as a… misunderstanding," Kohl said, and behind him DeBoer just managed to keep his wince from being too obvious.

For the first time I really paid attention to the fact that the Secretary of State seemed to have a better political instinct than the President: it was unwise, for instance, to open such an important conversation as this one with a declarative.

He had no idea why I was calling, after all. For him to make an offer without knowing what I was going to say… well, it was daft.

Fortunately, with Karen back, I was more sympathetic.

"You are a fool, Kohl. You're in no position to dismiss anything without me telling you to do so. This wasn't a misunderstanding, this was us being merciful, because good people up here convinced me not to kill all of you down there on your tiny little rock. But you know what, I'm reconsidering right now."

Wait. What was I saying about everything being back to normal?

I took a step closer to the screen, so I'd fill the viewfinder and thus loom larger before the President of the SAU: "We're leaving. We're going to go kill anyone who tries to protect your governor Madison. He has something that I need, and I'm going to find him and get it. If you send ships after us, we'll destroy them. And then we'll come back and kill you. And your family. Do you have children, Mister President?"

Kohl was staring at me, his nostrils flaring with barely-contained rage as I dared to speak to him so bluntly. He didn't answer, but that wasn't relevant.

"Well listen, let's assume you do. I want you to think about that, Mister Kohl. I want you to think about them, and how much you love them. Presuming you're the sort who actually loves them, and doesn't just appreciate them as good props in a photo op. I want you to think about what it was like the first time one of them really looked you in the eyes. Think about the time their tiny little hand closed around one of your fingers, and made you realize that whatever your faults, whatever your flaws, you'd created something wonderful. Your children, Kohl. The most important part of your life, the greatest gift you've ever been given. Think about them, and appreciate them. Because I'll cut their throats in front of you. And then I'll kill you, and every one of your people, freed or not, just to prove a point. Your ambitions out here are lovely, Mister President, but I am strong and you are of no consequence. Never forget that. And never try to make peace over a *misunderstanding* unless I give you permission to do so."

You could have heard a pin drop on *Wolf's* bridge. Looking back at the recordings of the Battlelink feed, Matt Baxter actually looks a bit pale.

Perhaps everyone had gotten their hopes up a little too soon. They didn't know it yet, but my rage had shifted… not disappeared. Now I had to go find Grant Merger… find him and cause him pain until he gave Karen her memories back. And if some President of the SAU thought he could get in my way, that notion had to be corrected.

Kohl's face was red — he was beyond speaking, and to me that was a sign that he wasn't very good as a President. You need to be able to think on your feet — or in his case, from his chair — when someone calls you out like that. But then what could he say?

Unsurprisingly, DeBoer had some idea: "Admiral Barron, I won't trouble you with moral statements of good and evil. I'm a practical man. You are stronger than us now, and there's no point denying it. But I hope you realize that your actions, your irresponsible anger today, has destroyed any chance of a positive relationship between your great state and us upstarts. We can't beat you today, but know that every waking moment in this Union will now be spent growing, building, striving to become the thing that breaks your Empire. And if you bother yourself with history, you will know that Empires do not last forever. We will be there at the end of yours. And it will be because of what happened today. What you did."

It was as good a comeback as anyone in the Union could have hoped to muster, but I was in no mood to lose the last word to some righteous politico from Etat Lexington.

One more step forward and I was filling the outbound feed completely, a smile fading from my face, "My dear Secretary of State, I know history better than you. Of course every Empire ends, and ours will one day. And maybe you will be there. Or maybe, like so many pipe dreams, your state will fly apart when its citizens realize it's largely defenseless. Time will tell. But you make it sound like my coming here will actually be a good thing… that it will help your people find purpose. So maybe you owe me, or maybe your indentured servants won't live up to your expectations. History doesn't do favors, you have to be smart. You have to work. And frankly, I don't know if you have it in you."

Kohl was completely out of it, but DeBoer was determined not to lose, so he came out around the President's desk for one last salvo: "When your Empire dies, you will be known as a foolish, petulant, self-absorbed monster responsible for the first cracks in its walls. History will remember you in infamy."

He was big on the history angle — something we might have had in common, had I not been predisposed to want to kill him and everyone he loved. Nevertheless, his words made me smile, "Mister DeBoer, you think people are going to have to wait until the Empire dies to start calling me a monster? I can get that title in six months or less. Just watch me."

I think that was the point where DeBoer realized there was no point continuing. He shook his head and turned away, then without any real parting words we ended our conversation. The link closed.

Obviously, someone taking so much delight in being a cold-blooded killer as I was warranted no debate. Breaking me out of old habits was not something a SAU politico could do under any circumstances, so DeBoer and Kohl and the rest had to simply be relieved that they weren't all dead.

And then, as the Secretary of State said, they had to begin preparing to compete with the Empire in the years ahead. There will be no cordial relations between us and them in my lifetime. That's my fault, and don't ever forget it when you read the headlines and wonder why they hate us so much. I acknowledge that there have been other contributing factors to our poor relations, and other people to blame on all sides… but I was one of the first catalysts. So blame me.

Anyway, when the screen blanked I took a great big breath and clapped my hands together again with a smile, "Excellent, so that's taken care of. We ready to cruise?"

My eyes turned to the other Battlelink screens, and again I failed to recognize the tension that had begun to wind back up.

Finally I took no reaction as a confirmation, and I nodded, "Excellent. Andrea, lead us out. Mark, if you could take last slot in line and keep an eye for chasers…"

I continued giving squadron orders, and eventually the familiar requirements of a cruise in contested space overcame the awkwardness. The Belt Squadron turned away from Etat Lexington, and aside from the crews on the SAUN ships we'd shot up, we'd left no dead bodies behind.

I was a little disappointed, but I knew we'd make up for it at Valcour. We were coming for Grant.

CHAPTER TWENTY-SEVEN
CONTINGENCIES

Charlie Peters found that *Wolf's* Special Branch armory looked a little different than it had back in 2233 — the last time he'd seen it during *The Mercury Assault*. There were more boxes of grenades lying around, clearly reflecting the preferences of his successor in the role of head Special Branch officer aboard… but that was to be expected.

It was undoubtedly a good thing, too — it was important for the Major in charge to put his or her stamp on a ship's Special Branch complement, and *Wolf* was now Rufus' ship, not Charlie's. Time marching on, and all that.

But Charlie hadn't come to the armory to remember his storied past on our fine frigate, and he hadn't come for a weapon either.

Rufus was sitting at one of the work benches in the middle of the armory, working on the grenade launcher slung under the barrel of his MAG-90. It didn't appear that our Chinese Major had noticed the arrival of our Hawke Lord Major, but of course he had — they're Branchers, for crying out loud.

"I cleaned out the Azure Horizon Community Centre for you. With prejudice," was Rufus' greeting, and while that might come out of left field for you, that place on Egesta had created lasting memories for these two.

Charlie nodded, "Thank you. I can't say I wish I'd been there."

"No one should wish to be there," Rufus agreed, continuing to fiddle with the launcher. "They put you back together alright?"

"Everything works, mostly," Charlie said as he stepped fully into the armory and closed the hatch behind him.

"And you got to spend a few months creating an excuse to end up the consort of Lady Hawke," Rufus said it flatly, but there was a hint of amusement under the words — if you knew what to listen for.

Charlie nodded, "Worked out for the best. Got to hear about all the good work you've been doing."

Finally looking up from his weapon, Rufus turned his mismatched eyes on his comrade from Mercury, "You miss it?"

For a second Charlie considered his answer. Then he grinned and shook his head, "Hell no. You kidding?"

Rufus actually smiled, then went back to work on his rifle, "I sort of was, yes. So you're probably up to date on what's happening out here?"

"I am. What's your read?"

"It's a mess. But so far he hasn't over-reached in any way that lost my vote. The kids on Concord was getting close to the edge, but he handled them alright in the end."

Rufus was, of course, commenting on me, and particularly on the way I was handling the situation. Taking a breath, Charlie moved over to one of the weapons racks and considered the row of MAG-90s standing there.

"What would happen if he started tipping over the edge?" my old friend asked, and Rufus shrugged slightly.

"I'll have to decide if I go with him," the Chinese Major answered.

It was a perfectly matter-of-fact reply, and Charlie wasn't surprised by it. Remember that together, these two had landed on Mercury, then fought for weeks until that explosion had wiped out their team. They could read each other pretty well.

Rufus knew what Charlie had come to ask, and Charlie was already starting to get a good sense of what the answer would be.

"You know if you try to stop him doing something, and he tells me to stop you from stopping him, it'll be a complicated moment," Rufus said, continuing to keep his mismatched eyes on his weapon.

The implications there were extensive — he was speaking about the possibility, however remote it seemed, that Charlie would try to intervene if I sought to do something horrific... and that I'd tell Rufus to stop Charlie, since I knew I'd have little hope of success if I were to try to stop him myself.

Imagine that. Two of the best Branchers ever to serve, suddenly set against each other because I was a petulant bastard looking to cause unjust harm. I've heard of no-win scenarios before, but that term hardly seems equal to such a situation.

It's important to note that Rufus wasn't saying he'd win such a duel — he said it would be complicated, and he meant it. Charlie was similarly unwilling to declare a victor, because both Branchers knew that they'd win, but that they could lose.

And that either way, they never wanted to find out.

But to answer one of my editor's questions, they couldn't actually promise each other that the time would never come — that they wouldn't put themselves in a position to be at odds. They were like two freight trains, running towards each other on converging rails and hoping the tracks weren't going to cross at an inopportune moment.

"Maybe we can work together, if the time comes, to keep things in hand," Charlie suggested absently, continuing to study the rack of MAG-90s.

"I hope that's exactly what we can do," Rufus agreed.

There was no animosity, no feeling of foreboding here. These two were simply too pragmatic... they understood that they'd be in the thick of whatever came when we got to Valcour, and it was impossible to fully predict the outcomes.

I suppose all of this tense and ambiguous dialogue makes for an unsatisfying chapter, but it was vitally important to them, and ultimately, to Karen and me. They both knew they might be able to change the course of what was to come, but it was impossible to foresee how things would unfold, and who I would have to overcome.

Too many contingencies, too many possible disasters.

Charlie and Rufus were together again, for better or worse.

CHAPTER TWENTY-EIGHT

THE OLD PEACE

I remember the day in September of 2222, when Karen got *Lady Grace*, and not just because it was the same day I got *Friendly*. It came after a rather active couple of months — Greg Noyce had detached us from *Alberta* to do special operations against a group of pirates known as the Rock Breakers. They hadn't lasted too long once Karen and I were on the case. We tracked them to Belt Seven, figured out where their leaders were hiding, and had gone in hard.

Lieutenant Charlie Peters had been with us when we did that raid, and Lieutenant Commander Wes Pellew had commanded the fighter patrol that kept the last of the Breakers from escaping by shuttle when we shot up their bordello.

A good operation, and for two Lieutenant Commanders it had meant promotion. New corvettes were coming out to join the Belt Squadron — the first of a new generation of warships which promised to make the job of chasing pirates that much easier. Greg wanted them in the hands of good young officers… he had good corvette Commanders in the Belt Squadron at that time, but they were different types of people.

Karen and I had followed the Daragh Ryan path to notoriety, and the pirates had no idea how to cope with us. So Greg brought us both into his office, then slid two folders across the table.

"My only regret," he said, "is that I have to split the two of you up."

Because the new corvettes couldn't hang together all the time — at least not at first. Once more of the *Noble*-class ships reached the Belt it might be possible for us to operate in tandem more regularly, but until that time Greg had to send us in different directions, to fly the flag in different parts of the Belt territory.

So Karen and *Lady Grace* were dispatched to the Coalition of Unaligned Asteroids, a group of miscellaneous free rocks that had banded together around the time the Hawke Protectorate had formed, and since then had been governing themselves in a haphazard manner. Theirs was a state built on mutual defense more than anything else — pirates could pick apart any single rock, but together these colonies had enough force to be a somewhat daunting opponent.

We liked the Coalition — both personally, and in diplomatic terms — so the decision was taken to send one of our newest corvettes out that way, to hunt a few pirates in their space and hopefully increase security for that plucky and determined ally.

Meanwhile, the Hawke Protectorate was going through a 'Naval renewal' — meaning Ian Hawke had finally decided that he did actually need to update the cruisers he'd kept in service with the Hawke Fleet. If he didn't, the pirates — who were increasingly moving towards his part of the Belt — would be able to do great harm.

So *Friendly* was going to see Ian, the first visit of several we'd make while the new Hawke Fleet was being brought online. Any pirates who sought to take advantage of the renewal would need to be reminded that the Protectorate was a close ally of the Empire, and Defense Command looked after its friends.

After we read our missions in our respective folders, and thanked Greg profusely for deciding to give us this chance to take command and go out into the Belt unsupervised, we'd left Greg's office and gone out for a celebratory dinner. No one cared — there were no cameras chasing us or fans coming up to our table. We just enjoyed our time together, and talked about all the crazy things we could get up to, and what it would mean.

The next morning, we'd packed our luggage and stepped off *Alberta* for the last time as crew, then spent the next few weeks in quarters on Belt Two base, choosing crews and getting our plans together. When September arrived and we went to Earth to collect *Lady Grace* and *Friendly* fresh from the Naval shipyards, we toured our two ships together.

It was a giddy time, and we were young and carefree enough to simply enjoy it. We didn't brood over the promise of being apart, because frankly we had no concept of what that was going to be like. We figured we'd see enough of each other, and that we'd have many stories to tell when we were together again.

We assembled the best crews in the fleet. You know mine pretty well by now: I had Kris Jacobs for my XO, Jim Hannigan at Sensors and Communications, Erica Martin at Helm and Navigation, Andrew Jenson for an engineer, Alicia Morgan running my med bay, and Matt Baxter himself as security chief.

And, of course, I had Charlie Peters — promoted to Captain after the Rock Breaker raid — running half a squad of Special Branch, including officers like Carly Henderson.

With people like that coming together on an elite new ship, you can probably understand how the enthusiasm fought off any anxieties. Confidence — sometimes arrogance — crept in.

But deep down, both Karen and I were mindful of one important fact: we'd be running our own shows, neither one of us chaperoning the other. We'd come a long way from the alley, and neither of us expected this would be a problem… but nevertheless, it would be a new challenge.

I remember that truth being in both our minds as we watched our shuttles land side-by-side in the Luna shipyard's main landing bay. Erica Martin had put *Friendly's* craft down on the left, and Helm and Navigation Officer Howard Purcell had landed *Lady Grace's* on the right. We watched them both as the space doors closed behind them, and then looked at each other with smiles that held back sighs.

"So, we're going to have fun, right?" Karen asked me.

I shrugged, "I hope so?"

She chuckled at that, and then reached out and hugged me. Because back then we could do such things without causing a media firestorm. I didn't need any convincing to put my arms around her in return, "Go destroy a lot of pirates. I hear the Coalition folks like entertaining kills."

Karen chuckled and squeezed me a little tighter, "And what if I like entertaining kills too much?"

"Make sure it's all legal, then get it on camera," I answered, squeezing her back.

Karen tells me she closed her eyes at this point, "I hear Hawke has a bitch of a daughter. Be careful she doesn't try to get into your bed."

Oh ha, how little we knew about Lia back then.

"You're not the only one who likes an entertaining kill," was my answer, and that was comforting to her — to both of us.

We continued our embrace for another moment, then gradually pried ourselves apart. Karen pulled her ponytail up onto her left shoulder, then crouched to pick up her travel case. I picked up my case as well, then we opened the hatch and headed out onto the landing bay, walking side by side as we stared at the shining new shuttles that had come to take us to our gallant futures.

Eventually we came to the place on the deck where we had to turn away from each other — me to the left, her to the right. We both stopped, and then we traded one long glance. To me, Karen's eyes said 'I think we've made it'.

To her, my eyes said 'I'm proud of you'.

Which makes no sense, because I had no business being any more proud of her than she was of me. But even if I had no right to be proud, I was in that moment.

Then we both took deep breaths and marched to our ships. Up the ramps, hatches closed, and out we went — cruising off to a future that was full of adventure, excitement, and saving the Empire a few times. So many possibilities... and I know now that despite some bad times, we absolutely got to live the lives we'd hoped for.

We'd become the people we'd been determined to become, we'd left behind our anger and our petulance and were forged into fine fleet officers. Karen especially.

I remember that, but as I watched Karen sleeping soundly on my bed, her brow creased by a frown brought on by a dream, I knew she didn't remember it.

We had been the best team in the history of Defense Command, and now we were both damaged. Thanks to Grant Merger. If he wanted us to leave a trail of wreckage as we chased him and his antidote, he was going to get his wish.

A long road lay ahead of us, but as I watched Karen continue to sleep I decided not to worry too much about it. She was sleeping uncomfortably, so I moved to sit beside her, then found her hand with mine. As our hands touched, she seemed to recognize me without waking. Her fingers laced through mine and she pulled my hand in close to her body. She held on for dear life.

Because as she slept, she was having a vivid dream — one about as strange as those I'd been having during the weeks of this mission.

She'd been sitting in the cockpit of the shuttle that was meant to take her to *Lady Grace*, but instead the craft was chasing my shuttle bound for *Friendly*. She knew she had to catch up to me... had to get back into step alongside me, but Erica Martin was flying too fast.

We flew past *Friendly*, and past *Wolf*, and we just kept going, and no matter how much she prodded her shuttle's engines, she couldn't seem to catch up.

She was stuck behind, and alone except for the shuttle pilot.

"What am I supposed to do? I can't catch up. He's ahead of me and he can't come back," she said, looking at the officer in the left seat.

This is where an otherwise straightforward dream takes a left turn, because Howard Purcell wasn't in that seat. Instead, it was the creepy personification of *Wolf* that I kept seeing in my dreams — the one that looked like a humanoid wolf in a uniform.

Now he cocked an eyebrow at Karen, and his ear twitched, "The whole metaphor of this dream is wrong. He's not ahead of you, he's holding your hand. You're not dead, you're with him. And while I know this dream is supposed to be about you finding your confidence, trust me when I tell you he needs you more than you need him. It will hurt, it will be confusing, and it will exhaust you, but don't stop. In the end, you'll have more than you ever did before."

And then, of course, she woke up. By the time she did I was asleep, fortunately not receiving the counsel of my ship, but Karen was not about to let a dream like that one go unshared. She prodded me awake, and I straightened up in surprise, "Everything was white."

No idea why I blurted that out, but Karen pulled on my hand to bring me back, "I just dreamt about a wolf."

I blinked a few times and then frowned, "Was he in uniform, and giving sage advice?"

Karen nodded, and then frowned, "You too?"

I sighed, "I think this ship has a soul. And a desire to do one of those self-help shows you see on TV."

It was meant to be amusing, and I suppose it was, but Karen was too disconcerted for humor. Her hand remained linked with mine, and then she reached up and put her other hand on my shoulder.

She didn't say anything, just seemed to be trying to get a grip — as if she wanted to make certain I couldn't go anywhere.

Detecting this, I spoke up, "You... just making sure I'm not an apparition?"

She stopped, then shook her head, "If I had any idea what I was doing right now, I don't know what I'd be doing."

It was a fair assessment of the situation. We were both, and pardon me for saying this, somewhat fucked in the head. Only way to explain it. But as she settled down and realized she'd been sleeping on my bed, we started to find our wits again.

There's no real easy closure to this chapter, then. The disconcerting feeling didn't end, and we didn't magically find peace. We just knew that, like our ship said, we were together and not dead.

We were bound for Etat Valcour, to find Karen's memories — the memories of angels, to invoke the book title (even though Karen should just be a single angel, singular) — and to kill anyone who stopped us getting them.

Stay tuned.

AFTERWORD

I've struggled with this book for many, many reasons. It's not the part about admitting my complicity in the many horrible actions that took place during the mission to the SAU — I'm obviously willing to shoulder all of the blame when it comes to our sour relations with those presumptuous upstarts. No, my reluctance has more to do with my attempts to come to grips with what Karen and I were both feeling.

Because I have to say, it wasn't rational, and the more I try to make sense of it as I tell you what happened, the less I can. What sort of man shoots his friend, and threatens to wipe out an asteroid of civilians? Me. But what about Karen coming back, shouldn't that help? Maybe. But it's none too clear, even now looking back, and I wish it was.

Some things just don't make sense. Dreams especially — apparently they're even contagious.

Anyway, you know what comes next: we're going to hit Etat Valcour with a sledge hammer, and Grant Merger is going to hit back as hard as he can. And the villain can hit.

The question is, who between the three of us is the meanest?

The sad thing: particularly in 2235, we might all have eagerly competed to win the title.

See you next time.

ACTS
OF
WAR

THE AUTOBIOGRAPHICAL REMINISCENCES OF
ADMIRAL THE LORD KEN BARRON FOR 2235

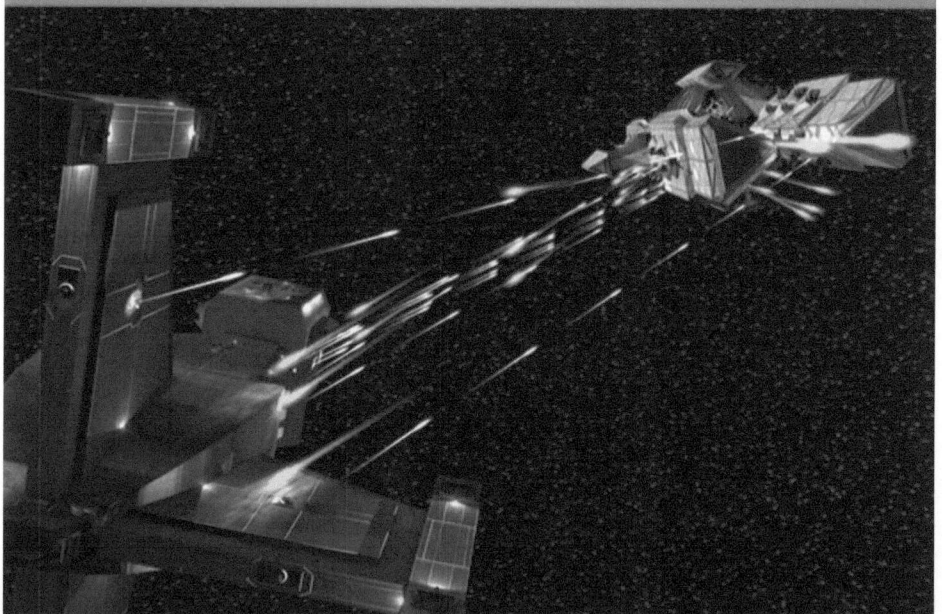

THE MARTIAN WAR - 19

KENNETH TAM

FROM THE AUTHOR

One-sided warfare might seem to some like an artifact from the days of gunboat diplomacy I talked about while introducing *Memories Of Angels*. However, I'd have to suggest that we today see far more examples of one-sided fighting than the great powers ever did during the height of their Age of Empire; consider how often the United States, or more broadly NATO, can take part in a massive campaign and inflict hundreds of casualties while suffering relatively few losses.

The recent wars in Iraq and Afghanistan have of course been bloody for every country participating, but recall the air campaigns waged in places like Libya. While I would never call the job of combat pilots easy, I believe it's fair to point out that their technological advantage gives them a comparative level of safety.

As science evolves our top-of-the-line weapons further and further, I suspect this trend will continue... at least until a conflict occurs where our highly-evolved weapons clash with similarly highly-evolved weapons. That will not be a kind day to anyone, and I rather hope it waits a few centuries to arrive.

Anyway, I make this point because I possess a dread curiosity about what a one-sided defeat feels like to those on the losing end. After building up their strength to such a high level, controlling their own affairs and perhaps even dominating their region, how must the elite warriors feel when rendered instantly irrelevant?

For the Earth Empire to learn the answer to that question, I suppose aliens would have to invade their solar system. Don't hold your breath.

But the Union is learning the lesson now... or at least they were. Because in the midst of such hopeless events, heroes can sometimes emerge. What if a man appeared who, like Churchill in 1939 and 1940, was determined to stand against the seemingly unstoppable tide of an enemy more powerful than any other seen in history? What if that man, unlike Churchill, had advanced notice, and was able to rally special resources to defeat that force?

What if, in fact, it had been that man's plan all along to draw old friends into a fight, and defeat them?

I suppose that man might come to wield a lot of influence among his adopted people. We might soon see how much influence... but first, my thanks.

As ever, to my friends who have provided the identities for so many of these characters, I am indebted. I hope they do you proud.

A special thanks too to Charles Chiang, because Rufus' mad plan owes him a lot. Of course Peter Caron remains my best friend and advisor, and Wes Prewer's countless contributions have made 2235 look better than any other year. Gentlemen: I'm grateful.

In our tenth year as Iceberg Publishing, I must continue to acknowledge my parents and partners, Jacqui and Peter. They are simply the most excellent people. As is Atlas, old friend.

– Kenneth Tam

Preface

When you get to flag rank, you're supposed to have some sense of responsibility, and proportionality. I know I've never been a poster child for maturity… for not doing stupid stuff, as Matt calls it… but I think through the war, and even before, I'd done reasonably well in maintaining an even keel.

Obviously, that didn't continue into 2235. My editors have kindly pointed out that I wasn't too outrageous in my actions. To quote one of them: "You'll still come off as the hero."

Right. Because that's how I should be judged: if [insert your favorite action movie star here] did what I was doing after having [insert unspeakable crime here] happen to his [insert important loved one here], I'd totally be the hero of an adrenaline-packed thrill ride sure to bring the audiences out next summer.

Socrates quakes before that sort of moral compass.

I'm very glad that, up until the events of this book, I'd confined my killing to those in the SAU Navy uniform, and to two assassins who had both directly been involved in Karen's poisoning. I'm glad that, for all my snarling and frothing at the mouth, I'd only managed to shoot one friend, and that he was expected to recover.

I'm glad that it wasn't worse.

But this is a book where, let's not kid ourselves, I more or less launch a war against an entire state for largely personal reasons. History has let me off the hook for this so far, and I continue to be baffled as to why. Maybe people who haven't nearly plunged the Empire into total war for the second time in a decade don't have the same perspective on it as I do.

What I did was not in keeping with the expected character of a flag officer. It was necessary, and it was brutal, but it wasn't the way an Admiral of Defense Command should operate.

I was wrong.

But — and don't mistake me on this — I have no regrets. Because the one man in the universe worth that much anger was my target. I would have launched an attack on his stupid rock by myself, if Daragh hadn't sent a squadron with me. I would have done all that you're about to read as a true rogue — not the plucky kind from *The Rogue Commodore* — if that had been the only way to manage it.

Grant Merger made a severe miscalculation when he attacked Karen and Mel Samuels at the new Emperor's ball, though: he'd set off Earth's new Irish Emperor, and in turn, I'd been granted more than enough resources to make Solar Asteroid Union weep for a decade.

This book is the story of the last great action into which I ever led the Belt Squadron. And the story of why, to this day, the SAU is not our friend.

Here we go.

CHAPTER ONE
CHESS

It may surprise you to learn that I'm a terrible chess player. I know that for a lot of people the game is considered the ultimate test of a person's strategic abilities, but I'm terrible at it. The only time I win is by accident, and for a number of years that really bothered me.

Why was everyone else so much better than me? Was I really so incompetent?

Well, I might say yes to that last question, but then I'd get yelled at for being self-deprecating. I did do *some* things sensibly to get to the rank of Rear Admiral... winning chess tournaments just wasn't one of them. As an old friend of mine could testify.

"Check in four moves."

I looked up from my white pieces — all six of them that remained on the board — and saw Grant smiling at me from across the table. We were playing an after-hours game in one of the Academy's student lounges, while Karen was sitting through a class on something... math, maybe. I don't remember.

Bottom line was we were playing chess, and he had twice as many pieces as I did left on the board.

"Sounds about right," was my answer to Grant's pledge of my certain defeat, and he shook his head slightly.

"Always assume you're just going to lose when you play me, do you?"

"I assume I'm going to lose whenever I play anyone," I shrugged back. "This isn't my game."

"Quitter talk."

At this point he made my last surviving rook — the castle-looking thing — vanish. His bishop was a real bastard, and I could never figure out how precisely Grant managed to make the piece so deadly.

"It's realism," I answered as I moved my queen to threaten the offending black piece, and Grant chuckled and sat back.

"No... just look at this board. Stop for a moment and look. Tell me what my next move has to be. Everything I can do, you can see. There's no hiding in chess."

He wasn't wrong. I think that's why so many people love the game as much as they do: it's a fair and upfront test of your ability to do battle by an agreed-upon set of rules. No one has a special advantage... neither white nor black pieces are somehow superior. It's pure strategy, and it separates the posers from the planners.

Proving this point, I sat back in my own seat and looked from Grant's bishop to his queen, then scanned the different avenues each piece might take. My own king was woefully unprotected — two pawns were staggered in front of him, like human shields in front of a shoulder laser. They knew the rain was coming. Pawns always do.

"Queen will move... here...?" I pointed to a square that would allow the black piece to threaten my esteemed monarch, but knew I was probably wrong.

And I was wrong. Grant looked a bit exasperated as he shook his head, as if he were trying to educate a hopelessly ignorant friend about one of the simplest concepts in life. Deciding it would be easier to show me than explain himself, he reached out and lifted one of his knights, then moved it into attack position.

"Check."

Of course it was check; the knight and its L-shaped assault vector put my king in direct danger… and at the same time put my queen in danger. I'd moved my queen to threaten his bishop, just as he'd known I would, and now I had no choice but to lose her.

Go ahead and make your own metaphorical connections there if you like.

"You have to see the moves before they happen. That's all this is… all it will ever be. You move your pieces around into the places you need them to be to do what you need them to do. To beat the pirates, or anyone else, you simply need to break things down this way."

As Grant offered that advice, I shrugged again, then moved my king aside so he'd avoid instant death. Not that he'd last much longer.

Taking my queen with his knight, Grant continued his coaching, "You have to see the plans inside the plans, too. I know they talk about all sorts of different strategies in our lectures, but it all comes back to these fundamentals. Master this game and you'll never lose."

He was speaking with the sort of certainty only the young and clever can muster — the knowledge of theory, and the confidence that theory can apply to whatever real-world circumstance you care to name.

In retrospect, maybe it wasn't all hubris. Consider all the damage Grant did after he left us… his plans and stratagems, moving us all around like pieces on his cosmic chess board. My friend was a genius — I knew that when we played chess, and I knew it when I chased him through the solar system.

But I didn't think his theory was completely accurate.

"What would you have done if my queen took your knight down with her?" I asked, eyes narrowing thoughtfully.

Grant was moving his queen to attack position as I asked the question, so there was a pause before he looked up and answered.

"How do you mean?"

I shrugged, "I'm not trying to argue with you. I know what you're saying is right, but my question is what'd happen if these pieces had the chance to be like people? To surprise you? What if the queen was a ship, skippered by you or me, and they told us that the knight coming in was going to defeat us — we had no say in the matter, it was just going to defeat us. Think we wouldn't try to find a way to prove them wrong?"

In the real world, I figured, people had the power to surprise — to defy the rules and to change the fate of empires. Grant listened to me, his own expression growing as thoughtful as mine. Then he shook his head.

"There are always exceptional cases… and you can have contingencies for those. But I don't think it's wise to plan on people being that good. I mean… look at the people we know. How many of the cadets in this place are really that capable?"

His question tugged at the sense of complete superiority both he and I felt over the vast majority of our fellow students. These young people were sometimes well-meaning, often not, and always inferior to us in terms of understanding and ability to execute.

Who among them could change the odds?

"If we're leading them, they can be that good."

Looking back, I think I'm surprised that I managed to come to that answer — surprised that I didn't just agree and start slagging our fellow cadets. My answer drew a frown to his brow.

"You really think that, don't you? Ultimately you think you can find the best people, and use them to tip the board in your favor."

I did think that. I thought it back then, and as it turns out, I lived it.

"Well let me tell you… no matter how good the people are, they have to live within the plans that are laid out for them. And if you can't plan properly… if you can't put them in the right place, at the right time, you'll just get them killed."

Though our game wasn't quite over, he started to reset the board. He didn't explain himself, but expecting that he was trying to make a point, I assisted. After a moment we were playing again, and within six moves he had his queen bearing down on my king.

"Checkmate," he said at that juncture. Most of my pieces were still trapped on the squares they'd begun the game on, helpless to intervene.

That seemed to be Grant's point, and he waved his hand towards them, "No matter who crews those ships, they can't help your flag now. So what's the outcome?"

I considered the situation for a moment, folding my arms, "I lose."

Grant began to nod at my concession… but I didn't give him much time.

"Or my king proves that flagships do have teeth."

"You can't change the rules…" Grant protested.

"Or maybe I could plant someone on your queen. Someone to disable her so we can get the upper hand."

By now Grant had flopped back in his chair, shaking his head with a sad smile, "Maybe, sure. If you're thinking and planning that far ahead, then you can have more intricate rules like those. But just be sure you're not waiting until the last minute, then saying 'oh I wish we had set this up before.'"

His was a prudent warning — relying on luck to bring you victory was a risky proposition. For him, every duel, no matter the scope or scale, was fought within a framework of rules — it was a puzzle that had a solution. He just needed to understand the intricacies of the system and then develop his answer.

"Guess we'll see when we're out there," was my cop-out of an answer to his lecture, and he gave up with a sigh.

He knew — truly knew — that he was a better strategist than me. He knew that one day I'd learn my lesson, perhaps the hard way. And I knew he was probably right.

But I also had a feeling that good people, brought together into the right sort of community, for the right sort of purpose, could make their own luck. Grant and I had competing systems of leadership and strategy, and perhaps they were both correct.

What neither of us knew as we reset the chess board… or at least I assume he didn't know… was that we'd be testing our theories against each other in a deadly way, both during the Syndicate years, and in 2235.

Time to see who wins — and whether victory means anything.

Chapter Two

Commander Karen McMaster

Walking through the corridors of *Wolf* was not a comfortable experience for Karen. There was no question that the people aboard our fine ship were welcoming her back with open arms and bright smiles — no one was unhappy to see her, and given all we'd been through together, I suppose that shouldn't come as a surprise.

But everyone also knew that Karen couldn't remember anything about *Wolf*, or most of its crew. Her plight had been explained to the skippers of the Belt Squadron, and our own ship's senior staff, and though there'd been no formal announcement to all hands, word spread fairly quickly after our departure from Etat Lexington.

It was important that everyone realized she wasn't going to be able to pick up conversations she had begun before her departure… that if they spotted her looking for directions to one part of the ship or another, they should just offer guidance without asking questions, generally be a supportive network for her, make sure she came to no harm.

There was a little bit of a double-edged sword in this additional care, though.

Karen wants me to explain this carefully, because it's not that she didn't appreciate everyone helping her. She did. And she was certainly grateful for the subtle way that assistance was coming — without anyone treating her like an oddity. But the fact that they were helping with a smile, instead of resenting the fact that she was basically wasting their oxygen (her expression) was somewhat uncomfortable.

She was supposed to be contributing, but she wasn't able to do much more than be a mascot, and that wasn't exactly a satisfying feeling for someone who set high expectations for herself, and never wanted others to see her at less than her best.

As she paced through *Wolf's* corridors, then, Karen did everything she could to keep a polite smile on her face. Sometimes she'd trade a few pleasant words with passers-by, and as much as she could, she tried to keep herself from looking confused.

It wasn't easy.

The most embarrassing moment came on the rec deck. She didn't ever remember seeing such a deck on a warship before — a whole level dedicated to crew recreation, with fitness facilities, cinemas, clubs for officers and enlisted, a dance floor… it was all there on one deck, and though she recalled vaguely hearing a designer speak of how all this would be a feature on the new *Predator*-class ships, she had a tough time believing it was real.

And navigating it.

She spent twenty minutes standing outside the swimming pool, wondering how to get back to the lift that would take her back to the rest of the ship. She'd gotten turned around going through the corridors, and didn't want to ask anyone how to make her way… so she stood and watched the pool, as if deep in contemplation about something, so that no one asked her if she needed help.

All she could think about during those long minutes was how lost she was… in every sense of the word. She was concerned she'd never be able to find her way around a new warship… that unless Grant had a cure, she'd be so far behind everyone else that she might as well just quit the Navy.

Irrational fears, of course — obviously Commander Karen McMaster, with all the talents she possessed, could forge herself into a leading combat officer at will. She just had to try.

But trying was hard. In moments when she couldn't find her way around her own ship, it even seemed impossible. And while I know there are many motivational speakers, and life coaches, and armchair philosophers who might get up to podiums and talk about accentuating the positive (or whatever), I won't listen to any of them unless they've experienced what it is to lose so much.

If Karen wanted to collapse into the odd bout of hopelessness, that was her right. She'd earned it because what she'd been robbed of was more valuable than just about anything else I can imagine.

Of course, having said that, I wasn't exactly going to *recommend* hopelessness under these circumstances.

"We swam the morning before the attack. It was very early, and I was grumpy."

Karen hadn't noticed me come up behind her. Now she looked back at me and I could see her chin sinking at the mention of something else she didn't remember, "I can swim?"

I shook my head, "Not really. You did a little, but mostly you just sank and coughed."

Making an effort to smile at that mostly-flippant comment, Karen looked back to the pool, "Some things haven't changed. Good to know."

Yes, that was a loaded reply.

I opened my mouth to start listing all the things that were indeed the same… but then I over-thought that perfectly logical reaction. Would listing all the things that hadn't changed just emphasize those that had changed… or call too much attention to the fact that she was looking for things that were the same, just to provide comfort… or… or…?

As you can tell, I'd be a shit counselor. This goes hand in hand with being the guy who doesn't know how to say comforting things when someone is in pain, or mourning… I spend too much time worrying about making certain I don't say something wrong, and then end up saying nothing.

So I stared at the side of Karen's face, watching the way the corners of her mouth seemed to tug down very slightly, and the way her jaw shuddered as it clenched. I did need to say *something*… but how could I broach the subject of memory without making it too overt?

What was the same… what had she cared about that was still on this ship?

I set my brain to work, and while we stood there in silence I came up with a couple of ideas. The first one seemed the best, so I went with it.

Reaching out, I closed my hand around Karen's forearm, drawing her to look at me. With a nod, I indicated the direction of the lift, "Let me show you something. Just one thing."

Karen blinked, then agreed, "Okay. I don't have anywhere else to be."

We left the rec deck.

+++

I suppose if you only know Karen and me from reading the books of this Martian War series, you won't realize quite how much flying used to mean to us. It was a love that we both found in our early years at the Academy, and that stayed with us for the first decade of our careers... up until we were seduced by the responsibility of warship command.

If you think about it, that probably makes sense: we graduated from having control of a single-seat ship to having control of a ship staffed with people... but in both cases, we had control.

Going back to our planes had always been a joy after we'd made the switch — you've seen how badly we could behave when we got into our Starlights, and maybe that's given you some hint of our earlier loves... but if it hasn't, then take my word for it: before she bonded with *Lady Grace*, one of the happiest places Karen could be was in the cockpit of her plane.

Her F-194 Starlight, in fact.

That's right, we'd come out of the Academy flying F-184 Starbursts, but when we joined *Alberta* and started hunting pirates, we were some of the first pilot officers in Defense Command to get the shiny new F-194s... the best fighter craft ever built. Twelve years later the Starlight still held that title, and *Wolf* had two squadrons embarked.

Including Karen's plane.

Watching her walk underneath the smooth-framed Starlight, I felt my heart rate pick up very slightly. The deck was alive with various bits of maintenance — we all knew we were cruising into action, so Adrienne Thompson had the deck crews prepping all of her planes to combat whatever Grant had in mind. But as I watched Karen, it was all in the background, just like in those movies where the music is about to kick in for an emotional crescendo.

I was close to hearing those violins because as she walked under her plane, and looked up and ran her open hand over its cool alloy hull, I saw her smile again.

This was obviously not the cure-all to her concerns — she was still missing twelve years of memories — but it was respite. Here was one thing that she knew... knew very well, in fact... and she was glad to see it.

"How many upgrades since our time?" she asked me without peeling her eyes away from her ship, and I smiled at her choice of words — 'our' time.

"Not many. I'm sure they've been tinkering with the flight control software... yes, actually, they did correct that over-boost thing we were... we're used to compensating for. But otherwise, still flies the same," I replied, and she simply nodded.

"Knew they'd be the best," she sounded proud, because she loved her Starlights.

She walked around for a few more minutes, looking in various openings and compartments to make sure everything was as it should be. After that she drifted back to me, her eyes traveling the length of the flight bay as she watched each craft in the squadron being serviced, "Guess we really don't need carriers with frigates loaded like this."

"Nope," I confirmed. "Concept proved... the *Bonnies* were a better use of our resources."

With a nod she turned back to look at her plane, then folded her arms, "Well you know I'm going to have to take mine out at some point. If nothing else, I'm still a pilot. A decent one too."

Confidence was trickling back into her voice, and I shrugged, "I don't see any reason not to let you out. But just promise you won't scare the shit out of the new pilots when you do. This latest generation didn't train the same way we did."

Karen frowned again — but this time out of interest instead of concern, "Really?"

"Yeah," I smiled. "John changed the training regulations because people were trying to one-up us, and they never managed to. Caused some serious crashes over Antarctica."

"Oof," Karen's smile came back, and I matched it because it was so good to see her warmth resurface. We both knew this particular boost in morale would probably be fleeting, but it didn't matter: we'd hold onto it for as long as was reasonable, and then deal with the next low point when it came.

At least we could console ourselves with the fact that answers would come soon. We were just a day-and-a-half away from Valcour, and Grant.

"I've scheduled a planning meeting for the attack," I eventually used that thought to drag me back to my reason for seeking out Karen in the first place. "Come sit in, will you?"

She looked from her plane to me again, and as our gazes crossed I could see a flash of uncertainty in her eyes. A planning session, presumably with the Captains she had once commanded…

"Alright," was her answer, and she ironed any anxiety out as she said it. "And can you please lead the way. Because I don't want to get lost again."

She had to fight for it, but she was in control.

Because even as a Commander, Karen McMaster was still a goddess. No matter what Grant believed — no matter how well he planned — he wouldn't be ready for her.

We hoped…

Chapter Three

State Of Emergency

"My fellow citizens of Valcour, the time we had most feared is upon us. The Earth Empire has just finished sacking Etat Lexington, defeating the defensive squadron there. We now find ourselves in their sights, and while I have summoned ships personally loyal to me for our defense, it is vital that we all prepare for the struggle ahead."

Grant Merger — or Governor George Madison, if you like — had developed a real knack for giving speeches. As his face was flashed up on every screen in the SAU colony he'd appropriated for himself, he wore a grave expression, and borrowed his cadence at least partially from Churchill.

"But we must not waver," he said, reading from a speech he had written himself. "I have faced the Empire before... faced them with much less than we have here... faced many more of their forces than they have sent. We can withstand them. There are nearly one million of us in this colony. Hearty men and women — citizens, freed men and indentured servants alike. If we all work together now... if we all struggle... we can stop the Empire. And if we do that... if we turn them back... then the message will be unmistakable. The Black Sun does not reign here. We make our own fate."

Oh yes, raise that oratory to the stars my friend. Make your people think they can win. Let's be honest, it's a little bit cute. Though I disapprove of the term 'freed men' — are women not allowed to be free as well?

I know, I'm being petulant. But come on, it's Grant. I'm allowed.

"Pay close attention to the instructions that will be broadcast on this channel by our civil defense wardens. If you wish to volunteer for service in the citizens guard, or the freed guard, you may report to the rally centers in Twain Stadium. And I ask all holders of indentured servants to consider offering time off their service, should they wish to join our militia reserve. Above all, first and foremost, we must work together — be true to each other. And we will prevail. Good day, citizens of Etat Valcour. You are mighty, and I am proud to be among you."

Slow. Clap.

You tell them, Grant. You sound profound. Good job.

Yes, that probably would have been a good speech, had it been given by someone else in a completely different context. But because I'm a jerk, let me fill in what happened next — after the camera's red light switched off.

Grant turned away from the viewfinder and first looked to Sonia Hart, who gave him a smile and a nod, then locked his gaze onto his top security advisor, Fletcher Karadzic, "Any of the wealthy notables getting out of line?"

"A few. We're picking up their children as collateral," the man who'd driven Julie Pichot into the spy killer's arms replied, and Grant nodded his approval. It was good when your subordinates could predict your wishes, and carry them out unprompted.

As the camera crew packed up and left Grant's office, the Governor folded his arms and moved to sit on the front edge of his desk, "When we get enrollment numbers for the civil guard units, let me know. They probably won't factor at all into the defense, but we might be able to use them to worry Ken when he gets here."

He was referring to the three different units he'd just suggested people join — the citizens guard, the freed guard, and the militia, which were formations made up of self-armed volunteers. They could all contribute to the defense of the Valcour main dome — ValDome, as Grant liked to call it.

Of course, he knew their contributions might amount to nothing more than service as cannon fodder. Even a thousand such volunteers wouldn't last ten minutes against a squad of Special Branchers who'd been let off the leash... hundreds would die in moments of hot fire, and the rest would flee. They were volunteer militias, that was all they were capable of.

But if they distracted our landing forces from his actual defensive garrison, that would be useful. Because while Grant was confident in the 7,300-man (almost exclusively male, by the way) security force he'd built up since taking office, he knew it would have to be spread out across all the domes of the colony... and that we could breach his dome at any lock we pleased.

Containment would be his main challenge. If he could stop us at the locks, then we wouldn't be able to touch him. If even six Branchers broke through, he'd have to consider escape — because Branchers on the prowl are hard to kill.

There were many possible outcomes, as you can see, and of course Grant had ideas for all of them. Plans and more plans, layers of redundancy. He knew this wouldn't be his last battle... he just hoped he'd be able to come back to this office when it was over. Or better yet, return to his quarters with Sonia and enjoy the honest pleasures of finally having a woman he loved at his side.

He didn't bother to think about the chance — the very slim chance — that I might get to Sonia before he did. That wouldn't happen. No harm would come to her.

"Think Caldecott's squadron is up to stopping the Belt Squadron?" that question came neither from Karadzic nor Sonia, but from another figure looming in the room.

Turning to Augustin Renault, the spy killer, Grant only shrugged, "I believe they have the capability, but we all know how handy Ken is with a squadron. And Pellew too. Between them I think they'll probably destroy Caldecott. The question is how much damage they take in the process. This far from home, they have to be conservative... but let's all be honest, it'll be a disappointment if they don't try to land."

He wasn't wrong — they all wanted their chance, however small, at getting to grips with us. And conveniently, none of us wanted to disappoint them.

Chapter Four

Rules

As the Belt Squadron burned towards Etat Valcour, many minds were hard at work. The problem we faced was fairly obvious: no matter how powerful and angry we were, Grant was going to be down in a dome, while were going to be up in space.

And because he might have the cure to Karen's memory loss, we couldn't just laser his rock to pieces, and take comfort in knowing that he was dead. We needed to take him into custody, get the information out of him, and then decide whether to kill him immediately or take him home for trial (and subsequent execution). Either way he would die — once in Defense Command custody, there was no way he, as an enemy of the Empire, could face any other fate.

Preventing orbital bombardment, though, might have been the reason why he'd left Karen alive. He was forcing us to chase him. But of course, as Wes recently pointed out to me, if that was part of Grant's plan from the first, he probably wouldn't have planted the false story about Karen's death — if we'd never found out the truth about her survival, lasering the dome is exactly what we might have done.

Unfortunately, nothing exists in the surviving intel recordings from Grant's office to explain one way or another — it's like accessing Martian Navy logs in order to figure out why decisions were taken... there's just nothing there.

But that's all a pointless aside: the bottom line was that we were confident (perhaps over-confident) in our ability to defeat the SAU Navy protecting Valcour... but once we won the space battle, we were going to be decidedly short-staffed when it came to doing a smash-and-grab dome mission to get Grant.

We didn't even know how many people were in the domes on the asteroid. Governor George Madison could have millions of loyal supporters. Our entire squadron had just seven Special Branchers with which to mount the operation.

Now, considering two of those Branchers were Rufus Chang and Charlie Peters, the odds were in our favor, but we still thought it'd be best to grasp for an innovative solution, instead of a blunt-force one.

Otherwise, I'd have to spend time in this book writing about how Charlie actually could kill you with half a proton. *Half* a proton. But Charlie hates those boasts, so it's a good thing we were being creative.

"There's a real argument to be made for us having a Marine Corps," Mark Gunney was up on one of the screens we'd wheeled into *Wolf's* briefing room for a brainstorming session on this subject, and his observation drew a look from both Rufus and Charlie. Unfazed by the glares, *Cheetah's* skipper shrugged, "Not saying you guys are no good. Saying if each ship here had at least a platoon of heavily-armed marines, we'd be able to send you down with more heft."

Obviously Mark didn't need to explain his remark — particularly given what Rufus would be doing after the war — but his point was fair enough. Marines would surely have been a help in this situation, instead of just seven Branchers and as many SF and crew volunteers as we could spare without compromising combat abilities.

"We'll have to make do," Kris Jacobs was up on a screen from *Lion*... and here's the point where I realize I've done it again — failed to set the scene.

On screens around the table were Kris, Mark, Matt and Rozy Young — the latter skipper still not particularly impressed with the rest of us. Rufus and Charlie were sitting at *Wolf's* briefing room table, with Andrea Kiley, Eugene Sengooba, Karen and myself. Both Karen and I were staying relatively quiet — Karen because she was honestly concerned about trying to provide advice to people who were wildly more experienced than her.

I was staying quiet because I didn't care. This is not something to be proud of — I just didn't give a damn how Rufus and Charlie intended to get Grant... or, sorry, that's not quite right. I didn't care how much *damage* they did when they got Grant. I wasn't going to rule anything out, because the people of Etat Valcour deserved whatever came their way.

"He's likely to begin in the main dome, in his Governor's palace..." Matt Baxter pushed us to more pertinent matters with his observation. He was the only Commander in this briefing, largely because it would have been idiotic to exclude him. The Briton had dueled with the Syndicate on the ground more than any other officer in the squadron save Charlie.

Now his words drew a nod from the Hawke Lord, "He didn't leave that mansion on Belt Four until we made him. And then he nearly went down with his ship."

They were recalling the old days of the Belt Squadron battling the Syndicate, times that taught us a few things about how Grant's ego influenced his command decisions. When you believe you're going to win, you tend to stay in your headquarters... so perhaps he'd do us that favor again now.

"But he's going to know we're coming specifically for him," Rufus offered the counter. "Do you think he's really going to wait for us where we know he'll be?"

It was a good question — a guess about the judgment of an evil genius. Could we really predict his intentions?

Of course we could. I need to stop asking such stupid rhetorical questions.

"Remember this is all a publicity stunt," I leaned forward for the first time in the meeting, and all eyes turned my way. "He needs us to do many things for him when we arrive. He needs us to stomp all over his innocent civilians, so that we prove how mean we are. He also needs to be seen standing up to us — not afraid, even when we storm his dome. If he runs, he's no better than Kohl, so he has to wait for us."

There wasn't any sign of doubt in my tone, because I was honestly confident in my conclusion. It was clear to me — as clear as a chess board was to Grant — that his agenda in this whole mess was going to guide his final actions.

"That's quite a risk," Mark Gunney was the most skeptical, and rightly so.

I simply shrugged, "It's what he has to do. Stay long enough to make sure no one calls him a coward. *Then* he'll run for it."

There was some finality in my words, and silence followed them as we all looked at each other.

"Suppose we'll just need to find his escape route, and make sure we're waiting for him when he makes a run for it," Kris said eventually, knowing that she was stating the obvious.

I nodded, as did Charlie and Eugene. Rufus' mismatched eyes were beginning to narrow as dangerous thoughts ran through his mind, and then Matt Baxter offered another relatively obvious point that still needed to be made.

"So, the question is how we surprise the man who plans for every contingency. He's going to know that dome inside and out — every way in, and how long it should take us to breach and reach him. Best case and worst case scenarios… we have to get around that."

Again I nodded, but remained silent because the first thing that came to mind was 'laser the dome'. I didn't care about the number of people that particular tactic would kill, but I wanted someone else to suggest it first. Otherwise Charlie might have knocked me out on the spot, and locked me in the brig for the duration.

In retrospect, maybe I should have spoken up.

"He's going to have superior decompression protection for himself. So we could laser the dome, force the defenders to worry about their SAR protocols, then fly in and grab him."

It was the first thing Karen said in the meeting, and I heard a pin tap-dancing like Fred Astaire after she spoke. Everyone looked at her again, and her expression was the stony and unforgiving sort that I'd seen many times years before.

She didn't sound hungry, at least… just eminently practical.

"Let's hold that option in reserve," Charlie said quietly. He didn't knock her out, of course, because she'd just *suggested* it. If she actually tried to act on it the way Andrea had back in *The Dark Cruise*… well, what happens when someone tries to kill a goddess with half a proton? That's what triggered the big bang, isn't it?

Sorry, stupid rhetorical question.

The room remained silent on the heels of Charlie's remark. I looked at Karen as she sat back in her seat, arms folded and a very slight crease forming on her brow. Her eyes revealed more about her unease… she knew she'd made an unpopular suggestion, but she also knew it was logical. Now she was unsure: was she really ready to pitch in at a meeting full of as much field experience as this one?

Well, to quote her, it was her marbles we were playing for so she might as well try.

Good thing, too, because her idea had one element that appealed in particular to Rufus Chang. As his eyes narrowed even further, he leaned over to Charlie and said something quietly — so quietly that none of the rest of us could hear. This was unusual for a briefing, and as Charlie frowned thoughtfully and began to nod, we all waited to find out what the Branchers were conspiring about.

But they didn't say anything; Charlie just continued to frown thoughtfully.

"What is it?" Karen was a little quick to prod, half-wondering if the two had been commenting on her idea. "I still recognize that frown… it's the Charlie Peters thoughtful frown. So… what's the idea?"

Charlie didn't dislike the idea, but it was complicated, and as such he needed a few seconds to translate it into something explainable.

"First," he said, "we should slow down. Second, we need to find ourselves… what, a Trojan Horse?"

He glanced at Rufus with that question, and the Chinese Major nodded: "Except, a ship. But a horse — like a ship."

"Not a ship shaped like a horse, but a ship playing the role of a Trojan horse," Charlie clarified — he just wanted to make sure we understood.

We did. Sort of.

The two Branchers then explained their idea. It was crazy.

Those are the best kind.

CHAPTER FIVE

OLDEST TRICK

"Wait, Trojan horse?"

Commodore Wes Pellew was not allowed to sit up in bed, because his burns were still very tender and some had been sealed, but he nevertheless did almost start to rise at Andrea Kiley's words.

Wolf's Irish skipper was standing beside his bed with a typically disapproving gaze as she relayed Rufus' plan from the meeting, and seeing him start to move she reached out to pin him down. He stopped himself before she actually had to touch him, which was probably just as well — it would only have been awkward.

Once she was satisfied that he wasn't going to leap to his feet and tear his own flesh asunder again, Andrea confirmed what she'd said before, "Yes, a Trojan horse."

It sounded crazy to Wes, for quite a few reasons. His expression reflected this, and he pressed the next question rather urgently, "And you say this *wasn't* Ken's idea. It was… Rufus? Who we know is usually pretty… sane."

Andrea nodded, "It was Rufus."

Hard to believe, but there was no reason for Andrea to lie, so Wes decided to just accept Rufus as the originator… and wonder whether he'd been hit on the head, or brainwashed, or…

"It's the oldest trick in the book. Well, not exactly, because this is a ship, not a horse… and the docking will be very different…"

"Not *that* different," Wes interrupted Andrea's half-hearted attempt to agree with him. "And you got it wrong: it's not the oldest trick in the book, it's the trick from the *oldest* book. Homer actually spoke of it before epics were written down, and someone else wrote it down *once written histories were invented*. But everyone's satisfied that Grant's not going to see it coming?"

With another shrug, Andrea repeated her earlier point, "Well it's a ship, not a horse. And the ship won't even be shaped like a horse."

Wes blinked a couple of times, staring open-mouthed at *Wolf's* skipper. At first he wondered if we'd all been drugged, or if somehow we'd been hit on the head simultaneously, and had lost our minds. Sure we needed to get past the first ring of security, and a Trojan horse would be a good distraction. But forcing the gates, so to speak, was going to be risky… perhaps even downright stupid.

We might even literally underestimate the gravity. What a mess…

But as the Independent Squadron Commodore's mind turned those facts over, another part of his psyche zeroed in on something Andrea had said.

He looked up at her, then repeated the words: "Not even horse-shaped? Was that… a joke?"

Andrea stared at him for a moment, her expression unchanging. She then tilted her head very slightly and replied, "Yes."

It had been a joke — one told with no real humor, but a joke all the same. Andrea Kiley was telling a joke, and that was... progress. It was also very weird, which both she and Wes acknowledge now... but let's focus on the part where it's progress. Because progress is good and important and such.

Wes smiled the way a parent smiles when a child brings in a picture of a pony that looks more like a brown box with streamers and a triangle attached at incomprehensible angles, "Good one!"

He over-sold that. He knows it, and Andrea knew it too.

"Don't hurt yourself with the sympathy praise," she answered, again almost invoking a little levity.

"Well I'm just glad you're not actually funny yet," Wes countered. "If I laughed now, my chest might explode."

"That would be messy," Andrea conceded, and then they both fell silent.

It was the most exciting exchange of repartee they'd had... perhaps ever. A sign of good things to come, once we had Grant in hand.

Now we just needed to find a horse...

"Sorry, what?"

Kate Levec was on one of *Wolf's* bridge screens, and on the next monitor over, Matt Baxter raised an eyebrow, "A Trojan horse."

The repetition of the words didn't help, and Kate's eyelids dropped slightly, "Yes, Matt, I did hear what he said. I meant *what the hell.*"

"Oh in that case," the Briton replied dryly.

I was standing in front of the bridge viewfinder waiting for my turn, and when they both remained silent, I looked back to *Lady Grace's* new skipper, "There are a few civilian ships around here. The transports are too small for what we need, but if you can find an ore hauler or a freighter... anything big... that'll do."

Like everyone else who had heard the plan so far, Kate simply didn't know how to react. I mean, it was an old trick wrapped in new clothes, and it was relatively insane... but at the same time, it looked good on paper. We'd get past their early warning defenses, let them think they knew what we were up to, and then hammer their dome from an unexpected flank.

Grant wouldn't have a plan for this... I was somehow very sure of that.

But it would only work if we actually found the right ship to convert for our needs. Commandeering such a ship would arguably be an act of piracy... but given what had happened during our time in the SAU so far, you wouldn't be wrong in guessing that we didn't give a damn anymore.

This was eminently clear to Kate, but as one of the two skippers being sent out to find us our giant metal space pony, she was still having a tough time coming to grips with the whole thing.

Seeing this, I offered a smile, "Look, just go with Matt and he can find the horse. You watch his back."

"No, I can find a horse. I just... well... really?"

I nodded, "Yes. Grant won't see this coming, I promise."

"But…" she stopped herself. "Yes, sir. We'll go find you a horse."

"No need to kill everyone on board either, Kate. Just the women and children," I tacked that on to see if she was paying attention, but apparently it wasn't funny.

"Shut up, Ken. Stay put until we get back or we'll have words," Matt's parental tone had returned — now that Karen wasn't dead, he was still angry but less divorced from his old morality. Perhaps another ally for Wes and Charlie…

That was the end of our conversation, anyway — both *Lady Grace* and *Friendly* soon turned away from the Belt Squadron and went looking for a ship to commandeer. I should have mentioned it already, but we'd slowed to minimum cruising speed — just 25 kps — to make sure we had plenty of time before we closed on Etat Valcour, and now my old corvette and Karen's would go add one ship to our arsenal.

As I watched the icons of those two veteran corvettes depart, Jim Hannigan stepped up beside me with a frown. I glanced at him as he arrived, then tilted my head, "You think it's a bad idea too?"

Wolf's XO didn't answer for a few seconds, then he shrugged, "I think it benefits from being so insane that Grant wouldn't ever expect us to try it. So that's a good thing."

Was it? If Jim was right and Grant didn't see it coming, then yes, it was a good thing.

But the problem with my old friend is he could see every piece on the board, even some that were hidden behind others and not yet in play. So while we were out looking for a ship that didn't actually have to be shaped like a horse, he was sitting at his desk, wondering what to do if someone knocked on his gate and offered him one…

Chapter Six

Moves

Dave Caldecott sat in the chair facing Grant Merger's desk, a smug look dominating his face. The round little bearded creature was sweating even though the room was cool, and his feet were tapping on the carpet as though good music was playing. We have both the sound and video recording from this conversation so I can confirm there was none.

Basically, the little sack of shit was nervous because combat was coming, and though he'd rallied the very best of the SAUN to the defense of Valcour, he knew he would be expected to lead those ships into combat.

And combat was a place dear Admiral Caldecott had never been.

Now I'll pause here for a moment in case you think I'm intent on slamming any officer who hasn't been in action. Not at all. I'm just slamming Caldecott because he spent so many years self-righteously preaching combat doctrine to those of us who actually had experience fighting pirates. Seemed he'd finally get his chance now to prove how right he'd been… and knowing it was the Belt Squadron he'd be seeking to prove himself against, he was starting to get anxious.

Come to think of it, I shouldn't criticize him for being anxious — you know how much I tended to worry before a fight — but basically I want to find any reason I can to insult this disgusting little Alcibiades troll. If that means I have to be unfair, so be it.

Anyway, sitting across from Grant, Caldecott was sweating like he knew his number was up, and Grant was basically ignoring him. Because while Caldecott was stupid and useless, my old friend was sharply deciphering the defensive situation.

"He's going to try to distract us, get you out of position and then land his strike force when we're looking the other way," the Governor of Etat Valcour said quietly as he frowned over the maps on his desk. "He's going to try to find another way in…"

Both Sonia Hart and Fletcher Karadzic were in the room, standing a ways behind Caldecott (probably to avoid the smell), and it was the security man who commented in reply, "Think he expects us to know his full squadron strength?"

Grant nodded, though said nothing. Karadzic was suggesting that we might show up with only some of our ships, then send the rest 'around back' to strike from the rear. But Grant had more faith in me than that — he knew that I knew that he knew how many ships had come out with us. If we showed up missing two or three, Grant would know to expect a flank attack.

So how would we distract the defenders, since Grant's people were clearly aware of the number of ships we had with us. Fighters? No, useless. Some sort of mines, like the ones Marlene Stoll had used against the Martian force that was meant to hit Earth, all the way back in *The Almost Coup*? Not likely, too static.

No, the only thing the Belt Squadron could do was find more ships.

It was the only option that made sense. Grant knew very well that I never liked to fight fair — that I always lost at chess because whenever he could see every piece on the table, I could never beat him. That's why he'd lost at Deep Black. We'd cheated and put a piece on the board he wasn't ready for (apologies to Mel Samuels for calling her 'a piece'... but she was totally the queen in that fight, and any fight she's ever been in).

Now we'd try to do it again (minus the queen, since Julie Pichot was still in *Wolf's* medical bay under heavy sedation). We just needed one more ship...

"I don't think Barron will try anything fancy. He's a brute, he'll just come in swinging and expect us to roll over because of his reputation," Caldecott picked the oddest moment to squeak out that prediction, and Grant looked up with a frown. If you read his expression, his thoughts on Caldecott are pretty clear: *Are you still here, using oxygen?*

But Grant needed the inept Admiral, so instead of voicing that thought, he smiled, "No, Dave, he'll try to use guile to gain an upper hand. Trust me, he's my friend."

It was meant to put an end to the conversation, but Caldecott takes hints the way a... um. I can't think of a simile here, but Dave Caldecott is stupid and I'm petty enough to keep saying it.

"Why do you keep calling him that? Whatever friendship you had cannot have survived all this time... he's just a disgrace."

Grant's expression hardened at the words, and he leaned very slightly forward across his desk towards Caldecott, "You really think that, don't you? I'll concede he's had a lot of luck on his side, and that's something I can never plan for... but the only member of your entire Defense Command Navy I *ever* worried about was him. Because he *is* my friend even if he doesn't realize it anymore. Because he's better than any of you, and that's what makes him dangerous."

That shut Caldecott's mouth, not because he understood the point Grant was making, but because he heard the sharpness in the tone and knew he should let the question lie. My editors are a bit more curious, though, and I suppose I can understand why.

You see things like this all the time in history, and in movies. Two enemies who respect each other deeply... see in each other qualities that they admire, and wish they could have been united under different circumstances. Hell, you've seen that in this very war, with Bort McWebsbert.

What was different with Grant and me was that we had those years of friendship, that bond from the Academy. We were so alike, did so many things the same way, and then found ourselves on opposing sides.

We'd then proceeded to do each other great harm (me more harm to him, up until the moment he landed his blow against Karen) but throughout all that, it was like a fight between brothers, or former-best friends. As much as we hated each other, we still shared a mutual respect... and some of our old bond remained. The nearer we got to each other, the more it seemed to come out...

It might seem impossible, but I did wonder whether, when I finally saw Grant face-to-face, I'd actually be capable of properly hating him. The connection between friends who saw the world the same way can be deceptively strong, and can sneak up on you even after you've spent years apart, antagonizing each other.

Caldecott didn't understand that. Karadzic had seen signs of this mentality before and so could simply accept it... and Sonia Hart recognized once again that his respect for me could put Grant in a great deal of danger. Because if it slowed him down, kept him from making that one timely decision that killed me… it could mean the end of him.

She filed that fact away in her mind.

"No," Grant took a deep breath and then sat back in his chair. "Ken was always bad at chess. He always hated playing by the rules, so I suspect what he'll do now is go out and find himself more pieces. Fletch, check with our intel folks, find out if any of the renegade pirates have been acting differently of late. Sonia, monitor all civilian traffic bound for us, or heading out. He'll probably slow his approach for long enough to collect whatever additional resources he's looking for… then he'll come in hard."

Those orders were enough to set Grant's staff moving, and they exited the Governor's office. That just left Caldecott quivering in the chair across from my old friend, looking confused.

Realizing he needed to actually explain his thought process to the dense little toad, Grant sighed, "He might try to round up some pirates to attack us… if he knows we have a pirate problem at all. Which seems unlikely, but you can never count him out. More than likely he'll try to capture a civilian ship, use it as a Trojan horse to get through our defenses. So we need to be ready for anything. And your ships will be ready for anything, won't they Dave?"

The last question was delivered in a most condescending tone, and on the feeds from the office bugs, you can see Caldecott puff up slightly and turn red. But he held back his spite, knowing he was in no position to deliver it, "Yes."

"Good. Get back to your ship and stay ready. We'll be needing you soon."

This truly was the end of the conversation, and without wasting any further time the Admiral who had been exiled by the Empire pushed himself out of his chair and waddled to the door. Watching him go, Grant's face soured. When the door shut behind him, he spoke to his empty office — as though he knew we'd need a little help figuring out his internal monologue.

"Ken's going to enjoy killing you, you bastard. And that'll be helpful…"

I still find it strange that Grant said that to the empty room, but hey, I'm not one to look a gift horse in the mouth.

Er. That almost qualified as a Trojan horse pun.

Anyway, Grant went back to looking at his maps. They were all displayed on a big screen built into the top of his desk, so he was able to spin them around, zoom in and zoom out. And thanks to the high resolution of the bug cameras, we can see now exactly what he was focusing on: all the airlocks that would give our Special Branchers access to his dome.

If it was a Trojan horse, then he knew our attack would be launched from one of four main columns, so he'd just have to make sure they were all well-protected.

He had thousands of men for that job.

We didn't… but we'd soon have a horse…

CHAPTER SEVEN

WILD HORSE

"Think it's big enough?"

Lady Grace and *Friendly* had only needed to travel a few hours away from the squadron to find themselves a perfect non-horse-shaped ship, and as the two corvettes loomed over that unfortunate SAU freighter, Kate Levec appeared on one of *Friendly's* bridge screens.

She still didn't seem entirely sold on this brilliant plan, but she'd gotten comfortably into the 'oh well, let's just do it' phase, and her expression was slightly eager.

I should probably point out again that this was Kate's first major cruise in command of a warship, so despite all the other implications of this whole mission, she was excited to be getting her first tastes of independent ship command.

Oh, and to answer another editor, yes I'm sure it would be very literary of me to draw a subtle comparison between Kate and Karen right now, since they're both theoretically in the time of life where they're taking *Lady Grace* into action for the first time... and yes their names both start with 'K' so that could seem clever... and yes it would have been awfully interesting if we'd given Karen command of *Lady Grace*...

Good God, I don't think I've ever received so many different thoughts from my editors about a single moment in this series. And as moments go, this is a pretty normal one. Anyway, sorry for the interruption. Suffice to say that Kate was new in the job, and eager, and maybe if you think hard enough, that means there are parallels between her and Karen.

But most important right now is that Matt Baxter nodded in reply to her question, "Yes it's big enough."

"Excellent. How do you want to play it... good cop, bad cop? Or bad cop and worse cop?"

I think she was intentionally playing up her youthful eagerness at this point, but Matt was having none of it; he folded his arms and put on his 'don't do stupid stuff' scowl, "Let's ask nicely first. I'll call, you keep an eye out for surprises."

Kate seemed a tiny bit disappointed by that, but she nodded. Then Matt turned to his Sensors and Communications Officer, "Signal them when we're in range."

After receiving a nod back, he waited. *Friendly* and *Lady Grace* were running down hard on the freighter they'd found, but they would still need a little more time to overtake the long, triangular-hulled hauler in space. It was doing around 154 kps — good speed for a cargo ship — and moving on an oblique vector that pointed it at Etat Valcour, so they just needed to do a standard intercept.

"In range and signaling," *Friendly's* Sensors and Communications Officer at this time was Lieutenant Svetlana Singh, and she made that announcement as soon as my old corvette crossed the threshold into comms range.

Looking up at the ceiling, the way we all do when we're watching the speakers in an audio-only message, Matt waited for someone to answer the hail.

It took a moment, and then this was what he heard: "The fuck do you want?"

Believe it or not, that's not the least friendly reply Matt (or any of us) had ever received from a civilian ship when we queried them. Back during the pirate-hunting days, we'd always be pestering traders for sightings, and they got fed up with us pretty quickly... right up until the moments they needed us because they were under attack.

Anyway, this fellow hadn't been friendly, but at least he hadn't opened with an empty threat.

Matt appreciated that, so he decided to begin by offering him some help with his comm gear, "I'm sorry, did you say 'The fuck do we want', or 'What the fuck do we want'?"

There was a pause on the line, and then the gruff master of the freighter came back: "The fuck do you mean?"

Raising an eyebrow, Matt looked across the bridge to Lieutenant Singh, then shrugged at her, "Well sir, either you don't know much about speaking English, or the first word of every sentence you say is getting cut off because of poor communications gear."

Another pause, then, "The fuck do you think you are?"

Some people.

"Sir," Matt decided not to waste any more time, "We are two Defense Command warships, from the Earth Empire. I'm afraid we have to commandeer your vessel for the purposes of capturing a criminal. You and your crew will be granted safe conduct aboard our ships until we put into a port that will take you."

If you put yourself in the shoes of any skipper in the solar system, a statement like that must be more hated than any other you could imagine. We're strong, you're not, so we're taking your ship and everything you've worked for. And we're not even going to say 'sorry'.

Again we were throwing our weight around, though at least this time we weren't killing people or threatening their children. That'd come later.

For now, the master of this freighter offered a predictable answer: "The fuck do you mean? The fuck do you think you are?"

Well that settled it, he just didn't put any of the five 'w's in front of his questions. And you think I'm a hack...

"Sir, we are two warships and we will board you with extreme force if necessary. If you comply with our orders, you and your crew will be safe and your ship will not suffer unnecessary damage."

He didn't add 'for now' to the end of that sentence, but he could have.

Matt waited patiently, listening to the silence on the line and wondering whether the freighter was armed, or whether it was contemplating a run. I should have mentioned this before, but both *Friendly* and *Lady Grace* were obviously at action stations — even when a ship looks as unassuming as this hauler, you have to play things safe. We didn't have much information about the pirates that Grant was apparently concerned about (so we couldn't make any jokes about the irony of the Syndicate's master now getting a taste of his own medicine), but until you know for certain what's aboard a ship, you're better off proceeding with caution.

In this case, the caution was wise, but ultimately not essential.

"Fuck you," said the ship's skipper. "Cutting engines."

The hauler stopped firing its drives, and as *Lady Grace* and *Friendly* drifted up on either of its flanks, Matt smiled towards the speakers in his bridge's ceiling, "Thank you for your cooperation."

"You'll pay one day."

Maybe we would, but for now Matt didn't care; by threatening in an amiable manner, he'd been able to get us our Trojan horse without so much as firing a shot. And it didn't even look like a horse...

Chapter Eight

A Horse's Mouth

It was rare for Rufus Chang and Andrew Jensen to sit down for a meeting, but the unique nature of our Chinese Major's plan required the assistance of an engineer with plenty of ingenuity. Obviously, that meant Andy.

Perhaps unsurprisingly, when *Wolf's* Chief Engineer learned what we had in mind, he was... er... skeptical.

"You're serious?"

Rufus was always serious, or at least I'd never seen him otherwise, so he nodded evenly in response to Andy's question. They were sitting in the latter's office in the engineering section, and as our elite Commander Jensen sat back in his chair, he whistled and shook his head, "The modifications... what you want to be able to do, that takes yard time to accomplish."

"But aren't these Union ships very modular? Seems likely that they'd need to have the appropriate membranes on their frames to accommodate their construction," Rufus was no slouch when it came to engineering, so he asked that question, and Andy shrugged.

"Could well be, but I haven't examined one. Even so, you're talking about a lot of new protection around the... airlock? And also, built-in lasers with enough power to crack armor. We don't have anything in storage powerful enough for that sort of operation. Maybe if we had *Artemis Agrotera* along we could find what you're talking about."

It may sound like Andy was being overly negative, but he was leaning more towards being practical. Rufus' requests really were unprecedented... turning a stolen SAU ship into an assault vessel designed for dome insertions... in deep space using the equipment found on ships within the squadron... in only a couple of days...

It was a tall order.

"So how are you going to pull it off?" Rufus asked the question flatly, stopping Andy's concerns in their tracks.

Our Chief Engineer stared at our Special Branch Major for a few seconds, then a smile crept onto his face, "By missing dinner. And you're going to have to sign a waiver, because if you all die I don't want to be fighting duels with vengeful families."

"Agreed," Rufus didn't smile in reply, but Andy could tell the Major appreciated the answer. Well, except for the waiver part.

Adrienne Thompson and Shelby McLaws were sitting together at a table in the Officers Club, both having just come off duty. As was their practice, they were meeting for drinks to discuss their days... though obviously the circumstances meant they were drinking little — if a SAUN squadron showed up suddenly, they'd have to be back on duty in short order.

So it was coffee in the Officers Club, and sipping her warm drink, Shelby listened to

Adrienne's report from the day. It was the most strained the Helm and Navigation Officer had ever heard the Fighter Group Commander.

"We're going to be close support in very tight quarters. I know Grant probably won't expect us to mix it up — there was no sign of fighters from that squadron we tackled over Lexington — but if they have mags like the ones those ships carried..."

She tapered off, and Shelby took a breath before reaching out to cover the pilot's free hand with her own, "You've fought Grant Merger up close before, haven't you? What was he like?"

It was a simple question, perfectly phrased and delivered (as usual) by our southern belle, and Adrienne took a deep breath before sitting back in thought, "Well... he was never the same sort of pilot as Ken or Karen. He seemed to get frustrated by fighters, but never really had the answer for us. Just counted on the fact that our weapons couldn't really hurt his ships. Because he built his ships strong."

That's a pretty succinct assessment of the way Grant saw single-seat planes. We all knew by this point that the Starlights were probably the high water mark of a dying breed — that soon our fighters would be good only for scouting, not combat, since their warheads simply lacked the punch needed for fighting warships.

But while Karen and I had tempered that knowledge with a love of actually sitting in the cockpit and flying our fighters into battle, Grant had dismissed the craft almost immediately. It was one of the first fissures in the trio we formed at the Academy... one of the first signs that perhaps we weren't all going to conquer the solar system together.

When he'd formed the Syndicate, Grant had carried that perspective with him. I don't know if you can remember all the way back to *The Rogue Commodore*, and particularly the attack of Belt Two that we ended with, but there were raiders in that fight... and raiders were as small as Grant liked to go in terms of combatants.

Big enough to be able to cruise long distances, heavily-built enough to resist anything smaller than a warship, and fast enough to outrun most warships. He was smart about building his Syndicate Navy, which is why they were so tough — why their attack on Earth was no joke.

Other pirates had tried to follow in his footsteps, but they'd lacked his central vision. Now the SAU was benefitting from his experience, but the question was how much he could have accomplished in evolving their pre-fabricated Navy during his years as Governor...

And whether he would have bothered arming his capital dome against the possibility of Starlights carrying out ground strikes. If, as Shelby was implying, he assumed his dome was impervious and simply focused on anti-warship defenses, then Adrienne and her small assault group might have the run of the place.

But if he'd learned from the past, and was determined to do harm, then Wolfstar Squadron could be shot to pieces.

For the first time since the war, Adrienne Thompson worried the adversary she was up against could do that to her flyers. Wolf and Wolfstar Squadrons were the best she'd ever flown with, but the man who had reached out and attacked Karen could do anything.

So Adrienne worried, as did Shelby... but they didn't waver. Because they're Belt Squadron, and that means they're the best. Yep, I said it again.

"I have a lot of faith in you," *Wolf's* Helm and Navigation Officer said eventually, with a squeeze to Adrienne's hand.

Smiling at her younger counterpart's confidence, our Starlight-driving Commander shrugged, "Well in that case, everything will be alright."

"Precisely," Shelby smiled perfectly, then sipped her coffee.

Those two were doing fine.

Eugene Sengooba was sitting at his desk in the security office, sorting through the names of the SF men and women who had volunteered to land on Valcour behind Rufus' assault team. Only two of his people hadn't stepped forward: one was six months pregnant, and the other was seventy-four years of age, and suffering from a nasty bout of back spasms. The rest... well, I could spend a paragraph telling you what you already know about Belt Squadron people, but I'll spare you just this once.

For his part, Eugene found himself shaking his head. Most of these women and men had done very long turns with him on Egesta... some of them had been there both times. They weren't hard-trained Special Branchers, or marines in the sense Mark Gunney had meant, but they were experienced, tough, smart and strong. There was no telling how many combatants would be down on Valcour, nor could he know whether Rufus' plan would have the desired effect in catching them all off guard.

But he could count on these people, and the rest of the crew besides. All told, *Wolf* had more than 100 volunteers asking to go down, and though not all of them would be allowed, that was a strong statement as to the ship's strength. It was up to our Master-At-Arms to figure out the best way to organize them all into their assault craft.

A knock on the frame of Eugene's open door drew his eyes up, and seeing the officer there he immediately came to his feet with a marvelous smile, "Lieutenant Khalid, welcome! Please come in!"

It was our Sensors and Communications Officer, Felicia Khalid, and as she stepped inside, Eugene quickly waved her to a chair, "To what do I owe the honor, ma'am? I rarely get to see you in these dismal parts!"

Eugene was a particularly gracious host, and though I fear I've never done justice to Felicia, he'd always been very warm with her — she was barely twenty-five at this point, young and capable, very much like his daughters. As she sat down and he did the same, he had no idea what to expect.

And honestly, I wouldn't have known what to expect either. Much to my shame, it wasn't until years later that I found out how this meeting unfolded.

"Master-At-Arms, I'd like to volunteer for the landing forces that attack Etat Valcour."

Eugene was surprised. Just like most of us would have been.

Let's review what I've related about Felicia so far in these books: we passed her over for promotion to Sensors and Communications Officer back in 2232, because at twenty-two we thought she lacked experience... and she did. But then when Kate Levec got shot (because of me) she stepped into the job and made it her own.

Since then, all we've really heard about her is how competent she was in that role... how she did Jim Hannigan proud. And that's how many of us saw her, I think — as the excellent bridge officer, smart and intuitive, never the sort to pick up a mag and go storming into a messy situation.

She hadn't been on Egesta, she hadn't been down to Mars with us, and she certainly hadn't been on the ground during the coup on Capital Island. Always the competent voice in the sky, but never the one in action.

And in a great disservice to her, I never really asked if she wanted something different. Most of the time I made an effort to understand the long-term goals of my senior staff, but Felicia had joined us after my time as Captain, so I suppose it just never came up...

Nevertheless, I'll use this as an opportunity to point out that I'm dumb. Take it as a general statement of truth, whether it fits this example or not.

"We do have a full roster of volunteers, ma'am... but of course I'll put you on that list," Eugene might have been surprised, but he's a very good man, and he didn't skip a beat in acknowledging her wishes. Then he asked the thing none of the rest of us had really thought to: "If you don't mind the question, why do you want to go in with the strike force?"

He asked that simply, not as though he was fishing for any sort of justification, and Felicia tilted her head very slightly, as though she'd been expecting to be queried — expecting to defend her interest.

"This landing may be the most important one in the history of our squadron, Master-At-Arms. This may be the day we take Grant Merger into custody. I've served from my consoles for the whole war... but I think now I have to be among those who take action, who make a difference on the ground."

It sounded like a carefully prepared statement, because it was. Felicia had been thinking about this request at some length, and she had anticipated pushback. But if there was ever a time to call in a favor, to get her way instead of being responsible and sitting on the bridge, this was it.

So her next line of reasoning — her next argument, frankly — was already waiting in the front of her mind, in anticipation of Eugene's impending expression of reluctance.

"Okay, I will recommend you to Major Chang as the commander of one of our volunteer units."

Felicia wasn't ready for his agreement. She opened her mouth to begin her counter, but being a Sensors and Communications Officer, she was fast enough to stop herself when she processed his message.

Eugene's smile grew wider and brighter as he watched her expression turn slightly confused, and then he explained himself, "You have earned your right, Lieutenant. You have sat at your post for so long, and if I can, I will help you. You must promise to take care, but you should have this chance."

There was no question this was dangerous. He could have pointed out that this was going to be a contested landing of an experimental nature... that every volunteer could be killed upon breach... that once on the ground, a Sensors and Communications Officer would lack the tactical experience to handle close-quarters combat with the best of Grant Merger's fighters...

Just like Karen and I had once argued, and concluded, that Felicia didn't have the experience to take over for Jim Hannigan. Sometimes, though, you have to let a person decide to jump in with both feet, and Felicia had earned her right to choose.

After sitting in silence for a couple of minutes, *Wolf's* Sensors and Communications Officer met Eugene's eyes, and then she smiled — something we rarely got to see her do back then.

"Thank you, Master-At-Arms, I truly appreciate your endorsement."

Eugene held up his hands and shrugged, "Thank you for volunteering, ma'am."

It was the right thing to say, and as her smile grew, Felicia got to her feet and shook his hand. Then she left, and walked through the corridors of *Wolf* with that bright smile, surprising many people who were used to a different side of her personality.

She would be landing against Grant.

Would he be ready… and would we?

CHAPTER NINE
THE QUALITY OF PIECES

As soon as *Friendly* and *Lady Grace* escorted the commandeered freighter into formation with our squadron, Rufus and his team boarded it, along with some of Eugene's SF, then kindly escorted the crew of seven back to *Wolf* to hang out for a while. After that Andy and his engineering teams went over, and were soon joined by the engineers from a few of our other ships. They were going to try to do within forty-eight hours what would normally take shipyards months of work.

But of course I had confidence in them. If anyone could make an airlock as tough as Rufus needed this one to be, it would be Andy and the engineers of the Belt Squadron.

Leaving those excellent minds to their work, then, the rest of the ships of the squadron focused on preparing for our part of the attack. There was nothing particularly special about what we had to do — it would be dangerous close combat, of course, but it wasn't as though we needed to be clever.

As we'd done at Lexington, we'd just show up and start hitting SAUN ships hard and repeatedly, and see how long it took them to break.

I wasn't worried.

That's the first thing my friend Charlie Peters noticed after I opened my cabin door for him. He hadn't joined Rufus' mission to the freighter — which was called *Hester*, by the way — and had instead been quietly surveying the crew, getting a sense for where everyone stood now that Karen was back.

Since Wes was down, it was up to him to read the situation, and now it was time for him to discuss things with me.

"We haven't had time to talk properly in ages, have we?" I asked as he stepped into my cabin and shut the hatch behind him.

Shaking his head, Charlie moved over to stand beside my wallscreen, then folded his arms and leaned against the wall when I returned to the chair beside my bed.

"Where's Karen?" was his question, and I glanced to the left — in the direction of her cabin, just through the wall.

"Cleaning up, she'll be over for dinner in half an hour or so. You want to join us? We could go down to the Officers Club..."

Charlie tilted his head slightly, then shook it. Being a keen observer of human behaviors, I could tell from his dour air that this wasn't a social call, so I gave up on pleasantries.

"I'll take heart in the fact that you haven't knocked me out and locked me up yet," I smiled instead, and recognizing that it was actually time to discuss the situation, Charlie took a breath and turned his stare against me.

"I'm sorry I wasn't at Egesta."

"You shouldn't be," was my answer. "Nor the coup, for that matter. You earned your right to be with Lia. It's one bit of good news we all get to hold onto."

"Doesn't seem like you've been holding onto much good news lately," he turned my point very deftly, and I shrugged.

"There wasn't much there to grab."

That had been true, and Charlie nodded in acknowledgment, "I see that. And I haven't knocked you out because you killed, if I have this correctly, the two assassins who attacked Karen… as well as some of the crews of that Union squadron at Lexington. And they were in combat. But you didn't kill anyone else."

"Scarred some children for life, I hope," my counter was predictably and pathetically spiteful, and Charlie's eyebrow climbed.

"I did hear that. You shouldn't feel too proud of yourself, though. You and I have both seen worse."

I think you can read that comment two ways — one being that I should be ashamed of myself for doing it, but consoled by the fact that others do worse things to children. That's not the meaning Charlie had in mind… he was telling me that I shouldn't think I was too much of a hardened cold killer just because I taunted a couple of kids. We both know that real monsters do a whole lot worse to children.

He knew very well the persona that I'd built around myself during this mission to the SAU… knew how much I needed to hold onto my anger and rage… and he wasn't impressed.

"We can't all be winners," my answer was an attempt to disarm Charlie's observations, but my friend wasn't having any of it.

"You shot Wes. I know Wes has an insight into this sort of situation that I don't, and I know he sees what you've done so far as analogous to what he went through with Sara. And you've continued to let him believe as much. But you and I both know what this has been. And why it needs to change before we storm Grant's rock."

I felt a frown beginning to crease my brow, and then tilted my head slightly before countering, "What has this been?"

Charlie stared at me, assessing exactly how much he needed to explain — wondering quite fairly, whether I'd been completely deluding myself with my need to hide from my pain by rolling around in it.

Choosing his tack, he then began to explain himself: "The righteous anger… the determination to get Grant because he killed Karen? I get that. There's nothing wrong with it, and that's why I'm here. But this nastiness you're clinging to… this desire to be the most terrifying psychopath in the solar system. Maybe people are buying it, or maybe they're just accepting that you're under unusual amounts of pressure here, and have been lashing out. But none of this is actually you."

Of course it was me. What was he talking about?

"You've never been a hardened killer. Whatever you and Grant told yourselves as kids was fiction. You just pretend to be monstrous — sometimes convincingly — because it's a helpful way to hide your pain, and your fear. That's it. Big lie to try to show the world how dangerous you are, so everyone will stay away. I never knew you back when you and Grant wrapped yourselves up in this silly notion… and I'm glad I didn't, because we wouldn't have become friends. But you and Karen give each other enough confidence in yourselves to not need to put on the stupid façade. That's why you're both so good together. You help each other *sort of* qualify as normal people."

He meant that last remark to lighten the heavy lecture, but it didn't. I was sitting in silence, staring at him, and he could see the wheels turning in my brain — despite my attempts to stop them.

"Here's the thing," he decided to press on. "You have each other back now. And whether Karen remembers the last twelve years or not, she remembers you. She remembers the tenth of September. There's no reason for you both to remain nailed to this spiteful position you picked. Because if we go after Grant with you acting like a fool, he's going to find a way to win."

Of course he would; that villain had been my friend, and was very smart.

Charlie was my friend now, though — my best friend. And he knew me better than Grant did.

My old juvenile rage had been a comfort when Karen was lost... but now that Karen was back, I didn't need it anymore. He was also implying (I think somewhat incorrectly) that I wasn't really as heartless as I let on when I was rageful... that I was, in fact, a decent person, just using a cold-blooded idiom as a façade.

Perhaps the heartless version of me was just an act... maybe it was a fiction I'd propagated to feel strong in a time when I was in so many ways powerless. The way I'd been as a kid, watching family members die far too young. The way I'd been at the Academy, before that girl in the alley had made an impression on me. The way I'd been since losing the girl from that alley.

This could all very much be the act of an insecure man, just trying to seem powerful. And if it was — if that's all it was — then my crimes are even greater, because I destroyed any real chance of a positive relationship between the Union and the Empire based on nothing but fear and spite.

Maybe you should remember me that way — not as some sort of hero.

All of those thoughts were playing out on my face as Charlie watched. He alone had been well-positioned to inspire this line of reflection; Wes had been cast in the role of opponent, and Karen was still trying to cope with her own mind. Only my friend, the Lord Major Charlie Peters, could make me listen.

And he had one more point.

"Also, before you go too far down the path of self-criticism for this whole operation, remember one thing: Grant Merger is here, this Union he's been cultivating is a genuine threat to the Empire over the longer term, and while I think you've been heavy-handed in your operations, you haven't done anything yet that makes me want to knock you out and jail you. However bad you think it's gotten, it hasn't crossed that line."

Friends like Charlie are very rare, and if you have one, you better make sure you're grateful — and that you're as good a friend in return.

Because his words threw the brakes on my self-scolding internal monologue. Changing directions yet again, my mind began ticking over the past weeks of chaos, and putting events into a different context.

Yes we'd shown up like the Imperialist monsters Grant told everyone we'd be, but in the midst of our demonstrations of power, we'd never descended to Sean Cook's level. We came close at Lexington, where it had gotten very touch and go at the end... but I believe to this day that I would have done much worse if not for the friends who'd intervened.

But my friends had intervened. And perhaps — just perhaps — I can take some solace in the fact that I'd had a hand in gathering those friends around me. Grant didn't believe that the quality of the pieces could change the rules of the chess game, and in a sense he was right.

They could, however, change the moves. And my friends had... Charlie included.

"You could spend months analyzing all of this," the Hawke Lord said. "Don't expect whatever revelation you're having now to automatically make everything okay again. Just hold onto it in the moments you need to be your old self, so we can put Grant down. Then spend a couple of decades making your peace. Maybe you'll write a book about it."

No seriously, he said this.

"That'd mean I'd have to learn to spell," I was finally able to get in a counter-shot, and Charlie smiled slightly.

"Well then forget the book idea."

He didn't have much else to add; he'd said his piece, and based on what he could see from my expression, it seemed to have worked. He was (of course) correct that his advice wasn't some sort of cure-all... it was really just the beginning of me starting to get a full grip on what was happening, and how I could wade out of this Union mess with some level of success, and perhaps a scrap of dignity.

That was vital, and I was grateful.

And as proof of my gratitude, I asked Charlie a question: "So what's it like being a 'consort'?"

Somehow my friend was ready for the rapid subject change. He shrugged and smiled, "Lots of politics, which I'm not used to yet. But I get to sleep with Lia every single night. Which is pretty awesome."

His smile grew at that, because those aren't the sorts of things you hear Charlie say very often, and he found it rather entertaining to voice them now.

But I wasn't having any of it, "Watch it, buddy, that's my little sister you're talking about."

He shrugged, "Well you can give her away at the wedding."

"Wedding?" I started to get excited but he held up his hand.

"Whenever it happens. For now we're just living in sin."

"Ah," I calmed myself again, then frowned slightly. "You're going to stop sinning after you walk down the aisle?"

Charlie paused thoughtfully at that for a moment, then slowly started to shake his head, "I want this marriage to go the distance, so we'll have to continue sinning. Enthusiastically and often."

"Sounds fair," I agreed.

And then we both nodded in satisfaction — not at the subject of our repartee, but at the quality of the back-and-forth. It had been far too long since we'd had the chance to trade quips like this, and it was good to see we hadn't lost all our abilities.

"Repartee still works," Charlie observed after a pause.

"It does," I agreed, then added: "Maybe all isn't lost after all."

"Oh don't say things like that, you'll ruin it," Charlie shook his head, and I didn't argue. He was right, and we'd just have to keep moving forward.

So we did; Charlie headed off to get dinner by himself, and I waited for Karen to arrive in my cabin for our supper together. Nothing was back to normal, but everything did seem a bit better nonetheless.

That's the power of good friends — of high quality pieces on the board.

CHAPTER TEN
THE DEFENSES

As comfortable as Grant had become in his Governor's office, he still did find it somewhat odd to be on the ground while preparations for a major space battle were being made. The fact that Dave Caldecott was going to be running the local defense squadron in this case made things even worse, so as preparations continued to receive our horse attack, Grant finally broke down and decided to tour the SAUN ships in orbit of his rock. Just to be sure.

Unfortunately the bugs in Grant's office didn't follow him on this particular tour, so I've had to piece together what he did and saw from a variety of places. But I think it's a convenient way for us to look at what we were facing — an 'elite' Solar Asteroid Union squadron. It did bear some similarities to the ones we're accustomed to seeing now, but it was different in a variety of ways too.

In orbit of Etat Valcour were eight ships, led by the battleship *Liberty*. You've probably seen pictures of *Liberty*; it's the only catamaran-hulled SAU ship from this period, meaning it has two of those triangular hull tubes attached to each other side-by-side, instead of bottom-to-bottom the way their other battleships were arranged. The result was a very mean-looking ship... though that meanness was definitely reduced by the fact that Dave Caldecott was commanding.

Along with *Liberty* were seven other ships (obviously), all of them the newest cruisers in the SAUN: *Constitution, Constellation, Congress, Captain, Chesapeake, Columbia* and *Capitol*. If you're getting an American vibe from these ship names, then you're obviously awake. When it came to building their fleet, these Unionists had been no more subtle about their appropriation of US culture than they'd been in every other part of establishing their state.

From a combat point of view, though, none of these ships were anything like those the American colonies had managed to put to sea in their first decades of independence. They also were quite different than the ships we'd faced at Lexington.

Again, when Grant had brought Dave Caldecott into the SAU, and had used his positive relationships with the Union's military to get the disgusting bastard installed as an Admiral, he'd gained even more control of the Navy than he'd enjoyed before. You might recall from the last book that Grant had been able to specify that the 'red group' defending President Kohl at Lexington was in fact made up of the oldest and worst-protected ships in the SAUN.

Guess what 'green group' — the Valcour force — consisted of.

The interesting point was that none of the ships looked noticeably different from those we'd faced at Lexington. I can't comment as to whether this was a clever part of SAU doctrine — have all our ships look alike, so enemies have to be generally wary of all of them — or if it was just a side-effect of the pre-fabricated manufacturing process.

Whatever it was, it meant that we might underestimate our opponents when we showed up. I don't think Grant was counting on us to make that mistake, but he certainly knew it was possible.

And as he took a transport up to *Liberty* and boarded the dark-hulled, highly-angular ship, he was able to get a closer look at what we were actually in for.

Both Sonia Hart and Fletcher Karadzic accompanied him for this tour, and as they marched around the battleship that wore Caldecott's flag, they undoubtedly got to look at many things that interested my old friend.

For instance, they went up into one of the disruptor turrets... recall that these triangular warships were covered in tank-style turrets, each with massive mags (they call them disruptors) that fire blue bolts of energy. Well, unlike Defense Command turrets, or even Martian EM cannon turrets, these disruptor mounts have crew spaces in them... so Grant and Karadzic went into one, and chatted with the gunners for a while.

Spirits among the crew were good, I should mention — Grant was a popular figure, and now that the Empire he'd warned people about was coming through (with all the arrogance he'd promised) the men aboard these ships were eagerly awaiting their chance to defend everything they'd worked for. One day, remember, they'd all have the chance to be voting citizens of the SAU... they wanted to make sure it was safe and ready for them when they got that privilege.

Because voting isn't a right. People are dangerous and the Union knows better than to let everyone have a vote.

Ahem.

After visiting one of the disruptor turrets, Grant and Karadzic joined Sonia in moving through the ship towards its bridge. Because they hadn't informed Caldecott of their plans to tour his battlewagon, the waste of flesh was sitting in his command chair upon their arrival. And because he was turned away from the entrance to the bridge chamber, he didn't actually see them enter.

The bridge itself was full of consoles and crew arrayed in a somewhat orderly fashion. It was nowhere near as elegant as a Defense Command bridge — there was no feeling that you were on the quarterdeck of a Nelsonian warship at sea. At the same time, though, it wasn't cramped and uncomfortable like the Martian bridges Bort has told me about.

Somewhere in between, then, and all of it had that pre-fabbed feeling... as though it was a cargo bay that someone had loaded up with command-and-control consoles.

And actually, that's exactly what it was...

"Good day, Governor!" Captain Rayne Archibald was the skipper of *Liberty*, and he greeted the arrival of 'George Madison' before Caldecott became aware of the delegation's presence.

As soon as Caldecott turned his chair and realized he had guests, he flopped to his feet and waddled in their direction, scowling mightily, "What are you doing up here? I have things under control."

Grant stared at Caldecott for a moment after those words, then smiled and looked away from the Admiral, to the rest of the SAUN's flagship bridge crew, "We know Defense Command is up to something... they're probably going to show up with a Trojan horse of some sort, that's why they're taking their time. So I just wanted to come up here and say to you all, personally, that I know this hard fight will be won by men with your character, and ships with the strength of *Liberty*."

We have to face it, my old friend was a complete fucking political ham. He loved his speeches, and this one earned him a cheer.

"Three cheers for the guv'ner! Hip-hip!" *Liberty's* Sailing Master called out

"Hooray!"

They did the hip-hip-hooray thing twice more, but I'm not going to write it. I do realize that it actually takes more words for me to tell you I'm not going to write it than it would just to write it, but it's a principle thing…

"How do we look for combat, Captain Archibald?" Grant purposely ignored Dave's fuming glare as he directed that question to the skipper of the battleship, smiling as the young officer stepped forward with his chest puffing out a little under this brown shirt.

"Very well, sir. It was rough what they did to red group, but they're going to get a surprise if they try to detonate our torpedoes with those beam weapons of theirs. And we're better shots."

Of course everyone in green group had watched the recordings made by Lexington civil defense, showing exactly how we'd defeated the unfortunate SAU ships under Group Captain Parm Harku… but as I said, *Liberty* and its escorts were newer ships, despite looking the same.

And the biggest difference was additional protection.

We were able to blow the hell out of a red group ship because one of our lasers had drilled into its submarine-style torpedo magazine. If we tried the same against these ships, we'd only hit more armor.

Survivability was going to be a major asset for the SAUN this time around, and that made for confident brown-shirted crews.

"Looking forward to seeing you and your ship in action," Grant answered Archibald, and while he was mostly speaking in political platitudes, there was some genuine truth behind what he said.

This was the first time since leaving the Defense Command fold that my old friend had a real Navy behind him. The Syndicate had been powerful — very powerful, make no mistake — and by the end there was definitely an air of professionalism around the pirates who were closest to the now-Governor of Etat Valcour.

But it wasn't a Navy. Ask Mel Samuels and she can tell you some of the stories… some of the very odd ways men and women served together on those ships. If you were to walk in on her explaining those relationships, you might be forgiven for thinking she was talking about Pion Rock.

As much as I will gladly belittle the pathetic Solar Asteroid Union Navy — which to this day is the butt of every joke in real military circles — it was trying to be a fleet. It was doing its very best to have people in uniform, with a hierarchical rank structure, run ships that were designed to defend the state.

And because this was the one thing Grant had given up in leaving the Empire (well, this and real bacon), he had a soft spot for his little toy fleet.

It was like he was a real boy. The villain was trying to get back what he'd abandoned…

Unfortunately for us, he'd built up some good toys here too. Because as much as the

SAUN was made of fail, it was actually not a pushover. I know that's entirely contradictory, but if you can't tell by now that I'm irrationally mean-spirited about the brave men who were fighting the SAU's ships, you might have some re-reading to do.

They were all idiots and completely useless... but they weren't to be underestimated. Perhaps that's something I learned the hard way. Guess we'll see soon enough.

CHAPTER ELEVEN

POLISHING A HORSE

"I'm honestly shocked it's going to work."

Wes was now allowed to sit up in bed, which was small comfort under the circum-stances. Andy Jensen and the engineers from the Belt Squadron had been working for only eighteen hours, and already their conversion of *Hester* was nearly complete. As Rufus had predicted, the fact that it was a SAU prefab ship meant it proved surprisingly easy to seal in the necessary sections of its hull, and install the equipment we needed aboard. And speaking of that equipment, more than enough cutting gear had been acquired from the frigates of the squadron to arm its airlock.

So we were only a few hours from resuming course to Etat Valcour, and Wes was still in no condition to command his ship for the fight. I was going to be in charge, and he was going to listen to the fight from his bed.

It was almost as bad as being shot all over again...

After expressing his genuine shock, Wes looked up at his latest visitor, and my friend Charlie shrugged, "I'm still not entirely sure it *will* work. But it has a solid chance, if we understand the gravity correctly. All I know is Andy guarantees the seal will hold."

"That's something," Wes nodded a couple of times and took a breath. "Well, glad you've got Ken seeing straight again. Gives us the best chance."

Charlie listened to Wes' hopeful words, then paused for a moment before slowly nodding, "Yes. We should be alright for the battle itself. But the question will be what happens when we get our hands on Grant. When we even get close to him, actually. That reunion is going to be... conflicted."

"Almost as complicated as if you or I had tried to kill Karen," Wes agreed. "This is why my English teacher always said the most drama happens when brother fights brother."

"Exactly."

Both my friends were correct, it was going to be an interesting day. And soon we'll see how right they were. But a few more stops first...

The Captains and Commanders of the Belt Squadron were having a quick summit. Every one of them — Andrea, Kris, Mark, Isoruku, Katya, Kate and Matt — were sitting in their day cabins with Battlelink up on their screens. Andrea also had an enhanced-cam view of *Hester* on her display. Two more hours and that ugly freighter would be ready.

"So we're expecting them to be tougher this time," Mark Gunney was saying. "That's helpful for me because I didn't face them last time."

He was being his usual sardonic self, and with a smile, Kris Jacobs reassured him: "We didn't miss you at all, either. But I'll be so much more comfortable knowing you're behind me."

"Comfortable isn't usually what I'm going for when I'm behind you," he didn't miss the opportunity, and Kris shrugged.

"Then you need more practice."

I should clarify that this summit wasn't some great planning meeting, it was essentially just a chance for the Belt Squadron's skippers to share thoughts (and banter) before the fight. This sort of thing happened a lot during the pirate-hunting days, but less during the war because… well, it was the war. It was different.

Now Andrea listened to the banter and found herself not entirely disapproving of it, which she later noted as potential progress. Not worth discussing now; instead I'll describe the more useful commentary she inserted: "We're going to have to expect the worst. Grant might have put paper tigers out for us at Lexington, so when Ken sends us in, we have to be ready to take real hits."

She was clearly the most serious person on the screens, but the other skippers were well-familiar with that reality by now, and they responded to her concern evenly.

"We'll be ready for that sort of problem," Matt Baxter assured her, leaning back in his chair on *Friendly*. "What I'm more concerned about is Grant trying to make his escape. He'll have something in the wings. I'm sure Ken knows this, and Charlie and Karen. They all know him well… Ken best of all. Grant will have something in place so that at the last possible minute he can escape."

As much as my old friend had kept his secret super-fast escape ship a secret, we all knew something like it had to exist. Perhaps that gave us a chance, even if the damned thing could purportedly do more than 300 kps.

"Intercepting him is part of Major Chang's plan, correct?" Isoruku pitched in from *Generous*, and both Kris and Matt nodded simultaneously.

"But," Andrea was again the voice of grim reality, "Grant knows how to slip out of our traps, so we all need to pay close attention. If he escapes we could find ourselves chasing through every rock in this Union. I'd rather just catch him and go home."

Everyone nodded, just as you'd expect, but no one seemed to really register the unusual nature of Andrea's remark. She wanted to go home? Why would she want to do that? It didn't fit with her recent mentality. When she realized later what she'd said, even she didn't quite know.

But it was a good sign.

Anyway, the skippers continued to talk amongst themselves, waiting for the moment when *Hester* would be ready to load up its assault force, and we could get underway again.

We were less than a day from Valcour if we burned at full speed.

Standing on one of the catwalks in the midst of *Hester's* forward cargo bays, Rufus watched the engineers from *Cheetah* who were working on the last of the new laser mounts at the front end of the compartment. The ship around him was basically a very crude, hopefully-airtight triangle made of pre-fab sections of plating.

But it would get the job done.

Folding his arms and leaning against the catwalk's railing, our Chinese Major took a breath and wondered whether his plan would work. It's probably not a great sign that, even as we were in the process of polishing up his Trojan horse (ooh, used the chapter title), he was still wondering whether the gambit had a chance of succeeding.

But it would work. The way things had to work even though there's no real evidence that they will, but you're depending on them so you tell yourself there's no question.

That might have been what Rufus was doing, because there were many things that had to go right with his audacious plan. He had only six officers with him this time — not a full squad of Branchers, and certainly no Colonel Ronald behind him with skiffs and reinforcements. We were assaulting a dome that could be every bit as tough as Mercury, and we were doing it on a shoestring (look it up). But — *but* — we were doing it with the guidance of a Mercury veteran, with another Mercury veteran pitching in.

Rufus and Charlie... those two knew better than most men still alive how dangerous it was when you stormed an airlock. They knew how vital it was to modify this ship, so that we weren't just trying to send twelve volunteers through an airlock at a time, to be slaughtered by whatever defenses Grant had waiting on the ground.

Hester was the answer. *Hester*, in fact, could change the face of modern dome warfare... if it worked.

And Rufus didn't *actually* know if it would. But it would.

Standing on a catwalk looking hundreds of meters down the massive empty cargo bay (which had been full, by the way, before we dumped its ore load into space), he just had to believe.

We all did.

Once *Hester* was made ready and the engineering teams had returned to their respective ships, our assault forces were transferred to the big, frankensteined assault vessel. This meant that Felicia Khalid — the commanding officer of *Wolf's* volunteers for the landing — joined Eugene Sengooba in taking two of our shuttles over to the SAU freighter. Adrienne said her goodbye to Shelby and took half of Wolfstar Squadron out of *Wolf's* bays as well — they'd be going with Hester as close support.

Rufus and his team had already been aboard, meaning I hadn't actually had the chance to speak to our Major with the mismatched eyes — to wish him luck or thank him. Most of the SF and volunteers went without me getting to speak to them either.

But as I stood on the bridge beside Andrea, and watched on the monitors as various small craft coasted towards the ugly triangular ship, one person who was to join the landing party did come to say his farewell.

It had been a long time since Charlie had worn a Defense Command tac vest, and as he said to me later, he was just damned glad it still fit. He hadn't been doing as much fitness training as a consort (no high-five jokes please), so he'd been entirely prepared for the possibility that he'd be somewhat out of shape... but being one of only seven qualified Branchers in the squadron, he'd have gone even if he'd needed to wrap two tac vests around himself.

Fortunately, it didn't come to that — didn't come anywhere close to it, in fact.

With a MAG-90 clipped to his vest, and his old battle gear wrapping him up for his first forced landing since getting blown up on Mercury, he was a welcome sight on *Wolf's* bridge.

"Ready to go?" I asked as he arrived beside Andrea and me, and he nodded with a slight shrug.

"Ready as we can ever be. See what Grant has in store for us…"

He let his words trail off there, and I nodded slowly before looking back to *Hester* on the bridge monitors, "Not much of an assault ship."

"It should get the job done. And we'll do the same. I don't think Grant will see us coming, not like this," my friend replied, his tone revealing that his mind was only half-involved with the conversation.

Already he was walking through the plan — looking at all the things that could go wrong, and all the things that needed to go right.

Even in the midst of all that pondering, he wasn't too worried. Rufus had come up with plenty of good ideas that were explicitly designed to keep the assault force alive, and Charlie truly believed that he was going to make it back… that most of the landing party would.

He also believed they'd have Grant in custody when they returned.

"Take care of yourself," I finally said after that bout of internal dialogue.

Charlie looked at me as I spoke, and we shared a very strange moment. Looking back, a lot of this was weird… because we'd parted ways before this, and now were back together again, like old times. We both seemed to have different lives, and yet somehow this moment was right out of the old days.

Anyway, that moment of strangeness ended with Charlie sticking out his hand, and me taking it.

"We'll get him for you. Have a good fight up here."

"Will do."

With that, Charlie left the bridge, and soon he was aboard the last shuttle bound for *Hester.* As we watched that SAU ship finish loading, and then gave orders to reset our course for Valcour, I remember being very glad that of all the people who could have been going down into Grant's dome, Charlie Peters was helping lead the way.

There's only one person who might have been more dangerous to Grant than Charlie, and she was waiting for me in her cabin, because it was nearly supper time.

As soon as we were closed up at cruising stations, I left Andrea in command and went to see Karen.

CHAPTER TWELVE

FINALLY

In case you're wondering, I'd never had any notion of being aboard *Hester* during this fight. Despite my history of doing stupid stuff, and my recent forays into completely irresponsible ragefulness, I knew that I had no business being involved in that part of the assault. With Wes laid up (thanks to my own stupidity), I was the only active flag officer with the Belt Squadron as we accelerated towards Etat Valcour, *Hester* cruising in our lee. I'd trust Charlie and Rufus to handle things. I had work to do, a role to play... and only by doing my actual job could I have a chance of beating Grant.

Karen didn't have a job to do. Just the opposite: she was entirely superfluous to our operations at this point. And as much as her presence was a boost to everyone's morale, it was torture for her to have to sit and watch from the sidelines.

It was something she needed to talk about, and as I stepped into her cabin, I could see that immediately.

"We're all set?" she asked her first question as soon as the hatch shut behind me.

She saw on my face that I realized she'd been waiting anxiously to get an update on the situation, and as soon as she knew that I knew, she groaned, "Sorry. I just... I want to be able to do something."

Karen knew the plan — she'd been in the meeting, obviously — but she was under no illusions that, in her current state, she'd be of much help to Charlie or Rufus when they hit Valcour's main dome. By the same token, our fully-staffed Belt Squadron wasn't missing a ship commander. She didn't even really want to be on *Wolf's* bridge — she was concerned (perhaps unreasonably) that if she was up there, and got too caught up in the action she was witnessing, she might try to get involved, and as a result disrupt us in the midst of some important combat evolution.

Sitting alone in her cabin and wondering what was happening... that's all she felt qualified to do in this moment.

Which was silly. Stupid, even. Downright wrong.

She took a deep breath and sat on the end of her bed, shaking her head as she did, "You should probably just keep your distance from me until this is over. If I'm going to be such a needy guest, I could get in the way when the shooting starts."

"Really?"

Karen looked up at my question — which she assures me sounded pretty incredulous — and then shrugged, "Well, yes?"

Of course it was yes — because we were in another low period. Another moment of wondering whether she'd ever again be fit for her job. One of those deeply annoying and later embarrassing fits of self-pity that defied reason, and were infectiously absorbing.

I wasn't immune to these, but since Charlie outlined the situation to me, I did feel somewhat better-positioned to deal with them. I therefore folded my arms and leaned against the wall beside Karen's screen.

Then I tried to think of something intelligent to contribute. Trying to follow Charlie's example is never easy — he sets a high bar — but this was Karen, so obviously I was obligated to try.

Karen sat on her bed and looked up at me with a frown, and then continued staring at me as I stood there, trying to think of the right thing to say. But as we've re-established lately, I usually have a tough time coming up with the correct words. So I just kept standing there.

After what had to be five minutes, Karen tilted her head slightly. Her expression now was both morose and confused — which is a very lovable combination of expressions for her, warranting again the comparison to a puppy being flummoxed by a new toy — and her words backed up that sentiment, "Um… is this a staring contest?"

"No," I definitely sounded defensive, and that just made her look more confused.

"Then… so…"

I shook my head rapidly, "I'm just doing what Charlie did when he came over to talk about my state of mind. It really helped."

Karen blinked a couple of times, shifted her weight slightly, "He… stood silently and glared at you?"

"No, obviously," I shook my head. "He said things. Gave advice. You know, stuff about my state of mind, and why I was being the way I'm being. So… that helped."

Clearly that explanation would answer all her questions. Because it was so well-thought-out and grammatically correct.

Karen added a gently-creased brow to her look of morose confusion, "But… you aren't saying anything."

She had a point there, and I nodded once, "Well, yes. But that's because it's tough to figure out what to say to you. I mean, I know you're feeling like a fifth wheel right now, and that there doesn't seem to be an obvious place for you. But there is a place. You're too good to be sidelined at a time like this."

I obviously didn't have Charlie's knack for getting the right message across, because a little bit of disappointment mixed into Karen's expression. Seriously, so many different emotions all present at the same time — her face was a work of art, painted with many layers of meaning.

Holy hell, that almost sounded literary.

But the disappointment was real, and justified. In response to my great morale-boosting speech, she answered: "Thanks coach."

She sounded defeated, and I didn't like it. That said, I didn't think it'd be right for me to tell her I didn't like it, because I didn't think I had the right to judge her in any way under these circumstances.

Well, you know how this ride ends. I'm an idiot, and you're probably sitting there just telling me to stop over-thinking things. More importantly, you're probably telling me to stop boring you with all this filler, and just get to the part where we attack Valcour. So fine, I'll wrap this up quickly.

Karen was surprised when, instead of trying to say something else, I crossed the floor to her bed, bent down and kissed her. She wasn't expecting me to push her back onto the

bed either, or to keep kissing her as one of my hands clasped the left side of her neck —
the place I'd once nearly cut through with a steak knife.

In completely surprising her, and carefully guiding her up the bed so that her head
reached her pillows and she could sink down into the form-fitting but still-unfamiliar
hollow of her mattress, I ended the conversation. For about four hours.

Now wait a minute... is this the first time Karen and I had kissed? Obviously not.
You read about us kissing at that press conference at the end of *The Pax Terra*. This time
there were no cameras, though — and I suppose we couldn't use the 'it was for the morale
of the Empire' excuse.

My editors have jumped to the conclusion that we did more than kissing, too. This is
logical on their part, because presumably four hours provides time for all sorts of things.
Several hands of whist, or perhaps a recitation of *Hamlet*, or a deep and meaningful
discussion about human history.

You'll be disappointed to know that we did none of those things.

You'll be even more disappointed to know that I'm not going to elaborate on what we
did do. Sorry, but a gentleman doesn't kiss and tell... and neither do I. You couldn't pay
me enough. Believe me, my editors have tried.

But in the interests of not being a coy and bastardly hack (just a regular, somewhat
uninspiring hack) I will admit this to you: we definitely spent those four hours together
in a rather intimate way.

Yes, like that.

Which means that Karen and I were *together* together. Now you can make your own
guesses as to whether that was the first time in all our years since the alley, or if it was just
the first time since she'd joined *Wolf* in Union space, or if it wasn't a first time at all. But
it was a time.

And it helped.

By the time we were both hungry enough to get out of bed and shower, our states of
mind had changed. Took us a while to get food out onto trays for a late supper, but as we
settled in and ate, we started talking again.

"So... like we were going to talk about earlier... where should I be for this?"

"The battle?" I asked for clarification between bites of fish sticks, and Karen nodded.

I chewed and swallowed, "Adrienne's left half of Wolfstar Squadron on our deck, and
they could certainly use a veteran pilot heading them."

Karen was looking at her plate as I made the suggestion, and she didn't stop scooping
up rice as she listened, "I think I can do that."

"I know you can do that," I replied immediately.

I didn't need to elaborate any further — Karen had been in the planning meeting,
so she knew that Adrienne and half of Wolfstar were going in with *Hester*, to protect the
assault dock. The rest of the squadron would be out screening for *Wolf*, and it wouldn't
hurt at all to have a veteran commanding.

Or in this case, a hot-shot pilot who'd just recently been promoted to her first
command, before being sidelined briefly by an accident.

"Okay. I'll do that," Karen looked up just before putting the rice in her mouth, and as she chewed I dropped my fork and knife to my plate.

"Really, that's it? You know you could have saved us both four hours and a lot of sweat if you'd just been less self-doubting earlier."

Yes that's what I said. Not my finest piece of dialogue, but true nonetheless.

Karen shrugged, causing the sheet she'd wrapped around herself to fall slightly off her shoulder, "Perhaps. But this was all part of my secret plan."

"No, it was part of *my* plan," I shook my head.

"My plan," Karen returned her gaze to her plate, pushing the food around rather disinterestedly. "I think we should fight about it."

You know, we did.

There's not a whole lot else I will tell you about this night before the battle. Some of you might be shocked by what you've read already, others disappointed that I haven't said more... and maybe some of you are just relieved that it finally has happened.

Whatever camp you fall into, let me just explain one thing: I hope you know by now that I don't tend to treat these sorts of relations casually. They have their time and their place, and it's not often that such a time or place is right before a major battle in which many lives are ultimately on the line.

But this was one of those rare occasions, like you see in the movies, where the night before the battle was the time for such connections, not because we were especially worried that this would be our last opportunity, but because sometimes there's no better way to... alter your perspective.

And strangely, Karen and I weren't the only ones finding ourselves requiring such a departure on the night before the final clash. It was just a different sort of experience for the other member of our old Academy trio...

CHAPTER THIRTEEN

PARALLELS

My editors remain baffled about the last chapter — delighted, I'm sure, but largely baffled. I had told them I'd never discuss any personal relations of this sort, but now I've gone and done it. One of them started reading the chapter while walking with a ceramic cup of coffee, and apparently that ended badly. Apologies to his cat.

Now we take a dangerous turn: we go to Grant's bedroom on the same night. I'm not about to start comparing notes in any way, shape or form. But the reason I bring this up... well, it'll become clear in a while. It's not a sudden bout of voyeurism.

Etat Valcour local time actually lined up perfectly with Imperial Standard Time — a choice that Grant had made shortly after taking over as Governor, and which he'd instituted as part of his anti-Empire defense strategy. There was nothing more dangerous, he'd assured his people, than facing the possibility of a well-rested squadron assaulting you at what was lunchtime for them, and midnight for yourself.

Fair enough, though I tend to think that time differences can hurt you or help you, no matter what side you're on.

Anyway, the effect of this policy was simple: Grant was spending the night with Sonia, and right around the time Karen and were I fighting over whose plan it had been for us to spend those four hours together, he was getting out of bed and wrapping himself in a robe, so he could go from his bedroom to the study in his residence.

"Where are you going?" Sonia interrupted him as he was about to leave, and he stopped at the foot of the bed and looked back at her.

"Just need to think," he answered.

Grant always needed to think, unsurprisingly, but Sonia didn't seem as sympathetic to that need as she usually was.

Instead of simply nodding, she summoned him back, "Come to bed. Hold me."

Now I honestly rolled my eyes the first time I heard on the spy logs, but I suppose I shouldn't have. She had the right to say whatever she wanted to say... and obviously it worked on Grant, because the villain sighed and then did as he was asked. Returning to bed, he put his arms around the Egesta survivor with whom he was clearly in love, and she seemed to draw comfort from his presence.

"You think they're going to be here soon, don't you?" Sonia asked him, and Grant took a deep breath before nodding.

It feels uncomfortable watching these surveillance feeds — not the ones where they're actually being intimate, I've never seen those, but the ones where they're being loving and human towards each other. It's very intrusive, to be able to see that look on Grant's face... the look I recognized from times long before, when girlfriends too immature to appreciate his deep and brooding concern had earned his protectiveness (for however long that lasted).

Holding onto Sonia in the middle of the night, wondering when the Belt Squadron was going to show up and whether he'd seen every possible outcome as completely as he believed he had, Grant was worried. He was anxious the way I was supposed to be anxious — he was like a real leader, concerned for the fate of those who'd put their faith in him.

Particularly concerned for Sonia.

"Soon?" his beloved asked him again, reminding him of her earlier question, and Grant nodded, pulling her closer to him.

"Tomorrow. Even early this morning. I can just tell."

He was guessing, but guessing well. There had been no indication of our approach thus far, so it really was just his gut telling him that we were nearby.

"It's going to be okay," Sonia promised him next, and his expression again twitched in a manner I was familiar with.

He didn't think Sonia was correct — he believed that, like many people, she wasn't as smart as he was, that she couldn't see all the angles the way he could. Grant's entire life had been plagued by the knowledge that he was the smartest person in the room, and that so many people simply couldn't comprehend the complex issues he was so easily able to cope with.

There was no question that he loved Sonia — his passion for her was deep and profound. He cared because he knew where she'd come from, and what she'd survived. He'd seen the scars on her body, and talked her through night terrors. He had fallen in love with a broken soul, and she'd rewarded him with unfaltering devotion, passion and companionship.

Things he'd never really had. Things he'd always desperately wanted.

But she just wasn't as smart as he was — couldn't see the whole picture as well as he could. And because of that, she didn't really know how dangerous the next twenty-four hours would be.

The realities of the situation were very much weighing Grant down, and as she read the heaviness in his expression, Sonia seemed to decide to follow the same path Karen and I had mutually decided to take — the physical one.

With Sonia expressing herself in that manner, Grant Merger's mind was well and truly dragged away from the dangers that were soon to come to his doorstep. You might not believe it's possible for an evil genius to be so easy distracted, but let me just assure you that nothing about this was simple.

Sonia was closer to him than any other woman had ever been, and that was the only reason she was able to clear his mind, and ultimately let him sleep for a few hours. It was not a matter of physiology but psychology, and it was for him a gift... a gift that I quite understand.

But as he slept, his arm draped protectively around the woman he loved (even in spite of her intellectual limitations), the Belt Squadron was hurtling towards Etat Valcour. With us was *Hester*, and an assault force determined to catch them both.

And if we got our hands on Sonia Hart, who's to say we wouldn't show Grant exactly how it felt to have that one person taken away from you in a brutal, unfair, uncaring way.

We needed my old friend alive for the cure to Karen's memory loss, but we'd have plenty of leverage with which to get what we needed.

That all being said, then, let's not wait any longer. Time to reach Etat Valcour. Time for the last big ship engagement of this series.

It's going to be a hell of a fight.

CHAPTER FOURTEEN

THE APPROACH

Many of the details of the battle we're about to relive have been repeated in countless formats — history books, popular novels, movies, documentaries, and even (confusingly) on the back of the box for a certain brand of cereal. As is always the case, some of the accounts you'll have seen are closer to the truth, and others are farther away. I think because of the significance of this action, many writers have taken license with it — done things to try to amp up the drama.

But it was dramatic enough without their ministrations.

Before we get too deep in, let me correct a few common misconceptions. First, Grant never took command of his fleet — not from a SAUN ship and not from his desk. He was overall strategic commander, of course, but you'd never catch him giving orders to aim specific turrets and fire at a certain time... that's for the skipper of a ship to do.

Also, there were no SAUN fighters in the picture. I think because watching Starlights do a deadly dance can be entertaining, many of the movies have invented SAU interceptors (or other comparable single-seat combat craft) to try to liven things up... and, memorably in a couple of cases, create more danger for Karen in this whole escapade.

There are a few other misconceptions, but I'll reference them at the appropriate points in the action. So for now, let's get started with *Wolf* leading the Belt Squadron into the Etat Concord local defense zone.

In case you're not familiar with the concept of a local defense zone, it's basically the sphere of space surrounding a base, asteroid or planet that's actively watched and defended by the local military forces.

We call them all sorts of different things... the bottom line is that as soon as *Wolf's* bow pod crossed this frontier, we appeared on the sensors of everyone waiting for us in Etat Valcour. Lit up their screens like Christmas trees.

Of course, we didn't know exactly when that moment came — unfortunately space isn't very good about providing dotted lines to let you know when you're in passive detection range of planetary scanners. That didn't matter, though, because as I waited with folded arms at the front of *Wolf's* bridge, I simply went on feeling.

"I think they know we're here," I said around 0100, and then glanced up at the screens. All the skippers were up on Battlelink, and they each nodded or showed their agreement in one way or another.

"Estimate we'll be on their doorstep around 0600," Shelby McLaws turned to me with that report from her Helm and Navigation consoles. "Maintain speed?"

With a nod in reply, I confirmed her assumption, "Yep. We'll kill them all at breakfast."

I may not have sounded quite so disproportionately vicious that time, though the sentiment itself was hardly diplomatic. Andrea was beside me on the bridge, and she cast a glance my way — a stare that was somewhere between matter-of-fact and slightly-but-not-too-judgmental — and then she turned away from me, to Lieutenant Gavin Nigh who'd taken over Sensors and Communications in Felicia's absence.

"Keep an eye out for scouts," *Wolf's* Captain warned somewhat redundantly. None of us expected the approach to Valcour to be as straightforward as our arrival at Lexington, so vigilance would be vital.

Who knew what tricks Grant would have in store.

It was that concern that led to my next order: "Squadron to General Quarters. Just in case."

Normally, you might recall, we could remain at standby action stations until we were much closer to a fight. Bringing our crews to full General Quarters five hours before we reached our target could leave them tired and worn... but since we were going after Grant, we weren't taking chances.

Besides, our crews were all Belt Squadron (or Independent Squadron in *Nova Scotia's* case), meaning a few extra hours at action stations weren't going to do them any particular harm.

As the men and women aboard *Wolf* hurried to their combat posts, I continued to watch the bridge screens, wondering what the villain was seeing, wondering what he'd have in store for us.

Surely it had to be something clever.

A very gentle knock on the door woke Grant. Despite Sonia's best efforts, he had still only managed to sleep quite lightly... but that still meant he had slept some. That was good for him — kept the mind sharp.

"Come," he called thoughtlessly as he sat up in bed, and as the door to his bedroom opened he saw Fletcher Karadzic outlined against the light from the hallway.

"They've crossed the outer perimeter," the security man announced gruffly.

Grant didn't react for a moment, but then he nodded and began to shift his legs out from under the covers, "Thank you. We'll start the civil defense alert at... 0330. Caldecott knows?"

"Yes," Karadzic answered. "And somehow it hasn't caused him to pop yet."

It was obvious that the security man liked Caldecott no more than anyone else, and Grant sympathized... briefly.

"Fine. I'll get ready and meet you in my office shortly. Let's make sure all the connections to the situation room are running smoothly."

"Already checked," Karadzic interrupted, his haste revealing some of the excitement he harbored about the impending battle.

"Check again," Grant didn't want excitement to disrupt communications, and his order was flat enough to brook no argument.

"I'll see you up there, sir," Karadzic nodded, and when Grant remained silent, he closed the door and restored the couple to complete darkness.

Sonia was struggling to wake as the conversation that had disturbed her ended. She rubbed her eyes and looked up at Grant, sitting in the bed beside her, then rolled onto her side and checked the chrono, "Are they coming already?"

With a nod, Grant put his feet on the carpet beside the bed, then took a few deep breaths, "This is the day. This is how it begins."

He was worrying one last time, the way I should have been.

He knew the importance of what was about to occur… knew that all the plans he'd implemented since the beginning of the Martian War… since sending his ships out after the Jupiter Squadron to stage that alien situation on *Idaho*… since stealing Caldecott and arranging the attack on Daragh's ball… all of that had been orchestrated to create the day that he was about to experience.

Soon there would be no more time for worrying — battle would be joined and certainty would take over. But sitting on the bed in pure darkness, he had one last moment of doubt.

Then he felt Sonia's hands on his back. Now say what you like about stereotypes or gender roles or whatever… in this particular situation, the greatest value that woman could provide was reassurance. She'd made it entirely clear over her years with Grant that she wasn't smart like Karen… wasn't a strategic equal (or superior) he could count on to make decisions and change the course of wars.

But she was the woman he loved, and her firm hands, coming from a past of violence, were able to impart calm.

"You're going to do this," she said to him as she pressed her whole body up against his back. "It hasn't all been for nothing. I believe in you. And whatever happens, we'll be together."

I have a fairly high standard for reassuring comments, thanks to a lifetime of being in a partnership with Karen McMaster, so I'm not really a fair judge of whether those words were good or bad. However, they made Grant nod.

He turned his head to look back at Sonia, and found himself pressing his nose into her cheek as she planted her chin on his shoulder.

Together they sat on that bed for two long minutes, sharing in silence the confidence that came from such a deep relationship. Eventually, Sonia released her man, and he proceeded to prepare himself for the day. She watched him dress and knew she'd soon have to join him… but he'd need to be alone first.

No more words were exchanged; Grant's mood began to change as he put on his Governor's suit. He'd be well-dressed for this battle, as was proper, and when he checked himself in the mirror after donning his attire, it was obvious the doubts were gone.

It was time to lead, and to lead alone. Sonia understood this, so she gave him space to go ahead, while she wrapped up in the sheets of his bed and watched. They'd be together again after the fighting ended… unless I got in the way…

Karen was sitting in the observation lounge for flight bay two, a pad in her hand as she reviewed again the changes to the HUD in her Starlight. There weren't many, but as always happens over a decade, software upgrades had come and gone, leaving some of the details she remembered behind. She was reasonably comfortable with her understanding of the latest-model OS XX flight control software, but since she had time to kill she figured it was worth reviewing one more time.

After another round of flipping through the IFF screens, she looked up quickly to check on the pilots of Wolfstar Squadron… or the half of the squadron that remained aboard *Wolf*, the rest having been shipped over to *Hester* to protect the Trojan horse from close-in fire during its assault docking.

None of those flyers seemed to be paying her much attention, and that was good for everyone. I've spoken to a few of the pilot officers, and their reaction to having Karen leading them has been consistent: *we didn't care if she remembered what it was like to walk a bridge, we knew she was hell in a cockpit.*

Maybe that confidence was the sort one becomes accustomed to from brash and bold pilots... but I think they were making a pretty safe bet. Like I said a little while back, in these books we've gotten to know Karen as a ship commander, but she got the promotion to her first bridge on the back of her stellar fighting and flying.

And because she'd forgotten everything that had happened since that promotion, the argument could be made that she wouldn't even be rusty.

Karen appreciated their silent acceptance — she'd been sure to introduce herself to each of them in as minimally-awkward a manner possible, and now she was certain they'd be the best backup she could ask for, on a mission that was more important to her than just about anyone else.

That was the thought that caused her to look back down at her pad — not to read what was on the screen, but to make sure none of her musings were revealed to her pilots through her expression.

She wasn't going in with the assault force. She wasn't going to be the one to lay hands on Grant, and neither was I. We were trusting Charlie and Rufus to get the bastard, and then once we had him, we'd need to find the antidote.

Karen didn't expect that to happen all at once — wherever the cure was (because it simply had to exist) it probably wouldn't just be a matter of storming into a lab and finding a vial marked 'Karen's Antidote'. There might not be samples of the compound... it might only be blueprinted somewhere, meaning we'd have to take it back to Earth and get it manufactured, tested and then injected.

Or maybe it wouldn't be a compound, maybe it'd be a specific course of treatment that would be detailed in documentation our landing forces would have to locate and seize. It could be anything... but she wouldn't be there to lay hands on it.

That was going to be a let-down, and she knew it. But she trusted the people going after the cure. She didn't know those people (aside from Charlie), but they were Belt Squadron, and they were my trusted officers... so she knew they were the best.

Blinking at that certainty, she adjusted her eyes and started reading the pad more carefully again. The IFF panel was definitely different, making it easier to re-code and transmit Identify Friend or Foe signals on the fly. That was a pirate-hunting trick — the ability to completely change the identity of your plane at the drop of a hat, to get close to pirates without them noticing. Karen thought it was clever, though she suspected (correctly) that in combat it was next to useless. Having your computer lie to another computer was fine, but rarely did opposition sensor officers fall for something so rudimentary.

Anyway.

Karen continued to review her pad, patiently waiting as *Wolf* led the Belt Squadron closer to the fight.

+++

A quick aside here to answer an editor's question: I suppose it might seem odd that Karen wasn't on the bridge waiting with Andrea and I, but it's not as abnormal as you might think. I mean, how often have you seen Adrienne Thompson waiting on the bridge for orders to put her planes into space?

Granted, Karen's very different in some elemental ways from our elite fighter commander... but in this situation, her command was Wolfstar Squadron, so it was her responsibility to wait with her pilots, as much as it was mine to wait with my skippers on the bridge.

So that's that.

Grant stepped into his office at 0141 in the morning, and found it bustling with activity. Karadzic had various members of the Governor's Defense Staff hurrying around, converting the mostly-posh space into a mini-situation room — screens were being rolled in, tables cleared for large charts to be laid out, and comm feeds hidden behind the faux-wood wall paneling activated so the entire colony could be commanded from one place.

Why Grant had decided to turn his office into the situation room for his mansion was a mystery to everyone — he had a perfectly good command and control centre in the basement of his swanky government building. But the decision had been taken during the remodel after his election, and because his acolytes have a habit of doing what they're told without asking too many questions, everyone just accepted his will.

Of course he knew, and Sonia now knew, his purpose was to make sure he was close to the access tunnel to his escape ship (the hatch was in his office bathroom, remember).

As he entered the room and stopped, Grant looked past all the commotion to the half-closed bathroom door, and to anyone who *really* knew him, the look on his face was obviously one of contemplation. Would he need to use that strange escape ship today, or would the Belt Squadron crumble? Either outcome would serve his ultimate plan well enough... but if he was honest with himself, he hoped he got to stay.

If the Belt Squadron was wrecked over Etat Valcour, with or without survivors, he'd be able to stay here with Sonia, and love her until he was elected President. Then she'd be at his side as he built the Union of Solar Asteroids into a force that could break the grip of the Empire, and shine a new light over human society — a culture that allocated power and resources based on merit, not some foolish notion that all people were the same.

Grant wanted that so much, because he believed we Imperialists were evil, and wrong. Today was the day we'd play chess for the fate of the solar system.

"Governor," Karadzic spotted Grant's arrival and moved to greet him.

"Fletch," the villain nodded back. "Preparations?"

"We'll be all up and running momentarily. Green group is at action stations, and awaiting orders. Ground defenses are standing by."

With a single deep breath, Grant smiled, "Then the board is set. Good work, Fletch... let's get the screens active so we can watch my old friend arrive."

Sitting in the copilot's seat of his assault shuttle, Charlie Peters rested his hands on the stock of his MAG-90 and closed his eyes. The shuttle was dark — sitting inside

Hester, it was empty but for Charlie, as the Branchers were all out in the improvised armory, stocking up.

I probably don't need to tell you how long it had been since Charlie had been aboard an assault shuttle — the last time had been back at Mercury, when he and Rufus had kicked their way into the dome ahead of the main landing and lost half their teams doing it. Given that history, it would undoubtedly have been quite understandable if Charlie was now feeling apprehensive. But he wasn't.

Don't take that to suggest that my friend Major Peters was somehow superhuman (even though he is). Even Branchers can get anxious, as Charlie had when he uncovered the location of the Blockheads' recreational facilities on Egesta. This time, though, my friend just didn't feel the need. A grim certainty had come over him — familiar as the certainty he'd felt before many other missions like this one, dating all the way back to times Karen could at this point still remember.

One last time, my friend was going to charge into a hostile dome, and on this occasion his prey was the most dangerous of all.

Fine, he'd deal with it, then go home and join Lia in running the Protectorate. This last loose end to tie up, and then he'd find peace for the rest of time.

Of course declaratives like 'the rest of time' are dangerous, but for a while at least.

That was an odd thought, and Charlie opened his eyes as it went through his head. Glancing sideways to the pilot's seat, he could have sworn he saw someone there... someone black and white and wearing blue... but the chair was empty.

Not yet.

Charlie wasn't one to be spooked by ghosts, but sitting in that cockpit my friend had to wonder if there were indeed some aboard this shuttle. It was the same craft that had ferried Carly Henderson's remains back from Pion Rock... that Chet Srisai had piloted for many missions that had ended with blood.

Was Carly here now? Were the rest of his old officers, who'd fallen during the war? Charlie once told me that 'there are no atheists in foxholes' — that sometimes, because of the places you go and the things you see, you're forced to *believe*. Maybe now there were ghosts with him, or old souls, or maybe humanoid wolves, cats and bears...

With such an internal monologue running in his head, you'd expect Charlie to jump when Rufus actually said: "One more run."

I mean, you're thinking about ghosts and having weird thoughts appearing in your brain, so you should jump when someone appears without warning behind you in the darkened cockpit, right?

Nah, Charlie simply blinked himself back into focus and nodded, "I look forward to this being the last one."

Rufus wasn't ready to leave the service behind yet (obviously), but he nevertheless understood his friend and counterpart's sentiment, "We'll make sure you get back to Lia safe and sound this time. I'm not going through that twice."

He was referring to nearly losing Charlie on Mercury, and my friend nodded to the Chinese Major, "Appreciate it. I think your plan will get us a long way, too."

Coming up beside Charlie and looking out the window of the assault shuttle's cockpit, Rufus tipped his head slightly and overlapped his hands on the stock of his MAG-90, which was dangling from his vest.

"Let's just hope they're not expecting a Trojan horse," he said.

Charlie frowned slightly, looking out the window in the same direction as Rufus, "Trojan horse be damned. Let's hope they're not ready for *Hester*."

That was fair, and Rufus nodded. Then together the two best Special Branch Majors I've ever known waited for their time to storm Etat Valcour.

"Looks like they did pick up an extra hull," Karadzic pointed to the additional icon beside our squadron, and Grant nodded.

We were all accounted for, and we weren't even attempting to hide the ship we'd stolen... so what were we up to? Was it simply a need for another vessel to carry out the landing while the Belt Squadron proper held off green group?

"Ken's not even hiding it..." Grant said quietly as he frowned at the screen.

"A decoy? He forcing them along so we'll think they're the assault ship, when he'll have landers come from a different direction?" Karadzic was largely an idiot, but he did have enough guile to imagine such a thing.

As his frown deepened, Grant took another deep breath and then answered, "I don't know. Order Caldecott to hold off opening fire on it immediately. Might be some sort of ploy to get us to kill our own people... try to turn the public against us, even if we win."

Karadzic snorted a laugh, "You think he's that stupid?"

Grant didn't think I was stupid at all (one of the premises he always got wrong when planning against me), but still, holding *Hester* unhidden in our lee was confusing indeed.

He couldn't dwell on it, though, because Sonia Hart appeared behind him, pad in hand, "General Mokotosos reports the ground defenses are all ready. The citizen and freed regiments are being held back at the rally points for deployment at your order, the militia is rallying at the stadium, and our units are all at their designated posts."

One thing Grant truly appreciated about Sonia was the way she could wall off her emotions at will. He knew that skill had probably been learned in a rape room on Egesta, and he thought that was a hellish way to learn anything... but it was vital. Because she wasn't the woman from his bed now; she was one of his key aides.

"Thank you," he turned back to her with a nod, then took the pad when she offered it.

The deployment was fairly standard: he knew we'd have to come in through airlocks, but didn't know which ones we'd try to force. If we went through the tower that jutted out of the dome, he'd have us trapped under fire in a maze. If we did what Rufus and Charlie had done on Mercury, and tried to force a service lock outside the tower, he'd drop militia on us to absorb our heavy weapons... then hit us with the volunteered and freed regiments, followed by real force.

There was no way we had enough SF to crack his ground defenses, but he knew we knew that too — and he knew better than to underestimate our cleverness.

"Alright, lock down the mansion now. They might have sent assassins ahead, so find Renault and have him wait on this floor. If anyone arouses his suspicions, make sure they don't get through that door," Grant gave that order both to Sonia and Karadzic, and as they nodded and left his side, he turned back to the main screen that had been set up facing his desk.

He knew I had to have some sort of gambit, because if I didn't, this was literally just a game of chess in which we could both see the other person's pieces the whole way. But one thing Grant always believed was that you could never counter a foolish attack until you saw it — until you had a moment to understand the mistake being made.

Since I was baffling him, and since by the very nature of his position he was on the defensive, that meant my once-friend was going to have to concede the first move to me.

"Signal *Liberty*, Admiral Caldecott. He is to hold his ships in orbit of this asteroid, not go out to meet the enemy," he ordered.

And with that, the game began.

CHAPTER FIFTEEN

SETTING UP THE BOARD

When we got the Valcour defense squadron on our screens, I folded my arms and studied the icons in silence.

"Eight ships, oh my," Kris was unapologetically condescending with that remark from her screen — and fair enough, considering how easily the Lexington squadron had folded.

But neither she nor any of the other skippers needed a reminder that Grant was behind these SAUN vessels.

"We're about half an hour from weapons range... about thirty-five minutes from the rock itself," Gavin Nigh reported from Sensors and Communications, and I nodded before Mark Gunney added his thoughts.

"One each... I suspect that'll be fine for the frigates, a bit more creative for the corvettes."

He was indicating that the cruisers might be a bit more dangerous to a smaller ship like *Friendly*, but would be easier work for *Cheetah* and the other bigger guns. This wasn't an unreasonable assumption, nor was he discounting the skill of our smaller ships — remember, he'd skippered *Honesty* at the start of the war, and had been a hell of a corvette commander.

"We'll find a way to make ourselves felt," Matt Baxter assured him, and Isoruku Togo and Katya Romanov both agreed with nods of their own.

From the bridge of *Lady Grace*, Kate Levec had started to look a bit less cavalier — this was going to be her first time skippering in a serious gunfight, and though things at Lexington had gone well, she expected this time would be harder.

"One of them is a battleship," Rozy Young was still an outsider in this group, so her interruption was surprisingly jarring.

I looked to screen three, where she was standing on Wes' bridge, "You're sure?"

If you'll remember, the ships of the Independent Squadron, despite being slightly older than the *Predators* of the Belt Squadron, had been kitted to the gills with tools that would help them fight pirates, and that included some sorts of sensors that, while not on the level of the mysterious corvette *Melbourne* — [all square-bracketed] — did give Rozy a clearer picture than we had on our screens.

"Definitely. Fourth from the left has a bigger profile," she answered, still not sounding overly impressed with me.

I didn't care; I knew Wes wouldn't have spent the war with her as Flag Captain if she couldn't fight, and I trusted her now.

"Alright, that'll be ours Andrea. Everybody else choose your opponent... eight of them and eight of us. We won't be seeking to disable this time," I gave those orders with a bit of a smile, and then waited as different ships started calling their targets.

Gavin Nigh kindly put different color halos around the icons of the SAUN ships as each of them was claimed, and he also coordinated with *Nova Scotia's* Sensors and Communications Officer to get us a better indication of the battlewagon — information that couldn't be easily transferred through the usual tactical Battlelink because it was a bit too advanced for our standard processors.

That all took a few minutes, after which we had our board laid out. There was no hiding now, so I gave one more order: "Rearrange squadron into line abreast to match them. Everyone face your date, and *Hester* can bring up the rear."

No hiding at all.

In his warehouse-like bridge aboard *Liberty*, Dave Caldecott was watching our deployment with a mix of smugness and panic. Those two things can go together; if you don't believe me, just watch the bridge feeds we appropriated for this fight. Dave strutted around his command deck in the oddest fashion, his hands intermittently wringing in front of him or linked behind his back. He was sweating heavily, to the point where you could actually start seeing dark patches on his uniform (which isn't supposed to be able to happen, since space uniforms should be atmosphere proof), and he wouldn't stop blinking.

"Range to target?" he asked in his squeaky, gruff voice, looking to his Sensor Officer.

"Twenty minutes to combat range for us, sir," that man answered, and Caldecott glared at him. Don't know why he glared, but he did.

Then the stupid bastard went back to pacing, and wringing his hands, and occasionally strutting. I suppose it's possible that he was thinking about two different outcomes for this battle: when he thought about beating us, and proving he'd been the better spacer all along, he strutted. When he was more realistic, and thought about us crushing him like the insignificant piece of shit he was, he was wringing his hands.

Like I say, don't know if that's exactly what was going through his head, but it's a safe bet.

"Range to target?" he asked again, turning back to the Sensor Officer.

"Um," the man looked up from his panels sheepishly, "nineteen minutes, sir."

You know how I say you're supposed to worry before the battle happens, so that by the time you get to the bridge nothing really surprises you, and you can project confidence to the people who need to see you calm? Dave Caldecott wasn't doing that. He wasn't capable of even trying.

That did nothing to help the confidence of *Liberty's* bridge crew, but fortunately for them they had a much better Captain aboard: Rayne Archibald. If you watch the bridge camera feeds closely, you can see people looking at each other and rolling their eyes whenever Davey decides to ask a stupid question. Then they cast glances to their skipper.

Archibald seems aware of every stare on those feeds, too — he obviously had a good rapport with this crew, and that's not to be discounted. Just because the Admiral ostensibly in charge of Grant's defensive squadron was a plaything of our old Emperor didn't mean green group was toothless.

And as proof of that, Dave asked again what the range to target was.

It was seventeen minutes at that point (I checked the time code), but before the Sensor Officer could answer Caldecott's question, Archibald had turned on the Admiral and approached. You can't make out whatever was whispered between the men, but

Caldecott looked none too pleased by the words.

Then he scuttled off to his command chair while Archibald returned to making the rounds of his bridge consoles, occasionally patting his officers and enlisted men on the back, reassuring them about what was to come.

As if he knew.

We didn't know at the time what ships were facing our squadron, but since I have that information now I figure it's important you have it too.

Obviously *Wolf* was going toe-to-toe with *Liberty*, which meant Andrea Kiley was going to be skippering our fine frigate against Rayne Archibald. That put us at a tactical disadvantage, because *Liberty* was a catamaran-style battlewagon with a ton of disruptors and plenty of torpedo tubes.

Lion had lined up to tackle *Constitution*, the first of the *Constitution*-class cruisers that we were facing — all of them, if I forgot to mention it before, were essentially the same generation, though because the SAUN was such a new organization, there were definite differences across the class. Putting *Lion* against the oldest definitely gave Kris the advantage over Captain Kerry Tennant.

Mark Gunney had *Cheetah* lined up against *Constellation*, the next oldest of those cruisers. Another mismatch in terms of firepower, this engagement was tipped strongly in Mark's favor by the fact that his opposing Captain was Ignatious Paul, a once-pirate who fancied himself a hell of a skipper, and wasn't.

While Wes was laid up in *Wolf's* med bay, Rozy Young was going to put *Nova Scotia* up against *Congress*, and that was probably the most even fight. Captain Casey Jenner was not completely incompetent, as far as anyone knew, and the ship was slightly newer than *Constitution* and *Constellation*... while *Nova Scotia* was obviously a bit older. Though that said, I'd tip Rozy as the favorite in any fight, especially with these idiots.

Isoruku Togo was leading *Generous* against *Capitol*, the newest of the cruisers skippered by Howard Haddad. Though a *Noble*-class corvette was undergunned compared to one of these cruisers, there was no question Isoruku had the upper hand here.

Kate Levec's first serious action in *Lady Grace* would see her dueling with *Captain*, and Captain Seymour Lidstrom. That fellow was undoubtedly more experienced in command than was Kate, but Kate had one of the best corvettes ever to put into space, and a lot of natural talent.

Also benefitting from a fine ship was Matt Baxter, because of course he had my old ship *Friendly*. His target was *Chesapeake*, a name he'd later find interesting because the original USS *Chesapeake* had been a frigate that, during the War of 1812, had a hell of a duel with HMS *Shannon*. The Royal Navy ship had ultimately won the fight, but neither vessel was in particularly fine sailing condition at the end of the encounter. Matt later told me he was glad he didn't know that going in, because it probably would have been in the back of his mind the whole time he was doing the hot work against Captain Po Kuma.

The hardest fight of the day, though, was to belong to Katya Romanov and *Sackville*. If you'll recall, that plucky corvette was older than the rest of the squadron and faced a frankly startling deficit when set against *Columbia*, under Captain Leroy Roberts.

So that's how it all stacked up. Don't worry, you don't have to memorize everything...

I doubt the names of the skippers of those SAU ships will even matter again in this book. What's worth remembering is that we had two duels lined up that were pretty much sure wins for our side, one contest that was mostly equal, and then the rest of our squadron was outgunned.

On paper, we'd lost this battle before it started, because as soon as *Sackville* died at the hands of *Columbia*, that ship could work with *Chesapeake* to erase *Friendly*, and then both those cruisers could pile onto *Lady Grace*, and so forth.

We didn't have a hope, unless we stood off and used our lasers to great effect while screening diligently against SAU torpedoes. If we played things cautiously, and fought in a coordinated and clinical fashion, then we could potentially win.

But that wasn't going to happen. I knew it, and Grant knew it.

So we'd see how the chess played out… after some barbs were traded over the comm.

CHAPTER SIXTEEN
ALCIBIADES

Another popular misconception about this battle is that before it began, Grant and I had some sort of discussion over the comm. Face to face for the first time in years, most movies have us trading either witty and razor-sharp insults... or some wince-inspiring dialogue. Here are a few different samples of what was never said, but which some screenwriter actually got paid to write...

Me: "I love you like a brother, Grant!"

Grant: "I hate you!"

Me: "Don't you realize, the Union of Solar Asteroids is, in fact, evil?"

Grant: "From my point of view, it is the Earth Empire that is, in fact, evil!"

Me: "In that case, we cannot be brothers anymore. I hate you too!"

I mean, I know I'm a bad writer, but honestly, that particular movie made a lot of money and I think we should all ask for some of it back.

It's all academic, of course, because Grant and I never said a word to each other before this battle. I suppose that's a missed opportunity for drama, but creating drama was hardly our priority.

The conversation that did take place between both our squadrons was far less... er... heart-wrenching than that fictional one. If anything, I found it delightfully amusing, and somewhat cathartic.

Because as we got down to five minutes from weapons range with green group, I looked across at Gavin Nigh with a question, "Think we can get someone on screen from their flagship, Gav? I'd like to give them the chance to run away before we have to kill them all."

Lieutenant Nigh raised his eyebrows at the suggestion, then nodded once, "We can certainly try, sir."

Gavin had done plenty of hours on the bridge, I should mention — he'd started his post on *Wolf* not long after Felicia had taken over, so he had a couple of years apprenticing with her to get comfortable with the idea of running Sensors and Communications for a flagship. Good succession planning by Felicia, I should add.

Now he tapped one of his technicians on the shoulder, and they set about sending a message across space to *Liberty*.

I waited beside Andrea, both of us looking up at the main screen as it showed the icons of our squadron closing with the icons of Grant's defenders. Two lines abreast of eight ships each...

"Think Grant is commanding that ship himself?" Kate Levec asked a bit anxiously from her bridge, and I shrugged as I shifted my gaze to screen six.

"Probably not. Governor taking command of the Navy sounds romantic, but doesn't leave him many options for getting out if there's trouble. That said, he did command at

Deep Black..."

I trailed off as a *WolfNet* buffering screen appeared in a window of the main monitor. Through Battlelink, every one of our skippers was tapped into the same signal, so we all fell silent as we waited to see who we were up against.

None of us were expecting to recognize the man who appeared... it was honestly a shock, or perhaps it might be better called a pleasant surprise.

"So, Barron, we meet again at last. Ready to be taught some manners?"

Alright, admittedly Dave's dialogue isn't much better than a crap screenwriter's. I heard the voice, and saw the puffy bearded face, but couldn't believe for a moment that it was indeed Dave Caldecott. There was no way. Seriously.

"Wait," Mark Gunney shifted forward in his chair, "Grant's the one who pulled him out of the Coalition? I didn't think the man liked incompetence."

"Explains how he got access to the comm ships, though," Matt Baxter's eyes narrowed thoughtfully.

"Right, they shoveled all of Caldecott's cronies into DCC during the war," Kris added, remembering her own crewing challenges from the year before.

But while my skippers were quickly analyzing the implications of Caldecott being on our screen, I was just gaping... and starting to smile. The fact that I didn't reply to him seemed to irk the former Second Lord, so he needled me with more of his exquisite phrasing.

"Prepare to die, Barron!"

"Oh my God this is too good to be true," I blurted it out, and grinned as I turned to Andrea, then looked back to the screen. "It's really Dave Caldecott. Grant must still have a soft spot for me. What a gift. Everyone, are you seeing this? We get to kill Dave Caldecott today too!"

I was positively giddy at the prospect, and I don't think Dave liked that very much. He's no fun, because he's a waste of oxygen, water and flesh.

"Presumptuous scoundrel. Today we'll see whether your Fiora Ring horseplay is any match for the discipline of a civilized Navy!"

In retrospect it's pretty clear that Dave was trying to puff himself up — you know how some supposedly tough characters need to get their wind up before they start trouble? But it was all just too laughable.

That said, if he wanted to get angry I wasn't going to let him down.

"So you try to stage a coup... was that Grant's idea?"

"I joined with Governor Madison after I was drummed out, not before!" he countered immediately, as if it mattered.

"I love that you're calling him by his alias. There's no way you don't know who you're working for... so he must have made you an offer while you were in the Coalition's hands. So cute. And now you're a big powerful Admiral. Working for whoever pays you..."

He was flushing very red, and starting to quiver with his righteous rage. This delighted me.

"Let me guess: he made you feel important. That's all it takes, right? Satisfy your hubris... you'll work for Defense Command, or the Emperor, or an enemy of the Empire. That's why you're an enemy of the Empire yourself, Dave. That's why you could never go home, even if you survived today."

"I'll have you know that I am going to—"

"Shut up, Alcibiades. Shut up and never speak again. Die in silence, because your voice itself is offensive. Alcibiades..." my tone dropped as I uttered the name again, and then took a couple of steps towards the viewfinder.

Of course, despite his supposedly profound intellect, Dave had no idea what I was calling him. He tried to speak again, but I simply yelled at him, "Alcibiades! Go away and die, Alcibiades. And in Hades you will never be anything more that a shade of a man, without accomplishment or meaning. No one will remember you. No one will care. Die, Alcibiades. You and your ships are about to come under our knife, and that will be your end."

Alright, so I was guilty of the bad dialogue too. When in Rome, I suppose... or more properly in this case, when in Athens, then Sparta, then Persia, then back in Athens again. I don't know if you'll remember back to *The Almost Coup*, but I compared our dear Dave Caldecott to Alcibiades then — a disgraced Athenian politician and General who, when he was driven out of that city state, went first to the enemy city state Sparta, then to the Persian Empire, in each case helping his former enemies against his former home.

Dave Caldecott's name doesn't have quite the same dramatic ring to it as 'Alcibiades' (pronounced Al-kibb-ee-ah-days by all the classicists I know), but he should be similarly remembered.

Asshole.

Anyway, after my rant — which I like to think was fit for Homeric epic, since we had a Trojan horse — I nodded to Gavin Nigh, and the link to *Liberty* was severed.

"I'd offer my applause, but I think we have to open fire," Matt Baxter immediately inserted his commentary, which drew a laugh out of me.

Altogether the wrong mood to carry into battle, but I didn't care. Why should I care? If Dave was leading Grant's defense force, then the only question we had to answer was why he wanted us to win so easily.

We were about to find out.

"Laser range in one minute," Gavin reported, and with that more somber notification I turned my eyes back to the main screen, then watched as the range rings around the icons of our ships came close to overlapping the SAUN markers.

"Ladies and gentlemen, please accept my thanks in advance," I said as my humor faded. "Now for today's labor."

The waiting was over. At last, Grant Merger was in our grasp.

And standing in his office, having just watched the feed beamed down from *Liberty*, my old friend smiled, "Alcibiades. Of course, very clever."

He then looked to both Karadzic and Sonia, who were quite confused. Folding his arms, he shrugged very slightly, "And the best part: Alcibiades won in the end."

Shut up Grant, no one cares about ancient Greece anyway.

Chapter Seventeen

Pawn To King Four

We expected Dave Caldecott's battleship to be the first vessel in this mess to open fire, but it wasn't. Despite being bigger and ostensibly more powerful than any other combatant in local space, it appeared that *Liberty* lacked any particular range advantage over its consorts, or over us. This was a surprise, but not one that we were going to complain about.

"Range in ten... nine..."

"All ships commence fire with lasers as soon as you have tracks," I looked up to the skippers on the screens as I gave that order, and instead of receiving nods in reply, I simply listened as every one of them passed along orders to their XOs.

Andrea did the same: "Jim, fire on that battleship at your convenience."

Jim Hannigan was working the laser controls with his staff at the Operations consoles at the back of the bridge, and he didn't bother looking up or even replying. We all knew he heard us.

"Three... two... one..." Gavin Nigh finished the count, and instantly Jim gave the order.

"Shoot!"

Wolf's laser one cut out into space, its angry red lance getting real work for the first time since the Fleet Clash. Our shot wasn't alone. We've been through this so many times during the war that I almost hesitate to dive in again, but I think that since this is the last Naval battle I'll write for this series, I might as well be thorough.

Every ship in the Belt Squadron was elite. We know that. And their elite nature meant every single XO hit exactly what she or he was aiming at — even at maximum range, there were *no* misses.

Considering we were racing down on Etat Valcour at 194 kps, that's not exactly a mean feat. It was helped by the fact that Dave's ships weren't maneuvering particularly, but nevertheless, for ships that hadn't been in a gunfight since 2233, I think it was an impressive first salvo.

What was more impressive, though, was the way the SAU ships shrugged it off.

"Eight shots and eight hits," Gavin reported for us... and then he followed with: "But no signs of obvious damage to the Union ships. They're accelerating towards us... energy readings climbing."

I nodded at the report, then turned my eyes back to the screen, "Seems Grant kept the tougher ones for himself."

"Sounds like him," Mark agreed from *Cheetah*. "We'll have to do it the old-fashioned way."

That we would; this'd be a shootout with no holds barred. And speaking of holds...

"Launch all fighters for anti-torpedo screening. We'll keep them in a defensive posture for the time being."

As I gave those orders, skippers across the squadron turned again to their XOs, and the launch sirens began to wail. Flight bay doors began to open, and as we sent out second laser shots, Starlights hurtled into space.

"Reduce speed to 150 and stand by for a knife fight."

Karen was first out with the crash launch, and as she hurtled from the flight bay's rear space door and turned her plane over to chase *Wolf* into the fight, she could feel the familiar pleasure of adrenaline flooding her system. Outside her canopy, the endless blanket of stars stretched in every direction... except just ahead of the squadron, where the squat and unpleasant-looking asteroid called Etat Valcour interrupted her vision.

Just ahead of that rock, Karen could make out the tiny shapes of the Union squadron, obvious only because our lasers were running red hot and pointing her to them.

"Wolfstar 825 clearing *Wolf*, squadron form on me and prepare for torpedo defense by section," she didn't let herself get too distracted, and as she gave the order she looked up at the underside of *Wolf*'s hull, watching as we slowed down to 150 kps to prepare for close combat. She matched speeds, then waited as the rest of the planes moved into position around her.

Wolf Squadron was forming up above us, Karen was below, and all those Starlights — together with the planes from the rest of the squadron — were in place to make sure none of the SAU's most dangerous weapons had a chance of doing us harm.

"*Wolf* fighter group in escort position," Karen reported as the formation became clear on her HUD.

She was looking forward to some shooting.

We've spent very little time with Katya Romanov in this series, in part because *Sackville* spent so much of the war away from us. Now she was back, and recognizing that her ship was the most vulnerable in the upcoming fight, she surged ahead of the rest of our formation — a move you might think was a bit crazy.

Standing on her bridge — which was somewhat more cramped than the bridge of a newer *Noble*-class corvette — she could tell I thought it was a bit crazy, because I looked through the screen at her with a frown, "Katya?"

"Indulge me," she answered simply, and I paused for a second before nodding.

Then she turned to her Helm and Navigation Officer, "They are coming out slowly. Go straight at them and close the distance before they turn their broadsides to us."

Katya was fighting with the cleverness that skippers of smaller, older ships need to possess. Mik Mikaelsen, for instance, had employed much guile when he commanded *Cyclops* against those monitors at Mercury... though it had cost him his ship.

Hopefully Katya would have better luck in this situation. No one here had battleship lasers, at least.

"Prepare for focused fire against turrets," Katya continued, obviously having thought this through ahead of time.

From my screen, I called to her again, "You're trying to get at them before they cross our 'T'?"

Katya nodded, but her eyes remained fixed on the screen showing her range to target — not on the viewfinder, which would have created the illusion that she was looking at me.

"Good call. All ships back up to 180. Keep pounding them until they turn, then break formation and see how well they can maneuver," I gladly took that idea from Commander Romanov, and suddenly *Sackville* wasn't advancing alone.

Katya paid the rest of us little attention; her eyes were locked on her main screen, her hand up holding fire until she was close. Her screen two was showing an enhanced camera view of her target, and as it came straight at her she started to see flashes of blue light erupting from it: the disruptor shower had begun.

"Maneuvers," she looked to her Helm and Navigation Officer again, and then abruptly felt *Sackville* begin to shift under her feet. Lights began to flicker.

"Some impacts, ma'am... power systems are being disrupted..." her XO called out that warning, and she nodded.

That was fine — just a little closer.

The rest of the Belt Squadron was firing like it was going out of style, but because *Sackville* was charging out ahead of the rest, and not firing, the line of SAUN ships seemed to take notice. A kamikaze run? Or a torpedo? If they didn't know corvettes of *Sackville's* era carried no torpedoes, that was perhaps a concern.

But no, just a laser, and now Katya was in range to use it, "Point blank, shear off those turrets!"

"Shoot!"

On the enhanced visual, Katya was able to watch the red beam from *Sackville's* number one laser gouge into *Columbia's* hull. At first the armor resisted, but as the beam dragged across its outer plating, and then struck the cruiser's forward-most upper turret, panels began to flake off. The turret jammed.

"Cease fire, target the next one!" Katya's excitement at her success was considerable, and rightly so — she was denying her opponent the ability to cover all the angles he might have liked. If her little ship couldn't outgun his, at the very least she could deny him the opportunity to spin his guns to easily hit her...

The lights on the bridge flashed again, going out for a fraction of a second longer this time.

"Shoot!" the XO called after the blink, and as *Sackville's* red beam dragged over the cruiser's hull, another forward turret was jammed. But the cruiser had eighteen turrets, and the closer *Sackville* got, the harder they hit back — especially because the little corvette lacked the underlying anti-mag shielding that the rest of us enjoyed.

"Severe power fluctuations!" the XO warned again, and as the lights blinked off for an even longer-seeming second, Katya looked up, then back to him.

"Peel off and maneuver violently. Continue to engage their turrets, but we will make them chase us."

Sackville peeled off.

Next over from *Sackville* was *Nova Scotia*, and given my orders to try to get at the Union ships before they'd finished advancing against us, Rozy Young decided to reveal one of her Independent Squadron ship's party pieces: its jump ability.

I've spoken of this before, I believe: Wes' ships all came with the rather fantastic ability to jump speed to over 200 kps for short durations, allowing them to close the range with pirates in an unexpected fashion.

As *Congress* tried to get *Nova Scotia's* range, then, Rozy turned to her Helm and Navigation Officer with a hungry smile, "Let's show them what *we* can do, HNO."

Then she turned to the back of her bridge, "XO, let's not spend time on the turrets. Stand by torpedo for point-blank launch."

Unlike Katya, Rozy did have a torpedo to spare… and unlike the Union models, our torpedoes consistently hit what they were aimed at.

It took a few seconds for everything to be made ready, and in that time Captain Young watched as *Sackville* peeled away, the corvette's aft laser jamming another of *Columbia's* turrets. The SAUN ships then seemed to begin shifting their fire, turning their disruptor bolts against *Wolf* and *Lion* in a bid to put us out of the fight.

That wasn't Rozy's immediate concern, though.

"Ready when you are, ma'am," *Nova Scotia's* HNO reported.

She answered with a nod, "Jump, Mister Richards. Hit them hard, Mister Weathers."

You haven't seen a warship move until you've watched *Nova Scotia* do a jump. I can't actually give you the distance covered or the miniscule amount of time it took (it's still classified) but it was a long way and it was quick.

Congress wasn't ready to have a Defense Command frigate just a few kilometers above its high drive pod that fast. Its turrets began traversing and the ship started to roll to present an upward-facing broadside… but too late.

Nova Scotia dropped its torpedo almost casually, and then chased that shot with mags, hoping to suppress any defensive fire. But there wasn't any point defense — *Congress* didn't have the chance. As Rozy ordered her frigate relatively 'upward', the torpedo drives kicked in at full burn. With only a few kilometers to cover, the impact came within a second, and *Congress* burst.

Better protected or not, a Defense Command torpedo will end your day.

That was our first kill of the battle.

Watching from the bridge of *Liberty*, Dave Caldecott howled with rage, but didn't change tactics.

"Ignore everyone else, concentrate your fire on *Wolf*, and on *Lion*. Those two ships are the leaders. Destroy them!"

Nice of him to narrate the reason for his tactical decision. Honestly, it was a good one — one that, had I been thinking more when I came into this fight, I might have mirrored. Why had I allocated just *Wolf* to take on the battleship in the Union squadron? Hubris?

That wouldn't be unusual for me in 2235, so maybe we should go with that.

Unfortunately, one guy was giving me too much credit.

"This is strange… why not focus all his frigates on *Liberty*?" Grant had fought me before, and played chess against me as well. He knew I was the sort to fixate on the queen — try to destroy her at all costs, even at the expense of too many important pieces.

So why was I now spreading my squadron out against his... it was as though I was playing not to lose... playing to keep all his pieces under threat and immobilized so that...

Oh yes, the Trojan horse.

"What do we know about the ship they brought with them?" Grant pointed that question at Karadzic, and the security man frowned and turned to one of the passing military aides, who called up the information for him.

"Freighter called *Hester*, overdue on an ore run here."

"Have skywatch hail it, warn it to stay off our locks or we will open fire."

Karadzic nodded, then departed to give the orders.

Folding his arms, Grant fixated on the freighter that was sitting back, seemingly unimpressed by the battle going on before it. Was it waiting for a gap to break through? Was it actually a hostage ship of some sort? Whatever it was, Grant meant to treat it with caution.

"As soon as one of our cruisers can detach, have it take a closer look," the Governor of Etat Valcour ordered.

Just one of his cruisers could blast *Hester* out of space...

But funnily enough, they were all occupied.

I know, because they were trying to swat me and my ship. Imagine how the gray-haired personification of *Wolf* must have felt at that rudeness.

CHAPTER EIGHTEEN

BISHOP TO QUEEN'S BISHOP FOUR

"Well this isn't very sporting," Kris Jacobs said as she tightened her hands around the railing at the front of *Lion's* bridge.

The lights were beginning to flash more frequently, and the deck was quaking slightly (not, as people sometimes think, because of the 'impact' of the disruptors, but because the surges they caused in the power grid resulted in brief punches in drive speed). There was no question that Caldecott's decision to focus all his firepower on just two frigates was having a noticeable effect.

On screen two, my face was occasionally distorted by the power ripples, but Kris could nevertheless see me agree: "Yes, seems dear Dave has a score to settle."

Of course he did, but his intentions were of little consequence; Kris turned from me back to her XO with a nod, "Let's maintain fire against our dance partner, no matter who else is shooting. Helm, make sure they have a tough time hitting us."

Those orders drew nods, and as *Lion* continued to spin, climb, twist and drop, the SAU gunners in their exposed turrets kept up as best they could... but as you'll recall, Karen's former frigate had been severely shot up once before. It was hell bent on not being ravaged in such a fashion again.

Kris held on and watched enhanced camera feeds as a seeming hailstorm of blue energy came sailing right at her ship. She knew some of it was striking the hull, and knew that the mag diffusion grid was obviously doing its stuff, because her mains weren't offline.

But with so much focus coming against her hull, she had to give a little back.

"Shoot!"

As that call came from the back of her bridge, Kris held her breath for just a second; the red lance of laser one crossed space to the elder *Constitution* — the cruiser *Lion* had picked to dance with — and cut into that ship's hull yet again.

Plating was beginning to flake off the older-built cruiser; it wasn't bearing up against danger nearly so well as *Columbia*... but a dozen of its turrets were still firing, and their anger was all focused on *Lion*.

"I get the feeling this is going to come down to survivability," Kris said as she looked back to my face on screen two. "They keep pricking us and we'll eventually bleed out... while we're trying to stab them through body armor."

That definitely seemed a fair assessment: the fact that the SAUN ships weren't devastating us with their disruptors was clear proof their weapons were underpowered and perhaps even conceptually flawed... but they'd paired poor weapons with stronger protection. Since we lacked battleship support, we simply had to chip away at them, while they chipped away at us.

If we could get torpedoes into the picture we'd have more success, but we weren't close enough yet — none of us were as nimble as *Nova Scotia*, and we didn't want to chance a long-range launch which would see our precious warheads destroyed short of their targets.

"Keep closing the distance for a torpedo strike," I called back to Kris through Battlelink. "Our ships won't let us down."

Lion seemed to tremor under Kris' feet when I said that, and she smiled at her ship, running her hand back and forth over its rail. She'd been in the frigate's heart — its reactor room — once after a nearly-lethal blow, and they'd both survived. These SAU bastards weren't going to stop them.

And they certainly weren't going to stop *Lady Grace*, since none of them were shooting at Karen's other old ship.

"We'll take some of the heat off you, Kris!"

Kate was starting to settle into her combat command, and as *Lady Grace* crossed our squadron line at a position relatively above the rest of us, the newest skipper in the squadron (not counting Karen) looked back to her XO.

"I can do what Katya's been doing, boss," he said. "We can cook some of their turrets, but I don't think I can drill out their torp bays."

"Turrets are fine for now," Kate nodded, then looked back to her main screen as *Lady Grace's* laser one heated up again.

"Shoot!"

Another red beam — you'll notice we weren't bothering too much with mags, since the SAUN didn't have fighters out, and no torpedoes had separated yet. Better to hit them with the powerful stuff, as their armor was probably keyed to protect them against electromagnetic bolts (since that was all they could shoot).

The shot from *Lady Grace* was rather more powerful than anything *Sackville* could put out, simply by virtue of age: obviously Karen's first command was only a dozen years old — in the prime of its life — while *Sackville* came from a previous generation, with less powerful reactors backing its less sophisticated laser emitters.

Not a knock against the long-time Belt Squadron veteran, you understand, just a fact of that ship's construction.

The additional power behind *Lady Grace's* beam meant it jammed up a turret much more quickly, and combined with *Lion's* next shot, it reduced the ailing *Constitution* to just ten of its disruptor positions.

"Close in and keep firing. Might as well take advantage, since they're ignoring us," Kate continued, and in so doing she ordered her corvette to surge ahead of our assault line, even as we were getting closer and closer to optimal torpedo range.

She'd get there ahead of the game, and make sure at least one more SAUN ship was in no way ready for that moment.

Unfortunately, as Kate moved *Lady Grace* forward and out of position, the opponent she'd originally planned to tackle — who was in fact now pounding *Wolf* quite merrily — was given new orders.

The relatively new cruiser *Captain* broke formation, and took a wide turn to find open space below the part of the line *Lady Grace* and *Nova Scotia* had been filling.

+++

Watching as the cruiser made its break, Karen turned her planes over and moved in for a strafing run.

"Chances of our missiles doing anything are slim, ma'am," Wolfstar 818, Lieutenant Hyujeong Trinh, observed as they made the move, and Karen nodded.

"Might worry him though, since they don't appear to have dedicated starfighter defenses. Close in fast and start lighting him up, see if we can convince him to back off."

The planes of Wolfstar Squadron, followed immediately by those of Wolf Squadron, peeled away from the light show that so far they'd just been observing. There was little point to their presence until the SAU torpedoes began to fly, and in the meantime this brute of a cruiser was headed straight for *Hester*, obviously with orders to figure out what the freighter was up to.

"Wolfstar 825 to *Wolf*, we're tailing the cruiser that's making for *Hester*… requesting assistance from any free warship to make him regret showing us his back end."

It was a typically cavalier sort of remark for fighter commander Karen, and I remember smiling when I heard it.

Unfortunately, she didn't get to carry through with her strafing run, because the next warning summoned her and all her planes back for urgent duty.

"We're not doing enough damage to stop them… it must be that new mag shielding they have," Grant was shaking his head and basically muttering to himself, but as Karadzic heard the words, he frowned.

"I thought Caldecott said it was worthless."

Grant's eyebrow went up, "I'm sure he did say that. There is a reason they threw him out, Fletch, and it wasn't because he was too intelligent… no matter what he tells you."

He tapered off after that, his frown growing ever-deeper as he watched the ranges close. Torpedoes could be unleashed at any moment, but with so many Starlights floating around with nothing better to do, there was little chance the warheads would reach their targets.

That was something he now regretted. Starfighters were largely useless, but some sort of Interceptor — much like the Martians had — might make sense in a situation like this. He'd keep that in mind for the future of the SAUN when he took over as President… though if he was able to make more of the technology that gave his escape ship such speed, perhaps small craft would again be potent.

For now, he just needed to risk it: each of his cruisers carried twenty torpedoes, and *Liberty* had forty, so it was time to start slinging them in massive waves — waves too big for the planes to shoot down.

Captain's move had drawn *Wolf's* fighters off station, so perhaps that was the best opening.

"Orders to Caldecott: flush all his tubes in one wave, focus fire on the frigates."

Okay, so maybe Grant did call some of the shots in this fight.

"Torpedo separation… twenty-four warheads in space!"

Isoruku Togo wasn't surprised by the warning from his Sensors and Communications Officer — he figured the torpedoes had to come soon. Now the first thing he needed to figure was whether any of the warheads were pointed at *Generous.*

So far, the corvette had been spared much attention, so he'd focused his fire on *Capitol* as planned. The cruiser had mostly been ignoring him, allowing him to cut up its drive pods — shooting which would hopefully reduce its maneuverability.

Isoruku, you see, was focusing his fire on propulsion systems because he believed (like another great Naval officer called Togo) that available combat speed ultimately controlled the engagement. If you look up the battle of Tsushima, you'll know what I mean.

"No torpedoes are tracking for us... all are bound right for *Wolf* and *Lion.*"

Nodding at the report, Isoruku considered his options for a moment; he could switch to mag fire, to try to shoot those things out of the sky... but doing so would have the dual effect of crowding the Starlights (whose job it was to bring down the torpedoes) and allowing the SAUN ships to get out another salvo of torpedoes unscathed.

"Switch targeting priority from engines to tubes... see if we can find a way through their launch doors when they fire next," Isoruku offered that order to his XO, then advanced towards the bridge screens.

"Since we can't get at their magazines, we're going to try to cook off their torpedoes in the tubes when next they try to launch," he announced as he looked up at the viewfinder at the front of his bridge.

He couldn't tell because of the Battlelink connection, but my eyes immediately jumped to him, "Excellent thinking. Everybody hear that?"

There were nods and sounds of affirmation from all the other screens, and laser fire tapered off as we waited and watched our enhanced screens for the signs of the next launch.

In space, our planes went to work.

Twenty-four warheads is a lot, but keep in mind that we had more than 100 planes in space, all of them crewed by the best pilots in Defense Command, and all of them with only one mission. It was overkill.

No matter how many torpedoes they had in their magazines, Grant's ships could only fire three at a time (six from *Liberty*). With *Captain* out of formation that meant their salvoes were manageable — as long as we didn't let them fire more too quickly.

Karen noticed the reduction in our laser fire as she led Wolfstar and Wolf Squadrons at full burn to the attack. Because she was only hearing certain combat frequencies through her headset, she didn't know if that was good news or bad — if our systems had been knocked out by all the disruptor fire, or if we were saving up for something special.

In either case, she had a job to do.

"Locking on Tango One," one of her pilots called out. "Going in mags."

It was a calm announcement, as she'd expect from the best pilots in the fleet. Our flyers always took their cues from the more reserved traditions of piloting — from the RAF in the Battle of Britain, not from the Top Gun school, if that makes any sense. They liked to be calm in times of stress, because they were so good they had no reason to worry.

Now one of the warheads disappeared... and then seven more — shot down by different squadrons across the front line. And as Karen lined up two more torpedoes which were clearly meant for *Wolf,* she realized she wouldn't get into range before several other Starlights had a chance.

And a chance was all they needed.

The whole salvo of missiles was blasted away.

"So much for their torpedoes," Karen muttered to herself, then banked so she could see where *Captain* had gotten to.

She turned away just in time to miss the incredible flash as *Capitol* blew up, one of its own torpedoes being detonated in mid-launch by a perfect shot from *Generous*.

Hell of a clever man, that Isoruku Togo.

However, before anyone could cheer, they realized another twenty-one torpedoes *had* been launched; they had to go again.

"Damn," Grant wasn't angry so much as disappointed; his ships were doing well — they hadn't been wiped out wholesale yet — but he was down two cruisers, with all his ships accruing noticeable damage. At the same time, we came on relentlessly, seeming to shrug off everything he sent at us.

He had to believe his disruptors were having some effect… we couldn't be completely immune to this onslaught.

And he was right.

I was congratulating Isoruku on his brilliant tactic when all the lights on *Wolf's* bridge turned off.

Then, standing there in blackness, I distinctly remember saying, "Oh shit."

That's what you get for standing off against a SAUN battleship.

CHAPTER NINETEEN

QUEEN TO KING'S ROOK FIVE

Mark Gunney hated commanding from his chair… but at least he was commanding.

"Keep us above him… don't let any tubes bear on us."

Though *Constellation* was *Cheetah's* dancing partner, the move by *Captain* towards *Hester* warranted immediate interdiction, and Mark was best-positioned to deal with the situation. Since Dave had ordered his gunners to focus on *Wolf* and *Lion* alone, *Cheetah* was entirely free to pursue… or in this case, reverse engines and try to back up fast enough to stay in touch with the SAUN ship.

The tricky part was avoiding the bastard's torpedo tubes, but by going high and staying out of the direct line of travel, Mark was able to accomplish that. And fortunately, because we mount our tubes downward-facing in the neck of the ship, being on top gave Mark some leverage in this situation.

You can do your own 'on top leverage' joke there if you like.

"We're almost locked," *Cheetah's* XO reported, and with a grunt our intrepid Captain nodded.

"Rain mags on him, don't let him forget we're up here," he ordered, and immediately the XO started the wash of golden energy that would have little effect on the SAUN hull, but which would be hard to ignore.

Hopefully the shooting would encourage dear *Captain* to back off and leave *Hester* alone… but mainly the torpedo shot would do that.

"They're opening up with their disruptors," *Cheetah's* Sensors and Communications Officer was next to report, and Mark nodded, steepling his fingers in front of him.

Enhanced camera feeds on the main screen showed the scene: a blue storm slashing back through space at *Cheetah* — bolts of EM energy from both sides passing each other as they traveled in different directions.

The fact that *Cheetah* had been free of injury so far meant the ship could undoubtedly withstand far more than *Captain* alone could throw, excluding torpedoes, so Mark wasn't worried.

He just wanted his own warhead in play.

"We have a solution. Firing!"

That came again from his XO, and Mark found himself holding his breath as *Cheetah's* torpedo dropped into space and fired its drive. The range wasn't nearly so close as that between *Nova Scotia* and *Congress*, so there was more time to shoot down this torpedo or evade it…

Captain started turning — twisting, really — and Mark could just imagine the scene on its bridge as the skipper ordered his Helm and Navigation Officer to evade with all possible speed.

It almost worked.

No, it *sort of* worked.

As the torpedo hit critical velocity and made its final dive, *Captain* spun just to port, and put one of its drive pods between its hull and the warhead. The flash was appropriately big, but when it cleared the ship was still largely intact, with two drive pods pushing it along, and at least eight of its turrets still in action.

"Bastard was clever," Mark grunted again, some genuine respect underlying his tone. This wouldn't be a quick kill, but the SAUN ship also wouldn't get to *Hester*.

"Lasers," *Cheetah's* Captain said. "See if you can shoot through the hole we just made."

The moment a warship goes dark in the middle of a battle is… apprehensive. Suddenly your super-advanced and highly efficient war room becomes a sensory deprivation chamber. After it happened to her aboard *Lady Grace* during the Fleet Clash, Karen had tried to explain to me how hard it was, but I didn't understand.

When *Wolf* went dark, I immediately got it.

There was something terrifying about the situation. *Wolf* went entirely offline — not even our backup systems activated — and aside from the sounds of people breathing and officers requesting updates that couldn't be delivered, we were silent.

That's what you realize most — how quiet it is. With the power grids and the weapons offline, there are no sounds of war to tip you off to what's happening — no reactors surging, no mags humming. There also aren't any sounds from outside, because it's a vacuum and noise doesn't travel well in those.

Well, there can be sound outside, but it would be the last sound you'd ever hear — metal twisting and shearing, just before the atmosphere carrying the sound vented.

No one wanted to hear that, though. That's what made the sudden plunge into darkness extra well-timed.

"Someone find the arms box and grab lights and comms," Andrea ordered into the blackness, her voice suggesting she was somewhere to my right.

Jim Hannigan started to make his way.

For Matt Baxter, the moment I disappeared from my appointed screen on *Friendly's* bridge was not a good one.

"What the hell?"

"*Wolf* just went dark… reactors read as normal but all other emissions are offline, must be an overload!"

Matt blinked twice at the report, then realized what that would mean: we'd be coasting right at the enemy, with no ability to slow down once we got to close quarters. We might drift right into a torpedo, if it wasn't shot down.

"Fighters, close up protection on *Wolf* and *Lion*," the Briton barked.

Even though he was by no means the most senior officer left with the squadron, no one disagreed. Kris' eyes went wider on the screen as she heard the orders, and she started to repeat them… but then Katya Romanov disappeared too.

The cumulative effects of disruptor fire were starting to take their toll… and suddenly, *Liberty* and its surviving consorts — *Constitution*, *Constellation*, *Chesapeake* and *Columbia* — had evened the odds again.

Lion, Friendly, Generous, Lady Grace and *Nova Scotia* were coming at them, and unless Mark could quickly finish off *Captain* and resume his position in line, the odds would be grim. How much more could we all take?

Grant saw *Wolf's* course begin to shift ever so slightly as our stabilizing thrusters went down with everything else. At first he didn't quite believe it — he'd almost convinced himself that the disruptors were a complete failure — but now he knew. Not only did they work, they gave him the opportunity to capture Belt Squadron ships more or less intact. A fast way to build up an armada, replace his losses and more.

"Looks like Caldecott is shifting focus to the next frigate... that'd be *Lion*," Karadzic was still beside Grant, and he pointed needlessly to emphasize those words.

His frown remaining on his brow, my old friend nodded, "I doubt they can take much more."

He was correct about that too.

Kris looked up at the lights in the ceiling of the bridge and swallowed. It was beginning to look awfully unlikely that *Lion* would be powered by the time our two battle lines got to point-blank range, but she had to keep trying.

Another wave of torpedoes was shot down, but more were coming, and if just one got through...

"Focus fire on our counterpart," she insisted again, resisting her concerns. "Kate, keep at him, we have to try to get the advantage again."

That was a message for both ships to renew their fire against *Constitution* — the oldest cruiser in the SAUN line appeared to be ailing, with only a few turrets left in commission. If it could be taken out of the picture, we'd regain the advantage.

Kris watched as another fine laser from *Lion* speared the triangular hull of the vessel... watched more plating crumple... and then could have sworn she saw a puff of atmosphere as a compartment decompressed. The ship listed suddenly to one side, then began to turn away from action, another laser shot from *Lady Grace* slicing into it as it went.

Out of the fight? Kris hoped to hell it was. At the very least it was falling back towards Etat Valcour, perhaps to lick its wounds for a while.

Whatever — just a tiny break would make a difference.

That's what Kris was thinking when the lights went off on her bridge. And stayed off.

On *Liberty*, Dave Caldecott was cackling with so much glee he very nearly started hyperventilating, passed out and died. He'd allowed *Constitution* to fall back, as it was never a bad idea to have a rearguard ship — especially if our Trojan horse, or whatever it was — made it past *Captain*.

But now three Belt Squadron ships were silenced in front of him, and the odds were very much in his favor, as far as he was concerned. The corvettes that remained — *Friendly*, *Generous* and *Lady Grace* — were not to be trifled with, but he had a battleship. They couldn't hurt him.

Cheetah and *Nova Scotia* would suffer the same fate as *Wolf* and *Lion*... there was nothing anyone could do to stop him now.

Then his panel lit up because *Hester's* engines boosted, and the freighter drove straight for Etat Valcour. It was only a dozen minutes away.

Nova Scotia had been focusing on *Columbia*, as that cruiser savaged *Sackville*. Without a torpedo left in its tube (reloading took quite a long time — an admitted design limitation on the part of our ships), Rozy Young had been forced to carve the Union ship with her lasers. Once *Sackville* had gone dark, she'd become tunnel-visioned. To let *Columbia* out of her sights would have left Katya Romanov to possible doom, and she wasn't about to do that.

When *Columbia* finally came apart — the first of these green group ships to die by lasers alone — and Rozy tuned back in to the rest of the fight, she realized what was happening and noticed that *Hester* was making its move.

As much as she would have liked to come to the aid of *Wolf* and *Lion*, she knew that freighter needed a close guard, especially because *Constitution* had begun to withdraw. Even ailing, that cruiser could blow the modified assault ship right out of space.

"Get us in front of *Hester*," Captain Young thus ordered her Helm and Navigation Officer. "We have to make sure it gets through."

"Wait for the next torpedo salvo and try to detonate them in tubes," Matt Baxter was indeed calling the shots now. Isoruku was officially senior to him, but the Briton still had the air of authority that leant to him natural credibility… and as three corvettes found themselves locked into a fight with *Liberty*, *Constellation* and *Chesapeake*, he knew they'd need guile on their side.

But laser shots down the torpedo tubes were by no means automatic, even as the distance between our two forces continued to close.

And the closer we got to each other, the more difficult it'd be for our planes to shoot down successive waves of torpedoes.

There was no easy answer to this, and Matt knew it. Perhaps we had bitten off more than we could chew. Perhaps the Belt Squadron wasn't invincible after all.

Cackling to himself on the bridge of *Liberty*, Dave Caldecott was convinced that was the truth. He had at last proved he was the better Admiral.

Standing in his office and frowning at the screen, Grant wasn't so sure. My friend the genius.

Chapter Twenty
Queen To King's Bishop Seven

As another wave of torpedoes went down, Karen found herself and her planes were getting awfully close to the ugly SAUN triangle ships. *Awfully* close.

And still the lasers weren't coming regularly. It looked as though both *Wolf* and *Lion* were drifting without full steering control — a fact that very much worried her, but which she was able to force herself to ignore because she was in a cockpit — but three corvettes were still in full flight. Why the silence?

Deciding to tap into fleet command comms, she targeted *Friendly* and sent a message, "Wolfstar 825 here… are we selective targeting?"

It took a moment for Matt Baxter's voice to come back over the line, "Karen, we're waiting for the warheads to get loaded into the launch tubes, and trying to cook them off with laser fire. That's how we blew up the last one."

Karen blinked as she heard the words, then looked again to see how close she was to the SAUN squadron.

Close.

And she had a ton of pilots with a ton of missiles and mags, all of whom could get right up close and aim carefully. How very convenient.

Without replying to Matt, Karen switched back to her fighter command frequency, "This is Wolfstar 825 to all star squadrons… let's see if we can't help our big ships cook off torpedoes in their launch tubes, shall we?"

There were some sounds of surprise, but pilots are a pretty clever bunch overall; they very quickly realized what was being asked of them, and for the first time in ages, they had hope of doing serious harm to fully-powered and largely-undamaged warships.

It was just a hope… but still.

Dozens of planes turned and burned, heading straight for the SAUN battle line.

Captain was doing everything possible to keep its wound away from Mark Gunney's lasers, but in so doing the SAUN ship merely allowed the frigate to gouge out other pieces of its hull. The damage wasn't so immediately obvious — compared to a torpedo detonation, nothing is terribly explosive about a laser strike — but the effects were adding up. Death by a thousand cuts is still death.

"We need you back here as soon as possible, Mark," Matt Baxter called over the Battlelink screens, and with a look up, *Cheetah's* seated Captain nodded.

"Alright. Hear that, guns?"

Mark's XO nodded, and as though he'd simply been waiting for the order to stop toying with his adversary, he put a laser shot right through one of the two working drive pods *Captain* had left. It wasn't a lethal blow, but it was sufficiently crippling; the ship began to tumble away from action, and without missing a beat, Mark ordered *Cheetah* around to rejoin our line.

Perhaps that precise gunnery would allow for a torpedo kill shot...

Dave Caldecott had been an advocate for fighters back in his time with the Admiralty, as you might recall. He advocated for them then, but had none now, because he was Alcibiades — he would become whatever was needed to win favor.

When the Emperor got hot under the collar about fighter planes and carriers, he did as well. Maybe he even believed the press about what planes could do. But when he got humiliated and exiled, he started to see reality — started to realize that planes were useless in modern warfare, and that heavy-gunned ships were the way.

Now, however, Dave must have been getting flashbacks to presentations he'd made in various places on Capital Island, about the *Ark Royal*-class carriers and why they were purportedly better than the *Bonnies*. As Karen led Starlights in against his three active ships, and he realized what their objective was, he panicked.

Was it possible that torpedoes could be set off in their launch tubes by mere fighter ordnance? Had he been right about the single-seaters before, or was he right now?

If you look at his face on the appropriated recordings, you have to delight in his horrified expression, because it's such a reversal from his cackling. It's as though he realized that he wasn't winning after all... that Karen was coming...

That he hadn't yet killed a single person in the Belt Squadron, while three of his cruisers were destroyed, and two others were limping (or tumbling) away from the fight.

And things were about to get worse.

In total darkness, Jim Hannigan managed to find me and Andrea and hand us both comms. Only after he did this did he bother to turn on the hand light which he'd retrieved from the arms box. This never made any sense to me, and to this day Jim doesn't know why he did that out of order, when having the light on immediately would obviously have made things easier.

Anyway, this certainly wasn't the time to even wonder such things — we were all waiting for the moment when we heard a torpedo tear through *Wolf*. With that fear in mind, I raised the comm Jim had provided and keyed it to an internal emergency frequency.

I needed to get Andy Jensen on the line. We had to find a way to fight the ship — even by auxiliary controls, the way Mik had done against the monitors at Mercury.

"Andy, you there?" I opened with that rather informal hail, and then heard nothing in reply.

"Andy, this is Andrea. What's the status of the mains?" it was *Wolf's* Captain's turn, and still there was no reply.

We had no way to know what was happening — the reactors could have cooked off and irradiated the entire engineering staff. We could all be receiving lethal doses as we stood on the bridge, and we'd never know because the radiation detectors were down with everything else.

As silence endured, Andrea and I looked at each other in the dim light cast by Jim's lamp, and then we made the decision. Andrea said, "I'll go."

I nodded gravely.

Then, in that exact instant (I swear) the lights turned on, and every sound of a ship that's supposed to be working came back. The screens at the front of the bridge were all blank, but as soon as the computer woke up and slapped itself on its electronic forehead a couple of times, the WolfNet loading screens started up as well.

And then, before we had any idea what was going on, every feed that had been up on screen before we crashed was back again — including Battlelink.

It was as if we'd never been down at all... because our OS XX operating system is that smart, and our hardware is that good.

The shock was complete, but people responded to the call of their duty stations with relief. And as Jim switched off his light and hurried back to his console, Gavin Nigh let out a sigh and looked to Andrea and me, "Engineering says they had to flip the breakers. Proverbially. Commander Jensen is emphasizing that the breakers are proverbial. But he says we're back to full operation."

Andy fucking Jensen, ladies and gentleman. Such a good engineer that I have anointed him with a rude word for his middle name, just this once.

Of course, Andy will tell you that the credit goes back the designers and builders who first imagined Wolf, and initially built the mag shielding grid underneath our armor. The fact that all that energy had been shivering through our hull, without melting so much as one critical relay, was incredible.

The only reason we went down — and you'll love this — was because of the failsafe modifications made to Wolf (and to just about every ship) after Lion's experience at Sinope. Remember how a surge from the secondary systems could have cooked off the reactors, caused a radiation leak and so forth? Well the system that disconnected the reactors from the grid in a situation like that had in fact been responsible for rendering Wolf unconscious.

Not, I should mention, because the SAU gunners hit us with so much energy we could have faced an overload, but because the software governing the 'breakers' had been set — fleet wide, at installation — at a threshold that we now realize was a bit too low.

Martian EM cannons had never had enough juice to alert us to the fact that we needed to raise the limit during the war, but the disruptors on Grant's ships did have the punch to break through the overall energy absorption threshold — barely.

So that was a learning for us. Would have preferred not to have discovered it in the middle of a battle with an evil genius, but no harm, no foul.

And now we were back in the fight.

Suddenly green group was very outnumbered.

Grant was fixated on the fighters charging his battle line, and as he realized their intent — desperate though it might be — he looked at Karadzic, "Order Caldecott to stow his torpedoes and focus on disruptors to get the corvettes out of action. Let's not make them the gift of high explosives."

That order went out, but by the time the Governor of Etat Valcour turned his eyes back to the sensor screen, he was able to see that Wolf was under power again.

He blinked twice, then realized what must have happened: the disruptors could have overloaded our power grid, but done no appreciable damage. Our crew had put things to rights, and now we were coming again.

While the ships he'd lost were truly lost.

The downside of focusing your offensive arsenal on EM weapons.

With *Wolf* back, *Lion* presumably on the mend, and *Cheetah* returning to the line after the distraction with *Captain*, it was suddenly six ships to three… and that didn't count *Hester* and *Nova Scotia* bearing down on Etat Valcour itself.

The landing had to be stopped. He knew I needed him alive to get the cure, which meant that we couldn't just laser the dome, but he had to stop us landing and then see if Caldecott could do better with a second chance, or if the escape ship would get to test its speed.

"New orders to green group: withdraw to orbital defense positions. Stand by to repel landing parties at all locks."

Grant had lost the battle for control of local space, but that was no great surprise. His plan was still working, the game would just change.

Caldecott looked relieved to get the order to pull back, but he was in too much of a panic to actually give the commands himself. It was actually Rayne Archibald who gave the orders, appropriately, as he was Captain. Old Dave could do little more than hug himself and whimper.

Yes literally. Sad waste of biomatter…

As laser shots again began to strafe *Liberty's* turrets, the catamaran-style battleship reversed its drives, as did *Chesapeake* and *Constellation*. Watching the move on *Wolf's* bridge screen, I smiled and took a breath, "Well, I suppose coming back from the dead makes people wary."

"They might think we're zombies," Mark Gunney offered from his screen.

It was perfect timing: Kris returned to the conversation in that moment, *Lion* having been restored just as easily as *Wolf* had been, "Brains?"

"Yours must be particularly good," Mark didn't miss a beat. "I hear redheads taste nice."

Singly the least appropriate thing I've ever heard said on Battlelink — and somehow it was Andrea who made the most of it.

"You *hear?* That ginger from Belt Four rejected you?"

Mark smiled at the quip from the Irishwoman — remember that, as corvette skippers, they'd been hunting partners. They knew each other well, and this was warmly received.

"She wasn't a natural redhead," he clarified.

At which point Matt Baxter — bless him — stopped us spiraling off into some schoolyard banter, "And we're all going to invade Etat Valcour now."

"Yes, immediately," I answered. "Starlight screen pull back, and thanks for the cover. Move us into position after *Hester*, we need to make sure the way is clear."

That was all that mattered now; we had Dave Caldecott on his heels, and now Charlie and Rufus had to be added to the equation.

Much of the battle remained to be fought.

Chapter Twenty-One

Checkmate?

Charlie and Rufus were waiting together as *Hester* approached Etat Valcour. Neither man was on the ship's bridge, where a skeleton crew of volunteers was guiding the big freighter into orbit over Grant's rock, but because of their comm connection they could hear the warnings coming in from ground control.

"Wave off, or you will be fired upon!"

"You are not authorized to approach our locks!"

"This is your final warning!"

It was all very desperate-sounding, and it certainly gave the impression that we'd won the battle thus far, and that *Hester* was being delivered to the perfect assault position.

"Think things are going to plan?" Rufus asked quietly after they listened to another round of warnings, and Charlie glanced at him and nodded.

"Sounds like it."

It was tough for both Branchers to be this disconnected from the action, but they could certainly cope. And they knew the quiet they were enjoying was soon going to end.

"Bridge to Major Peters and Major Chang," a hail simultaneously reached both men's ears, and Rufus was the first to answer.

"Receiving."

"We're closing on the dome with *Nova Scotia* running interference for us, but we might have to back off. Will let you know when we go for hard dock."

"Roger."

The update was appreciated, but it didn't lead to immediate action. With great self control, Rufus made certain that delay caused him no consternation, and Charlie did the same. They had to wait.

"This is a good plan, Rufus," Charlie said abruptly, glancing at his friend and counterpart. "It could change the way we go to war on domes."

With a slight frown, our Chinese Major with the mismatched eyes nodded, "Perhaps. Just taking a page out of your book."

There was some truth to that, so Charlie shrugged, but the fact remained that this assault by *Hester* was going to be remembered for a very long time, and the credit would deservedly go to Rufus for dreaming it up.

Hopefully Grant wasn't ready for it.

"Caldecott isn't answering directly anymore... but Rayne Archibald seems to be taking up the slack," Karadzic reported as he returned to Grant's side, and my former friend the Governor folded his arms and nodded.

"Fine — better that way, even. *Liberty* and the survivors are to rejoin *Constitution* and take up position over ValDome. If *Hester* comes close they must destroy it... they hold station until then, and fire at the Belt Squadron ships only if *Hester* is out of range."

The priority now was definitely to stop the landing, and it was so obviously coming from the freighter that Grant knew what he needed to do to interdict.

Unless the freighter was a decoy.

My old friend blinked at that possibility — was I clever enough for a double bluff? Or if I wasn't, was someone in my chain of command?

He was starting to see specters now, and he knew it... but caution was essential.

"Move regular force security teams to every service lock around the dome perimeter, in case *Hester* is a distraction and they start landing strike teams," Grant turned to his security man with that order, and Karadzic nodded again before turning away.

He brushed past Sonia Hart as he moved off, and it seemed obvious to her that both her lover the Governor and his most trusted personal guard were anxious now — perhaps things were starting to take a turn for the worse, even if no one was ready to admit as much.

Of course Grant's plan still held, but losing was never much fun.

Rozy Young watched as the remnants of the SAUN squadron withdrew ahead of her ship and *Hester*; because of relative angles, they'd easily take up a defensive position over the dome before she could get the freighter into position.

Looking up at my face on her screens, she asked: "Can we do something about driving those bastards off? They may not be much for us, but no way *Hester* can handle a pummeling."

I was watching the icons of the green group ships as well, and as Rozy asked her question I nodded, then let my gaze stray across the faces of the other skippers. Only Katya had failed to rejoin — unlike *Wolf* and *Lion*, *Sackville's* power grid wasn't easily reset.

That in mind, I frowned and then looked to Kate Levec, "*Lady Grace*, move over to guard Katya until she gets her mains back, then back up Rozy at *Hester*. The rest of us will push Dave's squadron off station."

It was a simple enough plan, and as Kate nodded from her screen and then gave orders to turn away from the fight, I redirected my attention to Mark, Kris, Isoruku and Matt, "Frigates will concentrate fire on the battleship, head for point-blank. Matt, Isoruku, pick the freshest looking cruiser they have left and carve it up."

Now that *Hester* was away from us, there wasn't much point in trying to shoot everyone at once, and of the four SAUN ships left in our way, there was no question that *Liberty* and the lightly-damaged *Chesapeake* were the ones we most needed to worry about. *Constitution* and *Constellation* would be hapless without their peers.

Karen pulled her flight of Starlights back into position underneath *Wolf's* bow pod just in time to hear Gavin Nigh's warning that we were altering course, and as she looked up through her canopy she was able to see our maneuvering thrusters fire as we began to accelerate.

Looking forward again, it was clear enough to her that we were headed for the dome, and that we meant to drive Caldecott aside once and for all.

Of course, moving into position for a fight directly over the asteroid meant we could be vulnerable to the ground defenses, be they more disruptor cannon, or groundside missile or torpedo batteries.

Either way, the close quarters meant the Starlights could have more work to do.

"Wolfstar 825 to Wolfstars, stand by for ground target sweep. Wolf Squadron, stay high and watch for torpedoes from the enemy squadron. We're getting awfully close."

We were indeed...

Dave Caldecott was starting to puff himself up again, but while he did that Captain Rayne Archibald was the one calling the shots on *Liberty's* bridge. The man's face was set — he probably knew his ship was our biggest target, and our toughest opponent... and he *had* to know that his mighty disrupters simply weren't causing critical damage.

He needed to use his torpedoes, but obviously thanks to Isoruku we'd found a way to use those warheads against him. Was the risk worth it? As he watched us come closer, he had to be thinking that a shorter distance meant less time for our fighters to interdict... yes, worth the risk.

"Send to the Governor, we have to engage with torpedoes and will do so at point-blank range," Archibald called to his Communications Officer, and the message was sent. Then he added, "Orders to *Constellation*... advance towards the enemy squadron and try to mask our torpedo attack."

That was a suicide order, and why Archibald chose *Constellation* for the job I'll never know. But his intent was clear: launch a spread of torpedoes and put a ship between us and them so as to mask the salvo. Clever, certainly, but would it work?

"One of them is coming out to meet us," Matt Baxter frowned as he saw the icons shift on his screen, then he shook his head. "Just one."

"Sacrificial lamb... or they're launching up his tailpipe," Mark read through the move, and I agreed with a nod.

"Mag storm, Starlights forward and knock down the torpedoes," was my command, and as our batteries started raining golden energy into space to make the life for any torpedo hell, I shifted my gaze to *Cheetah's* commander.

"Scratch my previous orders, Mark. You peel off and kill this one as quickly as you can — don't let him rejoin the line. We'll take the battleship."

At first Mark didn't understand why I was turning *Cheetah* away from the battlewagon, especially considering *Lion* and *Wolf* had both previously been rendered unconscious by the ship's disruptors... but then he realized exactly why, and he nodded back.

"Done."

"Have the torpedoes on scope now," Gavin Nigh called calmly from his station. "Starlights are on them."

This time the salvo was only a dozen warheads strong, and though the distance was shorter and the torpedoes thus able to fly a little faster (the closer you are, the more fuel you can burn more quickly), there wasn't much hope of getting past our planes again.

As I watched the markers of the torpedoes winking out on the main screen, I also got to see a red line cross from the icon of *Cheetah* to that of the cruiser coming at us: another fine shot from Mark's XO had disabled one of *Constellation's* remaining turrets, and realizing it was being singled out for a gunfight, the cruiser had begun vectoring away from the squadron, turning upwards to the position *Cheetah* had boosted to in order to draw it away.

That was clearly inexperience on the part of *Constellation's* skipper; being sent out in the first place was about as daft as it was clever, but then moving out of screening position just because you got tagged... that was either a lack of discipline, or a failure to understand the big picture... or hell, maybe the guy giving the orders hadn't explained the importance of screening to that ship's skipper.

Either way, four of our ships now had a straight run at three of theirs — and one of theirs was the much-ailing *Constitution*, no real threat.

"Dammit, orders to green group to get *Constellation* back in position," Grant was beginning to regret not directly commanding the squadron action himself.

But he had to disassociate himself from such frustrations. This battle was only for one part of the chess board, and he couldn't afford to become distracted from the broader strategic picture. Where was *Hester*?

Turning his eyes, he found that Rozy Young's frigate was holding that freighter just outside of the engagement, ready to pounce as soon as the coast was clear. Would Archibald or Caldecott be able to drive back the Belt Squadron now?

Unlikely.

Turning to Karadzic, Grant gave his next orders with that in mind, "Let the regimental commanders know they'll be deploying shortly."

The security man nodded, and then stepped closer to his long-time boss, "Sir, I've got a special convoy in the garage for you, and a fast shuttle waiting at a service lock behind the warehouse district. If the time comes that this mansion is threatened, I'm going to insist you leave."

Grant blinked, and then nodded, "Thank you, Fletch. But we're far from beaten."

The last part was true, at least, but as his security man turned away, the Governor couldn't help but think it was cute, even a little touching, that Karadzic had made those preparations... completely oblivious to the fact that Grant would leave him in an instant, by his much more secure escape route.

That thought drew the Governor's eyes across the room to Sonia, who was standing near the door to the bathroom and looking pale. She was a tough girl, but in the end she still relied on his confidence, so when Grant caught her eye he gave her a smile.

She saw that and smiled back, but it was very false. Didn't matter; she was right where she needed to be.

After a few more seconds studying her, Grant took a breath, then was drawn from his musing by a new voice, "I have a special hand-picked team of your guards ready. If anyone I do not like comes into the building, it'll be handled."

Turning at those words, Grant found Renault was standing close by, looking a bit smug (as was his custom). But he had a team ready, and that was good news — if anyone would be a match for Special Branch, Grant figured it had to be this man. The spy killer had a reputation in DCI that was truly horrifying.

"Thank you," Grant nodded to him. "Fletch has an escape shuttle ready, ask him about it. If this goes wrong, I want my best people clear."

At the very least, if his senior staff were able to use Karadzic's sweet little plan to escape, it would be of some benefit.

The question now was whether we'd get into the dome. Or perhaps: *how* we'd get into the dome.

Matt Baxter counted down from five in his head, and then as *Friendly's* lasers entered point-blank range of *Chesapeake*, he heard his XO say the magic word: "Shoot!"

I've been asked by my editors why 'shoot' is the word — not 'fire'. Naval history, that: when ships were at sea, and often made of wood, fire was a constant fear, so you only ever shouted 'fire' when someone needed to show up with a bucket of water. Saying 'shoot' left no room for misunderstanding, and Defense Command adopted the word for our own.

Now it was the command that sent a red lance into one of *Chesapeake's* drive pods, just as a second lance from *Generous* stabbed into another drive pod. Two corvettes, not usually hunting partners but certainly not strangers to each other, were spiraling towards the cruiser as it turned and brought its turrets to bear.

As blue bolts start slicing back towards the corvettes, Matt smiled to himself, "Not this bloody time..."

"Shoot!"

Like *Constellation*, *Chesapeake* began to peel away, leaving only *Liberty* and *Constitution* over the dome they were meant to protect. Very poor discipline now — clearly the sign of an inexperienced Navy. Either the skippers lacked the spine to hold their place and fight, or the doctrine they had been taught denied them the opportunity to do so.

Either way, *Constitution* began to reverse drives and turn towards *Hester*, leaving *Liberty* to hit us with the full brunt of its firepower.

Torpedoes launched from the catamaran-style battleship, but Wolf Squadron fell all over them like... hungry wolves... and they were blasted from space well short of us. Disruptor bolts filled the void with blue light, and started to tickle our hulls again, but Andy Jensen had overridden the software for reactor overload safeguards and put in a more realistic number for dangerous levels.

We weren't going dark again anytime soon, and as we closed to point-blank range I decided to make our presence obvious and arrogant, "Reverse drives. Drop our speed to 50 kps. Let them hit us."

It was a real bastard move — the big tough bully stopping and folding his arms while the smaller kid hit him for all he was worth.

Though considering how much bigger than us *Liberty* was, maybe that ship was the bully, and *Lion* and *Wolf* were the quiet kids who were tougher than they seemed.

"Point-blank lasers, start cutting out that strut connecting the two halves," was my next order. Because the ship was configured as two triangular hulls side-by-side, there was a strut connecting them which looked awfully vulnerable.

Wolf shot first, followed by *Lion*, and since we were closing bow-to-bow with the

SAUN heavy, our shots went right down its throat. In Nelson's day they called this raking fire, though back then it was rather different.

In this case, our beams just happened to converge on the hull outside the battleship's bridge, which was really far too exposed to our anger. The result was not good.

Dave Caldecott screamed his voice away when he saw Captain Rayne Archibald cut in two by flying shrapnel. Apparently there's a downside of having a bridge that is essentially a cargo hold with some consoles stuck in: the walls aren't designed to accept any more punishment than a standard crew compartment.

Now, I defy you to find a standard crew compartment on a Defense Command ship with walls that haven't been designed, right down to the molecular level, to resist throwing huge sword-like pieces of shrapnel... but in other fleets, these things can happen.

On *Liberty's* bridge, they happened with a bloody sense of timing.

I don't know enough about SAUN ships of that period to know why a laser shot caused such a profound explosion in the command center. I'm sure SAUN engineers puzzled over the same problem, determined not to let it happen ever again... one of the many lessons they had to learn from green group's experience against the Belt Squadron.

Anyway, the flying metal did indeed kill Archibald, and fully a third of the bridge crew either died at the same time, or suffered serious injuries.

This left Dave Caldecott in command, and as he staggered forward over the bodies of fallen men on his bridge, you could tell he was beyond panic, beyond shock. He was an enemy of the Empire, a legend in his own mind, and beyond that, he was about to die.

Some people don't believe this next part — don't believe I could be this cruel — but considering the year we're in, perhaps you won't be too surprised.

"Signal from their lead ship!" the Communications Officer was badly cut as he made the report.

Caldecott didn't have the capacity to speak in answer. He looked at that subordinate with wild eyes, and I suppose the young officer decided to take that expression as an order to put me through on the bridge monitor.

I appeared smiling, but because Dave Caldecott was too shocked to step into range of his bridge viewfinder, all I saw was smoky, dark, shaky chaos.

That didn't faze me: "This is Admiral Barron. We're going to destroy your ship now. But out of respect, we'll give you all two minutes to evacuate. Everyone except Admiral Caldecott. If he doesn't go down with the ship, we'll kill all the survivors we find. Thank you and have a nice day."

Still no response from Dave as the screen went dark, and then all the remaining officers and enlisted on the bridge started trading looks. They glared at the shivering Defense Command failure in their midst, they looked over their Captain's remains with sadness, and they decided they didn't want to die.

The First Officer was the one to hit the 'abandon ship' alarm, and then he started yelling for his officers to get out while he drew a sidearm and moved over to restrain Caldecott. After a few seconds of watching the former Second Lord's lack of reaction, this First Officer decided he wanted to live too, so he shot Dave Caldecott in the head.

So died Alcibiades.

That done, the First Officer moved over to what must have been his operations consoles, and launched the emergency beacon and ship's log buoy — standard SAUN procedure for a ship that's going down.

We only realized this because the log buoy inadvertently sailed right at *Lion*, and a Starlight had the good sense to catch it instead of blowing it away. Thanks for that, Mister First Officer — this battle would have made a lot less sense if we hadn't had those bridge logs.

I presume that man then evacuated, but since the bridge flight recorders we captured stop at the moment of ejection, I can't say for certain. What I do know is what we did next.

"Escape pods are still launching," Gavin Nigh reported as we watched the flood of small craft hurtling away from *Liberty* and down towards Valcour. Of course we weren't going to try to interfere in the escape... and even if Dave had slipped out on one of those pods and we'd found him, I doubt we were going to kill anyone over it (except him).

It was just a shot in the dark, to try to force him to stay aboard... and it worked. After a fashion.

"Alright, the rate is slowing down... they're probably mostly off," Gavin reported after another moment, and I nodded.

"Good. That was very nice of us. Doesn't everyone think that was nice of us?" I smiled a bit too callously, but no one argued — because it was good of us to let the crew escape. I suppose there might have been some respect there: *Liberty* was the only ship to hold its place, and face its obviously superior enemy over the dome.

Even now, *Constellation*, *Constitution* and *Chesapeake* were off fighting individual duels against *Cheetah*, *Nova Scotia* and the corvettes... though to be fair, *Constitution* was doing that to try to stop the landing... but either way, *Liberty* had fought determinedly, and its crew deserved a chance to survive.

I guess.

"Torpedoes when you're ready Kris, Jim."

Both *Lion's* skipper and *Wolf's* XO were completely ready, and because neither frigate had yet expended its warhead, we were able to send the SAUN battleship to its grave in dramatic style.

Grant shook his head as local-space cams caught the explosion of his flagship. That was the end of it; *Chesapeake* might survive, *Constellation* was already coming apart, and *Constitution* had basically nailed itself to the docking tower and was fighting *Nova Scotia* with every scrap of will it had left.

His ships had fought hard, as he'd known they would, but they were not cut out for this war. Not yet. That was something Grant admitted to himself — had to understand. No matter how good the theory behind their construction, no matter how well-trained their crews, these ships of green group were part of a young Navy, not one that had generations of experience behind it.

I know it's never wise to discount a newcomer simply for being new, but it's never wise for an upstart to arrogantly assume that being talented, or smart, means you'll automatically win.

Guts counts for something. Character and experience counts for a lot more. And this was the Belt Squadron. They don't make them any better.

Grant knew this. He'd watched us cut through his Syndicate fleet, and he'd known we could do the same here. But of course, he'd use that to his advantage. That we'd let survivors off *Liberty* would be twisted to fit his narrative: we toyed with the brave survivors of the battleship — made them dance and flee for our glee. And the fact that our ships had not sustained a single serious casualty, while inflicting such great harm on a SAU squadron… that would both shock the people of the Union into listening to his orders for better militarization, and emphasize how cruel we were.

To kill so many, when the brave SAUN — built to hunt pirates, not fight wars — was no threat to us?

See, when you're a genius like Grant, you can make anything work to your advantage. As long as you survive.

"What the hell is he doing?"

There was plenty of panic in that cry from within Grant's office, though I can't tell you exactly which one of his faceless acolytes it came from.

Blinking, my old friend watched as *Hester* turned away from *Nova Scotia's* wake, and then climbed up over the top of the dome, away from any of the service locks. Then the freighter spun so that its bow faced the top of the dome, and its drives fired.

It wasn't an assault ship at all… it was a ram. It was all suddenly dreadfully clear. To neutralize the many in-dome defenses Grant had prepared, I was going to ram the thing, decompress it, and kill thousands… maybe tens of thousands of civilians who were caught outside of atmosphere-proof buildings. Sure their microfilament bags would deploy, but they'd last less than a minute when sucked out into the frigid void.

"God help us," Karadzic whispered.

All Grant could do was blink and look for Sonia. He didn't see her at first, but then realized she was already in the bathroom. He'd have to follow…

"I sure hope we got the gravity right," Charlie Peters said it one more time, and then he braced.

Hester fired its reverse drives all of a sudden, and then very gently, its bow kissed the top of the dome. Grav clamps locked on, a docking membrane extended and pressed onto the outside surface of the dome, and laser cutters went to work on the shell of Etat Valcour's governing city.

Rufus Chang doesn't kill civilians, you see. But he sure knows how to win wars.

Chapter Twenty-Two

Gravities

What Rufus had proposed was something we all take for granted these days: that if it was easy for the enemy to defend the known locks in his or her dome, then the smartest thing an invasion force could do was bring its own.

These days, all our assault ships have this ability, but it was Rufus who first came up with it — after what he and Charlie had gone through on Mercury, he had no particular interest in trying to force a defended airlock of any kind, ever again.

Of course, full credit for making this a reality in such a short and improvised time goes to Andy Jensen, along with the other engineers of the Belt Squadron. They'd been able to fit an improvised membrane ring to a section of *Hester's* bow, as well as the grav clamps required to hold the membrane tight against the dome, and the laser cutters needed to make a hole to allow entry.

So *Hester* was now the largest and oddest-shaped mosquito any of us had ever seen — and as it was sticking its stabby-nose-thing into the dome, Charlie and Rufus were both sitting aboard their trusty assault shuttle in its hold, ready to fly through.

Everyone in the Governor's Office ran to the windows and looked up at the sky, which Grant liked to keep a welcoming shade of blue. Right at the top of the dome that blue was flickering — as the laser cutters sliced through relays that kept the displays on the inside of the dome alive, a gray patch began to appear.

Seeing it, Grant realized what was happening.

To confirm, one of the other acolytes in the room relayed a report from Valcour's dome control, "We're getting fracture alerts from the top of the dome… they're cutting through!"

"They're going to depressurize us — kill us all!"

"No, they'd have just hit us if they were going to do that!"

"But they're cutting anyway!"

So many panicked voices, but Grant just shut his eyes for a second, then opened them, "They're going to invade. That ship is carrying assault forces, so position our anti-armor batteries to cover the opening."

Karadzic was the only man in the room fit to respond to the order, and he nodded, "Yes sir! Come on, move, we need to get ready!"

Grant didn't know what we'd have in *Hester*, but he expected it wouldn't be a lightweight force. He wasn't entirely correct about that — we had only seven Branchers, remember — but still, he expected the worst.

Looking again to the bathroom door, my old friend found Sonia there waiting for him, as if pleading for him to follow her to safety. But he couldn't go yet. He needed to wait, even if this meant likely defeat on the ground. To flee as soon as the Defense

Command forces entered his dome would be an act of cowardice. He literally had to wait until the last moment... or until a moment that seemed 'last' enough not to be deemed cowardly... before he could make his escape.

That was how legends were made, and reputations built. And because he knew I'd probably leave people alive to tell the tale of what had happened, he needed his story to be as close to true as possible.

As soon as we got inside his mansion, he'd flee.

But timing would be everything.

"Get ready," Chet Srisai looked across at Charlie, who was sitting in the copilot's seat of the assault shuttle.

"All set," the Hawke Lord replied, and that earned a smile from *Wolf's* long-time Special Branch pilot. One last ride into hell with Major Peters... Chet was pleased.

The assault shuttle was floating in *Hester's* forward hold, along with five other shuttles and their escorts. The front airlock that normally allowed for the movement of vast amounts of cargo was open, but the gray top of the dome was all they could see... that and the flashes of light caused by the laser cutters as they sliced through it.

"Cut complete," a voice from *Hester's* bridge came over the comm, and the lights stopped flashing along the dome surface in the same moment.

And then, nothing happened.

Charlie sat there and watched... everyone from the assault force did.

The dome sat there and watched them right back.

"The cutters were set deep enough?" Charlie asked that question over the comm, and there was a pause before the answer came back.

"Six meters. I'd be surprised if the dome is even four," the engineer who'd been running the operation from *Hester's* bridge replied.

So the piece of dome should have been ready to fall... unless there was no *reason* for it to fall. Gravity inside a dome was controlled by the paneling that was laid in its foundation, and depending on the quality of that paneling, the artificial gravity field might not reach high enough to actually pull down a piece of the dome.

Indeed, there was little point to actually having gravity up as high as the top of the dome. It would make maintenance easier if people could just float along the underside.

"Maybe just a little nudge?" Charlie asked, looking at Chet, and the pilot officer shrugged and then smiled.

"I'll try it."

Reaching out to his controls, the Lieutenant flipped a couple of switches and then eased the assault shuttle forward. The bay was big, but not that big, so arriving at the dome took just a dozen seconds, and then Chet slowed his approach as though he was planning to dock with the surface.

As the robust nose of the assault shuttle pressed up against the dome, there was a thud and a gentle shiver through the craft.

"Ready to push," Chet said, and Charlie nodded.

"By all means."

With a grin, Chet hit the throttle.

♦♦♦

Grant was at the window when the piece of the dome that had gone gray suddenly dropped, then was captured by artificial gravity and actually fell towards the city far below. He also spotted the shuttle that had come right behind it, and that ship too was suddenly falling.

"Get ready!" Karadzic called out beside his Governor, and looking down briefly, the villain could see the companies of anti-armor troops he'd so carefully trained moving into position beneath the breach. They had a long way to fire, and a huge opening to cover, but surely they could still stop the invasion force.

The tricky thing you learn about assaulting a dome from the top, at least from an improvised assault platform, is that when you break through, you immediately go from flying forward to flying straight at the ground.

That's why modern, purpose-built assault ships tend to use belly locks, and drop forces through from 'above' — so there's no confusion about the gravity of the situation along the way.

As it was, Chet found himself accelerating face-first for the ground, and that was a bit of a shock.

"Pull up?" Charlie asked, planting his hands on the console in front of him as the ground approached rather quickly.

"Pull up," Chet agreed, hauling on the assault shuttle's controls and getting thrust pointed the right way so as to slow the descent. As the nose came up and Charlie's internal organs returned to a more comfortable orientation, he began scanning his surroundings with his eyes.

Etat Valcour's government dome was relatively nice, compared to a place like Io, but it was still brown. Something about the place felt needlessly industrial… almost Soviet, if the old reference helps at all. Which was very strange considering Grant's obsession with the fundamental inequality of humans.

What was also missing was immediate defensive fire — a positive sign, Charlie decided. If Grant's defenders had already been in place to shoot up the landing forces, it would have been disconcerting, since no one had ever used a plan like Rufus' before…

A laser shot passed the shuttle to the left. Charlie saw it and his eyes widened in surprise.

Right. Disconcerting indeed.

"Shit," he said casually. "The bastard is shooting at us already."

"Not for long, though," Adrienne Thompson interrupted over the comm.

"Get *down!*" Karadzic threw himself into Grant with that warning, but of course it was needless: the dozen Starlights that dropped out of *Hester* behind the assault shuttle weren't shooting at buildings.

Gun emplacements, however…

Grant forced himself back up to the window in time to see mags melt three of his prized anti-armor units, and deciding they were in no way armed to deal with Starlights, the men at the rest of the emplacements started to scatter.

Of course Grant knew that a simple shoulder laser could bring down a Starlight, if the shot was true, but these men had never conceived of single-seat fighters, let alone facing such craft inside a dome.

It was what Charlie had done to the Commandos at Io... except that, because of Rufus's idea, there was a separate lock for them to enter and exit when they pleased. *Hester* was our way in... and somehow we'd come up with it in just days.

How the hell did we manage that? I'm not asking, because I know... but Grant was starting to let the frustration show. He'd planned for years, controlled every factor, and now some goddamned improvised assault ship was changing the rules?

It was tough to win when the opposing pieces on the chess board got together and carved a new friend to join the fight.

Which, I believe, was my basic point all those years ago.

But Grant was still seeing the bigger picture. While the people in his office started to truly panic, he hurried to the bathroom door and took Sonia by the arm, leading her inside.

"We're going to be leaving soon," he whispered, and then he kissed her quickly. "Get down there now. I don't want to take any chances, so get down there and I'll follow."

He could tell Sonia was fighting tears. She wasn't ready for this — it was all too much, like the days on Egesta all over again. He could see that plainly, so with a furtive glance back through the door into his office, he made a decision.

Turning his back towards that door, he reached into his pocket and pulled out a small comm, "This is keyed to my personal frequency alone. Take it. If there's a problem, I'll call you. Just get down there, please. I need to know you're safe."

Gallant hero on a white charger... trying to spare his lady love from the brutality he knew was about to happen.

"You're going to die?" she whispered, her words breaking as tears started to flow.

Grant shook his head immediately and intensely, then kissed her forehead, "No. I'm going to make sure everyone sees what the Empire is capable of before I leave."

I think you'll agree that this scene could be right out of a heroic movie — the freedom fighter standing up to the evil Empire, and his beloved realizing that it was his destiny to risk his life for the greater cause, while she cowers in a secret bunker and prays for his survival.

Touching.

"Go," he whispered into her ear, then he turned back to his office, shutting the bathroom door behind him as he went. Wiping away her tears, Sonia turned and opened the hatch.

All of the kindly DCI bugs in the room followed her down.

As Adrienne and her planes — half of Wolfstar Squadron and half of Lionstar Squadron — maintained altitude and started flying orbits over the dome, Chet guided his assault shuttle towards the imposing three-story building with colonial-style columns and some reasonably elaborate lawns around it.

The convenient thing about Governor's Mansions is they're usually hard to miss, and figuring that's where Grant would be, Charlie nodded to his veteran pilot.

"This is Peters, we're rolling in on the mansion."

"Lieutenant Khalid here, sir, we are following."

Felicia was in one of the shuttles that had emerged from *Hester*, and together with four others, that craft full of volunteers now followed the Special Branch assault ship down towards the surface of the dome.

Because his ship was leading the way, Charlie didn't really get to see the shuttles following, but that was fine; he had plenty to focus on because there was a cordon of brown-uniformed figures surrounding the mansion grounds. Some heavy weapons too.

"Adrienne, it's Charlie. Looks like there's a perimeter around the mansion."

He waited for *Wolf's* fighter commander to answer over comm, but she didn't. Instead, being rather swept up in the moment, she guided her plane and her wingman past the Special Branch shuttle at high (relative) speed, then unleashed positively searing chain of mag bolts.

Her shooting was predictably superior, and as one of the disruptor emplacements went up like a pyre, Charlie could see the brown-uniformed soldiers begin to flee their positions. They'd probably be back as soon as the odds were stacked less against them, but for now their rapid departure provided a landing zone.

"I don't see any perimeter," Adrienne answered him after she pulled up, leaving long black scorch marks all over the lawns, and a few fires as well.

"Yes, I must have been mistaken," Charlie replied, and then he tapped his comm again to add Rufus to the conversation.

"We're about to touch down."

"Roger," Rufus confirmed, and then Charlie turned to Chet and patted him on the shoulder.

"Thanks for the lift."

"A pleasure, M'Lord," Lieutenant Srisai replied with another grin, then Charlie got out of his seat and headed back into the assault compartment with Rufus and the team.

It was a team Charlie had never operated with before, but of course his reputation was known. And besides that, if there was one thing Special Branchers could always do together, no matter how much or little they knew each other, it was storming a pirate base.

Clarissa Hutchinson nodded as Charlie arrived, "Sir."

"Captain," he nodded back, then came to a stop beside Rufus. "All set?"

The Chinese Major with mismatched eyes checked the grenade launcher under the barrel of his MAG-90, then answered, "Yes."

That was well-timed, because the feet of the assault craft touched down on the south lawn of Etat Valcour's Governor's Mansion.

"Hatch is facing the building, watch for sharpshooters," Chet's voice came over the comm.

"Shall we?" Charlie asked, like the gentleman Lord he is.

"After you," Rufus replied.

They went off to find Grant Merger.

CHAPTER TWENTY-THREE

INVASION

"Where the hell is our perimeter? House guards meet me in the lobby… we'll hold them back as long as we can!" Karadzic was yelling to everyone in Grant's office, and the man's loud and insistent tone bore enough of an edge to start the more jittery members of the Governor's staff panicking. A surprising number of these senior people began to really lose their heads…

Grant wasn't among them, of course. He looked out his window as the Special Branch shuttle's hatch opened, and he was sure that he saw Charlie Peters lead the way out, shooting three guards in three different directions at what appeared to be the same time.

Grant had a strange perspective on my friend, but that was irrelevant just now. Five more shuttles were landing even as the Branchers came down from their craft and established a quick perimeter. Soon a hundred, if not more, DCSF would be right here in his mansion.

And all the regiments and militias were elsewhere, not able to help.

"Order all regiments and militias to come to the Governor's Mansion! Right now!" Karadzic was still yelling — and still hoping.

Of course the loyal people of Valcour might come out and try to save their Governor — he'd been so good to these people — but there was no way they could cope with the Starlights. Those planes shouldn't have been the be-all, end-all in this situation, but he honestly hadn't planned for them inside the dome. Skiffs perhaps, even some tanks… but the planes were noisy and terrifying, and the pilots were good.

Any regiment that tried to come to the mansion now would be burned on the roads, or have buildings flattened on top of it. Eventually help might arrive, but when Grant could watch Charlie Peters coming towards the ground floor of the building, and he was only on the third storey, he knew he didn't have much time.

Karadzic grabbed him by the shoulders as he thought that, "You must stay here. We'll hold them off until reinforcements arrive. If we try to take the convoy now, the Starlights will burn it… but if we can stop their assault I can get you out through the sewers."

By God this man was loyal. Grant almost felt guilty.

"For now stay here. I'll come back and get you out, as soon as I see to the ground floor defenses!"

He really thought that if he went down to the ground floor, he'd make it back. There were probably 200 guards in the building — not counting those who'd fled from the perimeter — so perhaps he was right… but as Grant nodded and thanked his loyal old warhorse, he knew that was going to be the last time he saw the man.

Karadzic went to fight, and Grant watched from the window as SF in green tunics and tac vests started to surround his compound.

•••

Felicia Khalid had always done well in tactical training, and though her love was for communications and sensors (which, put like that, does sound a bit unusual), she was no slouch with a mag.

One of the brown-uniformed soldiers from Valcour learned this as she led the way out of her shuttle; using her sidearm, she shot him into a coma, without so much as blinking. Eugene Sengooba was right behind her as she emerged into the simulated daylight, and he watched the shot with just a little surprise.

He, like many of us, didn't know the full range of Felicia's abilities.

As she reached the bottom of the shuttle ramp, our Sensors and Communications Officer then stepped aside and started waving her volunteers forward, "Watch your surroundings carefully, establish a perimeter."

It wasn't her job to join Charlie's assault force — there were other volunteer SF who would follow the Branchers in — but someone needed to make sure no SAU soldiers attacked the insertion point from the flank.

With the SF fanning out around the building, and Adrienne keeping a watchful eye from high overhead, Felicia was doing quite well. And then, through sheer force of habit, she pulled out her comm and scanned for local frequencies.

She was looking for signs of local military chatter — anything she could glean over open channels that might help her predict when and where a counterstrike would appear. Instead, her comm lit up with something she certainly did not expect: a DCI communications frequency.

Detecting a friendly secure comm, all those happy bugs that had been wandering around the mansion began nattering, and because Felicia was close and she was listening, they all poured their information straight into her handheld.

Recognizing what was happening, Felicia did what any excellent Sensors and Communications Officer would: she immediately established an uplink to *Wolf*. And then she started detecting another DCI signal, which didn't make a whole lot of sense.

Frowning at that, she keyed a few more buttons and then tapped her headset, "Lieutenant Khalid to *Wolf*."

Gavin Nigh was just starting to process the sudden upload when he heard his boss in his ear. He turned towards Andrea and me, "Lieutenant Khalid calling... she's uploading a ton of information from some DCI source..."

I blinked, then wondered how many goodies Julie Pichot had left behind for us. Andrea answered her acting Sensors and Communications Officer while I wondered, "Put her up."

There was no visual, but we heard the telltale thud as a voice comm was piped up to the bridge speakers, "*Wolf*, I believe I have detected signals from a series of DCI observation bugs. Some are from inside the mansion... others seem to lead from the mansion, down through the asteroid. But I cannot scale the locations on my handheld screen."

Gavin was already working on this, so he put the asteroid up on screen one, and then started dropping markers on the wireframe outline of the squat, ugly rock. They led from the mansion in the dome... down through the asteroid...

Andrea and I both thought it at the same time, but I said it first: "Escape chute."

So before she was caught, Julie must have detected Grant's secret way out... or maybe her industrious bugs had kept looking after she left. Whatever. We knew now.

"There must be an outlet somewhere on the underside of this rock... send the information to Karen and get her to look for it," I passed those orders to Gavin, and he nodded.

Then Andrea asked a very good question, "Felicia, is there any way you can get access to some schematics of the mansion... tell Charlie where the entrance is?"

That brought a pause, and then Felicia replied: "I will find a way."

She was determined, and more than capable of following through.

Advancing into the lobby of the mansion was suitably dramatic; as soon as Clarissa Hutchinson was outlined in the double-doorway, every one of the forty-three guards either in the large open space or leaning in from surrounding corridors shot at her.

The stupid part was that they all missed.

Now I could be unfair and say that none of these soldiers knew how to shoot, but the reality was that Clarissa hadn't exactly been sauntering; she purposely silhouetted herself for a very brief second, so that watching from a window beside the door, Rufus could see how many grenades he needed.

The answer was just two — one for the left, one for the right.

Pulling the necessary magbangs off his vest, he tossed one to Charlie, and then together they keyed the nasty little bombs, leaned around the doorframe and lobbed. There were sounds of commotion for a second, then the loud hum of the mag charges going off, and then in the next second all seven Branchers swept in — just in time to watch most of the guards fall unconscious to the floor.

A few had managed to get to cover in time, and as they popped up again they were summarily shot. All in all, there wasn't much in the way of resistance.

"Lobby secure," Simon Keynes confirmed as he proceeded further into the open space than anyone else, and then just as Charlie was about to look to Rufus to talk deployment (or use tactical hand gestures, if they wanted to be quiet), my voice interrupted over the comm.

"Felicia has detected DCI bugs. They seem to be showing us an escape chute that goes from the mansion down through the rock and out the other side. Felicia's trying to find schematics to tell us where the entrance is, and Karen's looking for the exit. We'll let you know as soon as we know."

I didn't wait for a reply, which was good because one wasn't coming. Charlie looked at Rufus, and Rufus looked at Charlie, and they both had the same thought: tunnel meant 'down'. The place had to have a basement.

They didn't get a chance to look, because Fletcher Karadzic and a column of soldiers suddenly appeared at the end of a long corridor ahead.

"There they are, stop them!" he hollered, then leveled his pistol towards Charlie and started firing.

Before any Brancher could shoot him, the soldiers rushed forward with their impractical disruptor rifles and started punching holes in walls with erratic shots. Rufus dropped behind cover, as did the rest of the officers, and the building seemed to seethe fire at them.

Karen looked at the coordinates on her screen and frowned. An escape chute at the bottom of the rock? Sounded plausible, she supposed — if a little bit over-elaborate. But then, it was Grant...

Flipping a couple of switches, she patched her comm directly into *Wolf*, "Karen here... can you get me on with Felicia direct?"

Gavin obliged, so as Karen led her flight of Starlights to the underside of Etat Valcour, she got our Sensors and Communications Officer on the line.

Felicia had her comm in one hand and her mag in the other, and along with Eugene and four volunteers, she barged in through one of the mansion's side doors — well away from the main fighting in the lobby.

One brown-shirted SAU soldier swung out of an office to stop her, but she and Eugene shot him at the same time.

While she was doing this, she held up her comm, "I am here, Commodore McMaster."

There was a pause and then Karen came back over the line, "You want to try sending back to those bugs, get them to trigger a beacon or something?"

Karen didn't know what DCI bugs were able to do, but she presumed they had to be reasonably smart — they were being awfully helpful and intelligent so far.

Thinking it a good idea, Felicia agreed, "Of course."

She lowered her comm, then used her thumb to send the query back to the bugs (she did it one-handed to make sure he other hand was still on her sidearm). As soon as that was finished, she stopped because Eugene was in front of her; they were at the door to what appeared to be a maintenance office. Perfect.

"I am in a maintenance office and will connect the computer here for a downlink, *Wolf*," she said, and then she proceeded to put Gavin Nigh and *Wolf's* main computer in touch with the Governor's Mansion mainframe.

We got our blueprints moments later.

Rufus used hand gestures to let Charlie know what to expect: a grenade from his under-barrel launcher. Because Karadzic was storming down a single wide corridor with what must have been another fifty guards, he was very much vulnerable to such a weapon. Now Rufus would make him pay.

It was only another magbang, admittedly — not an HE or frag grenade that would have made an awful mess — but still, when thirty of the brown shirts dropped in a single flash, it was pretty impressive.

Also pretty demoralizing to the handful who remained on their feet.

With the flash over, Selma Koestecki and Bobby Franek popped up and started blasting again, and five more guards were down in a second. The rest did the noble thing; they turned and fled, passing Fletcher Karadzic as they went. Grant's loyal and hapless security man tried to stop them, standing there in the corridor and holding his own pistol high in the air as he called them.

"Do not flee, we can defeat them! Hold fast!"

Didn't work, they all ran away. Charlie and Rufus waved the team up to their feet to follow, figuring the guards might lead them to wherever Grant was, but as they entered the corridor facing Karadzic, they slowed and considered the man over the barrels of their MAG-90s.

Fletcher recognized Charlie from ages past, and that moment of understanding brought with it a flash of anger. For years, Karadzic and Charlie had sparred, not physically (because if they had done that, Karadzic wouldn't be alive anymore) but as respective heads of ground operations.

In the Syndicate, it had always been simple and brutal Karadzic sending out pirates to try to stop Charlie's old squad… now it was the last stand for the security man, and he knew he couldn't possibly win.

His scream was a defiant one as he leveled his disruptor pistol. That defiant noise gurgled to a stop when Charlie, Rufus, Selma and Maggie all simultaneously shot him in the chest. He dropped like a stone, and because of the range, it was entirely possible the shots killed him. None of the Branchers worried particularly about that; instead, they continued their advance.

Karen had split her squadron up completely as they flew over the rock to find the entrance to Grant's escape chute. She was frowning as she did both a visual and a lidar scan… but nothing was obvious. If they'd properly concealed the presumed airlock, it might be impossible to find.

Then her computer blinked: a DCI signal hit her plane's receivers, with both what appeared to be a location, and a sequence of numbers that looked like an IFF code.

"Smart bugs…" Karen muttered to herself, then spoke up to the rest of Wolfstar Squadron. "Checking out a lead, stay on course."

Gavin Nigh frowned over the schematics of the mansion, then tapped his headset to talk to his boss. Felicia was still sitting in the residence's maintenance office, pouring over the schematics as well, so she answered him immediately.

"Yes Gavin?"

"Are you able to see this, boss? Looks to me like the line of bugs starts on the third floor, in… in the bathroom off the big office."

Felicia was looking at the same schematic, and she nodded, "It looks like that to me."

"Roger," Gavin replied.

A second later, it was my voice that compelled Rufus to hold up his hand and stop his squad.

"Escape chute has a third floor entrance… behind a wall in the bathroom off Grant's big office. No telling if he's there, but hurry," I said.

Rufus looked up at the ceiling as I spoke, then immediately started translating my words into hand gestures. The squad, I should say, had just reached a bank of stairs that could have either taken them up or down; their first instinct of down (to the situation room) was not the one they needed to follow, and as he explained that, Maggie Joyce swung into the stairwell and started leading the way up.

They made it to the second floor in no time at all, and then up to the third. Stacking up against the wall behind Bobby Franek, they counted down fast and then exited the stairwell. Bobby went right, Maggie went left, and then the rest piled out covering all directions.

They discovered that they were in the outer office of Governor George Madison — Julie Pichot's desk was within reach, had they known it was hers. They also discovered they were expected, when a disruptor bolt knocked Maggie off her feet.

That shot went fully into the Lieutenant's vest, but it was powerful enough to knock her out and leave her with some serious burns. Clarissa Hutchinson pulled her behind a desk for cover, and then with Simon Keynes started laying down some merry hell in the direction of the shot.

Charlie had gone right, behind Bobby Franek, so before he could turn his attention to the shooters, he scanned that direction... and he saw Grant Merger. The villain was standing at the door to his office, looking out at the sounds of shots fired, deciding that now really was the time to go — that he might have left it too late.

Fire started to intensify to the left, and Charlie tapped Bobby on the shoulder to go join in. Selma Koestecki had already redeployed because she was the medic, and she was peeling Maggie's seared clothes off even as the desk over her head was coming apart under disruptor fire.

They had the situation in hand; they didn't need Charlie. They weren't his team anyway.

So my friend straightened up and advanced towards Grant's office, calling back because there was no time to make gestures to get Rufus into the picture, "Going after Grant!"

Those words drew Rufus' gaze, and he turned and spotted Grant backing away from the door. He'd be running for the chute, and while Charlie was after him, somehow Rufus knew more than one elite officer might be needed to pin the Governor.

"Clarissa, clear this floor. Charlie and I will get Grant!" our Chinese Major ordered, and without looking away from her gun sight, his Captain acknowledged.

"Go get him!"

Rufus hurried across the floor after Charlie, and caught up to him just as they reached the door to Grant's office. The sounds of the fighting got a little further away as Simon and Bobby started advancing against the guards who were still hiding in offices on the other side of the stairwell. The reduced noise made things a bit more unsettling as the two men pushed the half-open door and peered inside.

It was possible Grant had booby-trapped the otherwise-innocuous seeming office... chasing quickly could lead to disaster, and allow my old friend his ultimate escape. The question of how much risk to take flashed through both Majors' minds as they scanned the room ahead of them.

And then those calculations were stopped by some French-accented dialogue.

"Did you find Julie Pichot?"

The taunt came not from the office ahead, but from the desks behind. Both men looked over their shoulders when they heard it, and were treated to the sight of Augustin

Renault silently moving towards them. He wasn't finished being a disgusting bastard, either.

"Usually I do not cut up my fruit after I eat it, but she was so sweet to the tongue…"

Now remember for a minute how Rufus had felt about finding Julie Pichot, the gallant spy, on the runner bound for Etat Lexington. Remember how the torture she'd endured is an affront to certain fundamental tenets of how he lives his life.

If you recall that, then it'll be no surprise that our Chinese Major suddenly stopped thinking of Grant Merger, and instead turned and started to raise his MAG-90 in the direction of the spy killer. Renault would be very much killed…

Fortunately, Charlie inserted some reality back into Rufus' perception. There were a few relevant points to consider: Renault was unarmed, just taunting, and any delay could let Grant get away. Bearing those things in mind, the Hawke Lord pushed the barrel of Rufus' rifle down, and then he nodded towards the office, "Go after Grant."

Rufus' eyes were wide, and then just because he was getting a reaction, Renault licked his lips, "I loved sucking on her tongue. But you must agree, it was less attractive after it had been removed and put on ice. Yes?"

Of course Rufus' mismatched eyes widened, and he started to tremor with rage… but that was better saved for the more pressing matter.

"Go get Grant," Charlie repeated the instruction, seemingly unaffected. "I'll be down in a minute."

It is a complete testament to Rufus' self-control that he even heard those words. Even more of a testament that he finally turned his hard eyes to Charlie. The Hawke Lord nodded one more time… and then with a last deadly glare at the spy killer, Rufus stormed into the office.

We'll follow him in a moment; now for an event that so many movies have gotten so wrong. Charlie released his MAG-90 so it could dangle from his vest, then turned to squarely face Renault. The French killer sneered at him, then stopped himself as he finally recognized his opponent.

"It's… Charlie Peters. It has been a long time since I have heard your name, Major," he said with a slightly more respectful tone.

Charlie's reputation was well-known in the old Syndicate circles, just as Renault's reputation was known to my good friend.

"Augustin Renault," Charlie replied softly. "I'm not an admirer of your work."

That was the truth, and it made the spy killer smile. Suddenly he had more interest in this engagement than simple loyalty to Grant: Renault had a chance, at last, to go toe-to-toe with the one man everyone in the Syndicate believed could beat him. He could prove once and for all that he — the spy killer — was the deadliest man in the solar system.

Charlie was not possessed by any similarly childish desire to prove himself… but if a fight was what Renault wanted, so be it. Because while his anger was hardly evident, the Hawke Lord knew what this man had done to Julie Pichot. My good friend took serious exception to that.

If he was going to vent his many frustrations just once on this trip, now was the time.

Renault looked forward to his chance. He stepped out from behind the desk that separated them onto an open piece of floor, and then reached to the small of his back, drawing a dagger that had been sheathed there. He reversed he weapon in his hand, then smiled, "*Allez*."

Now, you know that Charlie Peters can kill you with anything. He doesn't like me saying it. He tried to make me stop. But the fact of the matter is, he could kill you with word association, or the color purple, or a butterfly's good intentions, or with your warmest childhood memories. He could kill you with your own immortal soul.

But there's one thing you never, ever, ever want him to use against you: his bare hands.

It was not an elegant hand-to-hand engagement, a bloody grappling match, or a duel that led to a rooftop chase. It was not a choreographed fight, or even a long one. It was none of the things the movies want it to be.

All it took was one fast hand.

Augustin Renault, the much-feared spy killer who had haunted the dreams of DCI agents for more than a decade, did not see, or even really feel the blow that collapsed his windpipe. As he staggered backward, hit the desk behind him and fell to the ground to suffocate, Charlie stepped back, unclenched his fist and watched.

That man would hurt no one else, ever.

And now Charlie was free to join the chase.

But, of course, things had happened in the meantime.

CHAPTER TWENTY-FOUR
REMATCH

When Karen positioned her Starlight to watch the coordinates provided by the DCI bugs, and then triggered the IFF code she'd been given, it was a good thing she was paying attention.

A section of rock that had otherwise seemed entirely inconspicuous suddenly retracted, revealing a small flight bay of some kind.

Then a black ship shot out of that flight bay at speed, whipping right past her Starlight and disappearing against the starscape so quickly she couldn't follow it.

"*Wolf*, do you have that... some sort of craft just shot out of here real fast... don't have it on my screen!"

Her heart started pounding as she realized what that meant — realized that Grant must have gotten away.

"*Wolf!*" she called more urgently. "If that's Grant, we need to get a track on him, *now!*"

Just the barest hint of panic around the corners of those words, but a calming reply came from Gavin Nigh, "They just spotted Grant up in the mansion... it shouldn't have been him..."

He didn't comment on the fact that all *Wolf* had managed to detect of the escape ship hurtling away was a brief flash of kinetic energy, and then a blur as it topped out around 372 kps. He knew that wouldn't have helped Karen in the slightest.

"Well... then maybe there are more ships in here. I'm going in," was her immediate — and I think you'll agree, entirely irresponsible — answer.

She turned her controls over and edged her Starlight into the tight flight bay. As she entered, the door shut behind her. Before Gavin could even turn to me with a warning that she was doing it, Karen had gone inside the asteroid.

As soon as I knew, boy did I ever call Charlie.

While my Hawke Lord friend was dealing with the spy killer, Rufus had focused his rage and moved straight into Grant's office. Boobytraps be damned: our Major with the mismatched eyes was going to bloody well get the Governor, and make sure there was no escape this time.

But the office was empty. Had Felicia not been so prompt in getting the blueprints, this might have bought Grant the time he needed. But instead of being confused, Rufus surged straight ahead, though the abandoned office and to the bathroom door.

It was locked, so he kicked it down. He then crossed the bathroom to the far wall — the only wall with enough space on it to suggest a hidden door. He knocked on that wall, and though it didn't sound hollow, he decided it was where he needed to go. Not knowing how hard it would be to break down, he simply swung up his rifle and set the charge to full.

If you ever want to understand the power of a full burst from a MAG-90, just watch the feed from the DCI bugs on the ceiling when that shot punched through the hatch. Granted, the door had never been built to accept fire — it wasn't on a warship — but the effect was still impressive.

And as the dust and smoke around the torn hole in the wall began to clear, Rufus was able to look through and see a long, bright corridor with a lift at the end. Grant wasn't in sight, but it was pretty obvious where he'd gone.

Without hesitation, Rufus dove through the hole he'd created, then hurried down the corridor with all possible speed. When he reached the door he keyed the hail button, and the lift helpfully returned just in time to open for him.

He was of course ready to shoot anyone inside, but it was empty, so he simply stepped in. Charlie appeared at the hole in the bathroom wall just as the doors closed, and Rufus plunged into the unknown.

My friend the Hawke Lord shook his head with a little bit of frustration as he saw that, then climbed through the hole and hurried to the lift as well, hitting the button as he arrived.

He had no idea how long the trip down would take, but he just had to hope that however late he was about to be, it wouldn't negatively affect the overall situation.

These were the thoughts he was having when my hail reached him from *Wolf*, "Karen just found some sort of flight bay at the other end of the chute, and she landed inside. We lost contact, so please tell me you're on your way."

Charlie blinked, then replied, "Rufus is on his way down, and I'll be following as soon as the lift comes back."

I think he heard my sigh of relief, but as far as he was concerned, it was premature. He looked down at the lift button, then pressed it again. Twice. Just to make sure it remembered to come back as quickly as possible.

As the space door closed behind Karen, an internal bay door opened in front of her… and revealed a small cavern with a platform, a lift door, some consoles… and a woman standing beside them looking awfully uncertain of herself.

Because the woman wasn't pressure-suited, Karen figured the atmosphere had to be breathable, so she popped her canopy and pulled off her helmet, then climbed from her Starlight. Her mag came out of its hip holster as soon as she got one foot on the frame of her plane, and then she looked away from the woman for a moment to climb down.

Of course, when her flight boots touched the deck and she looked up again, that woman — Sonia Hart — wasn't alone anymore.

"It's… you…" Grant raised a disruptor pistol as he came out of the lift, and to say he was honestly surprised was an understatement. Surprised for a lot of reasons.

Karen hadn't been ready for him, so she raised her own mag late, "You too."

Not the snappiest of dialogue, of course, because in reality we never manage to say the cleverest things in moments like these.

Sonia now hurried up to her lover's side, "Somehow she launched the ship. The space doors closed and then opened and when they did, the ship was gone and her plane was there."

Karen raised an eyebrow at that charge. It was unbelievably good news if somehow she'd managed to trigger an automated launch sequence with the info the bugs had provided — and thus had sent Grant's escape ship away.

And bad news for my old friend. Grant looked from Sonia to Karen and back, then realized the most obvious thing that was the hardest to grasp: he had no way out. He was about to be caught.

Unless... he took Karen's Starlight and made a daring getaway.

His mind began churning on that possibility — he'd never qualified on the Starlight, but he did know the fundamentals, and if he could just get out of Etat Valcour local space... find a surviving warship like *Captain*, or a civilian ship... anything.

It was a chance, and a chance was all he needed. He'd survived Deep Black with just a chance... now he could do so again.

If he could just get through Karen.

Sort of like saying he could get away if he could just get through the sun, isn't it?

"Stay behind me," he said quietly to Sonia. He could spare only the briefest moment to look at her face — her frightened eyes in particular. He didn't want to wonder whether she'd fit on his lap in the single-seat plane... it'd be hell for him to have to leave her behind...

"You know what I want," Karen interrupted his musing on that front, and as Grant put a hand on Sonia's leg and patted it to tell her to stay put, he advanced towards his nemesis.

"What's that?" he asked, honestly not remembering what her motive for being here might have been.

She didn't appreciate his lack of consideration and her eyes narrowed as real anger bubbled up inside her. Every fear she'd had, every insecurity, was trying to explode out of her in this one moment, and she had to fight all those emotions because this was not a time to lose focus.

Emotions were crucial to a good life, but there were times when they had to wait their turn.

"That compound you hit me with. There has to be an antidote, and you need to tell me what it is," she answered as evenly as she could manage, and Grant blinked.

Of course, her memories.

He had to use that for an advantage somehow... had to use that to get past her. He didn't know exactly how much she'd lost, but obviously she still knew how to fly, and that meant she could probably shoot too.

As he thought these things, he continued closing with her, step by step, and she didn't back off... she wasn't afraid of him, or being closer to him.

"I suppose striking a deal that allows us to escape in return for your memories is out of the question," the Governor tried a political approach first — nothing like a negotiation to end this sort of day, right?

Karen tilted her head, "You know me, Grant. You're bargaining right now for *her* life."

With that, Karen tipped her mag just enough to indicate Sonia... without moving her sights off his chest.

Grant knew that was exactly the bargain Karen wanted to make... that the vindictive bitch who'd steered me wrong was not beyond killing an innocent woman, just because that woman saw fit to love him.

Whatever I thought of her, Grant was beyond believing the psychopath in front of him was anything better than a self-righteous, petulant, and ignorant monster. He respected many of her abilities, and knew she was formidable, but that didn't change the fact that she was a danger. Not good enough for his best friend, as history had shown.

He just needed something — one thing — to let him get the drop on her.

Which is why Rufus' timing was either really good, or really bad, depending on your point of view.

When the lift doors opened again, Karen's eyes moved to see who was coming. She was understandably worried it was some of Grant's security... she didn't expect it to be one of her own. But that split second in which her eyes darted away, my old friend took advantage. He wasn't a God of hand-to-hand combat, but he was smart, and dangerous.

He knocked Karen's mag from her hand and swung his disruptor at her. Realizing what was happening, she turned and responded with a block that kept his pistol from lining up on her... then she punched him in the face. He lost his grip on the disruptor, and the two began a rematch of the tussle they'd once had in an Academy pub.

But this time, Grant was better prepared.

Rufus was still very, very focused when he stepped out of that lift. He saw Grant Merger, he saw Karen, and he started raising his MAG-90. This was going to end quickly, and then Rufus was going to go back to *Wolf* for a cool down.

Except that his MAG-90 was pushed down the second he raised it, and then it was somehow unclipped from his vest. He was well-accustomed to being able to let go of his rifle and have it stay at the ready for him, so when it dropped to the deck he was entirely surprised.

Trying to figure out what happened, he looked up and found Sonia Hart backing away from him, holding her hands up.

The Governor's girlfriend? Rufus didn't know the story — she could have been an elite former-Commando or something, so he decided to just handle her with gentlemanly prejudice. He came forward with his fists rising, and she waved her hands at him as if telling him to stop.

He didn't. Another one of Grant's super-killers... this one might be as good to put down as Renault would have been. So he swung, and she caught his fist and guided it past her, then blocked his next strike with her forearms, before pivoting and slamming her palms into his back, trying to knock him off balance.

That didn't work, because Rufus is like a stone pillar when it comes to hand-to-hand combat. He turned back and expected to have to chase Sonia again, but she came right in close as she sent her hands at him. She was fighting elegantly, like the wushu masters of China who had often impressed Rufus when he was young. But despite his fondness for kick-up films, our Major had trained mainly in Japanese-style martial arts, which was why he carried a tanto.

His strikes were close and powerful... and Sonia kept avoiding them, and then pattering her hands against his chest as though she were trying to knock him down.

But it just wasn't working, and he was confused as to why she didn't give up. She was clearly fast and smart — she'd learned somewhere how to survive — but did she really expect to accomplish much this way?

Then she slipped her leg around his, and planting her hands in the appropriate places, she pulled his legs out from under him and flipped him forward, so she could force him down to the deck on his face.

She did it slowly, as if she'd just learned how to do it...

And immediately Rufus understood what was going on. He countered the face-first drop as he'd been trained to do: arms up and legs reaching back to hook his attacker's torso as he went down. Sonia staggered to the side as he leapt back to his feet and drew his tanto from his vest.

He knew what he was up against now, and how it ended seemed entirely obvious.

The lift doors opened for Charlie, and he stepped inside and turned around, checking his MAG-90 and taking a deep breath as he waited for the thing to start moving. It seemed to take an awfully long time.

Karen groaned as she stopped a punch from Grant, then found herself off balance as he went low on her, hooking his arm around her leg and driving his shoulder into her stomach. It was a rugby tackle, and it drove her straight back into the landing gear of her Starlight — the same landing gear that, in 2231, had stuck while we were on Belt Two, and forced us to stay around and discover the plot to open the Martian War.

Now the rods and drums on that landing foot punched into her back in an explosion of pain, and she cried out as Grant pulled himself out from her crumpling body and wound up to hit her again. She could do nothing to stop his blow: it crossed her jaw and she felt blood erupt into her mouth as her teeth cut her cheek.

It was brutal, but Grant had no more time — he had to put her down and then find a way to kill the Brancher. Only then might he be able to get away with Sonia.

He wound up again, and as he straddled his adversary with his fists clenched and his face wild, Karen just stared at him. She'd been so angry, and so worried, and so everything else. She hadn't been clear-headed, and now Grant had the upper hand as a result.

In that second, she wished I could arrive, tackle my old friend, put an end to this mistake she'd made. But I was on *Wolf*, as much as I might have wished to be with her.

So she had to do it herself, which was less convenient but no less doable. She started by moving her head at the last possible minute, so his fist missed. The landing gear which had been unkind to her back cut Grant's hand right open, and he let out a wheeze of surprise as he felt the shattering pain go up his arm. Then Karen planted her feet on the deck and pushed herself into a sideways roll, forcing him over onto the platform and putting her on top of him.

Adrenaline and quiet rage were keeping her going now, because she was spitting out a fair volume of blood in a rather gruesome fashion. She pummeled Grant's face with her fists for a few seconds, and then he tried to do the same thing she'd done — he planted his feet on the deck and pushed up to the side, forcing her onto the deck beside him.

But Karen's blows had been strong, and he was too stunned to get on top of her once she was off him. Instead he looked back towards the lift, towards Sonia. His beloved was swatting at the big, evil Special Brancher who had come down the lift. His mismatched eyes were hungrily boring into her, and she was struggling and crying out for protection.

Grant had to protect her, that was his responsibility. She needed him. His beloved.

But the Brancher had a knife in his hands… a strange knife that was not regulation in any way. As Grant's vision hazed, he saw that knife turn around in the Chinese Major's right hand, and then he saw it swing around behind Sonia's back.

She looked surprise as it went in. She saw Grant's face and she almost seemed to smile, as if feeling like her death was some sort of kindness. He reached out for her, but then Karen got up on her knees, and with all the strength she had left, she punched Grant Merger on the temple.

With consciousness already waning, Grant let go completely. He let his vision cloud over as he watched Sonia's look of surprise… he let that all fade away.

He had not escaped.

"You could really hurt someone with that, you know."

Rufus was half-cradling Sonia in his arms as the butt of his tanto dug into her back between the fifth and sixth vertebrae. He had, of course, reversed the blade in his hand before hitting her with it, because it wouldn't have been right for him to actually kill her.

Now he frowned at her comment, and glared at her, "Not you, apparently."

"Was wondering how long it was going to take for you to catch on," she shot back, and as she felt the butt of the knife move away from her back she let out a breath.

She could have let go of Rufus at this point… but she decided not to. It wasn't that she had any special affinity for the Brancher, but holding onto him was comfortable. Because it was different… because he was certainly different.

Maybe she did have some special affinity for him.

Rufus had more practical concerns, though. He straightened up and let go of Sonia, then slid his tanto into its sheath on his vest before turning to Karen. She was on her knees beside Grant's unconscious body, spitting blood onto the deck and trying to catch her breath.

"You alright?" he asked, and Karen looked up uncomfortably.

After spitting more blood, she blinked a couple of times — one of her eyes was already swelling shut, "I don't think I'll be fit to fly back."

The words didn't enunciate clearly because her jaw was throbbing, but he got the point.

Then Karen looked past him at Sonia, and she pointed, "Should we shoot her?"

"She's DCI," Rufus answered.

"Oh. Okay," was Karen's response, and then she flopped back to sit on the deck, holding a hand to her face as the throbbing got worse. Adrenaline was fast leaving her system, and Grant had given her a bit of a beating.

Though obviously not as bad as the beating she'd given him.

Turning back to Sonia, Rufus folded his arms, "So you were protecting your cover?"

She nodded, "Been working on him long enough, didn't want to risk it. I got rid of his escape ship and sent that message telling you where he was, but just in case he did get away…"

It sounded to Rufus as though this spy hadn't been able to speak the truth to anyone for a long time — she was volunteering an awful lot in answer to a simple question.

"Were you able to save Julie Pichot?" was her next question, and Rufus nodded.

"She's in a bad way, but we should be able to make it right when we get home."

"Good," Sonia said with a quiet nod. "What's her name?"

Rufus tilted his head, then decided he could speak the truth, "Margot Messina. She was sent out to find you."

"I figured," Sonia nodded, and then she sighed again. "You know who I am?"

"A spy," Rufus replied. "I don't like spies."

Sonia frowned slightly, and tilted her head, "No exceptions?"

Rufus shook his head slowly, "No exceptions."

That was the moment, Haley Briand tells me, when she decided she had to marry Rufus Chang. Yeah I know I'm jumping way ahead here, but it was one of those situations where an undercover spy gets rescued by an unassuming hero-type, and it's love at first sight. Really. I mean, no one explained that to Rufus, which is why it took so long, but that's what happened.

Haley Briand had come back to us.

And don't worry, I'll pause to explain everything in a minute. For now, one more point.

The lift doors opened and Charlie stepped out, MAG-90 at the ready. In one sweep of the room he detected everything that had happened, and then made correct assumptions about Haley's identity, that Grant was unconscious, and that Rufus and Karen were both mostly fine.

With a nod to himself, he lowered his MAG-90, "Well, my work here is done. I'll go get the medics."

And with that, he stepped back into the lift.

Sometimes you just have to know when you're superfluous to a scene.

Grant Merger had been caught, and it was Karen who had done it — with help from our friends.

Chapter Twenty-Five

What Happened

Fool me once, shame on you. Fool me twice, and you know DCI has been involved.

Grant had done it to himself again. Well, I suppose we did it to him as much as he did it to himself, but either way, it was the same gambit and it worked a second time, because no matter what else Grant was, he was a romantic at heart.

Nothing wrong with that, just be aware that it can interfere with highly elaborate evil plans, especially when you trigger those plans by targeting another romantic-at-heart individual.

Just to be clear, Sonia Hart was Haley Briand all along. I'm sure many of you knew this, and some of you who didn't know it might have suspected. But indeed, Julie Pichot was not the master spy herself, just one of the agents sent by Thea Fostopolos to try to find Haley after she disappeared.

That's why Chapter 32 of *The Forge Fires* is so awkwardly written: because Julie… or Margot, I should say… spotted Haley immediately, but neither of them could actually be honest with each other about who they were. Having worked her way into Grant's inner circle, Haley figured she had a real chance at catching him… and with Margot coming into the picture, at least she'd have some backup.

The fact that Haley managed to get through Grant's guard is a testament to her skill as a manipulator, and her willingness to do the one thing that Mel Samuels never would: fake genuine love for a man she detested.

Being an agent like Haley requires you to compartmentalize many parts of yourself — even more if you're going to share the bed of the person you're targeting. But Haley had been willing to do it… or as she explained to me later, she'd started off arrogantly assuming it'd be easy, and then had been left with little choice but to continue.

I will be perpetually grateful that she held in there. Without a doubt, her efforts made the difference in us catching Grant at the last minute. Our super-advanced spy bugs hadn't been the ones who'd sent the information about the escape ship — not on their own, anyway. Haley had seen Felicia's request bounce back through their comm network and realized help was at hand, then sent Karen the information she needed to get the space doors to open.

It had also been Haley who triggered the launch of the escape ship — as much as she'd have liked to keep it for study (owing to its massive speed and its very unique tech), she knew the only way to be absolutely certain Grant couldn't escape would be to deny him any access to a spacecraft.

And then when Rufus had come down, she'd kept up the cover until she knew Grant was unconscious… because protecting a cover is never a bad idea, at least in the opinion of any good spy.

Rufus had figured out who she was as soon as she'd started acting like an instructor during Special Branch selection. Most superagents were required to go through Special Branch training, and the best spooks were as skilled as any Branchers when it came to hand-to-hand.

Some of the techniques taught in those courses are quite unique, and yet they're very familiar to those who trained on them. As soon as he figured out why his opponent was hitting him in all the right places to do a lot of harm, but was doing it with a suspicious lack of speed and power, it all fell into place. Despite being super-focused, Rufus had realized that his adversary was a spy, which meant he didn't like her... and he knew that if she was holding cover it was important for him not to just stop fighting and say, "OH, YOU'RE A SPY."

Grant was probably going to find out that he'd been duped again, but we'd save that surprise for later.

Hitting her with the tanto? That was just the conclusion of a standard knife training drill — one very unique to Special Branch, which was basically a silent message back from Rufus to Haley saying, "OH, YOU'RE A SPY."

Except without actually saying it.

So that's what happened. Haley Briand, who had ridden with John and Greg when they stopped the almost coup, and who had been in the room with Dave Caldecott back then several times, had come all the way out to the unexplored Belt, had trapped an enemy of the Empire, and had helped us pin him.

She was definitely looking forward to getting her cosmetic surgery reversed, and returning to Earth to either retire or perhaps take up a post at the Ministry of Agriculture. She heard that was nice.

Chapter Twenty-Six

Aftermath

Local space had quieted down considerably by the time shuttles started returning to *Hester* from the dome. *Constellation* had been thoroughly gutted by *Cheetah*, and was now adrift on its way out into unknown space. Rozy Young had put an end to *Constitution*; the old ship was in three pieces, and none of those pieces was fit to fight.

Perhaps most impressive, though, had been the duel between *Chesapeake*, *Friendly* and *Generous*. Those two corvettes had their work cut out for them against the Union cruiser, one of the only warships in green group that was honestly well-handled.

I could have spent all those chapters we were down on the dome recounting the story of cleverness and heroics, but unfortunately I missed that chance, so I'll direct you to Matt Baxter's own memoirs on the subject. Ahem. Shameless plug for my friend Matt.

When he and Isoruku pulled back into orbit, his question on the Battlelink screen was pretty wonderful: "Did I miss anything?"

I looked up at him, "Karen landed on the rock in a secret flight bay and beat Grant into submission with her fists. We found out that Haley Briand has been Grant's lover the whole time, and she led us right to him. We defeated all their in-dome defenses without a sweat because Rufus' plan worked. And Charlie killed Renault, the spy killer."

With that sudden flood of information, I suppose Isoruku or Matt could have started wherever they liked... but for the Japanese skipper of *Generous*, the last point was the one that warranted more information.

"What did he use?" he asked, referring to Charlie's defeat of Renault.

"His bare hands," I answered. "Mark's checking to see who won the pool."

That got a nod from Isoruku — it was a satisfying answer. Matt would have been similarly pleased, except he was still stuck back on some of the other stuff I'd said.

"Karen did what?"

Yeah, it was pretty inevitable that he'd fixate there.

"They're evacuating the dome now... she should be ready to withdraw shortly," Andrea helpfully added more context before I said anything, and Matt decided it was best to nod.

It sounded like the whole plan had worked flawlessly... because it had.

Charlie was holding Karen's head back as Selma Koestecki worked to patch her up. It was a bit tricky as the assault shuttle bounced around during its rise from the mansion, but tricky wasn't a problem. It would have been worse if someone had bothered shooting at them, but Adrienne's suppression of the defenses, together with the presence of so many no-nonsense SF and volunteers on the ground, had convinced the locals to just let us take their Governor.

It was, I suppose, anticlimactic. The worst injury suffered by any Defense Command person on this whole day had been Maggie Joyce getting shot by that disruptor outside

Grant's office. On *Wolf*, I think one of Andy Jensen's engineers burned his hand when he reached out in the dark and grabbed a hot pipe instead of the cool one right next to it.

And, of course, Karen had received a pummeling.

But compared to the destruction we'd wrought, our complete lack of casualties was almost obnoxious. After this whole war of us being hurt as much as we hurt others, it might seem a bit of a surprise, but I can tell you it wasn't that uncommon in the pirate-hunting days for us to turn up, trash a place, and leave with nothing more than cuts and bruises in return for lives destroyed.

We're the Empire. We're the best, and this is what we can do. This is why the Solar Asteroid Union hates us so much right now — because we swanned in and treated them very badly, and did so without remorse.

All because they'd harbored, and indeed lionized, a named enemy of the Empire.

Or perhaps this: all because my old friend, who was trying to take over the Union, had picked a fight with us in order to raise his profile.

Now Grant was cuffed to a backboard and lay on the floor of the assault shuttle, not far from Karen's feet. She didn't pay him any attention — she was suffering now, because her body (which wasn't as young as she remembered) wasn't bouncing back from the beating as well as she'd have expected.

One of those things that changes over time, I suppose.

Still, in spite of all the brutality of recent hours, Karen was feeling very peaceful as the assault shuttle climbed back into *Hester*, and gravity changed outside. A lot of her anger had been vented — and vented at exactly the person who most deserved it. Better yet, she hadn't even killed him, so she still had a chance at getting her answers.

Not a bad day.

As the last of the shuttles lifted off from the dome floor, Adrienne and her planes were extra vigilant. At no time during an operation this fundamentally crazy could you afford to be lax — a single shot from a shoulder-laser could cost a life, or even a dozen lives.

We weren't having that today, because one of us dying would be unacceptable in this circumstance.

"All ships are now off the ground, top-cover standing by to pull back into *Hester*."

I nodded at Adrienne's report, even though she couldn't see the gesture. Now the skeleton crew aboard *Hester* would be preparing to close the bow airlock behind our assault force, and open the stern airlock so the shuttles and planes could all fly out of the cargo hold to come on home.

This had not yet been tried, but we expected it to work... and after it did, we'd evacuate the crew from *Hester* and leave the freighter grav-anchored to the dome. The SAUN could figure out how to pull it off without decompressing Etat Valcour.

I could keep telling you all this, as if something interesting happened... but nothing did. This is the moment when there's supposed to be something dramatic — when something goes wrong and we lose someone. Maybe Felicia, away on her first mission, was to meet with an ill fate? Maybe Adrienne, who was preoccupying Shelby McLaws, would have engine trouble? Maybe the shuttle with Charlie, Rufus, Haley, Grant, Karen and the team would go missing?

No.

Everyone came home safe and as planned. One of the *Wolf* volunteers even went down into Grant's secret chamber and piloted Karen's plane back aboard. By the time the shuttles made it out of *Hester* and we took the skeleton crew off that freighter, Katya Romanov had even brought *Sackville* back to us.

This mission… this fight against the most intricate plans of a chess master… had gone off without a hitch. Because — and it's my turn to gloat for a minute — chess players can be brilliant strategists, but few things in the real world actually conform to the principles of the chess board.

You never see all the pieces, and no two pieces are intrinsically the same. When you have the best people — be it Katya closing the range fast and Isoruku detonating torpedoes in their tubes, or Felicia finding the DCI signals on the ground and Haley proving to be the greatest spy of her generation — you can leverage that into victory.

Plans are good. They help you move the resources you need into the positions you need at the times you need. And sometimes, despite what the saying promises, I suppose they do survive contact with the enemy.

But the villain passed out on a backboard at the feet of Charlie and Karen needed to learn that plans change with people, as much as they change with events. And as we'll really find out in the last book of this series, that was the biggest problem Grant Merger ever had.

For now, enough plot. Let's get some friends home safe.

CHAPTER TWENTY-SEVEN
FRIENDS

There were too many people for me to thank as the shuttles unloaded in *Wolf's* flight bays. I didn't even bother trying, because I knew we'd have ample opportunity to talk to all of them on the cruise home. My main priorities were to find Karen and Charlie, and also Grant.

That put me in bay two, and as my old enemy was unloaded by Selma Koestecki and Simon Keynes, I watched him come down the ramp. Actually, most of the deck crew watched — everyone was somber at the sight of our long-time foe finally being brought in.

The quiet didn't last — too many planes needed to be topped up and made ready for more combat in case we found ourselves in action again. That was for the deck crew to do; I wanted Karen.

She came off the shuttle with one arm over Charlie's shoulder, and a towel against her nose. As she hobbled to the bottom of the ramp, she managed to turn her head to see out of the corner of her eye that I was there. I frowned and tilted my head to try to look in under her towel a bit, but it was difficult — she was all sorts of colors, so finding familiar landmarks wasn't easy.

"I got him," she said, but because her face was mostly covered the words were just about indiscernible.

I looked at Charlie, and he shrugged, "I just got her back. What trouble she got herself into while I was waiting for the elevator is her business."

My friend.

It was impossibly proper, but I stuck out my hand to Charlie Peters at that point, and he took it. Manly handshake, as is appropriate under such circumstances.

"I'll go take our guest to med bay," he said next, but that actually stopped my warmth for just a second.

"Make it the brig. Alicia can visit him there, but I'll take no chances. He knows how to escape."

That was a good justification for throwing Grant into a compartment with far fewer witnesses around to make sure nothing happened to him… but Charlie bought it. For now. He nodded and then we carefully switched places; I got under Karen's arm and he went off to follow Grant Merger.

We stood there on the deck for a moment, Karen and me, and then I shook my head, "This really won't do at all."

"What?" she asked, again quite muffled.

"I was honestly planning on kissing you out here in front of everyone, to cause a sensation."

"Well you still can," she said, but I grimaced.

"No, that'd be gross."

She made to argue, but then she thought about it. Now this isn't some commentary on standards of beauty, or any other stuff like that. It's just a question: don't you think it'd be a little weird to go for a big kiss when someone's face is swollen up, covered in open wounds, and — and — she's spitting blood every little while?

Go ahead, you tell me you're game for that. I'll believe it when I see it.

But please don't send pictures. That's gross.

Wes Pellew was sitting up in bed, the sedatives that Alicia had quietly slipped him having worn off towards the end of the battle. Yes, he'd been so anxious about the outcome of the fight (and the way we'd conduct ourselves during the fight) that his blood pressure had been medically dangerous. So Alicia had fixed the problem, completely ethically I might add.

Now he was watching the preparation of a special bed for Grant Merger — the man had apparently suffered much during his capture, though Wes knew none of the details. He wasn't sure if he dreaded having the Governor as a fellow inmate of the med bay, or if he thought it was a good thing that he'd be nearby whenever Karen or I showed up for a conversation.

Either way, he was ready to deal with it, as much as he could be. He figured his presence could be important.

The hatch opened, and Wes figured that meant Grant was arriving. It was Charlie instead, and as the Hawke Lord Major stepped in, Alicia approached him.

"We're treating Grant in the brig. Bring anything you need, but I don't think you'll be allowed to leave much monitoring equipment with him. Ken's worried about escape."

It's a testament to how hated Grant really was that Alicia didn't object… she paused and then nodded thoughtfully, understanding well the point of being careful under these circumstances.

Wes caught an undercurrent of concern in Charlie's tone, though, and as the Major moved away to let the doctor collect her kit, the Commodore caught his attention, "Bad?"

Charlie shrugged, "Karen had to vent some anger, but she didn't kill him. Rufus says she didn't even come close. And she's pretty banged up."

"Think there'll be a problem with Grant aboard?" Wes asked the next question in a lower tone, and Charlie looked down for a second, then met the Independent Squadron Commodore's gaze.

"How could there not be?"

Shit. Wes needed to get out of his bed — soon.

Rufus showed Haley Briand to guest quarters, and as he opened the cabin door and led the way in, he offered his apologies, "It's modest, but comfortable."

The cabin was nice indeed, but compared to the finery of a mansion, he could have understood if she found it plain. Haley hadn't stopped smiling since she got aboard ship — she was, as she explained later, very glad to be back in a place where the rules made sense. Some agents who spend a long time in deep cover can became subsumed by their new identity, and the world it places them in… but not Haley. I suppose it helps that she'd been in the SAU, where she was mostly seen as a woman meant to warm the Governor's bed, while also having some abilities that were beyond secretarial when it came to organization and administration.

Just saying, the SAU bastards waste half their population, just like the Martians do. About as efficient as cuffing one hand to your belt at all times… idiots.

Anyway, Haley was happy to be back, and her quarters were just fine. She turned to Rufus as he waited at the door, then nodded and smiled, "Happy to be here. You want to help me figure out how the shower works?"

So it had been a while since she'd *actually* fancied a guy. Poor Rufus, he just wasn't in the right headspace for this.

"Blue means cold, red means hot. The computer will keep you from killing yourself."

Haley loved that answer, and I agree, it's pretty good. She then took a couple of jaunty steps towards our Chinese Major, and peered into his mismatched eyes. He leaned back slightly as she got into his personal space, then frowned quizzically at her, deciding that so much time under cover really must have messed up something in her brain.

"I'm going to marry you one day, Major Chang," she said. "Just you wait."

It seemed a ridiculous thing to say — and of course, it was entirely impossible as well. In order to be married, both parties need to sign the register, and there wasn't much chance of Rufus ever doing that at the behest of a spy. It wasn't personal; Special Branch and DCI just didn't mix. Superagent-types were so cagey… he liked to be direct, to go through walls if they were in his way, to use grenades…

Espionage was for other people.

Like his future wife.

Haha Rufus. He had no idea, but the best spy of her generation had just targeted him, and that's sort of like being caught in a black hole's gravity. It takes a while, but it'll get you.

Eventually, you'll even like it.

When one of Alicia's medics finished patching Karen up, I took her back to her cabin. She looked rather rough, it has to be said — the drugs did wonders to bring down the swelling, and sealant closed up the cuts, but she looked like she'd been in a bit of a fight.

Her back also had to be treated, because that collision with her Starlight's landing gear had actually caused a mirco-fracture in one of her discs. Easy enough to patch, fortunately, but she'd have to take it easy for a while to avoid re-injuring herself.

All of that being the case, she wheezed a little when I sat her down on her bed, which we hadn't made, and unzipped her flight suit.

"You're going to be all black and blue," I said disapprovingly.

"You don't like colorful people?"

"Yeah yeah be clever about it. You're going to be groaning all night."

"Promise?"

I poked her in the ribs for that, and she laughed until it hurt — which meant she laughed once and then groaned.

"See?" I said, and then finished peeling her out of her flight suit so she could start cleaning up. Before we headed to the shower, though, she put her hand on mine.

"We got him. That wasn't a hallucination because I got head trauma?"

I nodded, "You got him. Everything worked today… even when you landed without support in an unknown flight bay."

If she could have, she would have winced slightly at that, "I don't do that sort of thing anymore, right? I'm responsible now?"

Up until that question, I think I'd forgotten that Karen couldn't remember all our antics of the past decade — from the time she'd gotten off the shuttle to now, it had been not much different than getting her back after Pion Rock, or the fistfight in *The Mars Convention*. But this was still Karen missing twelve years of experience…

And you know what, she wasn't very different.

Because when she needed to deliver in combat, at the core she was the sort of person who made decisions, took risks, and ultimately made a difference. And as I thought that, I took a breath and shook my head.

"This is the most like yourself you've been in days," I said, and I was being honest.

She could tell I wasn't lying.

"Get up to a lot of trouble, still?"

I shrugged, "When it matters, and sometimes when it doesn't. But yeah, this isn't something you've abandoned."

Karen let out another wheeze, "Probably do it less, though. Because apparently I'm not as young as I used to be?"

"There is that," I shrugged. "You are sort of old now."

She didn't actually hear that at first, but then she frowned and whacked me, "Hey."

"Have to make fun when you're wounded. Fewer consequences."

"True," she answered. "Come help an old lady wash herself?"

I nodded, "Yes, ma'am."

We headed off to the shower, and no, I'm afraid this wasn't a repeat of something I didn't spell out for you before — Karen was in no condition for that, and neither of us was in the headspace for it either. She needed to bathe, and it hurt to move. Washing a banged-up goddess is not a glamorous job, but someone has to suffer through it.

For the record, Karen just read that line on screen over my shoulder, and slapped me in the back of the head.

CHAPTER TWENTY-EIGHT
OLD FRIENDS

When Grant woke up, he found himself on a bare cot in a blank metal room, wearing a flightsuit with no patches, no shoes or socks, and no restraints. He was under constant watch in our highest-security cell, but even with all of those provisions, one Special Brancher was going to be outside the door at all times, and the security desk a few meters away would have a screen constantly showing the feeds from within.

And, just in case that wasn't enough, the brig's normal staff of two on-duty SF was being doubled to four for the duration of the cruise home.

When I recommended heightened security, I hadn't been sure whether to expect pushback from anyone... obviously there had been none. What I didn't realize at the time was that the reason Charlie offered no pushback was because he wanted lots and lots of people around, to make sure I wasn't able to be alone with Grant without intervening forces close at hand.

That's also the reason he accompanied me on my first visit to Grant's cell, shortly after my former friend the villain woke up.

Now, when you visit our max-security cell, it's not a matter of opening the door, stepping in and chatting with the person. That would be stupid. No, there's one wall of the metal box which can retract slightly, and reveal a six-inch-thick transparent viewport that leads into a neighboring observation room. Thanks to comms in both rooms, you can talk back and forth, and see each other.

Perfect way to catch up when you're worried one person (or the other) might attempt murder on sight.

Charlie was pleased with this arrangement, but knowing that the crew of *Wolf* was fiercely loyal to me, he wasn't satisfied by that security provision alone. It was going to be a long, long cruise back to Earth.

For now, though, he simply leaned against the frame of the hatch in the observation chamber, while I moved over to the viewport and hit the key that opened it. Grant was looking the wrong way when the metal thunked back, but he turned immediately and caught sight of me, then locked eyes with me.

"Guess you got my note."

"Guess you ran into Karen."

We stared at each other for a second, and Charlie watched with folded arms, ready for just about anything he figured might come next. Not ready, as it turns out, for what actually happened.

Grant smiled — not the snide, annoying smile of someone like Howard Pedro Azuma III, but the smile of a friend who hasn't seen another friend in far too long, "She's still got a hell of a right hook. Thank God I didn't have any bar stools down there, or you'd be surgically removing one from my anatomy."

"I kinda would have preferred that," I grinned back, and in that moment I felt a great deal of tension uncoil from my shoulders. "Is it good to see you again? That might be perverse."

It's what I said — and what he said. And if you started reading here out of context, I completely realize it would not come across as the words of two people who'd been such desperate enemies as Grant and me. Were we joking with each other?

Yes.

Yes, and I don't know if I can adequately explain why. My first instinct upon seeing Grant should have been to shoot him, or kill him somehow. That's what Charlie expected. But for reasons outside reason, and well outside my control, I didn't do that. We had been friends, and as I'd suspected earlier, our reunion led almost immediately to a resurrection of the bond that had made us such a powerful duo in those early Academy years.

"It is perverse. But that probably makes it even more true," Grant agreed, taking a similar deep breath. This was perhaps less strange for him, given the arrogant way he'd hoped to bring me round to his way of thinking — the way he'd thought he could make us friends again, if I just saw the light. "How was the war?"

Not a loaded question, but an honest one, and still I couldn't help but answer like I would have years earlier: "About the way we figured it would be. Lots of repressing of concern, lots of serious times. Changes you, even more than fighting a renegade and his band of pirates does."

"I think this campaign you've waged made that clear to me," he replied, then waved his hand at the cell around him. "And my experience is ending on a down note compared to yours."

I shrugged, "You picked the wrong team."

That was the first thing I said that wasn't completely positive — took me long enough — and for the first time Grant's eyes narrowed just a little, "I think we're going to have plenty to discuss about that. Long trip home, isn't it?"

Now my brain started to work a little better.

"Very long. For us," I answered, and Grant frowned just slightly, turning his eyes over to Charlie Peters. It was the first time he'd noticed the Hawke Lord was present, and that made my comment make more sense.

"Aha, it's Major Peters. Lord Peters, now, I should say. Congratulations on the title... and well done with Lady Hawke. Particularly like how you've made it seem you just got together in that hospital."

There was an obvious edge in that greeting... the sort of low-level aggression that happens when friends meet friends of their friends, and don't end up getting along with them. Charlie simply tilted his head, "I'll tell her you said hi."

"Thank you," Grant smiled back, before returning his gaze to me. "Well, I suppose this will be an interesting trip, no matter how it ends. I expect you'll need to get back to Karen now, though. Tell her I'm sorry about the beating."

I started to nod, but now that we were speaking of Karen again, my mind was settling more completely into the moment. There was a vital question to ask, and no point wasting time before raising it: "And what about the memories. How do we get those back?"

Grant stared at me, then halted in thought. I could tell that he was calculating...

postulating… trying to decide what information he had, and how he could use it to his advantage. The wheels were turning, the plans for manipulation were being formed, and…

And I realized that if there was a cure — if there was any sort of treatment whatsoever — he wouldn't have had to think so hard to figure out how to use the information. It would have been the most obvious bargaining chip in the world… the one thing that might, theoretically, have improved his situation.

When I came to that conclusion, it must have been clear from my expression, because Grant's wheels stopped turning and his expression fell, "I won't be so disrespectful as to lie to you."

Charlie hadn't been party to my conclusion, because my back was mostly to him, but he still drew the correct interpretation from Grant's concession.

"There's nothing," the Hawke Lord said flatly, and the villain turned his eyes back to my best friend.

"We didn't design it to be reversible. You light a library on fire, Charlie, the books you burn don't reappear when you build a new one. You have to go find different books."

I stared at Grant when he said that. The man who had hurt the most important person in my universe. His remorse was as obvious as it was genuine — he did regret doing it, it's just that regret for him was different than regret for most people. But regret didn't matter, to him or to me. He'd done it, as part of a plan, and that plan had now ended. We both knew there would be consequences.

We just didn't know exactly what those were.

"Good night, Grant," I said, and before he could answer I turned and left.

Charlie followed me through the corridors from the brig until I stopped at the lift and waited for it to arrive. As he halted beside me, he considered my expression and asked, "Are you going to tell her tonight?"

"Of course not. She won't be able to sleep."

Charlie nodded, but he and I both knew that was a lie. There was no way I couldn't tell her. Recognizing this unspoken truth, my friend kindly walked me to Karen's cabin, and then shook my hand before I went in.

I don't really remember feeling anything when I stepped inside, or much beyond that when Karen sat up slowly and squinted at me.

Then I told her what Grant said.

Grieving is supposed to be a process, with a combination of anger and bargaining and fear and other things. Karen was so banged up that she didn't need any of those things right now. I'm sure logically this should have waited… but do you really think I could have managed to keep it from her somehow? And even if I could have found a way, perhaps by wrapping myself up in bandages so that my expression was obscured, and standing on my head to mask my posture, would it have been right to keep it from her?

No matter how much sleep it cost her, it had to be this way. Karen had waited long enough, suffered through enough, to deserve her answer.

And now with her face all battered and her body aching, she hung her head and felt altogether too tired to deal with the revelation.

I kicked off my boots and crawled into bed next to her, and kissed her on the forehead, then touched the left side of her neck. She stared blankly past me as I did this, and finally admitted what was going on in her brain: "I don't know what I'm supposed to feel."

"I don't think anyone knows what you're supposed to feel," I answered. "Just... sleep if you can? We'll figure it out."

"Right," she answered. "We'll figure it out."

The most amazing thing then happened: Karen went to sleep. Deep sleep — so deep she didn't notice when I left her bed, and her cabin. So deep that she was still down, not having moved an inch, when I came back two hours later.

She would sleep for nearly eighteen hours. It might have been partially due to the pain meds, but mostly it was because of her real, deep exhaustion.

There would be a lot for us to figure out on the way back to Earth... and we had an enemy of the Empire in the brig to help us through it all.

AFTERWORD

My editors were divided about where to end this book. Some thought we should stop it before I talked to Grant — before I found out about Karen's memories. They felt that was a 'downer', and that we should have ended this story on a more positive note — perhaps stopping just after we finally captured Grant.

I think this way works fine. And I think there's going to be plenty of ground for us to cover in the last book of this series... the last book in which you'll have to put up with my hackish crap writing.

Because the battles are behind us, and the SAU will be in our wake. But as you probably know, the single most controversial decision we ever made will be the focus of the final book. Everyone seems to have an opinion about what happened on *Wolf* during that voyage home, and it's about time I remind them of mine.

For now, though, thank you for hanging in — just one more, and then you're home and dry. Until then, take care.

ENEMIES
OF
EMPIRE

THE AUTOBIOGRAPHICAL REMINISCENCES OF
ADMIRAL THE LORD KEN BARRON FOR 2235

THE MARTIAN WAR - 20

KENNETH TAM

FROM THE AUTHOR

I've made this point in other places: I don't have many friends. The world may be full of good people, but each of us is limited in how many we get to build relationships with... and in my case, factors of time and personality mean there is a very small core of individuals to whom I am close.

As I've said in every book thus far, many of these people have lent their personalities to DC characters. You may have picked out some of them, and in this book I hope to lend credit to all of them... as well as those friends who have are purely fictional... because those people are clearly of profound importance to Ken Barron. Throughout the Martian War, the so-called Rogue Commodore was always kind to those he served with, not because it was polite, but because he truly believed those people were the best.

During his final battle with Grant, it was the officers and crews of the Belt Squadron who gave Ken Barron the edge over his former friend — who changed the rules on the chess board with their skill. Now it will be those closest to him who have the greatest impact on his choices, and Karen's choices, as they make the most important decision of recent years.

And, ironically, all those friends (save one) do so without knowing the greatest secret Ken and Karen ever kept. By the end of this book, they will know... and so will you.

But right now, I must take my final opportunity to offer warm regards.

On the subject of friends in these books, I now thank: John, Greg, Marlene, Mik, Sam, Mel, Keith, Brendan, and Matt, plus a few others who appeared for cameos. I'm indebted to you all for your indulgences, and for the texture your true qualities have added to the Defense Command universe.

Charles Chiang was singled out in the last book, and is so again here — with my apologies for the fate of his character. It's unkind to end on such a hopeless note, but I hope he understands why.

Wes Prewer has been specially thanked in every book of this series, because he's an immensely talented graphic artist, as well as a keen friend. If you haven't figured out that a certain Commodore might have something to do with him, well, take this as a hint. And as good a friend as Pellew is to Ken Barron, Wes is to me. Many thanks.

Then there's Peter Caron, who professes that he could not kill you with anything... but even if he could, he wouldn't. He's a gentleman, a scholar, an engineer, my best friend, and his contributions to this series have gone far beyond a certain Lord Major from Special Branch... though chances are, anything wise that Major says didn't originate with me, but with Peter.

And finally, my partners and parents, Jacqui and Peter. For ten years we've run Iceberg Publishing together; for seven we've worked on this series. Thank you forever... now I guess we have more editing to do. Atlas: one last time, with my thanks.

– Kenneth Tam

PREFACE

Hard to believe this is book twenty. I have to admit, I'm somewhat surprised that my publishers have put up with me for so long... and that I've put up with them. Though as you might have figured out by now, any threats I ever made to quit this project were entirely hollow. Indeed, I don't think I ever actually threatened these guys, which might be a surprise considering how cheap they've always been about maps, and how competently they spell 'Jupite(e)r'.

Pretty soon you'll understand why I stayed — presuming you don't know already. Because this is the last book, the last reminiscence I have to offer about the Martian War. And indeed, as my good friend Charlie has pointed out to me a few times, this last year isn't even really about the Martian War itself.

When you think about it... really look back and think about all the books we've been through... there are a few questions that I should probably take the time to answer. And because this is the big finale, I suppose I have to do it now. No more chapters for you to remember for much later, no more cryptic hints...

Or at least not too many.

Of course, this book is probably the most anticipated installment of the whole series. On that front, I'm sure my publishers are delighted — they know that, after all their patience and putting up with my abuse, they'll finally get the chance to uncover the truth about what happened on our cruise home from the Solar Asteroid Union.

I think more ink has probably been spilled about those eleven days of travel, and their aftermath, than anything else in my career. That's not the way it should be, but I suppose so many people have an opinion about what occurred, and whether a conspiracy is afoot, that it was inevitable.

I've never gone into detail about what transpired aboard *Wolf* in those days, and neither has Karen. There was never any appetite for an inquiry, and no journalist — not even Jessica Qing — could ever find a story.

But the speculation has been rampant and now, I suppose, is the time to bring it to an end.

Welcome to *Enemies of Empire*, the last book of this Martian War series.

Let's begin.

CHAPTER ONE
WHEN WE WERE FRIENDS

There are few days I remember better than September 10, 2222. That whole year was special — it was the first time since 1111 (Imperial standard calendar… previously known as AD or CE) that we had a year composed of four consecutive digits. But the oddity of the date aside, it was the year Karen and I both earned our first commands.

We'd take over *Friendly* and *Lady Grace* that September, and Greg Noyce had sent us home to collect both ships from the Luna yards. It had been an exciting trip, with several important visits on the agenda: we got to see my parents in St. John's, took care of a particularly important family event, and then we flew up to Terra Nova, to reunite with an old friend.

That meeting took place in an unimposing little coffee shop that no longer exists and it was supposed to happen at lunch. But because we'd been distracted during the morning, Karen and I ended up arriving late. That actually worked out fine; we didn't realize it until years later, but Grant Merger had been late too — just slightly less late.

Unsurprisingly, the reasons for his delay were nefarious: he'd stopped at the Imperial Archives, purportedly on an innocent mission to look up some service records for a research paper. Instead, he'd found a way to purge and replace some key data from his Academy files, including his DNA print. All part of his plan to go rogue, which wasn't discovered until years later, when it became necessary to pull that Academy file because he'd been revealed as a traitor.

Anyway, Grant had hurried over to the coffee shop after his covert mission, and perhaps because of the adrenaline that accompanied espionage, he was looking a bit grumpy when we arrived. Of course, he brightened when he saw us.

Coming to his feet, he shook both our hands, then we all sat down together, beaming and laughing in the only-slightly-awkward way friends do when they're reunited after a few years.

And it had been a few years. Grant had left the Academy at the beginning of his final semester, and while Karen and I had been hurtling up the ranks aboard *Alberta*, he'd been completely absent from our lives. Then we'd gotten a note from him asking to meet up the next time we were at Earth, and sure enough, we were following through.

It was good to see an old friend — even if he happened to be a friend who'd lost faith in the Empire as a political institution.

But that's too much exposition; as we sat and ordered our coffees (or in my case, orange juice) from the server, Grant sized us up.

"Karen, I do think you're glowing. Why exactly are you late again?" my British friend asked a bit cheekily, and even though Karen was never as warm towards Grant as I was, she chuckled.

"No telling," was her answer. "But you're looking well. What are you up to these days?

Getting into politics?"

It was a natural assumption — Grant had the brain for government, the ability to see all angles and plan in ways that would make most of Capital Island's operators go pale. I remember the look on his face as she asked the question, the way he seemed to keep any specific reaction to her words from playing out through his expression. At the time I didn't think much of that control, but now I know why he was being so cautious with us.

"Actually," my friend replied, "I've just put the funds together to commission my own private ship. I'm probably going out to the Belt soon. Private security for some independent asteroids who can't afford your fine protection."

Not the answer either Karen or I were expecting — because we hadn't seen Grant in years.

"What?" I didn't even manage to gracefully hide my surprise. "You been washing dishes all this time to save up for a warship?"

Grant smiled at me a little more freely, but shook his head, "Just have a wealthy benefactor who's tired of seeing the pirates get away with so much."

At the time I didn't think he meant that as a shot at the Belt Squadron, but Karen began to bristle slightly, "We'll stop them."

His eyes shifted back to her, and he calculated exactly how to respond before opening his mouth again: "And now you'll have some extra help. My ship will be called *Rapier*, and we'll be out there before the end of the year."

Of course he would. Karen didn't quite know how to respond to that boast — she wasn't keen on having Grant back underfoot again. My response reflected less prudent concern... all I heard was that my old friend was coming back into the fold, and he was doing so aboard a ship of his own, which would let him go places we couldn't.

"That's brilliant!" I didn't hide my enthusiasm any more than I'd concealed my earlier surprise. "You'll look us up when you get out there? Don't know exactly where we'll be posted, but I'm sure it'll be easier for us to catch up if we're all somewhere in the Belt."

Grant was getting what he wanted from me — blind excitement — so he turned his gaze away from Karen again, then continued with a nod, "Certainly. And if there's anything I can help you guys with... I won't have the firepower of one of your posh corvettes, but I'll still be able to throw a punch."

Karen distinctly remembers biting off a retort at that remark — something none-too-clever like 'I hope you've gotten better throwing those'. I simply grinned stupidly and then sat back as my orange juice was delivered.

"Well," I said after a swig of the drink, "we'll definitely talk to Greg when we get back... let him know we have a deniable asset nearby."

With another smile, Grant sipped his own coffee. Karen watched him as he did this, waiting for him to erupt into some sort of argument — to tell us, at the very least, that he wasn't going to be a tool of the Empire, just a helper to his friends if they needed it. After all, the entire reason he left the Academy, despite having a real shot at graduating at the top of our class, was because he started to believe the Black Sun as fundamentally wrong.

Had he experienced a complete change of heart since last we'd seen him?

"So you've come round to the Empire's point of view, I see," Karen decided to prod him, and she did it with less subtlety than I'd have liked.

I shot her a quick glance, trying to determine what she was about, but she and Grant were again locked into a stare. It was immediately evident that their initial friendliness was beginning to chill, even if they were both doing a respectable job of maintaining somewhat pleasant facades.

"Sometimes compromise is necessary," Grant answered, tilting his head. "I still think the basic tenets of the Articles are going to eat us away, but I don't see why the common people should suffer just because there aren't enough betters around to protect them. So that's where I'll come in to help."

It was a well-delivered explanation — not that I agreed with his premise (obviously), but he said it smoothly enough to avoid sparking an immediate clash. Still, seeing that my old friend and Karen were at each other, I decided to intervene — as an innocent young Commander, I had no interest in seeing this day spoiled by a poor reunion.

"Well, we'll see how you feel once you're looking at the situations we've been seeing. These pirates are a mob. No organization, nothing but lust and greed. The Empire is the only thing keeping them from pillaging and raping a lot of colonies."

Grant looked back to me, then shrugged, "Maybe that wouldn't be the case if more of us privately went out to make the fight against them. But you're right, the Belt Squadron is doing genuinely good work. No one can argue with that. And I'll be proud to help."

I was in too much of a happy haze to detect the artificiality of those words. I think that must have surprised Grant — he was probably worried that, of all people, I'd realize what he was planning, see that he was trying to get my endorsement for some purpose other than the protection of innocents.

Because he knew then what we know now: that *Rapier* was just going to be the first ship of many, and that when he got out to the asteroid belt and started catching pirates, he wasn't doing so to prevent raids… but to build an army.

Years on Earth, studying our then-poor defense infrastructure had convinced him that with just a few years of recruiting, he could build a force strong enough to blow Terra Nova off of Capital Island, and force the Empire to reshape itself into a new state altogether. This was not his best plan, but the fact that his Syndicate was ultimately able to attack Earth is proof of how dangerous he really was.

Our friend… my friend, the traitor. A future enemy of the Empire, and yet I'd promised to put in a good word for him with Greg Noyce. This was how it began, with a late coffee on September 10, 2222, the day so many things about our lives changed.

Thirteen years later, we would all have the chance to talk again, on the long trip home from Etat Valcour.

That trip would change our lives too.

CHAPTER TWO
HOMEWARD BOUND

We left the Solar Asteroid Union behind after Etat Valcour. Whatever other crimes the SAU might or might not have committed against the Empire, we obviously didn't care — we had Grant, and we'd destroyed his organization. I won't spend too much time dwelling on how we departed, but suffice to say our squadron withdrew in good order for a cruise in contested space.

No SAUN ships would get the drop on us as we left… not that getting the drop on us would have done them much good, as green group had discovered.

From the bridge of *Wolf*, Andrea was more or less commanding the squadron as we boosted towards Earth, following a course that would take us home in eleven days. Since Wes was still getting back onto his feet, she was senior because she was my Flag Captain… and for all the troubles she'd had throughout this war, she somehow was now at peace with the notion of going home, and fighting no more.

Good progress, I should think, and looking back she agrees.

As our ships formed a double-column for cruising, and our Starlight patrols flew out in a sphere around us to extend our detection range, our sensors did pick up one unknown hull far astern, seemingly following us. It made no attempt to close the distance with our ships, just shadowed us carefully. We figured that it had to be a SAUN scout, sent to make sure we were truly going home, or to provide advance warning if we turned against more of their domes.

Perhaps it's a testament to how satisfied we were with Grant's capture that we didn't bother this follower. If the SAUN wanted to watch us leave, that was fine.

No, most of our focus was inward. There was an undeniable sense of pride about what we'd accomplished — Grant had been our nemesis for so long, and here in the SAU he'd been stronger than ever before. We'd broken his defenses, shattered his plans, and done it all without losing a single member of the Belt Squadron family. Whatever tragedy we had caused to accomplish the feat, we were still proud of ourselves for taking him in.

But the question on many minds, not least mine, was whether my old friend would make it back to Earth. He didn't have to — the duty of an Imperial citizen is to *do harm* to a named enemy of the Empire. That's the law. If we took Grant all the way home, there would undoubtedly be a very public trial, not just for the attack on Daragh's ball, but for his previous crimes with the Syndicate. It'd probably take months, after which he'd hang.

If he didn't make it to Earth alive, well, we'd save the taxpayers some money… but possibly also deny the citizens of the Empire some catharsis.

Either way, Grant was to die, and soon… unless some of his friends in the Empire or beyond took steps to rescue him. It seemed impossible — anyone who in any way contributed to his escape would have been automatically named enemies of the Empire as well, no matter who they were or how much power they wielded — but one could never be too careful.

Still, no point building false suspense: the question was when he would be killed, and how. And in the end, that was up to me and Karen. Wes would do his best to play a part, and Lord Peters of Hawke would as well, but ultimately it came down to us two fine pillars of morality and humanity.

How badly had Grant hurt us, and what would we do to him in return?

It was a question that really began to preoccupy us on the first day of our cruise away from Etat Valcour.

"My library has been burned down."

Karen had woken up after a very long sleep, still looking a bit worse for wear after her brutal brawl with Grant, and she repeated that analogy — the one he'd offered me — as she stared up at the ceiling and kneaded her left palm with her right thumb.

"At least one wing of it. Not the whole thing," I tweaked the analogy with a half-shrug, and she barely nodded.

"Right. Just one wing."

I was sitting in the chair beside the bed, and when she fell silent again I found myself staring at her hands; she was still under the covers, but her hands were resting on top of the comforter as she fiddled with them.

She was kneading her left palm over and over...

"What do we do with him?" she asked, and her brow was creasing deeply as she voiced the question. "Is it too direct if I say I want to kill him? I would have done it in that flight bay if I'd known..."

I shrugged, "Don't see how it's too direct to *say*. Whether it's the way to achieve our ends, I don't know. We have other levers to work."

Karen was drawing a heavy breath when I offered that last observation, and she finally unlocked her eyes from the ceiling and turned them towards me in question... before realizing what I meant.

"The spy... Haley?"

I nodded, "Haley."

I didn't need to say any more for Karen, but just to clarify, Grant believed his lover was dead. She was, in fact, alive and one of DCI's best, and she'd gotten inside his guard so completely that he'd been denied escape.

Revealing the truth of his defeat would probably be devastating — he'd have to suffer through the knowledge that DCI had tricked him the same way twice, and that the woman he had been so determined to save was in fact more in love with Rufus Chang (after one day) than she'd ever been with him.

Knowing Grant, I expected that'd be hell for him, and Karen thought the same. Turning her eyes back to the ceiling, she nodded again, "Alright. I can go for that... but after we torture him for a while, the same question applies. Should we put him down ourselves, before we get home?"

That question did remain. Torture and kill my old friend, or let someone else do it?

I didn't know.

"I can't say, yet. Maybe we take it a step at a time, then decide."

It was all we could do, so Karen nodded, "One step at a time... and the longer we draw it out, the less I have to think about what I can't remember."

That was a slight left turn for the conversation, but I went with it.

"Fair enough. But in terms of things you can't remember… do you know why you're picking at your left palm there?"

Karen didn't immediately pay attention to my question, but then she looked down and realized she'd been thoughtlessly manipulating her left hand with her right. Perhaps that was a good sign, so she turned her eyes back to me with the question.

"A habit I used to have?"

I shrugged, "Maybe. You got a Pion spike through that hand a while ago. Before you put the same spike through a Pion's ears. It aching?"

Karen blinked, then looked down at the very faint scar she could see on her left hand, "I don't remember that."

"Is it aching or itching?"

She shook her head, "Not… not that I'm conscious of."

There was nothing more for her to say on the subject, but she did get a brief flash of hope, as did I. Maybe she couldn't remember why she had the scar, or what it meant to her after that day, but did her attention to it now represent a ghost of a memory? Something from a place deeper than her mind? Or just a subconscious need to massage a once-traumatized part of her anatomy?

We didn't know, and maybe it didn't matter… but little things like that were good to see. Karen was still Karen…

The question was how long Grant would still be anything.

CHAPTER THREE

SPECTACLE

We were not kind to my friend Grant; he was the talk of the squadron, and though it might have been cruel, we decided to let anyone aboard *Wolf* who wanted to observe him — the caged predator who'd once menaced our Empire — go ahead and visit.

As I described at the end of the last book, making a visit wasn't a matter of going to his cell and stepping inside — Grant was far too dangerous for that. Even his food was provided to him through a 'milk box'... basically a tiny airlock in the wall, where we put the meal in from one side, locked that side down, and then he opened an access port from the other to get it.

Grant wasn't a spy or a Brancher, but he was too smart to be careless with.

And so, the visitors who came and watched him wait for his fate were required to do so from the observation chamber next to his cell — the same place Charlie and I had been when we spoke to him at the end of last book.

It was like visiting a zoo.

All of these visits, and the conversations that accompanied them, were of course recorded by our surveillance feeds. There was no question of letting him say a word without it being recorded — everything that came out of his mouth would be analyzed, and re-analyzed, and re-re-analyzed by DCI when we got home.

The side effect of this recording is that we have records of some of the clearest and the most provocative discussions about his views of our Empire, and his motives for trying to destroy everything we've built here. And instead of trying to explain those in my own words, which would take effort, I'll just repeat certain conversations for your benefit.

The genius of a madman...

"You're... Jim Hannigan, correct?"

Grant knew all of *Wolf's* senior officers. He'd been studying our very best for years, even though he didn't really believe being good meant we could break his plans. Because of this study, Jim was immediately recognized when he stepped into the observation chamber beside Grant's cell. He was honestly surprised that the enemy of the Empire recalled his name... but no matter.

"I am," he replied, and then came to a stop in front of the glass. Grant rose from his cot to stand facing view port, and the two men stared for a moment, undeniably sizing each other up.

Jim had many reasons to want to see Grant. Of course *Wolf's* XO had been with us right back to the *Friendly* days, when Grant and *Rapier* had supposedly been helping in the war against the pirates. But since then, you might remember that his fiancée had nearly been killed aboard *Idaho* in *The Dark Cruise*... and a few of her closest friends had died as a result of that trap.

A trap set by the Connaughts, Grant's assassins who'd met with unfortunate ends at

Etat Concord. Kyle Stranks and a host of other Belt Squadron men and women had died on that cruise, the last time Grant had really hurt all of us until his assault on Daragh's ball...

But Jim's interest came back to Bunny.

She was with *Wolf* on this cruise — I haven't spoken of her much because, thanks to Jim's advice, she'd kept the camera off me the whole time. That's why there's so little record of my state of mind for 2235.

But now that she knew the monster was in our brig, Bunny was sick with anger. She is not a rageful person, you understand... but knowing who Grant was, and all he'd done, she was as close to wanting to kill someone as she'd ever been in her life.

Seeing that fire in his fiancée, Jim simply *had* to see Grant Merger, not with some particular agenda, but just so that he could try to make sense of the monster, once and for all.

"Is this the first round of interrogation?" Grant put the question to Jim after a moment of silence. "I'm waiting for someone to come here and demand answers."

The villain was not saying that smugly — it would have been out of character for him to verbally state how important he thought he was. Instead his remark was one of simple confusion: why was no one demanding to know every secret of every plan, past or present? Surely our first priority would be to make sure he didn't have more assets still in place... didn't have the ability to escape, or otherwise cause trouble in the months ahead.

But that wasn't Jim's purpose, so he folded his arms and shook his head, "Sorry, not my job. Just came to see you."

Grant tilted his head at the words, then took another step closer to the glass, his eyes narrowing as he went back into his mind and reviewed all that he knew about Jim Hannigan. It was a lot more than Jim expected.

"You... you're engaged to that media person. The one who nearly died on *Idaho*."

Of course Grant's intel on us was better than ours was on him — for one, we weren't in hiding the way he'd been. Still, those details very much caught Jim off guard, and he shifted his weight from one foot to the other.

"I don't enjoy those things, I have to admit," Grant spoke thoughtfully, which sounded particularly obnoxious under the circumstances. "I won't try to justify those actions, or pretend to feel remorse... but I don't *enjoy* them either, Commander."

I think the best word to describe Grant's tone was 'detached' — it sounded as though he was assessing strategies as they'd been played out on a chess board. Perhaps unsurprisingly, that mood wasn't on the level Jim wanted, considering he was talking about the near-death of a woman he happened to love. Just saying.

"You're so civil about it," *Wolf*'s XO held his building anger in check, then started trying to deconstruct his opponent. "I'm not sure what your angle is, but..."

"No angle," Grant interrupted immediately. "I won't deny what we did on *Idaho*. It was a war crime, and it was cruel to everyone involved. But it was necessary, and we did it. I will say that I'm glad that the one media person who survived from Jocko Kent's team has found a good fiancé, and realized how important it is to stay with him. That does me good to know. It almost makes that whole mess worthwhile."

None of that was said with the slightest hint of hubris, or smugness, just detachment, and at the end, even a hint of pride. As if everything he'd described was inevitable — facts that were impossible to change — and that somehow he deserved credit for the positive outcome. Implying that Jim needed to be grateful for the phosgene attack on *Idaho*, because without that traumatizing experience, he'd never have won Bunny's permanent affection.

All of those things were hidden in a handful of calmly and earnestly-delivered words.

Wolf's XO wasn't used to sparring with Grant, so it took him a few seconds to fully process why the villain's words made him as angry as they did. Stepping forward, Bunny's fiancé slammed his open hand against the glass of the viewing port, then let slip more fury than I've since seen from him: "You try to toy with me, Grant? You know I don't want any happiness for you, so you try to say my happiness makes you happy, and thus destroy it for me?"

Grant looked genuinely confused at Jim's seething explosion, and he began to shake his head, "No, I just... but..."

The confusion seemed so honest on the villain's face that Jim tapered off for a moment. He realized then Grant might just be baiting him for another attack, so he shook his head and stepped back, "I don't know if you're divorced from your humanity, or you're just manipulating me... but in either case I will be glad the day I hear you've died. So many of us will be glad on that day, and I hope you realize when you swing that we've beaten you."

That was all he had to say, and before Grant could reply, Jim left the observation chamber. Grant retained his confused expression for a moment after that departure... then smiled. He was a captive, but at the very least he could have fun playing with his captors' emotions.

Jim was seething the whole way back to his cabin, and when he got there it took Bunny a couple of hours to really calm him down and get him talking about the brief exchange with Grant. He'll be the first to tell you that he hadn't been ready when he went in to see our hated enemy. I've said it many times already: Grant's genius was more than most people were prepared for. You had to think things through when you were sparring with him verbally. You had to be ready for the ways in which he could bend reality — yours and his — to get under your skin. He never failed to find an implication that would mash your buttons, to drag you into a line of thought you didn't want to pursue.

It's difficult to really articulate what that looked like, or what it felt like... but it was a great challenge that Jim hadn't prepared for.

He would not be the only one of our officers to go speak to my old friend in those first few days of our cruise, and soon we'll see more.

For now, other friends of mine were concerning themselves with the situation.

Chapter Four

Allies

"You're not ready to be released."

Alicia Morgan was doing her level best to keep Commodore Wes Pellew from damaging himself, but my friend was hardly going to convalesce the whole way home, especially not aboard a ship with Grant Merger in its brig.

It wasn't so much that Wes cared about Grant; as you'd expect his focus was on what Karen and I were going to do about our old friend and enemy. Because although it was perfectly legal — indeed, perhaps expected — for us to do harm to the enemy of the Empire, Wes feared the high price Grant would exact from our humanity if we finally decided to do the damage we wanted to.

So when he put his boots on the floor and gingerly pulled a borrowed set of ship fatigues over his burned body, Wes was determined to hobble into position to stop us overreacting.

"I'll be fine," was his answer to *Wolf's* doctor, and when she came towards him to reinforce her point, he raised his hand. "I'm not going to shoot anyone, Alicia. I just can't be lying here and not able to... have discussions."

He was a Commodore, and he was lucid. It was theoretically possible for Alicia Morgan to confine him to her medical bay until she saw fit to release him... but it would be tough. Fortunately, he had a chaperone handy...

"I'll make sure there's no shooting."

Lord Charlie Peters was standing just inside the med bay door, arms folded as he waited for Wes to get ready to depart.

These two were perhaps the only people in the squadron who did not want Grant Merger to die before we reached Earth, because they understood the cost of killing from rage. Wes had an intimate knowledge of that particular vice, and Charlie's wisdom — his profound morality — simply transcended the scope of my limited conscience.

Together, they had to talk sense into Karen and me, and if that didn't work, they had to step in the way of whatever we intended to do.

This time, though, it would have to be Charlie fighting any duels.

Alicia finally gave up trying to convince Wes to stay, and after giving him a few terse instructions about what to do if he felt certain sorts of pain from his partially-healed burns, she let Charlie lead him out of med bay.

"So, Grant's not dead yet?" was the first question the Commodore of the Independent Squadron asked as they stepped out into the corridor.

Charlie shook his head, "Under heavy guard, including Special Branch... but you know if Ken and Karen decide he's not getting home..."

Wes nodded — he did know. No officers or spacers on *Wolf* would dream of refusing an order from their trusted heroes, even if the order was going to lead to the death of the villain. Hell, maybe 'especially' if the order was going to lead to the death of the villain.

"We have to get to them… we have to talk to them both and try to see where they're at," Wes had been reflecting greatly on the challenge as he'd been stuck in the med bay, and now he articulated his thoughts with a frown.

"And we'll need to speak with Grant," Charlie added, drawing a look of some surprise from the Commodore as they walked slowly along.

"Why?"

Charlie shook his head slightly, "We need to know if he wants to die here, or to make it back to Earth. If he wants to die out here, he's going to try to make them kill him… but it also gives us something to use to convince them."

It only took Wes a few seconds to catch on, "If Grant wants to die out here, they may bring him back home alive, just to spite him. So he can be tortured and humiliated in public?"

That was more or less Charlie's thought, though as it was repeated back to him it sounded somehow less positive than it had seemed in his head. Was it better for us to let Grant live so he could be tortured later… or to put him out of his misery now?

"Complicated mess," Wes added after his observation, knowing that Charlie was similarly displeased with the situation. "We just have to make sure… well, Grant wins if he turns them, doesn't he?"

Charlie didn't respond to that question for a moment; instead the pair arrived at a lift that would take them up to guest quarters and waited for it to arrive. My friend the Hawke Lord thought about the implications of our possible actions once again, then slowly shook his head.

"I don't know what circumstances let Grant win. I don't think we can afford to care if he's feeling satisfied with himself when all is said and done. What's most important is that Karen and Ken are something like themselves when we get to the end."

"Ah yes," Wes nodded. "Grant cannot set the agenda."

"Which is tough," Charlie confirmed. "Because he's a master at control."

They were right; everything so far had been done to Grant Merger's tune, even if we'd wrecked the beat a little. Now my two friends had to try to stop him setting the tempo, and that would not be easy.

When Rufus got our message asking him to join us in *Wolf's* briefing room, he wasn't sure what to expect. After leaving Etat Valcour, and having to spend far too much effort avoiding Haley Briand, *Wolf's* Special Branch Major had begun busying himself with an after-action assessment of the *Hester* landing. Since it had been such a success, he figured (correctly) that Defense Command was going to start considering the construction of purpose-built assault dock ships… and he wanted to make sure all his freshest thoughts were recorded on the matter.

That prudent use of time would also take him away from any issues to do with Grant Merger, a subject he certainly didn't mind ignoring. He'd helped capture the Governor of Etat Valcour; if there was to be a fight about the man's fate, he'd rather leave it to others.

No such luck, unfortunately for him.

I wouldn't say that Karen and I sought to involve Rufus on our side specifically to counter-balance Charlie's presence… but we were certainly conscious of the fact that having one Brancher with us was helpful. Not that we expected a clash of any dramatic sort… we were just being… forward-thinking…

Anyway, given all of this context it won't surprise you that Rufus wasn't exactly radiating enthusiasm when he reached the briefing room, and found Karen and I sitting there. The situation wasn't helped when Haley Briand turned her chair towards the door, smiled brightly and waved at him.

"Hello… Rufus," she greeted him mischievously, and the glare she got back was really quite romantic. No wait, sorry, the opposite of that. Neither Karen nor I at this point had an notion of the spy's intentions, so we just assumed she was needling a Brancher for kicks, as DCI people are sometimes inclined to do.

Rufus responded to that greeting by looking to the head of the table, where I was sitting, and to the chair beside me, where Karen was leaning back and playing with the end of her ponytail. His greeting was as follows: "What?"

Yeah, he was impressed.

"We need your help," I waved for him to take a seat and he grudgingly moved towards one… though the one he selected was as far away from Haley as possible.

"With?" his mismatched eyes locked on Karen and me with that question, and as he settled into his chair I nodded in Haley's direction. He decided not to look back to confirm that I was referring to the spy, he simply scowled.

"She doesn't need someone to show her how to use the shower. I'm not a chaperone."

Karen looked up from the end of her ponytail when she heard that, "What?"

My eyebrow went up as well: "I… agree?"

For some reason, Rufus had assumed that our reason for calling him to a meeting with Haley was to discuss her advances. He will tell you (now) that such a reason really wouldn't have made a lot of sense — why in the world would we care about a spy's interests? — but nevertheless, it was preoccupying him when he sat down, and he made a quick assumption that was unusually off base.

And let's face it, a bit funny too.

Fortunately, Karen and I were far too respectful of Rufus' character and abilities to take advantage of any opportunity for humor at his expense.

Unfortunately, we weren't the only ones in the room: "I can't get him to take a shower with me at all. I'll get him in time, but I really wish he'd come around more easily. I've been stuck with Grant for *years*, he should show me some sympathy."

Haley was definitely enjoying her liberty from the buttoned-up and somber role of Sonia Hart, so she made that declaration with a bit of glee. Karen and I immediately looked from Rufus to the DCI superagent, and read her intentions on her expression. My sympathies were instantly with Rufus, because I knew even our powerful Major was helpless in this situation.

It's tragic, really.

However, something neither Karen nor myself were particularly interested in commenting on. My eyes shifted back to Rufus, "That last part she said is more what we're supposed to be talking about. Grant thinks she's dead, and he cares a lot about her, so we want to reacquaint them."

"In as painful a way as possible," Karen added quietly, her attention returning to her ponytail.

Rufus blinked as he heard our purpose, then he quickly surveyed Karen's expression and my own, trying to determine what we'd consider most painful for Grant. Pretending to torture Sonia Hart to death while the villain was forced to watch immediately came to his mind as the worst possible thing… but before he could consider whether he'd be able to take part in such a fiction, Haley pitched in.

"Grant's a romantic. He really was trying to save me at the end, so I'm pretty sure that means he loves Sonia more than he's ever loved anyone else. The most devastating thing we can do is reveal to him that I'm a lie. But in order to make that most effective, we figure we should build up the moment with a couple of elements, and you're the main piece. He'll recognize you as the one who killed me, and that'll revive for him all the emotions of our wonderful years together. When he's at his highest, I can step in, and you can tell him who I really am."

It was all Haley's idea, but it's pretty much the same thing I'd have suggested had she not gotten there first. I don't know what you'd conclude about our superspy based on her seeming hunger to tear Grant's heart into pieces small enough to be fed to ducks… but she was without sympathy.

Part of that… a lot of it, I imagine… undoubtedly came from the fact that despite this whole awkward Rufus situation, she'd spent long hours in the med bay since her return, keeping Margot Messina (Julie Pichot) company, and assuring the younger spy that she'd be restored once they got home… and that her efforts had paid off.

I've never asked directly, but I have to assume that if Haley had felt any warmth for Grant after their time together, the knowledge of what he'd ordered Renault to do would have erased it.

So she was ready to cut his throat, destroy his heart, whatever.

And reflecting on the very same war crime, Rufus was willing to go along, "I can do that."

It wasn't a glowing endorsement, and he didn't appear particularly excited, but when he said he'd do something you could rely on him. Looking to Karen, I nodded and then took a breath.

"Good. I'm not going to be there, and neither is Karen. It'll be better if he doesn't think we had anything to do with this. I mean, we didn't… but if he thinks we put Haley in place, it might make him feel less of an idiot. We want him to realize it wasn't his old friends who played him… that anyone could do it. So feel free to reinforce the fact that he's not as smart as he thinks he is."

That didn't make a whole lot of sense to Rufus right then, and perhaps it doesn't actually make sense at all. But as much as Karen in particular would have enjoyed watching the look on Grant's face, we wanted him to know that it had been Haley alone — not with any advice from us — who had infiltrated his closest circle. He'd never be able to console himself with the fact that he was manipulated by old friends.

No, he was a fool, and that's why he failed. We needed him to know that, and stew on it for a while, before we could figure out what else to do to him on this trip.

With a breath, then, Rufus looked from us to Haley, and she met him with a wave and a smile, "Hey there, Brancher. Going my way?"

"I will go a different way, and meet you there," was Rufus' answer, because he hates spies.

It was good enough for Haley, so she smiled and rose from her chair, "As long as we get there at the same time... Admiral, Commodore."

With nods to each of us, and another smile at Rufus, she turned and left the briefing room. Rufus watched the door shut behind her, then shook his head and glared at the table. Even though he wasn't looking at us, he knew the second I opened my mouth to quip something — his hand shot up and he said, "No. Say nothing. I will deal with her."

Then he got to his feet and left the briefing room as well.

Sitting back and watching the hatch shut behind our Chinese Major, I shook my head and found myself smiling very slightly, "I fear our intrepid Major Chang is doomed."

Karen finally dropped her ponytail and shrugged slightly, "The way he seems to hate spies, you have to figure they'll have more sexual chemistry than a fertility lab."

Oof, sorry Rufus.

Chapter Five
Friends

Neither Wes nor Charlie knew Grant the way I did, but they were both well aware of his reputation, and the general danger he presented. That being the case, they did nothing to underestimate him when they sought intelligence about his desires, and their first tactical decision was to approach him separately. If he outmaneuvered one of them, hopefully the other would have a chance to get the information they needed without him realizing they were working to the same plan.

Wes was the first to go to Grant on this mission. I don't know why, and neither does he... he just offered to try first, and Charlie thought that sounded fine. So while Haley and Rufus were working through their plans to torture Grant with the revelation about Sonia Hart, Wes was hobbling into the brig, nodding to the officers and SF on duty there, and waiting his turn to go into the observation lounge.

In that lounge were a couple of spacers from the engineering section, whose agenda was far less sophisticated than Wes' — they were just taking the chance to stare at the caged villain, and to prod him with the occasional barb about his situation.

"I thought he'd be taller," one said to the other.

"I thought he'd be smarter," came the reply.

It wasn't the sort of dry and razor-sharp repartee that Grant appreciated, and if anything, that made it worse on my old friend. He was better equipped to handle challenges he deemed clever; he hated to simply be mocked. But he was prideful, and disciplined, and knew better than to let the words get to him. Wearing him down would take time... he hoped more time than we had on the cruise.

He didn't want to give anyone the satisfaction of seeing him truly frustrated.

So this would be interesting.

Wes let the engine techs finish, and as they both left feeling a little bit satisfied, he nodded to them before turning to the hatch and stepping in. Closing the door behind him, the Independent Squadron Commodore took his steps carefully as he crossed the small compartment to the viewing window (which was perpetually left open to give Grant no privacy) and laid eyes on the villain for the first time.

That's a good point, actually; Wes had never met Grant. Most of the officers of the Belt Squadron had never even seen him, because as much as he occupied our days in the pre-war times, he was never within reach. One more reason he was a popular attraction aboard *Wolf* during this cruise.

Grant was sitting on his cot, elbows on his knees, his stare directed at the floor as he waited for his next tormentor. He had no way to know his next opponent would be of any interest, so he remained in that position until words came through the speakers in his atmosphere-tight armored box.

"I've never seen you before."

Wes opened with those words, and as he spoke he reached out and planted his hands on the frame of the viewing port, using the extra points of contact to help him stay upright a little more easily.

Grant frowned and slowly looked up at the greeting, realizing that perhaps he had a proper distraction. At last.

"You sound as though you should have," came the Briton's reply.

Wes shrugged as much as he could with his hands braced, then watched as Grant got to his feet and approached the glass with narrowing eyes. He thought he recognized Wes as soon as he saw his face, though because the Commodore of the Independent Squadron was wearing a borrowed set of ship fatigues, with no flag rank bars on them, it took him a moment to confirm his first impression.

"It's... Commodore Pellew?"

"That's me," Wes concurred, and he was purposely trying to remain cordial as he spoke. He figured Grant would be most adept at getting under his skin, so he had to keep control, and not end up looking for a wrench. Or worse.

"You're on *Wolf*..." Grant stopped his advance towards the glass, beginning to nod. "I was thinking this whole operation seemed a bit neater than Ken. I was expecting more flailing around... and I didn't figure on him getting through Concord as efficiently as he did. But if you're aboard ship keeping an eye on him, that explains a lot."

Of course Grant didn't know about the help we'd received from Bort McWebsbert in getting to Etat Concord, and finding what we needed in the domes there. Wes was fully aware of the importance of that assistance, but he was hardly going to volunteer information about it to an enemy of the Empire. Instead he shook his head, and was honest.

"Ken actually shot me. I tried to stop him destroying Etat Lexington, and he shot me."

Grant blinked at that, then very noticeably scanned what was visible of the Independent Squadron's Commodore, "Obviously he didn't kill you. But that's interesting. He got some anger out of his system and was able to lock down again? Good for him..."

Wes found Grant's analytical tone to be rather frustrating, but he knew that was probably the villain's intent. As he'd done with Jim, he was trying to purposely sound disengaged from the emotions of a situation, and given another few moments, he'd probably have tried to take some positive credit for helping me and Wes work out our issues, or something...

But even though Wes hadn't spoken to Jim, or otherwise prepared for this sparring session, he knew he couldn't let Grant keep any of the initiative.

"Now he has you. And I don't know what his plans are," Wes interjected, driving the conversation back towards the intended topic. "He could bring you home for a humiliating public trial... or he might put you out of your misery here and now. You know as well as I do that anything he does is legal."

Grant seemed both disappointed and delighted by the pushback; it was no fun not being able to immediately get under Wes' skin, but the more difficult the challenge, the more satisfying the reward. He didn't miss a beat in offering his reply: "You're trying to stop him from doing something he doesn't want to do. Karen's here... as you can see from my face, she and I discussed matters already. She's here and she's not calming him down at all. You're worried the two of them are going to be a danger to me. And while you don't care about me, you don't want them putting me to death…"

Grant's voice slowly trailed off after he put it all together — the plan Charlie and Wes had developed barely survived a few minutes in secrecy, because he was too good at reading the situation. Wes had realized that might happen, but honestly hadn't thought it would happen this fast.

"The question is why you want to talk to me about it…" Grant continued, a small smile turning up the corners of his mouth.

Wes stared back, holding his frustration down firmly as he really got a taste of how difficult an opponent Grant was. I mean, it's easy for me to tell you how smart he was, or how well he saw plans or chess boards… but there's no better example of what he did best than this.

Combine that with all his other talents… well, as I've said, a dangerous genius.

And as Wes remained silent, Grant continued processing… continued figuring out what my friend was up to, and what his motives were. It didn't take long, because Grant knew about Wes' wife Sara, and knew some of the facts about Wes' involvement on Egesta. Here was a Commodore who'd once lived in darkness, and had been pulled out of the gloom by his comrades in the Belt Squadron.

"You're trying to stop Ken from making the mistakes that you made. Or I should say, doing the things that Ken told you were mistakes. It was Belt Widows you were killing, wasn't it? In duels?"

Wes blinked. He'd known it was likely that Grant could have a whole file on him, but the information was coming out too fast. And it was impossible not to wonder *how* our enemy knew some of the details. Frustration started to turn to anger, and pushed back against Wes' self-control.

Grant didn't give him time to dwell: "You think it's wrong to take revenge… or no, maybe you don't think it's *wrong*, but you think it can be *handled incorrectly*. And that there can be consequences if you do things incorrectly. That's fair. But I think… well, Commodore, let me submit an idea to you: when you were fighting duels, and flying your plane like a possessed killer, you were putting lives at risk. Lives of people you cared about. Correct?"

I don't know if I can describe the level of anger that can rise just from having a man like Grant be able to tell you things about your own past… things that only a few officers in the Belt Squadron had any familiarity with. Wes had kept his past, and Sara, very much to himself, as I think we've seen. Now his fingers started to grip the frame of the window more tightly, but he held onto his temper.

"Here's the flaw in your logic, Wes: if Ken kills me, it makes no difference to him, or to Karen. You think he's going to wake up one night twenty years from now in a cold sweat, remembering the day he slit my throat? Has that happened to you, ever?"

Wes continued to stare at Grant, but now the villain took another step towards the glass, "You've never woken up and regretted the look on their faces when they died, have you? You've regretted your loss of self control… but when you killed those gangbangers, you didn't end up haunted, did you?"

He hadn't. Wes tells me this was the first moment when his truth had been so clearly articulated to him. Not one of the Belt Widows he'd killed had stayed to haunt him. He wonders now what that says about his humanity, but he shouldn't, because he's a good man.

The point Grant was making was that Wes' regrets had nothing to do with those killings, and everything to do with how he'd let down the people he *did* care about. He'd put the lives of his officers and crew at needless risk, to serve his anger. And dammit, Grant had put his finger on the truth. Smart and subversive, and Wes clenched his jaw against the frustration.

Wes' silence was answer enough for Grant, and he shook his head, "No. The thing you must remember… is the trigger. The crime that caused you to lash out. You remember that because the victim was someone who mattered so much to you."

No matter how many thoughts were running through his head, Wes didn't want Grant to speak of Sara, ever: "Be quiet."

Grant didn't listen, "You might have had reason to worry about Ken going too far off the rails while you were coming out here… but by all accounts, he did keep inside the lines. Maybe you kept him there, maybe the price for that was you getting shot. But now… now we're headed back to Earth. Which means whether he kills me, or Daragh Ryan kills me, it doesn't make much of a difference. You know very well that if it's him, he's not going to be haunted by it… and he's not going to be endangering anyone by doing it. So why are you still trying to stop him?"

It was such a perfectly rational question — who really cared if I killed the enemy of the Empire in *Wolf's* brig? The heads of major vid networks would be disappointed by the lack of a show trial, but really, if I wanted to do it, why should Wes or Charlie or anyone try to stop me?

Wes didn't have an immediate answer, either. Grant was at our mercy, and there would be no consequences of any kind for killing him. So why bother trying to stop me? Why even care? Killing those widows had done him no harm, not in the end, so perhaps he should just wash his hands and consider it a victory that innocents in the SAU had been spared.

The worst sorts of enemies are the ones who can make sense. And Grant really knew how to do that.

Slowly releasing a breath, Wes dipped his chin and let his head sag for a moment as his brain grappled with the possibilities. Sensing victory, Grant let his smile grow a little larger. A more satisfying challenge, a more pronounced victory…

But Wes Pellew is no slouch.

"I've always wondered… have you had any friends, Grant? Real friends, since you betrayed the Empire?"

Wes looked up as he asked that question, and as his eyes locked onto Grant's, the villain clearly realized his victory wasn't complete. The question itself sounded loaded, but eternally confident in his abilities to win any exchange, he decided to answer honestly, "No."

Wes took hold of the momentum: "You're a lover. You had a woman you loved on Valcour… and you were trying to save her?"

Grant nodded slowly, feeling a stab at the memory of Sonia Hart, "I had her. So yes, she was a friend."

"But not… not an equal?"

It was a difficult question, but again Grant was confident he could maneuver around any point Wes was trying to make, so he decided to let the Independent Squadron's Commodore commit, "Not an equal, no."

"So here's a question," Wes straightened up slightly, his glare remaining strong. "You've never had good friends, but do you accept the possibility that others may have. That other people have had relationships, friendships in particular, that function in a way you haven't experienced?"

Grant realized the point that was coming, and he undoubtedly considered trying to evade it, but answered plainly instead, "I do acknowledge that."

"I thought you would," Wes continued. "Then you probably know the point I'm making. You probably realize that just because you don't know what it means to be a friend… a real friend… that doesn't mean others suffer from the same flawed character. So you must be able to understand that the reason I care what Ken does on this cruise has nothing to do with whether it'll keep him up nights in the future, or put crews at risk… it's because friends help their friends try to be the people they've always wanted to be."

Never assume you're going to beat Wes Pellew in a fight — even a rhetorical one — because this is him. He will beat you.

Grant had to admit that Wes had made that point well — that the Independent Squadron's commanding officer was no slouch. He offered one more rebuttal: "And what if your friend changes who he wants to be?"

Wes smiled very thinly, "Some friends change together, and some refuse to make the move. Those who don't change… don't grow… they get left behind. The way you were. You think you're Ken's friend now. Well maybe you were back then, but that was in a different time. He's changed. You haven't."

It was a cold and honest counter, and Grant actually let some discomfort flash onto his expression when he heard it. His rebuttal was weaker than he would have liked: "Maybe he's changing back."

"Or maybe you're all alone in your box," Wes narrowed his eyes, and then fell silent for a few seconds before making his final play. "I'm going to try to keep you alive, Grant, because that's what my friend Ken, who saved my life a long time ago, would have wanted me to do. Maybe that means I'll be in your shoes one day… maybe he's changing into someone who I can't be friends with. But I'll still do it, because I owe it to Ken. And I do feel sorry for you, because you were left behind."

It was all Wes needed to say, and as he delivered the final words he straightened up, pulling his hands from the ledge of the window. He stared at our villain for one more moment, then turned and left the observation room.

The first tiny chink in Grant's powerful mental armor had been made by my friend Wes Pellew.

CHAPTER SIX

LOVERS

"It'd probably be worse for him if he made it back to Earth."

Karen looked up at me when I said that, and shrugged slightly. She was lying on her bed, picking unconvincingly at her food as we waited to hear how Rufus and Haley's visit went. We'd both been entirely silent for our meal, clearly lost in thoughts about what to do with Grant… what would hurt him the most, and what would satisfy us the most.

It was not a cheerful subject to be dwelling on. I mean, there were moments of enthusiasm that would probably seem appalling to you — ideas we had that excited us with their brutality, in one way or another. But the problem about obsessing with destruction is that it stays with you. You get saturated by thoughts of doing violence, and causing pain, and at least I find, and Karen finds, that it darkens everything else and is tough to switch on and off.

Enough of that darkness, and you do start questioning yourself — not too seriously, but enough. Once your anger passes, and you're left simply with a feeling of darkness, you wonder what's happening to you.

That's why it's good when there are two of you, so you can help each other keep focused.

"You don't have to make him suffer just for me," Karen said quietly. "If you want it done cleanly… I'll be fine with that."

Her tone suggested that she would be 'fine' with that, but I got the sense she was trying to say the thing she expected she would have said had she not been missing a dozen years of memories, trying to sound more at peace than she was.

"Don't worry, I'm going to see to it he suffers in all the worst ways," was my answer, and something about the way I said it must not have sounded terribly convincing.

Karen turned her eyes to me, then narrowed them, "You realize on some level he's still your friend. It's no different now than when I remember last. You get him, and he gets you. And it sounds like you're not sure you want him to suffer."

That was an observation I wasn't entirely prepared for, and I frowned, "No, it's fine. I want him to pay."

I wasn't convincing enough, and Karen shook her head. That frustrated me, and I said so: "I've come out here, all this way, to get him. To kill him now that we know he can't help you. Think I won't finish him off?"

Karen tilted her head slightly, "I think it's easy to hate him from afar. But after Rufus and Haley do this, you'll have destroyed a lot of his hope. If that's where you want to end it, that's fine."

I didn't understand why she was saying this, and she seemed to realize that I was having a tough time making sense of it. With a deep breath, she looked away, "I don't know what it's like for us now. What it was like… whatever. But if I'm starting over, I'm not sure what instincts to trust. My mind is screaming that we should skin him... but I don't know if that feels right. I can't remember what I would have done if he hadn't done this to me... but I don't know if killing him feels right."

I stared at the side of Karen's face as she spoke. There was something in her voice... a texture that was definitely not reflective of who she'd been twelve years prior. But that texture had to be an illusion — she couldn't remember the weariness she'd come to by the end of the war, but somehow it was there under her words.

What did that mean?

After I didn't answer her for a few minutes, Karen slowly turned her eyes in my direction, "Sorry, I guess that was the wrong thing to say."

I blinked, then shook my head, "There are no wrong things to say when it comes to decisions like this. Let's just see how Rufus does."

"Yeah, that'll make things so much clearer," Karen nodded, and if I need to tell you she was being somewhat sarcastic, you might want to check your sarcasm detector.

How would our old friend handle the pain we were about to inflict?

Rufus has never, and will never, strike me as a cruel human being. There's no question he can kill, but to call him cruel would be like calling a wolf cruel for hunting... it's not cruelty, it's his nature.

That in mind, the gambit our Chinese Major was about to participate in might be the most devious and indirect thing I've ever known him to do, and it had been earned by Grant's treatment of the spy Margot Messina. *That* was true cruelty, and it made this plan more than acceptable.

Despite his hatred for everything Haley Briand stood for, Rufus had thus prepared with her carefully, and had learned from her a few finer points of manipulation — things he could use to try to get under Grant's skin, in order to further torture the villain. It was not natural for him, but he'd do his best.

Stepping into the observation lounge alone, *Wolf's* Major of Special Branch focused his mind and prepared to spar. This was later on the same day that Wes had visited, but instead of being seated on his cot, Grant was leaning against the wall, arms folded and eyes shut as he digested and expelled the taunts of the last group of visitors.

So many of the spacers and junior officers who came to assail him were so crude... so beneath the level of authority they held within society. It was trying for Grant to have to hear them all, but again, he wouldn't give them the satisfaction of seeing his frustration.

Now, as he waited for his next battery, he stood still and silent. Eventually this silence led him to open his eyes, and then to frown very slightly at the Chinese man with mismatched eyes who was glaring at him through the window.

Immediately Grant recognized Rufus from two places: he'd seen him in the intel files, because he was the Major of Special Branch who replaced Charlie on *Wolf*, and he was the man who'd killed Sonia Hart.

Grant had not thought about Sonia much since waking up in *Wolf's* brig. I know that comes as a surprise to some of my editors, but having reviewed all the log recordings from the brig surveillance cameras, it's pretty clear that aside from Wes' reminder, the villain had been preoccupied by the abuse he'd suffered at the hands of his audience. He'd spent no time grieving.

It seemed to Rufus that Grant only recognized that failure to remember his lost beloved at the moment their gazes met. It was as if he awoke to the fact that, current circumstances aside, he was supposed to be human — supposed to care that Sonia was gone.

Score one for the torturers.

"I'm Major Ruifu Chang." That was a fairly innocuous introduction, though it was made more formal by the use of Rufus' proper Chinese name. Folding his arms as he stared at Grant, our elite Major then narrowed his eyes, "I expect you knew that."

Grant took a few seconds to clear his head sufficiently to respond, then slowly nodded, "I recognize you, Major. Both from your file and from our encounter."

"With Miss Sonia Hart?" Rufus made sure to say her name, and the fact that Grant's face refused to so much as twitch at the reference was telling.

He did not want to allow himself to feel, so he came off the wall he'd been leaning against and paced towards the window, controlling his breathing carefully with every step. His hands were linked behind his back — the only way he could hide the balling of his fists — and his glare was sharp.

"Have you ever loved anyone, Major Chang? Your file, if I recall correctly, suggests not. So you wouldn't know what price I have paid at your hands."

It was an uncommonly direct assault from the villain — usually he liked to let his opponents come to him.

"I may not know. But then, you may not understand the things I'm responsible for either. It was me who planned the assault on your dome. The maneuver with *Hester*, the Starlights… that was all my work. I am the reason you are in this cell. And yet, you have never paid attention to me."

Obviously you know by now that Rufus is not a boastful type, but for the sake of this moment he had to play that role. It was another move in our plan to undermine Grant's confidence in himself; what did it say if a fellow like Rufus, who'd done so much damage, had been discounted by the Governor of Etat Valcour? Grant was losing his edge — was reading files on people but missing the details that explained how and why those people would beat him.

Grant was a fool. That's the revelation Rufus was trying to set up… the impression that needed to be created.

And Grant got the feeling he was being led down the path towards self-doubt, so he resisted, "Congratulations. It's always impressive when new talent makes itself readily apparent. Promotion should come quickly."

Clearly, my old friend was trying to hold to his discipline — to not give us the joy of seeing him lash out.

"Seems to me that all of your creative tactics… your intricate plans… they are very fragile. I'm not a complex man, Mister Merger. I do not play games, I simply go where I am needed, and overcome obstacles along the way. I don't know why you've been so successful for so long. Obviously you have been. But perhaps you are too convoluted for ultimate success."

Again, dialogue clearly designed to mash Grant's buttons, and though it was obvious that Rufus was trying to manipulate the situation, the enemy of the Empire was having difficulty keeping his cool.

"Major Chang, you and I come from different professions. I can assure you, that in the realm of government, I am the better man. That I am the better strategist, and the better operator. I don't grudge you your talents, but do not grudge me mine."

Rufus' assault was working. It was perhaps a testament to his more direct approach, aided by the torment Grant had suffered from visitors for the entire day. Fatigue, verbal abuse, and now a reminder of what he'd lost... or what he'd forgotten to care about...

"Better with women, I'll admit," Rufus said that in a conciliatory fashion, and then tilted his head. "It's interesting. I've spoken to people who've been here throughout the day, and none of them seem to remember you mourning the loss of your concubine."

Grant's breathing instantly shortened and sharpened, and he took two more strides towards the glass, "Watch your step, Major."

"Or?" Rufus shot back coolly.

"You do not call her that. She was a woman who survived *your* Empire's crimes on Egesta. She was strong enough and brave enough to fight you as well. So do not speak of her as if she was a whore."

At this point you could basically see a white charger appear in the cell next to Grant; he was up on his chivalrous high horse, which on one level I can appreciate, and on another level I know was complete bullshit.

The truth — the part he didn't want to admit even to himself — was that he'd put Sonia out of his mind so very easily when he had woken up in a cell. He hadn't asked about her, hadn't wondered if her apparent death had been an apparition or a trick of his mind as he fell unconscious, hadn't even dwelled on her after Wes brought her up.

He hadn't cared. After everything — the nights and breakfasts together, the escape plan, the years of building trust — she was just another minion, barely more memorable than Fletcher Karadzic or Augustin Renault, both of whom he presumed were dead.

Not something he wanted to admit to himself, but unfortunately his opponent here was inclined to make it clear: "You don't actually care. It's obvious that your defense of her is not genuine."

Grant hated that he'd been read so easily by some Major he basically knew nothing about. It was not right that he be upstaged by a Brancher without history or credentials, and the sheer nerve of Rufus forced him to clench his fists tighter still.

"That makes this easier for me, then, doesn't it?"

If there was a voice that Grant didn't want to hear, it was Sonia's. He chose for a second to believe that he hadn't heard it — that it was an illusion — but when he saw her enter the observation chamber behind Rufus, smiling brightly and swinging her hips... wearing black ship fatigues as though she was a Brancher...

As tormented as he was, Grant was still no fool. The implications were immediately clear; there was only the very slimmest chance that Sonia had survived, been healed, and had a change of heart to the point that she'd be allowed into the brig area of *Wolf*, unbound and wearing Special Branch colors.

And as she sidled up beside Rufus, and slid her arm around the Chinese Major's waist, Grant new that slimmest chance wasn't winning in this case.

When she reached up and cupped Rufus' jaw, turned his head and then proceeded to kiss him back into the Mesozoic era, Grant knew for certain that she was indeed a concubine... a paid DCI whore who had fooled him all this time.

For his part, I should add, Rufus was not expecting this kiss. It certainly had not been part of the planning process or rehearsals... nor had Haley's hand placement, which got a little ambitious. Of course, she wasn't above taking advantage of Rufus in these circumstances — she knew as a good Brancher, he wouldn't swat her hand away because it'd destroy the illusion for Grant.

So basically she took advantage of the most deadly Special Brancher she'd ever fought. Another sign of the sheer guts this young woman had — the guts that had destroyed Grant Merger.

My friend the villain's jaw clenched hard at the display of over-the-top affection. His mind started filling in all sorts of blanks — you could read every thought on his face. Rufus had planned the assault because somehow he was in secret communication with Sonia... whoever she was... the entire time. She'd stayed close to him, always batting her eyelids so innocently, feigning fear and past torment. How had she faked the cold sweats at night? How had she been so convincing every time she fell asleep in his arms?

Had that other girl... had Julie... been a spy too? Or was she just some innocent child he'd ordered raped and mutilated because she'd been made a scapegoat by a heartless professional?

Grant's entire framework for his years as the Governor of Etat Valcour shivered as he watched Haley withdraw her mouth from Rufus'. She turned to face him, smiled again, and then shrugged, "I don't need to tell you. You know. But take heart, you never actually loved me anyway."

It occurs to me now that Haley might come off as a bitch, and that you might wonder if it's such a good thing that she'd decided to marry Rufus Chang. I'm not going to delve into the psychology of a spy here, but I'd just advise you to reconsider any notions that the people who do that work — and do it as well as Haley — are inhuman. Inhuman manipulators certainly do exist, but usually to be able to be as convincing as Haley was, some measure of honest humanity is required. That fragment of humanity is often compartmentalized away from danger and affection while on the job, but it comes out again eventually.

When it does, the price of the work done — the soul-burning feeling — comes with it, and it takes someone like Rufus (or Marshal Samuels) to help cope with that deep-seated feeling in a positive manner.

For now, though, Haley was so close to the mission that she was still very much her compartmentalized and calculating self, and she threw one last dagger at Grant with some relish.

"I don't know what's worse," she said. "That you pretended to love me because you were so desperate to believe you were capable of it... or that your desperation to lie to yourself led to us bringing you down. *Again.*"

A lance with so many points: not only was Grant being called out for false affections, which might make him feel bad as a human... he was being called out for letting petty indulgences (like the desire to be seen as loving) bring down his plan.

For him that was the coldest assault, and his face finally broke, and fell. He knew he'd been a fool, and while the betrayal by Sonia Hart... by Haley Briand... hurt him on one level, it was truly his failure to hold to his plan that brought him down. He'd had victory within his grasp. Even after everything we'd done, that escape ship and its alien technology could have spirited him to safety.

But he'd trusted one woman. He'd been so desperate to put himself atop a white charger that he'd trusted one *woman*, and thus he'd been as much victimized as he perceived me to be.

This was too much for Grant, and without saying another word he turned away. It appeared to be all he could do to stop himself shouting... screaming... and he stormed back to the wall beside his cot, put his toes against it and leaned forward so his forehead rested on the cold plating.

"I'm going to go fuck Rufus now — and collect my promotion. I'll say hi to Mel Samuels for you."

It was an undeniably crude last note, and had Rufus not been in character he would have allowed himself a look of Special Branch horror (well, when Branchers get horrified, they usually just look grumpy). As it was, he was forced to keep his arm around her as they both left the observation lounge.

Looking to the SF on duty as they exited, our Major gave an important order: "Shut him in for five hours. Need to give him time to stew before the next round of visitors."

The SF guard nodded in understanding, and delivered that disappointing news to the small line of *Wolf* crew who'd been waiting to go in to observe the caged villain. Seeing that it was Rufus and the mysterious spy who'd left, those women and men were mostly approving, though — they seemed to figure that whatever had been said would have cut Grant deeply.

Obviously, they were correct.

Rufus and Haley left the brig behind, and as they walked towards a lift that would take them to find Karen and me for a report, the spy glanced up at the Brancher, "So... fancy a fumble?"

"No," Rufus answered.

Tough luck, Haley.

CHAPTER SEVEN
PEOPLE

"He raises good points. And while you're in that conversation with him, it's tough to break out of the frame he sets up, to get around those points."

Wes and Charlie were sitting down to a very early breakfast in the Officers Club on the rec deck — the place being largely abandoned because they were eating at 0300 in the morning. Both these fellows had tried to sleep after a late meeting to discuss their options, but neither had succeeded.

Now, if you ever needed a hint as to the gravity of the situation... at the importance they attached to Grant's fate... that's surely it. These two elite warriors had seen more than enough chaos and destruction, and had presided over the lives and deaths of people far better than me and Grant. They knew how to park their distractions and get the sleep they needed.

But they were friends of mine. Honest and good friends, and like others on this trip, that meant they actually cared about what happened. Something Grant didn't truly understand.

This disrupted their sleep, and I'm obliged to them both for their concern.

Wes had just been explaining his experience with Grant — his point being that the villain was such a skilled sophist that, in the midst of that verbal duel, the Commodore of the Independent Squadron had for a moment wondered why me killing my former friend would actually be a bad thing.

Charlie listened to Wes' warning as he chewed, then nodded slowly. Unlike Wes, Charlie did have more experience with Grant, and had seen similar abilities from the man before... but still he knew he'd have to be wary. It seemed almost absurd in a way, to fear the abilities of a prisoner locked in his cell... but Charlie was not about to lose his way after all this time.

He needed to get into Grant's mind — needed to be able to come to me and say, honestly, what Grant wanted. He had to be able to tell me that, and then convince me not to give it easily... convince me to stick to the principles I'd agreed to long before, and that Karen and I had helped each other uphold.

This was not an easy task, and Charlie knew it, but he would do it anyway, because my best friend was a Special Brancher as well as a Lord of the Hawke Protectorate. There was nothing he couldn't do.

"I'll be careful," he said after downing another bite of the eggs that had come with his breakfast. "I'll go see him right after I eat... middle of the night. Maybe I'll get more out of him because he's tired. And then we can go to Ken first thing, and spend the day if we have to."

Wes agreed with that assessment — it made a great deal of sense.

"Let's hope it works," he replied.

Charlie could only nod.

Hopefully indeed.

There was no sleep for Grant Merger that night, either. I should have been more clear about this, but the visit from Rufus came on the second day out of Etat Valcour — the afternoon after Wes' visit. That second night was sleepless for the former Governor, as his mind denied him any respite.

He tossed and turned on his cold cot. Memories of all his actions had to be flooding through his mind… from the first time he'd looked across the room at Haley, and seen a beautiful bird with a broken wing for him to mend… to the moment he took her down to his escape ship.

Every moment, every single thing that had not gone to plan… all of it running around his mind that night, and his anger at his own weakness grew with it. He had been fooled a second time — first Mel Fox, as he'd known her before her marriage to Marshal, then Sonia Hart. He didn't even get to know the second spy's real name.

All because of his desperate need to be seen as a loving figure — to be depended on by a woman he adored. To have someone who, in her final minutes alive, would want to see him, and him alone.

No real woman would ever want him that way. No real woman could understand him enough to be that person. People were too crude, and superficial, and unsophisticated. They lacked the ability to govern themselves, and to recognize what was best for them… which was why they'd needed him in the first place. Why everything he'd been trying to build in the Union was so important.

A place for philosopher kings… Grant had worked so hard to try to create that existence, away from the stupid moralizing of an Empire that legislated everyone into equality, even when it was so clear that no two people were ever equal, and that so many were unfit to decide for themselves.

How had he, one of the geniuses of human history, allowed himself to be fooled by a common person… or even a clever person… in the midst of such a great project? Even had Sonia been real, common and innocent, *why* had he let her so close? He was smarter than that… but twice now, he'd proven he wasn't.

This was his weakness — one born of the isolation that came with his knowledge of the failings of common humanity. He deluded himself into love, and it destroyed him.

The fire of his self-hatred was burning hot by 0400 when his next guest entered the observation lounge. Perhaps it goes without saying that by the time Charlie arrived, Grant was beyond smiles or attempts to compliment and wrong-foot his aggressive visitors. When he saw the lights go on through the view port, and turned his head to see who had arrived, he met the sight of Charlie Peters with something close to a snarl.

"Good morning," was the Hawke Lord's greeting, and Grant came to his feet in a flash, then stormed towards the glass.

"You. I know about you, Charlie. I really do. I know you're smarter than just about everyone else on this ship. And yet you protect them. They're common people, who will never understand your quality… but you protect them."

It was not a direct attack on Charlie — even in his rage, Grant was too clever and too arrogant for that. But it was a much more explicit statement of the villain's thoughts than others were likely to hear.

Charlie stepped closer to the glass too, his expression thoughtful, "You possess a real dislike for a lot of people, Grant."

Planting his hands on the frame of the window, Grant glared at the Lord Major, "You think it undeserved? You know what I see when I look at this ship, this crew... all these fools who have come through that lounge you're standing in to mock me? A mob. I know Ken loves them all... he plays down to their level, he lionizes them and makes them believe they're special. I understand that, and I've done it too. Many times. But the difference between him and me is that he believes himself when he tells them they're the best. He lies to himself, because he wants to belong."

It was a revealing outburst, and knowing that he had Grant over a bit of a barrel, Charlie decided to draw more out of the failed Governor, "Me too, I suppose?"

Grant dipped his chin, "Yes. You're a Lord now... a ruler in Hawke. That's good. I mean it, that's good. Because you're unlike most of these people. You can think. You have the quality, and that means you should reign. That's what I was building in the Union. That's why the Union, if it can struggle on without me, will outlive the Empire. Because we're a state built by leaders with merit."

Once again, here came the crux of Grant's great problem with the Empire — the one line in the Articles of Empire that ultimately turned him against us.

"You really obsess with this idea of... difference. You don't seem to understand the fundamental truth that we're all equal," Charlie knew better than to think such a platitude could be labeled a 'fundamental truth' in anything but the most simplistic of civics classes, but he said the words because he needed Grant to burst.

And burst Grant did.

"Don't toy with me, Charlie. You and I both know there are no equals among men and women. We're all different, and some of us are better than others. Smarter and faster and stronger than others. Tell me that the average career SF guard on this ship is as good as any of the Branchers you took through the war with you. Tell me an SF guard is as fast, or as tough, or as smart."

Again, Charlie baited him, "Anyone could be, given the right training, and the right opportunities."

"But not everyone gets the same training, or the same opportunities, do they?"

Now Charlie knew to fall silent and look studied — to make Grant believe he was starting to build momentum, to climb higher on that wooden box marked 'soap'.

"I don't care that we're all genetically the same species. That's simple stuff. Of course we are. But while being born poor may not be a crime, it's definitely a handicap. Being born stupid is a handicap. And there's no point denying that truth just because we want everyone to feel better. Charlie... Charlie think about it. How did Ken stop that almost coup? He turned up on *daytime vid*. Some show about grannies committing adultery with their step-grandchildren or something. You know how the media machine is turning you and your good people into celebrities because citizens with short attention spans only care about whether Ken and Karen are fucking, not whether their actions on a campaign might win or lose a war. People, by and large, are ignorant. Maybe they wouldn't have to be if they were all better educated, but we can't educate them all. Some will always be unfit to do anything more than breed and work. And it's our job — yours and mine — to lead those people in a way that lets them have their pleasures. And lets us chart a course for civilization from which they will ultimately benefit."

There it is — there is the reason Grant Merger left the Empire. Because you're an idiot, and he's afraid of what you'll do with your vote. He's afraid of a system that gives every one of us power, no matter how many wives or husbands we have... no matter how much trash vid we watch... no matter how many sports we're blindly obsessed with. He believed that system would ultimately self-destruct.

He believed that a civilization is more than the sum of its parts — that an Empire is more important than the people who make it up. And because of that, he believed we need to have leaders atop the ladder who exemplify the best qualities of our people, and who will save our civilization from itself.

With the Union of Solar Asteroids, Grant thought he'd found that system... or, at least, he figured he'd found the raw materials to build it. Because what he couldn't admit to himself is what we all know: that money doesn't always mean intelligence, and as such, those buying their way into power in the SAU were not necessarily any brighter than those running the Empire.

Indeed, I'd argue they were vastly stupider, because they decided to leave the Empire — where they could have any opportunity they wanted, provided they accept that we mouth-breathers also get to vote — and went to a shitty upstart state with a pathetic fleet and a couple of enemies of the Empire sitting in positions of power.

If you think back, you might see similarities between Grant's point of view and Luther Gregory III's — the fear of the common people in command. The fear of stupid men and women who were all, by the Articles of Empire, treated as equals.

If you think back to that moment when Christian Mikaelsen answered the Emperor's fears in *The Pax Terra*, you'll have one eloquent response — a response indicative of the wisdom Mik has brought to the House of Commons.

Sit back now for the words of my friend Charlie Peters, who is able to kill you with anything, and yet never will.

"Who decides who's stupid?"

Grant looked up with some venom at Charlie's words, then opened his mouth to launch into another tirade.

Charlie got there first: "I know what you fear. I know that you're trying to be practical, and trying to build a society with the best possible leaders. The truth of history... the truth of humanity... is that no political system will ever guarantee the *best* people are leading it. Perhaps you can control it for a little while... force good people to the fore... but eventually privilege and nepotism will break through, or some other factors will bring you down. A civilization is not a chess board — it is not a fixed and unchanging thing. That's why you've failed at derailing ours. You fail to realize it's an organism, that it's living and can adapt. So while at one moment, by your design, your Union might look better-led than our Empire, our Empire will *always* give more opportunities to those who can excel, and lead. They will always be treated the same as the people you call stupid, and if they're real leaders, if they're truly excellent, they'll take advantage of their chance."

Grant leaned back from the glass, and Charlie leaned forward, "You can say someone is stupid, Grant. That's your right, under the Articles of Empire. You can think whatever you want. But you cannot build a system to hold people down based on one definition of stupidity, or raise others based on one definition of intelligence. And you're right, we're at risk if people who don't pay attention vote for things they don't understand… but I'll take that risk, because it comes with the opportunity for new definitions of intelligence, and progress, to take hold in years ahead. Whether I agree with them or not is my problem; the Empire is for everyone, which means everyone gets to help choose. Not everyone can be happy, but the opportunity will always exist for *anyone* to be great. And that opportunity makes our society better, because it gives everyone something to strive for. It created you, Grant — it raised you up to believe you could build your own state. What would have happened if you were born poor in the Union? Do you really think you'd have had the chance to create so much havoc, for the greater good?"

The glare from Grant nearly shattered the glass separating him from the Hawke Lord, and seeing that he'd gotten through, Charlie simply shook his head, "And even standing here, looking at you… looking at the worst aberration our Empire ever created… I still wouldn't rather be in your Union. It's true that our mandated equality created the one villain who nearly destroyed us. But it also created thousands of people able to stop that one villain. Thousands of people, from thousands of places, with thousands of dreams… all of whom *chose* to come here, and to be the best they could be. We won, Grant. We beat you. It wasn't pretty, or well-planned, but it happened. So maybe you should ask yourself whether you were right when you chose to dismiss us all as stupid."

In so many ways, Charlie Peters killed Grant Merger right then, with eloquent truth. On the camera feeds you can see Grant break — hunched down and barely holding onto Charlie with his glare. After a night of questioning himself he was being greeted in the morning with cold truth from someone wiser than me, or Karen, or himself.

And there was a last blow: "I came here because I wanted to know what your hopes were. I wanted to know if you wanted to die in this cell, or if you wanted to go home and face those stupid people. Now I'm going to do everything I can to make sure you face them. Look them in the eye. See them for who they are. And maybe for just a moment you will really doubt yourself. Then those people will hang you."

As Charlie fell silent again, Grant finally lost the ability to hold his stare. Gaze collapsing to the deck, the villain turned away from the glass and staggered back to his cot. Under other circumstances, it might have come across as melodramatic… but truly, it was evidence of a grievous wound that had been delivered by the most formidable champion in the history of our Empire.

My friend Charlie Peters, in case you hadn't somehow noticed, is a philosopher, a warrior, a Lord and a friend. And right there he delivered the coup de grace that destroyed Grant Merger.

CHAPTER EIGHT

DECISIONS

Charlie's and Wes' success gave both my friends plenty to work with. Together they figured they had a line of argumentation that would blunt even the hottest determination to kill Grant. Being able to tell Karen and me quite honestly that death after a public trial would be the worst fate Grant could imagine… that would be a compelling and hopefully convincing case. If we wanted him to suffer, then the best thing to do was *not* give him the satisfaction of being killed by people he perceived to be his equals.

But while my dear friends were collecting that same information, Karen and I were questioning one of the very fundamental points upon which their case was based: what *did* we want Grant to suffer?

This is probably a surprise… or maybe it isn't. At this point I couldn't really comment as to what you think we should have wanted. I just know that the heat of our anger was fading — that after Rufus came back to us to report how poorly Grant had taken the news about Haley, we were left silent in my cabin, distinctly avoiding eye contact with each other as we digested the news.

I'm not going to tell you everything we said to each other once we finally locked eyes. It was a long evening of discussion, and I could probably fill one of these books with a transcript, but too much of it warrants no repeating.

What was most important came shortly after 0100 hours — the very early hours of the morning — as Karen sat cross-legged on the end of my bed, eyes down as she picked at the scar in her palm.

"What would I have done? What would Commodore McMaster do?"

It was a question that I had been deliberately skirting as we discussed our options — as an angrier, younger Karen asked me about all the things Grant had done with the Syndicate, and since. About the crimes, the destruction… about everything Grant-related that she had forgotten, and which proved beyond a doubt how dangerous he was.

How cruel he was.

The more we talked about those things, the more I should have become angry. I remembered every injustice, every incident, every betrayal. I should have been fuming by the time we reached 0100, at the very thought of a friend who'd turned against us, and done so much harm.

But I wasn't. By the time Karen asked that question, I just sounded exhausted — just sounded as though weight had been piling up on my shoulders, pressing me down and keeping me from thinking. It was Karen whose anger had begun to build, not that she was overtly acknowledging it — she didn't want to come across as out of control. No, I could see the tension mounting in her shoulders as she listened, and detected the old hallmarks of forced self-control as she spoke.

Her anger built, she points out now, because the last she'd remembered, Grant had been her 'friend'. Of course, he wasn't really her friend, she just tolerated him because he was mine... but imagine. Imagine having a bad feeling you could never fully understand someone in your social circle. Imagine waking up one morning — tomorrow morning — and discovering a decade has passed, and that your suspicious friend turned out to be a serial killer.

Imagine too that you're the sort of person who's had to work really hard to get a handle on your anger... and that you're also very self-confident. You're the sort of person who makes changes happen, because you are a leader to your very core.

The question that might come to your mind, and which definitely came to Karen's, wasn't 'why did he make me forget', but 'how did I miss this until it was too late'?

Why couldn't she have stopped this a decade ago?

It was a completely useless question, and she knew it... but still, it was the fuel that burned hottest in the fires of her frustration. All she wanted to do was walk into Grant's cell and shoot him in the head, or better, take her time and really make him suffer.

She hadn't seen the crimes — the assault on Earth by the Syndicate, the countless pirate attacks, or the rape of *Idaho*. But her imagination was sturdy, and it filled in the gaps... with pictures of what happened to Margot Messina. Grant was ruthless and she wanted him to die in agony.

But as that rage built within her, she couldn't miss the fact that the opposite was happening to me.

It's not that I disagreed... not that I somehow thought what Grant had done wasn't wrong. It was. But I suppose it's like the old adage about boiling a frog: you drop a frog into a pot of boiling water, and he turns into a prince. Put him into the water and turn up the heat, and Saturn explodes.

I think that's the gist of it, anyway. Look, the point is that I'd become numb. It's not that I'd stopped caring, it's that I didn't have the energy to deal with this anymore. Taking Grant back, killing him... whatever... I just wanted it decided, so that I could get under the covers with Karen, and fall asleep with my head on her shoulder, breathing her air and feeling the reassurance of her heartbeat.

Maybe that sounds needlessly sentimental, but it's the truth.

Karen wasn't yet ready for me to be so easily mollified. The Ken she knew from her time would have wanted to answer such betrayal with slow and agonizing torture... would have wanted to make a point, if only to Grant, that he was by far the most brutal, most angry, most dangerous.

And she would have wanted the same.

So she wasn't quite ready for this decision. This complex — perhaps needlessly convoluted — choice that lay before us.

Hence her question. Hence her wanting to know what she would have done as Commodore McMaster, instead of Commander Karen.

When she asked the question, eyes down and fingers plying a scar she didn't remember getting, she drew my stare, and finally, my answer.

"Commodore McMaster would sit here and ask me what she would have done twelve years ago," I said, not really sure why it was my response, but trusting in whatever instinct formed the words.

Karen stopped her fingers against her palm for a moment, then looked sideways at me. It was either a daft deflection, or simple honesty... and from my face, she decided the latter.

"You're saying decisions about life and death never get easier?"

"They might. Decisions about killing are always complicated, though... and if you don't check them against yourself... don't wonder what you've turned into, and how you arrived at them, maybe you make poorer ones."

It must have made some sort of sense, because Karen looked down again, "You think it's possible I could have looked back at who I was... who this version of me *is*, and wondered how I turned out so bad, with such a shining start?"

"I think you might have looked back and wondered what I'm wondering," my answer was immediate, and almost as much a revelation for me as it was for her.

Karen turned her gaze back to me, and realized what I was getting at. I knew my hunger to torture and kill Grant was less than what she expected... and I didn't know if it was good or bad that I was so indecisive about his fate.

But I didn't know if that uncertainty represented progress in my humanity, a loss of my edge as a killer, or more likely a loss of my sense of bravado.

For her part, Karen didn't know either. She wanted to be calm, and in control, and always reliable... to be all the admirable things Commodore McMaster had become. But she wasn't. The question for her was who to act like: herself now, or herself then.

Which, as I read it back, is about as confusing a sentence as I've written in these books.

Fortunately, Karen decided to voice her internal divide: "So we have to choose. Either we allow my anger to dictate our actions, which is the same kind of anger you'd have had back when Grant first betrayed you... and we spend time in his cell cutting little pieces off him until he dies. Or we act the way you want to now, and I would if I hadn't forgotten who I've been... and let the people hang him."

That was it. That was the whole challenge we faced: who were we? I'd done so much to go back to the furor of my youth when I lost Karen... while she, as a younger woman, was surrounded by proof of how good she could be, and why it might be wise to strive for that again.

Talk about conflicted. And confused.

"I should try to be like... me," Karen decided aloud after a few moments of thought. "We should just let him rot. Spend our time together."

I began to nod slowly... but then I stopped. There was a deep down part of me that disagreed with that option. The thought of letting Grant get all the way to Earth... to be killed by others...

If it was a simple decision, we would have made it quickly. But we couldn't.

"I don't know," was my conclusion then. "I feel like we're framing ourselves into a choice. To be what we were twelve years ago, or to be what we were twelve months ago."

"Without figuring out who we are now," Karen picked up my direction immediately, because down a decade of memories or not, her mind was still far swifter than mine.

That was the point: who were we now?

"I think I know who can help us figure it out," I said as the question played in my mind. "But we should wait until morning."

We both agreed to that, and by 0200 we were under the covers. She got her head on my shoulder first though — still faster than me. The air was the same, and that's all I really cared about as we slept.

Much depended on the morning.

CHAPTER NINE
CLASH OF INTELLECT

Charlie had been expecting me to be asleep when he and Wes knocked on my hatch at 0600. The fact that the door opened almost immediately after the hail caught both my friends off guard, and then as they stepped inside and found the bed made, me in full uniform, and all signs pointing to me being ready for the day, they exchanged a look of some confusion.

They'd come to make their case… to present their evidence that Grant needed to be allowed to live to go to trial… but both of them got the distinct feeling all their hard work might be irrelevant.

"Decided about Grant?" Charlie didn't waste any time going right at the central issue, and Wes backed him up with some teasers.

"We were working on him yesterday… Charlie really got to him last night. He's losing his faith in himself, we think…" the Commodore of the Independent Squadron trailed off after getting that far, watching my face for any signs of reaction to his words as I stood a few yards from him. But my face remained neutral, so he gingerly produced the kernel of his recommendation, "It would be torture for him now… if we took him all the way back for trial."

Wes and Charlie fell silent after those words entered the air. Their gazes remained fixed on me, both friends doing their best to read my expression and trying to figure out my ultimate intentions… whether their words were garnering any interest.

For me, it was simply a return to the conversations of the night before. Certainly, it was good to know that two of my closest friends did care enough about this matter to intervene for Karen and me — to go to Grant and bring him down in a controlled fashion so we could step back.

But the insight they provided wasn't a great surprise to me, and it didn't change the course Karen and I had set.

"Keeping him alive could be torture. Killing him could be a different kind of torture. We don't know what we want, so we're going to ask him."

I said it all too easily, I think. They probably should have had to work for it, or at least to be patient while they finally circled the issue sufficiently to get a solid hint of our intentions. But there was no value in deceiving my friends about this. We had not decided which course to take, and so speaking to them about our options would have been senseless.

"Ask him? Ask him what he wants?" Wes sought clarification.

"Or what we want."

There was nothing else for me to say — I wasn't about to launch into a summary of the hours of discussion Karen and I had shared, or our concern that we were trapping ourselves into a bad decision-making framework. My silence endured for a few moments before Charlie and Wes exchanged a glance, and then the Hawke Lord vocalized the awkwardness of the moment.

"So, I guess there's not a lot we can do right now."

I answered by shaking my head, "Nope."

"Just so we're clear, we were going to try to convince you to keep him alive so he can stand trial," Wes put in helpfully.

"Figured that," I said. "If we decide not to follow that advice... well, I can't promise that we'll tell you in advance. But we're making a decision here based on all the clarity we can muster. I appreciate your efforts on our behalf, and I know Karen does too."

Reading that back, it sounds like a pretty callous brush-off under the circumstances, but apparently the way I said it reflected my genuine appreciation for their concern. Had I wanted to be properly disrespectful, I would have simply lied to them — told them they had nothing to worry about, or that we'd consult them before we took any action... anything that might mollify them.

But I was honest. Charlie locked eyes with me for a few seconds after I spoke, and then he took a deep breath. He realized that it was really in our court now — Karen's and mine. He and Wes hadn't made much of a case, but then they didn't need to. It was clear what side they were on, so now it was up to us to determine what to do.

And we'd take that question to Grant.

As silence retook control over the conversation, Charlie remembers distinctly hoping that between his efforts and Wes', enough had been done to shatter the villain, so that Karen and I wouldn't feel the need to put him down ourselves.

But he'd have to wait and see... because that's exactly what I was doing.

Wait and see what Karen learned from her mind-to-mind with Grant Merger.

By the time Karen arrived in the observation room off Grant's cell, my dear old friend was no longer making any effort to seem composed. Charlie had proven his reputation as the fiercest of enemies, and with no real hope ahead of him, it seemed as though the villain had stopped caring about how his visitors would perceive him.

He certainly wasn't ready for Karen — or at least, not ready in the way he would have been before the Wes-Rufus-Charlie gauntlet. In point of fact, he wasn't even facing the observation window when Karen arrived. Lying on his cot, facing the wall and almost in the fetal position, he was a pathetic sight.

And Karen wasn't having any of it.

"You just going to sulk?"

Her opening question was sharp, and she meant it to be. She's asked me since whether that sort of direct attack was in character for her Commodore-self, or whether being so aggressive was a reflection of her Commander years. I honestly don't know... think back to how Commodore McMaster was on Egesta, or Pion Rock, and I think the aggression would fit. Maybe it didn't come out as often, but it was always a part of her... a part that Grant so loathed.

He recognized her voice immediately, and the insolence in her tone, but he didn't acknowledge her in any way. It was obviously too much for him to have a woman he considered to be such a low creature gloating over him.

"You can lie there and pout all you want, but I came here for answers. One way or another I'll get them."

Karen folded her arms after that, her glare driving through the viewport and boring into Grant's back. The villain maintained his silence, wrapping himself in it as though it was a blanket. And yes, that does sound a bit too literary. Apologies.

He simply didn't want to speak — didn't want to give Karen any chance to slice at him...

"You know I never really trusted you. Not deeply. Of course we had our niceties, we had our friendship. But that was for Ken's benefit — because he was your friend, and if he saw something in you, I figured it must be there."

If you watch the surveillance feeds, you can just make out Grant's head beginning to turn at those words. She'd piqued his interest.

"What I didn't realize is that his attention was really a sick fascination. He saw that you were so much like him... like a mirror image of himself in so many ways. But whether he recognized it or not, he knew you were on a different trajectory. You're very smart, Grant, just like him. But you had a different kind of chip on your shoulder, and a lot less understanding of humanity... and he knew that could lead you to becoming what you became. He was fascinated by that. I don't know if he wanted to try to keep you on our side, or if he just wanted to watch the wreck... but he saw you as the dark reflection of himself. I didn't realize that then, but I see it now..."

She trailed off with that, and Grant rolled onto his back, eyes turned to the ceiling as her words were digested. His mouth remained shut, though, and that was encouragement enough for her to continue.

"He still doesn't really want to kill you. I'd cut your throat in a heartbeat, but he still sees too much of himself when he looks at you. There but for the grace of God, he thinks. He wonders what he'd have done if he'd been in your exact shoes. And the worst thing is, the reason he figures he's not in your shoes is *me*. He thinks I saved him. He thinks I spent all these years with him to keep him from turning into you."

It was those words that caused Grant to finally look at Karen through the glass. He wore a deep frown, and quickly he rolled to sit up, then stand. Karen was speaking about herself. He wanted to hear. He wanted to be proven right.

"What have you been doing all this time, if not *saving him?*"

Karen restrained a smile at the bitter question — and at the fact she'd gotten Grant to engage. She shot back sharply: "Well I don't remember exactly, because not so long ago your people wiped out a swathe of my memories. But I don't imagine it's changed since we first got together in the alley. I'm with him because he's the person I've always needed to keep *me* from turning into you."

Grant's frown deepened into a scowl, "Into *me?* You couldn't ever."

It wasn't clear whether he meant she wasn't smart enough to have turned into a villain like him... or that she'd never see the wisdom of his cause and decide to turn against the Empire for the supposedly noble reasons he had. It was, however, perfectly obvious that this notion represented a series of buttons Karen could mash.

"I could. I'll admit, I wouldn't have been calculating or cold like you. I read all about the Syndicate, and I'm sorry I forgot taking it down... but bravo. You did very well, for a pirate. I wouldn't have been so accomplished, but I'd have killed myself, and others. For no reason."

Shaking his head, Grant pressed a counterattack with all the spite he had left: "But he sacrificed his future on your altar, because he was infatuated with you. Does it give you comfort to know that your peace of mind, your being saved, cost the human race a leader who could truly have made a difference?"

Big and mighty challenge, that, and Karen smiled gently, "Does it occur to you, that if you hadn't been so self-absorbed and unwilling to listen, that maybe you could have been a real part of the team that *has* made a difference?"

"What you've done is not—"

Karen held up her hand, and to her surprise, Grant actually fell silent at the gesture, "We're never going to agree on who made the difference, or whether it was the right difference to make. Neither of us is ever going to win the argument. One of us is simply going to die. My question for you is when, and how, you want to go."

Grant hadn't been ready for the turn in the conversation — especially not because it had been Karen who had essentially started the previous line of discussion. Now his mouth fell open with surprise, and he actually took a step back from the glass.

He knew he was going to die — he had to. But for whatever reason, it was Karen's question that rammed it home for him, and he undoubtedly realized that his attack on her, and the time he'd stolen from her mind, was potentially going to worsen his fate.

Simply taking away memories had seemed like a good idea when he'd been certain of victory — when he'd needed to be able to honestly tell the people of the Union that he had not killed any of Defense Command's heroes, and that my incursion into their space was over someone being wounded in a random attack.

But now he was faced with the cold reality that leaving an enemy alive always puts you at risk of facing him or her again. Perhaps he'd have been better off just wiping all of Karen's memories... leaving her neutered, maybe even giving her a chance at living the remainder of her life in a condition more fitting her simplicity.

Now he was at *her* mercy?

"Just in case you're wondering, that look on your face is answer enough. You're really terrified."

Karen was purposely needling him now — his expression hadn't really changed, but lacking a mirror, he didn't know that. Upon her prompt, color started rushing to his face, and he struggled to hold onto what dignity he had left.

"You want me to suffer. You prove my point about everything you are, because you're here gloating over my death. Whatever you were before doesn't matter... though I don't think you changed in twelve years, or that you can ever change. You're an irrational killer, a bitch who always has to be right, or protected, and you're going to kill me because I make you ask questions about yourself when you look in the mirror. Whatever you do, keep that with you. Realize that you're nothing more than a scared girl in an alley, hoping someone will think she's beautiful."

And with that little soliloquy complete, he turned away and stormed back to his cot, where he lay down again facing the wall. Karen was so wrapped up in her pleasure at tormenting him that his attempts to unravel her bounced clean off — she didn't care if killing him proved his point, because a dead man couldn't tell her 'told you so'.

But as she stared at his back, she did realize that he'd confirmed one important truth for her: every decision she was making was still coming from the alley. Perhaps every decision she'd ever made started there — Commodore, Commander, or anything in between... she would always have to live with the fact that she'd nearly let me kill her, because she'd been so wrapped up in her self-pity.

That was the main thought that stuck with her... that dug itself into the surface of her mind. She took it away with her as she left Grant behind, and returned to my cabin to talk about what she was feeling.

The decision had not been made yet.

CHAPTER TEN
REAL FRIENDS

Karen and I spoke of her conversation with Grant... and of that last thought about who she was, and what had been fueling her. I didn't have an answer to her question about whether she'd moved beyond the motivations of the alley. How could I answer a question that was implicitly based on the idea that the goddess with whom my entire adult life was intertwined, was simply running from who she'd been?

I didn't know, and because talking to someone who understands you is usually a good way of helping you get your head around a problem, I decided to do exactly that.

"You know better than anyone how bad I could have gotten without her around. Why didn't you tell her that?"

Perhaps not the question Grant would have expected me to open with as I entered the observation chamber and moved over to the glass. He was still on his cot, still looking at the wall as he sulked and anticipated the end of his life.

Hearing my voice he turned around, and I could immediately read the tension on his face. Perhaps this was the first time he was feeling his own mortality — the game was over, and he'd truly lost. Charlie had made that point, but he hadn't been able to drive it home quite the way Karen had. My Hawke Lord friend had made it all too clear to the villain that his reasoning had failed, and that his principles were at odds with reality.

Karen had established unequivocally that his personal defeats were going to cost him his life. It was just a matter of how, and when.

In the midst of all those grave thoughts, it might seem somehow perverse that he was relieved to see me... but he was. The tension in his expression began to ease; a friend was visiting in his darkest hour, and he was glad of the company.

That I was the friend who was responsible for that hour somehow didn't matter.

"I don't want to argue anymore about this," was his answer as he came to his feet, and moved towards the glass. "I'm going to be killed soon. I don't care who was right about Karen."

He was, at least, being honest, and I folded my arms and slowly shook my head as I watched him approach. Quickly I realized we were past the point of sparring, or trying to tackle a question like Karen's new identity, or her old one... all the years that had passed disappeared and it was as though we were friends again. We were people who'd been as close as brothers once, and then had split far apart.

Together one last time before the end.

Wondering where it had all gone so very, very wrong.

I couldn't help but ask that question: "Why couldn't you just have stayed with us? I know what you think, I know what your *reasons* were. But you could have stayed with us. We would have been the team... we'd have sewn up the Belt so much easier, and we'd have beaten the Martians so much faster..."

Grant came to a stop as my words trailed off, and his sigh was heavy, "I couldn't believe in the cause."

"Don't give me that bullshit. You and me, we're too smart for causes. If you'd wanted to, you could have found a way to rationalize it, and stayed. You could have been the one commanding the Belt Squadron. Imagine how much you could have done to change this Empire from the inside, if you'd just stayed. If you hadn't run out on us."

My stare had locked onto Grant's, and at my words I could see all those possibilities start to play out before his eyes. What if he'd stayed and leveraged all the talent he clearly possessed to become one of the celebrity cadre of officers. If he'd been a hero of the war against Mars, and had been able to go into government with the power of public confidence behind him, ready to change the Empire into a state which better reflected his vision?

Instead of years on the run, he could have been home, eating real bacon, loving women who weren't spies. He could have had everything. He could have been whatever he wanted to be.

Or at least in that particular moment of thought, it seemed as though he could have.

"I never understood why people hated hindsight," he said quietly after his thoughts finished playing out. Then his eyes fell, and he shook his head, "I was close to making this all work. It wasn't completely the wrong decision."

I heard that attempt to save face and blurted out an answer: "Yes. It was completely wrong."

My firm reply drew his eyes up again, but without a hint of fight in them.

"Not wrong because of the people you killed, or the damage you did, or the state you tried to build... I think those were wrong, but I know you wouldn't agree, and I don't have the patience to try to bring you around to sanity. It was *wrong* because you're my friend, and now, one way or another, I have to kill you."

Those thoughts of what might have been came to a sharp halt. Grant's face drained of the little color it still had, and he started to shake his head — to protest. It was even more real when I was saying it. It was too real. His death was coming soon... the true consequences of everything he'd done.

"I don't have a choice. Don't even pretend you think I do. You forced us into this position. You made the wrong decisions when you were young, and they destroyed our friendship. This, right now... this is the wreckage," I pressed. "Not even you can argue with that."

He was still fixated on the point that he had to die, but was smart enough to try to counter, "You could have come with me. If not for Karen, you would have come with me."

I don't think Grant was trying to argue with me there — his tone was wrong. I think he was focusing on Karen to try to justify to himself one more time why he was in the cell. It was because his partner in crime had fallen for a siren, and he'd been forced to fight the good fight alone.

Listening to that pitiful contention once more, I suddenly realized I didn't need anyone to tell me who Karen was, and that I really didn't give a damn about what part the alley played in any decisions she made.

This wasn't about either her or me being perfect. It was just about our willingness to work together at being whoever we were.

And Grant's unwillingness to do the same — his refusal to be anything more than an angry boy who believed he was right, and never allowed any hint of humanity to interfere with his plans and presumptions.

I don't think he was ready for the fierceness of my reply: "Stop trying to make her the excuse. Stop trying to pretend that somehow this is all a melodrama. I didn't come with you because I didn't need to believe, so desperately, that I was better than everybody else. And that's why Karen and I have been together all this time. Not because she's holding me back, but because finding someone you fit with, and sticking with that person, is just what smart people do. Just happens that she's as good as me, or better than me, at a lot of things… so the partnership worked out pretty well."

Grant was uncharacteristically silent at those words. His mind began grappling with what I was saying — with the idea that he had cause and effect out of order in his assessment of the impact Karen had on me. She wasn't holding me back; my flaw was that I actually approved of people like her.

It was logical, but somehow he didn't want to believe it — didn't want to give up on his hope that I really was like him.

I could read that hope on his face, and with no patience for this debate, I shook my head, "What you should be asking yourself right now is why you were incapable of being open to us. To being part of the team."

Grant looked up, "No, I was willing to—"

"You weren't. It was your way or you weren't playing. Your rules or you'd go it alone. And that's exactly what you did. You could have found a place, made it work with us, but you decided that it had to be your trajectory, one you set as a boy in an Academy, and which has *defined your life*. You decided to be alone forever… and now you're going to die alone. Superior to the rest of us in no ways at all."

That, honestly, was the crux of it. To say he hadn't evolved since his bitter youth would be entirely wrong — much about the villain had truly changed — but he'd held to the one tenet that defined him: that he was better than everyone else, and that no one deserved his true loyalty as a result. It's that last part that was so devastating; being exceptional is no crime… indeed, it's a good thing… but to believe that makes you more powerful than the rest of your race is dangerous.

And now he knew it. He really, truly knew it. That was actually hard for me to see — there was no satisfaction in this 'told you so'. Because Karen was right, I did see myself in that cell. I did wonder what I would have been like if Karen hadn't appeared that night, and forced me into an alley, and helped alter the course of my life away from Grant. If it had just been him and me, where would we have gone? It probably would have turned into the most villainous buddy-cop-style story you ever heard.

Or maybe I would have found a different chance to begin to break away from him. Maybe I was just wired to be a different man, and Karen was simply the catalyst who proved that to me. I can't imagine any other catalyst would have changed my life in quite the way that she did… but at least I'd like to believe that for all our similarities, that fundamental isolation which set Grant apart from me would have ultimately caused a divide.

It didn't matter, though, because I had Karen, and Grant had nothing. He was a terrifying image of what I might have been, and now the Articles of Empire dictated that he had to die.

"What will you do? Will you do it… or will you make me stand trial?"

He didn't want to know, but he had to ask that question about his fate. I think most people with the chance to have some input on the means of their death would. And as I listened to his question, I knew I couldn't answer it.

"I don't know. Karen and I will have to hammer this out. We'll decide, and then you'll see."

In itself, that lack of clarity was a particularly cruel kind of torture. Grant's chin dipped, and his head slowly shook as he turned away. I could have tried to say something else, but what? Tormenting him any further would simply have been a case of burning the ashes.

This old friend was destroyed. Everything he had done, every assumption upon which he'd based his life, would haunt him for the rest of his days.

With that grim thought in mind, I turned away from the glass and left the observation room. Karen and I really did need to talk, because this would be a difficult decision… and because for the first time this year, I was beginning to achieve some clarity around who we were, and what we were about.

How would Grant die?

CHAPTER ELEVEN

FOCUS

Wes had been assigned guest quarters since leaving med bay, and now he sat alone in his cabin, carefully watching a blank piece of wall as he waited for some word of what was to come next. He and Charlie both knew they had no alternative but to give us time and space to reflect, both of them hoping we'd circle back with them before we made any decisions. Neither of them certain we would.

All Wes could do, then, was wait and see.

As morning drifted into afternoon, he continued to sit and watch the wall, reflecting on everything that had happened over the course of the year thus far, and wondering about what had brought him to this place — to a borrowed cabin on *Wolf*, and to regular medical check-ins due to burn wounds inflicted by a mag shot he'd taken from a friend.

He'd been so determined for so long to be the voice of good — he'd carried that with him through the war, through Egesta, through everything since the rampage he'd gone on after Sara had died. In so many ways that segment of his identity had come to define him, and as he waited and considered what Karen and I might do, he did have to ask: why was it such a concern for him?

So many other people in the squadron — good and sensible people, who he respected and would forever call his friends — seemed totally at ease with leaving Grant's fate in our hands. He wasn't so casual because he was ashamed of his own loss of control... but he'd obviously turned out alright, so perhaps his concerns were irrational?

It was a serious question for the Commodore of the Independent Squadron... one he could entertain only in silence, and only in private — where men like Grant couldn't know he was actually wondering about it.

Because he was so deep in thought, Wes really doesn't remember hearing a knock at the hatch of his guest quarters, though he did notice when the door slid open. Looking up, he expected to see Charlie with news. Instead, he saw the unexpected face and form of Andrea Kiley. *Wolf's* Captain has been largely absent from this book so far; she'd been making sure we — our ship and squadron — made a safe escape from the Union.

But as rumors spread about the division between Wes and Charlie, and me and Karen, she began to wonder about the Commodore of the Independent Squadron. She didn't know if there was going to be a fight between the heads of the Belt Squadron... if Grant's fate would be so divisive... but if there was a clash, she knew whose side she'd have to take.

And as had been the case at Etat Lexington, it wasn't going to be mine.

"Andrea?" Wes greeted *Wolf's* skipper with a note of confusion, and she stepped into the cabin without answering. As the hatch shut behind her, she leaned against it, then fixed her eyes on him again and took a breath.

"I hear there's a chance that you and Charlie, and Ken and Karen, are disagreeing over

Grant's fate?"

Wes wasn't really surprised that the rumors had gotten around — on a warship, rumors always did. The crew of *Wolf* was exceedingly intelligent, whatever Grant believed, and it'd only take a few sightings — Wes and Charlie having breakfast at 0300, plus each of them going to see Grant — for interpretations to be made, and narratives constructed for circulation.

"I presume you don't want anyone to kill him on this cruise?" Andrea asked next, unconsciously beginning to fiddle with her hands as they hung in front of her.

With a shrug, Wes shifted in his chair, "I don't really want them to kill him, but they don't know what they're going to do yet. I hope they agree with me, but if they don't... well, I don't think we can actually stop them if they're determined. I mean, it's Ken and Karen... and Grant's the bad guy. There is no living member of the human race who is more deserving of death. Maybe they'd be right to do it."

That very last part was not what Andrea expected to hear — she figured she'd be treated to one of Wes' more moralistic speeches about how we all needed to be better than the ruthless enemies we faced, Grant especially. But not at all, and that made her frown.

"You're doubting your resolve?"

Wes looked up at her, then nodded, "I killed a lot of Belt Widows, Andrea. I killed them in cold blood and I came back from it. So... maybe it'd be hypocritical of me to try to stop them putting an end to that villain on their own. Maybe there isn't a rational argument to stop them. I... hope they don't. But..."

As he trailed off, Wes cast his eyes down and shook his head. He was feeling rather conflicted, now that the thoughts he'd entertained in solitude were being voiced to someone who seemed to expect better from him.

Andrea approached Wes, and then sat on the corner of the bed so that she was obliquely angled to him in his chair. She laced her fingers together and dropped her hands into her lap, then shrugged, "Seems to me, wanting irrational things is normal. Being hypocritical can be normal too. If your gut tells you killing Grant would be wrong, then maybe it would be. You don't need to be rational all the time."

Wes looked up again, caught Andrea's eye.

With a gentle shrug, she went on: "It would have been rational to let me rot, wouldn't it? Some damage is too much to fix. But you're a humanitarian, Wes. Maybe killing the Widows turned you into one. I don't know. But whatever caused it, it's who you are now, and whether that's rational or not, you keep being that way until you don't want to be anymore. Some of us might be counting on you."

It helps to have someone who has faith in you. Andrea Kiley was on a long road back, but for the first time she was starting to see clearly where she was headed, and she wanted to make sure Wes was still there when she arrived.

He would be. He's a good fellow, and she was fortunate. They both were.

Unfortunately for Charlie, Lia Hawke wasn't within communication range of *Wolf* — he surely wouldn't have minded the chance to see her, and speak to her. He missed her a lot, and he looked forward to going home to the Hawke Protectorate and to putting this chapter of his life far behind him.

Now he just had to hope for a positive ending. He wasn't going to try to stop Karen and me the way he'd once stopped Andrea on her way to the brig... there was no point. He knew if we wanted to kill Grant, we'd find a way. He just had to hope that if we remained as conflicted as we'd appeared, we'd come to him for counsel. That would be his one real chance to help us preserve the humanity he knew Karen and I had once held very dear.

Charlie had done all he could. And as he sat alone in his own guest quarters, wondering about the different possible outcomes to this mess, Karen and I were making our decision.

"This sounds like something new. But I'm probably not the person to judge."

Karen was lying back on her bed as she spoke, picking again at the scar on the palm of her hand. I listened to her words from the very comfortable position of also lying on the bed, but using her stomach as a pillow. She calls this 'wolf rest', not for the name of our ship, but because you can always find pictures of real wolves in the wild, lying all over each other when they're tired.

Looks peaceful for them, and it certainly was for us. Having a pillow that breathes is generally enjoyable.

To her comment I made a sound of disagreement, "You're one to judge. You know if it feels right or wrong."

Karen took a deep breath when I said that (I could obviously tell), and then she nodded, "It does feel right. Which in itself is probably weird, but..."

"Let's not overanalyze this. Be too easy to convince ourselves we're wrong."

We had made a decision. It was not a decision that would please anyone, and the way we would do it certainly would not please our friends. But it was necessary.

"It feels right," Karen affirmed then, and dropped her hands so she'd stop obsessing over the scar. One of her hands landed on my face, and she started to trace her fingertips over the lines in my brow, seemingly fascinated by the fact that I was older and uglier than she remembered. "I don't feel like I'm making this decision because I'm trying to be who I was... or who I used to be. So that's good. I feel like... this is who I am. Not trying to be who I wanted to be... or who I was... but just who I am now..."

I turned my head slightly and looked up at Karen's frowning face as she tried to explain herself. Seeing my raised eyebrow, she moved her hand down and covered my eyes.

"Shut up," was her answer, and I actually smiled.

"We're making this decision without basing it on what we think we'd have done before the ball," I clarified for her, and though I couldn't see, I got the sense I'd said exactly what she meant. "Maybe we'd have done this same thing if you had those years back... maybe we wouldn't have. Doesn't matter. This is what we do based on what feels right to us now."

It really was that simple. Clear all the arguments, all the complicated debates and possibilities and the influence of friends... the fear that we're not making the right call because the events of this year had changed both of us... get rid of it all, and realize that the only people who can make the choice are those in the moment, as they are in the moment. Perhaps it would be a mistake, but that was irrelevant. Karen and I both had to trust our instincts... and our instincts said Grant could not survive for trial.

It was such a relief to have decided. Maybe we'd regret this later — maybe we'd be haunted by it. But the decision was made.

"You're definitely okay with this, right?"

Karen's question, and the slight uncertainty behind it, was less a reflection of her lost years in reading me, and more an indication of how alien this choice was to everything I'd done so far in 2235. I wasn't making this decision out of rage… it wasn't about killing Grant the way I'd killed the Connaughts.

I reached up with my hand and covered the hand that Karen had put over my eyes.

"Yes," was all I said, and that was enough to satisfy her. She took another deep breath — a real struggle because my dense skull was pressing down on her stomach — and then uncovered my eyes. As her hand travelled elsewhere, I took a breath too. We didn't need to rush, now that we knew. Indeed, it would be important to take our time, so as to avoid clashing directly with those who wanted Grant to make it home alive — good men like Wes and Charlie would be watchful.

Step by step, a methodical preparation, and then a callous encounter.

"You want to look at the Schedule 1 compounds, or Schedule 2?" I asked quietly as Karen's mind turned in another direction.

She didn't want to think about that for the moment. So many long hours had been spent in darkness on this subject; for now, she wanted to absorb the relief of just having decided.

"We'll figure that out later," she said softly, and I noticed her breathing change. We had our answer for now, and preparations to make.

One step at a time…

Chapter Twelve

Silence

As the days wore on, our cruise towards Earth seemed to lose a tiny bit of tension. Of course neither Charlie nor Wes intended to relax their concerns about Grant's fate, but the fact that they heard nothing from us, and that we did nothing for twenty-four hours, and then forty-eight hours… that did bring about a certain level of calm.

Of course, it shouldn't have — both Wes and Charlie knew very well that killing Grant could take just a moment, and that there were many moments left before we got back to the Empire. But even these two, powerful and vigilant, were starting to let down their guards.

As they shared lunch on the fifth day out of Etat Valcour — the day before we were expected to get back into range of a DCC comm ship, and thus gain the ability to report to Admiralty House — they were both a little less tense.

"If we make it to tomorrow, we could be okay," Wes said as he loaded up another spoonful of soup, and Charlie nodded without looking up from his own beef sandwich.

"Maybe. But if they're thinking the same, that could make today even more important. Their last chance to get rid of him unobserved," the Hawke Lord pointed out.

Wes 'hmmed', then had more soup. They both remained silent for a few moments, and then the Commodore of the Independent Squadron finished his lunch and dropped his spoon into its bowl, "What if they actually do it? Have you thought about what that'll mean?"

Charlie had thought about it, but it wasn't a conversation he was terribly inclined to have. Respecting the question, he answered succinctly, "No."

Narrowing his eyes, Wes considered challenging the answer — the implication that somehow a Lord as wise as Charlie would have let all the possibilities go unanalyzed.

But then he realized what the word actually meant: that there was no point discussing it. This was different than worrying about all the possible paths a battle might follow — when worrying ahead of a battle, your primary concern was to make sure you, as the person who could change the course of events, were ready for any eventuality.

Neither Charlie nor Wes could change anything now — worrying would do them no good.

They just had to wait and see.

And somehow Charlie knew they wouldn't have to wait for very long.

The preparations were not inconsiderable. Appropriating supplies from Alicia's med bay was the toughest — she was there all the time, and for obvious reasons, dangerous substances (particularly those compounds listed on Schedule 1 and Schedule 2) were kept under lock and key.

But Karen had been plenty crafty in our pirate fighting days, and a visit to see Margot

Messina provided all the cover she needed to slip into the drug vault and retrieve one of Alicia's full bottles of Ketsan. It also gave her the opportunity to see what Grant had ordered done to the young spy who'd backed up Haley; though Margot was more lucid now, and her spirits were improving daily at the promise of returning home and being made whole again, it was still horrific to see a young woman without fingers or tongue, brutalized and under close care.

Such sights made it altogether clear to Karen why we needed to be so elaborate... because Grant clearly deserved a fate as thoughtful (and merciless) as the ones he had inflicted on his enemies.

While Karen went for the tools, I cleared the field of possible interruptions. It was no less simple for me to get to the alarm controls on the brig deck. By crawling into a service shaft just a few corridors over from the brig itself, I was able to re-route the scanners and klaxons that would have alerted the whole ship to our protracted visit to Grant's cell, therefore buying us all the time we needed to make certain the occasion could be handled with appropriate reverence. I should mention this was not the cleanest of rewiring jobs, and I remember distinctly thinking that Andy Jenson would probably be very displeased when he had to make it right... but that was a small price to pay for the opportunity.

The rest of our murder kit wasn't difficult to put together. We had some fun party pieces. A first-aid kit had been acquired because it included an old-fashioned syringe — not an injector gun, but the sort of syringe that's tipped with a needle, and has a plunger to deliver the dosage. Such crude technologies work fine even after an EMP pulse, so you can sometimes find them in older aid kits. We got our hands on one.

We also collected other miscellaneous items. Karen's favorite was a nose-job-in-a-box kit, with its chemical that could be used to make biological material soft and pliable for reshaping. If you happened to use that stuff without the included painkiller, it was reportedly quite agonizing. We weren't above finding out.

A case of rations was acquired too, because we didn't want to have to leave for a meal if we decided to take our time. You'd be surprised how hungry you get when torturing someone, and while many people would probably forget to bring the food necessary to sustain them in the room, we were smarter than that.

Nothing was going to interrupt us when we were in the brig with Grant. And as Charlie suspected, it was going to happen on this last day before we regained contact with Earth.

When Karen and I arrived on the brig deck, me with a small duffle in my hand, the spacers and officers lined up out into the corridor to see the caged villain all watched us approach. Everyone quickly realized the significance of our visit.

There was an SF guard standing in the corridor, so I waved to her as I arrived, "Spacer, we're going to need this deck cleared from drive section to bow pod. No one in or out. Those are my orders."

The guard was undoubtedly surprised by my command, but she nodded after a second, "Yes sir."

"Sorry folks, you're going to have to miss the show," Karen was smiling at the spacers in line, and a few of them smiled back.

"You get the bastard, ma'am!"

"Wish I could watch!"

There was no question that an appetite existed for revenge, or justice, and soon that appetite would be sated. As Karen and I stepped into the outer security office which led to the brig, the officer on duty came to his feet, "Sir, ma'am?"

"We'll be clearing the deck, drive section to bow pod. Please make sure it's locked down for us, Ensign. Everyone out, including your staff."

The young officer looked at me with some surprise — he hadn't expected to be excluded from his post, but then, it was a Rear Admiral telling him to go. Just strange that this order hadn't come down the chain from Eugene.

"It's alright, Ensign. Go ahead, clear the deck," Karen reinforced my orders, and even though everyone knew her memories were missing and she was in some sense just a Commander, that familiar voice was enough to push the young man to action.

"Yes ma'am."

From that point the Ensign began giving orders to the guards on duty, who in turn moved away from their respective posts and started escorting crew out of the waiting area. One SF went down to the observation lounge, collecting the last member of *Wolf's* company who ever spoke to Grant Merger.

As those people started to move out, Karen and I proceeded down the long corridor into the cells, heading all the way to the end of the line, and Grant's isolation unit. Only one obstacle remained in our path: Lieutenant Bobby Franek. Remember, Charlie had insisted that Special Branch have an officer on duty in the brig at all times... both to make sure Grant couldn't escape, and to stop anyone getting into his cell.

Now the young Lieutenant watched both Karen and me approach, and he took a step away from Grant's cell door, keeping his hands overlapped on the butt of his MAG-90 as it dangled from his vest.

"Good evening sir, ma'am," the Brancher nodded to us both, and as we slowed to a stop a few meters from him, he followed up with a question. "Can I help you?"

His eyes tracked from Karen's to mine, and when our gazes met I nodded, "Bobby, I know your orders. Right now I have to countermand them. Need you to clear this deck, from drive section to bow pod. No one in or out."

Like a broken record (look it up) with those orders, but unlike the SF guards who were naturally part of our chain of command, Bobby was more resistant. He was, of course, bound to obey flag officers... but Rufus and Charlie were fellow Branchers, and they'd both told him that his job was to keep the prisoner alive.

It was just bad luck for him that he was the particular officer on shift when Karen and I came gunning. An hour later and it would have been Selma Koestecki.

But it was Bobby, and now he took a deep breath and shook his head, "Not so sure I can do that, sir."

"I'm sure you can, Lieutenant," Karen's own tone was firm, and it drew the young Brancher's gaze.

Before he could add anything, I stepped forward, closing the distance to him, "Bobby, you have to leave. Go get Rufus if you like. But leave. You can't be here for this. No one can."

There was something insistent in my voice — I was giving an order with technical authority, and with what almost sounded like moral authority. It wasn't entirely what he'd expected, but it was enough. For so many reasons he had to do as we said, and though his face reflected his displeasure at being sent away, he took one more deep breath, then started moving.

Karen and I parted to let him escape up the corridor between us, and then we were alone in the brig — and alone on the deck. How long that would remain the case was difficult to determine. Our orders for privacy had been clear, and because they had come from me, not even Wes could officially overturn them.

But we still didn't feel like we had time to waste.

It was just a few more steps to Grant's cell, and we took those strides evenly. When we arrived there, Karen reached out and punched an unlock code into the panel, and then we looked at each other one more time.

This was it, we were going to kill Grant. My editors want me to call it an execution, since it was legal, but they weren't there. It was murder.

And because we hadn't disabled the cameras, everyone was going to have a chance to see.

We opened the hatch.

Chapter Thirteen

This Is What Murder Looks Like

When Grant watched us walk into his cell, it was obvious he was trying to keep his expression neutral. It was a very noble effort, but it didn't really convince either Karen or me, because we knew that he knew the significance of our arrival.

The previous visitor's time had been cut short, the window to the observation lounge had been shut, and of course, Karen and I were stepping into the same compartment with him, carrying a duffle.

I dropped that duffle beside the door, then crouched and drew a mag from it as Karen watched Grant. It was arguably quite dangerous to bring a weapon into close quarters with my old friend — he was no slouch with his fists, as we've established, and now he knew this was his last chance to fight for his life.

But with Karen ready to handle him again, it was a risk we'd take. And if it got messy, that was just fine.

"You're here to kill me," Grant finally blurted out the obvious, backing towards the wall opposite the now-open hatch. Karen watched him as he moved, knowing it would be altogether logical for him to try to make a run for it.

I knew the same, so I checked the settings on my mag, and shot him in the knee. He just managed to bite off a cry as he collapsed back against the wall, hitting his head against the alloy frame in the process.

"We're here to kill you," Karen confirmed his suspicion as he went down. "It's just a question of how long we take."

There was no deviating now; we were in the room and things were going to happen to plan. I think that was obvious from our expressions, because Grant looked up at us both with more desperation than I'd ever seen.

This was his nightmare — *we* were his nightmare.

"Should be a fitting end to an enjoyable stay, I hope," I smiled at him, and his glare back was toxic.

Unfortunately for him, it wasn't as toxic as the stuff we had in the duffle. Karen and I crouched on either side of that bag, making a show of sifting through all the toys we'd brought along for fun.

"Oh good, you got the bacon rations. I hate the simulated stuff," I smiled as Karen piled the meal kits on the floor.

It's funny what sort of impact a simple line like that could have — because if you'll recall, Grant hated simbacon, and loved real bacon. In itself, seeing that we had good rations shouldn't really have affected him. But it wasn't the food that mattered, it was the idea that he'd never, ever, get to have real bacon again. That he'd never, ever, see his home again. That he'd never see anything outside of this cell ever again.

That was what we wanted him to realize — in all its crippling brutality, we wanted him to know that there were no more chances, no more moments of joy left.

Everything between now and when he stopped breathing would be misery, and if we had our way, there would be plenty of moments separating him from his death.

"Oh, a nose job kit… going to use the face-melter stuff without a painkiller?" Karen asked as she pulled the box out of the bag, and placed it on the deck facing Grant. Of course she knew what we'd use the kit for, but again she was telegraphing our intentions to my old friend.

"I prefer the dental drill… do we have a dental drill?" I asked.

"In here somewhere," Karen said with a frown, even though we didn't have one — unfortunately, I only thought of it on the spot.

We kept sifting through, and Grant kept watching, broadly shaking his head and beginning to despair. It was all about to end, in the worst sort of way, and he knew it.

"I had a plan…" he started to say, then hammered his fists impotently against the floor. "Ken, I had a plan! When I attacked Earth. I promise you, I was going to make sure your parents were off Capital Island safely before we bombarded! I promise you!"

It didn't matter whether that was the truth or a lie. I don't know why Grant felt compelled to say it in that moment — whether he thought it would help his situation, or whether he just wanted me to know. It was nice enough. I appreciate that he didn't intend to kill my family when he mounted his attack on Earth so many years before.

Wouldn't save him now.

"Karen… I'm sorry," Grant was getting desperate. I suppose I could call him pathetic again, but I don't know if I'd be any different under these circumstances. Maybe he was trying to bring down our guard so that he could jump us when we got close to him… or maybe he really was just losing the very last scraps of his dignity.

"That compound… yes, Karen, the compound you were injected with. I didn't come up with it. We found the biomatter. It's *alien* biomatter. *Idaho* was transporting it home from the lab on Io. We don't know where they got it, but they must have saved it when the Martians attacked… along with that *creature*. My people found that thing and the biomatter samples in *Idaho's* hold. It was too dangerous, we took the samples and set the trap. I'm sorry about the trap… but the compound… it's alien and it's inside you, so be careful…"

Now he was simply descending into delirious fiction. Neither Karen nor I paid much attention. Whatever truths Grant wanted to expel were his own business.

As he finished his fiction about the aliens from Jupiter, Karen finally closed her hand around the most important item in the duffle: the small bottle of Ketsan. If you don't know, it's a chemical compound found on Schedule 2, specially designed in the earliest days of space travel to fortify people against decompression aboard a spacecraft. Fortunately, today, we have microfilament bags to protect us against a loss of atmosphere, but in the old days, if you were on a ship that was opened to the vacuum, a Ketsan shot was your only hope. A full dose would sweep across your body and fortify your cells, keeping you from boiling for as long as a minute. The compound, however, did nothing to keep ice crystals from forming in your body.

Still, if you were trapped in a decompressed compartment and you took Ketsan, you might live long enough to be rescued. It had only ever worked twice in the recorded history of space travel, and one of those two people had suffered terrible brain damage because he'd taken a double dose in an attempt to survive longer.

Ketsan was reportedly incredibly painful — the feeling of the compound racing through the body, infesting every cell, has been likened to being burned one molecule at a time. It also has the delightful added benefit of more or less compelling consciousness, because it disrupts the brain and the body's normal pain responses. No matter how bad it gets, you're forced to feel every second of it.

In huge doses it can also kill someone.

That last part was the most important. After a person was sufficiently saturated with the compound, it could begin to cause permanent and irreparable damage to the bonds between cells. You might have seen a couple of horror films, particularly old ones, in which massive Ketsan overdoses cause a person to dissolve like a pillar of salt. This is obviously bullshit… think more of a body melting into itself, as different cells fragment one at a time.

This happens while the person is conscious, meaning he gets to feel every piece of his anatomy break down until he's a puddle of goop.

As far as Karen or I could find, no one had ever actually used Ketsan as a weapon for that purpose. Indeed, as a weapon the chemical was generally useless — the process of dying could take many hours indeed, and most of the time weaponized chemical agents are required to act much more quickly.

But for our purposes it was perfect. And we had a whole bottle of the stuff — more than enough to turn Grant into a puddle.

"What is that?" he asked us both, his words growing feral as he saw the bottle of clear liquid. We'd unkindly turned the label away from him, which I only realized when I looked down. As I placed the old-style syringe on the deck next to it, I felt charitable and turned the label in his direction so he could read what it said.

His eyes widened and his head shaking grew more violent, "No… this isn't right…"

"It's turnabout," Karen disagreed, getting to the paper-scrawled note at the bottom of the duffle and deciding there was no point pulling it out. She started re-packing all the contents, shaking her head as she did so, "I know we were supposed to do all this other stuff, but I really want to start with the Ketsan."

"No… No…" Grant was beyond controlling his reaction now. I can only imagine what it must have felt like for him, knowing this was the end. Knowing there was no hope and that his years were about to be destroyed.

I stood up slowly — crouching for too long had actually started to make my legs ache — and then I approached him, mag still dangling from my hands, "I suppose this seems cruel to you. But at least we're using a compound that's on the Schedules. You didn't give us that luxury on *Idaho*."

"You didn't give me anything close to that luxury either," Karen stood more nimbly, and approached Grant as well. "I don't know how much it hurt when your man hit me at the ball. I can't remember how much pain there was because of that shit… what did you call it, *alien*?"

"You've been infected with an alien plague," I added, glancing at her. "Will the grandkids have gills? Maybe antennae?"

Grant kept shaking his head, and pounding his fists on the deck, "You have to be… stop this. Let me go to trial. Let me die some other way. What will happen if you do this? You two… you two are going to marry one day. You're going to walk down the aisle and marry. Do you want to see this moment in your minds on that day? Do you want to know that the thing that brought you back together was torturing me to death?"

It was unabashed begging. Grant was struggling to find anything to stop us — any words, any ideas that might slow us down. But he had nothing left. He was shaking his head and trying to get a grip on some sort of verbal weapon. He was watching the open hatch, and hoping Charlie or Wes would arrive.

But he was alone in a room with Karen and me. And it was the end of him.

Moving over to my old friend Grant, I crouched beside him and took his hand. It was balled into a fist, so I pried it open and took it properly, squeezing it tight.

"You don't want to kill me. Neither of you do. You've become better people than that."

"Maybe I had," Karen shook her head. "But thanks to you, I've bounced back."

Grant gave up on her, but he still felt my friendship through my grip. He turned his eyes on me — a desperate gaze, as much terror as I've seen in any human — and he pushed his face at me.

"You have to stop this. You are a better man, so be that man for her. For everyone. People like you and me… we don't do this to *each other*."

I frowned gently, "We just do it to the people we think are inferior?"

"This is for them. We're officer class," Grant made his last plea, and I met it with a smile.

"Maybe it's time people like us start killing each other, instead of people who can't fight back."

It was probably that moment when Grant realized his hope was gone. He looked away and his eyes started to tear, so it was easy enough for me to wrench him from the wall. He began to struggle as I got behind him — writhing like a desperate animal as my arm circled his throat, and I pulled him tight back against me. I was restricting his airway, and his hands were trying desperately to get a grip on my head, but I had him at a bad angle.

"Shh," I said softly to him. "Quiet now."

He wasn't quiet; he screamed and flailed like a man about to die. Funny, that.

Karen knew this was her cue, so she crouched again, took the big syringe and stabbed it into the membrane at the top of the Ketsan bottle. It was a huge needle, and as she pulled the plunger back, Grant was able to watch the clear liquid occupy the vacuum inside its cylinder.

He kept crying out, "No… no…!"

Because apparently that word will stop you being killed.

Once the syringe was absolutely full, Karen held it up in front of her nose, tapped it a couple of times like you see in old movies, and then smiled at Grant.

"Shh," she said. "It's okay now. Just relax, and it'll all be over soon."

"Soon?" I asked, my voice basically going straight into Grant's ear.

She crossed the floor to the vicinity of Grant's flailing leg (one was immobilized by my mag shot) and shrugged at me, "Well, *soon* in a geological sense. A dozen hours of our time is just the blink of an eye to planets."

"Right. But if you're a human suffering in agony?"

Another shrug, and a grin, "Well then. It'll probably seem a lot longer."

Grant flailed hard, but I had him pinned. His one good leg tried to swing at Karen, to knock the syringe from her hand, but she came up on the side of the wounded leg. He tried to grab for her, but I got my free arm around his, and held it still so Karen could roll up his sleeve.

"Just going to feel a pinch," she said soothingly.

"I'm sorry. Please. I'm so sorry. Please don't do this. Please…"

It became a mantra of begging from my old friend.

"Please… please…"

Karen's smile didn't stop; she just leaned forward with the syringe and pushed it into a vein, "Sorry Grant."

He became very still in that second, his eyes locked on hers in a haunting way that she says she does remember to this day. Then I said one more thing to Grant Merger: "Goodbye, old friend."

Karen pushed the plunger, and the Ketsan powered into Grant's veins. The compound was fast-acting by design — of course, if it was meant to protect someone against decompression, it had to be. Grant's body immediately stiffened, and then began to tremor as a wail escaped him.

I released his throat and slid back from him, letting him tip sideways onto the floor. Karen backed away as well, withdrawing the massive syringe and looking at it one more time.

Neither of us were smiling any longer — we had no need to be.

"Best start packing up the kit," I said after a moment of watching Grant quake on the floor. His screams grew louder, but were unintelligible.

"Yeah," Karen answered, and then we both got to our feet and moved back over to the duffle. All our unused tools went back inside — the rations with real bacon, the nose job box, the rest of the bottle of Ketsan… it had been ambitious of us to think we'd use it all, when indeed, that one compound could inflict all the pain and death we needed.

Grant was the victim of the same sort of attack he'd twice mounted on Karen, and that was about as fitting as it got.

But, of course, there remained one problem. Because if someone found him with that much Ketsan in his system, and started purging his bloodstream, that person might be able to save him from his fate. Not that we expected *Wolf's* crew to go against our wishes like that… but, well, it was better to be safe.

This was how Grant Merger died. No one else would have a chance to participate, and that meant we had one more step along the way.

Closing up the loaded duffle, I slung it over my shoulder and then nodded to Karen, "Grab his feet?"

"Of course," she concurred.

We picked up Grant Merger and carried him to his coffin.

CHAPTER FOURTEEN

KILLERS

Charlie was sitting in his cabin when the knock came at the door. He looked up when he heard it, and immediately knew what it had to be. Rising from his chair, my friend approached his hatch and keyed it open, and there he found Bobby Franek standing beside Rufus Chang.

Wolf's Major of Special Branch looked grave, but he didn't delay his words: "They're doing it now. Are you intending to intervene?"

It was one of the most difficult questions Rufus had ever had to ask, or perhaps it would be more accurate to say the implications of the question were more damning than most. Because if Charlie immediately flew out of his cabin with the intention of keeping Grant alive, the Chinese Major would be forced to a decision: would he protect the orders of his Rear Admiral, or instead try to save my soul?

But Charlie didn't respond immediately. His eyes drifted to a spot between the shoulders of the two men at his door, and his expression saddened. No one could pretend that Charlie hadn't killed many people in his time, but it had always been for good reasons. He was proud to be able to say that never had he squeezed the trigger, or slid in the knife, or triggered the explosion on someone outside of a real fight... outside of a real necessity.

He would have feared for his own soul if he had done otherwise.

Now... now his best friend was among those who could be damned. And it was one of the most disappointing moments of his life.

"I'll go in a while, Rufus. We should give them time to finish."

It was a defeated statement, and as he spoke, Charlie turned and strode back to his chair. He would wait, and not be party to this. He had done all he could, and had failed.

Wes was a guest on *Wolf's* bridge. Unable to relax in any way on such a dangerous day, my friend had petitioned Andrea for the chance to be somewhere comfortable, and she had not denied him.

That's why the Commodore of the Independent Squadron was present when Jim Hannigan — still smarting somewhat from his encounter with Grant days earlier — frowned at his console, and then looked up at one of his operations staff.

"Gunter, see if you can pull up the log for the escape pods on the brig deck."

Jim didn't say that loudly — it was delivered like thousands of other brief orders from a department head to his staff on the bridge of a warship. But despite its familiar delivery, Wes immediately detected it, and his heart rate began to climb as the possible implications became clear to him.

He turned slowly as he waited to hear if Gunter could find anything, and when his eyes reached Jim, he knew there was something amiss.

"What the hell... I have a pod launch on 8-7..." the spacer reported back to Jim, and immediately all the people at the operations console were abuzz.

"Pull up alert logs... someone get on internal cameras for that corridor..." Jim passed those orders along quickly, before calling up to Andrea: "We're missing an escape pod, but we received no warning when it launched. Brig deck."

Andrea hadn't noticed that Wes had turned, so she was surprised to see that he was already facing Jim Hannigan when she looked back, "How long ago?"

Looking to Gunter, Jim found the answer: "About... five minutes."

It seemed impossible. Launching escape pods creates quite a racket — that's by necessity, because if one person is trying to get off a ship, typically many other people might have reason to do the same.

Unless... unless something had happened and Grant had gotten out of his cell and made a break for it...

"Felicia, scan for a beacon. Order squadron to all stop and stand by to redirect our Starlight patrol to find that pod," Andrea didn't need much time to figure out the best course of action; if a pod had gotten away, it was important that it be found. Because she couldn't conceive of any reason why a pod sent from the brig deck *shouldn't* be retrieved.

"Registering all stop on drives... beginning reverse thrust deceleration," Shelby McLaws reported from her station, not having needed a specific order to carry out the necessary actions at Helm and Navigation.

Five minutes cruising at 190 kps meant only 50,000 kilometers of separation from launch point. The pod could have gone in any direction after being shot away from the ship, so that added another wide range of variables into the search grid... but with a whole squadron looking, there was still a solid chance of finding it.

It was that knowledge that led Wes to speak for the first time, invoking the authority that everyone sort of knew he had, but which he hadn't used much at all on this cruise: "Squadron to General Quarters. Bring up Battlelink and order all ships to launch Starlights for a grid search. We don't have much time."

"And get Rufus on the line, I want him on the brig deck immediately," Andrea added, glancing at Wes just once.

Apparently it felt right to her, giving orders alongside the Independent Squadron Commodore — felt like they were actually a team. Not that Andrea was fully capable of processing such a feeling... yet.

Both their orders began to take hold; with speed and precision, the Belt Squadron went to General Quarters, and Starlights on every ship started powering up for a search. The patrol planes that had been circling our ships the whole way out of Valcour were already tracking back to the launch point, so they could look for clues.

Then the bridge hatch opened and an SF Ensign entered. At first, he didn't draw anyone's particular notice, but as he quickly hurried over to Jim and reported in low tones, it became obvious to Wes that the junior officer knew what was going on.

Jim's eyes widened slightly at the report, then he opened his mouth to pass it along to Andrea and Wes, before deciding not to let the whole bridge hear. He patted the SF on the arm in thanks for bringing word, then hurried out from behind the ops consoles.

Wes put a hand on Andrea's shoulder to draw her attention as Jim neared, and so they all faced each other at close range as the XO passed along the orders I'd given in the security office.

Andrea took a few seconds more than Wes to realize the implications, and then she took a breath, "I don't care what he said… we need to get down there to make sure the wrong people weren't in that fucking pod."

That was a good point, so Wes nodded. They wouldn't sit back and wait — if that was Grant getting away, or if he'd piled Karen and I into a pod and shot us off into the black, something had to be done quickly.

"Call Rufus, tell him there's been an escape pod launch and we're going to the brig to confirm it's suppose to have happened," Andrea directed those orders to Felicia, but our Sensors and Communications Officer frowned.

"Having trouble getting Major Chang on the comm," she said, and that made Andrea worry even more.

"Intercom, then. Major Chang… and Major Peters, to meet us at the brig. There has been an escape pod launch," Andrea ordered as she began moving, Wes right in her wake.

They left Jim in command of the bridge and went to find out what was going on.

Rufus and Charlie were in the lift heading to the brig deck, neither of them armed but both of them ready for trouble. Though the two had traded no words since being forced into action by Andrea's message, they'd communicated enough in silence to know the next few minutes had the potential to be incredibly awkward.

Or dangerous.

What the hell was going on with the escape pod? That part made no sense, unless Karen and I wanted no evidence of how much harm we'd done to Grant. Or unless we'd done something so inhumane to him that no one on *Wolf* would tolerate it, and we wanted to leave him time to slowly die.

Neither prospect particularly pleased Charlie as he thought about it, nor was Rufus especially thrilled. But together they hoped that it was indeed Grant in the pod — not an escaping Grant, but a dead one. Because if somehow he'd overpowered Karen and me, and sent us out into the black where we might never be found, that'd be a loss of an entirely different kind.

There was no point speculating; they were close to actual answers, so both men waited as the lift came to a stop on the brig deck and the doors opened.

Karen and I were standing there, and it looked to Charlie and Rufus both as though they'd caught us in mid-conversation.

In mid-causal-conversation, because we were both chatting with the usual ease that we tended to share. There was no sign of tension on either of our faces… certainly none of the great darkness that had been hanging over us.

Rather it was as though a great weight had been lifted from both of us, and now we were bouncing back to who we'd been.

Neither of us seemed to notice the two men in black ship fatigues standing in the lift we were about to enter… but it didn't take long for Charlie to make himself known.

"You've done it, then?"

I looked towards the lift first, and I noted the presence of both Branchers, "Charlie, Rufus, good evening."

I stopped there, and saw an uncommon look of frustration appear on Charlie's face. My friend had no appetite for clever games, so Karen took the reins and immediately gave him his answer: "It's done. His remains have been jettisoned as well."

Charlie had been expecting to hear something like that, but he still felt somewhat unequal to commenting. Rufus, on the other hand, was less circumspect, "You're pleased with yourselves?"

Though he hadn't been party to the efforts to stop our killing, or to the killing itself, he still clearly wasn't overjoyed by what we'd done — or by how we'd gone about it. Sending his officer away, skulking into a cell on our own...

"Just relieved it's over, Rufus. And now we're going to get away from this place and get some rest. Thanks both for checking on us," I reached that conclusion in a flat tone — I had no intention of standing on this deck any longer than I needed to. Not on this day.

Both Rufus and Charlie picked up on that, but they remained in the lift as their eyes moved from Karen to me and back again. They were men who knew about killing, and they were trying to get a read on our states of mind.

"You getting out?" Karen pointed that question at them, and the two black-clad Branchers both seemed to straighten at her words. Then, almost reluctantly, both Majors stepped out onto the deck, thus unblocking the door for us.

As we entered and turned around, I offered parting instructions, "Somebody should call Andy Jensen and let him know some wiring needs to be fixed up in service shaft 8-1-4. And it sounds like we're at all stop, so tell Andrea to get us moving again. No search for the pod."

Neither Major moved. They stood there, only just far enough out of the lift to keep the doors from closing... and then down the corridor behind them, we spotted Wes and Andrea coming out of an intersection at a very fast walk.

As soon as those two spotted us they hurried down the hallway in our direction, looking at once relieved to see us and concerned to know what had happened.

"There's the Captain herself," I said. "Direct orders, Andrea: recall any search flights for the pod, and get the squadron moving immediately."

Both Andrea and Wes were slowing just beyond the lift, and my orders brought frowns to their faces. Realizing they didn't know what had happened either, I clarified: "We've killed Grant and dumped his body in the pod. Just let it go."

"You didn't..." Wes blurted that out, but found his words fell away as our expressions answered his question.

"We did," Karen replied, just for reinforcement.

So that was it. Whatever we would be after committing cold-blooded murder, we clearly were now. Karen and I knew we were no different than we had been before we'd done this task, but for the four people facing us — four of our most loyal friends and officers — it was the beginning of a new era in our relationships.

That was for them to grapple with; Karen and I had done enough for one day, and were due to put our heads down, to close our eyes and sleep in the midst of the peace that came from knowing the greatest villain we'd ever faced — the specter from our past, the man who'd been determined to end our Empire — was dead and gone.

And I was in no mood to wait any longer for that release.

"Recall the fighters and get us moving, Wes. Don't make us give the order twice," I nodded to my friend, and he opened his mouth, but failed to speak.

He could resist that order... could insist on seeking out Grant... but for what purpose?

"Good evening to you all," Karen preempted any further questions with that farewell, and with decent timing, the lift doors closed. We were left in beautiful solitude, just Karen and me, and as we were carried back through *Wolf's* hull to the safety of our cabins, our friends were left to try to piece together exactly what we'd done.

It wouldn't be difficult: we hadn't switched off any of the cameras.

CHAPTER FIFTEEN

CRIME SCENE

When Charlie, Wes, Andrea and Rufus arrived in the brig, they were met by nothing but stony silence. There was no particular smell of gore, but somehow the place seemed darker to them than before. It was as though a great moral wrong (which, ironically, was a legal right) had taken place within its walls.

Of course that was melodramatic and stupid, but perhaps it was inevitable. They'd come here to see how and where Grant had died, and frankly, as Charlie led the way towards the cell door, he expected to see blood.

That's understandable, I suppose. If you consider what Andrea had done to the captured assassin back in the palace — essentially cutting her to pieces in order to secure information — blood seemed logical. Bodily fluids, maybe body parts... surely we wouldn't have had time to clean things up, so the whole murder scene would be pretty raw.

It was a shock — indeed, a disconcerting one — when Charlie stepped into the cell and found no signs of death. The air did smell slightly of a recently-fired mag bolt — that's a scent that only a Brancher would really recognize — but beyond that, it was disturbingly clean.

"What... happened here?" Wes stepped past Charlie as he entered the cell, then turned around as he looked for signs of what had happened. "Did they kill him somewhere else?"

Charlie was wondering the same thing, but then my friend had a thought — a thought that others seem to have had, which has become the source of many rumors ever since this cruise. I'm going to address it thoroughly over the next few chapters, so that we can put it to rest once and for all.

Here it is: Charlie wondered whether we'd actually killed Grant Merger.

But of course he didn't say that, because even though he wondered, he knew the notion was quite ridiculous.

"Must have been somewhere else," Rufus pitched in at that point, staying just inside the cell door as he surveyed the room for any signs of bloodletting. "No smell of cleaner... no sign of a struggle. I saw what Ken did to those assassins on Concord. There was no way Grant was getting away clean."

That point drew nods from the three other officers present, Andrea remaining silent as she looked over the room with folded arms.

"We'll go take a look at the pod," Charlie said after a time, locking eyes with Wes. "Andrea, you should go follow Ken's orders. Whether we like it or not, we need to leave."

Those instructions seemed a little odd to both Andrea and Rufus, but with a slight frown, the Irish skipper decided to follow them. For some reason she had little interest in being in the place where one of the good people she'd helped corrupt (at least by her own reckoning at the time) had done harm.

She was on the road back to humanity, bless her.

With a nod to Rufus, *Wolf's* skipper left the cell, and once the footfalls were far enough behind, Wes moved over beside Charlie with a frown of his own, "You're thinking something?"

"We need to look around more. Check out the pod lock... and see if they left the cameras running in here."

"Sure," Wes nodded, and with that they set off.

Their first stop was the lock that had launched the escape pod. I've never described one of these in this series, because fortunately I've never needed to use one, but essentially a pod is a small craft attached to a pressure hatch. The whole assembly sits beneath the armor of a warship's hull, and at launch, the armor swings open and the pod hurtles away. Once the pod is out, the armor flips shut, and the void where the pod had been repressurizes

Any evidence from inside the pod would obviously now be gone, but if we'd dragged a bloody corpse into the small craft, it was likely we'd have left blood or tissue or *something* on the frame of the hatch. That in mind, Wes and Charlie did their best imitation of crime show investigators as they looked for any sign of a mess on the otherwise well-kept deck, all the way from the brig to the hatch.

No blood though — blood being the thing they expected to see most.

"I'm really starting to wonder. Did they just walk him out here and throw him into deep space with no beacon?" Wes was getting on the hopeful train as well.

Charlie refused to be optimistic, so he answered simply: "I think there are a lot of possibilities."

"A mag shot on full power theoretically could kill him with no gore, right?" the Commodore of the Independent Squadron asked next, as they both moved up to the lock door for a closer look at its control panel.

"No gore... or a small enough amount to clear up easily," Charlie agreed. "But that'd be awfully quick. And you have to wonder about them wasting a lifepod. Isn't there an airlock on this deck? They could have just thrown his body out there."

Though Charlie had served in *Wolf* for many years, he'd been off the ship for a while, and had never been expected to memorize the exact locations of every service lock aboard.

Wes, having skippered *Cheetah* for years and being a Navy man by trade, was exactly the one to answer that question... and as he straightened up and frowned, he had to shake his head.

"No lock on the brig deck. Think it's meant to make jailbreaks tougher."

That did make sense to Charlie, so he nodded — were he trying to rescue someone from a frigate, he would probably have thought it awfully convenient if the ship had an airlock on the brig deck.

Escape pods, though, were necessarily ubiquitous.

"So if they were looking to dispose of a body without hauling it between decks, an escape pod was the only way," Charlie said slowly.

"Afraid so," Wes concurred. "But that still doesn't mean anything."

It didn't. My two friends wanted to believe that we hadn't killed Grant, so they were going to keep up their search.

After deciding there was nothing at the lock, they headed back to the security office, to see if they could make any use of the recordings from the brig camera.

Andrea stepped out onto a bustling bridge with every screen at its front alive with Battlelink feeds. The skippers of the Belt Squadron were all there, looking duly concerned about the missing pod and its implications.

The rest of the bridge was tense too — Shelby, Jim, Felicia and all their staffs wanted to know what was going on, and Andrea decided there was no point wasting time filling everyone in.

"Grant Merger has been executed. His body was disposed of by lifepod, so we're going to call off the search and get back on course. Those are orders from Ken."

Andrea was just stepping into range of the viewfinder when she started talking, and as she paced closer to the screens she saw the looks of surprise on the faces of the skippers there. Some were less pleased that others, and Matt Baxter looked positively severe.

"Who exactly did the executing?" he asked, and Andrea met the question with a tilt of her head.

She didn't need to say anything, Matt just understood. His expression reflected a couple of layers of conflict; on the one hand, he was glad to know the bastard he'd fought for so long was dead, and that Karen and I had been strong enough to do the killing.

But on the other hand, he just got a feeling from Andrea… a feeling that something was amiss.

"Are they alright?" that question came from Mark Gunney, who frankly wasn't too worried about Grant's fate. His concern for us was appreciated, though, and Andrea decided not to sugarcoat her answer.

"They appear to be fine. We're still not sure of the details, but they seem to be relieved it's finished."

Of course we were. The villain was gone, and we'd found our own way to do it — one that was poetic justice for a man who'd tortured so many, and stolen so much. The grave brutality of our method was still unknown, though — no one on the bridge screens could do more than imagine what sort of horror we put Grant through.

That would soon change. As the squadron recalled its fighters, and returned to cruising formation on course for Earth, two detectives were finding incontrovertible proof that Karen and I had murdered our prisoner.

"They didn't turn off the cameras."

Charlie was sitting at the main console in the security office when Wes drew his attention with those words. Standing at the observation station inside the room, the Commodore was rolling back through feeds to try to find relevant camera time… and because they were so close after the event, it didn't take him long.

As the vid started to roll on the screen in front of him, he waved to Charlie and the Hawke Lord came to his feet and moved over to Wes' side. They kept winding back the feed until they reached the moment just before Karen and I entered the cell, then they turned up the volume to make certain they could hear every word.

This feed has long been declassified, and that means you can watch it yourself, just like they did. I don't know why you'd bother, unless you like to see men die in humiliating ways. What I described to you a couple of chapters ago is exactly what happened, and it's disgusting to watch.

That was sort of the point. If it makes you uncomfortable to look at, imagine how terrible it was for Grant.

And imagine how crushing it was for Charlie and Wes. They should have known better than to hold out hopes about Grant's fate. The very notion that we'd somehow set free the monster who had done so much harm both to us and to the Empire was patently ridiculous. Indeed, it would have been a hanging offense — to set him free so he couldn't be tried? Doesn't matter who you are, you get the noose for that sort of silliness.

But they had hoped, and I think the hoping made watching this worse. Because they weren't just watching Grant die… they watched us commit murder. A cold and heartless destruction of a man, ending in agony as Ketsan tore him apart.

They also saw us goad him, and watched him plea. They saw all sorts of things that reminded them of places like Egesta, but this time being done by people they called friends.

It was time for them to give up on me. They knew it, but as they watched Karen and I take Grant's body out of the cell, they *still* held out hope. My friends are wonderful people, but they were wrong this time.

"Let me… pull the feeds from the other cameras…" Wes offered, and Charlie chose not to argue.

He waited as the vid from the brig hallway rolled, and I think they both secretly hoped that it'd show Grant hopping to his feet, shaking our hands, and running for the pod.

It didn't.

They went to the feed from the corridor outside, and all they saw was Karen and me struggling as we tried to angle Grant's shuddering body out of the brig door. It was as though we were moving a convulsing sofa.

Every feed along the way to the lock — all of them declassified, and checked numerous times by numerous experts — showed the same thing: two people dragging the body of a dying man. And then, when we got to the lock, two different angles showed us toss Grant into the lifepod like a rag doll, and hurl the duffle after him. No point keeping all that shit now that we didn't need it, Karen and I believed in cleaning up our own messes.

Take that however you like.

When Wes paused the feed after watching Karen key the launch trigger into the escape pod's control pad, he let out a breath and slowly shook his head.

"Well… he was clearly still alive when he was thrown in there. And they didn't deactivate the cameras, so that means they could have faked the whole thing. To get him out?"

Even to Wes, that was starting to sound pretty flimsy. There was just no motive for us to try to save Grant, and if we were going to do so, why would we go about it in this brutal way? Of course there were other things to consider. Charlie was no mean detective, if you'll recall from *The Mars Convention*, so he knew he was going to spend the rest of the trip back to Earth doing more homework… checking other feeds… seeing if there was any hint of what we were up to.

But Occam's razor was starting to shine. Because no matter what he wanted to believe about me, I'd killed my former best friend.

Let me say that again for all of you people reading this who are desperate to believe a 'good man' like myself can't do something properly cruel. I killed Grant. End of story.

Unfortunately, Charlie still wasn't ready to close the book.

CHAPTER SIXTEEN

NEWS GETS HOME

When the first signal from *Wolf* reached Admiralty House, it caused exactly the sort of sensation you'd expect. Everyone was called to John Fiora's office — soon-to-be-named Second Lord Greg Noyce, soon-to-return-to-Venus Admiral Marlene Stoll, along with Mel Samuels, Marshal Samuels, and Christian Mikaelsen.

Once all these people had gathered, John played my message for them, having seen it only once himself: "John, everyone, I must report the death of Grant Merger. Karen and I executed him yesterday in a cell aboard *Wolf*. He had been known as Governor George Madison, of the asteroid Etat Valcour. There's a whole Union of Solar Asteroids out here, trying to masquerade as the new United States. We destroyed half their fleet while we were capturing Grant, but mostly they fired first, so it's their responsibility. But sorry, I get ahead of myself. Grant seems to have moved out there and set up after we stopped him at Deep Black… he's been building his own little empire since. He also had Dave Caldecott running his fleet, which explains how he was able to get into our communications so easily all this time. Don't know how long Dave was working for him, but he's dead too, we're pretty sure. Blew up his battleship."

Talk about an avalanche of information. The fact that Grant had been killed in his cell left a bad taste in everyone's mouth, but I'd buried that news amongst so much other information it was hard to process any one thing at a time.

"I've bundled a lot of data into this message. Some of it is straight from the Martian Intel file on the Union… I don't know if you have that already, but it's solid. The rest is from our experience. John, you might want to talk to the PM and Craig Macdonald about whether, in light of what I've done out there, we want to send a diplomatic mission. I doubt it'd be well-received, and I'd say send it with a lot of firepower, but I suppose it's always an option. In the meantime, we're bound for Earth with a full squadron and no casualties. We also picked up a couple of DCI agents, one of them being Haley Briand. She was in Grant's inner circle and she's the reason we were able to catch him right at the end. She's fine. The other was one of the people Thea sent out when Haley went dark. Her name is Margot Messina, and she's less fine; we'll need our best restorative surgeons ready for her when she gets back. Details and my chief medical officer's report are appended."

Again, so much information and so many ideas that no one could completely absorb them all — different people zeroed in on different pieces of news.

"Oh, and Karen's fine. Down a dozen years of memories, and that might have implications for her next assignment, but otherwise she's the same. Thanks for letting her come out after me, because God only knows what might have happened if she didn't."

That was true. Getting over what we'd done to Grant was a bit sticky, but if Karen hadn't shown up and I'd started forcing my crew to laser domes, that would have been worse. And don't doubt I would have done it.

"Think that's all for the moment. We'll be resuming regular comm checks now that we're back in range, and there shouldn't be any further security concerns with Dave floating in pieces in deep space. See you all in five days, and talk to you before then."

With that, my face froze, and John let out a breath and turned away from the screen. As his eyes crossed the officers he'd assembled, he shook his head, "I haven't had the chance to look through the attachments he sent us, but there's a lot of data. I'm going to have DCI open an official file on the Union, and we're going to have to start assessing their military abilities in light of a possible reprisal for this…"

"Sounds like Ken cruised in there and took one of their senior Governors," Marshal interjected at that point. "If it were us, I'd expect a lot of trouble as a result."

That was exactly the problem — the sort of thing a sensible officer sees, particularly when he has the benefit of distance.

"If he could break half their fleet, I'm sure we'll be fine… but the last thing anyone wants is another war," Mel added to her husband's assessment, then slowly rose to her feet. "I'm going to go bring the news to Thea Fostopolos."

John was surprised by the rapid movement, but it was Greg — now effectively in charge of Defense Command personnel, since he was soon-to-be-Second Lord — who turned in his chair and looked back at her, "You might want to tell her to start packing her office as well. And you should choose paint chips if you want her place redecorated."

It was not the most formal announcement of promotion ever, and Mel sounded confused when she responded, "Wait… are you saying that I'm taking over as the head of Defense Command Intelligence?"

Greg smiled at her — one of the few reasons anyone in the room had to smile just now — and nodded, "How long have you known?"

"I've already had her office repainted. I'm sure she's been wondering what the cleaners were thinking, but now I'll be able to tell her. And I'll get our analysts ready to go through every scrap of data Ken sent us. Snap briefing first thing tomorrow, and subsequent updates every Monday, or special ones if we find something important."

That posting was good news for everyone; we needed a professional at the head of DCI who could make good use of our resources, so that we never got blindsided this badly again… and we always knew what we were up against.

Marshal got to his feet beside his wife, mainly so he could give her a congratulatory kiss on the cheek, and then she kissed him back and departed.

"Marshal, you want to come with me when I brief the PM?" John put that question to the soon-to-be-MP for Belt Two, and he nodded. It only made sense that the man who was likely soon to be the Minister of War be in on the first official discussions of a new potential adversary.

"Sure," Sam's answer was simple and direct.

"Good. In the meantime, Mik, could I put you in a spare office to start reviewing Ken's tactical data? Be helpful to have someone experienced collate an executive summary for us," the First Lord directed that question at the Belt-born Commodore, and with a stroke of his goatee, Mik nodded.

"I'll have a look."

With that, both Mik and Marshal came to their feet and nodded to the other

Admirals in the room before leaving. As they departed, John looked to Greg and Marlene — his two most trusted and most senior officers since the beginning of the war — and folded his arms.

"Thoughts?"

Marlene sat back in her chair and looked again at my face frozen on the screen, "There's a lot about that report I wasn't fond of. But what's most important will be how much damage was done to this Union, and whether they have the will or the ability to come after us."

That was a particular concern for Marlene, as she was shortly heading back to resume command of the Venus defenses. An assault on Earth would be met by the whole might of the Home Fleet, but if the Union people decided to go after a more isolated target, it could easily be her... or, of course, the Belt colonies.

They'd need to analyze our data carefully, and determine how likely such a reprisal was.

"I think our concerns in sending Ken in the first place were correct. Time will tell whether the consequences will include further fighting," Greg added evenly from his own seat. "For now, we can at least rest assured that Grant Merger is out of the picture. As much as we may have preferred for him to be brought back for trial, it's an important development."

"True," John agreed — a development that no one could underestimate. Grant had been too great a danger for far too long... no one who genuinely cared about the fate of the Empire could be unhappy to see him dead. With a sigh, then, the First Lord of the Admiralty shook his head, "Let's hope we've seen the worst of things for a while. And let's make ready to welcome the Belt Squadron home."

The three great Admirals of Defense Command all shared that sentiment — they were relieved that the Belt Squadron was returning, were concerned about the consequences of our actions, and were ultimately focused on a much bigger picture than the one we were preoccupied with aboard *Wolf*.

Soon enough, we'd be home to see them.

CHAPTER SEVENTEEN

LETTING IT LIE

Charlie Peters was sitting in the chair in his cabin when his screen lit up with a new message. This was a day after we crossed the threshold into communications-friendly space, and his first act after finding out we were in range of a DCC ship was to send a message through our network to the Protectorate, so that he could let Lia know he was coming home.

He'd also informed her of what had happened, because she'd have wanted to know.

He hadn't heard back instantly — as much as he might have liked to have her reply in near-realtime, the reality was that the message had a long way to travel, and even when it arrived, it would have to be accommodated within the schedule of a Lady running a court government.

The fact that he was seeing a response on the same day was pretty telling as to how much Lia wanted to talk to her consort, and while Charlie can never be called a selfish or self-important fellow, he was privately pleased at the promptness. Made him feel good, and rightly so.

As he quickly manipulated his screen's remote, he called up the message and was greeted by Lia's face. She still had the more mature look that had seemed to come with her father's death, and the eyes of a woman who'd been to war and had scars to prove it. But she was smiling brightly.

"So glad you're back, and can't wait for you to get home," she said. "I'm getting all lonely without my consort."

She then proceeded to describe some of her expectations for his return — what many people call a 'honey-do' list, a lot of which you wouldn't be interested in, and some of which you'd be very interested in. After that was done, Lia turned her mind to the situation we'd found in the Union, as Charlie had described it, and she began shaking her head.

"I'm really surprised at what you said about Ken and Karen, though. I don't know what it is, but something just seems odd about the whole thing. I get killing Grant, but the way they did it…" She tapered off, then shrugged. "I guess they had their reasons. Maybe they were just playing it up for the cameras, because obviously those vid records are going to have to be released to the public sometime. When they don't bring a body in, everyone's going to want proof that he didn't escape, and that the Empire's not just trying to cover up a botched recovery mission."

Charlie honestly hadn't made the last connection. The benefit, again, of an outside perspective — especially the perspective of a wise woman like his Lady, who might have had a history of playing with sock puppets, but who was clearly a better leader than her father ever had been.

Sorry Lia, I don't mean to slam your father unduly, but it's true.

"Playing for the cameras…" Charlie wasn't in the habit of speaking to himself, but in this case he made the exception.

He watched the rest of Lia's message, and became somewhat uncomfortable when she reiterated a few points from the honey-do list, but once it was finished he took a deep breath and began to turn possibilities over in his mind.

My friend still refused to believe his eyes.

Later that evening, Wes was back in the med bay for another check up. He and Charlie hadn't spoken that day — after what they'd watched in the security office, they felt there was really very little to discuss.

Sitting on the medical bed that he'd been confined to for days, the Commodore of the Independent Squadron appeared to be in a rather unapproachable mood, but his expression was positively sunny compared to Alicia Morgan's.

As *Wolf's* doctor came over to begin checking the burns on Wes' chest, he greeted her with typical politeness, "Evening, Doctor."

She didn't so much as answer him, just reached out and pushed him on the shoulder to get him to lie down. He'd already shed his fatigue shirt, so Alicia started checking the dressings without a word, and Wes found her bedside manner to be altogether unpleasant.

"Look, I've been taking it easy," he decided to speak defensively on his own behalf, and it earned him a glare from Alicia.

"Just keep your hands where I can see them, Commodore."

Wes blinked, then frowned at her, "Excuse me?"

Alicia was clearly pissed. No politer word for it: not angry or livid, *pissed*. Because she was a doctor, and no matter what, she was not the sort to have any hand in killing. Now that rumors had made their way around the ship that Grant Merger had been tortured to death with a chemical agent that came out of her restricted drug lockup… well, she wasn't pleased.

Especially because she thought Wes was the one who lifted the Ketsan. Yeah seriously — Karen had been that good at getting it out without raising suspicions.

Wes didn't understand why he was getting the poor treatment at first, but as his mind started to roll over possibilities, he floated a comment for clarification, "You know how Grant died?"

Alicia was carefully peeling back a dressing, and I suppose had she been less of a professional, she could have been cruel and ripped it off. Of course, while that might look like a good and petty way to gain revenge, it actually could have medical consequences, so she didn't do it.

Instead she just locked her eyes onto Wes, "I don't like my lab being used that way."

The way she was saying those things, as if they were directed straight at Wes, caught him by surprise. Finally he put the question back to her: "You think *I* took the stuff?"

Alicia continued to glare at him, then nodded her head towards the store room that was just across from the foot of his bed, "You saying you didn't notice it was over there, all those days spent convalescing?"

It was an unusually hasty conclusion for a doctor as fine as Alicia, and Wes decided to put an end to it. His hand reached up to Alicia's arm, "I'm in here because Ken shot me, and you think I helped him kill Grant? Of course I know what's in that room… but everyone does. You're looking in the wrong place."

To this day, Alicia quite regrets that case of mistaken blame, and she still doesn't really know how she got it into her head that Wes would be so callous, especially considering his reason for being under her care.

Her expression started to mellow, though residual anger meant she didn't offer an apology. She was still responsible for the chemical that had killed Grant.

"How secure is that stuff anyway?" Wes asked, trying to bring Alicia around to consider who had taken the Ketsan.

With a sigh, our doctor shook her head, "Secure. It's a Schedule 2, so it's in with the rest of the dangerous compounds."

"You keep much of that stuff on hand?" Wes continued with an easy tone, and Alicia raised an eyebrow as she turned her eyes back to his dressings.

"We're not a weapons lab. There are a few dozen compounds in that lockup… most of it for use against a radiation leak, or other situations like that…"

Wes nodded, "Situations when the danger is more toxic than the drug meant to stop it."

"Exactly," Alicia confirmed, continuing her work on one of the bigger dressings. "Any of that stuff, when you overdose on it… it's a painful death."

Though we often take the safety of space travel for granted these days, I think it's worth remembering that there's a lot out in the black that can kill you… some that's native to that place (like the vacuum of space), and some that we take with us (like the radiation from reactors). When such unpleasant things come to kill you, much of the medicine… if you can call it that… that stands between you and death is pretty toxic.

Wes had always known as much — it was one reason he was glad he'd never been in Kris Jacobs' shoes, because the sheer volume of anti-rad drugs she'd been injected with at Io would have undoubtedly forced her into gene therapy, regardless of the radiation dose she took.

All of those thoughts were occurring to Wes as Alicia continued to check him out, and along with them came a question.

"So… was Ketsan the most painful one? Or were they being humane?"

It was a macabre question, but Alicia answered it anyway, "If they wanted to be humane, there's half a dozen compounds in there that would have killed him instantly. I wouldn't have pointed them out, but I'm sure they did research. They weren't as cruel as they could have been, though. They could have just gone down to Andy's storage room and gotten and injector full of irradiated coolant. Would have taken him a week to disintegrate from the radiation poisoning, and there'd be no way to stop it."

Wes frowned at those words, but tried not to show too much reaction as his mind churned over possibilities. Why go after a controlled medical substance when Andy had uncontrolled lethal fluids that were even crueler?

"I've never heard of Ketsan being used… it's bad in an overdose, though, obviously…" the Commodore continued to prod, and as Alicia finished peeling off his dressings and turned to collect the necessary paste to apply to his burns, she shrugged.

"I'm glad we've stopped using the stuff. There's only one OD recorded in the medical history. Freighter Captain must have thought he was going to double the time he had to get out of his bridge after a micro-meteor… this is back in the early 2100s, right. He doubled up but survived."

That last word made Wes involuntarily attempt to sit up, but Alicia put a hand on his shoulder, "Not done."

"He survived? Does that mean Grant might actually survive?"

Alicia hadn't been party to any thoughts, hopes or other silly notions that we might not have killed Grant — at this point, that fiction was contained to just Wes and Charlie. That being the case, she answered with a frown and a shake of her head, "Oh no. They used that full bottle… he'd have taken hours to liquefy. In agony and conscious the whole time."

That sounded about right, but Wes wasn't convinced.

"They used a syringe… the kind from the first aid kits. Would that amount kill him?"

Alicia still didn't know why he was asking these questions (she was having a bad day, cut her some slack), but with a frown she thought about the syringes that were normally packed in med kits for use after an EMP pulse.

"The whole syringe… it'd probably actually take him a bit longer to die. So even more painful."

Not what Wes was hoping to hear. How could less hurt more? Well, as with many things, letting a person die slowly just lengthened the time spent suffering. In the end, the hateful thing about chemical weapons (as we learned in *The Dark Cruise*) is their effects are in no way compassionate. Either you have a lethal dose or you don't… but some lethal doses take longer to kill than others.

"Yeah, any more than half of one of those syringes and he's done for. And even if they just doubled his dose, the consequences would be pretty dire," Alicia's words were dark. "That freighter skipper had huge amounts of brain damage. Lost a lot of motor skills… though that might have been due to the cellular destruction caused by the ice crystals. The cold cost him two legs and a hand, and they didn't have gene therapy to fix the damage back then."

Another part of space travel Wes wasn't a fan of — he didn't envy Mark Gunney all the therapy he was having to do just to get walking again, though it was fair to say *Cheetah's* skipper was better off than if he'd been hit with a proper dose of Ketsan. Microfilament bags really did work… though they weren't perfect.

"He also had total and permanent memory loss. Didn't know who he was. Never recovered," Alicia shook her head as she added that fact, and for a second Wes didn't process the meaning of her words.

Of course, after that second my dear friend Wes — with his desperate need to believe that Karen and I had not killed Grant — seized upon their possible implication.

"Total memory loss?" he asked.

"One of the side effects. Don't know how extensive… I suppose it's in the journals, but I haven't looked since med school. Still, not a good way to be."

Not a good way at all, Wes thought to himself. And if anyone on *Wolf* could speak to the harm caused by lost memories, it was the person who had stuck the syringe in Grant Merger's arm.

It was all Wes could do to stay still on the medical bed for the remainder of his treatment; he wanted to go talk to Charlie. He wanted to hope.

CHAPTER EIGHTEEN
PUBLIC OPINION

While Wes and Charlie were putting their heads together to try to find ways to believe that Karen and I had not killed Grant, Daragh Ryan was drinking a fine glass of scotch whiskey in celebration of the fucker's demise.

Sitting in one of his over-sized offices with the Prime Minister and the Foreign Secretary, the mad Irishman was feeling more than a little relieved at the outcome of the mission — particularly since a day of analysis from DCI had suggested that no immediate threat existed from the Union of Solar Asteroids.

"Looks like we taught those fuckers their fucking fuck lesson!" the Emperor was obviously pleased with himself, and Craig B. Macdonald made a face.

"I'm *Scottish* and I don't even know how you get that many 'fucks' into a sentence."

"Practice," Daragh countered, and sipped his scotch again. "This whiskey of your people encourages it, you bastard."

"I think the question put forward by John Fiora is a good one," Douglas Pope wasn't about to involve himself in a Celtic rivalry, so he moved the conversation forward. "Do we reach out to the Union now, and offer more formal relations?"

It wasn't on option our Prime Minister was terribly enthusiastic about; he couldn't imagine how a relationship could realistically begin on any positive terms after what had happened. Sure, there was good news inasmuch as the collateral damage was light... but to try to send an Ambassador at this point would be incredibly awkward.

'Oh sorry about that, we didn't mean to wipe out half your fleet, but you *were* asking for it. Would you like to purchase our cheaper manufactured goods?'

"They helped the Martians, and knowingly or unknowingly, they sheltered enemies of the Empire. Still can't fucking believe that stuffed stocking full of shit was out there." Daragh meant Dave Caldecott in that case, and just to punctuate his observation, he added: "That little bastard had a very uncomfortable taste in chairs. When I moved into his office I started to lose feeling in my fucking legs."

Yes, I think you can tell that Daragh was generally pleased with the outcome of the mission. He was a mad Irishman whose hospitality at that ball had been abused, and now the fools responsible had their comeuppance.

But the important thing for us to understand was that Daragh wasn't alone in his enthusiasm. I'm not sure if this proves Grant's point about the nature of the 'common people' in the Empire or not, but as soon as news was released indicating that Grant Merger had been executed, approval for the action seemed universal.

Literally — and I'll never understand this — people started gathering outside of government offices, and Defense Command bases, cheering and sharing in their common sense of relief. It was by no means as widespread an outpouring of joy as the one that came after the wartime ceasefire... but it was still a lot more pronounced than I would have expected.

The media bought right in as well — every broadcast channel was showing retro-spective documentaries on the menace Grant had posed, throwing in the limited information that had been released about his attack on Karen at the ball. Some of the most interesting (occasionally humorous) pieces that were running included speculative stuff about what the Belt Squadron had found when we went hunting him. I think one fanciful news station even did a simulation in which Charlie and I had to slay a dragon to get to Grant. I suppose that was just imagery for something more tangible, but still, a dragon. Imagine the sass of that.

The general elation was catching politicians like Douglas Pope slightly off guard — not that they had reason to be defensive, but largely because like so many of the responsible people in charge of our Empire, they had spent days worrying about what could occur if things went horribly wrong on the mission. Now that it had mostly worked out, they could afford to feel some relief... but for those people who knew only the few details that had been widely released, it was a triumph.

Tarnished only by the fact that we weren't bringing home a body for them to stare at.

"My office has had several complaints that they're not bringing the body back for a spectacle," the PM said eventually. "I think there's an appetite out there to make sure this is big... but we won't have a prop."

Daragh nodded, "Bad luck."

Craig B. Macdonald was a little less psychotic than the Emperor, so he shook his head, "Maybe not. No body means less time to keep this whole mess in the news cycle, and fewer opportunities later for people to obsess. Could be the best decision Ken made on the whole damned mission: don't give us too many tangible things to hold onto and make it easier for people to move on."

That was the right perspective, as far as I was concerned. Though the spectacle of a public trial or the display of Grant's remains might have served the vid channels well, it seemed better to just let everyone get back to more peaceful thoughts.

Of course, Grant would have said that the fact that we had to control the message to avoid inciting violent passion in the minds of our voting citizens was a sign of the weakness of the Empire. He'd be wrong. It's a sign that the Empire respects the right of every living body to participate. And it allows those who excel the equal chance to lead.

Managing the death of this villain was a chore — the three leaders in this room knew that better than most. But it was a small price to pay for the greatest Empire that has ever existed.

"Well here's to peace at last. For now. Hopefully," Daragh was still in too good a mood to be brought down by talk of spectacles and public opinion. He raised his glass, and with a glance at each other, the PM and the Foreign Secretary did the same.

Earth would welcome Karen and me home, because the good common people of our planet had no problem with what Karen and me — two other common people — had done.

Unfortunately, we had to deal with one last stab of denial.

CHAPTER NINETEEN

LIES

I think we've already established that the thing Grant never benefited from, which could truly have changed so much about his life, was the presence of good friends — the sort of people who saw the good in him. I had been his friend, but I had left him... so perhaps by some twisted definition, I was partly to blame for all the destruction he wrought.

But really, he had left Karen and me... and had left himself alone. Because of that, he never had the people he needed to build his faith in humanity — never had a reason to think that maybe not everyone was as stupid as he desperately wanted to believe. That was a great disadvantage for him in life. However, as is often the case with disadvantages, they do come with silver linings: namely, Grant never had to endure the awkward conversation that arises when two of your best friends come to you and insist you didn't actually kill someone.

Two days before we were due to return to Earth, Karen and I had just finished supper in my cabin when the knock came at the door. She looked at me, and I looked at her, both somewhat surprised to be interrupted during supper (me especially, because I remembered how rare such an interruption was).

Pushing her tray aside on the bed, Karen swung her legs over the side, hopped to her feet and went to the hatch... then opened it to reveal Charlie and Wes standing there with odd expressions on their faces. Maybe the right word is hopeful. They looked as though they were carrying good news — as if they could tell us something we didn't know, that would make the day better than it was.

Since it had been a pretty decent day, it was hard for me to predict what that news might be.

"Can we come in for a minute?" Wes asked Karen almost formally, and she shrugged and stepped back to allow them through the door.

"Okay," was her answer, and then she turned to me with eyes that said 'what the hell are they doing here?'

Since I didn't know, I asked: "So. What the hell are you guys doing here?"

I made sure to ask it positively — so that the 'hell' sounded ironic instead of rude — and as the hatch shut behind them and Karen returned to the bed, Wes and Charlie both planted their feet on the deck facing the bed and the chair. Then they both folded their arms, which was a bit dramatic, and proceeded to just stare at us.

Wes points out to me today that despite the hours they had spent discussing their theories, and checking them against the evidence that had been recorded, they hadn't actually figured out how to initiate this discussion. The fact that two of the finest tactical minds I've ever had the privilege to serve with — let alone call friends — had overlooked such a detail gives you some idea as to how distracted they were by this particular situation.

Finally, though, Charlie opened fire: "We know you're faking it."

My eyebrow went up, and both of Karen's eyebrows went up. Then, bless her, she demonstrated how not-seriously we were determined to take this conversation: "I never fake it."

Read what you like into that.

"Sometimes I fake it, but I don't think that's what we're talking about," I added.

That earned me a glance from Karen, and she was full-well ready to follow that tangent into an oblivion where decorum doesn't exist... but Wes interdicted.

"Oh you can try to deflect. But we know what happened."

Sorry Wes, but that was a pretty big claim. Karen was still looking at me as he spoke, and her expression changed slightly before she responded, "Is that so?"

Wes glanced sideways at Charlie, and that seemed to be enough of a signal for the Hawke Lord to begin: "You had to decide what to do with Grant. And after our last meeting, it was pretty clear to us that you weren't as inclined to kill him as both Wes and I had assumed. But you didn't have any choice... you had to do something... so what about a chance to turn the tables? Do to him what he'd done to you, Karen? Take away the one thing that he cares about most?"

As if scripted, Wes picked up at this point, "I talked to Alicia about Ketsan. It's a hell of a way to die, but there are more painful ways to kill someone, and some of those ways are much more convenient than a medical compound kept under lock and key in her storeroom. No, you'd only choose Ketsan if it had certain properties that you needed. Namely, the ability to cause brain damage in an overdose."

"It's a perfect scenario," Charlie was next. "You choose a chemical that *will* kill a man, if a significant dose is administered. You take enough to deliver that lethal dose, and you use an injection device that is manually controlled, so that you can administer as much or as little as you like, with no evidence left behind. Then all you have to do is stick him with enough to wipe his brain and cause pain... but not enough to kill him."

"And then," it was Wes again, "you pile him into an escape pod, along with rations, a facial reconstruction kit, and the rest of the Ketsan, so that no one knows exactly how much you gave him. When he wakes up, he'll have no idea who he is, but you probably could put a note in that duffle to warn him that he needs to change his face, and never be seen again. It's the perfect way to get rid of him while you *look like* you're killing him."

Charlie again: "Because, as my consort pointed out to me, you had to play this whole scenario for the cameras. You knew that if you didn't bring a body back to be turned into a spectacle, there would be a lot of questions about where Grant was, and whether he was really dead. So you had to stage a very brutal execution so that people could look for themselves and see that you had truly done it."

"And if something went wrong," Wes finished up his part, "you could always just blame the Ketsan — say you read the instructions wrong, and that you expected to kill him. But really, you didn't expect to kill him. That was never your plan. You rigged the pod to launch without alarms to try to give him enough time to get away free. You came up with plausible-sounding excuses to steal supplies for him, and you voiced those reasons on camera to dismiss any challenges from observers. Then you tossed that duffle into the pod with him, ostensibly to get rid of the evidence..."

"But really, you were just giving him one more chance to be a different man. It's not a sure thing the Union ship that was tailing us would pick him up, or that he'd ever be found… but you gave him a real chance. It was a very crafty plan. I commend you both. But we've seen through it," Charlie had the last word, and then they both fell silent, honestly seeming a bit proud to have pieced it all together.

It was very convincing too — this theory (or conspiracy theory, if you like) — has chased Karen and me around ever since we got back. Of course, it took time for it to find its way into more public circles, either through rumor or because other people outside the squadron did the same sort of homework Wes and Charlie had, and reached the same conclusions.

They were so desperate to believe we hadn't murdered Grant, they were doing all they could to cast doubt on the murder that we had so very clearly put on camera for them. And now it looked as though they expected us to confirm their suspicions.

Glancing again at Karen, I saw the rather amused expression on her face. She looked at me too, and apparently my face reflected the same sentiment.

"Jesus," she smiled, "I told you we should have kept his head on a pike."

"Only way people believe you these days. I thought vid would be enough," I agreed.

Charlie and Wes weren't impressed by our deflections.

"Come on now, you're caught," Wes shook his head. "Don't be coy. Why else would you throw him in that pod?"

Karen answered that one: "Because if we didn't, and you two came down, you might have been able to get him to Alicia in time to get the Ketsan out of his system. Or even just to put him out of his misery."

"Yeah, and shooting someone off into deep space is a pretty good way to kill them most of the time, anyway," I added.

Wes' brow creased, "Yes, but you threw in rations. Bacon. He likes bacon."

"And the facial reconstruction kit," Charlie added. "You have to admit, the contents you pulled out of that duffle on camera did seem like a getaway kit for a spy."

"Well if I was trying to help him get away, why would I have pulled them out on camera?" I countered, and that good question quieted both Wes and Charlie for a moment.

But Wes wasn't done, "The Ketsan. Why the Ketsan when you could have gone down to one of Andy's unlocked storage lockers and gotten irradiated coolant? Would have taken longer for him to die, and it probably would have been more painful."

"Because making someone radioactive is usually a risky thing and should be avoided," Karen made that rather good point.

Wes blinked and looked at her, then shook his head, "No, you wanted the *only* compound available on this ship that would be guaranteed to cause memory loss."

I shrugged, "Well it sounds like you talked to someone smarter than us. We wanted the only compound on this ship that could cause that much pain, and compel consciousness, while still not making Grant's corpse a danger to anyone."

"Why would you care if it was radioactive if you're shooting him into deep space?" Charlie asked that pointed question, but Karen caught him on the flank.

"Deep space? Hell, I'd be more worried about getting dosed while I dragged him to the airlock. The chances of a dangerous level of exposure were low, but why take the risk when we had the right tool at our fingertips?"

Both Wes and Charlie had expected us to give up by this point — to simply admit that they'd caught us in a lie, and that Grant was soon to wake up, confused and alone in a lifepod with plenty of rations, the ability to change his appearance, and a note containing instructions about how to begin a new life that reflected none of his bad old habits.

But obviously we couldn't admit such a thing to our friends, because it wasn't true. And there were good reasons it wasn't true.

As both our interventionists fell into silence, going back over their own theory of the crime in their heads and wondering why we were so resistant, Karen piped up with additional rationale: "What would we gain by keeping him alive? Even without his memories, what if he stumbled back to Earth and was genetically printed at any point? The alarms would ring and people would discover that the man we said was dead, was in fact alive."

"Grant tampered with his own DNA samples before he started the Syndicate," Wes pointed out — and sure, he was right. Remember that on 10 September, 2222, just before we met him on Capital Island, the villain had infiltrated DC's central archive, and replaced the genetic prints from his Academy file with false ones.

Of course, Karen didn't remember that now because we'd only discovered it after his failed attack on Earth. There would have been absolutely no reason for me to explain it to her before this moment, so she looked to me with the question: "That true?"

I nodded, "He was a clever boy. That's why he was on Capital Island the day we met with him in 2222."

"Interesting," she answered, clearly demonstrating that she hadn't learned that fact while we'd been planning Grant's death.

"So there," Wes was insistent. "You knew that he couldn't be identified if he changed his appearance... you decided that you could spare him and reset him, and now you're just perpetuating the lie."

The Commodore of the Independent Squadron was still pretty gung-ho about this theory, though Charlie had gone quiet, and seemed to be alternately reading the expressions on my face and Karen's. He was coming to his own conclusions...

"What I don't understand..." Karen decided to put an end to this fun discussion, though she looked at me as she spoke, "...is why the two of you are trying to invent a story that will get us hanged."

Charlie didn't respond to that, but Wes did with a frown, "What do you..."

Then it struck him. However, even though I saw the realization on his face, this was one time I wasn't going to leave the obvious unsaid. It was rather vital to both Karen and me that everyone — our dearest friends included — were left in no doubt of the fact that we had murdered Grant Merger, in cold blood.

"Grant was an enemy of the Empire, correct?" I asked as I came to my feet, and both friends turned their eyes in my direction.

"Correct," Wes helped me out with that answer.

"What you're suggesting is that, instead of killing him, or bringing him back for trial... either of which would be our duty as Imperial officers who had him in custody... we basically helped him escape."

That exact thought was the one that had come to Wes' mind, and he tilted his head, "Without his memories."

"Memories or not, he was an enemy of the Empire. It was our duty to kill him, and we did that," Karen reinforced the truth.

"If you guys were right, and we let him go, maybe that would mean we were better people than we are. But that's not the case," I persisted. "We all know that deep down, Karen and I are cold-blooded killers, and that we tortured Grant to death. Because if we didn't — if we helped him escape — that would actually mean we'd aided and abetted an enemy of the Empire. And under the Articles, that would make us, Karen and myself, enemies of Empire as well."

"Us and anyone who knew about it, and didn't turn us in," Karen added helpfully.

Wes looked from me to Karen and back. Then he looked at Charlie.

Charlie was staring at me, and his eyes were slightly narrow.

"Do you think that we'd really risk the rest of our lives, and our careers, and the lives and careers of everyone on this ship... of both of you... just to give one more chance to the son of a bitch who tried to destroy Earth, who killed the crew of *Idaho*, who attacked me?" Karen asked gently. "Why would we do that?"

Wes opened his mouth to say something, but he stopped himself. He looked again at Charlie, who was studying me carefully, and whose mind was working through everything that had been said.

The Hawke Lord didn't believe us, and neither did the Independent Squadron's Commodore. But now he had a good reason as to why we couldn't admit what he believed to be the truth; because while every moral argument in the cosmos might have concluded that we — Karen and I — had the right to give Grant a reprieve, the Articles of Empire allowed only one possible fate for him: death.

There was no way any officer of the Empire could capture Grant and then knowingly punish him with less than that, without being condemned along with him. There was no statute of limitation on treachery; if we'd let Grant go, and he'd ever resurfaced, Karen and I would face death. Charlie understood that, and he believed it was the answer to the question — the answer he could never hear from us, but which he felt had to be true.

"So," Lord Major Charlie Peters of Hawke said, "we have to decide if you two would be willing to risk your lives, and the lives of the people you command, in order to do the morally right thing."

Charlie Peters is a fucker. This means you, Charlie. Fuck you. Stupid believe good things about me.

"You might have to wonder that," I narrowed my eyes at him. "But we know the answer."

Karen now slid off the bed and got to her feet, coming around to stand on Charlie's other side. He didn't so much as move to acknowledge her, he just kept his eyes on me. He figured he had his truth, but obviously he was wrong. We killed Grant Merger — I can't say it enough, I can't offer more proof. Killing Grant was the right thing to do, and my only regret is that I didn't cut out his heart or something, so people would never have started this stupid rumor that he's alive, that we let him live.

Because obviously we *wouldn't do that*.

"They killed him," Wes said with a smile, and placed a hand on Charlie's shoulder. My friend from the Independent Squadron didn't believe what he was saying, but he knew it was what had to be said. "Well done. They killed him, Charlie."

The Lord Major said nothing… he just started to smile.

Then, with a very slight nod, Charlie ended the conversation, "Alright then, we'll leave you two alone. Have a good evening."

"A very good evening," Wes agreed.

Both those fine fellows seemed a good deal lighter when they left, and to this day they'll tell you they felt like they had their answers. Since then, of course, they've both come to terms with the fact that we truly did murder Grant in cold blood. The conspiracy theorists have occasionally found ways to ask them directly, and in all those cases their answers have been clear: Grant Merger is a bloated corpse somewhere.

But then the theorists, being theorists, just assume that Charlie and Wes are lying to protect me and Karen. It's a never-ending cycle of disbelief — and no amount of evidence will break it. Not that there's any more evidence than the vids. Sorry about that, I guess Karen and I were just too neat when we murdered Grant.

By me repeating it over and over — that we murdered Grant — are you believing it? Fine, believe what you like, but if you try to bring charges you'll run straight into a brick wall. Because he's dead and we killed him.

"Do you really fake it?" Karen had to end this whole conversation with that question — asked just after the door shut behind Charlie and Wes.

I'm not going to tell you what my answer was, because that would start a conspiracy theory too. We spent the night determining an answer.

CHAPTER TWENTY

HOMECOMING

Though we'd been in safe Imperial space for days, it really was a relief for everyone when we finally got home to Earth. Seeing the whole fleet there — the *Bonnies*, the Independent Squadron, the Heavy and Light Squadrons, all the might of Defense Command — was always a reassuring thing for us fleet types. No matter what had gone on, or who we'd picked a fight with, we knew there was help at hand.

And that we were home.

Those hours as we pulled back into Earth local space were some of the only ones of the entire mission that Karen ventured to *Wolf's* bridge. Even though she had no particular sense of belonging in the command chamber of the frigate we'd shared for the war, she still thought it important to see out the final leg there. And it was appreciated.

"Good to see you up here, ma'am," Jim nodded to her as she arrived, and then both Felicia and Shelby moved to the edges of their banks of consoles to shake her hand in turn.

It was a warm welcome for Karen, and she quite appreciated it... though it left her (unsurprisingly at this point, I suppose) feeling a bit odd.

She couldn't put her finger on the reason for that strange feeling — at least not right there — but she filed it away for future consideration, then spent a bit of time surveying the bridge.

Up on the main screen was an enhanced-cam shot of Earth, and all across the secondary screens were the faces of our skippers. With the whole fleet laid out in orbit, the effect of the visual was astounding — all the power of the Empire arrayed to welcome home weary travelers who had gone forth and done right by the Articles of Empire.

I was with Karen, I should have mentioned, and as we approached those screens, the skippers up on Battlelink greeted her with smiles.

"Look who's come for dinner," Matt Baxter said warmly, referencing (poorly) some movie I've never seen.

"If she's lucky, she won't remember what a pain in the ass I am," Mark Gunney pitched in.

Karen didn't miss that opportunity, "I learned that on the way out, remember Mark?"

"I thought we weren't going to speak of that," *Cheetah's* skipper grinned.

It was all very friendly — as though life were back to normal. But (and I undoubtedly don't have to point this out to you by now), it wasn't normal. Maybe we should start a drinking game for those alcoholically inclined: every time I say something had changed, you drink one liter of spirits.

My editors think that would be a bad idea, because we might be liable for a lot of drinking-related deaths. Fine, skip the game.

The point is, Karen was watching everything happening on the bridge, and feeling the same sense of wonder that she'd always had about command decks. One of the absolute highlights of her career had been standing watch on *Alberta*, not during combat or anything fancy, just when the ship was cruising. She'd stood watches for Greg back then, and thought she was in absolute heaven.

Now *Wolf's* bridge was even newer, shinier, and more impressive than that of our old *North America*-class ship. It was like being in the future… I suppose it *was* being in the future, and Karen marveled at it.

And still it felt strange.

Why that was, we can talk about later. For now we were getting into realtime range of the planet, and we had no exact idea of what to expect. Would we have a welcome fit for heroes, or just a standard approach?

Before we were to find out the bridge hatch opened again, admitting both Wes Pellew and Charlie Peters. Strictly speaking, neither of them belonged on *Wolf's* command deck, but what the hell, we were home and they deserved to see it too.

"Closing to realtime range," Felicia Khalid reported as we crossed the comm threshold. "Signal coming in from Admiralty House."

That report was directed officially at Andrea Kiley, even though with me, Karen, Charlie and Wes all crowding around her (all of us much taller than she is, she'll be delighted for me to point out) it was almost difficult for her to respond.

"Window in screen one, please," she answered unseen.

With a tap on the shoulder of one of her techs — her deputy, Gavin Nigh, in fact — Felicia prompted that window to open, and a *Wolf*Net buffering screen to appear. Because we were just talking to Admiralty House, the signal didn't take long to load. We all waited to see who we'd get — John Fiora, the PM… the Emperor…

Not at all lofty, our expectations, were they?

When the feed glowed into life, it turned out we were massively right on all fronts: the signal was being directed through the Admiralty House transmitter, but it originated from one of the chambers in the Terra Nova Palace. Daragh was there, along with John and Douglas Pope, and they were all making a point of smiling.

This immediately indicated to all of us on the bridge that the feed had to be open — broadcasting live to everyone on the planet, and eventually out to the rest of the Empire. Good thing I'd shaved.

"Welcome home to Earth, *Wolf*. Bring the Belt Squadron into orbit over Capital Island and make ready to come down to see us. The whole world is looking forward to your story," the fact that it was Daragh who offered the first greeting was even more telling. This was a complete exercise in political capitalization, and while I suppose that sounds like a terrible thing, remember that Grant's attack had come on the heels of the first attempted coup in the history of the Empire.

After people had seen the throne and the House of Commons basically start a mini-shooting war on Capital Island, here was a visual that would represent the unity that now bonded our two halves of government. The throne was welcoming home the Belt Squadron, and we were going to be political footballs for a while.

I suppose that's insufficient penance, considering what we'd done. And yes, by all means go ahead and wonder what it must have been like for the SAU people, when recordings of this heroic welcome got back to them. In their minds we were monsters and criminals — pirates who had captured and killed a beloved Governor on charges we'd never properly substantiated — and yet the whole Empire was welcoming us home.

It's all about where you're sitting, I suppose.

For now, my old media instincts kicked in. I looked to my left at Karen, and then to my right at Andrea, Wes and Charlie. Then I looked back to the viewfinder (very squarely, knowing that would give the camera people the shot they needed), and smiled.

"We read you, Emperor Ryan. Thanks for the welcome, it's good to be home."

I may have lifted the wording and the inflection from an old movie about a disastrous flight in the early days of the American moon landing program, but sorry, I was caught a little off guard.

With that the feed cut, because apparently they didn't need anything else.

"Looks like we'll be the circus for a while," Wes said, though he didn't sound as glum as he usually did when the media was poking into his affairs.

Apparently, convincing himself of that lie about me and Karen not killing Grant had brightened his spirits.

"Well, you heard the Emperor: squadron into orbit over Capital Island," I looked up to the screens, and Andrea simultaneously nodded to Shelby McLaws.

It was the homecoming for the Belt Squadron, and we'd do it right one more time.

Karen watched with interest, and wondered how many times she'd done this over the past twelve years. She figured, rightly, that the answer was probably 'a lot'.

We were home.

Chapter Twenty-One
Rebuilding

In a way, it was very helpful that Charlie and Wes had grilled us so thoroughly before we got back to Earth, because of course the first thing we had to endure upon our arrival was a press conference. And it was a long one. According to some histories I've reviewed, it was actually the longest press conference that was ever broadcast live, from start to finish, in the history of the Empire... and nothing was sacred.

People wanted to know about Grant, whether he was really dead, whether we'd secretly put him in an evil Imperial prison where he could be tortured into eternity (wish we'd thought of that one, actually, but alas no such prisons exist), whether the Union was a threat, whether Karen was still in shape to command a squadron, whether Karen and I were lovers, whether the injuries inflicted on Wes Pellew were truly a result of my shooting, and whether there would be diplomatic repercussions.

They wanted to know how it felt to kill the assassins, whether I expected to see the children of the Connaughts on a vendetta in the future, whether the wounded and at that time anonymous spy would recover, and whether the spy who had brought Grant down had survived (unfortunately, she 'hadn't' — just a white lie to protect Haley). They wanted to know if any of the old Syndicate organization still survived in the Union, if more expeditions would be sent to bring the SAUs to heel, if I'd be remaining with the Belt Squadron, and if Karen was beginning to remember anything yet.

And that was just the first hour.

Even with all my media experience, I found this marathon of questioning to be quite a trial. And Karen, now having lost that experience, was entirely overwhelmed. Of course she bore up under the onslaught, because she's still a goddess, but it was a long day.

By the time we were able to retire back to Admiralty House, we were glad of the respite, though I wasn't looking forward to discussing the entire situation with John. I'd burned him by going to Daragh with my request to command the mission, and I hadn't conducted myself in a manner that, frankly, would have made him proud. This was no great joy for me, and it wasn't for him either, but we were long-time friends, and I'd learned a great deal from him over the years.

As he settled into his chair and shook his head, he opened the conversation with an observation that no one could disagree with, "I hate those things."

John was no rookie when it came to dealing with the press (obviously), but it was fair to say that conference had been something else. Pouring himself a glass of water from the pitcher on his desk, and then offering glasses to Karen and me, he shook his head.

"Glad the news you brought back was well-received. I didn't expect problems, and there's nothing that was beyond the threshold people will accept right now... but still, good that we've cleared the first hurdle."

The way he put that said everything I needed to know: John was glad we weren't dealing with a complete mess, but he wasn't exactly happy about where I'd gone, or how I'd acted while I was there. It was not a good feeling for me, I must be honest — to disappoint the man who, as the Commandant of the Academy, had done so much to help get both myself and Karen on a track that shaped our lives.

It was not something I thought about much during the cruise to the Union — I suppose such thoughts are easy to leave behind when you're in the midst of so much chaos — but now that things were settling again, I did have regrets.

But there was nothing I could do to change my actions. Indeed, an apology in itself would seem inadequate. Honesty was all I could offer.

"I think we'll find our way back," was my answer to his comment — an answer which admittedly had little to do with what he'd said. John looked up from his glass of water with a frown at those words, and then began to read my expression.

Then, worthless or not, I said it: "I'm sorry, John. Truly."

The First Lord of the Admiralty continued to stare at me for a moment, his mind replaying everything he'd thought but not said about my actions. Nearly plunging the Empire into a war, killing an enemy of the Empire in cold blood... I'd certainly gone off in a different direction than he'd have wanted. But there was a lot more to our friendship than commonality of action, or unity of thought. It wasn't going to be automatic, or easy, but he and I both knew we would find our way.

"Okay," he answered simply — a single word laden with meaning. "For now, we need to start looking at new deployments. Mik has been reviewing the tactical data about the Union for us, and he doesn't see much of a threat in the short term. That your assessment?"

Right back to business — an Empire to protect — and relieved at the change in direction, I nodded, "Not for now. They're not building specialized warships, and they don't have convincing main armaments. We'll need to worry if their mags... disruptors, they call them... get better. And if their torpedoes improve."

John nodded again, "DCI is going to keep an eye. Mel Samuels has taken over, by the way, so I expect we'll have a much clearer picture. Right now her people estimate we have a five-year buffer... but we're not going to take that for granted."

Of course we wouldn't; John was as much a student of history as I was, so he knew about some infamous five-year buffers from Earth's past. For something like a decade, American intelligence had been convinced that the Soviet Union was five years away from going nuclear... you do the math on that sentence and explain to me why the Americans were surprised when one day the Soviets ended up with nuclear weapons.

'But I thought we had five years!' was the cry.

'Yeah, that's what we told you ten years ago!' was the answer.

"It's going to be important to keep strong formations out on rotation. The PM thinks the political will now exists for that — the people are keen to ensure Grant's cronies don't come looking for revenge. So we'll be able to maintain Naval strength well above pre-war levels... mainly in battleships."

I nodded, "Good. One battleship would probably decimate their whole fleet, so keeping them out on station wouldn't be bad."

"Our thoughts exactly. We'll be sorting out the deployments... I'll sit you down with Greg and Marlene to help with that... but for now, we need to talk about you," John shifted his eyes from me to Karen. "And *you.*"

You might have noticed Karen's conspicuous silence in this meeting so far — she had said not a word, and indeed, had no idea how to contribute. Keep in mind that she had no experience dealing with fleet or even squadron deployment, and she'd never sat in the First Lord's Office and been solicited for an opinion.

Her silence had been nice and safe, and as she listened to John and I go back and forth, she understood what we were saying, but didn't feel at all comfortable contributing any opinions to the mix.

But now the spotlight was on her, and she shifted slightly in her chair, "Talk about me?"

John nodded slowly, his face beginning to cloud, "We will not reduce your rank. That'll never happen. But we need to be practical about your appointment, because your experience..."

"I'm a Commander, but somebody typed it wrong and it came out 'Commodore,'" Karen nodded. "No need to sugarcoat it, sir."

She called John 'sir'.

That actually set the First Lord back for a second, but he pressed on: "The best option might be to keep things simple. If you two retain command of the Belt Squadron, and the services of Captain Kiley as *Wolf's* skipper, it could be a good opportunity for on-the-job training."

Quite a generous suggestion, it has to be said. John had been struggling with the options for Karen for quite some time, because as much as it would have been nice to simply say she was ready for whatever role a Commodore, or a Rear Admiral, could be granted, that factually wasn't the case.

If he took advantage of the fact that having a Commodore working under a Rear Admiral in command of a squadron like ours was sort of superfluous, he could justify putting her back into the role. And then, together, Karen and I could find our new way, and get her up to speed for squadron command.

Because it was Karen, I knew she could do it — knew she'd be better at it than me in just a few years.

So it was a perfect posting, a testament to John's deft handling of his best people.

"I don't think so," was Karen's answer.

I was surprised — honestly shocked — and the frown that sunk onto John's brow revealed his reaction was the same.

Knowing that she needed to explain herself, Karen took a breath and then shifted in her seat, "I've been thinking about this... and I think I should go on the sick list. I'm not sure where the right place for me is anymore, and I don't think I should fill a post just because of who I am. Or, more properly, who I was. Let me stay ashore here on Earth for a while... get my bearings and see what I want to be good at. Then I'll find a way, either in the Navy... or out."

She hadn't planned to say that — but then, she hadn't planned to say anything at all. It just came out (rather eloquently, because it's Karen and she's perfect) when her subconscious finally decided to confront why she'd been feeling strange on the bridge back aboard *Wolf*, and in this office now.

Why go back to the fleet? Just because that's where she'd been before? Our decision about Grant had stemmed from a determination to make choices based on what felt right for who we were now… and this is what she had in mind.

This course of action made perfect sense to her in that moment; the only question she had was what I'd think. Even with her twelve-year memory gap, she knew how rare it was for us not to immediately be on the same page, and when she looked at my expression, it was clear to her that I hadn't seen this coming.

But that was okay, I had time to consider her words…

"Ken?"

By time, I mean about four seconds.

Karen McMaster wanted to be put on the sick list — removed from active fleet duty so that she could spend some time rediscovering herself, in a safe place where the lives of others wouldn't depend on her. I had an offer for squadron command, or indeed, command of Belt Two station. I could go on with another step in my promising and heroic career. I could go do that, while she recovered… or maybe I could stay with her.

If you think that was a hard choice for me, GET YOUR FUCKING HEAD CHECKED.

Sorry, that was an overreaction.

"You need anyone to mop up around here? Or get the coffee? I don't drink coffee, but I could run and get it for you," I asked, my eyes fixed on Karen.

John didn't get the joke at first, "What?"

Turning back to him, I spoke through gritted teeth, "I'm trying to come across as gallant. Please find me a posting on Capital Island so I can stay with her."

"Oh," John responded. Then, as though he'd thought of this contingency, he nodded, "I'll make you Fifth Lord."

I blinked at that… an Admiralty Lordship (even the stupid placeholder one) seemed a lot more than I deserved. Nevertheless, it was a perfect position — a role that, as I've said before, was usually just used to park someone who didn't have a proper assignment, but who needed to be kept at the ready in case future requirements demanded his or her talents.

Since I had no talents to speak of, I could expect to sit in that chair for a long, long time.

Karen smiled, and I smiled, and then — and I'm glad about this — John smiled.

Our immediate future was not with the fleet, it was on Earth. And that meant there would have to be many other changes.

CHAPTER TWENTY-TWO

NEW HOMES

When Greg, Marlene and I sat down the following week to discuss the state of the Empire, it really was with a completely different perspective on things. My decision in John's office — to leave squadron duty behind — had been as much a surprise to me as it was to Karen, and everyone else who later found out. But it felt right.

For me, it was the end of more than a decade of work on the bridge — all those years fighting pirates, and then the Martians. A whole lot of life spent pacing back and forth in front of screens, making decisions that literally could change the fate of whole colonies, and knowing the wrong judgment on my part could cost lives.

Had I been good at it? I'm told I was, and I'm past the point of arguing. But now I had an excellent reason to try to be good at something else. Leaving on my own terms thus felt right. It also gave me a chance to really help shape the course of things to come after my departure.

That was the purpose of the meeting with Greg and Marlene. Like John, they'd both had their reservations about the events of 2235, but with the passage of time those concerns were subsumed. That's not to say either Greg or Marlene would have approved of the decisions I made in the Union — don't think I'm trying to invoke them for any sort of moral support. It just means that, as we moved forward again, our old rhythms returned.

And there was a lot to do.

"Belt Squadron," Greg was sitting at the head of the table in one of Admiralty House's briefing rooms, and the first file in front of him was, of course, for the Belt Squadron. That formation had once been his, was officially still mine, and soon it needed to be passed to another officer.

There was really only one person I could recommend for that job, and I said the name with no reservation: "Wes Pellew."

Greg looked up from the file, then nodded, "Wes Pellew. And we'll make him a Rear Admiral."

Wes had certainly earned that, and I don't just mean because I'd shot him. I knew he'd be reluctant to leave his Independent Squadron — he'd truly turned that formation into something incredible, a fine partner for our Belt Squadron out in the asteroids. But now he could come home again, to the bridge of *Wolf*.

"Should we put a Commodore with him?" Marlene asked that question, again invoking the point that Karen had been a Commodore aboard *Wolf* when I'd been Rear Admiral.

But that had been a bit superfluous, and we were so short of good squadron commanders as a result of Mik and Marshal both preparing to leave, there wasn't really room to have one yet.

"Not for now. We would have to promote a Captain," Greg pointed out in reply. "First, we need to determine who takes Wes' place with the Anti-Piracy Force."

If you'll recall all the way back to *The Independent Squadron*, the 'Belt Anti-Piracy Force' was actually the technical name for the formation Wes headed, not that anyone ever called it that, except for Greg this one time.

The question was a good one, though: I knew Wes thought highly of Rozy Young, his Flag Captain, but I was really in no place to gauge her abilities, because our only real encounters during the mission to the Union hand been punctuated by me shooting her commanding officer.

Marlene was looking at the Independent Squadron file as we pondered the question, and as she scanned the information about the formation's Captains, she was shaking her head, "Not seeing anyone there for right now. Wes gave a lot of Commanders their start in 2232."

"Anyone more senior available?" Greg glanced back to me. It might have seemed at this point a tradition to place a Belt Squadron Captain in charge of the Independent Squadron, in order to give him or her squadron command experience before bringing them back. That sort of makes the Independent Squadron out to be a 'farm team', which I think is unfair…

But then, if anyone was ready to take the step up to Commodore, it might be one of the Captains with the Belt Squadron.

And the most obvious one, despite her time out of action, was Kris Jacobs.

"Kris did a good job managing the coup. Good initiative and a hell of a skipper. Wes might not like losing her when he takes over, but we could move Matt Baxter up to *Lion*, and Jim Hannigan over to *Friendly*, and Felicia Khalid or Shelby McLaws up to XO on *Wolf*…"

I was going way too far way too fast; first of all, it wasn't the role of Admiralty House to unilaterally tell Wes who to move around within his squadron once he took over. Of course we'd have the authority to do so, but as you've seen before in these books, the brass usually tries to leave those sorts of decisions to the officers closer to them, to make sure the best fits are found.

Moving a skipper from one squadron to another, though, was fine… and as Greg held up a hand to stop me reassigning the whole of *Wolf's* crew, he got back to the central question, "Kris Jacobs. We'll pencil that in and consult with Wes."

"It's a shame Mik isn't sticking around. The Independent Squadron would be a perfect fit for him, even for just a year or two. Give us time to make sure things settle in nicely at the Belt…" Marlene made that suggestion, and Greg raised an eyebrow.

We all liked Mik — it was impossible not to. And while it was clear he did intend to leave the Navy, and that naturally inclined us not to put him in a position where he'd bond with his people just in time to have to go, maybe it made sense.

"I'll talk to him," I nodded, making a mental note. It wouldn't be hard; he was working out of Admiralty House on the SAU files.

"We'll have to give Wes command of the Belt Station, as well as the squadron," Greg returned to that point. "I think he'll be able to manage both."

"You did it just fine," I pointed out, and Greg smiled.

"Glad you thought so, since we'll be working together here so much going forward," he said. "And on that point, do you have any particular agenda for the role of Fifth Lord? We can probably find a project for you, but if you have something in mind, I'm sure it would be welcomed."

I paused at the question, then leaned back in my chair. Of all the things that had come up over the course of the war, was there one issue that I felt was so significant to the effectiveness of Defense Command that I'd be willing to throw the considerable administrative might and paperwork snowstorm of Admiralty House at it?

Of course there was.

"Well, considering I just invaded Union space with six Special Branchers and a Doberman, and that I didn't really have a Doberman, I think it might be worth studying the possibility of a Defense Command Marine Corps."

Greg liked the sound of that, as did Marlene — the experience of Mercury, and having to coordinate with so many boorish war criminals (by which I mean the Imperial Army) just to be able to launch the invasion, left no one in doubt about the possible benefits of Defense Command having its own strong ground force.

"I'd support that," Greg nodded. "Start thinking about a study team. We'll find a time to put the idea in front of John, and then start the discussions."

It's funny: as a line officer, and especially as a junior line officer, you can often find yourself wondering where some of the bright ideas that dictate your life come from. Sitting in a briefing room with Greg and Marlene, I now had clear proof of the answer: the idiots in charge just have brainwaves, open their mouths, and things start happening.

The reason Defense Command has long been successful is because our idiots in charge aren't actually idiots, with the notable exception of me. And with this Marine Corps thing, I was obviously fluking into a good idea anyway.

For now, though, I'm going to stop this chapter. The key points are already covered — Wes was taking over the Belt Squadron, and we were either going to con Mik into sticking around to run the Independent Squadron, or steal Kris to do it.

And I apparently needed to put a team together.

It was a productive meeting at Admiralty House, and it helpfully sets the stage for the rest of this book. Because now, after all these pages, it's time to start seeing how we said our goodbyes.

CHAPTER TWENTY-THREE
CHARLIE LEFT FIRST

It's perhaps surprising that my best friend was the first to leave, but he was desperate to get home to Lia — or at least as desperate as a Hawke Lord can be. We weren't back a week before he'd found passage to the Protectorate, booking himself a cabin on a tramp steamer.

Well, as soon as we heard that he was leaving in such an undignified manner, we inquired as to which Defense Command ships might be heading out that way, and realized that Sela Kinder's frigate *Guangxi* was set for a cruise of the Belt, leaving just around the same time. Couldn't be a better ship to take a Special Brancher home.

Charlie packed up his cabin on *Wolf* quite easily — he'd travelled light, as Branchers can, and was already waiting for a shuttle across to *Guangxi* when I caught up to him in the observation lounge outside landing bay two. Karen came with me for this — she was in the midst of packing up her own cabin, in fact, but this was a very good reason to stop.

As we entered the lounge, Charlie was looking through the glass at the deck crew in action. They were waving a shuttle in through the space doors, which meant none of us had a lot of time to say anything... we wouldn't hold up his departure for the sake of sentimentality.

"This is the second time we're saying goodbye-goodbye," I said as I came up alongside him.

"Just goes to show what our goodbyes are worth," he answered, not missing this chance for a bit of repartee.

"Suppose that means we'll see each other again," was my unimpressive strike back, and Charlie shrugged.

"At some point I'm going to ask Lia to marry me and she's going to say yes. And then you're going to be best man, and Karen's going to be maid of honor."

That was a terrifying prospect, for many reasons. I picked the most obvious for my next quip: "Imagine the bachelor party. We'll all sit in wingback chairs and complain about the state of the economy."

"With dancing girls," Karen interrupted, completely breaking our rhythm, and forcing us both to look at her with frowns.

"What?" she defended herself ably, "I happen to like dancing girls."

"You'll plan Lia's party. You can have as many dancing girls as you like," I replied.

"There are *never* enough dancing girls," she huffed with all the disdain she could manage... then abruptly slipped past me and gave Charlie a big hug.

That changed the mood instantly, because this hug had a great deal of meaning. Charlie was still a friend she remembered from before, and he'd been the one who'd taken her out to the Union. He was every bit the hero the history books make him out to be, and every bit my best friend.

Even if he has to lie to himself about me in order to keep up his side of that equation.

"Thank you," Karen's final farewell was simple, and though Charlie is easily as aloof as me under certain circumstances, he hugged back.

"No problem. Take care."

Knowing that we didn't want to waste too much of his time, Karen slowly released him, and then stepped back to give Charlie and me room to hug as well. Seriously, she thought we were going to hug. It was funny, because she stood there and watched expectantly, and then nodded slightly after we remained still, "Go on. Hug."

I frowned again, as did Charlie. We both looked at her with our frowns, and then it was Charlie who said it: "Hug?"

"You don't hug?" Karen asked.

"Manly handshakes," I shook my head. "Much more... manly."

"I'm not very secure about my manhood, so handshakes it is," Charlie agreed, and I nodded an extra time to emphasize the point.

Karen looked from Charlie to me, then back, and then she laughed, "Okay then."

That was it, so I extended my hand to Charlie, and Charlie took it. We smiled at each other, shook hands in a manly fashion, and then released our grips.

"Have a safe cruise home. My regards to Lia."

"You take care," Charlie replied, then looked to Karen. "Both of you. Enjoy your peace. You've earned it."

The space doors had closed by the time he finished speaking, so the timing really did work out perfectly. With nothing more to say, my friend Charlie Peters, Lord Major of the Hawke Protectorate, consort to Lia, and the single greatest hero I've ever served with, stepped out the hatch and crossed the deck to the shuttle.

It obviously wasn't the last time we'd see him; he'd become a ruler of the Protectorate, and that meant we'd get to run into him plenty. But now was the time when, finally, he was putting his Defense Command life behind him, and beginning anew.

That was something not dissimilar to what Karen and I were doing, and as we watched his shuttle clear the deck, the truth that everything was soon to be different affected us both, albeit in different ways. More on that later.

For now, there were more people to place.

CHAPTER TWENTY-FOUR

MIK, MEL AND MARSHAL

Commodore Christian Mikaelsen was working out of Admiralty House, so it was no trouble for me to find him when the time came to convince him to take over Wes' old squadron. I'm not going to hold you in suspense: he agreed to run the Independent Squadron for two years, and after that we gave the formation to Kris, and did everything else I'd suggested.

But I didn't know he would agree when I knocked on the door of his borrowed office, and he looked up at me over his pad.

"Admiring your handiwork," the Belt-born Commodore said, then stroked his goatee. "But I was expecting more collateral damage."

I shrugged, stepping through the door and then shutting it before Mik waved me into one of the chairs opposite his desk, "I probably wouldn't have been so cool if not for good officers. Like Wes. Who's taking over the Belt Squadron."

Mik raised an eyebrow at that, and didn't stop stroking his beard until the rest of the conversation had played out in his head. Of course the man who'd once assaulted Mars with Greg, fought the monitors at Mercury and then had managed the disgraced Emperor and his ship throughout 2234, was able to read all the implications of what I said with very little effort.

"How many years can we convince you to give?" I asked, knowing Mik was already far enough ahead of my words to correctly interpret the question.

The first number that came to his mind was just one, but he realized that wasn't really enough to justify his posting. If he was going to the Independent Squadron, it wouldn't just be to keep Wes' chair warm until we found a permanent solution. He'd need at least two years in the post, both to get the experience he wanted and to make sure he left the formation in good shape.

"Two," he said. "Two and then I'll leave the service, and head for the hustings."

"You want me on any campaign trail for you, I'll be there," I smiled in reply, and Mik actually laughed.

"Do you even know what my politics are?"

I shrugged, "Do I look like I'm anything other than a blatant political opportunist? Point me at a camera and tell me who you're trying to impress."

"And then you'll try not to accidentally burn down their buildings?" Mik knew he had to clarify my vague promise, and I nodded.

"I'll try really, really hard."

Mik laughed again, and I joined him. This war had given us the chance to become friends, and I was glad of that. Now he would follow Wes in command of one of the fleet's greatest squadrons, and would build a reputation for safeguarding the very Belt colonies that, just a few years later, he would represent in the House of Commons.

Yes, he did take me up on that endorsement offer. And no, there were no people or animals harmed in the filming of the commercial in question. That cat was computer generated, and so was the falling building. Witnesses contending anything to the contrary are liars paid by Mik's political opponents.

Just clearing that up.

My friend Christian 'Mik' Mikaelsen may now leave this series of reminiscences in peace.

Also politically-bound was Marshal Samuels — and he was similarly destined to represent the Belt, even though he hadn't been born there. Of course, Marshal's trip to the Commons was set to be rather different than Mik's, in part because his politics put him squarely in Douglas Pope's cabinet, and partly because his wife was getting an office on Capital Island long before he was.

I met Mel and Marshal for a drink at the *John Guy* again, not long before the Commodore was to ship back to Belt Two, along with the Belt Squadron. As planned, Marshal would wind things up at the base, but now instead of turning command over to me, he'd pass it to Wes. They'd spend plenty of time on the cruise out figuring the best ways to make the switch, so no detail would be left without careful deliberation.

Then Marshal would prepare to stand in the next election, when veteran MP and deputy Belt Party leader Twinkle McDonough retired from her post representing Belt Two Dome Two. No matter who the Belt Party put up for that riding, there was very little chance of Marshal losing... he had rightly become a hero in the Belt (and the wider Empire) because his convoy system had kept the trade of the Black Sun flowing throughout the war.

That may sound dull when you read it in a history book... but when it means the products you manufacture and the ore you mine gets purchased and paid for (instead of being stolen and paying you nothing) it actually counts for a lot.

No point being coy: Marshal would win that election, and would be named Minister of War the very next day.

Mel, of course, was required to remain on Capital Island. This was a separation that neither of them particularly liked, but they knew it was necessary and wouldn't last too long. Marshal would be able to return regularly even before his election... and then when he got in, he'd obviously live on Capital Island for a lot of the year anyway.

It would be a good fit, just a bit of a juggling act to begin with.

I don't know why I'm telling you all this. I suppose I should actually paint the scene, and remark on the conversations I had with Mel and Marshal... but I don't remember anything we said to be especially special — not grand enough, at least, for this occasion, the last time I'm going to bring them into these reminiscences.

I suppose this is the best part — the one that matters most. It came not at the table as we shared laughs and stories of old times, but right as we left the pub after dark. Mel and Marshal were arm in arm, and I was facing them.

Said my friend Marshal: "My regards to Karen. You two did great work out there, and it's good to know that you'll be here when I get back."

Mel added, "You two really should get married."

And then she smiled in a very strange way, which led me to raise my eyebrow.

"I have absolutely nothing to say to the head of DCI on that subject. But you two take care… see you soon."

It was a fine way for us to part that night, and again, we'd see each other soon. And if you want to know more about their remarkable deeds, just turn on the news or pick up a book. You want to talk about power couples, then Mel and Marshal Samuels are definitely a pair to pay attention to.

There were more good friends yet to place, so let's not stop.

CHAPTER TWENTY-FIVE

RUFUS CHANG WAS DOOMED

"Seriously. She was *in my hotel room* when I landed. I stayed under an alias in a hotel, instead of a barracks, because I didn't want her to find me. I booked three rooms in case she figured that out, but when I randomly selected one at the last minute, she was there. And she was not fully dressed when I arrived."

Just take a guess as to what Rufus was complaining about as he and I drove a hovercar up the main lane into the Terra Nova Palace. My friend the Major was being besieged by a beautiful spy (cosmetic surgery now reversed) who wasn't ever going to let him off the hook.

Like a horror movie, really.

"What did you do?" I asked as we approached the front doors and slowed, and then Rufus answered completely flatly.

"I jumped out the window."

I looked at him, and my jaw dropped, and then I very nearly ran straight into Schwartz T. Babcock. Fortunately, I saw the young Emperor's Secretary just in time, and I didn't in fact run him over… though he says it was close.

"I landed okay, obviously. But I had to jump out the window. I think I'll bunk in the woods tonight," Rufus wasn't just deadpan, he was *serious*.

I blinked a couple of times as I shut down the car and popped my door, "Rufus, I've met her. She's not exactly Medusa. I think you can just give her a chance."

"She's a spook," he said gravely. "I'd rather she was Medusa."

I just shook my head as we both climbed out, and Schwartz was there to greet me with a nervous smile, "Threatening to kill me again. Good one."

"Yeah, I just don't like you Schwartz, you know that," I grinned, and we shook hands.

It was good of the EmpSec to come out and meet both Rufus and myself, and he wasn't the only one to greet us; the Imperial Gamesmaster and former employee of the Ministry of Agriculture, Keith Pine, was waiting on the steps.

"This is why I don't wait for cars by standing in the street, Schwartz," Keith said, then grinned as he shook my hand. Rufus scowled at him, but the man with the goatee and the ponytail… and the axe tucked into his belt (still)… just smiled back. "Good to see you, Major Chang."

Rufus then grumbled something about the Ministry of Agriculture, and its hiring practices, before we all gathered together to walk into the palace. The place was still being guarded by SF, I should point out — the Imperial Army was restricted to its bases, and there was no timeline to suggest when that might change. Again, much of what Daragh was doing now was rooted in public relations; he had to overcome the public distrust of the throne, particularly while the Egesta Inquiries were getting off the ground.

Defense Command was the only safe armed force to put in front of the camera, and go figure, our Emperor was only too happy to oblige.

In point of fact, that whole question of armed forces was the reason for this dinner meeting… and the reason Rufus had been reassigned off *Wolf* and attached to Admiralty House whether he liked it or not.

"The Emperor is rather interested in hearing the case for the Marine Corps," Schwartz said as we walked deeper into the palace. Then he thought about what he said, and corrected himself, "Let me rephrase that: he knows he wants one, and he's interested to hear what excuses you'll provide the public and the government so they'll let us do it."

I liked Schwartz T. Babcock. Then and now, the wonderkid was a real good operator, and yet somehow he still had a soul. I suppose he's a freak of nature.

Anyway, he pretty much spelled it out right there: we were going to dinner at the palace to get the Emperor's official blessing on our plans to start the 'Commission To Investigate The Creation Of A Defense Command Militarized Ground Force', or CTITCOADCMGF. Yes, someone did try to coin the acronym. No, Rufus didn't actually harm that person physically — that's a myth. It ended up that we called the whole project the 'DCMC Viability Study', which was much more manageable.

Important point: the study was to be run by the Fifth Lord of the Admiralty (yay me), with the field direction of Colonel Rufus Chang. For the time being, our Chinese Brancher with the mismatched eyes was hanging up his MAG-90, so that he could figure out the best way to evolve a Marine Corps that worked for Defense Command. Without growth in that area, we'd face shortages after any future ground campaign, just as we had after Mercury, so Rufus was the guy to find a solution.

And considering what he'd come up with on the fly with *Hester* in Union space, and the resources he'd have at his disposal at Admiralty House, we all knew to expect great things… after we got the Emperor's buy-in. Remember, under the Articles, militarized ground forces are the preserve of the throne… orbital defense was considered an extension of domestic policing, which was why Defense Command encompassed ground constabularies and space, and spread that authority out to the solar system.

Technically, Special Branch and SF were all just constables (under the constitution), but that wasn't going to fly for something called a Marine Corps, so we had to twist Daragh's rubber arm and get the approval to start making it happen.

Now, sorry, that's been an awful lot of political talk, and none of it is terribly exciting. Let's just skip ahead, after a ten-minute walk to one of the palace's dining rooms, where the Emperor was waiting.

Though waiting might be a bit of a misnomer, because when we finally arrived, he was sitting at the head of a long and ornate table, eating a leg of fried chicken.

"Glad you saw fit to wait for us," Keith Pine called to him as we entered the cavern.

Daragh grumbled something, then said: "Took you too long to get here. I was hungry."

Schwartz pitched in after that, "We need to get some sort of hover transport inside this place. It's too big to cover on foot."

"Look into that, I might be entertained by having races in the corridors," the Irish Emperor agreed thoughtfully.

Rufus and I both hung back slightly as the two trusted staffers for the Emperor crossed the floor, rounded the table and took up seats near their boss. Then Daragh looked up over his fried chicken and nodded to us, "Come on over. The chef will make anything you like. And fast, too. He's really good."

"There are actually eleven chefs, that's why it's so fast," Keith corrected, and Daragh shot him a glare. The Irishman didn't like being reminded of the opulence that inevitably came with his stupid throne.

"Get over here. And meet this person who's been keeping me entertained," Daragh kept his attention on us, and we gradually approached the table and sat down.

Now this was impressive: the tall-backed chair at Daragh's right had its back towards us when we came into the room and sat down. I took the chair next to it, and Rufus the one next to me, and we both studied the back of this chair and wondered if it was actually empty. There were no legs visibly dangling down in front of it, so we figured Daragh was just making some sort of joke.

"Miss Connie Ramilles. Did I get that right?"

"Yes sir," the answer came sweetly from the chair.

"From the Ministry of Agriculture," Daragh said, returning his attention to his chicken. "I found her in my bathroom. It was awkward but luckily I was wearing pants."

This is the part of the movie where you hear the screeching sound that means THE MONSTER IS IN THE ROOM WITH YOU RUN AWAY!

The chair turned, and sitting there with a lovely smile, her legs pulled up so they wouldn't dangle down in front and reveal her, was Haley Briand.

Sorry, Connie something. Whatever, it was Haley, and Rufus shot to his feet, "You!"

She waved at him and then shrugged girlishly, "Didn't know if you saw me before you jumped out the window. I would have followed but it took too long to get dressed."

"He jumped out a window to avoid you?" Keith asked, and Haley nodded.

"Third floor."

Only a Special Brancher can walk away from that, in case you're wondering.

"She tells me there's an awkward situation going on..." Daragh looked up from his chicken again, frowning. "Something wrong with your chair, Rufus?"

The Major looked from his stalker to his Emperor and back, then huffed and sat down.

"She says you're not appreciative of her affections. That's why she decided to break into my bathroom," the Irishman explained, then glanced back to Haley's chair. "How'd you do that again?"

"I've done it before," she said, turning back towards the Emperor.

"How'd that turn out?" Daragh asked.

She shrugged, "The guy who was Emperor then isn't any more."

Pausing for a moment, the Irishman made a big deal out of pretending he had to remember his predecessor, then he pointed at her, "I think I remember that. Pretty good job you did."

"Thank you!"

"So Rufus, I hate to do this to you, but I'm going to insist you have a private dinner with this girl… whatever the hell she's calling herself. I'll have one of my fifty fucking chefs—"

"Language," Keith interjected immediately, and Daragh glared at him.

"I'll have one of my fifty chefs make you two whatever you like. And you're going to sit down and have a quiet dinner. If you agree to that, you'll have my full support for the Marine Corps."

Honest to God, this happened.

Rufus leaned forward and shot a glare at the Emperor which unsettled even the Irishman, "You are telling me that she breaks into your bathroom and petitions you to help with her hopeless romantic agenda, and you agree?"

Daragh lowered his chicken, "Thought it was pretty obvious. Power corrupts, don't you know?"

I don't know how I didn't laugh. Schwartz just managed to keep it together, but then he's a master politician. Keith simply seemed disapproving.

"Marine Corps support?" I interjected at this point, and Daragh shrugged.

"Well you'll get my support either way. But don't tell Rufus that."

"I won't," I agreed, and then turned to Rufus. "What's the worst that can happen… just have dinner and hear her out. Maybe the beautiful, capable, and inventive spy will have a redeeming quality."

Rufus switched his glare to me, "She won't."

But as he said that, he stood up. He would do what was necessary for the good of the Empire. And just to protect his honor, Daragh turned his attention back to Haley, "Now child, if you so much as put a hand on him, I'll have you thrown out of the Ministry of Agriculture. You only get to talk. It's up to him if he wants anything else. There's a water bed. But only if he says so."

Haley put on a very serious frown, "Yes Emperor. Of course."

"And no mind control," Daragh pointed at her with a half-eaten chicken leg.

"Of course not."

"Good."

With that, Haley leapt to her feet and was rapidly approached by one of the serving staff, who would lead her away.

Rufus looked at me, took a centering breath, and then said, "It's been an honor serving with you."

With that melodramatic statement, the Chinese Brancher left the dining room with Haley, never to be seen again. Until the following morning, when he came into Admiralty House complaining that she was evil. But that they had dinner plans anyway.

I think she spiked his drink.

Daragh, Schwartz, Keith and I got on with talking politics, but really, you don't care. This was what the Emperor could do now: abuse his power to compel happiness. I can think of no better way to leave these three fine fellows for the final time.

And as for leaving Rufus on this note, I suppose he might want to kill me for it, but I figure Haley has my back. They're excellent people, who between them brought Grant Merger into our hands. Whether the things that happened after were right or wrong, they both did a great service to the Empire, and I'm glad to call them friends.

All of these people have since served with great distinction, so keep an eye out for them — you'll see them around.

CHAPTER TWENTY-SIX

THE BELT SQUADRON

We waited to do the ceremony which transferred command of the Belt Squadron to Wes until the very day that elite formation was set to boost for Belt Two. We figured that was the best time, because we knew we could coordinate everyone's schedule and get them together for the simple but incredibly significant ceremony.

Though there wasn't really enough space, we decided to stage this event on the bridge, and I'll remember the occasion for a long time.

Karen and I were there, in our dress uniforms, and Wes, Andrea, and the entire senior staff were on the command deck, along with Rufus' old team (now five officers under Major Clarissa Hutchinson). On the bridge screens were all the skippers of our Belt Squadron, along with John, Greg and Marlene standing together in John's office.

There was no media (aside from Bunny, who was standing back at the operations consoles with Jim because she was one of the family), and there were no speeches. We all just wanted to be together one more time, to officially mark the end of an era.

I don't know if this seems strange to you, especially considering the squadron wasn't disappearing, just going back on patrol at the Belt... but it mattered because it was us. All of us. Maybe it wasn't going to be the last time we were all together, but it could be, so we had to do this properly.

From the main screen, John was the master of ceremonies, "Ladies and gentlemen, I officially transfer command of the Belt Squadron from Rear Admiral Ken Barron, Fifth Lord of the Admiralty, to Rear Admiral Wes Pellew. Congratulations."

I know it sometimes seems silly for friends to applaud other friends, when there's no audience other than friends, but we did it anyway. On the bridge, Wes and I were standing face to face. I stuck out my hand, and he took it.

"Sorry I took your other squadron away," I said with a grin.

He shrugged, "I think I'll survive."

"Ladies and Gentlemen," John said from the screen, "your Belt Squadron has consistently and ably defended the Empire for countless years. It represents the highest traditions of the service, and it will continue to do so as you return to your cruising station. Godspeed."

"All the best, everyone," Marlene added, and as last mentions go, I feel like that one doesn't do her enough credit. This whole series I've never managed to include Marlene as much as I wanted to, but maybe the fact that I keep trying, even though she and I rarely served in the same place at the same time, tells you how important she really is.

Now she smiled, and waved to us all one more time.

Finally, it was Greg who took a step towards the viewfinder in John's office. He had been the commander of this Squadron — he had won at Deep Black. Now he was watching it turn over to new leadership once again, and he was proud.

In fact that's what he said, in his final appearance in these reminiscences: "I'm proud of you all. I look forward to word of your successes. Safe journey."

With a smile and a wave from him, and from Marlene and John, the feed to Admiralty House cut. Of course I'd see them all shortly, when I went back to my office, but as a final appearance for them in these pages, I hope this is enough for you to realize their importance.

And speaking of final appearances... the whole crew of *Wolf*. My crew.

Alicia hadn't really forgiven us when I shook her hand and hugged her on the bridge... but she already missed us. Don't know if that makes sense. Andy Jensen criticized my rewiring job when he shook my hand, and he told me if I ever needed an engineer, just to call. I kept that in mind.

Adrienne Thompson gave me a hug, and actually got a little teary. I shook the hand of every Brancher: Clarissa Hutchinson, Selma Koestecki, Maggie Joyce, Simon Keynes and Bobby Franek. Bobby in particular; I thanked him and he nodded to me.

Felicia Khalid thanked me for the opportunities I'd given her, which was kind but hardly right; she'd made her own way, overcoming any doubts.

Shelby gave me a hug, in as proper a fashion as any southern belle could, and promised to visit whenever she got a chance to come home. Eugene Sengooba gave me a big hug too — a manly hug, of course, which I returned. It was impossible to resist the newly-promoted Lieutenant's good spirits, and his laugh filled the room.

By the time I worked my way back around to Andrea, then standing beside Karen (who was simply leaning against the front railing as I said farewell to all these strangers), the Irish skipper of *Wolf* was almost — just almost — smiling.

"Have fun at your desk," she said. Then she looked at Karen, "Take care of each other."

I hugged Andrea (she was getting a hug whether she liked it or not, now that Eugene had opened the floodgates), and then Karen did too. That just left my friend Wes to bid farewell to on the bridge, and as I approached him he stuck out his hand one more time.

"No hugs," he said, and I grinned.

"No hugs," I shook his hand again. "Go do what you do best, my friend. I look forward to hearing the stories."

With that, I turned to the screens. Lots more people to say farewell to there, and I called them all by name: "Kate, Katya, Isoruku, Mark, Kris, Matt..."

"We'll do plenty of stupid stuff," Matt Baxter said with a grin. "Now that you two aren't around, we'll have plenty to make up for."

"Speak for yourself, everything I do is smart," Mark Gunney disagreed.

"Can you take him with you, Ken? His flirting gets on my nerves," Kris completed the circuit, and all I could do was smile and shake my head.

"You all, are the best. Listen to Wes, visit when you can, and try not to start any wars without asking," I said, and for some reason that was met with a cheer.

I was starting to get emotional by this time, and though now she lacked the bond with all of these people that she had once enjoyed, Karen did know it was time to get me to the hatch before I embarrassed myself. With a last pat on Wes' shoulder, she guided me towards the exit, where Jim and Bunny were waiting to escort us down to our shuttle.

Perhaps it's telling that we hadn't flown up in our Starlights.

As we went down, Jim and I nattered about something which I can't remember, and Bunny chatted with Karen about something neither of them can remember. All we do know is that when we got to the landing deck, and stopped in the observation lounge, Bunny hugged us both and said her goodbyes, then Jim Hannigan shook our hands.

"Thank you for getting us all back here," my friend the XO said.

That statement was simple, but it meant a lot. As I've said before, Jim was with me from the beginning on *Friendly*, and he'd come so far since them. He had, and we all had.

"You're the very best, Jim," was all I managed to say. "Take care."

With those parting words, I turned and joined Karen at the hatch. We soon withdrew from our ship.

"Shuttle is away and we've got clearance to break orbit," Jim got back to his consoles just in time to make that report.

Nonessential personnel had cleared from the bridge by that time, and striding to the front of the command deck with Andrea at his shoulder, Rear Admiral Wes Pellew folded his arms. Around him, the best crew in Defense Command all waited a little expectantly, looking up at their new-but-familiar commanding officer as they prepared to cruise.

He took a moment to gaze back at them, and feel some pride as he saw Jim, Shelby, Felicia, and Eugene all at their very best. On screen there were Mark, Kris, Matt, Kate, Katya, and Isoruku. He had left behind a wonderful squadron, but he was where he belonged.

And that's what he had to say to these people who'd followed Karen and me through a war: "I'm glad to be back… I'm glad to be *home*."

My friend Wes Pellew sees out his time in these reminiscences with those words, as do the rest of the finest officers I've ever served with. As they all smiled to each other like the excellent people they are, Wes nodded to his Flag Captain, and Andrea Kiley gave the orders.

"Shelby, we'll lead out, 190 kps."

Wolf turned away from Earth, for the first time leaving on a campaign without me on its bridge. Behind followed the elite of the Defense Command Navy, and as I watched from the window of the shuttle that was taking Karen and me back to my office, I felt a sort of sadness, and a sort of joy.

A chapter in my life was over, but as Karen squeezed my hand, I had no doubt that the time was right to move on.

From here out, things could move only forward.

Well, except for one more visit. Because you don't honestly believe that I couldn't give my best friend Charlie the final sendoff, do you?

CHAPTER TWENTY-SEVEN

HERO OF THE EMPIRE

By the time Charlie Peters made it home, he wanted nothing more than to see the Lady he'd eventually marry. Go ahead and groan if you want, but Charlie has earned the right to want that — he earned it then, and he's earned it ever since.

You name me one time when Charlie didn't step up and do more than was asked of him. From the first day on *Alberta*, when he decided he should probably keep a certain crazy pair of pilots from getting themselves killed, to every step along the way with the Belt Squadron, to Mercury, to that hospital at Venus where he uncovered the Egesta crisis, to absolutely everything about 2235. You find me one minute in there when he was less than the best, and I'll let you groan about him being happy to get home to Lia.

Of course, the only person who can find fault with anything Major Peters did in the service of the Empire is this idiot called Charlie Peters. But don't listen to him, because he's always wrong about himself. He's the best friend I've ever had, except for Karen, and he was going to marry a Lady who was pretty much my little sister.

That makes him my brother, and I'm lucky to have him.

So as you might expect, what follows will be a very sappy and emotional tribute to my friend Charlie, beginning with the moment his boots hit the bottom of the chute at the government locks on Hawke One. He pulled his duffle down out of the transitional gravity with him, then walked out into the quiet and slightly posh receiving area where he saw his uniformed beloved waiting for him.

Lia had one hip thrust slightly forward, a frown on her face and her arms folded. He went to her, and dropped his duffle so he could put his arms around her.

When he got close, she took a breath, opened her mouth, and said, "I'm pregnant."

If you've never heard the screech that comes when a needle is abruptly ripped off a vinyl record, just go look it up and I'll wait. Get it? Okay, play that sound, and picture Charlie freezing in place.

"What?"

Lia looked up at him with big eyes, and he immediately started to re-shape his mental framework. Pregnant? That meant he was going to be a father...

Then he looked down at Lia again, filling up with all sorts of loving and meaningful thoughts... and she smiled.

"I'm lying."

Charlie discovered that his lungs could actually take in oxygen, and as soon as they did he gasped, "What the hell, Lia?"

"Sorry, I just figured if I didn't say something you'd get emotional on me."

"Well... maybe. But I... that's. You shouldn't joke about that sort of thing," Charlie shook his head. "What if we try and it doesn't work? Then... then you'll be cursing the karma thing. With the... the karma."

Only Lia knew how to do this to Charlie — to make him babble incoherently. It was excellent. She shrugged, "Well if it doesn't work the first time, we can try again. Maybe even try several times. I hear the mechanics of it are pretty repeatable."

"That's not what I mean," he protested, which made her smile even more, because obviously that's not what he meant.

"Well let's not worry about that now. I'll go say my prayers and ask for forgiveness. Can you please embrace me so that I swoon now? I meant to avoid us having an awkward moment, but a girl still needs some affection."

"I don't know if I want to," Charlie shook his head, trying to throw some of Lia's game back at her, but she obviously wasn't going to let that stand.

"Oh we'll see," she stepped right into him and hugged. It was not a manly hug, either... though considering it was Lia, that would have been strange. She's not very manly, and I don't care if she hears me saying it.

Charlie decided to accept that hug as an apology, even though he wasn't certain one was warranted, and even though it absolutely wasn't one.

Deciding to be a little bit romantic, he leaned back with her in his arms, so that her feet lifted off the ground. Then he spun her.

"Don't do that," she said. "I don't want to get morning sick on you."

He put her down on her feet immediately and pulled back, "Wait, you're actually pregnant?"

Lia wore a look of disbelief, "Oh my God, did Grant hit you with an anti-sarcasm gun? Is your brain okay?"

Just to be clear, it was a joke. And no, despite her poor taste in humor, Lia never had trouble having kids when circumstances demanded. I think she and Charlie both had paid enough dues to not have karma cause them trouble for that.

Anyway, Charlie scowled and then lifted Lia back into his arms, "I'm not taking any more impromptu trips ever again, so that we never have to do this awkward reunion thing ever again."

He wasn't lying about that, and Lia knew it. For all her silliness, she finally hugged him for real, and then she whispered into his ear, "Welcome home. Love you."

At this point they did kiss, and then Charlie collected his duffle from the floor and they left the receiving lounge, to get back to their life together.

They are my family, and so it is on this final note that they depart from these reminiscences. I'm just glad that I still get to see them regularly in my life.

Thanks Charlie and Lia. For everything.

CHAPTER TWENTY-EIGHT

OUR SECRET

And so we come to the end of these books, with just one last secret to tell. This is the story of how Karen and I found life on Capital Island, her on the sick list and me as Fifth Lord of the Admiralty.

The short version is simple: it was perfect.

There were all sorts of things that weren't perfect, of course — Karen was still trying to find her way outside fleet duty, and struggling to recover as much as she could of the years that had been lost (not as memories, but to literally just understand the events that had taken place). We spent time with my parents on Capital Island, and fortunately she still remembered them, which made things easier.

We spent a lot of time just exploring, if I'm honest. When we had days off — and frankly, we had as many of those as we needed (perk of being Fifth Lord) — we'd venture off to parts of the island that were quite remote.

Terra Nova itself is surrounded by a great nature preserve, which had once been a national park in Canada. We spent time near the city exploring, finding a rocky beach and then climbing through the arduous woods up to a clearing that looked out over a bay. It was a peaceful place, and one that resonated with some sort of meaning… somewhere meant to comfort those who had been at war.

That makes no sense, of course — we were just assigning meaning to a place of beauty and solitude — but it was still wonderful. We did all of these things together, and gradually we learned not to wonder what Wes was up to at any given moment, learned not to miss the feeling of a ship's deck under our feet.

I had expected that freedom to come only after years away from the squadron, but it actually came within months. I don't know if that was because of the places we were visiting, or the fact that it was just us, alone in a world that seemed empty.

Either way, I was glad of it — glad to find a way to leave it all behind.

I might end this series of reminiscences there, in that serene way… but I can't, and I'll tell you why. When I was first approached by this publisher to do these books I made a few promises, and one of them was to reveal a secret of great importance.

Now, you know by this point that I don't really think a lot of my editors. Well, I say I don't. Maybe I actually respect them a lot, because that would explain why I keep writing books for them. Well, it *might* explain that — we can revisit the question later.

But I did give my word, and Karen and I decided it was right. So there's one more thing to tell you, because you've suffered with these books for so very long. And it's a truth that you'll find on Capital Island, in a place no one ever looks.

On the morning of September 10, 2235, Karen and I decided to wake up early and have a big breakfast. By this time we had a very nice condo in Terra Nova, which was convenient to Admiralty House and had a beautiful sea view. Of course, that view was only good on days when the place wasn't completely awash in fog, and on this particular day it was indeed gray and the visibility was non-existent.

That didn't matter; we had our big breakfast, got dressed, and went down to the parking garage to our hover rover. We still had our planes — we'd been sure to take them off *Wolf*, and now they were parked at the Admiralty House landing field, kept ready for us whenever we wanted to use them (yet another shameless perk).

But we weren't going to use them today. Instead, we piled into the rover and switched on, then programmed the guidance computer to take us to the city of St. John's. Long before Capital Island had been chosen as the seat of power for our Empire, it had been a province of Canada... one that was barely wanted by anyone, except for those souls born upon it, or those who found it and fell in love with its remoteness.

The fact that it was stuck out in the middle of the North Atlantic, with a tiny population and difficult terrain, had made it a good compromise when Luther Gordon the Great was seeking a place to put his government — neutral ground where nations of the world could meet safely, and build their international government. But before that time, St. John's had been the capital. In 2235 (and today) it was a small town built around a wonderful harbor, overlooked by headlands so high as to take your breath away, and on a clear day, show you a horizon of ocean so vast it makes space seem inconsequential.

Alive and welcoming, St. John's is the place I call home — and that's why we were visiting.

We laughed and nattered as we floated our way towards the city, over its outskirts, and then down into its winding streets near the harbor. Karen and I had been here many times, so it was good to be getting back, even if we could see none of it for the fog. We knew where we were.

Of course, the fact that we had a computer and satellites helping was good, because the streets of this town are in no way linear — some of them date back around 800 years, and believe me, there weren't many urban planners among the poor starving explorers who beached themselves on the rock back then.

Our rover helped us find the highest ridge looking over the harbor (still seeing nothing in the fog), and then we traveled up Bonaventure Avenue until it turned into Military Road. We barely spotted the parking lot, but when we did we floated up and over the pedestrian walk beside it, then touched down.

As we switched off I got a little fluttery feeling in my chest, and I looked at Karen. She was decidedly excited, so we wasted no more time. Opening the doors, we hopped out of the rover and locked it up, then looked up at the fog all around us. It was beginning to glow a bit, which suggested it might burn away... we hoped it did.

But the fog was no barrier for us now; we turned in the direction we knew led towards the structure we sought and began to walk across the small parking lot. Only when we neared the foot of the steps leading to the centuries-old front doors did we finally see the two great grey stone towers reaching up into the foggy sky.

This was the Basilica Cathedral of St. John the Baptist; a Church, if you're not familiar with the jargon, that had been in St. John's since the middle of the nineteenth century. Its two mighty towers, which now rose up and vanished into the fog, had been a landmark in the city for all that time; ship pilots taking their vessels through the narrows into the harbor would always look to them for guidance when navigating.

I don't know what you think of religion, but as Churches go, this one was doing exactly what it was advertised to do: helping people find their way home. If that's what the ads said. Come to think of it, I never checked. Anyway.

Climbing the stairs, we proceeded through the arched entrances and went inside, to be greeted by all the finery one must expect from a Catholic Cathedral of its period. There were pews (rows of benches) covered in red velvet, stretching all the way from the door to the altar at the front. Plenty of Christian imagery surrounded this chamber, and of course the ceiling was so massively vaulted it would put one of *Bonnie's* flight bays to shame.

Again, whatever your view on God and religion, you have to admire some of the world's places of worship, and though this Basilica was known to few, it was still magnificent.

As we stepped inside, Karen and I were greeted by total silence — undoubtedly typical for a Thursday morning — but we nevertheless advanced slowly, even cautiously. As our eyes swept the great chamber for signs of activity, we saw only two people sitting in the pews right at the front on the left side; otherwise, there was nothing.

With a glance at each other, we began advancing up the aisle, side by side as we looked around at the stained glass windows, all of them glowing a little brighter with each passing moment. We were in no hurry, but by the time we reached the steps up to the altar at the front, we found there was still no one there.

No priest, at least. And that was the man we needed to see.

It never pays to be impatient in a Church, so Karen and I simply waited, taking the chance to look around again. It was really interesting. For about half a minute. But we weren't going to go storming into the offices behind the altar — this wasn't a raid on a pirate bodega, it was a visit to a respectful religious institution that meant a great deal to many people. We weren't carrying mags for that very good reason.

Unfortunately, though, life without mags required patience.

"Are you waiting for the Father?"

That question interrupted our very patient waiting, and both Karen and I turned to face the two men sitting in the front row of pews. They were both wearing blue uniforms that we didn't recognize, and they looked quite old... if well-kept for their age. One had gray hair, the other's was white with black streaks... and they both had an air about them, as if they'd fought wars together.

It was the gray-haired one who seemed to have asked the question, and now he came to his feet, his friend doing the same a little more gradually.

Glancing at Karen, I nodded for us both, "We need to see a priest, yes."

The way I said it implied pretty clearly that I didn't know the name of the particular Catholic Father who was now in charge of the Basilica, so I figured these two — who were probably regulars — had me and Karen spotted as out-of-towners from that point on.

But the gray-haired old man smiled, which looked very strange for some reason. He had a comically big nose, and giant ears too, for that matter... but his amber-colored eyes were plenty wise, "Well, Father Conroy is just out. I think he might be on a run to the alcohol store, if I'm honest. I don't like to say that, because I understand there's a stereotype, but I think it's true."

"You could have said he was going to a food bank," the white-haired old man elbowed his friend quite spryly, but the gray-hair shrugged.

"I suppose I never got good at lying. Unless there was a good reason. But is there some way we could help you? We're familiar with this place, and old Father Pat... left us in charge."

That last part sounded like a lie, especially knowing that the old man was no good at them. Still, I had no problem with a little bit of guided mischief, and looking to Karen, I found her smiling too. These old fellows were sweet... but she also found something strange about them, particularly when she looked right at them. But that wasn't reason enough not to let them have a bit of fun too — smuggling a couple into the back offices of a Church would probably be their most exciting adventure all week.

Oh my, scandalous.

With a conspiratorial look between them, the two old timers led us past the altar and through a door towards the Church's back offices. This was by no means a fancy or secret place — it was the workspace where the priest and the Church volunteers and staff did their jobs. Just in case you were under the misimpression that we were searching for the Holy Grail, or something...

The old men in blue led us to the record room, which I don't remember instructing them to do, but which I must have because they never asked. As we entered that rather straightforward office and switched on the lights, we were confronted by a whole wall of bookshelves, all of them containing ledgers and file boxes that stretched back decades, even centuries.

Paper still really does have its place in some institutions, and indeed, I believe the move of certain Church records back to written ledgers was one consciously made sometime in the twenty-first century, during a period of concern over the protection of data in the event of an EMP.

Not that that's terribly relevant.

Karen and I both stood back and looked up at the massive shelf full of records, and started trying to figure out where to begin. The bad thing about paper is it lacks a search feature — you have to do it the old fashioned way, with your eyes.

But the gray-haired old man was way ahead of us. Sauntering over to a specific section of shelf, he reached out his hand and started running his forefinger over the spines of books until he stopped on one in particular. Pulling it down, he walked back to us with it, smiling all the way.

"Start here," he said, handing it to me.

I frowned as I took it from him, and saw that it was exactly the book we were looking for. Lowering it with a frown, I started to shake my head.

"How did you know?" Karen asked, and the gray-haired fellow shrugged.

"I trust my instincts," he smiled, and his white-haired friend groaned. I didn't understand the joke, and neither did Karen, but it made the gray-haired man chuckle... before turning to Karen and approaching her with an outstretched hand. "We'll leave you to it. But I just wanted to say that you remind me of my wife. I lost her a long time ago. She was a doctor. I know you're a flag officer, but you remind me of her."

Karen was caught entirely off guard by that, so her mouth dropped open and she frowned a little before taking the old man's warm, apparently gloved hand, "Thank you."

He shook his head, "Thank you. For everything you've done, and will do."

With that, he released her grip and turned to me. I just had time to shift the ledger from my right hand to my left so I could take his gloved hand in mine. Said he: "It's really a pleasure to meet you here."

"You too..." I said with a frown of plain confusion, that made him smile even more.

Then his friend approached and quickly shook Karen's hand, "It was wonderful to meet you, Karen."

And to me, as he shook my hand, "We'll see you again someday."

Old men are strange. I know this because I've turned into one, but even so, these two were extra strange. As they turned for the door, they started chuckling to each other about something I couldn't hear. Moving over beside me, Karen called to them, "What were your names? In case the Father comes back and we need someone to blame?"

The two old timers stopped and looked at each other before turning halfway back.

"There's probably no harm in it," the white-haired one said, and the gray-hair nodded.

"I'm Caine. And this is Felix. You two... take care."

With parting smiles and waves, they wandered out of the office, leaving Karen and me genuinely baffled.

"This is why I don't usually go to Church," she said after a moment, and I shrugged.

"They seemed nice enough."

"They're crazy," Karen shook her head, turning back to the ledger. "And who wears fur gloves indoors in September?"

That was a good question, but it didn't matter. Deciding to put the two strange fellows out of our minds, we returned to the purpose for our visit: the ledger. Moving over to a clear desk I set it down, and then we both read the year marked on the cover: 2222.

Without further ado, I flipped it open and leafed through the pages until I neared September. As every old, glossy page passed, Karen and I both fixed our gaze on the same section of the paper, looking for the familiar marks. It didn't take long until we could stop.

"There it is," Karen said, and a smile slipped back onto her lips.

Her breathing changed, and mine did too. I put my finger down beside the date and time — 10:11 AM, on September 10, 2222 — and then slowly glided it across the page. First there was my signature, and then there was Karen's, and then the signature of Father Morry, who had presided. Then the signatures of my parents, the only witnesses.

"See, it's still there," I smiled, and then took a breath. "We're still married."

Karen's smile got bigger, but her eyes also got a tiny bit wet. She remembered that day, same as I did. If there was anything that saved Grant Merger — and obviously nothing had, because he was dead — it was the fact that when Karen woke up without being able to remember twelve years of her life, the blank period began *after* that morning, when our secret wedding had made us late for coffee in Terra Nova.

Yes, in fact, we had been married this entire time. Bet you didn't guess that.

Of course you know we're married now... but that's because, shortly after this, we registered our marriage with the Imperial Revenue Directorate, so that we could take advantage of the tax breaks that come with a spouse.

Everyone assumed we had a secret, private ceremony before that tax registration, and everyone was right. It's just that no one knew *how long* before the registration — no one except Father Morry, who had agreed to keep it secret, and my parents, and eventually my friend Charlie Peters.

All the rest, even Karen's family, had not known. We wanted it that way — we wanted it to be for us, recorded only on the rolls of a Church, which made it valid but not public. We didn't want pirates or criminals to realize how close we were… to try to hold it over us. And eventually, we didn't want the media to know, or even the Navy to know, because it was better that everyone wondered, instead of realizing.

And we'd been proved right, because remember even Grant hadn't known.

Now it doesn't matter — now I'll tell you, and thank you for staying with these reminiscences for so long.

I'll do that in a minute, anyway, because first I should point out that it wasn't Father Pat Conroy who found us, but a secretary named Eudora, who wasn't too impressed that we'd broken into a Church. We even tried to explain to her why we'd done it, but she threatened to drag us out by our ears. I don't care how many Martians or pirates you've faced, when a Newfoundland woman named Eudora gives orders like that, you obey.

Neither of our old trouble-making friends were in the pews when we fled out the front of the Basilica like a couple of ne'er-do-well teenagers (they probably knew the fate that awaited them, and scrammed), but that was fine: as we burst out the front doors we were greeted not by fog, but by a beautiful, bright, blue-skied morning.

Go ahead and tell me I'm lying if you like, but the weather satellites will confirm my story: as always happens on Capital Island, the weather changed in just minutes, and the glory of the place was revealed all around us.

Catching our breath, Karen and I linked arms and found ourselves looking skyward, on the verge of laughing endlessly with youthful glee.

"This was a good idea," she declared as we walked — perhaps stumbled — away from the door.

"I agree wholeheartedly," I concurred, and slowly we descended the steps from the cathedral's entrance.

"I don't know what I've lost… I mean I really, actually don't… but still… it doesn't feel like that happened a few months ago. It does feel like it's been a dozen years," she continued, shaking her head and smiling. "How's that possible?"

I shrugged, "Long term exposure to me is noticeably toxic?"

She laughed and then let go my arm so she could turn around and look up at the blue sky between the twin steeples of the Basilica.

"Maybe the mind can forget, but the soul can remember," she said, and then she looked down and just about laughed at herself.

"The *soul* can remember?" I put some absurd emphasis on the word, and she stepped on my reply with hers.

"The soul *can* remember!" she grabbed my arm again and pulled in close. This was Karen. This was, I can finally say, my wife. Had been this whole damned time. She asked me: "Do you think I have a soul, Ken Barron?"

Nice touch — she said my whole name at the end. It honestly made me a little swoony. If you don't like it, shut up. This is my time, with my wife. Get your own.

"I think," I stared into her eyes, and thought about it for a moment. "I think you are full of light, Karen McMaster."

She liked that too, and I could tell by the way the smile on her face flattened out, and then grew again. If you've never seen it happen, you may never understand what it means, but it said more in a second than twenty of these books have said in five years.

Her eyes drifted down for a moment, and then she took a breath and pulled away a little, "Well I don't know about that. But I do know what I'm full of: *alien biomatter!*"

She said the last two words dramatically, and I groaned, "Really, you're going to bring that up again? It was ridiculous."

Karen shook her head, instantly looking serious — too wonderfully, absurdly serious: "No, I mean it. I can feel it. It's like... like it's going to burst right out of my chest."

"Indeed," I cocked an eyebrow, and felt my ear twitch. "And I suppose you expect me to help you with that."

"I really wish you would," she nodded again, and then we pulled ourselves closer together — right into each other. We were face to face, and as a cool wind blew, Karen McMaster kissed her husband, and I kissed my wife.

And that, my dear friends, is how I close my reminiscences.

AFTERWORD

Before we end, I must confess one great lie to all of you. If you remember all the way back to the beginning, to *The Rogue Commodore*, you might recall that I spent a while explaining why we were starting the story of my career in the middle, with the Martian War. I trotted out a few excuses — that it was like starting a biography of Nelson at the interesting part, and that the anniversary of the war meant it'd sell well.

That's all plausible, but it's really just a good lie. The secret that not even my publishers knew until they read this is quite simple: I was never writing these books for history, or for them, or for you. Granted, they gave me the chance to say many things that I've always wanted to say about the war... to give credit to good men and women who did so much for us all. The process of writing let me reconnect with old friends, helped me learn a few lessons, and I hope allowed you to get to know people who history has unkindly overlooked.

All of those things are bonuses — great benefits of which I can be proud.

But the truth is that these books started where they did, and when they did, because they are meant to recount the story of what Karen and I did together... for her. The publisher who pitched this series to me might wonder why I finally gave in and agreed to do it... it was because one night after his proposal, Karen said to me: "I'd love to read them. I'd always be able to remember what I missed."

I called him the next morning and said yes. Then we had to wait until I learned to read and write (poorly), but that was the start of it.

And here we are now, at the end. I can never tell the stories that came before 2231 — not Karen's stories, anyway. Maybe one day I'll tell my own from that time, or others that have happened since... but none of them matter so much as these. These days, as good and bad as they were, are the ones that needed to be remembered for Karen.

So here they are.

My apologies to any of you who feel cheated by having spent time and treasure to read twenty books that amount to a love letter from a man to his wife. Admittedly, a love letter with a war in the middle of it. But I've used you all without remorse, and I'd do it again in a heartbeat.

Gladly, I don't need to, because Karen is sitting right here, with me and our children, and we are happy. I hope you can say the same, now and in the future.

Thank you for joining us for this trip, and until next our paths cross, take care.

THE
EQUATIONS NOVELS

The Earthers evolved after humans were driven from the Earth by an intelligent bio-weapon dubbed 'Omega'. They are faster, stronger, smarter, wiser, *better* than humans, and they are the only hope for the survivors of the human race as an interstellar war between two great alien powers absorbs the galaxy. But all is not as it seems, and the humans and the Earthers face challenges that overshadow the wars of alien empires and threaten to destroy their civilizations...

The Equations Novels by Kenneth Tam

Book One: THE HUMAN EQUATION (Oct 2003)

Book Two: THE ALIEN EQUATION (May 2004)

Book Three: THE RENEGADE EQUATION (Dec 2004)

Book Four: THE EARTHER EQUATION (July 2005)

Book Five: THE GENESIS EQUATION (July 2006)

Book Six: THE VENGEANCE EQUATION (July 2007)

Book Seven: THE NEMESIS EQUATION (July 2008)

Book Eight: THE DESTINY EQUATION (July 2009)

The Equations Novels are complete, but there are new stories in the Earther universe still to come!

For more information, please visit
www.earther.net

ABOUT THE AUTHOR

Born in 1984 in St. John's, Newfoundland, Kenneth Tam holds both a Bachelor's and Master's degree in history from Wilfrid Laurier University in Waterloo, Canada. His MA thesis examined the creation and operation of the Caribou Hut, a hostel for Allied servicemen in St. John's during the Second World War.

In 2006, Kenneth received a prestigious Canada Graduate Scholarship from the Social Sciences and Humanities Council of Canada. He was also awarded a Balsillie Fellowship at the Centre for International Governance Innovation during 2006-07. In that capacity, he worked for Mr. Paul Heinbecker, Canada's former ambassador and permanent representative to the United Nations. He has served as a Communications Consultant for Kitchener–Waterloo's federal Member of Parliament, Peter Braid, and is presently an Advisor with Sun Life Financial.

Since releasing his first novel in 2003, Tam has promoted his books across Canada, speaking with junior and high school students, delivering writing workshops, and doing book signings at bookstores and Iceberg-organized events. He frequently appears as a guest author at science fiction events across the country.

Kenneth is a partner in Iceberg Publishing, the company he and his family started in 2002. He has authored many of the company's existing titles, and is also responsible for graphic design, including the company logo, website, banners, advertisements, and other marketing materials. He acts as a primary contact with printers and suppliers, and is also key in new author development and recruitment.

He remains very lazy about writing his author bios. When they told him to make this one longer, he mostly copied and pasted it together from the Iceberg website, www.icebergpublishing.com.

www.ingramcontent.com/pod-product-compliance
Lightning Source LLC
Chambersburg PA
CBHW030746030726
47497CB00001B/160